Pilcrow

ADAM MARS-JONES

Pilcrow

{ novel }

ff

faber and faber

First published in 2008
by Faber and Faber Limited
3 Queen Square London WC1N 3AU
Published in the United States by Faber and Faber Inc.
an affiliate of Farrar, Straus and Giroux LLC, New York

Typeset by Faber and Faber Limited
Printed in England by Mackays of Chatham, plc

A CIP record for this book
is available from the British Library

978-0-571-21703-8

2 4 6 8 10 9 7 5 3 1

Dedicated to the Patient Ones
Holly, Keith and Lisa

and in memory of

The Net Book Agreement
1900–1997

unglamorous defender
of my trade

I'm not sure that I can claim to have taken my place in the human alphabet, even as its honorary twenty-seventh letter. I'm more like a specialised piece of punctuation, a cedilla, umlaut or pilcrow, hard to track down on the keyboard of a computer or typewriter. Pilcrow is the prettiest of the bunch, assessed purely as a word. And at least it stands on its own. It doesn't perch or dangle. Pilcrow it is.

1

The Taste of Dirt

The spring I learned to drive, the cherry tree in front of our house in Bourne End flowered as never before. It was 1968. Driving meant a lot to me as an idea. I felt that mastery of a car was a big step on the way to mastery of a life. I had my grandmother to thank for the car, a red Mini, licence plate OHM 962F, which cost £670 that year (new). I had Dad to thank for the gruelling lessons. I got started with the British School of Motoring, but Dad finished me off. He could be rather a remote figure, but I had nothing to complain about on that score while he was my driving instructor. He was relentless.

The Mini was the fun car of that decade – everybody liked it. Granny said, 'People seem to be able to do everything these days,' a vague sort of remark not at all characteristic of her. Generally Granny was vague as a razor, vague as a cruising shark. It turned out that she was confusing Issigonis, designer of the Mini, with Annigoni, who did Old Masterly portraits of the royal family. Granny was wrong only rarely. She didn't enjoy it. She felt it didn't suit her. It was always best for everyone to pretend it hadn't happened.

I made a modest contribution to the car from my savings. That was the way things worked with Granny. It wasn't her practice to buy things for people outright. I hadn't yet grasped that Granny's bounty always had a bit of spin on it – if she was helping one person, then she was almost certainly putting another one's nose out of joint. I was callowly grateful, not understanding that Granny's family interventions were like snooker shots, the ambitious kind where what you bounce off and how you scatter the cluster of balls – what you make impossible for the other players – is as important as the obvious aim of racking up points. All her charitable transactions tended to have that kind of ramifying quality. She wasn't exactly rich, though she was rich compared to Mum and Dad, and she had the knack of getting value out of money even after she had given it away. It went on working for her somehow.

It took time for me to learn there were other attitudes to money. When I was about ten, and Mum and I were out shopping, a bus stopped for us. We hadn't hailed it. We weren't even at a stop. We were looking in a shop window. The driver got out smiling and asked Mum for my name and address. She hesitated and then gave it to him. Years and years later, it turned out that this same bus driver had died and left me £100 in his will. Mum and I were touched – it made up for the embarrassment of the original situation, with the passengers staring at us or grumbling about their interrupted journey. But Granny was unimpressed and even disapproving. Perhaps she resented competition, even of this unrepeatable kind, in matters of largesse. She seemed to be repelled by the idea of giving without strings attached, as if this was a missed opportunity for controlling events. Or perhaps she sincerely thought that generosity to someone you didn't know could only be vulgar and sentimental.

Still, Granny must be thanked for her gift of the Mini, however many strings were attached, and however many different directions they pulled in. Every life needs an acknowledgement page – but this isn't it. The beginning isn't necessarily the best place for such a thing.

As a toddler, I had come up with my own pet name for my maternal grandmother. I was her first grandchild and I christened her. To me in my childhood she was Granny Annie. Anne was in fact her first name, something I couldn't have known. Anne Mildred Hanway. In any other family the name would have stuck. But somehow Granny was covered with an invisible protective coating, like the anti-climb paint which deters vandals. No pet name could get a grip on that treated surface, no endearment would leave a mark.

With her cheque for the balance of the car's price Granny included a note. Even her most casual communication was carefully thought out. I gave it due attention. Her hand-writing was crisply formed, her punctuation had the force of law. 'Promise me, John,' she wrote, 'that you won't pay too much attention to the road. Look around you; don't waste the privilege of the view. People who keep their eyes on the road become bored, and boredom is the foremost cause of accidents.' I wrote back to her with the promise that my driving life would be led according to her watch-word. I would not fall victim to boredom.

Dad wasn't thrilled that his mother-in-law was subsidising my independence, but there wasn't much he could do about it. Except that I'd only been able to afford four lessons with the British School of Motoring, so Dad supplied the rest. There may be an exception to the rule that you shouldn't be taught to drive by a family member, but Dad wasn't it. I drove the Mini tentatively and he drove me hard, though I tried not to show my distress. I didn't want him to see my tears any more than he would have tolerated being shown them.

After a gruelling lesson Mum could see how near the end of my tether I was, and then she'd give Dad a good carpeting. She never learned the knack of standing up for herself, but she was all cudgels on my behalf. This was a peculiarity of her temperament. Then of course Dad would feel put out that his expertise was being so little appreciated.

During those lessons I was exposed to a rich sample of his personal slang, a largely war-time compound. 'Gently Bentley,' he would say when the gear-box gave me grief. 'Don't get *agitato*' was for my moments of panic on the road, when obstacles threatened. 'Don't take *umbriago*, I'm only trying to pass on my skills' played its part when the pain in my shoulder made me sullenly silent. 'You'll thank me when you pass first time,' he said. He seemed very sure of that. For me Italian (or near-Italian) will always be the language of fancy ice cream and driving instruction that amounts to a form of torture.

As the lessons ground on, Dad got a little of his own back on Granny through me, in his rôle as a driving instructor. Acquiring the car might have been made easy for me, but he made sure that learning to drive it was no picnic.

Dad wouldn't allow me to nose the car into the garage at the end of our sessions – I had to reverse it in properly, 'according to Hoyle'. I cursed Hoyle, whoever Hoyle was. Heartily I hated Hoyle. There was a section of the Highway Code which Dad cited in justification, prohibiting the reversing from a minor thoroughfare into a major one. He gave away his forces background by this passion for regulations. Not many fathers would apply the rules so strictly, on a driveway which was technically a private road, with a son prone to weeping. It made the end of each lesson a bitter experience. Of course, if Dad had told me that one day I would be chased out of the house by a couple of maniacs, and that I'd gain valuable seconds if the car was pointing

3

towards the garage door, I might have been convinced that the elaborate manœuvre was worth all the trouble, instead of ignoring it from
the very moment I had passed my test. Though when the day came,
and I had to make a get-away just as fast as I could, one of the two
maniacs would turn out to be Dad.

We spent long afternoons doing three-point turns in the drive
despite my aching arms. The cherry tree shed so copiously on the car,
as I ground through my manœuvres, that I had to turn on the windscreen wipers. The meagre motor strained to clear the mash of blossom. I love the vegetable kingdom in all its provinces, every canton
and palatinate. I have a particular tenderness for *Prunus avium*, but
just this once I found myself thinking of the pink clods of petal on the
windscreen as a sort of morbid discharge. Flowering pus, supremely
ugly if only I had the knack of seeing it that way. It was a double
cherry, scentless, cultivated for the blowsy show it made. Every year
when the blossom got messy Dad would threaten to cut it down, but
really only to get a rise out of Mum, who loved it and had a terrible
suspicion it was vulgar.

I liked the cherry tree better earlier in the year, when tiny caterpillars let themselves down from its branches on the flimsiest threads.

Brain surgery without a knife

Granny had warned me against keeping my eyes on the road, and I
did my best to oblige. Dad with his affinity for machines and vehicles
had a different priority. He wanted me to develop a 'feel' for the car.
This mystical union was beyond me. Gradually I acquired a competence, but my imagination wasn't touched. A shrewder instructor,
more attuned to my character, might have tried telling me that driving lessons are really exercises in neurological processing.

First you have to learn a set of routine actions with the apparatus of
steering-wheel, gear lever and pedals, and then repeat them so often
that they migrate from the right lobe to the mid-brain and become
automatic. All you're doing, inside your skull, is transferring material
a couple of inches to the left, to a place where consciousness can safely
leave it. That's where the action is, inside your brain and not on the
road. From that point on, driving is something you won't need to be

aware of until there's an emergency on the road. Then actual thinking steps in again – usually too late. When a crisis looms, when the windscreen is full of onrushing wall, control reverts to the conscious mind, with its more highly developed capacity for making excuses.

The pilot and the autopilot only differ by a whisker, but how we insist on the distinction! We make quite a meal of that whisker. Consciousness is a useful technique and even an entertaining hobby, but a little goes a long way. It doesn't do to make a fetish of it.

It would have comforted me to think of my driving lessons along those lines, as a sort of slow and rather wonderful brain surgery performed without anything as crude as a knife. Instead I experienced it as an ordeal which gave me a frozen shoulder, and aggravated the emotional weather inside the house, the frozen alliance between a husband and wife who weren't really intimate enough to have rows on their own account. They needed stand-ins like me. And all along it was driving that was supposed to be the thing that got me out from under. I had to learn to drive if I was ever going to drive away, from Mum, from Dad, from the whole bang shoot.

After you, Gerald

I had my fair share of adolescent clashes with my parents, but there is one thing I never said: 'I didn't ask to be born.' It's a sentiment teenagers express very often, as a way of magnifying their sorrows and making the world take notice. I disapprove. It can't be good to blaspheme against your own existence.

'I didn't ask to be born.' That's the bass note of every whine, the fundamental. The drone underlying the moan. It's the sloping foundation on which nothing can be built true. Because there's no proof either way, is there? And I prefer to think that I did. I did ask to be born, knowing more than I do now. I made my choice. It isn't even necessary, as life goes on, for me to understand my reasons.

Souls await a womb. That's from the *Tibetan Book of the Dead*. Every religion contains at least one true thing, and this seems to be Tibetan Buddhism's. Souls await a womb, and I waited for my mother's. I knew what I was doing. I have to trust the judgement I had before I looked out of this one pair of eyes only.

I chose the womb as surely as the Duke of Westminster chose his — and who's to say I wasn't offered that one first? Perhaps I gave it up, like a seat on a train, in favour of someone who needed it more. Perhaps I decided to wait for one that would suit me better.

Admittedly the etiquette involved is hard to fathom. *No thank you, I think I'll pass. After you, Gerald, I insist. You be Duke this time. I'm in no hurry. There'll be another one along in a minute.* There's a system of short-listing in operation, obviously — not all wombs available to all souls. That's where karma comes in. Your past lives affect the range available. Karma winnows, karma restricts the possibilities. But there's still plenty of scope for the choosing agent, in a subset of infinity. The short-list being infinite in its own right. Between lives the soul moves with a special caution, gingerly as a cat in snow. Try to see your original face, as the Zen koan puts it, the one you had before your parents gave you birth.

Eight curves

I sat quiet in the womb I had chosen. I made no erudite statements from the darkness of my becoming. If I'd spoken out, if I'd intervened in the world before I was part of it, then surely Mum or Dad would have mentioned the fact. Even in a family like mine, where there were so many blockages of communication, news of that sort would have got through. Uterine speech is the province of a few highly developed souls, incarnations out of my league.

There's a great sage in the *Mahabharata*, Astavakra, who spoke out before his birth. Out of the womb he piped up: 'Father, through your grace I have already learned the Vedas, even lying in my mother's womb. But I am sorry to say you often make mistakes in your recitation. Allow me to correct your Sanskrit.' I don't know what the equivalent of the Vedas would be in Dad's life — maybe the home pages of the *Telegraph*. It's a fact that I love to be right. I can imagine floating there in the dark and picking my father up on his bad habits. I might have announced, 'Father, the *Telegraph* is confirming every assumption you have already. Can you find no better guide to the world?'

I might have taken issue with his odd habit of playing Switzerland in matters of family conflict, saying, 'Father, why do you not side with your wife against her mother? This is the great struggle of her life, and you are not entitled to neutrality.'

Or I might have taken a longer view, saying instead, 'Father, the men of your generation were unfairly accelerated by the War you grew up into. Even from here I can see that there are still trapped bubbles of childishness in all of you. Are you sure you are ready to be a father, however much you want the completion of your family? Are you sure you meant to give me my opportunity?' I might have had the option of resolving back into dew, never to be born, in a spiritual abstention. Perhaps this is the origin of miscarriage, in fœtal second thoughts.

I might have added a few words to Mum, in a lower tone, my voice reaching her directly through her bones and mine. 'Mother, I must ask you to pronounce *vegetarian* properly. The word is not *vegeteerian*. The avoidance of meat is an enlightened choice. There is no call to sneer at it, by your pronunciation of the very word.' If I'd been given the option of some such amniotic lecturing I would have chatted away pedantically nineteen to the dozen.

Astavakra's dad cursed the baby in the womb, saying, 'May you be born with a twisted form.' And in fact Astavakra was born with disabilities. The name means *eight curves*. Dad didn't curse me, though over time he may have come to see me as some sort of judgement, on him and the choices he had made.

Nursery world

I was a text-book healthy baby, a magazine-cover specimen of infant. I don't exaggerate. The magazine for which I was the cover star was *The Nursery World*, Vol. 41, No. 1,290 – the issue for August 31st 1950, when I was eight months old. I was the sort of bonny baby who provokes knitting frenzy in susceptible persons. The publishers have detected this matinée-jacket-provoking aura of mine, and have linked my image to a commercial slogan: *Wise knitters aim for . . . Target Cherub baby wool!*

They knew full well what bait they were dangling in front of the knitting public. They knew what a marketing tool they had in me. I'm adorable. I'm enough by myself to start a craze for bootees and tiny cardigans, pale blue with matching pearlised buttons.

I wasn't always so groomed and wholesome. I remember playing in the garden, as a baby, as a toddler, and loving to eat dirt. It's one of my strongest early memories. When Mum caught me doing it, she would scold and even shout. It was the first thing that I learned was wrong. Not that I stopped doing it. I liked the taste too much. Eating dirt was the first thing that I learned to do when Mum's back was turned. It was the secret vice which turned the withdrawal of her attention into an opportunity rather than a bereavement.

Mum hated dirt, though she also hated cleaning. The garden with its necessary dirt was unattractive to her. Dad took charge of all outside chores, until (much later) she discovered the joy of herbs, and a way of planting them which let her keep her shoes clean. Of course she kept a pair of old shoes to wear in the garden, but even those she hated to get dirty.

Inside or outside the house, creating order was a burden to her. Dirt was her enemy, cleanliness not altogether her friend. There was something brusque and aggrieved about her housework. Every flick of the duster, every pass with the broom, every guilty glance at the cleaning lady (when we could afford one at last), was part of a life-long dialogue with her mother, with Granny, whose attitude to domestic hygiene was passionate and entirely single-minded.

In Hindu cosmology it's said of Krishna that he too ate dirt as a toddler. A playmate told on him to his mother. But when Krishna's mother went to scold him and demanded that he open his mouth, he did – and then she saw that all the stars and the planets were held there in safety also. That was her revelation of her boy's Godhead, when she saw the cosmos whirling in his little mouth, a mouth that still had its baby teeth. If Krishna's mum had been mine, of course, he'd have been sent to bed without supper just the same.

There's a theory that children, when they put the wrong things in their mouths, are incorporating necessary impurities, building up their defences for later encounters. Mum took a more social view – eating dirt was common. When I put nasty things in my mouth I was showing her up, even when there was no one around to witness my vulgar behaviour.

8

Cave of all pleasure and knowing

Once I found a red Spangle in the garden. It was caked with dirt, but I wiped it roughly clean and ate it. It was delicious. Afterwards I didn't feel so good. When the taste wore off, there was nothing left in my mouth but fear, telling me that I'd done something terribly bad and wrong.

The mouth, being at that age the cave of all pleasure and knowing, refuses admission to nothing. Another time my imaginary friend Peterkin and I ate some little black-and-yellow caterpillars we found in the garden, not for the flavour but to feel them wriggling in our tummies. Peterkin said that nobody could see him but me, but that was just him being silly. I only pretended to eat my caterpillars, but Peterkin didn't notice and wanted to show he was as brave as me, so he swallowed his down. He said he could feel them moving for a long time afterwards. It wasn't half as much fun as I'd said, but I knew he'd do the next thing I told him to do just the same.

Vomit of truth

Near Christmas, I saw some holly bushes in full berry. I had Peterkin with me, and I told him they were the tastiest of all berries. 'And now, Peterkin,' I announced, 'we're going to eat tasty holly berries like the ones in the carols.' Even after the berries had been heaved up on the kitchen floor I tried to talk my way out of trouble with Mum. I wasn't ready to come clean even when my guts had made a full confession. 'I only ate one,' I said, 'but Peterkin had lots and lots.' There was no chance of my getting away with it, since Mum could see the undigested berries shining in what I had thrown up. My vomit was more truthful than my story.

After that I ignored Peterkin, pretending I couldn't see or hear him. I made him cry. He didn't like being reminded he was imaginary.

Of course Peterkin wasn't really my imaginary friend, he was my little brother Peter. Peter on his birth certificate, Peterkin to the family (I think the diminutive comes from *Treasure Island*). I was told I should love him. I didn't want to. I didn't want a brother at all, I wanted a friend who could run and maybe fly. Instead there was this dull bundle who spent most of his time on the floor even after he had learned to stand. Perhaps it was my job to teach him to fly. I helped him up onto a chair in the kitchen and told him he could do it, but he had to wait until I had counted to ten before he took off. Then I went into the garden, still counting. There was no sense in being too near the scene of the spell if the magic didn't work after all.

When Dad came in from his work, he would turn his hand into a flat blade and use it to deliver a soft chop to his forehead. He did this to Mum, he did it to me, sometimes he even did it to Peterkin. It was called a salute, and other people's daddies didn't do that. My daddy flied for the King. My daddy was a Squadron Leader. Mum made a smile with her lips while I saluted back.

We were allowed to roam pretty freely. I said to Peterkin, 'I know exactly how to get on the runway where Daddy keeps his plane. I'll take you there if you like.' Then there they were, all the flying men. From the start I liked uniforms always. The men stamped together and saluted. 'That's all for us, you see,' I explained. 'This man is coming to see us. He wants to know if we liked it.'

Of course when he came closer I saw that it was Dad, and all he wanted to know was what the hell we thought we were up to. He was jolly cross.

To feel myself being washed away

It was Mum's choice to call me John, but Dad was delegated to choose my middle name, as a consolation prize. Originally I was going to be John Draper Cromer, after one of Dad's Air Force heroes, Kit Draper, but Mum dug her heels in. She hadn't met him, but she certainly didn't like what she had heard about him. Yes, he'd served in the War – yes, all right, both wars – but he wasn't what you could call a war hero, was he? He kept wrecking planes. He was a show-off and a liability, if not worse – some said he had been lucky not to be tried as a traitor and a spy. Dad said that was all nonsense and drivel, but she insisted on his second choice instead, and so I became John Wallis Cromer. After Barnes Wallis, of the Dam Busters and the bouncing bomb.

Somewhere in Dad's papers I expect there's a list of possible names for his first-born, written in small caps:

JOHN DRAPER CROMER.

JOHN BARNES CROMER.

JOHN TRENCHARD CROMER.

JOHN BADER CROMER.

JOHN CHESHIRE CROMER.

JOHN GIBSON CROMER.

As if he imagined them looking well on a war memorial, if it came to that. Of course the War still cast its shadow, over him and over everyone. There was rationing still. 'Cheshire' would have been for Leonard Cheshire, war hero and witness of the bombing of Nagasaki, 'Gibson' for Guy Gibson, who led the raid on the Ruhr when the bouncing bombs were dropped.

The earliest pattern of sound I can remember is Mum saying '*Dou-asíss – Dou-asÍSS!*' I didn't know what it meant at first, but she always made that sound in the same set of circumstances.

Sometimes it sounded like '*Móndou-asíss*'. Some sounds were fuzzy and others were clear. Some were said so quickly I missed them all together. There was almost certainly a little 'k' before the soothing, pleading phrase, but I have no memory of it. *Dou-asíss* was familiar and friendly, and sometimes Mum stretched out the final 's' for onomatopœic ages. *Siss* was Mum's word for doing a wee. We were playing a game, Mum and I. She wanted me to have a wee so I would drop off to sleep right away, and I didn't want to, for exactly the same reason.

The next memory after Mum saying '*Dou-asíss*' is of Dad saying, 'You should blow on it, m'dear!' That was his stock form of address to his wife, a phrase so stylised that it hardly counted as an endearment.

Under the hood of my big black pram it was almost as dark as the womb. It was wonderful to be wrapped up in swaddling clothes with my face breathing in the cool air. I would wait for the blissful warmth to creep up all around me. It was impossible to maintain this bliss for more than a second or two without falling into sleep, but I wanted to enjoy sleep as a conscious condition. I was a precocious investigator of states of mind. I wanted to stand on the shore, on the very edge of the tide of sleep, and feel myself being washed away. I was drawn to examine the moment that consciousness gave way to one of its opposites. I wanted to freeze that moment, to savour my awareness as it slipped from me, and my secret weapon in the quest was a full bladder. That focus of discomfort kept me on the edge of nothingness, preventing me from dropping off. Then when I could hold it in no longer I would relax and let it all flood out. It was bliss to feel the gentle warmth seeping into my swaddling clothes, before I fell properly asleep, for the few moments before Mum woke me with an exasperated sigh.

It must have been very frustrating for Mum, who had to keep changing my clothes. 'He's being impossible today – I'm at the end of my tether. I've only just put him into fresh clean clothes and now look! He's soaked them again!' That was why she was so keen on making me 'go' before putting me down to sleep, and why Dad came up with his crucial suggestion: 'Blow on it, m'dear!' I didn't actually hear Mum say, 'Dennis, I'll do no such thing!' but with my later experience of her I can absolutely guarantee that she would have used that form of words. In the end she didn't have to do it. Dad would do it for her. I remember the feeling of the cool air flowing over my body, and seeing Dad with his cheeks puffed out, as he blew cool air over the clenched bud of my infant equipment.

His tactic was sound. I let go immediately, and on this first occasion I hit him right in the face, while Mum shrieked with horrified laughter. After that he managed to dodge the jet. Mum and Dad made gratified noises.

I was happy to be the cause of such sounds, even though it meant I was being cheated out of a few precious seconds of nirvana. From now on, when I was wrapped up I had no way of indulging in this delicious game, playing Grandmother's Footsteps with oblivion. I just drifted off. It wasn't long, though, before I began to enjoy Dad's blowing technique in its own right. I remember seeing the jet of water rising high into the air, and being very proud that I'd managed to achieve this. How they managed to catch the proud stream I don't know.

I soon discovered that any source of fresh air could act as a trigger, so when I came to toddle I started to experiment. Even opening the little flap of my dungarees was enough to start the tingle of release.

I have a separate memory of sitting in a shaft of sunlight and real-ising that everything around me happened by my say-so. Everything was conditional on me. Logically, of course, this is a memory of suc-cessful potty-training. The potty has been pushed out of the picture, but I know it's there. I'm a little king, and I'm sitting on a foreshort-ened throne. My gross happiness is the immediate radiant aftermath of being told I was Mummy's clever boy for doing my siss or my 'tup-penny' (the family word for defæcation) so beautifully in the right place. That's something that disappeared early on – excretion as one of the pleasures of life, expressive as a smile, not some dark duty that dominates the days.

My fascination with my personal squirting device didn't stop in the cradle. As soon as I was fully mobile, I wanted to aim, to stand and point. I came to think that potties were dreadful silly things, use-ful only if you needed to do a tuppenny in them, and I would head straight for the garden instead. Whatever Raff station we were at, West Raynham, Waterbeach or Hayling Island, as the family moved home in my early days, I would soon be toddling around in the gar-den seeing how far I could make my siss go. The desire soon spread to the road. The attraction here was there were other houses and those other houses contained little boys. I'd practised my sissing skills in private, so by the time I was ready for the road I was quite advanced, and it wasn't long before I was taking part in tournaments. None of the other little boys was quite as good as me. I was the champion of siss. Mum and Dad told me I wasn't allowed to go into the road, but there was no rule to say I couldn't do my best to project a stream of urine from one side of it to the other. After I ate beetroot once my siss turned red, which was thrilling and gave an extra flair to my display.

I was a good little boy, always meaning well, so it follows that a lot of my memories are about doing wrong. There's no contradiction there. My iniquities were striking enough to be remembered. When I was naughty Mum called me 'Bad King John', and if I grizzled Dad would say, 'Pipe down, Johannes R.' Both of those were from a poem. But it was understood between us that I was a good boy.

Once when I was staying with Granny, though, I saw her changing the bulb on a bedside lamp. After that, I had an idea about how I too might shine. I wanted more than anything to glow like that.

Granny had given me an idea about the electric light and how I could make it work in a different way. I knew the switch had to be on to make the light work, and I unscrewed the bulb and put my finger in its place, switched it on and duly got a burn. I knew I'd been naughty, and I tried to hide the place for as long as I could, till it had quite a blister. There's probably not a necessary link between being scolded and the smell of vaseline, but there is for me.

I don't know where Mum was when I went to stay with Granny in her old house in the country. Perhaps she was there too. Mothers are so constant, so irreplaceable in early life that they tend to disappear from the picture somehow – just as Mum, as well as the potty, disappeared from my memory of seated happiness, though her approval was what created the memory in the first place.

Granny's house had thatch on it, which hung very low. She had to stoop to get in her own front door. There was a painting of a cat in Granny's house, hanging over the fireplace. She lifted me up so I could see it properly. I tried to stroke it. It was funny that Granny had a painting of a cat, when the animal she kept was a dog, her lovely boxer Gibson. I don't know who or what he was named after. There's a make of guitar by that name, but I think we can rule that out. There were 'Gibson girls' who danced, but I don't think Granny would name a male dog after females. It certainly wasn't Guy Gibson the raider of the Ruhr. I plump for the Gibson cocktail, a dry martini garnished with a pearl onion instead of an olive.

Looming angel

Gibson's colouring was so pale he looked spectral, other-worldly, with one eye a warm and cloudy brown, the other stony blue. Boxers aren't clever dogs. They're famous for it, the not being clever. I don't mean that any dog is exactly brilliant – they're never going to show up on *Mastermind* – but it's a fair bet that by the time poodles are being made heads of university departments, boxers will still be nosing their alphabet blocks around with big frowns on their foreheads. All the same, Gibson was a very thoughtful dog. His great pastime was to pick up his ball in his jaws and carry it upstairs. Then he'd sit at the top of the stairs, nose his ball forward, and watch as it bounced all the way down. Then he'd repeat the performance, without limit. He'd do it until the ball was taken away from him. As I say, he was a very thoughtful dog. It took just the one thought to fill him.

Gibson loomed over my toddlerhood like a guardian angel, tolerating with patience the fist I thrust in his warm wet mouth. I would lean in fearlessly as far as my shoulder, like a plumber probing a drain, and he'd just let it happen, while I dredged his mouth for marbles or simply explored the walls of gum in which his teeth were set. Dogs can smell fear, as we're always being told, but on me Gibson must have smelled something very different, trust and love. It's the simplest explanation for his long-suffering ways. According to family tradition he let me learn to stand and then walk by supporting myself on his ears. I clutched tightly onto those velvety flanges, while his breath came out and warmed my face.

Mum told me his breath stank. She didn't know how I could stand it. Simple – as far as I was concerned it wasn't bad breath, it wasn't even dog breath, it was Gibson's breath and it smelled fine. I don't remember smelling his tuppennies but I dare say I would have liked them too. I certainly liked mine.

Something about Gibson reminded my senses of Granny herself. He smelled a little like her, which seemed only right, though she never smelled quite as good as he did. Dogs' ears smell of mown hay.

I couldn't know then that Granny, fastidious but well aware of the damaging effect of frequent baths on dogs' coats, sprayed him fairly regularly with her own perfume. Gibson, the thoughtful friend who taught me to walk, had a depth of aroma, all the way from mud and glands to high floral notes, worthy of a court lady from the time of the Sun King. Gibson must have been one of the few boxers ever to wear *Je Reviens*.

Gibson lost his hearing quite young. White dogs tend to be deaf. Deaf dogs tend to be white. These things converge. In Gibson's case, with my granny as his mistress, it was always on the cards that he went deaf as a husband might, for the peace it brought.

I loved and admired Gibson more than any person in my life, except the mother whom I only noticed when she wasn't there. I formed a passionate attachment to him. He was my totem animal, yet I could learn nothing from him. He wouldn't even let me take his ball. Dogs know what the nose knows: *this* and *here* and *now*. That, yonder, tomorrow – none of these carries a smell. Animals can't show us how to live as they do. With their enclosure in the present they offer examples we're disqualified from following.

When I put my finger in the socket of the lamp where the bulb went, I was in search of light, but my deeper interest from the start was fire. I loved it that both Mum and Dad could make smoke with their faces. Dad was a serious smoker and Mum was a frivolous one, restricting herself to three du Mauriers a day.

The du Maurier packet was a lovely piece of design, red with an odd black pattern like a modified swastika or cubist sphincter – there was definitely a suggestion of engulfment, of being hypnotised and drawn into the oblong void if I looked at it for too long. On special occasions I was allowed to pull the rip-cord of cellophane on a new packet, though Mum might have to raise the edge of it for my benefit. It gave me great joy that the top of the box opened upwards from a hinge on one of its long sides.

Mum and Dad demonstrated their incompatibility not only in the way they smoked – he absently masterful, she nervous – but in the way they lit the necessary matches. I watched closely, loving to see fire in all its forms, even this transitory one. Dad would blow out the flame when it had done its work with a single smart puff, without really even looking at it. Mum would wave her hand around, not quite rapidly enough to extinguish the fire she held, slowing down and wavering in a kind of panic, until she finally worked up enough velocity with her hand to strip the little stick of its flame, a fraction of a second before Dad muttered, 'For God's sake, m'dear! Is it so difficult? Is it strictly necessary to burn the house down?' She was addicted to something other than cigarettes. Her air of being at odds with her surroundings was something that she insisted on, somehow. It wasn't something that simply happened to her. Meanwhile I registered the beauty of flame, and the way it could be summoned by the agency of matches.

Adults worry too much

When I was three I made a bomfire – that's bomfire with an 'm'.

'Bomfire' always held a promise of devastation for me, smouldering away in the middle of the word. I used grass cuttings, lit with matches supplied by an older boy, who cuddled me. He sat with his legs apart, which left room for little me between them. Perhaps there wasn't really an older boy – perhaps I stole the matches from home and he was just a story I told when everything went wrong, with the detail about him cuddling me just a bit of wish-fulfilment put in for my own benefit. If I'd made up an older boy for the purpose of spreading the blame, I might as well get some extra enjoyment out of my excuse. In my mind that was a very natural position for me, between a big boy's legs.

Even if there really was an older boy, the bomfire was all my idea. I did the talking, calming Peterkin's doubts. I said, 'I know what I'm doing. I've seen how it's done.' Adding with grave assurance, 'Adults worry too much.' Then I burned the greenhouse down. Well, that became the family story. In the struggle for survival of rival versions of an anecdote, 'John almost scorched the greenhouse' has no chance against 'John burned the greenhouse down.' My memory of the incident is of triumph not disaster. It gave me joy to release the smoke and flame lurking inside an unpromising heap of cut grass. The word normally attached to such feelings is pyromania, but I don't really think it covers my case. It misses the aspect of worship, the sense of a sacrament. I feel 'pyrolatry' comes closer to the truth.

My love of fire affected my feelings about the days we celebrated. Nothing about Christmas could compare with Guy Fawkes. For a born pyrolater like me, December 25th couldn't hold a candle to November 5th, and not just because someone with a birthday on December 27th was bound to feel his own nativity over-shadowed. Bomfire Night was a festival with no moral improvement to offer, a gala of unholy combustion that had its own sort of holiness. It was also something that our family did rather well.

Dad never used milk bottles as rocket launchers for our family fire-work displays. He built his own, using broom handles sharpened at one end so that they could be driven into the ground more easily, with eyelets screwed in at intervals along the shaft. Eyelets of different sizes could accommodate different diameters of stick, without the sloppy angle that comes from a loose fit.

I suppose all this was an extension of his identity as a pilot, his sense of a general command of the air. Milk bottles were out of the question because the size of rocket he favoured would have tipped them over. Dad didn't ordinarily enjoy spending money, but he never begrudged the expense when it came to fireworks, and perhaps a sense of family pride came into it. Even if he'd bought the same titchy little rockets as everyone else, I don't think milk-bottle launch pads would have been good enough for the Cromer family fireworks. Not for us the 85-degree angle – 72°, even – of rockets that loll in the mouths of milk bottles before the moment of ignition. The family projectiles were never less than fully erect. Our rockets must ascend in a perfect vertical, as if they really were meant to escape the earth's pull.

Those home-made rocket launchers were the only bit of do-it-yourself I remember Dad doing. They fitted his definition of manly activity while serving the purpose, for once, of something wonderfully useless.

I wasn't allowed to light fireworks or handle sparklers, and I can see the sense of that. The pyrolatrous glint in my eyes can't have been much of an inducement to take a chance on me behaving responsibly.

Mum and Dad both smelled of smoke even when it wasn't Bomfire Night, but underneath that Mum smelled like me and Dad didn't. Mum and I had marked each other, as dogs mark lampposts. I smelled of the milk she had made inside herself, and she smelled of the milk I had taken in and then burped softly over her shoulder while she patted my back. Dad smelled different entirely.

I remember being held in my father's arms at a fruit stall in a market. I was reaching out towards a bunch of bananas and saying the word 'Gee!' with a hard 'G'. My word for bananas. What I meant when I said 'Gee!' was partly 'lovely bananas, want bananas' and partly something else. It was partly 'I love my daddy's smell and the feeling of being in his arms.' It was only much later I wondered if the brand name Geest had been stuck onto the bananas, so that I was instinctively reading the word, remembering my letters from a previous life. *Geest* of course being the Dutch for ghost or spirit.

Baby Bear bounce

One day when I was three Dad borrowed my favourite red ball, flew over the garden and dropped it down to me from his plane. This would be the house in Bathford, outside Bath, at the top of a hill. Perhaps it was his farewell outing in a Tiger Moth, a training biplane manœuvrable at low speeds which was coming to the end of its long service life around then. Can I really have caught my red ball cleanly, without help, on the third enormous bounce? There was a Daddy Bear bounce, that seemed to go right back up into the sky it had come from, then a Mummy Bear bounce, up to the level of the tree-tops this time, and then a Baby Bear bounce which was just right, at hedge height. A bounce for each of us, and into my waiting hands. This was an extraordinary happening, needing to be replayed again and again in my mind until it took on a dark varnish of meaning.

I feature quite strongly in the early pages of the family album. Later on I'm relegated to the sidelines. I become awkward supporting cast for other people's birthdays and holidays. But Mum and Dad had quite a lot of photographs taken when I was three, by *Cyril Howes of Bath / Abbey Churchyard / Telephone 60444*, so I go out in a blaze of glory as a photographic subject. Then later they couldn't bear to sort through them critically, getting rid of the ones that weren't so good. Knowing that my life from that point on had nothing in common with what went before.

As a three-year-old I was a cheerful active child, happy to play with my bricks while the photographer worked away, with a little gallery of memories that didn't need chemicals to be developed and fixed – the happiness of a good session at potty, the pride of peeing a winning arc, and the physical stimulation of being in Dad's arms, reaching for the suggestive fruit *par excellence*, all too obvious object of desire. Unzip a banana.

Then my life began. My life acquired its *sruti*-note – the fundamental drone that underpins a raga, the part of the music that isn't even part of the music. The Sanskrit word has come to mean 'authority'. Hindu cosmology is particularly compatible with musical analogies. It's not so much the Big Bang as the Big Twang, a primal throb underlying every variation of pitch and timbre.

My life began with a fever. The pain came only at night, to start with. Starting in the knee. Hot and dizzy. At two in the morning I'd be screaming, then by breakfast-time I would almost have forgotten. All childhood illnesses are dramatic, but this was more dramatic than most. I would scream for quite a while without stopping, and I couldn't bear for my knee to be touched. Mum gave me aspirin, so many that once I saw two Mums coming into the room.

The fever played hide-and-seek with doctors. Mum would take me to the local surgery, but by then I was fine again, running around merrily, impatient to be read Beatrix Potter, to start fires, to eat dirt when I could get it. The doctor may have wondered if this was an obsessive mother making too much of things. He said, if you're really sure, call me out the next time it happens. If you're really sure.

We didn't have a car, but we did have a phone. Not everybody did, but we did, though it didn't get much use in daily life. So the next time it happened she phoned him, her heart pounding as much from her own daring at disturbing a doctor's sleep as from the screams of her first-born. When he came he could see for himself how inflamed it was, how much pain it gave.

It was beyond him. I needed to be seen at a hospital, where they would do tests. I'm taking you to a nice hospital, Mum told me. What's that? A place where they stop you being ill. But I'm not ill. I'm a good soldier. I've only got a sore knee sometimes.

I was taken to a place called Manor Hospital, where they prodded and poked. It wasn't a nice sort of place at all. When we arrived, I asked if my mum could stay as well. Because I asked that, it was put into my notes – as she later saw – that I had 'an unnatural attachment' to my mother. What would have counted as a natural attachment, in a three-year-old full of pain being left to be poked and prodded by strangers?

Mum came with me to the ward, but the moment I was put in bed she left, not saying a word. I watched her grief-stricken as she walked away. Her shoes made a sharp clopping noise on the floor, and the tight skirt of the period required her to take short steps, so that she seemed to take ages to abandon me. She didn't even turn round at the last moment to give me a little wave, as love would have compelled her to do.

I felt deserted by her, and aggrieved by the hospital's ways of doing things. They had put me in a bed with sides, a hospital cot. Did they think I was a baby? And now Mum who could have explained it all to me had gone away.

She came to visit the next day, and when I sulked and wouldn't speak to her she cried, explaining that she was only doing what she had been told to do. The hospital said it was for the best to leave without saying good-bye. Mum had trained as a nurse, which may have made it harder to argue with hospital rules. She had no training in how to be the mother of a patient.

Spiritual carbon monoxide

A clean break was prescribed as the least distressing procedure. It avoided the heart-ache of protracted leave-takings – tears, pleading. It prevented Scenes, and Scenes never did anyone any good. Better for the children in the other beds, certainly, if Mum walked off without a word, as if she couldn't wait to be shot of me.

There are things, though, which clean-break theory ignores. A child who imagines himself delivered into the hands of cruel strangers, for no fixed term, has an altered body chemistry. In his sleep he breathes out dismal vapour – spiritual carbon monoxide. Better for my ward-mates to have witnessed a scene of squalid sorrow, with me howling and begging Mum to stay, than to have taken into their lungs the low fog of desolation and abandonment which I exhaled that first night.

Mum tried to cheer me up. Did I like it here? No I didn't. I wanted to go home. Children cried in the night. I didn't like the cereal. There was only Corn Flakes for breakfast and fried bread, which I hated. Why couldn't I go home, where there was Weetabix?

The third day she brought along some Weetabix, to give me a taste of home. A little bit of continuity between my new life and the old. When she asked a nurse for a bowl and some milk she was told that Weetabix wasn't allowed.

Mum argued the toss and made a little headway. It was agreed that it would be all right for me to have some Weetabix just this once, but it wouldn't be right to make a habit of it. There were other children being looked after in the hospital who didn't have mummies to bring them in Weetabix. It wouldn't be fair on them. There was socialism of some punitive sort evident in the hospital's thinking about cereal.

Manor Hospital doesn't get many marks from me, as a giver of care. Some of the procedures they subjected me to may have been medically sensible, but as no one explained anything they were humanly degrading. They kept putting swabs down my throat, looking for streptococcus, I suppose. Before the swab came the spatula. The spatula was horrible because it made me retch. I remember the feeling of being about to be sick, and also trying to work out how far back in my throat the spatula went to produce that hideous sensation. So I took the straw they gave me with a glass of water and practised taking it into my mouth as far as possible. When the sick feeling came I learned to overcome it. It was a sort of game. Soon it was easy.

The doctor didn't play along, though. When he came in again, I didn't retch, or even flinch, when he got to what had previously been the point of my gagging reflex. He gave me a funny look, as if he didn't enjoy being outsmarted, and pushed the spatula further in, until he got the painful, humiliating reflex he seemed to want so much.

It was a useful discovery, that there were other factors in the world of doctors and hospitals than the welfare of the patient. However much I trained myself to accommodate his probings, this particular doctor would keep on pushing until he got the desired paroxysms. Other children on the ward gagged the moment the spatula entered their mouths, and the doctor was perfectly satisfied. If I'd had any sense I'd have done the same, from the beginning. As it was, by the time he came to scrape his swab against the back of my throat, the tissues were so tender it felt as if he was trying to strike a match there, to set my throat alight.

There was another doctor who came in at one point to carry out the same procedure. His hands smelled of the same soap, but they followed a different code. They were gentle. His voice and manner were full of love. His spatula wasn't pushed any further than the minimum, and my body reacted as if it was a different organism entirely. My throat opened like a flower to his swab.

There were also bone biopsies, which no doctor could have made painless. They involved scraping the bone of the conscious patient with an instrument that had a little hook attached to it, to gouge out a sample. It's hard to describe pain, even to compare one pain with another mentally, all you can say is pain or no pain. This was pain. The scraping was deep inside me. I cried out for 'Suzie' and the nurse asked, 'Is that your sister, dear?' No, Suzie was a straw dog, given to me by my Uncle Roy for my first birthday.

Many years later, reading accounts of tortures used on political prisoners in South America, I came across a very similar technique, which went by the grimly poetic name of 'tickling the bone'. If I'd known that what the doctors were doing was a form of torture, though carried out in my own best interests, I might have tried confessing my meagre sins, crying out, 'I ate a red Spangle that I knew was dirty! I saved up my tuppennies and did them in the bath! I wanted to see them float!'

I was as incidental to what was being done to my body as the abductees on television programmes, when aliens probe and scrape. No one is actively drilling for pain, in the hospital, on the mother ship, but it spouts from its bottomless wells. Perhaps the writers of those shows had hospital experience as infants, and are using fantasy to work through their traumas. Good luck to them. I find such things hard to watch. I find such things hard to turn off.

They stuck sharp things into my bottom and they pushed blunt ones up it. The sharp things were the needles that administered injections of iron, and the blunt ones were enema nozzles. I squealed as the funnel was inserted and the liquid began to flow. I remember the smell of the rubberised sheet beneath me mixed with the smell of my opened bowels. There was someone at each corner of the sheet holding it up, so as to prevent my helpless slurry from spilling onto the bed or the floor. Not quite the four angels, one at each bed-corner, that I had been encouraged to visualise in infant prayers, who were to guard me as I slept. The slurry formed a shallow pool with me at the centre. The whole event was shaming, with no explanation given. Why was I being made to go to the lavatory in bed? 'It's only soapy water!' said a nurse in a rather cross tone, as if there had never been such a fuss made over nothing. And as if the exact composition of the warm liquid that was being driven into me, reversing the proper direction of travel, was something I could be expected to know. I was baffled as well as humiliated. Holding on was a relatively recent achievement for me, and now the right and clever thing seemed to be letting go. I just wished they'd make up their minds.

The only good thing to come out of my Manor Hospital days had nothing directly to do with medicine. From my bed I could see a chimney on one of the hospital buildings which was pouring out black smoke. It was a windy day. A gust of wind suddenly snatched the smoke and whisked it past my window. I knew I was stuck where I was, but the smoke rushing past the window produced an optical illusion – as if the whole ward was moving at speed in the opposite direction. Objectivity went on the slide, just as it does when the train next to yours starts moving, and for a while you don't realise that your own is still waiting at the platform. I lost my bearings in a way which amounted to revelation.

This was a glimpse that stayed with me, a mystical inkling. One suggestive thing about the experience was that its materials were so humble. It wasn't frankincense taking on a meaning beyond itself, only smoke from incinerated hospital refuse. A sense of the meaning of life can be constructed from any material however unpromising, from whatever lies to hand. Perhaps burning was a necessary aspect of the experience, from the point of view of getting my attention, since I've always been so attuned to combustion.

I don't know how long they looked after me at Manor Hospital. It was long enough for Mum to bring me Suzie the straw dog eventually, who gave me some comfort. When I came home I was no better but I had a diagnosis attached to me: rheumatic fever. It wasn't an uncommon condition in those days, a side-effect of streptococcus infection. Three per cent of individuals with untreated streptococcus go on to develop acute rheumatic fever, when antibodies are generated which attack the membranes in joints – the synovial linings. It was thought that I might have had streptococcus without any noticeable symptoms. So perhaps there was a reason for them to be so keen on pushing swabs down my throat.

At three I was well below the usual age of onset for the disease (six to fifteen), and the arthritic pains I was experiencing didn't really fit the definition of 'migratory'. They seemed pretty stubbornly resident. New areas were beginning to be inflamed, but not because old troubles were clearing up. There were squatters in my knees wrecking the premises, and they showed no signs of moving on. In fact somehow they were inviting their cronies to join the party, to occupy my hips and elbows, ankles, wrists and shoulders, until there was a general involvement of the joints in misery, pain and swelling.

I had my diagnosis, or rather Mum and Dad did. But diagnosis without cure or even treatment is cold comfort. There was nothing to be done for me. To be more accurate: nothing was to be done by me. I was to do nothing. In rheumatic fever it is the heart that gives concern. Permanent damage can be done to it. Additional strain must be avoided.

If you're a patient who isn't positively going to die, so that sooner or later your condition is likely to improve, then the chances are you'll be on the receiving end of whatever treatment is currently the fashion. In the seventeenth century I would have been bled. In the 1950s the prevailing wisdom required no special equipment. I was simply put to bed. Bed with no supper was a punishment. Until you say you're sorry. Bed rest till you're better was doctor's orders, however long it took.

2

Butter Melon Cauliflower

My bedroom wallpaper was yellow roses. I turned my face to the wall
and I stared at the yellow roses.

Every joint was swollen, and pain came in leisurely waves and sudden spasms, the spasms riding on the waves. I couldn't endure the
contact of the bedclothes, even a single sheet on a warm night. Mum
had trained as a nurse, even if she didn't have anything you could call
a career, and she knew about things like cradles devised to take the
pressure off skin that couldn't bear to be touched. She improvised one
by fetching the fire-guard and putting it over my legs. Then she
draped the bedclothes over the fire-guard. It had the right curved
shape, and provided a good gap above my legs. The gap had to be
small enough for the volume of air underneath to be heated by my
legs relatively quickly, so they didn't get cold.

It wasn't just the bedclothes. Even the lightest hug brought as
much pain as comfort. In my chosen family, hugs were emergency
measures, not for every day. I wasn't used to them. I'd hardly experienced them, or seen them happen. Dad would say, 'Cheerio, m'dear,'
in exactly the same way whether he was going out for five minutes or
on a tour of duty which might last months. Hugs might just as well
have been kept in the medicine cupboard, so as not to lose their effectiveness by over-use. They were like the little bottle of brandy that
lived in the kitchen cupboard, dire treatment for shock, shocking in
itself.

I kept myself mentally occupied for most of the first week in bed by
playing my favourite game, which was quite an achievement, since it
was 'I Spy'. I must have driven Mum mad. It was a bare room. Apart
from the wallpaper and the curtains (a design of vintage cars) there was
no ornamentation to engage the mind. There was a wardrobe and a
chest of drawers with a mirror on top of it, but there were only two
objects in the room which could honestly be said to reward attention:
a night-light in the form of a sailing ship and a miniature brass ashtray

with a farthing set in the middle of it, which both lived on a bedside table. The sails of the night-light were made of a sort of primitive plastic that was textured like vellum – the bulb shone dimly through them. S for Ship, S for Sail. With my little eye. There was a little cabin, with a little low railing round the top. The ashtray must have been brought in from another room to tickle my visual palate, since smoking in a sick room was discouraged even then. I liked the little wren design on the farthing. A for ashtray, R for Wren.

I wasn't allowed to feed myself – Mum had to do it for me. The only self-feeding I was allowed to do was drinking milk from a 'feeder'. It was like a teapot with a spout and no top. Mum would bring it to me and put it on my chest, and then I could drink without having to get up. She would say, 'Drink it all down, John, there's a good boy,' but I didn't want to. I'd take a little sip, but that was all I wanted. For some reason I thought that if I drank from the feeder all the way to the bottom, the way I was supposed to, something terrible would happen. I didn't have an idea of dying, but that was the feeling, of death as the dregs in the feeder. It was as if I was losing my trust in Mum. The feeder had milk or Horlicks in it. I didn't like milk or Horlicks. What I wanted was what Mum drank, was tea, but I wasn't allowed it.

Mum had a few hours' domestic help every week. This was 'the girl'. The girl who 'came in'. She was 'the girl who came in' from the village. She was a teenager who came in and changed her smart shoes for some shabby ones that were all worn down at the back, then put on a housedress that must have been her mother's.

I got these details from Mum, since the girl changed in the kitchen. I soon got used to being satisfied with second-hand information. The other sort was in short supply, although one day the girl came into my room in the act of pulling a dressing-gown cord tight round the house-coat, redeeming its shapelessness by giving her narrow waist some definition. She winked at me then. She told me her name was Polly. Mum didn't seem to know her name – or at least she would say to her friends, 'I have no help at all, except for a girl who comes in.'

I pleaded with the girl who came in to let me have tea, but still it wasn't allowed. One day I was particularly upset that I was going to be made to drink from the feeder until I got to the bottom and died.

The girl came in with the feeder full of hot milk. I pleaded in tears for tea, but she said in a loud voice, 'I'm not allowed to give you any!' This was torture, since I could hear the clink of a tea-cup in the kitchen where Mum was drinking it, though she was probably crying herself.

Then a marvellous thing happened. The girl bent down and whispered in my ear, 'I've put a splash of tea in it, just to stop you moaning. But don't say a word, or I'll get a big telling off from your mum!'

I thought she was probably fibbing, but even so I was grateful. The little conspiracy between us did me good. It meant she was on my side, and it meant that even when I was very ill I could still make things happen just a little bit. And when I sipped from the feeder, I found Polly had been telling the truth. It was milky all right, but somewhere in it there was the tang of something else, something that must have been tea, and I drank it to the last drop.

After that the girl would give my milk a boost of tea on a regular basis. I would hum a tune to tell her what I wanted. The tune was perfect because it kept what she was doing a secret. It was just a tune, and anyone can hum a tune. The tune was 'Polly put the kettle on'. And we'll all have tea.

It may even have been that Mum was in on the whole thing. It's hard to believe that she would have come down hard on a drink that was still largely milk.

Fairy cabbages

As for food, I didn't have anything that could be called an appetite, and Mum had to coax me to swallow every mouthful. Even before I was ill, I'd been a fussy eater. Meat in particular I instinctively disliked. The idea of chewing it disgusted me, so I would spit it out, politely if possible, if not, not. This was the heyday of the British Sunday joint, with leftovers in various forms being made to last much of the week, but if I hated the theme then I could only hate the variations on it. It was still hateful meat, however behashed or enrissoled.

It wasn't likely that I would work up an appetite while I was lying still all day, so Mum became expert at working one up for me, using presentation as much as the promise of flavour. She learned not to put too much on the plate, which was sure to put me off. I could eat maybe a quarter of a boiled egg and a single finger of toast, a solitary soldier cut off from the company. Half an egg on a good day. An egg was a special thing in the domestic economy so soon after rationing, but I didn't know that, and its aura wasn't enough in itself to stimulate my appetite. An ice lolly, though, was a tremendous treat, well worth the trouble of licking. I couldn't bear anything heavy – a little mouthful of sponge pudding and custard would be the most I could manage. Mum learned to tempt rather than scold, and to resist turning the whole subject of eating into a psychological minefield by striking too many bargains (if you finish your egg I'll brush your hair – that sort of thing). She told me Brussels sprouts were 'fairy cabbages', knowing that the nick name would draw me to that disregarded vegetable. She was like an advertising executive, trying to crack a one-child market.

Mum would put a Mars Bar in the 'fridge to chill, and then cut it into thin slices. That worked pretty well. It wooed me. I could usually manage two or three of those little slices, and the daintiness of the presentation was a pleasure in itself – its elfin picnic aspect. Or its laboratory overtone, I suppose. Mum made meticulous cross-sections of those Mars bars as if she was a lab assistant preparing slides for the microscope. She even took the trouble to chill the saucer she served it on, so that the slices didn't warm up too quickly, and lose their satisfying firmness of texture before they entered the cavern of my mouth.

Mum was enough of a traditional housewife to bake cakes, but I took no notice of them. They all went down Dad's throat. I loved to eat the scrapings from the bowl, but I set my face against the finished cakes. Cakes were fine until they went into the oven, as far as I was concerned, and then they were spoiled for good, done for.

Theory of eating

I had pretty much given up on the practice of eating, but Mum didn't stop educating me in the theory. She explained that the correct and best way of eating, which didn't apply to me for the time being because of my hands and so on, was to sum up the whole meal in each mouthful. So: suppose I was going to eat 1) Sausage, 2) Yorkshire

Pudding, 3) Roast Potato, 4) Garden Peas and 5) Gravy, first I would have to survey my plateful, assessing the elements at my disposal. The gentle art of eating started with the setting aside of a building area on the plate. This was why it was never correct to fill a guest's entire plate. Although it would not actually be wrong to assign the centre of the plate for this job, this course of action was less than ideal. A blank sector to one side of the plate was a better choice.

Then the job was to build an entire miniature meal on the convex side of the fork. Convex, not concave. If some of the food was awkward, for example peas, then a little mild mashing was allowed, but only as much as was needed to help the peas to stay in place while mouthful-building was completed. 'Why?' I asked. Why go to so much trouble? Because the delight of mixing is to take place in your mouth – as long as you don't open it for all the world to see.

Mum gave a demonstration, and it was fascinating to watch her at work. First she mashed and moulded a tiny piece of potato onto the rounded side of the fork. I guessed that this was to be her foundation, a moderately squashy substrate for the cornerstone of sausage which would still leave room for the addition of Yorkshire pudding in a small but unprocessed chunk. There must be room left for a bonnet of lightly crushed pea. I was fascinated to watch the whole edifice grow, tottering a little but never in serious danger of falling.

Finally it was time to crown the forkful with gravy. This was the moment of truth, a test of the cook as well as the diner. Mum carefully rested her loaded fork on the plate. A suitable puddle of gravy would be waiting to one side of the perfectly balanced forkful. Providing the gravy was properly viscous, she could coax it with a swoop of the knife against the urgings of gravity so that it ended up on the top of the potato-sausage-pudding-pea amalgamation as a savoury varnish.

'With practice it soon becomes possible', she told me, 'for one to have an intelligent conversation about something entirely different at the same time. While working in this way it should never appear that any particular effort is required. Food must always be incidental to the pleasures of conversation.' In this way her atomic theory of the forkful melted into a fantasy of gracious dining. In fact the whole little demonstration of microcosmic eating may have been the only meal I ever saw her eat without anxiety.

Mum had a cunning way of serving bananas. It wasn't so very long since bananas had become available again at all, and those with memories of rationing greatly prized the yellow fruit. Mum could hardly believe it when I showed no interest in a fruit so rare and distinctive, so curved to the eye and creamy on the tongue. There was no trace of the excitement I had shown before I was ill, snug in Dad's arms and seeing the yellow hands hanging from their hooks.

Then one day Mum tried again. She would never give up. She waved a banana in front of me and when I said I wasn't hungry, she said, 'This one is different. This is a special banana.'

I stayed silent just as long as I could, but curiosity was spreading over my body like a rash, as Mum had known it would. 'What's so special about it?'

'It's a magic banana.'

She had me. This was irresistible. 'What makes it magic?'

'What makes it magic, John, is that it's already in slices. Inside the skin. Just open it and you'll see.'

Already in slices inside its skin? Now I was in the palm of her hand. She held the banana where I could see it close up, and revolved it slowly so that I could see that there was no blemish on it of any kind. Finally, with me still watching very closely and ready to halt the operation if I saw anything at all fishy, she tugged on the hard stalk on the top of the banana until it broke open with an alarmingly definite noise. It was as if she had snapped the neck of a sleeping yellow bird. Then she peeled back a strip of skin, far enough to show me that she was telling the truth. The flesh was cut into even discs. I was baffled and thrilled. Impossible for the skin to have been peeled and then put back in place.

'Where did you get it? How did you do that?'

'Eat it and perhaps I'll tell you.'

'I won't eat it unless you tell me.'

'You'll have a long wait. *Patience is a virtue*,' Mum chanted, presumably re-hashing one of the many bitter lessons of her childhood, '*Virtue is a Grace. Grace is a little girl – who never washed her face.*'

The prestige of the magic banana was so great that Mum won an argument at last. I ate it. From then on magic bananas appeared at regular intervals, when my indifference to food became actively alarming. Mum knew how to keep the magic going, too. Sometimes she would produce a banana and I would ask, 'Is it a magic banana?' And she would say, 'I'm afraid not, John. This is just an ordinary banana. There weren't any magic ones in the shops. It's a very short season, you see.' And it sometimes happened, since human nature is perverse, that I would eat the ordinary banana anyway.

It was years before I learned how she did the slicing, and how she discovered the method in the first place. While I was in bed I obviously didn't attend parties, and my own birthday celebrations were muted to the point of inaudibility. But Mum had heard from a neighbour about a magician who performed at children's parties and had amazed everyone – the adults perhaps more than the children – with the banana trick. Mum managed to get his address and sent off a letter begging to be told the secret. She enclosed a ten-shilling note. A letter came back sharing the secret, but also returning the ten-shilling note. With all the heart-rending details she included in the letter, the return of the money was practically certain. Sometimes there are worse ways of getting what you want than her life-long technique of milking the world for the sympathy it contains.

The secret was laughably simple. All you need is a pin (needle, miniature bodkin). What you do – what Mum did – is to push the pin into the banana at one of the seams of the peel, and then work it back and forth until the improvised lever, pivoting where it enters the tougher tissue of the peel, has carved a slice through the flesh. Withdraw the pin, leaving no more trace than a pinprick, and repeat at intervals along the fuselage of the fruit. Abracadabra! Magic banana.

So much for food. Mum's training as a nurse helped her to deal resourcefully with a number of other difficulties. I couldn't use the lavatory, but the bedpan was a non-starter. I had to lift my bum from the horizontal to use it, and this was agony, so Mum devised a different method. She taught me to 'go' on my side, sissing into a bottle, tuppennying onto a kidney dish. Our teamwork improved, until every drop went into the bottle. The bladder-hooliganism of my earlier days had been properly tamed.

For a short time it was actually thrilling to be a baby again, praised and rewarded for a level of dependence that would have brought stern looks and impatient words only weeks before. But regression is an unstable pleasure, all the more so when no choice is involved.

The head of the bed was by the window, so I couldn't see outside, though I could hear things. Nature filtered in, but not in any form I could interpret. I could hear birds scuffling on my window-sill in the mornings. I thought of them as wrens, because of the farthing ashtray which I was sometimes allowed to hold and explore with my eyes. In ornithological fact they were almost certainly tits. Sometimes I would hear a big galumphing noise which could only be a stork depositing a baby under the gooseberry bush at the bottom of our garden, the little girl Mum had always wanted to make the family complete.

From a distance in time it's easy to say that Mum and Dad could have turned the bed round, the moment an indefinite sentence was passed on me, so that I could at least see out of the window, though my view from that angle would have been only sky. It wasn't even the bed that needed turning round, just the bedclothes. It wasn't a major engineering project. It could have been done in five minutes. Even so, I understand quite well why they didn't. Every adjustment to my new state was a step backwards for them. Turning the bed round would have made it harder to pretend that I was going to get up any time soon. I only had my situation. They had something much worse – knowledge of my situation. I was not their son in the way I had been, and there was nothing they could do to re-connect me with what they had lost.

If Dad was at home then of course the radio was his preserve. No one questioned his need to hear the news whenever it was on. If he was away, Mum would sometimes lug it in and set it up in my room. I liked listening to the *Billy Cotton Band Show*, though Mum thought Billy himself was very vulgar, and his opening cry of '*WAKEY WAKEY!*' really got on her nerves. It was the pronunciation that got her goat particularly. What Billy Cotton shouted was actually 'WHYky– WHY– *KEE!!*' and he stretched out the second 'WHY' so that it seemed to last for ever. I wonder if Mum guessed how much I loved it.

I was told not to move, and I was a good boy. I had to move something, and if it wasn't my body then it would have to be my mind. I learned my numbers. I got Mum to teach me to count to a hundred. Then I'd reel off the tally, time and time again. Counting up, counting down. Mum was very patient. She didn't baulk even when I upped the stakes and went as far as a thousand, not even sighing when I asked, 'What comes after a hundred, Mummy?' If I had known about times tables I would have made short work of them. I loved every little number. I didn't let her read the paper or do her sewing while I did my counting. I made her say, 'Very good, John,' or 'Correct!' after every single number. I made her concentrate on me absolutely. She was never allowed to be off duty.

Mum would soothe me by brushing my hair. As a special treat she would use Dad's brush, a Mason Pearson with no actual handle, a military oval of manly grooming, the bristles set in a bed of dark pink rubber. My own brush was softer but conveyed no electrical tingle to the scalp. Sometimes she would leave Dad's brush with me when she left the room. On some primitive level it seemed wrong that my hairbrush had a handle and his didn't.

When she was out of the room, counting lost its interest, and I explored the few movements I was allowed, things that didn't count as moving. There were various activities that could be managed while lying perfectly still, as the doctor had ordered. It counted as keeping perfectly still as long as you didn't move any bones. There were no bones in eyes, for instance. I rolled my eyes until I felt a sort of dizziness, although I was flat on my back and there was no danger of falling. I could fool myself I was falling while remaining perfectly still. I learned to cross my eyes. I practised breathing in different ways, concentrating on one nostril, for instance, at the expense of the other.

A Great Big Figgieman

Some of the rules of the house were suspended in my interest. If I retrieved a crumb of snot and rolled it between my fingers, Mum would pretend not to notice. Talk about making your own entertainment! The privilege of my situation, in which boredom lay so close to over-excitement that there was hardly any space between, was that snot qualified as a toy. The home word for such a crumb was Figgieman. In the days before I was bed-bound, Mum would say, 'I can see a Great Big Figgieman!' in a tone of ominous triumph. When my life thinned out, she just looked the other way and let me get on with it. She took pity on my dirty little ways, even when I accumulated a whole gallery of waxy snowballs. When they dried out I would flick them at the wall when nobody was looking, or else amalgamate them into one revolting whopper with a little supplementary spit.

My tongue was a rich source of games. I would tickle the roof of my mouth with its tip. It didn't quite make me burst out laughing, but it brought laughter to mind. Anybody who says that tickling yourself is impossible, and that the sensation depends on someone else doing it, hasn't tried tickling of this type. It's not perfect but it works, and that made it a precious game for me then.

Then I stuck my tongue out and started rotating it very slowly at full extension, feeling the wet trail I left on my chin or my cheeks or the groove above my lips as it slowly evaporated. I learned to touch my nose with my tongue, gradually improving its flexibility. I discovered for myself that the tongue is a muscle, by straining it. Then it was back to eye work for a while. When the speaking muscle had recovered, I would combine the eye-rollings and the tongue sweep, sometimes synchronising the movements, sometimes making them contrary, even contrapuntal. When Mum came into the room and surprised me while I was engrossed in my little theatre of grimaces, she was shocked. She thought I was having a seizure. A fit, on top of all her troubles. Even then I understood that they were her troubles.

Mum was my jailer, but she was also the Entertainments Officer, even the Escapes Officer. It was her responsibility to see that I didn't break the rules of my confinement, but also to fill my time with any amusement small enough to be smuggled between its bars. On top of which she was necessarily my fellow prisoner, though there was no one to organise entertainments for her.

Once she brought the local bobby to pay me a visit. He was wonderful in his uniform. She left us alone, after warning him not to sit on the bed. He said I'd been in the wars, hadn't I? I said that I had – in fact I was still in the wars.

He said to keep my chin up and called me 'sonny'. He let me hold his whistle. I blew down it for all I was worth, without asking permission in case he said no. Mum came running – her heart was in her mouth, she said. But then her mouth was where her heart mostly lived.

Metaphysical teeth

In my spare time I invented a game I called Teeth. All my time was spare. This was the opposite of the eye and tongue games, and more sophisticated. Teeth was metaphysical. It involved keeping still a body part that wasn't actually under the ban on movement. I suppose I was asserting a sort of freedom by adding a voluntary freezing to the one that was imposed from outside. I put my teeth together lightly, not grinding them but just letting the tips rest on each other, and let them grow together in my mind and become huge. My teeth turned into a sort of cave, and I could disappear inside it, clenched inside myself. Escaping to the interior, knowing that nobody in the family home would ever know what had happened to me. Once again Mum was worried by my frozen state, and even called the doctor in. There seemed to be nothing, in the narrow range of activities that was left to me, that couldn't be interpreted as a symptom. Any behaviour on my part might be the prelude to a crisis.

I spent a lot of time looking at the yellow roses on the wall. They were a comfort and a temptation. By crossing my eyes I could make one flower coincide with its identical neighbour, and so produce the optical illusion of space opening up. I knew I was supposed to keep absolutely still, but squirming didn't count. When I was only inches away from the wall and the yellow roses, I would cross my eyes so that the wall seemed to recede, leaving the flowers floating. Then I would slowly, naughtily, reach out a finger, and come up short, prevented from entering the space that my mind could see and yearn for.

When I gazed at the yellow roses and let them float freely while the background colour of the wallpaper fell away I was scratching primitively towards transcendence, towards an understanding of the unreality of what surrounds us. The experience was at that stage desolating, and I turned against it. One day I tore the wallpaper away from the wall, at the edge of a seam. After that it wasn't possible to superimpose two flowers and open up a space that wasn't there, since the torn and curling strip broke the illusion. I knew I was being naughty when I tore the paper: I waited for punishment but none came. It gave no pleasure that illness kept me safe from disgrace. I had the evidence of my crime permanently close, and that was punishment enough. For the time being it put paid to any mystical inklings.

It may have been partly for the protection of the wallpaper that one day the bed was moved away from the wall, like the ones in a hospital, so that I could be attended to from both sides. This was a milestone of more significance for the carers than the patient, and not just because it made their tasks easier. It defined me actively as an invalid, rather than someone who happened to be ill without an end in sight.

Blizzard of attachments

In the meantime, the long meantime, even Peterkin wasn't allowed on the bed, small as he was, light as he was. He would inevitably jump up and down, and cause me pain without meaning to. Until I was sentenced to bed rest he might just as well have been a made-up creature. I had tyrannised the poor soul, with no thought of his having a life outside the parts I made him play. The age gap, seventeen months, was just right to set him on a track of slavish devotion to the first-born, and to delay the time that he learned to know better. Only when I was immobilised and Peter was out of my power did I begin to absorb the fact of his separateness. Before then he had only been a small (and reversible) step up from imaginary, as far as I was concerned.

He had been another person all along, potentially a sidekick rather than a rival, an asset not a liability, but in my infant egotism I hadn't thought of that. Luckily he hadn't lost his desire to please me, and would bring in treasures from the garden that was now his exclusive domain.

I hadn't noticed him enough to feel threatened before I was ill, and we weren't in direct competition even now. The prisoner in his bed, having his meals brought in on trays, cajoled into eating each modest mouthful, and the toddler in the high chair left to feed himself, could hardly resent each other. There was none of the enforced sharing that brands brotherhood on the older party. It's the appropriated toy that does the damage. The loved object forges a bitter bond, when it turns up missing an ear. The favourite comic is the culprit, defaced with an alien crayon. It's the blocked path to the breast, usurper smugly at suck. None of this applied to us as brothers. Fashions in motherhood played a part in the area last mentioned. By the time Peter came along, Mum had been persuaded that bottle was best. The nipple remained my symbolic possession even when I'd been weaned from it.

Peter would come to see me but keep on the other side of the room, as if any closer approach would be too stimulating for me. He would wave at me rather solemnly, from the far side of the crevasse which divides the sick from the well. Some days he would steal up to me with his hand clenched, and then open it to reveal one of his toy soldiers, which he would slip between the sheets with me where Mum wouldn't see, before trotting off to explore his wider world. He was leaving one of his troops with me as a sort of hostage, a kindness which almost made me forget my stubborn lack of interest in games of conflict. Normally the only soldiers I liked were the ones to be dipped in my egg.

I wish I could claim that illness sheltered me from the blizzard of attachments, so that I freely recognised Peter's claims to equality, but it isn't so. Later on I would have to invent techniques to hold onto my dominance, but for the time being Mum belonged to me without question. I was her priority. Silence on my part could bring Mum to my side at least as quickly as Peter's cries could draw her to his.

Sometimes Mum read to me, poems and stories. All my time was bed-time and every story was a bed-time story. More than once she read me a poem about a little girl who didn't eat properly. She grew thinner and thinner until she was as thin as a piece of paper. Mum read it in the ominous tones suitable for a cautionary tale:

> Oh, she was so utterly utter!
> She couldn't eat plain bread-and-butter,
>> But a nibble she'd take
>> At a wafer of cake,
> Or the wing of a quail for her supper.
> Roast beef and plum-pudding she'd sneer at,

A boiled leg of mutton she'd jeer at,
   But the limb of a frog
   Might her appetite jog,
Or some delicate bit that came near that.
The consequence was, she grew paler,
And more wishy-washy, and frailer,
   Ate less for her dinner,
   Grew thinner and thinner,
Till I really think,
If you marked her with ink,
   Put an envelope on her,
   And stamped it upon her,
You could go to the office and mail her!

Perhaps this was her way of blackmailing my appetite, on days when I was sated by half a boiled egg, or a quarter, or a single teaspoonful, days when I was disenchanted even with magic bananas.

Something in my character stopped the poem from working on me as Mum must have hoped. At first when she recited the poem and added at the end, 'You wouldn't want that to happen to you, now *would* you?' I was terrified by the thought. But as the days inched by, the fascination of the idea grew on me in secret. Then when Mum said, 'You wouldn't want . . .' at the end of the reading, I whispered 'Oh no!' but I was secretly infatuated. The idea of dwindling to nothing held a strong attraction for me, which I now see as the magnetic pull of austerity in a previous life.

There was one story that made us both weep: Paul Gallico's *Snowflake*. There was plenty of food for Hindu thought in that story of transformation and essence, if I'd noticed, but I took my cue from Mum and wept. How sad and how beautiful it was, the story of the little Snowflake and her pear-shaped water drop of a husband, her progress from snow bank to river to millstream to estuary to the sea. And however much the Snowflake was jostled or scalded, she was aware of a backdrop of love. When Mum reached the end of the story, her voice vibrated in a way I had never heard before.

Eight physical signs

Here the story reached out and held hands with the poem about the girl who dwindled to nothing. The idea of simply evaporating from life was exquisitely beautiful. Its tingle gripped me from head to toe. We were both of us melting in sympathy with the fated life cycle of H_2O. As Snowflake's life ended the Sun said to her, 'You have done well, little Snowflake. Come home to me now.' We felt the hairs on the back of our necks standing on end, the very shiver of divinity. Without any idea of what was going on, we were visited by four of the eight physical signs of the presence of God. Horripilation (specifically *nirvikalpa samadhi*, the horripilation that precedes enlightenment), trembling, tears, faltering of the voice. The other signs of divine presence being perspiration, changing of body colour, inability to move (even the limbs), holy devastation. I really appreciate having a technical vocabulary for religious states. It's one of the great advantages that Hinduism has. When you think about it, there are sodding great holes in the Christian descriptions. Even Paul Gallico, if he had witnessed the glory-babble of Pentecost or St Teresa hovering in the chapel on jump-jets of grace, would have struggled to put it across without a precise vocabulary to hand.

I pestered Mum to get other books by Paul Gallico from the library, and she came back with *The Snow Goose*. I hated it, perhaps because it was about war. It was also full of dialect, oddly written out, along the lines of 'We was roustin' on the beach between Dunkirk an' Lapanny, like a lot o' bloomin' pigeons on Victoria Hembankment, waitin' for Jerry to pot us. 'E potted us good too. 'E was be'ind us an' flankin' us an' above us. 'E give us shrapnel and 'e give us H.E., an' 'e peppers us from the bloomin' hatmosphere with Jittersmiths.' Mum couldn't seem to extract the desired accent from this orgy of apostrophes, and we both felt that it wasn't proper writing somehow.

We went back to *Snowflake* any number of times, and it always affected us the same way. Mum and I had a strange taste of that sublime state in which the ego melts, to return as a shadow if it returns at all. On the basis of that one little book, Paul Gallico is a great magus and swami, and that's flat. The image of death as a merging resonates so deeply. People understand that the drop merges with the ocean, but they sometimes forget that the ocean also merges with the drop.

Mum would sometimes leave *Snowflake* or another book with me when she'd finished reading. I would take it under the bedclothes, understanding that this was a more precious hostage even than Peter's toy soldier. A boy who was only allowed to move his head and his hands wouldn't long resist the lure of print.

My favourite book at that time didn't have words at all. It was a book of *What I Want to Be When I Grow Up*. It had pictures of various professional uniforms and styles of dress, each with a cut-out circle where the head should be. Mum had mounted a picture of my face at the back of the book, so that I could see myself looking proudly up through a porthole cut in all the pages of rôles and careers. She must have done that before I was ill. I was always excited by the obvious uniforms, soldier sailor policeman, but I was more deeply drawn to the curative, investigative or spiritual professions: doctor, scientist, priest.

Engine of hope

It was in those days that I started talking to God, making prayers. Even the most selfish prayer is a little engine of hope. I prayed for small improvements rather than drastic transformations. At a time when I could only squirm from one side of the bed to the other, I'd pray that some day I'd be able to inch from one side of the room to the other. That would be enough for me. No sense in being greedy.

When Mum wasn't reading to me, she would look at the fire. I could understand her fascination when the gas was lit, with my own pyrolatry so incandescent. I liked the way the honeycombed panels behind the grille glowed orange and pink as they grew hot, and held those wonderful colours, yearningly, nostalgically, for a long moment after the flame was extinguished. Perhaps I had a memory-inkling that *nirvana* in Sanskrit means the state of having been extinguished or snuffed – otherwise it's a mystery that I should have been happy to see the fire I loved so much die down. Nirvana isn't 'extinction' with all its ominous overtones, more an extinguishment (an indispensable word I've just made up) welcomed by the flame. But Mum would sit

42

there for what seemed like hours on a warm evening, with her knitting on her knee unthought-of, looking at the fire when the honeycombed panels were pale and dead.

One of the games I played, Itches and Scratches, needed another player – Mum. It was fun, though the itch could often get out of hand. Any itch I had was likely to be in a part of the body I couldn't reach, and I would have to ask Mum to scratch it. Having the itch scratched was sheer Heaven, but it wouldn't be long before another itch broke out, and then Mum would have to scratch that one also. After three or four such itches, I seemed to be itching all over and would be wondering whether the game was so much fun after all.

Sometimes the game took on a new twist. It would happen that when I had an itch and Mum came to scratch it, the itch wasn't affected in the slightest. Then Mum said, 'Shall we try scratching bits of your body which don't itch at all? Somewhere quite different.' I could do a certain amount of scratching myself, and I discovered that if there was an itch somewhere on my right leg near the foot, then scratching part of my left arm completely cured it. The same trick only worked less well on the other side because I found it harder to scratch my right arm. What's more, the phantom itch, when treated by remote control in this way, was much less likely to break out again.

I pestered Mum to tell me how this piece of body magic worked. She said she didn't really know, but I could ask Dr Duckett next time he called. Dr Duckett was the local doctor, portly and fierce of eyebrow. He smelled of the little cigars he smoked, pungent little things. Weren't they called Wills Whiffs? They were certainly whiffy. Once I heard Dad say, 'Why can't he smoke cigarettes, like a normal doctor?', not meaning a joke.

Dr Duckett was a very good explainer. He thought for a moment after I asked him about the itches and then said, 'John, you know how sometimes a light bulb has two switches, on different sides of the room?'

'Oh yes!' I had always been fascinated by such things.

'If you turn on a switch near the door, the ceiling light comes on. Yet you could turn off the same light' (well, I couldn't, couldn't have reached even if I was allowed out of bed, but I had seen it done) 'by using a different switch right over on the other side of the room.

43

Well, itching is to do with nerves, and in a way nerves are the body's "wiring". The wiring of the body is a much more complicated business than the wiring of a house, but sometimes you can put your finger on an itch-switch in a place you wouldn't expect.'

Dr Duckett gave me so much to think about. No wonder I loved him. I decided that I'd try to understand house wiring as soon as possible. In the meantime I marvelled at the thought of all those little wires running through my body carrying every sort of command. Most of my wires, barring the odd sparky fluke, were connected properly and working well. I didn't need to think of myself as completely ill. It was only part of me that was ill. I was partly well.

One day I would have a house of my own, a cheerful house much more colourful and full of life than the one I was stuck in now. I would have a house built entirely to suit my needs. I talked about it with Mum. She warned me that planning a house was a lot of work, and I was grateful for her ideas, but I made a secret alteration to her suggestions. When it really happened I wasn't going to hire an electrician. I knew someone who would do it so much better. All the wiring was going to be done by Dr Duckett.

Dad was away a lot. It wasn't a priority for the forces to give young fathers time at home. They weren't feather-bedded. Sometimes he would send postcards, usually of æroplanes, but one he sent me was of a restaurant somewhere abroad. On the back he'd written:

> Ate here last night. Funny sort of place. None of the plates
> matched, none of the cups belonged with their saucers. Saw a
> beautiful green praying mantis trying to escape by the window,
> tho'. Right up your street. Love Dad.

He knew I liked everything that crept and crawled.

'Love' wasn't part of Dad's normal vocabulary, but he seemed to be able to write it down, though he did have to be abroad for the trick to work. As if the very word was in a foreign language, the custom of another country. A body of water had to intervene between us before the risk could be taken, the words 'love' and 'Dad' brought into startling proximity.

Dad wasn't away all the time, and my nose was sensitised, even through several closed doors, to the strongly medicated smell of his beloved Wright's Coal Tar Soap. In the flesh he could sometimes show a muted tenderness. I remember him sitting in my room once, resplendent in his uniform, and I couldn't take my eyes off him. Mum asked me, 'What do you want? Is there anything you want?' I couldn't say anything. Five times she asked me, and I wouldn't speak. I just shook my head. Finally she knelt by the bed and leaned over so that her ear was near my mouth. I could smell her hair. Even so, a whisper was too loud for what I wanted and I wanted to put my hand over my mouth when I made the whisper. 'I'd like to sit on Daddy's lap.' And very gently she picked me up and carried me over to my daddy and lowered me onto his lap. Gingerly he put his arms around me. I stayed there for a minute or two. I could feel a faint bunching in the muscles of his thighs, first one and then the other, as if he was suppressing an impulse to rock me. To dandle his first-born. It was absolute Heaven, to rock on the big warm muscles I didn't yet know were called quadriceps.

The waiting-room pounce

He was away the first Christmas I was ill, and Mum had a guest, a young Canadian airman. Jim Shaeffer. He had hairy wrists, and he brought presents of an extreme generosity.

I don't know how to account for Jim Shaeffer's presence at that Christmas. I assume he was a contact of Dad's, and there may have been charity involved in the invitation. But was it Mum who was showing charity, by taking a stranger in for the festival, or Jim Shaeffer, persuaded to offer the stricken mother a shoulder to cry on? If it was Jim, he made a good job of it.

I resisted him to some extent, partly because he called Mum 'Ma'am' not 'Mrs Cromer'. It was too close to my own name for her – it seemed to place us in competition. I was sensitised to male presence anyway, in Dad's absences. If anyone was going to be tall, if anyone was going to make a glass vibrate with the low register of his voice, it was supposed to be Dad.

Mum brought a couple of upright chairs into my room, and she and Jim had a glass of sherry together there. The Christmas tree had been put up in my room for a change. I had wanted an enormous tree, right up to the ceiling, but Mum had pointed out that we didn't really have many decorations, and a tall tree would just look bare. Better to settle for a smaller tree properly dressed. She was right, and in any case the real pleasure of the tree came from its smell of outdoors.

I expect the sherry in the little glasses had a dusty taste from being opened the Christmas before and not drunk since. Jim hadn't wrapped the presents he brought. I imagine he'd been told I wasn't allowed to exert myself, even to the extent of fiddling with paper, but still he'd given thought to presentation. There was a proper grown-up gramophone, covered in snakeskin. This was already a wonderful gift – it would have been generous as a gift to Mum, let alone me – but he had gone one better by putting a further present inside it, so that even the gramophone became a wrapper for something else. He'd filled the inside of the gramophone with sweets. Even better: not 'sweets' but *candy* – thrilling alien sugar treats, when I had had little enough exposure to the British varieties. While the sweetness flooded my mouth, Mum started to unload her tragic troubles on Jim. Though I gazed at the Christmas tree in a sort of trance, I was familiar with what Mum was doing.

It was quite in character for Mum to recruit a stranger to share her griefs, spilling secrets and living off all the sympathy she could cadge. Chatting about her problems was a deeply ingrained habit, even before she had any problems to speak of. When I was a healthy toddler, she hadn't hesitated to use me as bait.

Later she specialised in the waiting-room pounce, reaching mothers through their little ones. She had a fixation with babies, not entirely because they couldn't keep her at a distance. Her love for small children wasn't put on, it was perfectly genuine (and the younger the better), but she knew the strategic value of baby-worship. Mothers with babies couldn't keep her at bay so easily, and once a tiny finger was curled round one of her own she was there for the duration. Then it would all come out: how lucky they were to have a normal healthy child. The mothers wouldn't quite have the nerve to grab their babies and run. They were stuck with the long sad story.

She was a classic Heather type, as defined by the system of the great Bach. I know there are other contenders for the title of 'the great Bach', but as far as I'm concerned J.S. can't hold a candle to Dr Edward, the father of modern herbalism. If it came to a choice between the *Well-Tempered Preludes and Fugues* and the *Twelve Healers* of 1933, I'm afraid I wouldn't hesitate. In my book, the 'Twelve' are worth ten of the forty-eight.

The Bach guide sums it up perfectly, though Heather wasn't actually one of the Twelve Healers in the original book. There were sequels which added nuances to the system of remedy and character type. *HEATHER: Those who are always seeking the companionship of anyone who may be available, as they find it necessary to discuss their own affairs with others, no matter whom it may be. They are very unhappy if they have to be alone for any length of time.*

There's more up-to-date wording in one of the newer manuals, which lists positive aspects as well as negative. The positive aspects are: *A selfless, understanding person. Because of having suffered, is willing to listen and help. Can be absorbed in other's problems and is unsparing in efforts to assist.* That's Mum on a good day. It's just that she didn't have very many good days. The negative description runs: *'Obsessed' by ailments, problems and their trivia. Always wanting to tell others about them, and about themselves. Sometimes weepy. Comes close – speaks close into your face – 'button-holers'. Saps vitality of others, consequently is often avoided. Dislikes being alone. Makes mountains out of molehills. A poor listener – has little interest in problems of others.* That's more like it. That's the Mum I knew.

She wasn't obsessed with ailments in the sense of being a hypochondriac – or rather, the element of hypochondria in her wasn't to do with illness, exactly. It took the form of superstitiousness, which is really only a hypochondria of the spirit. Superstitiousness is entirely self-defeating. In Mum's case, it did the opposite of what it was supposed to. It sealed in the dread it was devised to seal out.

So for instance she had the wooden outline of a magpie on the kitchen window-sill. It was her insurance policy against bad luck. If she ever saw a single magpie – 'for sorrow' – she could interpret it as really being a pair with the one on the window-sill. Two for joy. The old formula, tipping your hat to Mr Magpie. That's superstition for you.

Of course it's not mathematically possible to see two magpies as often as you see one, so the odds are stacked against joy. The wooden magpie was there so that she could cheat. She could tip her hat to joy, not sorrow, when there was just the one magpie in the garden. She managed not to notice that her little stratagem had installed a sorrow-bearing magpie right inside the house. If the wooden cut-out could count as a magpie for a second, then it was a magpie always. Despite her best efforts, sorrow was the resident emotion, joy the visitor that caught her unprepared. It came close to frightening her with the clap of its wings.

Incabloc

That Christmas, Jim's lovely hairy hands held my attention even more than the baubles on the tree, but even at that age I knew you couldn't just say, 'I like your hands. Your hands are nice.' It wasn't a possible thing. He was wearing a watch, though, so I asked him what time it was.

In its way this was a trick question. Jim said, 'It's five twenty-five,' and then I knew he wasn't as important as my dad. My dad always said, 'I make it five twenty-five.' That was his power. He made the time, and Jim only told it. But I said I liked Jim's watch, so he wouldn't feel bad – and after all the watch was near the hairy hands. I didn't so much covet the watch as envy it for its closeness to the hairy hands. Then Jim Shaeffer said, 'It's yours, pal. Happy Christmas!'

Mum looked shocked, and said something about it not being possible – it was just too much. Of course she was right, but I saw my chance and said, 'I have a birthday in two days' time! It could be a birthday present.' Why shouldn't the unfortunate timing of my birth work in my favour for once, enriching the harvest of presents? Instead of bilking me out of them in the usual way, when people made one gift do double duty.

So Jim said, 'Happy Birthday then!' I held my breath. I couldn't imagine I would get away with it. Miraculously, Mum didn't scold me for my greed and the generous impulse was allowed to stand, even

if she was quietly embarrassed by it. I still have that watch somewhere, though it doesn't run properly. Incabloc. But I do wonder
what he would have given me if I'd said straight out that I liked his
hands.

There was something wrong about that Christmas which I dimly
noticed even at the time. There were too many presents, for one thing,
which should have rung a warning bell, if not a full-change Treble
Bob Major. Normally Mum was very definite about the risk of children being spoiled. In that she was a mother of her time.

It was long afterwards that I realised Mum was taking the brakes
off the giving for a reason. Not because she was playing a part in front
of someone she wanted to impress, or too shy to over-rule a guest. The
hectic giving had a simpler cause. I had lost a lot of weight and
seemed to be more or less fading away. Mum thought I was dying and
wouldn't see another Christmas. She relaxed the rules so as to make it
really happen, not just as a figure of speech, that all my Christmases
came at once. There was still just time for me to die spoiled, now that
the damage it would do to my character didn't matter so much.

Mellow fraud

There was a record that Jim gave along with the gramophone that
Christmas which we played again and again. It may have been a present for Mum, but it stayed in my room with the gramophone. This
was a strange piece of music, it seemed to me, with at its centre a
sound that was grotesquely rounded, obscenely comforting. I was told
that it was Mozart's Clarinet Concerto, and I'm sure it's a masterpiece
from first to last. And I liked the advantage it gave me, later in life,
of knowing it was Con-chair-toe without being told, rather than Con-
sir-toe. But it soaked up too much of the hysterical mood of that
Christmas, all that terrible going-on-as-normal while things were
falling apart. Whenever people came near me, I got electric shocks
from their fear, though they seemed to imagine they were reassuring
me.

I've never really taken to the clarinet as an instrument – all that
mellowness is a fraud, as far as I'm concerned. The first person to pick
up a clarinet sucked up a syrup of lies right up into the mouthpiece,

and from then on no one's been able to get a truthful note out of it.

The watch, though, was marvellous. I had plenty of time to get to know it in detail during the weeks after Christmas. Below the twelve o'clock mark on the dial it said RELIDE, with a swash 'R' which travels as an underline through ELIDE to the end. Then in small caps it said WATERPROOF and under that INCABLOC, also small caps. Then above the 6 it said AUTOMATIC, also small caps. On the left side of the 6 below it said SWISS and on its right MADE. Best of all, best till last, it said 25 JEWELS in *red* small caps, below AUTOMATIC and above the 6.

This bit was utter magic. Mum said the best watches were Swiss, and they had real jewel bearings. I imagined diamonds, rubies and sapphires spinning away under the bonnet of the machine, winking as they worked. It was also such a clever present for Jim to give. I couldn't say 'I like your hands' to Jim, but I could think it, and he had read my mind and made his reply by giving me jewels.

The grown-up watch looked funny on my wrist, with a new hole made in the strap a long way from the ones punched in it when it was made. I didn't mind the way it looked. Most things were either too big or too small or too high or too low or too hard or too soft for me, which was partly why I loved the story of the Three Bears. In real life something exactly the right size for me would actually have looked wrong.

Another way in which it was a really clever present was the AUTO-MATIC bit. You had to shake it to wind it. When you shook it and listened really carefully you could hear a tiny rasping sound. The watch thrilled me, and it seduced Mum into over-ruling herself twice. First when she let me keep it, and then when she said I must keep it well wound, entirely forgetting that I wasn't supposed to move at all.

To start with I had to take the watch off and pull the winder out with my teeth if I wanted to change the time. The winder was a little stiff in the beginning, but I spent so much time playing with it that it loosened soon enough. I wore the watch on my left wrist, because the right elbow still had a bit of play in it and I wanted the freedom to fiddle with it, but this arrangement had a practical flaw. There wasn't enough motion in my left wrist to keep it charged. Without movement from the elbow I couldn't get a decent wrist-flick going.

The watch was only properly self-winding when it was on the arm with the decent range of movement, so every day I would have it swapped to the other wrist for some gentle shaking to prevent it dying in the night, when its presence and its ticking were most comforting. On my abnormally restricted wrist the automatic winding mechanism, which was supposed to be so blissfully simple, actually took a certain amount of work, but it was well worth it. The Relide watch was luminous, and the radium markers on its dial glowed beautifully in the dark. Whenever I opened my eyes in the night, the figures and the hands shone with a steadfast glow.

After Christmas I was no better physically, but I started to show signs of a new mental strength. This manifested itself as asking the same question again and again. The questions I wanted answered were, 'If my new gramophone is covered with snakeskin, then what happened to the snake? Did it mind having its skin taken off? Was it a giant snake, to stretch so wide?' I wouldn't leave these matters alone. Mum said that many snakes had gone into the cover, not just one giant. That made the middle question even more urgent. I saw an entire clan of snakes in my mind, mum and dad, grannies and grandads, aunties and uncles all living perfectly happily together, and then some man comes along and kills them all and turns them into my gramophone.

I really upset myself. I was fretting as well as wasting away. Mum had to work hard to reassure me. She said soothingly, 'They didn't kill any snakes, JJ.' She'd started calling me JJ. It began about then. 'When they have to get bigger, snakes just crawl out of their old skin and leave it behind.' I cheered up mightily, relieved that there was no blood-guilt on my Christmas present. I sucked the sweet lie right up, no better than a clarinet. No one was telling me the truth about important things at this point. Everything from Christmas to my gramophone was wrapped in a nasty secret.

It's entirely in character that I don't remember Peter at all from that Christmas. Years later I asked him if he remembered Jim Shaeffer, the nice Canadian airman who came for Christmas, but the name didn't ring a bell with him. He remembered me being given the gramophone and the watch, though, when all he got out of it was a handful of sweets. Even so, he wasn't a neglected child in any real sense, except by me. Mum smacked him a fair amount, but smacking isn't exactly neglect.

Perhaps it was Dad's choice to be away that hectic Christmas, but I doubt if he had any say in the matter. He was often away for as long as a month at a time, and the armed forces didn't go in much for compassionate leave in those days. Even if they had, I imagine Dad would have preferred not to ask for it. It would have been more in character for him not to ask for special treatment. That was very much a virtue to his generation's way of looking at things.

With the help of herbalist hindsight, potent tincture, it's pretty plain that Dad was a Cerato, which is one of the original Twelve Healers of 1933 and a fundamental character type. His buried keynote was indecisiveness. Surprising in a military man, or perhaps not. Where better to hide an inability to choose than in a chain of command? In the forces decisions are handed down, and servicemen are routinely relieved of the burden of initiative.

It's mysterious that this fundamentally lukewarm soul should attach itself to a long line of strong believers – preachers and pastors – whose only previous aberration was a fairly distinguished Victorian architect, his piety well up to par.

When Dad was a young man his own father kept quizzing him about whether he had yet been visited by Jesus the Christ, as if this was positively a stage of adolescence, the spiritual equivalent of starting to shave. Dad had to admit that no such visitation had been granted him.

Of course they aren't all sheep in the armed forces. There are occasional mavericks, and one of them was his friend Kit Draper, the one he'd wanted to middle-name me after. Hence Draper's nickname: the Mad Major. Yet even Dad's worship of this senior airman (who had seen action in the First War as well as the Second) didn't break the pattern. *Has tendency to imitate* is also part of the herbalist picture. Dad admired the Mad Major for daring to break the rules, but didn't even get as far as imitating him. He just muttered, 'Good old Kit. *He* showed them.' Kit Draper did his rebelling for him, at a safe remove.

Promiscuous sympathy

In daily life Dad hated to be asked to make choices, and the more trivial the alternatives with which he was presented the less he was able to choose between them. The rolling incompatibility that was my parents' marriage can be described in many ways, but one of them is herbalistic. They were a Heather and a Cerato bound together, one sapping the other's vitality by demanding sympathy, the other sapping right back by needing to be told what to do. The whole situation was made worse by the fact that he had no sympathy to give her, and so she sought it promiscuously elsewhere. He, of course, as a man of his time, would happily take advice from a male acquaintance, however slight, but never from his wife.

Tempting to say that if someone had been there to administer the relevant tinctures, those four drops in water four times a day, they could both have been brought into the positive ranges of their characters, so that Mum could sympathise with the uncertainty that Dad tried so hard to hide, and he in turn could tap into the large-scale emotions which she could bestow as well as demand. But I chose the womb as it was and must accept the life it led to, without getting out my portable dispensary of herbalist hindsight to tamper with the givens.

I myself seem to be a Vine, another secondary character type, as infallibly sketched by Dr Bach, when he came to round up the stragglers after the Twelve: *they think that it would be for the benefit of others if they could be persuaded to do things as they themselves do, or as they are certain is right . . . Even in illness they will direct their attendants . . . may be of great value in emergency.* The layman's term, I suppose, would be bossy-boots.

I had been patient for a long time, but now I was beginning to chafe against the restrictions of my bed-bound life. Mum had to step up her efforts at diversion without excitement.

Abstraction of wrestling

When children are very young, their parents find styles of rough play that won't cause any harm. If one adult hand is pushing against the chest of a delighted toddler, the other arm is poised behind his back, ready to catch him when he falls. The joy of play is intensified by a tiny infiltration of pretend-fear, pretend-risk. Mum had a harder task when it came to rough-housing with me. She had to carry the risk-monitoring approach much further. My level of agitation had to be carefully measured. She would climb carefully onto the bed so that she could support herself on her elbows and knees, poised above me. Then she would blow on my face, shake her head so that her cheeks wobbled, make menacing noises in her throat, roar like a lion, and raise each hand from the bed alternately, to waggle her fingers thrillingly in front of my face.

The whole performance was a wonderful treat. I think we both forgot that this was an abstraction of wrestling, taken to such a stylised extreme that no physical contact was involved. It was closer to an art form like Noh drama than to actual rough-housing. Then one day while she was crouched over me like a tenderly devouring spider, her weight shifted on the bed, and that was enough to make my back click. The pain came shuddering and stabbing into the facet joints of the spine. The immobility of bed rest was encouraging my ligaments to weaken, so that tremors of the facet joints could happen more or less at any time. Mum climbed off the bed in slow motion, trying not to make things any worse, and weeping bitterly at the failure of our mime of normal fun. Even this charade of roughness was too close to the real thing. From then on we had to find other forms of game, less risky than horse-play even at its tamest.

Mum racked her brains to devise new pastimes for me. One huge treat was a candle set on a saucer. She gave me a knitting needle, which I used to heat up and poke into the wax. She kept the flame of my pyrolatry from flickering out in those dark times. Peter and I were even allowed, under close supervision, to hold scraps of food in the flame to toast them. It need only be a modest square of bread, toasted in the flame and then dipped in tomato sauce. We became adept little chefs, and produced quite a range of toy snacks. We wanted to feed Mum and Dad with our one-candlepower barbecue. It was our turn, after so long being looked after, to play host.

One day Mum said she had a surprise for me. When I asked what it was, she said I'd just have to wait and see. Otherwise it wouldn't be a surprise, now would it? She went out and I heard murmuring in the hall. She came back in. 'Shall I tell you what it is? Perhaps I better had.'

'No you mustn't. You said it was a surprise!'

'I know I did.' But she was having second thoughts, remembering the risks of over-excitement. What if it was all too much for me? So she whispered, to take some of the shock out of the scene she had engineered, 'It's a surprise *donkey*.' At last she called out, 'We're ready.'

It must have taken quite some organising. She must have persuaded or bribed a rag-and-bone man, or someone from a fair. A fair is more likely, I suppose, since the animal wore ribbons. There were rags tied round its hoofs so that the surprise wouldn't be given away by clops.

What I saw first was its master walking backwards into the room holding a parsnip and backing slowly towards me. He made clacking sounds of encouragement with his tongue against his teeth. He wore a hat, also with ribbons, which he swept off with an awkwardly dramatic gesture as the animal advanced into the room. I think his showmanship must have been cramped by the lack of space, the difficulty of steering a sizeable quadruped with a mind of its own. Under the hat he had bright red hair, worn rather long for the period.

The donkey was comfortably lower than the lintel, but almost too wide to fit through the door. There was a strong bodily smell which fascinated me. As they came nearer I realised that it came from the man and not the beast. The man manœuvred himself towards the bed and crouched down so that the donkey would be almost beside my head when it got its reward. I could smell the donkey now – it had an intense burnt smell, harsher than the whiff of bonfires. It reached down and took the parsnip with a series of astounding crunches. The man said, 'Want to pat him, sonny? He likes that ever so,' but my tensely smiling mother was already calling out, 'Better not, John.' As if the surrealist tableau she had laid on would be pushed over the edge by actual contact with the wonderful animal, into something that would squeeze my heart to bursting.

The man made slow shunting gestures with his hands. Again his tongue clacked against his teeth, and eventually the donkey backed out of the room. It left no trace of its visit except a little patch of drool on the worn carpet by my bed, which soon dried up. I would almost rather it had left one of its droppings, a shocking log or a scatter of pellets which my mother would have rushed to clean up, though I don't suppose it would have smelled any worse than horse-shit does, which is wholesome enough. At least that would have made the episode less like an apparition or a dream about a magic animal, about a clacking noise and a series of deafening crunches, about a man whose red hair I would have liked to touch at least as much as I would have liked to stroke his donkey.

I had few other visitors. I remember a troop of local children coming to sing their carols one Christmas – though not perhaps the first, the indelible Christmas of candy and gramophone, of hairy hands and suspect clarinet.

The carol singers would traipse round knocking on doors, singing their two carols alternately. 'Away in a Manger'. 'Hark the Herald'. They came into my bedroom and sang their whole repertoire to me, first one and then the other. They brought the cold in with them. There were six or eight of them, mostly girls. A great crowd in my room. They clustered round the bed, but they didn't look at me while they sang. Only a couple of the little ones, the ones closest to my age, couldn't resist lowering their eyes and sneaking a peek.

What had Mum said to them? Here's a few coppers for you, if you sing to my poorly boy, only be sure not to stare. It was a treat. It was certainly meant to be a treat.

They stood very near the bed. They breathed over me. Perhaps Mum was getting extra value out of her handful of coppers by asking them to expose my system to every bug that was going. She'd been a nurse, it was her way of thinking. Otherwise I would be a sitting duck for every cough and sneeze, if I ever managed to find my way back to the lively world of germs.

After so much under-stimulation, such a rationing of sensation, having this multitude burst into my room and sing at me was like an assault. It was a shock seeing runny noses and bright scarves, open mouths and chapped lips, all in a bunch and from close to, after so little variation of solitude. My heart raced and didn't slow down for a long time after they had gone.

It seems obvious in retrospect that I must have been bored, but boredom doesn't really describe my experience. Small events resounded with more significance than I knew what to do with, and attempts to vary my surroundings didn't always have the intended effect. When Mum brought some buds in from the garden and put them in a vase I found their presence on my bedside table disturbing. Some of the inflorescences fell off in a day or two, the little catkins, and they looked like slugs dusted with yellow powder. It wasn't the resemblance to slugs that bothered me (I'd always liked slugs) but the invasion of known space by an alien element. I was happier, perversely, with the unchanging roses on the wallpaper.

Only lightly agonised

Treats and surprises were one thing, but what my morale needed was some regular occasion to look forward to. Mum had enough nursing expertise to know how to forestall bedsores by changing my position, but my mind was always lying in the same dull trench of thought. It was agreed with Dr Duckett that one expedition per week, properly supervised, was compatible with the sentence of bed rest.

It wasn't much of an expedition. I only went as far as the hall. Our local grocer offered a delivery service, for which orders could be taken by telephone. It became my weekly treat to play a part in the chain of retail command. Mum would write out her list in diagram form, in the days before my reading became fluent. A sketch of two oblongs meant *Two pounds of potatoes please*. A red stick was *A pound of carrots*. Wiggly strips meant *A half of streaky bacon*. I even learned to understand the hieroglyph that meant *a quarter of field mushrooms if they're not too dear – ask how much*. Then Mum and 'the girl' would set me up on a chair, well supplied with cushions, only lightly agonised, within reach of the phone in the hall. Mum would hold the receiver while I relayed the family order into the cold black curve of the mouthpiece. I loved doing that, feeling that I was at the nerve centre of the household. I manifested a character trait for which there was little scope at the time, obscured by pathos on this first appearance. The desire to be useful.

How did Mum cope? How did she save her sanity? One of the things she did was to get a dog, a golden retriever, our lovely Gipsy. If Gipsy was company for Mum then she was a sort of nurse for me, just as Nana in *Peter Pan* is more nanny than dog. Golden retrievers are frisky, lolloping creatures, but Mum trained her to stay put on a chair next to my bed. I would only have to say, 'Hup!' and Gipsy would jump up onto her chair and curl up to watch over me. I couldn't really pet her. There's a picture of the two of us taken the year after I became ill. I'm terribly skinny – it's not surprising that Mum devoted so much energy to making me eat. I look like a monk on hunger strike. My face is like a worn-out mask, at the far end of life. Gipsy wears an expression of the most soulful worry. You would think she has just taken my temperature and is wondering when my fever will break. She slept in my room, adding her night voice to Mum's and Dad's. Every now and then she gave out a distinctive grunting sigh.

I remember one day when a neighbour came to call, bringing her own dog, a low-slung terrier. Gipsy jumped down from her chair and the two dogs went around in circles, sniffing each other's bottoms. They were of such different heights that they had to get into the strangest positions. I thought that was the funniest thing ever – I really laughed, but being careful not to let my head go back or my shoulders shake.

Afterwards I asked Mum what Gipsy was doing with that other dog. She explained that long ago all the dogs in the world went to a special party, and they hung up their bottoms on pegs as they arrived. But then there was a fire at the party and everyone left in a rush, taking any old bottom down from the pegs. And ever since then, dogs have sniffed each other's bottoms, trying to join up again with the lower half that had once been theirs. This fable says almost nothing about dogs, but it explains a great deal about Mum. During that fire alarm she might not even have looked for her bottom half. She would have managed without, and never looked back. Perfectly happy to wipe other people's bottoms as long as she wasn't expected to have one of her own.

Yet she often discussed my stools, with enthusiasm and technical knowledge. One day I asked, 'Why was my tuppenny black today?' I must have caught a glimpse of the kidney dish while she was carrying it away.

'That's because the doctor has been giving you iron. You need iron because you're anæmic.'

'Is it just iron that makes a tuppenny black?'

'No, charcoal does it too. I expect a piece of burnt toast would be enough . . .'

'Next time I have my half of boiled egg, can you burn the toast? I want to see if it makes my tuppenny go black.'

'Yes, but you must finish the iron tablets first.'

'Do tuppennies come in other colours?'

'Oh yes, many! Ever so many.'

'How do you know?'

'I saw many different colours of tuppenny when I was a nurse.'

'What colours did you see?'

'Babies do tuppennies that are yellow. Yours looked just like scrambled egg. And I've seen tuppennies that were red.'

'I bet you never saw a white tuppenny!'

'Oh but I did!'

'When?'

'I told you. When I was a nurse.'

'Was it a man's tuppenny or a lady's tuppenny?'

'I can't remember.'

'Why?'

'Because I just can't.'

'Why was the tuppenny white?'

'Because he'd had a barium meal.'

'What's a barium meal?'

'It's like porridge. You eat it and the next day they X-Ray your tummy and your botty so they can see if it's all right.'

'Have you had a barium meal?'

'No. But your granny has.'

'What did they see in Granny's tummy and botty?'

'Oh they were both fine.'

'Remember when you saw the white tuppenny?'

'Yes.'

'You said you didn't know whether it was a man's tuppenny or a lady's tuppenny.'

'No, and I don't.'

'But then you said, "Because *he'd* had a barium meal." So it must have been a man's tuppenny!'

'Then I expect that's what it was . . .'

'What do you mean, "*expect*"? You should *know*. You're supposed to know nearly everything. Well, I don't expect you to know *everything*, but if you remember the white tuppenny, you should certainly remember whether a man or a lady made it!'

'Yes, I should, shouldn't I? I would certainly have made the effort to remember if I'd known you were going to be so interested.'

'So was that the only white tuppenny you saw, or was there another one?'

'I can't remember . . .'

'Why ever not? When you saw a man's white tuppenny didn't you want to see a lady's white tuppenny as well?'

'No, not really.'

'Why?'

'Well I don't expect there'd be much difference really.'

I was learning to make a little conversation go a long way. Mum, meanwhile, was becoming increasingly resourceful in manipulating my appetite. If she could turn a conversation about black excreta into a piece of salesmanship for burnt toast she was well and truly getting the knack.

She knew when to give way about food, strategically. I started to insist that all I would eat was a teaspoonful of raw cake mix. She said she couldn't make such a small amount. I said why not? I might even eat two. I think she was beginning to be alarmed by my will-power. Immobility was the hallmark of my days, and now it seemed to be invading my character. So the next day she came in with half a dessertspoonful of raw cake mix. I wolfed it down.

Half-heartedly she warned me about the danger of worms but I wasn't put off. Why not feed them too? I couldn't believe that worms were nasty. The ones I could remember from the garden had seemed perfectly nice. She said they would tickle my botty from inside and make me want to scratch it. I quite liked this idea of having an itchy botty, but only if the reason was worms. I would want to be very sure that it was due to the presence of worms. Then I would want to see one, and keep it in a little dish for a while and then I would ask if I could feed it something else, or should I put it back into my botty to make it happy. Having something that enjoyed living in me seemed rather an honour. I would only take a worm-killer tablet if the worms got too itchy or bred too fast. First I would give them a good talking-to about how we should get along together, a worms' rule-book or Highway Code. If they were sensible and behaved themselves I saw no reason why we couldn't get along perfectly well together. I didn't tell these secret thoughts to Mum, but hoped that eating cake mix might give the opportunity of putting my theory into practice. I never even caught one worm. It was a great disappointment.

Tomato flotilla

Mum also knew when to go to town with the catering. Bomfire Night was a treat I could no longer attend. The family did without fireworks for the duration, though Gipsy and I could hear the whoosh of joy, the crackle of exhilaration, from other gardens than ours. Gipsy whined miserably and I did my best not to join in.

Still, Mum was shrewd enough to exploit my love of the fire festival to boost my intake of food. She had always made 'Scrambled Egg Boats' for Firework Night, and there was no reason to change the menu just because we weren't having any fireworks. Like many of her best and worst ideas, the recipe came from a magazine.

Mum hoarded the recipes from magazines, but was afraid to try them until she had scanned subsequent issues in search of corrections of misprints. She had once been tempted by a recipe for home-salted beef, only to read in a later issue that the amount of saltpetre required had been over-stated by a factor of ten, making it potentially toxic. We might all have been killed by a typographical error – except that I wouldn't have touched it. I alone would have been left alive, to charge *Woman's Own* with manslaughter by misprint.

Mum would make the scrambled egg in advance. Nearer to the time of serving she made toast, then buttered and trimmed the slices into a graceful curving point at one end. While the toast was under the grill she took fresh tomatoes (neither too firm nor too soft), quartered them and scooped out the innards. Taking each tomato quarter she cut them into narrower, more graceful wedges. These were the 'sails' of the Boats.

She spooned a dollop of scrambled egg, to which she'd added a few chopped chives and a dash of pepper, onto each shaped piece of toast, and then put an eviscerated tomato wedge on top of that, neatly attaching the sail to the buttery, scramble-freighted hull with the mast of a cocktail stick.

She came into my room with a whole flotilla of them, arranged in naval formation on a large plate balanced proudly on the upraised fingers of one hand. I didn't say no. The creamy egg and fresh tomato played such a lovely fanfare of aromas. Reluctantly I dismasted the savoury boat and wolfed down the ambrosial snack. The flavours danced and blended on the taste buds. Somehow the toast kept its crunch despite the moistness of the scramble.

The only shadow on the feast was my knowledge of the next day's menu. The innards scraped from the tomatoes in the process of sculpting the sails had to go somewhere, in those thrifty 'fifties. In the wake of those delicious boats the abomination that was stuffed marrow, that dismal barge, would be slowly surging towards me.

Stuffed marrow was as disgusting as the Scrambled Egg Boats had been delightful. It wasn't the tomato innards that I minded but the mince part of the stuffing. That I wouldn't eat. Fasting was a doddle when you knew in advance it was going to be marrow for lunch, and could prepare yourself. The treat was balanced by the going without. I didn't consciously thwart Mum's plans to feed me up, but something in my forming character applauded the symmetry of this arrangement.

At some stage Mum realised that there were such things as indoor fireworks. It would have been poor tactics to lay on a display inside the house, necessarily very muted, on the same night that everyone else was letting off rockets galore just outside. Indoor fireworks are to outdoor what tiddlywinks is to the pole vault. Mum waited for my birthday instead.

One advantage of the indoor fireworks was that I was actually allowed to light them, with a long spill. They were brought in on a tray and laid on the bed. I particularly liked the ones that looked like pills on square pieces of cardboard, but produced a writhing snake when touched with the taper. A serpent made of some grey and fæcal ash would rush from the ignited pellet, and I watched in raptures while it writhed in coils of silent agony. The smell of indoor fireworks is harshly beautiful. I hated for it to dissipate and would plead with Mum not to open the windows. She grumbled that she didn't want to be smelling that stink on her curtains in a week's time, but still she agreed to wait for a few minutes, chafing, after the show was over.

Perhaps that was the day when I solemnly announced, 'This is a very special birthday. Today I am the same age as all the fingers on one hand.'

I had yet to understand the spiritual significance of a birthday. The spiritual significance of a birthday is nil. She who fills a cradle fills a grave. I had yet to read the verse which describes celebrating a birthday as a sort of necrophilia:

> Of all days
> On one's birthday
> One should mourn one's fall [into entanglement].
> To celebrate it as a festival
> Is like adorning and glorifying a corpse . . .

The left hand which I held up to demonstrate the special significance of that birthday was becoming strange to me. The wrist was twisting of its own accord, and the fingers were losing the knack of staying parallel. Dr Duckett the GP recommended that I wear splints at night to minimise the distortion of the joints.

Collie Boy

Now that my age corresponded to the number of digits on a hand, however well or badly shaped, it was time to think of my education. Not a school, of course, but schooling none the less. A teacher coming to the house several times a week. An elderly school-teacher earning a little money in her retirement. Miss Collins.

There must have been a lot of work behind the scenes to arrange it, but Mum only gave me the news a little bit before Miss Collins arrived for the first time, so that my excitement wouldn't become dangerously magnified by a long wait. I had time to ask, 'Is she a governess?' Granny had had a governess, who had marked her nose with a piece of chalk if she got her sums wrong. She hated that, and so would I. Granny's governess would tie her thumbs behind her knees if she fidgeted. Would Miss Collins be allowed to do that?

Once I was reassured that Miss Collins wasn't a governess, I was mad keen for lessons to begin. Someone was coming to the house with only one object in mind: to teach me everything she knew. I couldn't wait. There was never a pupil so willing.

After the first lesson, though, I asked Mum, 'Is Miss Collins a lady or a man?' I was genuinely puzzled. My tutor was at a rather mannish stage of later life. She had whiskers of a rudimentary sort. Mum laughed rather uneasily and said Miss Collins was definitely a lady, but she could see why I needed to ask. After that we gave Miss Collins a nick-name which we used with much guilty pleasure. To us she became the Collie Boy.

This wasn't the first time I had been puzzled by the marks of gender. For a long time I worried about the status of nurses, who seemed to be in some strange way intermediate. Finally I asked Mum, 'Are nurses ladies?'

'Whatever do you mean, JJ?'

'Are nurses ladies or are they men?' I wasn't thinking in terms of male nurses, not yet knowing that such things existed.

'They're ladies, of course! Why would you think anything else?'

'Well, nurses have ears and ladies don't.'

'What on earth are you talking about?'

What I was talking about, really, was that nurses were the only female persons I had seen who wore their hair pinned neatly back, so that I could see their ears. I had always thought the hair-do was all part of the lady. Normal ladies wore their hair permed and shaped, so that they had waves of glossy hair where their ears would have been if they had had them.

'Men have ears, but I've never seen a lady's except a nurse's so are nurses ladies?'

'Everyone has ears. I have ears, you know I do.'

'Will you show me?'

'Of course I will, silly. There's one, see? And there's the other.' So the nurse question was settled, just as the Miss Collins question would be. It turned out that nurses and Miss Collins were all really ladies.

Not long after that Mum told me the facts of life. She was remarkably direct about it. She warned me that people would try to tell me about babies and everything, 'and they'll get it wrong'. So she told me. This sudden surge of frankness represented an underside of her character, the medical professional in a hurry to dispel ignorance. Other children were kept in the dark, even when they were obsessed with knowing where babies come from, and here I was being overwhelmed with knowledge well ahead of schedule, and without having to ask a single question.

She used family words for the parts involved, saying 'taily' rather than penis, but otherwise she was fairly frank. I was outraged. I thought she must be making it all up. 'But you told me it was all to do with storks and blackberry bushes!'

'No, John, I never did. I said that some people *say* it's to do with storks and blackberry bushes. That's what some people pretend to believe, but now I'm telling you the truth.'

She might at least have come up with a better story.

'But that's *rude*. Why do mummies and daddies have to be rude to make a baby?'

'Well when they do it, it's nice. So if it's nice, it's not rude.'

'Nice? *Nice?* What's *nice* about putting your taily in a hole between a lady's legs? I bet it hurts!'

'No, it doesn't. The lady likes it.'

'*I DIDN'T MEAN THE LADY*. I meant, I bet it hurts *the man*!' My concern was all for him, in this desperate transaction. 'The poor man! He must love the baby terribly to do that with his taily.'

'Oh no, the man likes it!'

'How do you know? You're not a man!'

'No, but I told you – Daddy says it's nice.'

This was where her lying was blatant and I became incredulous with anger. 'Daddy would *never* say it was nice to stick his taily in a hole between a lady's legs.'

'He says it's nice.'

'Bring him here. I have to hear him say it.' I was almost in tears. 'He won't say it, he *can't* say it because it's not true. You're fibbing!'

'I'm telling the truth. And one day you will find out for yourself . . .'

'Do you mean that one day I'm going to take my taily and stick it in a hole between a lady's legs?'

'Yes, I expect so.'

This was the last straw. This made me so angry she must have regretted, for the sake of my immobility and my health (which seemed to be the same thing), that she'd ever started discussing human reproduction. I shouted, 'Well I won't won't *won't*! It sounds really horrid and I'm never never *never* going to do it! And I don't want you telling your rude lies to Peter!'

Where the baby comes out

She bustled out of the room but she was back in a minute or two. 'I've asked Dad. He says it's very nice and not rude at all.'

'What sort of nice? How can it be nice? It must be horrid.'

'Let me think of something you really like. That'll help you understand.'

She fetched Dad's Mason Pearson hairbrush and softly brushed my hair with it. 'When Daddy does the thing with his taily, it's even nicer than this.' How could it be nicer than this? Then she spoiled it by saying, 'He puts it in where the baby comes out.' Both of us had lost track of the fact that there was a lady involved, and that she had a place for Dad to put his taily, and that the lady in this case was Mum. I tried to concentrate on this important part of the absurd story. Making an effort to sound like Dad myself, no nonsense, all business, I said, 'I think I'd better see this pocket where the taily goes.'

'Well, I'm not going to show you!'

'You can't tell me and then not show me. That's not fair.'

66

'You just have to trust me.'

'Well I won't. You showed me your ears, remember.' If she'd exposed the one hole, surely she could do the same with the other. 'You're just going to have to show me where the taily goes. Or else I won't believe you ever again.'

'You can believe what you like. I'm just trying to save you getting into a muddle later on.' I wondered why she was so shy about showing me the pocket, *really*. Perhaps she had a little taily of her own.

The only bit of the story I liked at all was the idea that the bag beneath my taily (the family word was 'scallywag') was full of seeds. Otherwise it was obviously rubbish.

Dot-ditty-dash

From Miss Collins's point of view I must have been a faintly alarming child to teach. Teachers usually like a responsive pupil, but in me the hunger for knowledge had got entirely out of hand. Mine was a desperate case. It wasn't just that I wanted to know everything. I wanted to know anything, anything at all.

Miss Collins brought a little portable blackboard with her, which I thought was a thrilling piece of equipment. I loved the dot-ditty-dash noise the chalk made as she wrote, and the way she wiped the board with a hanky tucked into her sleeve. The noise of her dancing chalk was like the tapping of Morse code. Dad had a proper Morse tapper which he let me use, until Mum said that I was getting too excited. He said that to be really good at Morse you actually had to think in the code. He was probably thinking in Morse the whole time.

Miss Collins was rather set in her ways – not a surprising thing, considering that she had spent most of her life in charge of rooms where she was hardly likely to be intellectually challenged. Her lessons were set pieces, well rehearsed and forcefully delivered. I remember one rather dramatic lesson, about the family life of a vowel.

It went like this: baby 'i' used to be taken for walks by his parents. They held his hands on either side as they strolled along. Then one day the wind came along and blew off his hat – his hat, of course, being his dot. To demonstrate, the Collie Boy puffed up her slack cheeks and blew on the blackboard, while she wiped off the dot with the board-rubber. Twice more she blew, and with each puff she wiped away the letters on either side of baby 'i'. The wind blew away his parents!

Hatless and abandoned, baby 'i' was engulfed by shame, and there his childhood ended. His hat was lost for ever, and his parents weren't there to hold his hand any more. He was doomed to grow up into a capital letter – that is, an adult – and to make his way in the world alone.

It's not the most obvious way to think about the alphabet, is it? I don't think I've invented the element of trauma and isolation – little 'i' as part of a joined-up world, then when maturity strikes having to come to terms with bereavement and solitude. *I* stands alone. *I* stand alone. Italics convey an extra emphasis on disgrace, the stricken capital staring down at its feet.

Apart from the Freudian scenario, there was something close to bad taste in Collie Boy spelling out this little drama to me. I was taking a bit of a break from standing up, myself. It was a treat even to be propped up, so that I could see the blackboard properly. Was it tactful of Collie Boy to remind me that even lower-case letters led a more active life than I did? She was teaching a standard lesson, not going to the trouble of tailoring it to the pupil.

The challenge of mashed potatoes

My writing was hopeless, but my devotion to books was intense. In fact Miss Collins became alarmed by how quickly I learned. My reading age was galloping ahead, since I had so little else to do. It couldn't be good for a five-year-old to be rattling through Beatrix Potter, or so she thought. She would intervene. It didn't seem to occur to her that normal development was no longer a possibility, and she must build on what she found. If I was racing ahead in one area, she should be glad rather than place obstacles in my path. In most respects I was falling far behind, and would never catch up.

Miss Collins's treatment of my rampant reading was very much in keeping with the doctors' treatment for the underlying condition that caused it. The remedy for the excessive stimulation I was creating (to replace the stimulation that had been taken away) was to take it away. I hope this philosophy has fallen into the contempt it deserves. Miss Collins decreed that my access to books should be rationed, and the appetite for reading which worried her so much indulged for no more than half an hour a day.

It was absurd that mental inactivity should be supposed to be beneficial, but then it was also an absurd proposition on the physical level. I was being kept in bed for reasons of fashion. Bed rest was the panacea of its time. Just as there were people with certain specific conditions who happened to benefit from blood-letting when that was the vogue – people with hypertension, gout, polycythæmia – so there may have been people who benefited from bed rest. I wasn't one of them.

The 1950s was a period which put a lot of faith in the healing powers of tedium. Taken to extremes, of course, this principle yields a mystical insight, but I don't think that was the idea at the time, the hidden wisdom of the system. So patients with mild digestive troubles, for instance, would be put onto a bland diet, religiously avoiding roughage until their systems could hardly deal with anything more challenging than mashed potatoes.

The fad for prescribing bed rest in hospitals and convalescent homes didn't really pass until the late 1960s. Even then, it was phased out for economic reasons, not because the professionals lost faith in its effectiveness. It simply cost too much to keep people horizontal and in limbo. It was expected that mortality figures would go up when the beds were cleared, freed up for patients with acute and actual needs, the only doubt being how much. In fact death rates went down. It turned out that bed rest had been killing far more people than it saved. Pulmonary embolism was murdering people in their beds.

So much for physical bed rest. The arguments in favour of mental bed rest hardly exist. I don't believe that imposing inertness on the mind as well as the body would have improved the well-being of a single patient. My mental vitality had been forced underground by physical inactivity, and rather than rejoice that the current was still strong Miss Collins tried to pump concrete down into the culvert where my life now ran.

After the rationing of books time passed more slowly. I think time passed slowly in the 1950s anyway, for everyone, not just for me. Still, I had *The Tale of Two Bad Mice* safely memorised, and odd stretches of *Pigling Bland*.

Beatrix Potter revealed new aspects of herself when I considered her with my new style of attention, without the book in front of me. I was less involved, and saw things from a greater distance. Tom Thumb and Hunca Munca, the anti-heroes of *The Tale of Two Bad Mice*, are confronted in their own way with the illusions of the world. Exploring a dolls' house, they find food aplenty in its kitchen. Hungry, they settle down to eat, but the ham, the lobster and the bread are all made of plaster and stuck to their plates, a discovery that the mice greet not with religious resignation but with vandalistic fury.

Pigling Bland's name was delicious in itself. Those clustered consonants – *gl* – *bl* – had a globulous poetry to them. My favourite sentence went 'Pigling Bland listened gravely, but Alexander was hopelessly volatile.' I didn't know what all these words meant, but still I felt I was being nudged towards something. I wanted to be one of those who listened gravely. When I was allowed my daily ration of reading, of course, I preferred to tackle books that I didn't already know. If ever I'd been dilatory in my reading, idly browsing from story to story, then that time was in the past.

Even when reading time was up I liked to have books near me. They became symbols of themselves. After the Collie Boy my love of books was deeply ingrained, and I would never again take them for granted.

There was a pattern set by her edict. There have been times in life when people have pointed the way for me, but more often I've only been able to find my path by spotting the pile of rubble in front of it. The roadblock was actually a signpost. Every time I've been told that some activity was unnatural, I was actually been being shown that this was where my nature lay.

Latent pigment

In the meantime, there was printed matter which didn't need to be read. I loved the paintbooks which were printed with tiny dots of latent pigment, waiting for the stroke of a wet brush to make their colours appear, like cactus flowers. In fact Magic Painting of this kind was the only painting I was competent to do. My elbow had more or less seized up, and my wrist felt the loss of that movement. The wrist joint itself was no great shakes in terms of flexibility.

I loved the 'Spot the Difference' puzzles in comics. They were like a more sophisticated continuation of the beloved old games of 'I Spy'. The puzzle page was always the first one I turned to, the moment the comic was in my hands. I never had the patience to save it up, to ration it so that it would last for the whole of the week. Sometimes as a special treat Mum would draw me a home-made one, to tide me over between publication days. I didn't mind the fact that in a puzzle drawn freehand, there were always more differences detectable than Mum had meant to put in.

There was a picture in a comic that made a deep impression on me at this time. It was the simplest possible image, of a boy sitting on a roundabout in a playground. There was nothing special about him, but in my mind he was the Sit-Upon Boy. He could sit on anything, whenever he liked, while I could only lie. It was a sort of crush of envy. I felt such pangs of yearning, to be him, to do what he did.

In my daily half-hour I wanted to read proper grown-up books. Far from protracting my childhood by putting the brakes on my reading age, book-rationing drove me further forward into precocity. I didn't always want stories. My favourite books were ones which explained the world, preferably all of it. Over several months I absorbed great swathes of *The World We Live In* by Arthur Mee. I would often lavish my whole half-hour on that book, as long as Mum sat by me to help me with the harder spellings and tell me what words meant. We had a little routine about the book before we started. I'd say, 'Who wrote this book, Mum?' And she'd say, 'It's by Mee,' and I'd say 'Clever Mummy!' We never tired of that – at least I never tired of that.

When the half-hour was up (and I could hardly pretend that I didn't know the time, with Jim's outsized radioactive watch permanently on my wrist) Mum would read to me from the book I loved so much. I listened gravely. She held up the book for me to see the pictures. It was absolutely thrilling. I loved the pictures of trilobites and wanted to keep one as a pet. There was a section called 'The Pageant of Life', which was a phrase I loved, even before Mum explained that a pageant was a sort of procession with everyone dressed up. The best chapter of all was the one on the sun. It had a lovely pull-out bit that showed just a wedge of the sun and how big (how small!) the earth was in comparison. I loved the pull-out pages in *The World We Live In* and dreamed of a book whose pages would fold out again and again, till the pages were bigger than elephants' ears, and then fold back neatly to be put away. A book that was huge and tiny at the same time.

I felt my mind stretching, as my body was forbidden to do, when I imagined how big the picture of the sun would have been if they had shown more than a wedge. The book would hardly have fitted in the room!

My body was subject to pinpricks and broadsides of agony, but from time to time my mind had pains of its own. Growing pains, perhaps. One night I woke up terrified that the sun was going to run out of fuel. I screamed for Mum who said of course it wasn't. There was nothing to worry about – but I remembered the open fire at Granny's house in Tangmere, and how she had to add coals to it every few minutes, using a wonderful tool like a giant pair of sugar tongs. I remembered that at Granny's house I wasn't allowed to touch the coal tongs because they were dirty, nor the sugar tongs because they were clean.

If Granny's fire couldn't burn for more than a few hours without going out, how was the sun any different? *Nothing* could burn like that and not get smaller. But Mum said our gas fire was different from Granny's open fire, which was old-fashioned. She asked me if I had ever seen her having to add gas to the fires in our house? I had to admit that I hadn't, but I stuck to my guns. Arthur Mee specifically compared the workings of the sun to a domestic coal fire, so it would have to run out sooner or later, wouldn't it? Mum picked up the book and showed me a wonderfully reassuring sentence: 'The Sun has enough fuel to go on burning indefinitely.' Of course I was only reassured because I thought 'indefinitely' meant 'for ever'. It's a good job I didn't know I was being kept in bed 'indefinitely' myself. Neither state was strictly speaking everlasting. One day I would leave that room and one day the sun would run out of fuel, too. Bed rest wasn't going to be for ever, but it came close enough. It gave me a good working model of eternity.

When the half-hour of my ration was used up, and Mum had things to do so she couldn't read to me, I would ask her to twiddle the knob of our big valve radio until it picked up words in a foreign language. Then I could find my own stories in the unfamiliar syllables. I loved it if there was a foreign radio play on, with unfamiliar speech-rhythms, dramatic music and mysterious sound-effects. I would come out with my own brand of rapidly-spoken gibberish, gabbling away and chortling all the time. I asked if I could learn to speak foreign, and Mum said, 'No you can't!' which didn't disappoint me as much as I made out. I wasn't searching for sense but for magic. I didn't want to understand so much as surrender, to something beyond knowledge with which I felt affinity.

The invalid's friend

I always tried to keep a bit of my reading time reserved for the Ellisdons catalogue. This was one of my great weapons in the war of attrition against boredom. I expect Mum came across an advertisement for it in a magazine. It seemed inexhaustible. Postal shopping is the invalid's friend. Catalogues can tickle an appetite that would otherwise die. I found the notion of sending off for things miraculous. The Ellisdons catalogue turned the letter-box into a magical opening, through which any number of wonderful, tawdry things could flood in. I was only just beginning to get the hang of spelling, but SSAE, for Stamped Self-Addressed Envelope, spelt Open Sesame as far as I was concerned.

Ellisdons had some astounding things in their catalogue. A Magna No-Flint Lighter, which I wanted even at the exorbitant price of twenty-five shillings. Whoopee cushions and stink bombs, though I had enough sense to realise that a stink bomb only worked if you could run away from the stench yourself. I was much less mobile than my intended victims, and while they were busy running off I would inhale a dose which (given my apparent fragility) would probably kill me. It was probably the slogan used to advertise the stink bombs in the catalogue which made me so keen on them, with its mystical inkling of the way our everyday categories can change places under the right circumstances: *'gives off a smell you can almost see . . .'*

73

There were fire-breathing lessons also, which I actually sent off for. The trick involved a wick (with potassium nitrate) and some hay. Like most of the tricks that really attracted me, it was incredibly dangerous.

Of course there was the occasional dud. I couldn't imagine why anyone would waste good money on a wooden paddle with THE BOARD OF EDUCATION inscribed on it. Drawn on the paddle next to that motto was a cartoon of a boy bending over to have his bottom whacked. It was crudely drawn, like something on a sea-side postcard, showing blown-out cheeks and air rasping out of the mouth. It seems strange that an implement of physical punishment could count as a novelty item in the 'fifties, however jocular the presentation. I wasn't tempted. My pennies went towards tricks and treasures.

When I sent off for things, I wanted to use my money, not to rely on Mum's. I knew I had some money in a Post Office account, thanks to Granny. It was a shock to learn that I couldn't take any money out until I was seven. To me that was the same as the Post Office robbing me. They had taken my money and now they were refusing to give it back when I asked nicely.

Seven seemed an awfully far-away age, well over the horizon. The way things were going, I decided my body was going to be dead long before, and I wanted the money before then. I remember asking if I could make an early withdrawal because I was so very ill, but Mum said, sadly, no. The whole thing was definitely a swizz. The next thing I wanted to do was to make out a will, so that the Post Office could be made to cough up after my death, but I was told I wasn't old enough to do that either. Swizzed all over again, swizzled and reswizzled. It seemed hardly possible that a boy who couldn't go anywhere, hardly even to the other side of the bed, could be ramped and cheated by the world in so many ways.

In the Ellisdons catalogue there was also a joke camera, a Home Hypnosis Kit, a ventriloquism course, some little worms which grew in water, a See-Back-roscope which showed you things behind you, a magical flowering shell, and many sorts of indoor fireworks: fairy ferns, snakes-in-the-grass, Bengal Lights and the star turn, Mount Ætna, which spat fire and sounded almost as good as the outdoor kind.

I loved the little mummy which wouldn't stay in its tomb (unless you knew how to tap the secret hidden magnet), and the magical fish which curled up in your hand and showed you how much life force you'd got in you. If an Ellisdons toy didn't do anything it was no good to me, though I made an exception for the Java Shrunken Head. It didn't do anything but hang there, but it had had no end of things done to it to make it so small, which was almost as good. It would have been a nice spooky treasure to have hanging from my ceiling in darkest Somerset.

Jiggling her big fat bum

In the end I sent off for the whoopee cushion. I couldn't wait for it to arrive, and the postman became a figure of commanding fascination, though I'd never given him much thought before. In the end, though, it was a bit of a disappointment. It worked a treat on Mum, who hated it. In her book the only thing which might be worse than a real blow-off (the family word for fart) was an artificial one. But it didn't whoop for the Collie Boy, who had been the prime target all along. At first I thought Mum must have tipped her off, but I suppose you don't have a career in education without some experience of pranks. I knew she was in on the joke because she kept jiggling her big fat bum on the cushion, and nothing at all happened. Somehow she knew how to disarm it, to silence the rubber lips that gave the blow-off its rasping voice.

My next Ellisdons acquisition was a trick camera, and I certainly got her with that. I asked if I could take her picture, but the camera was really a jack-in-the-box. When I pressed the button a toy mouse flew out of the apparatus and hit her on the nose. It was marvellous! Exactly as the catalogue promised. She fell off her chair. She didn't see that coming! I suppose it was a prank that she hadn't come across during her time as a school-teacher. It was news to her. It came from nowhere and biffed her right on the conk!

Her own sense of fun was wholesome and even childish. I remember her giving a little cry of joy at Christmas when she saw our decorated tree. She couldn't keep her hands off the ornaments. She blew all the little trumpets and rang all the bells, rapping every glassy bauble with her knuckles to make it sound.

Dad always said I could wrap Mum round my little finger, which was a delicious image. I pictured a mother shrunken and made pli-

75

able, a plasticine woman I could wear like a toy ring or a sticking plaster. Dad himself was less amenable, and I was exposed over long periods to two female intransigents, the two styles of sovereign will embodied by Miss Collins and Granny.

When Granny came to stay, she would sometimes sit with me while Mum went out. She would sit formally facing the bed, elegant in a way that indicated long practice, the grace whose school is time. Granny had been sitting beautifully for years, with a steely poise not always designed to relax her companions. In Bach terms she was very much a Water Violet, except perhaps for the bit about her serenity being a blessing and a balm to all those she encountered. Granny could use her serenity like a jemmy. I showed her the little fish from Ellisdons which rocked in your hand to show the life force, or else rolled over or curled up at the sides (all of which had different interpretations in the little booklet that came with the fish), but it just lay still in her palm. 'I suppose this means I must be *dead*,' she said.

Before she sat down she would inspect the seat of the chair and invariably picked up a long stray hair of Gipsy's, which she disposed of without comment. She wouldn't read to me or give me lessons as such, although she couldn't help giving me a certain amount of schooling in her special subject of unarmed combat, or conversation as she called it. Sometimes she taught me tongue-twisters, and songs she called rounds. These weren't rounds like a doctor's rounds but special songs which you didn't both sing together but in relays.

When Granny was coming to stay, Mum would spend hours cleaning the house from top to bottom, with murder in her heart, using the white-glove technique to find dust in out-of-the-way places. By the time her mother actually arrived she was exhausted. Granny would wake her up bright and early the next morning, fresh as a daisy and bearing a cup of tea, with the words 'You take the upstairs and I'll take the downstairs, and we'll soon have everything ship-shape. I don't know why you insist on paying that girl. She's worse than useless.'

Granny and Mum did everything differently, down to the smallest detail. When she passed the mirror on my chest of drawers Granny would straighten her back and raise her chin, while Mum cast her eyes down and to one side.

'Granny' has always seemed to me a powerful word. It's odd for me to hear it on other people's lips, referring to some irrelevant or ornamental presence. Certainly for Mum, and even perhaps for Dad, Granny was a thin grey cloud which would always blot out the sun. I remember when I learned that 'Granny' only meant 'Mum's Mum' – it was rather a letdown. Somehow there seemed much more to her than being Mum to the power of two. Mum squared.

It must have been clear to everyone she met, as it was to me, that Granny had very particular reasons for being born, and for every link in the chain of decisions that followed on from there. Of course I can't reconstruct her beginnings. The place Granny chose to be born is three wombs distant from me, and each womb is a wall of metaphysical brick which no mundane thought can penetrate. Each birth is an absolute new beginning (on the level of the organism, if not the cosmos). That's the whole beauty and virtue of the system.

Granny was always a vivid figure to me, though not in the oppressive way that she was to Mum. I stood up to her sometimes. I knew no better.

In superficial terms, Mum made a very odd choice of womb. In a way she never managed to get free of the womb she had chosen. She was like the baby bird that can't peck its way out of the egg.

I remember Granny squashing Mum flat one day just by re-hanging the washing while she was out. Granny went out into the garden and calmly unpegged every item, putting it back up the way it should be, without argument or mercy. Mum came and told me about it. She almost cried.

For one of my bed birthdays Granny gave me a doll. I'd said I wanted one, and of course what I wanted was a doll in a pretty dress, with lovely long hair and eyes that opened and shut, framed by long dark lashes. At the time this was not what boys were supposed to want, and my birthday wish was greeted with a certain amount of discomfort.

Granny made herself busy, and fulfilled my wish in a way that was more than half a thwarting. I got my doll, but it wasn't at all what I had in mind. It was a little soldier in a tartan kilt. Thinking about it now, I realise that this was an unusual plaything for the period, perhaps even a specially ordered object, certainly not something that you would find on a shelf in the newsagents. Granny had gone to the top man, or to some toymakers *par excellence*, to secure what she wanted me to want.

I sort of liked it. I didn't hate it. I didn't cuddle it very much. I went through the motions, rather. No one had the vision to give me the ordinary thing that I wanted, without substituting their own version of what I should have asked for. It's funny, really, that family members should stamp on the only faint manifestation of interest in the female body I ever had. Question of bad timing, I suppose.

What I wanted was a female doll I would call Mandy. Mandy would wet the bed. She would share my shame over that lonely malady, over which I cried so often. The boy doll didn't do that. Dolls of the period were rather unstimulating in general. I also wanted my doll to do a tuppenny, and I wanted to watch her do it. I was ahead of my time. The market wasn't ready for defæcating dollies.

Educational dud

Another reason, the most secret reason, for wanting Mandy instead of Hamish was to get a chance to see the hole where a man put his taily. The boy doll, being tailyless, having hardly so much as a bump beneath his kilt, was an utter dud from the educational point of view.

Granny's manner with me in conversation was formal but not condescending. 'Laura always suffered from the fidgets,' she said. 'I'm glad to see that you are different.' Laura was Mum, and I wasn't different at all, I liked nothing better than a good fidget, but it seemed a bit of a waste when there was someone in the room.

Talking to Granny was very different from talking to Mum. It may have been true that I could wrap Mum round my little finger, but Granny was not to be moulded, by me or by anyone else. She lived by her rules, and expected everyone else to abide by them too.

At home she kept bees and grew strawberries. I said that I loved strawberries, quite innocently, with no idea that I was asking for trouble. 'John,' Granny said, 'you should love your parents, but you can only *like* your food.'

I was enjoying our conversation, and decided I'd have a go at getting round Granny. 'Granny?' I asked. 'Can you like food *lots and lots*?'

She hesitated. 'Well,' she said, drawing the word out to three times its normal length. 'I suppose one *could.*'

'But if you can like strawberries lots and lots, it's almost the same as loving them, isn't it?'

'Almost. But not quite – and remember, a miss is as good as a mile.' This was one of the most serviceable proverbs in the adult armoury. Granny wasn't going to any great trouble to keep me in line.

'But if it's almost the same as loving it, why can't you just say you love it?' This was where I played my little trump card. 'You always say don't ever waste anything, and I'm only trying to do what you say. I'm being careful with words. Look! *"I-like-straw-be-reez-lots-and-lots."* That's wasteful compared to saying, *"I love straw'bries."*'

There was some shameless cheating going on here. To make my case stronger I dragged an extra syllable out of 'strawberry' in the wasteful example and contracted it back to two in the economical one. Eight syllables as against four. Surely I had her on the run?

It's true that she was very much taken aback. But then she said, 'Rules are rules. There are lines that need to be drawn.' When I asked, 'Why?' she snapped back, 'They just must.' In fact the rules had changed. It was no longer legitimate to argue back, no longer a good thing to stick to your guns and use logic. Now the game had to stop, just when I was starting to enjoy it. For form's sake I protested, but I knew I wouldn't be able to dodge the strongest rebuff available to the adult brain and tongue: *'You just can't, and that's an end of it!'* Logic was out of the window, logic had its back to the wall and so did I.

Even so, I admired adults like Granny for their ability to impose arbitrary limits, to say 'so far and no further' without having to give a reason. I decided to stop being a child as soon as possible, so that I could do the same, being reasonable when it suited me and jamming on the brakes when it didn't.

I'm cheating even now, as much as I did then when I squashed and stretched 'strawberries' to suit the case I was making. When I had the argument about syllables with Granny, I didn't actually know the word 'syllable'. Miss Collins hadn't got to them yet. Instead I made do with the term 'word-bits'.

I had asked Mum what the right name was for word-bits, but she said words were made up of letters. That was all there was to it. I said there must be another word. For instance, I explained, Mum has one wordbit, Granny has two and cauliflower four. The number of letters in a word was something different.

Mum couldn't think of the word. Her education had been extremely patchy, and her younger brother – Roy – was the one who had been designated as clever. Mum would never be able to earn Granny's respect by using her brain, and I think she just stopped trying. Now she became flustered at her inability to retrieve the desired term. Perhaps I should have noticed with sorrow that she didn't feel able to hold her own mentally with a five-year-old boy, but I was too frustrated by not getting an answer to my question.

Any fool can mind a child

The way my mother had been brought up by Granny could just as accurately be described as a keeping down. When Mum was little, Granny hired domestic help, at a time she could hardly afford it. There was a curious patch of no-money in the family history. Mum had coincided with it. Some nights Granny would crawl upstairs to bed on her hands and knees, not just because the house was old and the stairs were steep, but because she had starved herself to feed everyone else, and she was too dizzy to stand up. Only much later did Mum realise there was something perverse about Granny's domestic arrangements, and when she did it really wounded her. Bad enough to be raised by a father who barely seemed able to see her, having eyes only for her younger brother. It was worse that her mother paid someone to come in and look after the children, freeing Granny herself to concentrate on the more important business of cleaning the house. Mum grew up in a household where there might just as well have been a motto in cross-stitch over the fireplace, reading HOUSEWORK IS A SERIOUS ENTERPRISE, and a companion piece on the opposite wall declaring ANY FOOL CAN MIND A CHILD.

Dad must have been away at the time of 'word-bits', but when he came back he told me the word I was looking for was 'syllable'. It was great to have it confirmed that words had bits, and the bits had names. Proper names. And 'syllable' itself had three syllables, which was an extra pleasure for some reason.

Dad and Granny had a strange sort of relationship, a pact of mutual invisibility. For the most part they just walked past each other. They didn't approve of each other, but they couldn't seem to be bothered, either of them, to hide the fact or else to spell it out.

Granny cast a strange spell over the household, magnetising assent without lowering herself to ask for it. She didn't hold with drinks at mealtimes. By drinks I mean 'fluids', she wasn't talking specifically about alcohol. Sherry before a meal was permitted, as long as it was dry and not sweet. Granny's was a theory about digestion: don't dilute the gastric juices. Let them do their work. So when she came to stay everyone meekly went without.

Granny rarely cooked, but when she did it was a bit of a performance. I remember one evening when she made scrambled egg. There was a definite overtone of masterclass, despite the humbleness of the dish, and spectators seemed to be welcome.

I imagine Granny made sure that her visits coincided with the times that Dad wasn't there, but this was one occasion when they overlapped. I have no idea how the sleeping arrangements were worked out, in that small house. Only one possibility seems thinkable, either practically or in psychological terms, and that would have been for Mum and Dad to hang by their heels from the rafters like roosting bats, while Granny took possession of the marital bed.

I know Dad and Granny were both there because I was allowed to witness the ceremony (almost the sacrament) of scrambling, and my expedition to the kitchen took a lot of planning. First Dad moved the armchair from my room to a spot in the kitchen with a suitable view. Then Mum carried me. It wasn't a long trip, but had its hazards even so. Dad was much the stronger, of course, but he hadn't had much practice and he lacked the necessary sense of my vulnerability. I was so immobile that I had become a little statue of myself, though I was as sensitised to pain as a violin strung with stretched filaments of nerve instead of catgut. It wasn't just that banging my feet against the doorframe would have me jangling with agony. Even the fear of an impact would set off the same detonation in my joints. I trusted Mum to make the transfer, and she didn't let me down.

Mum's carrying was reliable but her lap wasn't a suitable place for me to sit. It was too bony. Not that I really sat – my posture was closer to leaning, but even with the padding of a cushion Mum's lap offered no comfort. That was where Dad excelled. Of course I was magnetised to his lap in any case, but I think this really was a medical necessity rather than a preference. Mum padded Dad's lap with a single strategic cushion and then I could lean there perfectly happy while Granny got to work.

Officially Peter had recently grown out of his high chair, but on this special occasion he was wedged back into it, so that he had a sort of tennis umpire's vantage-point.

I wouldn't have thought there was a special implement needed for scrambling eggs, but apparently there was. 'Don't you have a spirtle, Laura?' asked Granny. She made it sound like something absolutely basic, like a cooker or a bath. A spirtle turned out to be a spoon without a blade – no more than a rounded stick – used in Scotland for the proper agitation of porridge. Granny made do with a wooden spoon held upside down, so that what entered the egg mixture was indeed nothing more than a round stick, a cooking dowel.

Glossy suspension

Granny had laid the table before she started (no drinking glasses of course, our internal juices must be at their keenest), which gave us the impression that eating was imminent, but there has never been anything less like fast food than that pan of scrambled eggs. She set the flame on the stove at its lowest, and stirred indefatigably. Nothing seemed to happen, and it kept on not happening for a very long time. No curds were forming at all, as far as I could see from my perch, in the glossy suspension she stirred so constantly. Her activity seemed designed in fact to protect the contents of the pan from any changes that might be brought about by cooking. Yet the long-delayed transformation of the texture must have happened all at once, spreading in a yellow instant from a million specks of ovonucleation. Suddenly the eggs were scrambled, and yet *scrambled* seemed too casual a word. Granny took the pan off the heat, and ground pepper onto a saucer, then tipped it into the pan. I was relieved that we had a pepper-mill if not a spirtle, since she regarded that as essential – almost as if there was no point cooking eggs without it. Dad himself was a pepper mill fiend who ground thick specks densely over everything. His plate at mealtimes had the look of something unearthed at Pompeii.

I realise now just how rare an item was the table-top totem of a pepper-mill in a 'fifties kitchen or dining room. Mum behaved as if ours was a loaded weapon, never so much as touching it if she had the choice. Granny treated ours with grudging respect – no doubt hers was an heirloom that lived in a monogrammed case on a bed of velvet, like the pistol which it must have resembled in Mum's mind.

It can't have been easy for Dad and Granny to ignore this node of affinity in the matter of their shared addiction to the dried berries of *Piper nigrum*, but they rose to the challenge.

I was puzzled that the pepper had to be ground onto a saucer and only then scattered on food. When I asked Granny why this was, she explained that over time the steam rising from hot food would corrode the mechanism, as if it was something everyone should know from an early age. It was high time I learned.

The moistly solid savoury cream she now spooned reverently onto plates was barely palpable to the tongue. It melted there. It was barely particulate. We ate it in wondering silence. Part of Granny's success was to have made us wait so long that she led us to a contemplative state on the far side of hunger. It was as if we'd been starved to death and then brought back from the grave for a light meal.

For once Dad ate what was put in front of him without taking his own turn with the pepper grinder. It occurs to me now that he didn't like spicy foods or strong flavours. He liked roast meat – the ritual joint that needed a family to justify it – accompanied by potatoes and runner beans, the only green vegetable whose claims to edibility he accepted, and served with redcurrant jelly, a condiment he honoured with its own acronym ('pass the RCJ, will you, m'dear?'). Really what Dad liked was bland food that he could grind pepper over until it almost disappeared. His pepper habit wasn't to do with taste, it was to do with showing the food (and the cook) who was boss. Granny's scrambled eggs, though, he ate without insisting on the usual black top-dressing.

In the kitchen Dad was essentially helpless. According to Mum, he couldn't even boil an egg. The only time he had tried it he boiled it in milk, thinking that was how you would make it turn white inside.

I wonder, though, if he wasn't just making a point. He had more than enough scientific knowledge to avoid such a mistake, but there were other factors involved. It was almost a matter of principle in those days for men to be as incompetent in the kitchen as they were supposed to be competent everywhere else. And perhaps Mum was making the same sort of general statement about men and women, and their proper spheres of competence, when she so consistently fumbled the shaking-out of her match flame – she who, with her nurse's training, could flick the recalcitrant mercury back to the bottom of a thermometer with two brisk movements of her wrist.

Family trigonometry

I suppose Mum's ultimate priority, if she had been able to formulate it, would have been to set me against Granny. Granny meant money, though she also meant somehow being above money, and Mum had conflicting feelings on these important topics. Her ideal solution would be to set me against Granny at a mathematically precise angle: just enough to send the message that we couldn't be bought, but not enough for us actually to be written out of The Will. There was some vengeful family trigonometry Mum would have liked to get exactly right, but she wasn't quite confident enough to make the shot.

In the meantime she was short of allies, and the best one would certainly have been Dad – if she hadn't been running her own campaign against him. She kept on asking me which of them I loved more. I didn't know the word 'comparison', and hadn't yet picked up the skill of refusing to answer a question. The best I could do was to say, an orange is a norange (I loved 'noranges', the word more than the fruit) and an apple is a napple. The rules that govern 'a' and 'an' were easy to learn – I picked them up from Granny. Oranges used to be noranges, apples used to be napples, until the 'n' popped across the gap and never came back.

Oranges were oranges and apples were apples, and how could you say which was better? Better didn't come into it. I loved Mummy with all my heart and I loved Daddy with all my heart, and when I said 'Mum' or 'Mummy' I always inwardly intoned, 'The best Mummy in the world.' Wasn't that enough for her?

84

It was not. She wanted a definite answer, one way or the other. Day after day she worked on me. I was to take sides. There must be schism. She said I should think it over, and not forget all the things she had done, the things she was still doing for me. Dad was away most of the time – I should remember that when I gave my answer. Then she would leave my bedroom with her head held high, leaving me to sadness and guilt. I was not to be allowed to love in peace.

Later Mum would make an entrance and come over to 'hug' me, being careful to let me feel mostly her aura rather than her body. She would have put on fresh scent while she was out of the room. I loved *Intimate*, which Dad had been trained to buy her for birthdays, not anticipating that it would be used as an instrument of brain-washing against him. I would reel from the beauty of the smell. Then while she had me spellbound she would drip the words 'Who do you really love most, me or Daddy?' into my ears and I'd rouse myself out of my trance to say, 'The same!'

For a while she would go easy on me, till it almost seemed that I had got away with my crime of being equally attached to both parents. Then she went back onto the attack. Finally one day, when she came over to hug me, I caved in. I did what she wanted. I whispered into her ear that I loved her more than Daddy. She was my darling. At the same time I sent off a prayer, begging forgiveness for telling what I was almost positive was a lie.

Perhaps it was as a reward for my knuckling under that Mum came up with a new sort of treat. To be fair, she and Dr Duckett were always putting their heads together to come up with some form of entertainment that would somehow fall within the proper bounds, warming the brain without heating the heart. Being in charge of a telephonic grocery order was no longer the privilege it had been.

'I Spy' had lost its charm, and our games were becoming more sophisticated. The family re-jigged Grandmother's Footsteps to suit me – I would hold a hand-mirror up, a little one from Mum's handbag, instead of physically turning round. I always had to be Grandmother, of course, there was no taking of turns. In the family version, it wasn't at all easy for anyone to get within reach of the bed (to give me the lightest possible tap), even after Gipsy had been sent out of the room. She had to go, otherwise she would bark. There was something about the heightened atmosphere of the game which set her off.

The only way for me to lose was by consent. I would relax my vigilance just long enough to be tagged, otherwise I was invulnerable. That may have been the whole virtue of the game, that it humoured me by giving me some experience of humouring others, while Gipsy softly scrabbled at the door to be brought in from the long seconds of exile.

Pelted with woven snakes

A more exciting game, with a definite element of transgression, involved one of Dad's treasured accessories, the Brummell Tie Press. It could only be played while he was away and Mum out of the room. Peter would fetch the Brummell Tie Press from Dad's dressing table. It was a box of dark-toned Bakelite resembling a small radio, except that it had an opening on the sloping front panel and a single large knob on one side. You turned (or rather Peter turned) the knob and carefully fed a tie into the interior, where it was wound round a central drum and kept free of creases. When you wanted to retrieve the tie, you pressed a lever on the front which released the spring. The tie was projected out of the opening with great force and a loud whirring. Properly aimed, it could cross the room.

I wasn't able to do the winding, but Peter scrupulously gave me turns at the exciting part, the dramatic discharge of Dad's formal neckwear. Illness hadn't deprived me of seniority, only the means of enforcing it. Peter never challenged my status. He would aim the loaded Brummell, and all I had to do was release the catch. If we aimed the tie towards Gipsy, she would bark madly at the noise and the fright of being pelted with woven snakes, and then the game acquired a hectic second phase. Peter must dash out of the room with the tie press, and return it to its place on the dressing table before Mum came to investigate.

Windfall panorama

One morning Mum asked, out of the blue, 'John, how would you like to go with Dr Duckett on his rounds?' Any child would be thrilled by such an offer, surely, let alone one who had been living in horizontal exile. I was all agog. Between them, Mum and Dr Duckett padded the front seat of the car for my benefit, and Dr Duckett drove very slowly. Gipsy rode in the back seat. I didn't mind about the slow speed, though. 'I've never been in a car before,' I told Dr Duckett, and he smiled at me, though it can't quite have been true. I didn't walk all the way to Manor Hospital to have my bones scraped, did I?

I liked being close to Dr Duckett, who was sort of a dad away from Dad, though he was much more likely to touch me. I was disappointed, though, that when Dr Duckett actually arrived at a patient's house I was left in the car. I'd thought that I would be involved in the consultations. Not that I would be giving advice or choosing medicines, but at least I'd be able to frown and nod my head in unison with the doctor, as I had been so plentifully nodded and frowned over in my time. I wouldn't talk about what was wrong with people. I could keep secrets.

I took advantage of my novel surroundings for the rest of the trip by playing 'I Spy' with the doctor. B is for Bus, P is for Puddle. I was growing too old for the game, really, but it would have been mad to waste this windfall panorama.

There were things I would have liked to ask Dr Duckett, things I couldn't talk about to Mum or Dad. I had been thinking about the unchanging 'I' burning deep within. The body went through states of pain and ease, of nice and nasty, well and sick and sicker still, but the 'I' didn't change. It was like a brown candle, or like the bulb of my sailing-boat night-light showing through the deckled parchment sails. By 'brown' I mean the colour you get when you close your eyes and take in the light that filters through the lids. I understood that I would still be John if I lost a finger, but did that mean I would still be 'I' if I lost my whole body? Yet I must have sensed that this was not truly a medical question, because I never actually raised it with dear Dr Duckett.

At the end of our rounds Dr Duckett taught me a long word and a useful exercise which wouldn't hurt me. The word was *quadriceps*, which meant the muscle at the top of the leg, and the exercise involved flexing it. He put my hands on his quadriceps, so that I could feel the movement involved, and his hands on mine to see if I was imitating him. We flexed our leg muscles together. He said I should do this several times a day – whenever I was bored. Through the cloth of his trousers I could feel the edge of his pocket, warm and swollen with coins. I liked touching Dr Duckett's leg. It made a deep impression on me. It was intoxicating, that broad leg with the power in it, at a time when I was on only the most distant terms with touch. Whenever I did my dutiful flexing, I thought of the warmth of his leg through the thickness of his trouser-cloth.

The style of exercise that he taught me that day later became generally popular under the name of isometrics. These were exercises you could do at your desk or while waiting for your bus. I never saw the appeal, for those who had the option of actually using their limbs in real life, but it was the only sort of exercise that I was allowed.

Not the king of hugs

By this time, my left hip was entirely fused, and my right hip had only the ghost of movement, though there was still muscle there. Dr Duckett's flexing game wasn't actually called 'Let's Not Get Atrophied!', but that was very much the thinking behind it.

If I remember Dr Duckett as being tactile, I'm only recording the fact that he touched me more than Dad did. Touching the patient is a diagnostic requirement, so it doesn't follow that Dr Duckett was an intrinsically tactile man, and it's no sort of reproach to Dad that he was not the king of hugs. Strictly limited horse-play may have had a rôle in some boisterous, high-spirited families, in privacy, but in the 1950s, men didn't touch their children except to smack them, ruffle their hair or carry them from burning buildings.

The first time I tried Dr Duckett's quadriceps exercises I somehow wet myself for a second or so, until I regained control, and was terribly ashamed. I was moving the wrong mental lever, the one connected to the bladder. After that I was in control. At home I treated myself to one more round of 'I Spy' with Mum. I might be getting too old for the game, but that was no reason to pass up the pleasure of stumping her with Q, that rarity of an initial letter. Q for Quadriceps. A new word for something that had actually been in the room all along.

Sometimes peace broke out between my parents, when their temperaments dovetailed for once. Mum had always been a skilled and adventurous knitter, but there were times when a pattern didn't work out. Sometimes it looked very much as if there were mistakes in the instructions, but Mum said that as a rule the pattern was right and the knitter wrong. On some evenings she and Dad would put their heads together to find out why a particular pattern was running into trouble. I loved those evenings, because Mum and Dad were likely to stay up late – past their bed-times. Finding the cause of the problem took as long as it needed to take. During the investigation, time took a back seat. There was an unwritten rule that the error must be run to ground on the day the problem was discovered. If that entailed a late night, then so be it.

I loved knitting-pattern-problem nights. Something was really happening. There was activity in the house, and a warm and busy feeling. Mum and Dad were happy without trying for it or even necessarily realising it. Their characters meshed for once and I basked in the glow. Dad became absorbed in the quest for a solution and forgot that by definition he had better things to do.

Knitting-Pattern Man

The idea occurred to me that God had sent along this problem as a way of uniting them, and I started to pursue some promising ideas about Him. When I visualised Knitting-Pattern Man I had always given him a big beard and white robes anyway. Not a badger-coloured beard like Dr Duckett's but a proper snowy one. I knew that it would be God and not Jesus who would do this sort of thing (I could never get to grips with the Holy Ghost). God was older and knew a thing or two about the way people worked. His Son was greener and less sure of himself, more like a big brother or youthful uncle, really. He was even quite chummy, almost to the point of being a playmate, and you could talk to him about anything without being made to feel silly. He said, 'I don't know,' to a lot of my questions, but always added that we would find out together, which was all part of the fun.

The usual outcome of Mum and Dad's battle with the knitting-pattern was that though everything looked terribly wrong, it all fell into place if you just kept going and completed the design. It was difficult to tell which was the greater triumph: Mum being Right and the Pattern being Wrong, or the other way round. At first sight, it was fantastic if Mum found a flaw in the Pattern, but then Dad would say, 'You should make your own patterns and sell 'em, m'dear!' Which was supposed to cheer her up, but unsettled her instead. 'Oh Dennis, don't talk like that, *please*! The Pattern just can't be Wrong. It's probably only a slip-up at the printing stage. And I bet the Maker was absolutely furious when he found out!'

The Pattern just can't be Wrong – The Pattern just *can't* be Wrong. How close Mum was coming to a genuine mystical experience at that time. How narrowly she dodged enlightenment. She was only a step away from realising that she had been handed a key to the apparent miseries of her life. If something as simple as a knitting pattern could look wrong and yet be absolutely correct, then why shouldn't the same be true of larger matters, of her life and mine?

One day Mum came back in floods of tears after a horrible conversation with an Indian gentleman at the bus stop. She'd been in Heather overdrive, pumping her miseries into a virgin ear at a terrific rate, when he said exactly the wrong thing. 'Dear lady,' he said, 'you are so lucky. God must have a special purpose for your son.'

'How could he be so cruel?' – the Indian gentleman she meant, not God. Mum fed on sympathy drained from strangers and here was starvation. The last thing she wanted was to be offered a fresh perspective. She didn't take kindly to being comforted, at the expense of her tragic prestige.

Despite her immediate distress at the time of meeting the Indian man, Mum rapidly re-jigged her attitude. She calmed down after a while and even managed half a smile. 'Well, maybe he knew something we can't see,' she said. The incident even became part of her repertoire, for all the grief it had brought her when it was fresh. It gave her a way of ending the story on a wise and reconciled note. She began telling everyone that maybe this man could see something we couldn't. There might be an Unseen Hand working, to push together this valiant mother and an enlightened Asiatic. Providence was always busy behind the scenes, wasn't it? Mum developed a new, far-away look to accompany this new repertoire of ideas.

Since I spent so much of the day in a half-state of under-stimulation, it was inevitable that I should be much awake while others slept. It was always frustrating when Mum and Dad went to bed and left me to the watches of the night. To the night and Jim's watch, whose glow never failed me, and the vigilant dozing of Gipsy. However much she was brushed, she brought a welcome whiff of the outdoors with her. I would pray to God very hard at night, and was sometimes saddened when I didn't seem to get an answer. In the morning Mum would say, 'I expect he's very busy – but he'll see to it sooner or later, that's for sure!' Then she said perhaps I should try praying to Jesus specifically, since he had more free time and was generally easier to approach.

I tried to interest Jesus in my questions about the 'I', but they weren't really his cup of tea. He was more involved in relieving pain and suffering, which was all very well, but just relieving the pain didn't solve the problem, did it? If we could find out how the pain had got there in the first place, we could stop it from even starting. But I suppose that wouldn't leave much for Jesus to do, it would virtually be handing Him his cards, so then I'd have lost a useful friend of last resort, and it would be back to me and God, Who was far too busy and didn't seem terribly hot on the milk of human kindness side of things, which was why Jesus got the job in the first place. It was all very confusing. I couldn't seem to get the hang of the Trinity.

I could hear trains but not see them. Trains started early in the morning and ran till very late at night. There was a different rhythm every seventh night, which I later learned to call 'Sunday service'. Perhaps inactivity was sharpening my hearing. I could certainly tell Dad's night noises from Mum's. His snoring was dry and enquiring, hers sounded like a throatful of bees.

The night splints on my hands were supposed to keep my fingers reasonably straight despite the skewing heat of the fever. You'd think I'd be sick of rigour and restriction, what with willed immobility by day and splints by night, but perversely I wanted more. I wanted to go to sleep with my left arm straight – not only straight in the sense of unbent, but straight up in the air. Straight up, like a flagpole waiting for a flag to fly. If my arm was going to stick in one position I wanted to decide which position it would be. It looked as if I was going to have to live with a useless arm, and I wanted to exercise my power of choice as much as possible. There was something obscurely satisfying about that particular posture. Naturally Mum and Dr Duckett said, 'Bring it down or you'll stay like that,' which of course was the whole point. 'You have to bend it,' they said, but I didn't want to. I wanted there to be at least one part of me that wasn't out of true.

Die-hard little Nazi

It can't have helped that my chosen position had overtones, however innocent, of a lying-down Hitler salute. I must have looked like a die-hard little Nazi, waiting for my Führer to bring me a bunch of grapes and read me a story. Of course they were right to discourage me, even if it sounded like being told that if the wind changes and you're pulling a face, it'll set there rigid for ever. But still I wanted to sleep with my arm straight, even if it meant I'd wake up unable to move it. And this turns out to be an old and rather austere yoga posture. There are ascetic mystics who have kept their arm straight in that posture for years, without any help from stiffening joints. It's a recognised practice, and there's even a special stick some yogis use, called a *dhandam*, to help them with the task of fixing their limbs.

When I could get to sleep I dreamed vividly, and it's not surprising that my night-pictures should have been of movement. Running, soaring. Dreams take up the slack of the day, and in my case there was much to play with, basic fantasies to fulfil. There was a lot of grey existence to balance with floods of colour, a lot of powerlessness to redress. Mum had told me once about the Indian Rope Trick, and I had seen it in my mind and loved it. Now I dreamed of doing it myself, shinning up a hawser that writhed like a snake and vanishing while Mum looked on goggle-eyed.

I dreamed of lying in bed, obeying doctors' orders to keep still, but at the same time using magic power from my hands to make a massive steel ball move around the room, landing anywhere in the room, until I became famous for my abilities and people queued up behind a rope to watch and wonder.

I had other, stranger dreams, seemingly quite wrong for my situation. They were nightmares of health. I dreamed of running in the garden, without pain, of pushing Peter over and making him cry, and being fiercely told off for that, in a way that made me cry too. I dreamed of refusing to go to bed, for fear that if I did I'd never get out of it again. I dreamed of actually hiding under the bed so that Mum couldn't get me, despite which she hauled me up and plonked me roughly down on it. I dreamed that she locked me in my room then, and that I lay on the floor rather than the bed and woke up shivering. All this seems curious night-time traffic in a mind that didn't have to worry about those particular things.

One day Granny came to stay, bringing honey from her own hive. I liked bees. I liked wasps too. In summer, when the window was open, bees or wasps would sometimes fly into the room, and I didn't mind. I let them walk on my face if that was what they wanted. I even opened my mouth so that they could walk around inside. I really quite wanted them to sting me, but they never did. My appetite wasn't for pain but for drama, and I didn't raise the stakes by closing my mouth while they were walking around inside it.

There was some comb in the honey, which she showed me was made up of little regular rooms. Late at night she sat on the chair opposite my bed and told me her cure for sleeplessness. She was wearing a dressing gown which made a luxurious rustle quite unlike the anxious swish of Mum's. I assume she was sleepless herself, wandering the house, and found me in the same state.

Polyhedral infinity

What she did when she couldn't sleep, she said, and what I should do also, was to imagine herself being inside one of the cells with a little brush, a brush as soft as a whisper. Only when my brush had done its work and the little chamber was perfectly clean and shining should I move onto the next cell with my whispering brush. In this way the mind might be calmed and sleep invited. I liked the idea of polyhedral infinity, my mind as an empire of cells, needing proper maintenance. It was entirely in character that Granny's cure for sleeplessness should be vicarious housework. It was still hard, though, to associate Granny with either sleep or the lack of it. I already felt that she would resist being mastered by unconsciousness. Why would she give in? Capitulate to that soft siege. Equally unthinkable, though, that sleep wouldn't come running the moment she snapped her fingers.

Granny let her guard down a little that night we pooled our insomnias. 'I remember when your mother was starting to grow up, John,' she said, 'she would go out to dances and such things. I would tell her very strictly to be back by nine, ten at the absolute latest. Sometimes she would not return until gone eleven. On one occasion it was after one.' Children love these revelations that Mummy and Daddy weren't always good little girls and boys themselves, and in that respect I was no different. I was utterly normal.

Between louche and lozenge

'I would sit at the window,' Granny said, 'watching for the lights of the car of the young man who was to bring her home. Mostly all I would see was the ghostly outlines of trees. When there was a car, I became very agitated, thinking that this must at last be her. It never was, but during those moments I realised how much I really . . .' The word *love* almost leaped from her lips under these special circumstances, but even sleepless and confiding she was able to choke it back. '. . . How much fondness I had for her.' Love was a word that had been fiercely edited out of her conversation. There was a gap in her personal dictionary somewhere between *louche* and *lozenge*.

'Then my son Roy – your Uncle Roy – asked me what I was doing. I said, 'Worrying,' and he said something that was not just sweet and clever but wise. He wasn't fully grown up himself, in some ways still a child, but he knew what he was saying. He said, "Well, why don't you just get on up to bed and I'll sit up and worry for you?" I really valued that in him. So I say to you now, if you have a worry that is keeping you awake, just tell Granny and she'll do the worrying for you, while you get some sleep.'

What kept me awake was more like a disappointed appetite for events than worries of any kind. Since my life was being kept so free of content, I would have to import things to occupy me from the few people I saw. It wasn't that people volunteered their inmost secrets, exactly, but they certainly said more than they would have to anyone else in my age group. Baby talk is a performance, even if you're a baby. Prattling becomes a chore. Sooner or later the adults I spoke to tired of the effort it took to talk down to me.

I dare say the people around me felt a need to compensate me for my deprivation, as I floated month after month in a clumsy 1950s prototype of the isolation tank. They chatted on, and I encouraged them with every inducement I had. I didn't always understand but I always remembered. I had nothing else to do with my time. If I was precocious, at least I was innocent of swank. It was pure survival strategy. Who else was I going to talk to, if not adults? For practical purposes I had no contemporaries. Peter was younger and unavailable, intent on exploring his surroundings in ways I no longer could. He didn't share his discoveries, either out of innate tact or because Mum had warned him not to rub it in that our destinies had diverged so markedly.

From Mum I wanted to know if we had other 'home' words, like 'siss' and 'tuppenny', which I had needed to explain to Dr Duckett. I wanted to know the proper outside word for things as well. It's the doctor-and-nurse word that really counts. Then when she said that the proper word for tuppenny was 'fæces', I thought it was priceless. I made up a rhyme which went 'My sheep have got fæces in their fleeces.'

Besides 'taily' and 'scallywag' there were words for female parts. 'Boozzie' was the family word for 'bosom'. There was no home word for the lady's hole where the taily was alleged to go, which struck me as rather suspicious, but there was apparently a doctor-and-nurse word, which was 'vagina', which had a nice poetic sound to it.

Not all home words came from Mum and Dad – some were from me. 'Snort', my improvised baby-word for 'nostril', had passed into currency, so that Mum herself sometimes used it.

One day Mum let slip that she had been brought up with a different set of home words. I piled on the pressure till she told me what they were. At last she gave in, but she made me swear not to use them even in the house. The pleasure for me in learning this archaic vocabulary lay not only in imagining Mum having to use the words but also Granny teaching her them. Mum's childhood word for 'milk' was 'ookkies'. What we called 'tuppenny' was 'jobs'.

Jobs had been a dark word in Mum's childhood. 'Have you done your jobs today, Laura?' Granny would ask her every day, and if she hadn't the sentence was castor oil. Mum's voice throbbed with ancient trauma. 'That is something you *never* want to take, John.' I thanked my lucky stars that however ill I seemed to be, I had never been subjected to castor oil. 'Tuppenny' must have been her light-hearted antidote to to the fearsome 'jobs'. Spend a penny, spend two while you're at it, no need to make a fuss.

In Mum's childhood 'sick' was 'ikky', or (even better, I thought) 'ikky-boo-ba'. If you'd been sick in the lavatory you had to say, 'I've been ikky-boo-ba down the slobber-pail.' Mum could hardly bear to say the words even as a grown-up. Now I hear an extra element in all these silly words, a posh archness and glee which reveal a younger Granny than the one I knew. Granny had been very comfortably brought up, as she told me more than once, with fruit from the glasshouse reserved for her, and a goat milked for her benefit because she had once been ikky-boo-ba after drinking cow's. She didn't claim to be allergic, just indulged.

By this time there was a sort of pressure differential between me and anyone who sat by me or came to visit, which made information flow in my direction almost irrespective of the character and intentions of my companions. It was a form of magnetism, or electrolysis. I learned to generate a current which would produce a transfer of microscopic anecdotal particles from them to me. I was a scavenger living on molecules of gossip.

Some of this was imitation. Mum herself was good at getting things out of people and would rise to the top of any social gathering of service wives. She was a bit of a queen bee. When she came in from the shops, if she so much as said, 'Oh, I saw Doreen Parsons, she asked after you,' I'd milk her for every last drop of gossip and aimless service-wife conversation. I who had no memories of ever being in a shop learned that 'I always say you get what you pay for' was a valid contribution to any discussion of value and price. I learned to give the proper cues myself. And what did *you* say? And what did *she* say to *that*?

I tired Mum out with my talking. I exhausted her modest store of small talk, and still I wanted more. Tell me about *anything*. I absorbed all her prejudices. U and non-U, I suppose. Well-bred people say 'sitting room' not 'lounge'. Never 'lounge'. You can lounge about in the sitting room, John. That's different. There were no limits to the traps that lay in store in language. When referring to weather or a room that is uncomfortably hot and airless, you must say 'stuffy', not 'sultry' or 'close'. And I still don't know why.

There was an etiquette for everything, even elevenses. Mum was very particular about morning coffee. A little dip of the biscuit into the coffee was acceptable, though best avoided. She showed me the way it should be done, if the temptation grew too great. The biscuit went in and out of the tea in a flash. It didn't have the time to become soggy. That was the nightmare, the loss of texture and form. If the biscuit showed signs of bending when held at the horizontal, a point of danger was being reached. 'Never let a dip turn into a dunk,' she would say. 'Don't do what your father does. When he dunks a biscuit in public, there is absolutely nowhere I can look.' Just because I was ill didn't mean I was allowed to be common. She didn't fully close her mouth while she ate the dipped biscuit, so that I could hear that it retained its crunch. She broke one rule (she whose lips closed round a mouthful as if sewn shut) so as to underline the importance of another.

If you said 'sultry' or 'close' you were something worse than common. You were suburban. Being suburban was much worse than being working-class, because suburban people had their roots in the working classes, and were denying their own people just as St Peter did to Jesus. Suburban people were not 'our sort'.

Being working-class wasn't really bad, in fact it was often fine. Really it was heroic. These were people who loved to have things the way they used to be. They knew their place, and liked it. They looked up to you. They were marvellously free of pretence.

Poor Mum. She herself was under-stimulated. It wasn't as if her life was full of incident. She had barely enough on her own plate without being made to dish it up again for two. She was missing out on some vitamins essential to healthy mental life. So she'd end up saying things like, 'Doreen's not really on our level, but she's terribly sweet,' or 'Barbara is terribly suburban, but a *lovely* person. Really lovely. You know me, I take as I find.' All of which I would store away for later pondering. She was my captive audience, and I was hers.

I must have been a bit older, I suppose, when I started to see Mum's snobbery as no more than a dutiful shadow of her mother's. It had the air of something learned by heart rather than felt in the bones. She lacked the maddening confidence which allowed Granny to break her own rules. Funny that it should be harder to forgive Mum for a bad habit than Granny for a vice – I suppose because the vice had a sort of magnificence.

Mental mantelpiece

Some of the things Mum said to me were a little more substantial than the social stratification of vocabulary. She enlightened me, for instance, about the day of the red ball, Dad's ceremonial domestic fly-past and dropping of an innocent projectile.

That red ball had been given pride of place on my mental mantel-piece all the time I was in bed. It was an official happy memory, proof to the world that my life had once been full of drama and life out of doors, impulse and play. As such it was a group project as much as an individual effort of recollection. It was like a big jigsaw done by the whole family, where the grown-ups establish the border, and the chil-dren fit in a few straightforward pieces and are heartily praised for their cleverness.

Even so, I have to say that I couldn't make much sense of the inci-dent when I thought about it from the vantage-point of my bed. What did it mean, that Dad dropped a red ball to me out of the sky?

The flying aspect I took completely for granted. Flying was magi-cal, of course, but it was magic my Dad did every day. I wasn't sensi-tive to the level of skill involved, the sheer difficulty and daring of hitting as small a target as a child's hands with an object dropped from the moving cockpit of a low-flying Tiger Moth. It was a piece of marksmanship worthy of the man who invented that other bouncing bomb, the Barnes Wallis I was named for.

Something bothered me about the choice of object to be dropped. A red india-rubber ball – wasn't that in a poem I knew? Of course it was. The poem was by A. A. Milne and it was about Bad King John ('King John was not a good man – / He had his little ways. / And sometimes no one spoke to him / For days and days and days'). The poem soothed me because of its rhythm and the pleasure of its story, but it was also a tease because I was John, and the poem was somehow about me. When Mum said, 'King John was not a good man . . .' I didn't know whether to be pleased or scolded. And when Dad said, 'Pipe down, Johannes R.,' I knew that was my last warning. That was from the bit of the poem where King John writes his Christmas list, addressed 'TO ALL AND SUNDRY – NEAR AND FAR – / F. CHRISTMAS IN PARTICULAR', and signed 'not "Johannes R." / But very humbly, "Jack".' He takes the list onto the palace roof and leans it against a chimney-stack.

Perhaps I had already shown an aversion to Christmas, understandable in someone whose birth-date was the 27th of December, in competition with incarnate God from the outset. Perhaps I had mistaken the whole festival as my tribute and been disappointed when I was told I still had two days to wait for that other big (bigger) day. It turned out that the presents under the tree weren't all for me. The unwelcome news, so hard to take in, that there are other people in the world.

Bad King John in the poem gets the present he most wants, a big, red india-rubber ball, even if it comes through one of the palace windows by accident, propelled by a peasant child's foot, and I got my ball too. Except that it had been my red ball in the first place, and Dad was only borrowing it.

Theme of A. A. Milne

That was as far as I got in my understanding of the big scene, based on the information I had. But there were things I didn't know about the tiny drama, that aerobatic variation on a theme of A. A. Milne.

There was a larger cast of characters than I appreciated at the time. 'You'll have heard Dad talk about that awful Major, JJ. Mad Major Draper. I've always thought he was a terrible influence on your father, though I haven't met him and I've no wish to. He does the sort of madcap stunt that might be amusing in a child, but he's a grown man and old enough to know better.'

The Mad Major couldn't resist stunts like flying low over water, so low in fact that the wheels of the plane were made to spin by the contact, a stunt made all the more difficult by the fact that the undercarriage couldn't be seen from the cockpit. Dip the wheels just a little too deeply in the water and the nose of the plane plunges in also. As the Major eventually found out. The onlookers couldn't even necessarily see when the stunt had gone right, but nobody could miss its going wrong. 'Dennis always hero-worshipped the man, which was bad enough when he was just an ordinary eccentric sort of person, but then suddenly he was in all the papers. I thought it was the silliest thing ever, but Dad was pleased as punch, proud of knowing such an outstanding individual. He kept on saying, "Good old Kit! He showed them!" but no one could tell me what it was he'd shown them – whoever "they" were.'

The Major had hit the headlines in a big way, nationally and even internationally, in May 1953, which must have been a little while before Dad asked to borrow my red ball. Kit Draper was no longer a serviceman, and he did what he did entirely off his own bat. He hired a plane and then flew underneath all the bridges over the Thames from Waterloo to Kew, including Hammersmith (the lowest) and Westminster (the narrowest), missing out only Hungerford, Fulham and the Kew railway bridge. Fifteen bridges in all. After that he was known to the whole world as the Mad Major.

'I was worried sick,' she went on. 'I was at my wits' end.' That was when Mum's worries began, back when she didn't have to worry about me, when she could worry about her impressionable husband. 'I started thinking that Dennis would try to beat that stupid Major at his own game, by doing some mad stunt with the whole world looking.' By bad luck Dad was shortly going to be in the public eye himself. What if he did something silly? 'Your father has a very good record – there was the time he took off without checking his fuel and had to make an emergency landing, but nobody made too much out of that. I asked him, "You're not going to do anything silly on the big day, are you?" but I should know by now he'll never give a straight answer. He just said, "A fellow needs some fun, m'dear." You know yourself what he's like, and how maddening it is.'

The big day she was referring to was big by any standards – the new Queen's Coronation Day. Dad was due to take part in a mass fly-past over the Mall. What if he took it into his head to loop the loop in his Meteor, with millions watching on the television? She would die on the spot, that's what.

The poultice of indulgence

Mum had already headed off Dad's attempt to pay tribute to the Major on my birth certificate, and she hadn't softened her attitude since then. But perhaps she had learned some tactics. She decided to humour her husband, whose maverick streak was deeply buried. Better to give him his head than risk him doing something Draperesque on a grand public occasion. Best to get the mischief harmlessly out of his system, to have him pull off an authorised transgression with no official ripples. She would draw the poison of self-will with the poultice of indulgence.

If Dad had been a heavy drinker, Mum might have tried to curb his excesses by accompanying him to the pub, having a drink herself by his side, forcing herself to have just enough fun to kill the adventure for him. She applied the same technique in a different area. 'It was Mum that came up with the idea of your red ball, JJ,' she said. 'I thought he could have some fun without risking his career.' Her voice went very quiet. 'We didn't know it was one of the last days you'd be running around the garden.'

'It's all right, Mummy,' I said. 'At least I got my ball back.'

Mum's stratagem of letting Dad break the rules in a setting that was comparatively tame seemed to do the trick. Perhaps he was just playing with her by hinting that he had some dramatic misbehaviour planned. Dad played his part in the celebrations as scripted, though weather conditions were uncertain until almost the last minute. When Group Captain Wykeham-Barnes, the commanding officer of RAF Wattisham, near Ipswich, made a reconnaissance over the route in mid-afternoon it looked unpromising. Cloud was so thick over Biggin Hill that he couldn't see the ground from 900 feet, but

moments later, from near Crystal Palace, visibility was almost unlimited. He could actually see the procession moving through the West
End.

He telephoned Air Vice-Marshal Lord Bandon, stationed on the
roof of Buckingham Palace, who gave the go-ahead but vetoed the
tightly packed 'arrowhead' formations which were to have been used
for the first time. The seven wings of aircraft (twenty-four in each,
arranged in six 'bunches' of four) flew in line astern instead, with
thirty-second intervals between the wings. They reached a speed of
340 mph – the round trip from Wattisham only took fifty minutes.
Dad played his part in the Queen's special day, and didn't spoil it by
saying, 'Hang the weather, let's give the arrowheads a go anyway. Let's
give that pretty girl the bunch of flowers she deserves on her big day.
Isn't she a smasher?'

My childhood ego, undiminished in illness, perhaps even subtly
inflated, took a little bit of a battering from having the incident
brought down to earth. What had seemed a mystical episode in the
family saga was only part of Mum's campaign to keep Dad in check.
Operation Killjoy. It turned out that I had only a bit part in my own
big scene.

My imaginary photograph of the cryptic event slipped down from
the mantelpiece, and I lost track of it somewhere out of sight over by
the fire-surround.

Silent Perambulator

Just by virtue of lying there, under doctor's orders, I made my visitors unearth any scrap of their pasts that might entertain me.
Granny, for instance, taught me by rote an advertisement for patent
medicine dating from her childhood, or even earlier.

Learning by heart is a discredited technique, I know, but I loved it.
There's something rewarding about the process of learning first and
understanding later, even if my first real experience of it was *If you
want a really fine unsophisticated family pill, try Dr Rumboldt's liver-
encouraging, kidney-persuading Silent Perambulator, twenty-seven in a box.
This pill is as thorough as a fine-toothed comb and as gentle as a pet lamb. It
don't go messing about but attends strictly to business and is as certain for the*

middle of the night as an alarm clock . . . Memorised formulas work on the mind from within, as if they were pills themselves, slow-acting pills which do their work over time.

I wanted to understand things. I wanted family history. I asked Mum how she and Dad met. It was an idea I found exciting, that there had been a time when these people whose job was to make me and love me didn't even know it! Her answer was distinctly vague. 'Oh, at some dance or other. I don't remember exactly.' Disappointing. 'He was based near your Granny's house. RAF Tangmere.'

'And when did you know you were going to get married and have children?' When did your mission to make John become clear to you?

'Oh, when he asked me, I suppose.' I had absorbed the prevailing ideas about love and marriage, not yet realising that the coming child does the choosing, and I wanted something a bit more full-blooded. I needed more details, and reluctantly she provided them. 'We were on a train. He was eating a sandwich. He said, "How about it?" and I said, "How about what?" He said, "Getting hitched." I said, "That's no way to ask such a question! Aren't you going to go down on one knee, at least?" He said, "Don't see why I should – there's a lot of muck down there. Take it or leave it. Either you want to or you don't. Just don't expect me to ask again." I said, "At least put down your sandwich," and he said, "I've almost finished. Hang on a mo." And he finished eating his sandwich, and then he shook the crumbs off the greaseproof paper and folded it up neatly. So I can't say I wasn't warned. He was never lovey-dovey. And he's always been tidy – I'll say that for him. There aren't many men who are.'

The London Derrière

The high point of Mum's marriage, to hear Mum talk about it, had been the wedding itself. I suppose it marked the point when she passed out of Granny's direct power. That was something, that was quite a lot. And if Dad wasn't lovey-dovey, then neither was Granny.

Her bouquet was yellow roses. She pointed them out on my wall-paper. 'They were always my favourite flowers. I had a favourite tune, too, and I wanted it played at my wedding, so I asked the organist, but I was shy about saying its name. I was being so silly. I thought the name was rude! So I asked if I could write it down instead of saying it, the name of the tune. What I wrote down was "The London Derrière". *Derrière* is French for botty, you see, JJ. I knew that much. But the tune isn't really called that, only I never knew. I had never seen it written down, I was going by ear. It's really called "The Londonderry Air", and it has another name as well. It's called "Danny Boy". It's Irish, and the tune just pulls at my heart, do you know how that feels? But then a marvellous thing happened. It turned out that someone had loved the tune as much as I did, and he'd turned it into a proper hymn, so we could have it at the wedding. Not just the tune on the organ but everyone singing along. Shall I sing it for you, JJ?'

'Oh yes, please!' Mum wasn't confident about her voice, so it was a treat to be sung to.

She opened her mouth and sang,

The day Thou gavest, Lord, is ended,
The darkness falls at Thy behest . . .

By the time she had finished, her eyes were shining with tears. 'Your Granny said it was a bad song for a wedding, but I told her it was my wedding and I didn't care what she thought. I was very brave then, wasn't I, JJ?'

In my mature judgement (if that's what I have now) Granny was bang on the money. It takes some kind of Anglican genius to turn the Celtic keening of the original – 'Oh Danny boy, the pipes, the pipes are calling / From glen to glen, and down the mountain side. . .' – into such a desperate trudge, so unsuitable for a wedding as to be positively ominous, making the marriage-bed sound as welcoming as a warm grave. Asking for trouble, really. But yes, it was brave of Mum to stand up to Granny on this point or any other.

The pink limit

I decided to ask Granny about the wedding. I was beginning to feel like a sort of human Dead Letter Office, where unsent messages between these incompatible women could be safely left, picked up at the addressee's risk, but I was also free to follow my own curiosity. I was building up a more complete picture by putting different versions together. 'Did you go to Mummy's wedding, Granny?'

'Of course I went to the wedding, child. What a question! It couldn't have happened without me, and I don't say that just because I paid for it. I told Laura, "Many girls plainer than you are getting married to perfectly nice men. If this war had been like the last you might have had something to complain about, but there's really no shortage." Even so, I had to put in some work to make it happen. And then that wedding! Your dear mother has no taste in music whatever, and she chose a hymn like a funeral march. I told her, "If you're going to have that dirge for your wedding, what'll it be for your funeral – 'All Things Bright And Beautiful'?" But she would have her way, and I thought it best to let her. The last thing I wanted was for her to blame me for spoiling her day – as if she needed help! Have you seen the wedding photographs, John? She's cut herself out of most of them, and do you know why? She got the idea into her head that there were thirteen yellow roses in her bouquet, and so the whole thing was jinxed. Can you believe it? She's always been superstitious, Heaven knows why, but that to me was the pink limit.'

Perhaps it was more than the pink limit. Granny and I should really have wondered if it wasn't a sign of something beyond superstition for Mum to take the scissors to herself, even if it was just in photographic form. But Granny was too set in her ways, and I didn't really have ways yet.

Of the three available witnesses to the wedding, Dad was by some way the least forthcoming. He did at least confirm the fact that Mum had had 'a bee in her bonnet' about thirteen roses in her bouquet, when anyone with eyes could see that she was counting her thumb as the fatal bloom in the picture.

Otherwise he kept his counsel about marriage, saying only, 'Anyone who gets married is buying a pig in a poke, John. You can't get your money back.' I could have told him that. That's what comes of wanting to put tailies in ladies' holes! Besides, you get what you pay for. 'Still,' he said without enthusiasm, 'it's best to be settled.'

In my conversations with Granny I had exhausted her small talk, and all that was left was the serious side of things, from which I might have been kept. In effect I had drained the ornamental lake of Granny's trivial lore, and there were strange shapes to be seen in the mud. She liked spilling the beans, did Granny, one illuminating parsimonious bean at a time, but I'm sure this time she told me more than she meant to. 'Your father was a catch in his way, or so everyone said, but he didn't altogether want to be caught, if you follow me. He came from good people, not well off. Generations of vicars, one rather good architect in the last century – your great-grandfather. The Air Force made a man of him, and uniform certainly brightens up a wedding. It was all arranged, and very suitable. Then your father sent me a letter.

'Possibly the most remarkable document I've read in my life. I dare say I should have kept it. Quite astonishing. He said he was sorry, but he was unable to marry my daughter because of a "private peculiarity". Luckily I knew exactly what to do. I sent him back a letter of my own, saying, "You do not say in what way you are peculiar, and I greatly prefer not to know. I will however give you the name of the top man in this field. You will see him, in his rooms on Harley Street, and you will have him send his bill to me. If treatment of some sort is required I will pay also for that. You have not had the good manners to deal with my daughter directly, and now you will be guided by me. You will not tell her of this correspondence or this consultation, either before your wedding or afterwards. I congratulated you when I was told of your proposal and Laura's wish to accept it, and I see no need either to change my mind or to repeat myself."' Granny may have found Dad's letter remarkable, but I can't help feeling she rated her reply even more highly. I have no doubt that she kept a copy of that.

Of course I was burning to know in what way Dad was peculiar. Perhaps then Granny realised that she had gone too far. She hadn't been able to resist the temptation of letting me know that my existence was all thanks to her intervention. I racked my brains trying to think what else had been referred to as peculiar in my hearing, without much benefit. One of the Air Force wives liked beer, and kept up with her husband when she drank it. That was peculiar. One of the husbands handed round peanuts and crisps when entertaining company. That was peculiar, not the serving of snacks but the man rather than the woman (in that fiercely asymmetrical world) handing them round. I didn't have a lot to go on.

Granny wasn't going to retreat from her words or apologise for their unsuitability. Instead she simply changed the subject. I might have stuck to the scent of Dad's peculiarity if she hadn't suggested that we sing together, something we did sometimes and which she knew I loved.

She taught me a new round. I had come to enjoy these odd songs, where one voice after another joined the music and counting was important. We sang them together. 'London's Burning' was bound to appeal to a boy who loved fire. 'Frairer Jacker' was another treat. If Mum came into the room Granny would try to get her to join in, to thicken the texture of the round, but Mum never would. Now Granny told me to start singing 'Frairer Jacker', and she'd join in with different words. When we'd finished she'd teach me the new words.

'Frairer Jacker' was in French and I'd learned it by rote. The new words were English of a sort. In her voice that was sweet like faded roses Granny sang:

Life is butter, life is butter,
Melon cauliflower, Melon cauliflower,
Life is butter melon, Life is butter melon,
Cauliflower, Cauliflower.

I concentrated on singing my French words, but I liked the new ones right away, even if Granny had to work a bit in the second line, to fit 'Melon cauliflower' into the same space as 'Dormay Voo'.

Granny explained that the new words were a sort of joke, or perhaps more of a riddle. A play on words.

'Do you see, John? Life is but a melancholy flower. Not "a melon cauliflower". A *melancholy flower*. That means a sad flower. Do you see?'

'Is it true, Granny?'

'Is what true?'

'That life is a sad flower.'

'It's not a question of true or not true. It's a riddle. What's called a play on words.'

'But is it true about the flower being sad?'

'For Heaven's sake, it's a round! It's a song! It's amusing because of how the words fit together. Don't ask again about it being true – you'll only get the same answer. We can sing it again if you like, but I won't discuss it any further.'

After that, we sang the round often with the new words. I'd let her start, and then try to force the tempo when I made my entry. Sometimes she'd insist on keeping to the pace she had set, but sometimes she indulged me and we turned it into a sung tongue-twister, racing harum-scarum through the syllables until laughter overcame us. Mum would come in with a rather disapproving expression, whether because I was over-exerting myself, though without moving, or because we were playing a game from which she had chosen to be excluded. Family history ruled out what musical sense demanded, the completion of the round. I imagine Mum had taken enough stick about the shortcomings of her voice as a child to be wary of singing in front of her mother ever again.

Self-abolishing magic

The new words to 'Frairer Jacker' were my introduction to a particular sort of power that lay in words. Not the obvious power of a spell, but the self-abolishing magic of a mantra. Something which becomes meaningful only when the meaning has gone from it. It was plain that Granny didn't subscribe to the melancholy-flower idea. Life for Granny was a nettle to be grasped, grasped and then made into soup. I learned to do as she said, to relish while we sang the silly music of the words.

If I didn't really get the joke in the new words, I wasn't offended that it wasn't funny. Not many jokes are. It's optional. Most jokes are like the ones in Christmas crackers, and produce only bafflement or groans. But it did bother me a bit that a whole phrase could mean two things. What I could enjoy in a single word I feared as a larger principle. When things meant more than one thing, a process was set in train that would end in them meaning nothing at all. It was the same with the biscuits that Mum dipped in her morning coffee. They came from a tin bearing the words 'Peek Frean'. 'What does that mean?' I asked Mum, once I'd learned to read it. 'It doesn't mean anything, John, it's just the name of the makers.' Peek Frean seemed more freighted with meaning than a mere name should be, but I couldn't pin its significance down. Then the name became a series of nonsense shapes and sounds. Peek Frean Peek Frean. The words dissolved in my mind just the way the biscuits lost their texture when Dad dunked them, so that a crisp edge became a gummy flap.

Flakes of metal fur

Dad didn't spend much time with me, and when we played together there was likely to be a practical lesson involved. His mind was attuned to experiment rather than pure entertainment. He placed a magnet under some cardboard and showed me how the iron filings fell into a fated shape. Then he moved the magnet under the card. I loved the way the flakes of metal fur crawled into new arrangements.

He played me musical glasses. He brought wine glasses into my room on a tray and made them sing at different pitches, by filling them to different levels and rubbing the rim with a wet finger. He taught me to see the agitation of the water in the glass, throbbing in little surges as the note was produced. I couldn't decide whether the particles in their focused swirl were chasing the finger or trying to run away, but I was fascinated. This was science and music and magic all rolled up in one. Mum came to hear what the eerie noise was, and Dad tried to show her how to make the glasses sing. Even though he gave her precise instructions, she couldn't produce a note, which annoyed Dad or gave him satisfaction or both.

I knew better than to ask Mum or Dad himself about his being 'peculiar'. Dad had got married, hadn't he? – which meant he was cured of his peculiarity. Or if he was still peculiar, then at least he was a peculiar married man. At the time that counted as a sort of happy ending. Marriage being curative in itself, the end of the journey. Marriage didn't solve everything, but in those days it did at least contain everything. Bachelor and spinster were larval forms of life, and only married people could claim to be grown up.

Mum and Dad never knew anyone divorced, socially. There were no bad marriages in those days, none so bad they couldn't be endured. None that were talked about as failures or allowed to unravel in public. There wasn't trial separation and giving-it-another-go and staying-together-for-the-kids, there was only marriage.

Marriage was the rest cure then, for relationships between men and women. Marriage was bed rest for couples. Lie down as man and wife and wait to feel better. If after a while it doesn't seem to be working, then keep trying for another few years. As long as it takes, in fact.

Later Mum told me that while I was spending those years in bed she had many times considered gassing us both. The way she talked about it, she was almost apologising for her failure of nerve. She didn't feel she deserved any credit for resisting suicidal temptation. She still thought it would have been better for us both to be dead. Speak for yourself, Mum! But at least I understood then why she was so fascinated by the gas fire. She wasn't mesmerised by the grille and the colours of its combustion. She wasn't looking at the fire at all, nor the colours of its fading. What drew her eyes was the stiff little tap in the pipe that came out of the wall.

Looking back on those years, it isn't Mum I feel sorry for, even if she was playing with thoughts of suicide, but Dad, so little a part of the household. His projects were so peripheral, apart from his moments of glory lighting rockets on Bonfire Night. The pleasures of the house happened in his absence, even when his belongings made them possible, like the Brummell Tie Press, so that we played in the shadow of his outrage if our games were found out.

One day Mum sat on my bed softly crying, and I tried to find words to reassure her. 'It's all right, Mummy,' I told her. 'I really don't mind being ill.' I even think I was telling the truth.

Net profit of joy

Mum was starved of activities that didn't centre on me. One thing that kept her sane in those years was breeding budgerigars. From knowing nothing about it she rapidly became something of an expert, even an authority. She got the idea from a magazine, I think. The article promised 'hours of pleasure for a modest outlay', which turned out to be no more than the truth. Those birds produced a vast net profit of joy. It must have been wonderful for Mum to find a world in which she excelled, and which she didn't have to share with anyone else, though she chose to share it with me.

If I'd been consulted I would have preferred a pet anaconda or else some baleful insect. I wanted to create a relationship with a very alien creature. Knowing Dad's unsentimental love of nature I tried to sell him on the idea of a pet scorpion, but he said gently, 'I'm afraid even I draw the line somewhere.'

It was probably a minor joy of keeping birds for Mum that Granny feared them. Perhaps it was even a major incentive. Granny said birds were dirty, but really she was afraid of them getting tangled in her hair. She would make sure that Mum checked the cages before she came into a room, and she'd disappear if Mum announced that the birds needed to be let out to stretch their wings. Mum didn't exactly tyrannise the tyrant, but it was a treat for her to have Granny at her mercy in any way. It was something she never got tired of.

Budgies gave us a lot more to talk about, but they also extended Mum's world without the drastic step of taking her out of the house. As word got round that Laura Cromer knew what she was doing, budgie people would telephone for budgie advice. It was a wonderful change for her to be giving out support and information, after becoming so knowledgeable in such a remarkably short time. The satisfactions of budgie breeding even took the edge off her life-long need for sympathy. When she did find herself in a waiting room full of strangers, she might go down the new and sunlit path of budgie happiness rather than the muddy pot-holed track of tragic children and their illnesses.

I learned a few things myself, from picking up the conversational crumbs from Mum's bird table. I learned that if budgies got out of their aviary they almost never got back. They starved because they had never learned to find food for themselves. Being fed by man had stunted their instincts, and so an aviary must have both an inner and an outer door – to act as a sort of air-lock. I remember a weekend of banging and frayed tempers which must have been the time that

Mum and Dad built just such an air-lock. The intoxicating smell on Dad's hands, for which I had no name, can only have been sawdust.

Mum liked the blue birds best. They were the best talkers, and they looked heavenly. Literally heavenly, as blue as the blue of Heaven. 'What's more,' she said, 'they match your eyes exactly. God has not taken your beautiful blue eyes from you . . .' Up to that moment I hadn't known that there were illnesses which could make your eyes change colour.

Budgies, unlike ladies, really didn't have ears. Mum showed me by manœuvring one of her birds, gently stroking his feathers and down against the grain until I could see the tiny little hole where the sound went in. The bird in her hand was very good and didn't mind at all, but I felt sorry for him. I thought that hearing something with a hole instead of a proper ear would be like eating tomato soup with a fork.

On special occasions, if the weather was warm, I would be allowed to spend part of the day in the garden. Dad would carry me out there to enjoy fresh air and warm weather. He settled me comfortably, but then he looked at me with a rather sarcastic expression and said I was lolling there 'like a pasha'. I thought I'd better not ask what a pasha was. Some sort of slug perhaps. He must have been in a good mood all the same, because he volunteered to play 'I Spy', even if there was a catch. All the 'I Spy'-ing he did was of plants, and since he knew all the Latin names as well as the common ones, I had no chance of guessing them. Dad loved plants and was good at making them grow. If he'd gone to university (if the War hadn't come along) he'd have studied biology, specialising in botany.

I remember one particular day of lying out in the garden. Mum told me that the sky that day was a special colour, not just blue but *azure*. The word tasted beautiful in my mouth. I didn't need a perfect sky to entertain me, though. It was pleasure enough to connect up dim sounds that I heard from my room, particularly when the back door was open in warm weather, with the activities that produced them. The scratchy whisper of a rake from the garden two doors down, the bite and chop of the same man's hoe.

I don't know if Mum had been distracted on her last visit to the aviary, but there was a sudden flutter and we saw that two budgies had escaped. They didn't waste time. Soon they were soaring upward,

and it became difficult to pick them out from the sky which so perfectly matched them. It was extraordinary to see their ascent into freedom, and I imagined I could share the exhilaration they felt.

Mum was naturally very upset, and I tried to reassure her. I found
it very hard to believe that those glorious soaring birds would not survive. I couldn't disregard the hard logic with which Mum had
described their fate, but I was somehow convinced that this was a special case. It wasn't even that I selfishly wanted them to return. I just
felt that in this one case the birds would be discovered, captured and
cared for all over again. The moment was so happy for them. It just
couldn't be death they were escaping into.

The blue cere

When her birds started to nest in their boxes, Mum was trans-
ported. Our small world was greatly enlarged when she officially
became a Breeder. She loved all her feathered babies, and yet blues
would always be her favourites, being the best talkers. They made the
best pets and the best friends – females had a tendency to deliver
painful nips. Mum loved to talk about the 'blue cere', a phrase I
instinctively loved myself without knowing what it was. It sounded
such a wonderfully grown-up word. Mum couldn't wait for the Blue
Cere to come, and nor could I. All I knew was that it would be a great
day for our budgies when the Blue Cere arrived. Their lives would be
changed in some way I couldn't imagine. I visualised the Blue Cere as
a sort of springtime Father Christmas, wearing blue rather than red.

Mum had a deep connection with her birds and even with their
eggs. She could tell the signs that meant a clutch was about to hatch.
She would become very keyed up. The excitement even rubbed off on
Dad, who would pop in to tell me the news every time a hatching was
taking place. Hatching wasn't always a happy event. One day I could
hear that an argument had started between them, even if I could only
hear snatches of it:

'No, I'm not going to *chuck it out*! How can you even suggest it?'

'If it can't get out of its egg, the bird will never be a good breeder,
and most likely . . .'

'I don't care, Dennis – for me that is *murder*.'

'You're far too sensitive, m'dear! Quite ridiculous . . .'

'And don't tell me about your blasted kittens. Just don't!'

During his childhood Dad had become used to drowning unwanted kittens in buckets of water. 'Nothing to it, m'dear. Just do it the moment they're born, though, or then you'll get attached to them and you'll never be able to do it . . .'

The argument I overheard had been about one particular egg. The bird inside had managed to crack the shell, but had been too exhausted to get any further. It had lost its fight to be born. It was very scrawny and weak, and it had been rejected by the mother. How would it find its way back to life after that? Dad insisted nature knew best about survival, and from what I saw of the condition of the bird it was easy to feel he had a point. Newborn budgies aren't exactly pretty at the best of times. They're scraggy little pink things, but this one was positively unsightly.

Mum paid no attention. The baby had rights, and if it had been rejected by its mother, then she would take the mother's place. Dad pleaded for her to be sensible, warning that her attempts to hand-feed the runty chick with special food were doomed anyway. It would all end in tears (one of his favourite phrases). She dismissed his arguments, making out that she wasn't really going to any trouble. Since she so often got up in the night for me anyway, what was another little creature to care for?

And then the little bird failed to die, even began slyly to thrive. Little by little it grew, until there was no doubt that it had turned the corner. It loved Mum, and chirped in its little rasping voice whenever she came near. Never was imprinting more richly deserved. The baby bird had been rejected not only by its mother but by the other birds in the aviary, so it became my companion by default. The little bird had nobody, and so the little bird had me. 'Is it a boy bird or a girl bird?' I asked Mum.

'I don't know.'

This was rich. This was marvellous. Much as I wanted to know the answer to my question, I was vastly tickled by Mum's inability to decide the issue. Sorting creatures into the right categories was so much her special subject. She had cleared up my confusion over nurses not being ladies, and she had tactfully led Miss Collins away from the goaty group to which I had assigned her, returning her to the rightful sheepish company. And now she had been stumped by a little bundle of chirping fluff!

Mum explained that you couldn't tell the gender of a budgie until later. That's where the blue cere comes in. The cere is the soft, waxy swelling at the base of the upper beak, which develops as the bird grows to maturity. Blue for a boy, tan or brown for a girl. Of course I couldn't wait that long. I wanted to give the bird a name, and I wanted to call it 'him' until the case was proved the other way.

'I really don't mind if it's a girl, Mum,' I said, 'I'll love him anyway. Him or her. Even if it's a girl and it pecks. But can it be a boy for now?' Mum must have thought it likely that our bird was a boy, because he bobbed his head in the way that is characteristic of males. If he was female he would have been quieter, but bossy. So we assigned maleness to him for the time being, 'on approval', as it always said in the Ellisdons catalogue.

Dad made out that he was indifferent to the bird's existence, but he was the one who came up with the name that stuck. The bird became Charlie. Then it was only a question of waiting for the blue cere to confirm or invalidate our assignment of gender. The change happens at between eight months and a year old, but Mum was looking long before that. Dad said, 'You're being ridiculous, no one can tell so early,' but Mum said she knew what to look for. She had an eye for such things, and said she didn't care what the books said. When the blue cere appeared, it was visible only to Mum at first. Then it became as plain as the beak on his face. There was no doubt about it. Charlie was still a boy and still Charlie.

Tail-end Charlie

It occurs to me now that there was a hint of whimsical tenderness in the name that Dad suggested. Consciously or not, he had gone back to his memories of the War. 'Tail-end Charlie' was RAF slang for the rear gunner on a plane, the airman with the shortest life expectancy. The sitting duck. It was uncharacteristically good shrewd psychology on Mum's part that she let Dad, who wasn't that keen on pets, have a hand in their naming. It made him part of their lives.

Who knows? Perhaps Gipsy was named after the Gipsy Moth, his favourite biplane.

I knew quite a lot about budgies by this time, and although I was happy about Charlie's miraculous survival I was sad to realise he would never be a dad himself. You can't breed if your own kind rejects you, and it wasn't clear if Charlie even knew he wasn't human. All my objections to the business of reproduction melted away in this case. The bond between us tightened as we shared our disadvantages. I became attuned to the faint whirr of his wings and the high humming of his heart.

Charlie was a talker, and an excellent one. Since he had been rejected by his own kind, talking to humans was the only sort of communication he had. His repertoire included snippets of songs and nursery rhymes. He would be let out of his cage to fly around the room, but when I called 'Charlie', he would always come and sit on my finger. He gave me love-nibbles on the lips without ever going so far as to bite. Sometimes he would hop across the pillow and whisper secrets in my ear.

Charlie would have been a fine companion for any child, but he was tailor-made for my needs. He responded to a word, to the merest movement of the lips. No agitation of the bones was required to set him in flight towards me. Charlie responded also to Peter, but if I called to him while he was in flight he would change course and come to me. The summons was answered almost before it was formulated, as in the ideal working of a prayer.

Sometimes I would close my eyes when I called him, for the slightly spooky heightening of sensation, feeling the wind from his wings and the little blurting noises he made as he landed. His feet, which were hard and warm, gave a feeling exactly half-way between tickle and prickle.

It gave me a great feeling of intimacy with creation to feel Charlie's warm beak rubbing and brushing against me, and to feel the tiny bursts of slightly warmer air puffing out of the slits in his nose. 'Birds can't have nostrils,' said Mum, though. 'Not even noses really.' I thought that was unfair. For a while I hated dictionaries for being so killingly exact. When she went out of the room I spoke to Charlie about his non-existent nose, telling him that it's what you can do inside that counts. As far as I was concerned, there were no nostrils wider or more flarable than Charlie's.

Charlie was fascinated by Gipsy. There could be no question of restricting Charlie's movements after all he'd been through, so Mum clipped the dog's wings instead. Before she opened the cage, Mum would raise her hand and say, '*YOU DO!*' to Gipsy, who instantly froze and stayed motionless. Charlie would land on Gipsy's head, talk to her and fiddle with her ears. This was great fun for Charlie. Gipsy was furry and silky and she had wonderfully satisfying ears. With humans you could go straight to the hole in the ear and tell your secrets, but with Gipsy you had to burrow and pull up the flap. When Charlie seemed to be climbing bodily into the poor dog's ear, Mum would step up her vigilance. She would call out a stern warning ('*CHARLIE!*') if she thought he was probing too deeply.

Dad thought all this peace-keeping between the species was ridiculous. 'Let Nature sort it out' was always his principle. If it had been up to him Charlie would have ended his first mission of exploration as a fluttering snack, since that is generally the way Nature Sorts It Out.

Then one day 'the girl' forgot to close the window of my room, and Charlie escaped. I remembered those other blue birds flying off into the doom of the even bluer sky, and I wept. Surely God could not be so nasty as to take away the one thing I really loved and could actually play with? My dear friend kept me cheerful and never got sad himself. He was a playmate who weighed so little that he couldn't hurt me even if he flung his whole ounce-and-a-bit against me. His play could never get rough. I prayed like mad to God at least to look after him. My praying style was crude and I hadn't yet learned to add 'If it be Thy will' to every petition, but just as I was getting to my 'Amen' the door opened and in came Mum with Charlie in her hand.

It was a miracle. I had to hear the whole story from Mum. I made her tell me time and time again. How she had watched him landing in a tree, how she had climbed the tree stealthily like a cat. How she had laddered her stockings but didn't care. How she climbed right up to him until she was ready to pounce, all the time making tiny *tch* . . . *tch* . . . noises with her lips. Tell it all again, Mum. From the beginning.

Charlie's disability must have added to his disorientation at being outside. All birds were hostile to him, even other budgies. It had been Mum who had coaxed the orphaned bird out of his egg in the first place, so he was only going home when he chose to land on Mum's hand. We weren't keeping him against his will. Ours was the only home where he could thrive. And soon Charlie was chirping and dancing again, making additions to his vocabulary.

The twenty-seventh letter

The Collie Boy and I had a bit of a barney one day, about the twenty-seventh letter of the alphabet. I memorised the order of the letters to her satisfaction, which was the sort of thing I enjoyed, but then I started asking about the letter that had been left out. I knew there was one more. One more makes twenty-seven. But did it go before the A, or after the Z? Or somewhere in the middle? 'Nonsense, John,' said the Collie Boy, 'there's no such thing as a twenty-seventh letter. Twenty-six is plenty.'

'Shall I draw it for you, Miss Collins?' I offered politely. 'I know exactly what it looks like. I just don't know what it's called.'

I suppose I was a faintly alarming child from the word go, in terms of curiosity and oblique obsession. Illness had intensified my mental life without feeding it. And I had always been the sort of child who looks troubled – as his mother notices – during tellings of 'Goldilocks'. Always at the same point in the story. Something puzzles him about the details.

Then he tells her what he wants. They must do an experiment. He wants her to go into the kitchen and fill vessels of different sizes from the hot-water tap. He is trying to reproduce experimentally the conditions of the Bears' interrupted breakfast. Fairyland is in breach of the laws of physics. This offends him. It doesn't make sense. Baby Bear's bowl is the one which must by rights lose its heat the fastest. If any of the helpings of porridge is to be 'just right', not too hot and not too cold, then it can only be Mummy Bear's. Why has the story gone wrong?

On the day of our alphabet quarrel Miss Collins humoured me at first, by bringing the little blackboard in range and handing me a piece of chalk, so that I could draw the twenty-seventh letter, but her expression was not indulgent. Perhaps she thought I was being cheeky. I did what I could with the chalk, to reproduce a letter shape that I had only seen in print – and only as a capital. Collie Boy hardly glanced at my drawing before saying, 'There's no such letter, John. Perhaps you'll allow me to know best. The English alphabet has twenty-six letters in it. No more and no fewer.'

'I can show you in a book if you'd like, Miss Collins.'

'What nonsense you're talking, John. Who is the teacher here, may I ask, me or you?' Somehow my eagerness to learn registered with her as pathological. She was a particular character type, the teacher who doesn't much care for responsive pupils, part of the strange group which includes the librarian who prefers the books to stay on the shelves and the bus driver who would much rather not pick up passengers.

'It's in the Ellisdons catalogue, Miss Collins.' My Bible. 'I know the page number by heart. If you pass it to me, please Miss, I can show you.'

'Very well, John. You have one minute to find this wonderful letter that no one else has ever heard of. But be warned, I don't take kindly to cheekiness, from whatever quarter it comes.'

The passage I was looking for concerned a subject dear to my heart, indoor fireworks, and there it was: the pride of the box, miniature volcano which at the end of its display gives birth to a snake from its cone. *Mount Ætna*. Containing a letter which was neither *A* nor *E* but a glorious hybrid, a marriage or mutation. I was hoping for a creation myth from Miss Collins like the one she had for baby 'i', explaining how *A* and *E* came to be so lovingly interlaced.

In fact I'm sure that Ellisdons only went in for this bit of typographical fancy-work in an attempt to raise the general tone, just as it described a remarkably wide variety of toys and devices as 'educational'.

Miss Collins was flustered for a good long moment. Then she said firmly, 'That's not a letter at all, John. That's just a way of writing things down, quite different.' She must have felt she was on weak ground here, since what she had said described letters precisely. They're just ways of writing things down. 'What I mean to say is it's old-fashioned. We don't write like that any more. It's correct to write

Mount Etna, E-T-N-A.' I wasn't in the slightest bit convinced, and I have to say that I took the whole thing rather personally. Miss Collins should never have tried to make a liar out of the Ellisdons catalogue.

In fact I had a funny sort of love-hate relationship with spelling. At that stage I could have gone either way, towards pedantry or indifference. I remember how silly I thought some of the spelling rules were. Why did we need rules anyway? I verry much wonted to rite things owt the way they sownded, and then evrywun wood no wot wee wer torking abowt.

Still, I applied myself to the task of learning the rules, despite a few despairing moments. The spelling of 'meringue' was so impossibly distant from the sound of *merang* that I thought it just wasn't fair. And there were more exceptions than rules, which offended my sense of things. Why wasn't the curved returning stick which aborigines threw, as featured in the Ellisdons catalogue, called a boo-meringue? Once again Miss Collins couldn't give me a satisfactory answer.

A saltation of tits

A year or two after I started to be ill, someone had the idea of fixing a mirror to the end of my bed, a swivel mirror adjusted to an angle that let me look out of the window. At last I could see the birds that squabbled on the window-sill in the early morning. They were blue tits and not wrens at all. I wish I had been able to observe them more closely, since this was the time that blue tits were making a remarkable breakthrough. There's a word for this: a saltation, a sudden evolutionary leap within a species. Not an exultation of larks but a saltation of tits. Admittedly the word is usually applied to appearance, whereas the breakthrough was one of behaviour, as birds adapted to the human environment.

It was like one of Æsop's fables, which I enjoyed being read so much. 'The Fox and the Grapes'. 'The Ass and the Grasshoppers'. I didn't know at the time that the name could be spelled using the rare Siamese-twin vowel I loved so much, which would have been useful corroborative evidence in the case of Ellisdons *v.* Collins.

In Æsop's version it would have gone like this. 'Here's one you'll like,' Dad would say. '"The Tits and the Robins".'

It would have to be Dad telling me the story because Mum had no real interest in natural history. Dad, though, was a good observer and loved the Latin names of things.

'Once there were some tits and some robins living near a village. The tits (*Parus cæruleus*) lived as couples when they raised their chicks, but when that was done they spent the summer in groups of eight to ten, flitting from garden to garden. The robins (*Erithacus rubecula*) stayed where they were, fiercely defending their territory. The tits chattered about everying and nothing, while the robins kept themselves to themselves. The tits thought the robins were stand-offish and the robins thought the tits were suburban.

'Both groups of birds, the tits and the robins, drank milk from the top of milk bottles, where it was really cream. This was years ago, John, when milk bottles didn't have tops at all. The cream was much richer than anything nature provided for the birds' tummies. Not all of them could digest it, but it was such a potential advantage for the birds to exploit this resource that natural selection favoured those who could.

'You see, John, birds are really nothing more than little æroplanes. And here was an unlimited supply of aviation fuel.

'Then one day the birds found that they couldn't get at the cream. There was a hard shiny film sealing off the rich treat they liked so much. It dazzled them and frightened them too. Nature is hard, John, and human beings are unsympathetic. They wanted all the cream for themselves. They didn't want to share it with any of the birds, not with the blue tits and not with the robins either.

'Those were hard times for the birds, both *P. cæruleus* and *E. rubecula*. Winter cost them dear. They hadn't forgotten how to feed themselves, but they were close to starving without the rich food in those bottles. Not all of them lived to see the spring.

'They were resourceful and clever birds, both species equally. They kept returning to the milk bottles with the shiny tops. By summer they weren't afraid of them any more, but they were no nearer to getting the cream again.

'But it is in the nature of birds to peck, and to be fascinated with their own reflection. It turned out that the shiny bottle-top was not only a mirror but a drum, returning a fascinating echo. Every now and then a tit or a robin pecking at the surface would make a tear in the silver foil. After that, with the cream so near and smelling so sweet, it was an easy matter to enlarge the tear and get at the creamy treasure.

'The difference was what happened after such a happy accident. The tits, spending their time as a group, chattered and spread the knowledge amongst themselves. Soon they all knew how to get at the cream. They called out to their neighbours, "Peck at the shiny place – soon your beak will be full of cream!"

'But when a robin happened on the cream he kept the knowledge to himself. And when other robins heard the tits calling they sang back, "Keep your distance! Clear off! Come no closer! You're no robin, but if you don't clear off I'll give you a red breast you won't forget in a hurry!"

'And that is why all tits and very few robins know how to get at the cream they all like so much. The tits keep the secret alive by spreading it far and wide, but the robins lose the secret by keeping it to themselves.

'And the moral of the story is: *Never be too proud to listen to gossip.*' Not something that Dad would have come up with in a thousand lifetimes, but I can't help that. A fable needs a moral. It was one thing I particularly liked about Æsop's fables, that the morals were so explicitly pointed. I was at the age for that.

I myself was experiencing something like a saltation in reverse. The mobility of my joints was so impaired by this stage that I could hardly even lay claim, for practical purposes, to an opposable thumb. Garden birds were making breakthroughs, but I was backsliding.

Thanks to the mirror I could watch Mum going shopping down the lane, and I could watch for her to come back. Bathford was a steep street, and we were at the top. I could see all the way down. The address was actually 5 Westwoods, Bathford. The street sloped so steeply down from where we were that I thought that 'ford' must mean a very high place. It was only much later that I learned there was a connection with water.

The mirror was a comfort in some ways, a reprieve even, but in another it only made me more anxious, as I waited for Mum to come back with her shopping basket full. I worried about her. I was afraid that she wouldn't come back, not because she would run away but because she would be run over. She always seemed to be looking at the ground as she trudged off. She wasn't paying attention.

For a boy deprived of childish company the wireless was a handy stand-by, either when Mum had to go out or when there was a programme we could listen to together. There was one programme which was specially for us, called *Listen with Mother*. The lady always asked, 'Are you sitting comfortably?' which was very well-brought-up of her, but to start with I didn't know how to answer. I knew that it was always wrong to tell a lie, but it was sometimes rude to tell the truth. I was neither sitting nor comfortable. I lay there squirming in a cleft stick of manners and morals while the lady waited for my answer. It was always a bad moment. Then she took pity on my embarrassment and said, 'Then I'll begin.'

Later Mum explained that the lady couldn't hear me and I could say anything I wanted to as an answer to her question. So I would shout out, 'No! I'm lying down and it hurts!' and sometimes Mum would even join in with the mockery of dear Daphne Oxenford.

You've won fair and square

My mind had only two gears, and one of them was idling, though 'instinctive rudimentary meditation' sounds more flattering. The other gear was overdrive. My brain raced wildly when there wasn't enough to tax it. There were things on the wireless which set off chains of thought that flailed and skidded, giving my mind no traction. There was one song that came up every now and then on the Light Programme which I loved to pieces, though it was so strange on first hearing that I struggled to make sense of it. A man and a lady were singing together, but they weren't being sweet to each other. They weren't being what Mum called 'lovey-dovey' (something she didn't like). They were singing and fighting at the same time. It wasn't the singing that was beautiful – the lady was really only shouting in tune. So it was a quarrel as well as a song. They were being rude, in a way, but they sounded happy at the same time, and they sang in turn, waiting for the other person to sing the next bit, so in another way they were being polite even while they were fighting. It was a real puzzle.

The song didn't come along on the radio every day, it didn't even come along every week, but sooner or later I would hear 'Anything you can do I can do better', and then Mum would know to turn the wireless up right away, without being asked, even before the song got as far as 'Sooner or later I'm greater than you'.

I concentrated as hard as I could. There was a bit in the middle of the song which I found particularly baffling, though being baffled was all part of the thrill of the song. 'Can you make a pie?' the lady asks the man, but when he says, 'No,' she says '– neither can I.' I couldn't stop giggling. It was heavenly.

It was so terribly funny, but why, exactly? First of all because of the singing and fighting, which made it different from any other song. Then because they sang so fast. That was clever and it was fun for me to try to copy them.

The whole song was quick. But the bit that I learned to listen out for was very *very* quick. It was so quick that 'quick' wasn't really a quick enough word for it, whatever it was they were doing. There would be a word for being more quick than quick, but I didn't know it.

It was dazzling. I was following the quick argument in my mind, wondering who would be the winner. Then when the lady asked, 'Can you make a pie?' I applauded her in my mind. I didn't really mind who won, but I had a lot of sympathy for the lady. She couldn't win a physical fight with the man, so it would only be fair if she won this one. Ladies have different ways of winning. When she mentioned pies I gave her the crown in my mind.

The line that went 'Can you make a pie?' was obviously the clincher. Everyone knew that ladies knew how to make pies (Mum specialised in cakes but she could certainly make a pie), and so I applauded her silently, saying, 'Bravo, Madam! You've won fair and square!' to myself. The matter was all settled and jellified when the man said, 'No,' and I thought that now the argument must be over for good.

Except that I wondered how the song could go on if the argument was over? It couldn't just stop in the middle, but I didn't see how it could go on either, with the pie question settled so conclusively.

So when she said, 'Neither can I,' it was a total opposite surprise. It took me completely aback, and I couldn't stop giggling. I was laughing and also a little sorry for her, thinking to myself, 'Oh you poor lady! You're supposed to be winning this argument, oh dear! Yes I know it was very fast, and you had to think of all those things quickly, I really don't know how you sing so fast and so clearly – I wish I could do that! – but surely, surely you're supposed to think of something you *can* do if you want to win the argument? I suppose, like me, you thought you were a general sort of lady, and that as a general lady you could make pies because that's what ladies generally do. So you asked the pie question without thinking about it properly first.

'Then as soon as you had asked it, you realised that whereas most ladies could make pies, you for some reason could not. That was sad, and also a little dangerous. If you weren't a general sort of lady and couldn't make pies, he might not be a general sort of man and maybe he *could*, and then the argument would go right the other way and then you'd be well and truly dished. But once he'd given his answer, and it turned out he was a general sort of man and clueless about pies, don't you think that under the circumstances you could have told a very small lie? The man would never know, and wouldn't be likely to want to come and watch you cook one, and even if he did, he would have to make an appointment like we all do when we go to hospital or the doctor, and if that happened you could learn to make a pie in an hour or two, couldn't you? Someone like my mum could give you a lesson. So if you had lied, nobody would ever have known!

'But you were a very honest lady, weren't you? Like an angel, you couldn't tell *any* sort of lie, however small it was. . .'

All this convoluted reasoning took place in a flash. It can't have been conducted in words, because so much verbalisation wouldn't fit into the second or two it took the people to sing that bit of the song. In my imprisoned and restricted body, I was having an intense session of mental gymnastics, and hearing the clever-quick-fighting song made me feel on top of the world.

I tried to explain all this to Mum, but it didn't work. I couldn't make her see what I saw or hear what I heard in the song. I was a chatty enough chap, but my tongue lagged far behind my thoughts. Each thought seemed to come faster than the last one, but each word arrived with more and more of a delay. What was going on in my head

125

was like a disembodied squash game, with the balls having minds of their own. It was like a chain reaction of mental particles. The way each ricochet had more pace and spin than the last one would have been frightening if it hadn't also been exhilarating.

Of course I had entirely missed the point that if the lady hadn't told the truth the song wouldn't have been funny, so perhaps I wasn't being that clever after all.

There was something else I got from the song, other than the experience of having my thoughts bounce so nimbly from lobe to lobe of my brain. The lady said, 'Neether can I,' not 'Nigh-ther'. And nobody scolded *her*. Mum smiled along with the song, as if that was perfectly all right. If anything, the lady was the one doing the scolding. She had the last word and won the argument.

The knowledge that some proper people said 'Neether' was bound to come in handy for a later argument of my own. I didn't make the mistake of coming out with it right away. Patience is a virtue, virtue is a grace. I was learning to have a few tactics, and to keep my powder dry. So all in all I got a lot of ammunition from *Annie Get Your Gun*. I'm sure I learned more from Irving Berlin than I ever did from the Collie Boy.

Invalid privileges

Two things happened towards the end of my years of bed rest which had a knock-on effect on my future, although I wasn't really party to their importance at the time. One was that my dad sat down on the bed, and the other was that Mum picked up a magazine while she was waiting her turn at the dentist.

Sitting on the bed wasn't done. Granny didn't do it because it suited her sense of formality to sit elegantly on a chair facing me. After the failure of simulated horse-play Mum only did it very rarely, and when she did she was careful not to rest her full weight on it. She would perch on the very edge instead, with her legs braced, so that she almost hovered.

Dad wasn't so careful. To some extent he thought I was putting it on. Well, he did and he didn't. I could hear him saying to Mum that I had everyone running around me in small circles, and when were they going to stop letting me have my own way about everything? It didn't help that he had lost his own invalid privileges from the time I became ill. Mum would no longer make him tempting little dishes when he was under the weather. I monopolised the nurse in her, so that there was no one left over to fuss over him. I hogged her help-meet side. It didn't help that with her rather perverse sense of family drama, Mum sometimes used me against him in their marital quarrels.

One awful morning, after a row which had culminated in Dad throwing the marmalade pot at her (the crock and the preserve it contained hit the wall with a double impact I could hear and interpret very easily), she came in and coached me with reproaches to make on her behalf. It wasn't a job I wanted, it wasn't a game I was eager to play, but I couldn't stand against her for long. I put up a small fight, and then I was parroting to my father, 'I'm really quite cross with you, Daddy. You mustn't make my mummy cry.'

Disgraceful. Shirley Temple stuff, really, to which I wasn't suited, and to which Dad responded, quite rightly, with a look of disgust. His wife was hysterical and his son was a malingering ventriloquist's dummy.

Even then he didn't turn against me. Another day I was looking at my old *What I Want To Be* book, and went through doctor, scientist, priest as usual, but this time on impulse I added actor. Mum was busy pouring cold water on this fourth crazed ambition when Dad pitched in to back me up.

'I say let the lad be an actor if that's what he wants.'

'Oh Dennis, *please!*' she said. 'As if things aren't difficult enough already. Can't you act responsibly for a change? Surely you can see he worships you? Now I'll never get the idea out of his head.' I think Dad and I were both taken aback by the idea of me worshipping him, but certainly I was full of adoration in that moment when he stood up against her and defended me. 'Be realistic, Dennis . . . what part could he possibly play?'

'Well,' said Dad, 'he could be an old lady sitting in an upright wing chair in the corner.'

'But what sort of part is that?' she pleaded.

'Oh, I would say it's quite a good one!' he shot back. 'For one thing, he could direct operations, like a general in a battle. He gets it straight from his Great-aunt Molly, of course. Anyway, it's really only a slight twist on what he's doing now. There would be nothing for him to learn. Being thoroughly selfish is what he knows best, and I must admit he does it quite superbly. Even better than your mother, m'dear.'

I was beginning to see the less enjoyable side of being championed by my father.

'The only snag is that he couldn't sit in a wing chair because his hips don't bend, but I dare say that'll all be sorted out by the time he's grown up.' He may only have been using me as a weapon to get back at Mum, as she had used me to make him feel guilty about throwing the marmalade, but at least my father was holding a possibility open, while everyone else was busy shutting up shop on any bearable future I might possibly have.

So when he sat down on the bed one cold night there may have been a hint of hostility in the heaviness of his movements. In any case I had learned to over-ride the reflex of tensing up in such situations, which only brought the pain-spasm on, and to relax whether I felt like it or not. There was no real ill will driving his body weight down onto the bed. Nothing bad need have come of it.

It's just that he sat down on the hot-water bottle, and it burst. It was an old item, which had come through the War (I expect) and was at the very end of its useful life. People of a less thrifty generation would have replaced it long since. It was entitled to fatigue, to perishing. Still, if only Collie Boy had sat down so squarely on the whoopee cushion lying in wait for her! Surely then it would have sung its vulgar song.

Dad leapt to his feet as if he was scalded, though of course it was me he was worried about. The water wasn't close to boiling, I doubt if it was even very hot. He yanked the bedclothes off me and threw the leaking hot-water bottle into the corner. Then he must have started to lean over me, reaching for me with his hands, signalling his intentions. His course of emergency action was to scoop up the entire disaster area, the boy in his steaming pyjamas, and carry it to Mum for her to sort out. That's when I must have said what so wounded him, to discourage him from bringing so much movement and excitement to a body that had been insulated from events for such a long time. I said, 'Please fetch my mother.'

It was the formality of the request that was so wounding, the implication that he might not know instinctively who my mother was, and apparently I made it with a hideous sort of grin on my face. As if he was nothing to me. So Mum was duly fetched to sort things out, to soothe me, to peel the pyjamas gently from me, to dry me, to change the sheets and bedclothes without disturbing me too much, so that the whole alarming incident ended as a sort of accidental bed-bath. Very little water had reached the mattress. It really wasn't serious.

Except for what I said to Dad, and the nasty grin I wore while I said it. Dad's great love was biology on a small scale, dealing with miniature organisms that revealed themselves under the microscope. He wasn't much of a mammal man. I don't imagine he had read Darwin on facial expression in the animal kingdom (which would certainly have been a set text if he had gone to university as planned), and he interpreted my grin as a sardonic rejection of him and his attempts to remedy the small disaster he had caused.

What he saw on my face was a changeling expression, something looking out of a child's face that was not the child. Of course the primate grin can express a number of things, submission sometimes, aggression when the lips are lifted defiantly off the teeth. In my case the rictus had a simple cause, physical pain, as my brain filled up with signals from spinal joints inflamed and in spasm. I suppose I had the option of screaming, which might have been more reassuring to Dad (though that could go either way), but filling my lungs to scream would have jarred my back more and made the pain worse, so all I could think to do was grin and bear it. Unwittingly I offered him a grinning fox mask of pain.

I'm reconstructing my part in all this. I have no memories of that evening, I who memorised so much. You'd think that after so much inactivity my mind would seize on something as dramatic as a scald. Life was visiting my sick-bed with a vengeance. But I think the events of that evening didn't stay with me for exactly the same reason. My idea of a major event had been re-calibrated since the days of my mobility. By now it was a big thing if two wet leaves of different colours, one red, one yellow, happened to be plastered against the window, just like that, one two, by a gust of rain, while I was watching in the mirror. Like the paw-prints of some window-walking animal.

It was headline news if Dad hung up his trousers in the bedroom upstairs without taking the change out of his pockets, so that coins rained down on the floorboards. After years of becoming accustomed to the rhythms of the day-to-day, fragments of gossip about people I hardly knew, scrupulously neutral lessons, excitement banished, a real event flashing its teeth and barrelling towards me from the cloud of plankton would simply burst the fine mesh of my attention. There is a fuse-box in the brain, and under the impact of such charged events I think a traumatised filament blew in mine, saving the rest of the organism from shock.

It would have been better, though, if it had happened the other way round, if I had remembered and he had forgotten.

As for Dad's changeling idea, I have to say that he wasn't altogether wrong. The look that he saw on my face, the construction he put on my words, neither of these expressed actual rejection on my part, but there's no doubt I was leaving his world. I was being changed away from him, and I could no longer be expected to carry the weight of his hopes. For Dad the fantasy aspect of parenthood collapsed early. It became clear before I reached school age that my life would be no sort of extension of his, and he went into an angry mourning.

Usually parents have the feeling that their children are stolen from them when they're bigger, almost grown. The current word that has something of the flavour of 'changeling' is 'adolescent'. It carries that sense of malign substitution. Nowadays children are abducted not by fairies but by their peers. Only a poor copy of what was taken is left behind.

I was already a poor copy. Dad forfeited his due as a father – the knife box brought home from carpentry class, the girl-friend brought to dinner who would look at him slyly and tell him she could see where I got my looks. The thing which happens between fathers and sons happened early in our case. He never stopped being the father who threw a red ball to me from his æroplane – whatever the reasons he had for that – but I soon stopped having anything in common with the son who had caught it.

As for Mum and the dentist's, what happened was that she went to have two teeth out. She read an article in a magazine while she was waiting to be seen. She had always been more of a magazine person than a book person, even away from waiting rooms. Over time magazines had rewarded her with household tips, recipes, sensible opinions and even the idea for keeping and breeding budgies – that fulfilling pursuit, that life-saver. Now the world of magazines punished her with something it normally kept at arm's length, brute fact, not to be bargained with. Not to be cooked, cleaned, common-sensed or hobbied away.

Mum was going to have two wisdom teeth taken out – only the upper ones, which isn't normally traumatic. It's pretty much in and out. The dentist was only going to use a local anæsthetic. It's the bottom ones that give the grief. Mum was half-way through reading the article when her name was called. At that moment her whole world was going smash. She didn't even think of cancelling the appointment. It was something people just didn't do in those days. She would keep her appointment with the anæsthetic needle and the extraction pliers, but as she stood up to go through into the surgery she slipped the magazine into her handbag. She was only stealing a second-hand magazine that no one else was likely to want anyway, but this was by her standards a steep descent into lawlessness. The abandonment of morals showed that she was in shock. She held the handbag tightly against her, despite the dentist's cajoling, all the way through the raid on her mouth.

The dentist injected her in the gums, each side, and also in the palate. When he does that it feels as if someone has stuffed a shoe in your mouth. He tells you that you'll feel as if you're unable to swallow, although if you try you'll find you can.

He tested the inside of her mouth with a probe, to make sure that the anæsthetic had taken hold, while she held the magazine against her heart.

I don't think dentists enjoy inflicting pain any more than any other health professionals. I quite enjoy my own sessions in the chair. I find the dentist's working position comforting, leaning over me from behind, so that I can sometimes rest my head against his chest. I enjoy the warmth transmitted through his smock to the crown of my head. There's a soft connection there, where the bodies touch, as well as a harsher one where the scientific illusion makes its investigations, usually with something sharp, into the 'I-am-the-body' illusion.

The anæsthetic deadens pain, but it has no power to muffle the disconcerting sounds of extraction, which are transmitted sharply along the bone to the ears so close by. The groans of the gums are silent, but the teeth creak and crack under the pressure of the pliers in the moments before they give way. The sounds they make are very much like iceberg calvings, frozen sunderings. Cracks echo from an arctic distance as the dentist consolidates his grip on the condemned tooth and starts to pull, yanking its roots from bone.

Mum's dentist was a competent one, and he didn't take long to perform the extractions. He asked her if she wanted to see the teeth he had removed, but she didn't hear him. She was already pulling the dog-eared magazine from her bag. He showed her the teeth anyway, with a touch of professional pride, explaining that one of them had been infected and would have given her grief before too long. Between his pliers the crown of the tooth was mush. She barely glanced at it. Her eyes strayed only for a moment towards those shattered trophies before they returned to the pages in her hand.

The dentist asked Mum to open her mouth, and when she obeyed him he popped in a little cotton-wool bolster on each side, to absorb the blood. Her mouth was still numbed, and she found it hard to close her mouth round the cotton wool. Then she wandered into the waiting room again. She sat there, as if she was still waiting for her appointment, until she had read the article to the end. Her legs had received no anæsthetic, but she didn't trust them yet to carry her home. Normally she was the one who did the pouncing in waiting rooms, with sad or happy stories, bed rest or budgies, but now she had been pounced on herself.

Horribly perfect

The article she read was about a special hospital where they sent sick children, children whose joints swelled and then locked, whose first symptom was a pain that kept coming back at the same time of day. As the article described them, they were children exactly like me. They didn't have rheumatic fever. What they had was systemic juvenile rheumatoid arthritis, known as Still's Disease after George Frederick Still (1868–1941), the professor of pædiatrics who first described it.

She read the article again and again, trying to find something in it that didn't fit my case. The fit was horribly perfect, the symptoms identical. The only discrepancy was the diagnosis. The only thing that didn't fit was what the doctors had told us. Lightning had struck twice in exactly the same place – in my joints. The first strike had been destructive enough, but this second strike was worse. It seemed to blast with a sort of irony.

Mum rolled the magazine up without looking around and put it in her bag. She was smoother in the business of stealing now. She was hardened. She passed her hands over her face, and braced herself against the chair to stand up.

Only on the way home did unnatural calm give way to hysteria in its other form. Granny was sitting in the kitchen with a cup of coffee when her daughter came flying in, her swollen mouth stuffed with blood-soaked swabs, hardly able to speak, making sounds that were more like howling than anything else.

Mum should have remembered who she was dealing with. It was a point of principle for Granny not to be taken by surprise. She said, 'Laura, dear, whatever's the matter? You look like a molested guinea-pig.' Mum spat the swabs out into the sink, making fastidious Granny wince, and she tried to explain, though the anæsthetic did her articulation no favours. She was trying to master a new language.

'I can't understand a word you're saying,' said Granny impatiently. 'Calm down and then start from the beginning.' Instead Mum thrust the magazine at her, stabbing at the fatal article with her finger.

Granny didn't like wearing her reading glasses, even in front of close kin. Her eyes flickered over the pages, but it may even be that she didn't take in the full details. She gained an impression, and that was more than enough, usually, to enable her to marshal her forces.

'Oh *that*,' she said, pushing the magazine back to Mum. 'The daughter of a very dear friend got that. I sent them both along to the top man. She's cured now, quite cured.' Granny couldn't break the habit of knowing best, however little she knew. *Send along* was a very characteristic phrase. She popped people with problems into the post, making sure they were properly addressed to the Top Man, and then everything was sorted out.

Mum pushed the magazine back in her turn, and this time her finger was jabbing down onto one word out of the many in the article. Granny put her face near the paper, then pulled her head back and looked down from an angle. And still the word was *incurable.*

Sidelong Heather monopolising

The sensations in Mum's mouth began to alter, as the pain that had been postponed returned in instalments to take the place of chemical numbness. She waited for her tea to grow cold before she drank it, and then, fortified by the national drink, she set off for Dr Duckett's surgery. Mum practically barged in, which wasn't at all her usual hating-to-bother-you style, her sidelong Heather monopolising. She was beside herself, adding queue-jumping to the crimes of the day. Duckett was simply baffled when Mum produced the fateful pages. 'Oh it won't be that,' he said. 'I can set your mind at rest. That's just something they teach you about at medical school, for completeness' sake. You never actually see it.' But I suppose somebody has to have it, if someone has gone to the trouble of naming a disease. It simply hadn't occurred to him. As Dad put it when he heard, 'It wasn't on his radar.'

Granny got to work on the Top Man angle. A week after Mum's appointment with the dentist she put in another appearance. She took a piece of paper out of her handbag, and also, this time, her glasses case. She put the glasses carefully on her nose, now that there was something worth reading, a name written in her own hand-writing. 'The top man in this field, Laura,' she said, 'is a Professor Eric Bywaters. As it happens, the friend of a distant friend.' Mum just stared at her. It was the same Bywaters who was heavily featured in the fateful article, and he held out no hope of a cure.

After that first time, Granny made no further reference to knowing someone whose daughter had had Still's but was now cured. She didn't admit to having been wrong – it wasn't quite such a crisis as to call for that. She certainly didn't apologise for holding out false hope at a terrible time.

The emotional weather outside my room went through some convulsive changes, but I can't say I noticed at the time. Despite Dad's kind words about the prospect of me commanding the scene as an actor, all this drama took place while I was off stage. Mum had explained 'the facts of life' to me very promptly, even prematurely, but now she held off from telling me what turned out to be the facts of my own. I learned things in small doses over a long period. There was a slow process of filtration. Information entered my system by a sort of drip-feed.

Rheumatic fever and Still's Disease weren't as different as chalk and cheese. They differed as one cheese differs from another. In one way they were much of a muchness: there was no cure for Still's Disease, any more than there was for rheumatic fever, so Mum and the doctors hadn't missed out on some magic potion to make me better. One day (the day Mum said good-bye to her wisdom teeth) she had woken up the mother of a pain-ridden, immobile child, and she had gone to bed that night the mother of someone very similar. Eventually both diseases die down in their chronic forms, leaving different types of devastation.

There's a certain distinction, too, in suffering from a condition that has a personal name attached to it, like Still's Disease – to be afflicted with a condition that someone had to go out and *find*. An outcrop of illness that an explorer planted his flag on. It feels more adventurous, somehow. A named disease seems more select, less suburban in Mum's terms, even if a few named diseases are rather common, like Parkinson's. There was an additional distinction that Still could claim: he had named a disease on the basis of an MD thesis, an achievement he shares with only a tiny handful. Raynaud, Tooth (though Howard Tooth only managed to hitch his name onto Charcot-Marie-Tooth Disease with the help of a hyphen).

Mum cared nothing for cachet at this point. What she cared for was a crucial difference between the two conditions, and that was the palliative treatment suitable for each. That was where she was entitled to feel guilt and regret, rage and despair.

A boy with rheumatic fever would have been doing exactly the right thing by staying as motionless as possible, as I had, for those years. A boy with Still's Disease had different obligations. His job would have been to keep his limbs in constant gentle movement, so as to minimise the seizing up of the joints. As his joints became caked with rust, he should have been keeping them oiled as best he could, with continuous mild activity. I had done nothing of the sort. I had been lying down on the job, and bed rest had let the disease's effects run riot through my body. Still's Disease had taken away my power of movement without meeting even token resistance.

My years as a bedbug

My years as a bedbug left me with a diminished stature and a defective apparatus. When I went to bed, Peter was comfortably smaller than me. By the time bed rest had done its work, my imaginary friend was not only real but taller than me.

The effects on my legs and arms were different. My legs are more or less standard in their proportion, while my forearms are distinctly short, in relative as well as absolute terms. By this time I had almost no movement in my left arm. The wrist and elbow were fully ankylosed, so that any motion had to come from the shoulder. I pay the price for such efforts in the form of a frozen shoulder, particularly if I get cold at night.

My right elbow has a certain amount of movement, so my right shoulder is spared problems of that sort. Nobody has explained to me how this discrepancy between left and right came about. If I choose to think that my right elbow would have gone the way of the left, if I hadn't kept it moving with my daily shakes to keep Jim Shaeffer's watch wound (I fight the temptation to acknowledge his contribution by giving him the honorific spelling *Shæffer*), then likewise there is no one to over-rule me.

Below the waist mobility was long gone. The hips had a little play in them, but knees and ankles were locked. As ornamental objects my legs failed to redeem their deficits as instruments of walking. They were thin, thanks to the wasting of my muscles, though the joints were enlarged. The right knee was bent forward, the left to one side.

I had indulged in no wilful contortions, and still the wind had changed and I was stuck with their skewing.

Despite all the damage, I can't manage to regret the years I spent in a particularly intense state of isolation. That period of under-stimulation was very important for my development. I was thrown back on resources that I might not otherwise have discovered for many years. Health impels us toward the outside world, sickness brings us home to ourselves – that's something Aldous Huxley says.

I was forced inwards, and so started to make experiments in self-enquiry at an unusually early age. I soon became bored with my own personality, as much as with my surroundings. I decided there must be more to me than the 'John' who felt pain and hunger and the desire to make mischief, just as there was more to the world than the room which confined me.

In the course of mundane education, children learn to ask the question 'Who am I?' only in the narrowest contexts – whose child? Whose sibling or friend? Whose pupil? We push children outwards towards the world, and demand from them nothing less than full participation in illusion, from the earliest possible moment. *They're going to hang that blonde lady because she shot a man who wasn't her husband, but also because she isn't really blonde and no better than she should be. No, darling, a mushroom cloud isn't made of mushrooms.* We defend children from the reluctant inwardness of tedium. Terrified of their boredom, we make them fear it themselves. We addict them to distraction and then feel better.

Less like melting

One thing that many people have noticed, though, is that children die well. Children are better at dying, as a rule, than adults, but then adults react to this fact with sentimental wonder. No one ever asks why it should be that dying should become harder as people grow up – as the world interprets growing up. What is it that makes dying less and less like a melting, more and more like a tearing? It has to be the way we come to accept the conditions of life.

I got only a mild dose of this conditioning. The great obstacles to enlightenment are the 'I-am-the-body' illusion, and the 'I-am-the-doer' illusion. The years I spent in bed were an apprenticeship in pain. The pain wasn't always intense, it had its moods and its tides, but it never wholly went away. To see myself only in terms of my body was to define myself in terms of pain. I wasn't tempted. Looking for an alternative was as natural as any physical reflex. When pain is continuous you come to realise that you have an aspect that pain doesn't touch. Without conscious effort I started to construct a different mental organisation, in which I might be able to live continuously where pain was not.

I had every incentive to develop a sense of myself that wasn't dependent on sensation – since my sensations were so overwhelmingly negative. The road to satisfactory sensations was blocked by the piled-up wreckage of my health. If pain prevents us from remembering ourselves, then it is a great obstacle. If pain keeps us in the present then it is a great advantage.

In the whole of the Western tradition there's only one text, as far as I am concerned, that has any illumination to offer on this subject. It's a poem actually, and it goes,

> There was a faith-healer of Deal,
> Who said, 'Although pain is not real,
>> When I sit on a pin
>> And it punctures my skin,
> I dislike what I fancy I feel.

A limerick, in fact, and not on the surface sympathetic to my philosophical position. It sets out to lampoon quackery and to champion common sense. It has no time for the transcendent. I get it, really I do. It's droll. But how easy it is to draw the teeth of the satire! All it takes is some additional punctuation in the last line, leaving every word intact. The last line should read, "'I' dislike what 'I' fancy 'I' feel.'" That's all it needs. Just a little re-pointing dissolves the mockery, and the final meaning is straightforward Hinduism.

As for the second illusion: I was able to do so little for myself in those years that I likewise loosened my ties to 'I-am-the-doer'. If I was the doer, I was making a bad job of it.

When I tried years later in life to do yogic breathing exercises, *pranayama*, I found that some specialised respiratory patterns were already familiar to me. I had learned how to calm myself using only the body's untapped resources. I knew how to raise or lower body temperature with different styles of breathing, and when the *pranayama* exercises called on me to inhale or exhale through a single nostril, I found that the knack was easily acquired or recovered. I'd already been practising in all innocence.

It may be that I was also meditating in an amateurish way, without benefit of a mantra, seizing on any remembered object for contemplation until I had worn it smooth, turning it into a mental pebble cool to my mind's touch. If the main obstacle to successful self-realisation is uncontrolled thought, then I had a head start. There was so much less for me to shut off, only a dripping tap rather than the unperceived daily waterfall of distracting sensation.

From my bed I sniffed the wind and could smell the weather changing. I just couldn't decide what exactly was happening. The emotional climate around me was complex and hard to read. There was change on the wind, undoubtedly, but the change didn't correspond to the workings of a single season. It was as if the trees were shedding their leaves and coming into bud at the same time.

Then Mum told me I would be going to school. Decisions had been made. It would be a school *with other boys and girls in it*. I tried to bank down my excitement, but still it came fizzing up. Going to school! I could wait a lot longer without moving, if that was to be my reward. I could wait another year if I had to, so long as school happened in the end.

Mum and Dad didn't spell out the exact character of the education that awaited me. They knew the things to say which would keep me happy. Yes, there would be teachers, many teachers and many other children. There would be books – any number of books – and there would be blackboards. There would be as many blackboards as I wanted. There would be chalk and learning, maps and sums and foreign languages. There wouldn't be the Collie Boy. Her work was done.

In fact her life's work was done. Soon after she stopped teaching me Miss Collins ate some contaminated tongue and died. There must have been something quite hard and cruel inside me at this time, because I didn't mourn her. My main regret was that she had taken with her, as she departed from the earth, one of the few delicacies that I would reliably eat. She had been wise to the whoopee cushion on her chair, but not the sliced tongue on her dinner plate. That got her good.

Tongue had been just about my favourite food, being so silky and tender, and now I learned that it could be poisonous. From then on I could only look at it wistfully, knowing that if I was tempted to eat it again I would probably die. I hadn't fully realised that tongue *was* meat until then – let alone what it really was. Compressed bovine lingual flesh. The possibility had never occurred to me. I knew that this silky food had the same name as the talking muscle in my mouth, but it looked nothing like. I assumed that there were two different words that only sounded the same. There are plenty of words like that. Like *pain* hurt and *pane* window. They might even be spelled the same, like *bark* a dog's voice and the *bark* that was a tree's skin.

I tried biting my own tongue, even chewing it a little, to see if it had the same sort of flavour, but again there was no resemblance. Mum had worried so much about the weevils in flour, the worms that never grew despite my hopes, and all along she had been feeding me something really dangerous, something close to poison. I'd never take that chance again.

So Miss Collins was out of my life, and her own, and there was also another good-bye that was harder to say. No pets were allowed at the school where I was going, so Charlie would be staying with Mum. This bit of news gave me a pang, but I got over it. Charlie was my best friend, but that had a lot to do with his being my only friend, and if I stayed at home with him I'd never get another. And besides, wouldn't I be coming home at weekends? Yes, John. Every weekend? Not every weekend – some weekends. Now and then. And will there be holidays? Yes, every now and then there would be holidays. Then I'll see Charlie on my holidays. Cheerfully I sold out my only friend in the interest of getting a proper education.

At that age I wasn't able to frame the crucial question: is that in fact what I will be getting, a proper education? What I wanted, really, in the way of education, was to watch boys wrestling without antagonism, wrapping their legs round each other and rolling back and forth. It stood to reason that school was where that would happen, if at all. What Mum didn't mention, until just before I was due to go, was that there wouldn't only be teachers and books at the school. There would be doctors and nurses and needles. Some of the needles might have tiny hooks attached. There might be invasions of my mouth and my bottom. Soapy water might be introduced there until I made a tuppenny mess. I would be going to school, yes – there was no real deception involved. There would be lessons, certainly. But I wouldn't exactly be going to a school. I would be going to a hospital, and the school was tucked away somewhere inside it. The hospital would be there all the time. The school would put in an appearance now and then, as and when.

She told me the truth eventually, in her own way. 'You're going to school soon, John dear, but it's a special school. You see, this is a special hospital that is also a school. So they're going to make you better and make you clever – all at the same time.'

In fact I would be living in a hospital. To be specific: I would be living in the hospital mentioned in the famous article, the Canadian Red Cross Memorial Hospital, Taplow.

Interlude: Great Western

First I had to get there, to be schooled and hospitalled. Mum and I would travel to Taplow by train – but first we had to get to the train. A special ambulance would take us to the railway station. Before that, though, we had to get out of the front door, and that meant packing. I think the last day or two before I went to Taplow were the ones which taxed my patience most, in all that time of bed rest. Officially the sentence of bed rest might have been lifted, unofficially it went on, since there was so little I could do any more apart from lie down.

Those last few days were my homely introduction to Zeno's Paradox, the rule that nothing can ever happen, because something else has to happen first, and something else has to happen before that . . . I truly thought I would go mad in those days, just when my seat was booked on the Sanity Express to Taplow, wherever that was.

I tried to think that packing was an adventure in itself. By 'packing' I mean watching Mum put things in a case I would never carry. She laid the things I would be taking out on the table and showed me them before she tucked them away. Spare pair of pyjamas, toothbrush, toothpaste, Mason Pearson brush with a handle, flannel and soap. Most important, as far as I was concerned, was a stack of pre-paid postcards, more important even than the sweetie tin filled with treats like Milky Way. Mum had addressed all the postcards to 'Mrs L. M. Cromer' at 5 Westwoods, Bathford nr Bath, Avon. I laughed at the sight of that bundle of cards, all of them under strict instructions to find their way right back to where they were now. It was a boomerang bundle! My hand-writing was atrocious if not actually non-existent, but Mum said it didn't matter, I must write to her anyway and she would understand.

If I dreaded the labour of writing, I was still in love with numbers, and I worked out the aggregate cost of the postcards in the bundle. I still had several unreachable pounds in my Post Office Savings Account. I felt in my bones that those pounds were as good as gone. The Post Office would probably pass a law that you weren't allowed to withdraw money if you lived in a hospital, just so they could hang onto my (Dad's lovely word) spondulicks.

All I had in cash was 8s 5d, saved up from little gifts. Doing the sums in my head, I told Mum that I wouldn't be able to write more than once a week or it would be too expensive. We had a bit of an argument, with her saying that I could write as much as I liked – it wasn't going to cost me anything. In my own small way I reasoned back, using the argument that the money for the stamps would have to come from Dad. If it came from Mum, she would only have to get more from Dad when it ran out. Dad had quite enough to do already, without having to work even harder to pay for stamps for postcards to be sent home by me, a boy who couldn't even write properly.

I reassured Mum that the family money problems would soon be over. After all my health problems were sorted out I would run a jeweller's shop. Mum could come along and have any watch in the shop she wanted, absolutely free. It was only for now that we'd have to be careful about things like postcards. Finally Mum pointed that the money had been paid already, so it would be Wasting Money not to send all the postcards. Then I gave in, quite pleased for once to be over-ruled, after putting up a good fight on behalf of Dad's solvency. I regretted it soon enough. I never heard the end of it, about John's jewellery shop and how terribly sweet it all was.

As far as I was concerned the postcards were the most important things in my little case, but Mum said my toothbrush and paste were vital. I must ask Nurse for a kidney dish, and I must remember to brush my teeth morning and evening. 'And I do have ways', she said darkly, 'of finding out whether you've been using your toothbrush. You've been well brought up, and if I asked you now, you would certainly tell me the truth. But you may find out in hospital that advantage can sometimes be gained – just for a little while – by fibs.'

I asked Mum if the train was going to be special, like the special ambulance that would be laid on for us. 'Not really, JJ, but trains are always special to me. I'd live on a train if I could!' All her life she had a fascination with trains. Roads terrified her, but trains were somehow soothing as well as thrilling. If she had her wish, there'd be more trains everywhere, more trains and more lines and more stations. Wouldn't it be wonderful if there were no cars and only trains, no cars anywhere except taxis to take people to the station? Being proposed to by Dad on a train hadn't crowned her obsession with the permanent way, but it had fallen short of putting her off the romance of the rails.

Any train was special for me, too, just by being a train, by not being my bedroom and by going to a place which also wasn't my bedroom. That was specialness enough for someone whose experience had been narrowing, over the previous years, almost to a point. It didn't need to go anywhere. Even a train that just sat there in the station without moving would have been enough to fill my dreams for weeks.

The sick room

I left the Bathford house with no regrets. That rather austere room had done as much as it ever could do for me. Its bareness embodied the philosophy of the period, that it wasn't right to make a sick room too bright and cheery. Perhaps it was thought that if the room had a sick look in its own right, it might spur the patient on to get better! The steep down-pointing road outside my window showed no signs of doing anything interesting either. Beautiful things had happened to me there, but apart from Dr Duckett (who was still around) and Jim (who had gone) the experiences were internal, and I was taking 'me' with me.

Even separation from Mum didn't really worry me. My prayer to God to 'have the ability to move to the end of this room, or possibly even a little further' was being answered in a big way! Taplow and the Canadian Red Cross Memorial Hospital sounded modern and futuristic beyond belief. Everything would be there: doctors, nurses, friends, children to play with both mentally and physically, and because it was a famous hospital, it would be connected to everything in every conceivable direction of time and space. There would be people who were better connected with God than Mum and Dad were. There would be sure to be a doctor or scientist to tell me what this mysterious sense of 'I' was, this entity which burned in the reddish-brown space of consciousness, and didn't weaken when the body weakened. So I would be sure to find out all about that!

The ambulance was enormous fun. After I'd been on board about ten seconds I started thinking that if Mum could happily spend the rest of her life travelling on trains, then I could just as happily spend the rest of mine travelling in ambulances. It was quite an exciting world, there was much more life in it than the room in Bathford. Every new face was a feast, and here there were two at once, the driver and his friend, who would be riding in the back with me and Mum. Every face was a feast, but the friend's was more of a three-day banquet. He had green eyes, something which I had never seen before, and hair so pale it was almost transparent. He had freckles. I didn't think boys could get them. I'd only ever seen freckles on girls, but then I'd hardly even scratched the surface of the world.

There was a container of water with a glass attached to the wall, so I asked for a drink of water. Mum started to get some out of her bag but I stopped her, saying, 'I want a drink of *that* water.' I wouldn't rest until I had tried some special Ambulance Water, special water for the people who travel in a special ambulance. After that I spotted a sign saying OXYGEN and wanted some of that too. Mum said, 'That's only for sick people, John,' beginning to be embarrassed, and I said, 'I'm sick so I want some.' I hadn't been out of the nest for an hour yet, and I was already turning into a full-fledged pest.

Mum was starting to look a bit thin-lipped so I asked for Martin to come over. I'd picked up from their conversation that Martin was the man in the ambulance and his friend Mick was the driver. At some point Mum must have used the phrase 'properly trained' about the people in charge of the ambulance. I said I wanted Martin to come and sit next to me because he was properly trained.

I had to have Martin sitting right by me. Close contact with Mum wasn't a novelty, but the sudden nearness of a man made me feel as wildly excited as if I was about to discover Africa, Venus or London. Martin was wearing a uniform, but even without it he would have been exciting because of his male aura and vibrations. But there was undoubtedly something transcendent about the properly trained vibrations of a man in uniform. I snuggled up to him as closely as I could, and I relied on looking as sweet as pie. The plan was to get to know him really well, and then ask for what I wanted. Then if he said 'No' it wouldn't really matter. The snuggliness was much more than a means to an end, even if I planned to use it to get my way.

Mates

I explored this man as far as my limited reach would allow. I pressed his thigh and told him to flex his quadriceps and he laughed. I told him he could feel mine if he wanted. Then I said I had something I wanted to whisper in his ear and I asked, 'Martin, can I have some oxygen please?'

I didn't get any, but the snuggliness was a wonderful consolation prize. And there was one more thing about the rest of the ride that I stored away in my memory. Martin called the driver 'Mikey' and also 'mate'. The lingo went so well with Martin's manliness and fresh properly trained male scent, and the word 'mate' made a great impression.

I remember the ambulance pulling up at the train station, and wondering why we couldn't just stay in the ambulance all the way from Bath to Taplow. But that was it for ambulances for the time being. Any disappointment I felt didn't last. A new wave of excitement rose inside me as I realised I was about to make my first journey by train.

Nothing in my straitened experience prepared me for the railway station. My view of everything was skewed since I was carried on a stretcher. I could see people's heads from below, some of them jerking down to look at me with an expression that was almost angry. There was a wonderful high ceiling, with pigeons fluttering under it. I remember thinking that this might be a good place for a church if it was only a bit quieter. Perhaps it became a church at night? There was certainly enough of an echo.

The concourse was full of activity, with people running and announcements blaring. Being inside the station was like being born all over again, the impression of light and confusion. It was a good job Mum was so enthusiastic about the train, because I wasn't so sure as the stretcher came near to it. It looked very dirty and it made an awful lot of noise. Then I realised that the dirt was probably caused by smoke, which cheered me up. Smoke was a mystical substance as far as I was concerned, just by being so little like a substance. I some-times thought I would like to be smoke because then I could be every-where at once and nowhere in particular. Smoke was like mist, only it was man-made, and mist was mystical. When I learned the word *mys-tical* it seemed positively to smell of smoke and misty devotions.

From my position on the stretcher I couldn't see anything of the rails beneath me. Probably just as well. If I'd caught a glimpse, I doubt if I'd have agreed to go on something which looked and felt so dangerous. Being carried on board was like flying, but not nice. I felt fluttery and afraid. I knew what railway carriages were, from toy trains I had played with before my illness, so I knew I was in a car-riage. I was being carried though to a compartment.

I'd hoped that there would be other travellers on the train to talk to, but those hopes came to nothing. Although the train wasn't spe-cial, Mum and I did have a compartment to ourselves. I had to lie flat across two seats, while Mum sat opposite with all our things. I sup-pose we were also given so much privacy as a way of protecting the public from distress, the distress of seeing this sick and unsightly child, but that didn't occur to me at the time.

When we had got settled Mum put some of our things above our heads, where there were shelves called luggage racks. I must have looked worried, because she said, 'It's all quite all right up there. You don't have to watch it. You don't even have to think about it. It just gets carried along with everything else!' My neck had very little play in it, but I could nod to my own satisfaction, if nobody else's, so I nodded now and said wisely, 'What a relief!' It was a phrase I had picked up from Mum. She always seemed to look and feel a little bet-ter after saying it. What a relief!

I wasn't quite as convinced as I made out, and I kept asking how she knew that the things up there would not come down when we met a rough bit of journey. Wouldn't they come down and bash me right where it hurt? Mum said, 'Don't be silly! It's all quite safe,' and

I said 'What a relief!' again, wondering why those words didn't seem to work as well for me as they did for Mum. Perhaps if I kept on saying them, the effect would come on gradually. Then the whistle sounded, meaning that the doors were about to be slammed shut and I suddenly panicked.

'Mum, are you sure you remembered my Siss-Bottle?'

'Quite sure!' she said, opening her bag and letting me have a peek at it.

'And the kidney dish?' I added, which was silly really. If the answer was 'No', then they would hardly have held up the entire train while Mum just popped out for a few seconds to grab a quick kidney dish for John. But if I had a whole compartment to myself, then I must be fairly important, so perhaps the train would be held after all.

Mum let me have a glimpse of the kidney dish too.

What a relief!

Watery leaf

I fell into a sort of doze after all the excitement and forgot to notice everything that there was to see as the train pulled out of the station. The train's wheels sang a song as they rumbled and slid along the tracks. *What-a-relief, What-a-relief, What-a-relief . . .*

On the edge of sleep I thought, 'Now the train is agreeing with Mum.'

What-a-re . . .

LIEF WHAT-A-RE, LIEF-what-a-re,

Lief, watta-ry

LEAF, watery, leaf watery, leaf watery leaf, watery leaf . . .

I should say in my own defence that I had never been on a train before, but I knew plenty of Enid Blyton's books, and the trains in her books were always making words like that. It was life imitating art, the Great Western Railway's trains imitating Blyton's. Their speech pattern was different, though. Blyton never tried to render the way trains pass with a clatter over points on the track, ratcheting up the volume and the urgency of what they're trying to say.

My eyes were absurdly heavy. I knew I should be looking out of the window, to see the sights that had been kept from me for so long.

There would be rabbits nibbling at lettuces at the edge of fields. What was the beautiful word Beatrix Potter used about the effect of lettuce on the Flopsy Bunnies? *Soporific*. Enid Blyton never mentioned that travelling by train was so soporific.

When I woke up I was very thirsty.

Mum was nodding, but she always told me she slept With One Eye Open, so I didn't seriously suspect her of having a little nap of her own. I called out for water. 'Thirsty, Mum, want water . . .'

She sprang to life right away. It was really true. She did sleep with one eye open.

'Well you can have water if you really want it, darling, but I thought perhaps you might care for some of *this*.'

With a flourish Mum produced a huge Thermos flask from the depths of her basket.

'What's it got in it, Mum?' I asked. When she told me it was tea I thought Father Christmas had popped by with an extra present. By now I was allowed to drink tea occasionally, but it had never lost the romance it had had in the days of 'the girl' and the feeder. Today Mum said I could drink as much as I liked. She wouldn't have been Mum if she hadn't stepped in to damp down joy the moment she'd aroused it. 'Before you get carried away,' she said, 'you'd better realise that "as much as you like" means "you can't drink more than there is in this flask". They don't hold anything like as much as you think!'

It didn't really matter, because the amount left in the flask would surely still be huge – enough to get us to Taplow station and half-way back as well, I thought. Coming back on the same train on the same day was an option I still secretly had in my mind. In case the famous Taplow hospital didn't live up to expectations. Mum and I had managed on our own before and we could do it again.

Mum got out a cup for herself, and instead of the hateful spouted feeder, a proper cup for me too. A supply of pillows had materialised from somewhere, so I was half-sitting, and with a little more expert plumping I was half-way to perching in my mobile bed, and starting to feel very chirpy.

I told Mum I was looking forward to the tea very much, and then asked what the taste would be like, because she always put the milk into the cup first and then poured on the tea. Wasn't it going to taste funny after being mixed in the flask with the milk for so long? Mum's tongue did some clicking in her mouth and then she said, 'Jay-Jay-eee! You don't think Mum would forget a thing like that, do you?' She pulled a little bottle out of the basket.

I watched in rapture as she poured out the milk and then the tea. Mum was always saying she needed to keep her blood sugar levels up, and so she dropped two sugar lumps in each cup. It turned out there was a limit to the elaborateness of her preparations. 'When you're having tea on a train,' she said, 'bringing tongs along is just showing off,' dusting her hands together to shake off any lingering grains.

Mum had propped me up so expertly that I needed only a little extra help to drink my tea. She also helped herself, took a ladylike sip, sat back, closed her eyes and said, 'What a relief for this cuppa!' *Leaf for this cuppa, leaf for this cuppa*, agreed the train. My whole world became more highly coloured, and my mind rushed off in a number of directions. Mum's system was hardened to tea, but mine wasn't really, and despite her nurse's training she had forgotten that tea is fundamentally a stimulant. I was used to much smaller doses.

God the puzzle-picture

God featured largely in my thinking. This was inevitable, given my basic cast of mind. God was indeed the basis of all things, and I could see now that whenever I had been afraid and doubted Him, it was merely lack of vision on my part. God was like those puzzle-pictures we played with to pass the time, where you had to see secret things – spinning tops, banjos, cats and books – hidden inside a picture. I also knew that getting to know Him was going to be hard work, and a long journey, but I felt I was on my way. Once Paul Gallico's Snowflake had begun her trembling descent from the sky, there was no turning back for her.

Soon I learned that it wasn't just Snowflake that couldn't turn back. After the first cup there was only enough tea left for half a cuppa for me and the same for Mum. She had been right in saying that the flask didn't hold much. And it wasn't long before I remembered that I didn't hold much either. I wanted to have a siss. I was grateful that Mum had arranged me with the aisleway to my left, because I could only use the bottle if my taily was pointing that way. A lifetime of weeing to the left has fixed my taily so it points in that direction, though I seem to be the only one who has noticed.

On the way into the train I had noticed that the carriages were connected by something that looked like a concertina. It looked very worrying and I was frightened. I had been glad that when they had laid me down we hadn't needed to pass that point. I'd thanked God that I didn't have to pass through the sinister concertina. When the train began to move the concertina became even more terrifying, bucking and plunging, emitting squeaks and groans.

After the siss was comfortably managed I felt my bowels begin to stir, and then I couldn't get my fears out of my mind. I told Mum that I needed a tuppenny, so could she please get out the kidney dish, but she went all strange, and said she would have to ask about it first. She made me secure in my bed and then disappeared. She was back after a few moments with a rather fixed look on her face.

'Sorry,' she said. 'But it just isn't allowed. Out of the question. I'm going to have to get you to the lavatory. Somehow.'

'But you can't!' I wailed. 'We've got the kidney dish in your bag, you showed it to me yourself!'

'Yes I know, JJ, but we're just not allowed to do it here. It's against the rules. But don't worry, I'll carry you carefully. The way only Mum knows how.'

'But that means I'll have to go through that concertina thing, and I'm scared and you know if I knock any bit of my leg it'll hurt for days and weeks. I *won't* go through the horrible concertina thing.'

'Well you'll just have to get used to it!'

I decided then that I hated trains and I wished we'd never got on this one.

'But you *know* I can't. I'll *never* get used to it!'

Now the train was siding sneakily with Mum, going against me and joining in with her scolding. *Used-to-it, used-to-it, GET-USED-TO-IT . . .*

'But you *tricked* me! You *lied*! You showed me the kidney dish! If you make me go to that lavatory through the concertina thing, I can never trust you or love you ever again!'

Ever-again, trust-her-again, ever-again, love-her-again . . . The silly train really didn't know when to shut up.

I had been deceived by Mum, deceived by the mystic enchantment of the train, and finally deceived by the God to whom I had prayed with all my heart. The concertina thing was bucking and rattling madly. My terror wasn't entirely irrational. I had never seen a storm at sea, but I grasped instinctively that some such collision of almighty forces was involved, a war between the elements. All the mechanical tensions in the train, the parts struggling to go in different directions, or (worse) trying to be in the same place at the same time, fought themselves out in this dark and rickety area. It was tricky enough for Mum to carry me from my bedroom to the kitchen as a special treat – how could she hope to manage when the very ground under her feet was lurching and plunging?

I shut my eyes as tight as I could and prayed for everything to end all at once, even if it meant I was back in my room in Bathford, but when I opened them again, everything was still there – and Mum was folding the bedsheet back and sliding her right hand under my shoulders and her left hand under my legs. She was preparing to lift me up and take me on the worst journey of my life.

I made the worst fuss I could possibly imagine, and I had some talent in this line. I made quite a commotion. I couldn't prevail over Mum's superior strength, and Gandhi wouldn't have recognised my demented squirming as passive resistance. He would have disowned me. Soon Mum realised that it just isn't possible to carry a seriously ill child, one who is determined to wriggle and cry out, any distance along a train corridor. She put me back down on the bed and covered me up again, looking very thoughtful.

What I want to be when I grow up

When she spoke again it was in a bright cheerful tone which immediately made me suspicious.

'JJ,' she said. 'Do you remember what fun we used to have reading the *What I Want to Be When I Grow Up* book?'

'Ye-es . . .' I said rather warily, wondering if she could really have changed her mind so completely about making me go to the train loo.

'Well, do you remember which of the jobs you liked best?'

'Of course I do!' I said defiantly, still on my binge of misbehaviour. 'Why will you never listen!' I was close to angry tears. 'I've told you I want to be either a doctor, or a priest, or a scientist! I've told you *time and time again*!'

'Oh yes, so you have!' said Mum calmly. 'So why don't we talk about which of those jobs you could probably do?'

I needed to have that tuppenny more than ever. I couldn't make out why the subject had shifted to the career I wasn't going to have. The pressure on my insides was fierce, and it was hard to think of anything else. It was making me wince. 'Any of those jobs would suit me.' I tried to think of a proper grown-up phrase. 'Suit me down to the ground.'

'Well let's see,' said Mum. 'If you're a doctor, you have to be able to do operations and go round and visit sick people and give them medicine to make them better, and unless you can get completely better yourself, that doesn't sound very likely, does it?'

Looking at my fused left wrist and ankylosed elbow, it was hard to deny the force of what was being said. But I did my best. 'If you're ill yourself you know what it's like. Some things make you feel better and some things don't do any good at all. There could be junior doctors sent round to visit the sick people and then they would come to me and tell me what was wrong. I would think what was best and then say what the treatment should be. I could do it all from my bed . . .' My voice trailed away as I tried and failed to visualise this scene. If I couldn't convince myself I wasn't going to convince anyone else.

Mum saw her moment. 'I think it's a bit the same with priests. Priests can't deliver sermons from their sick-beds, they have to be in a pulpit where everyone can see them. Climbing the steps up to the pulpit is actually part of the job.'

So that just left being a scientist.

'What was the other career, JJ?'

If she went on telling me about things I'd never be able to do, I would do a great fat tuppenny right where I was, and then Mum would be sorry that she hadn't brought out the kidney dish the moment I'd asked her for it.

'Scientist,' I said sulkily.

'Mmm. That might be a problem too. The pieces of laboratory equipment are so big and heavy, you see, and the scientists need to be able to move them around.' Then perhaps she took pity on the desolation her words were making in my mind. 'But by the time you grow up, JJ, I'm sure modern science will be carried out with very small pieces of equipment. Scientists will be able to conduct experiments with only a little movement of their fingers. But JJ . . . Remember that the real scientific work is carried out in your head. You can't be a scientist on the outside, without being a scientist on the *in*side as well.'

'But I *am* a scientist on the inside!' I said. 'That's just what I've been telling you. You know how I always want to know how things work!'

'Yes,' said Mum, 'I do know that. But you see, darling, it just isn't enough to want to know how things work. First you have to learn how things work, and after that you have to think of ways of making them work better. You have to think of it all by yourself, and if you're that type of scientist, you become what is called an inventor.'

'But I *do* try to think of ways of getting things to work better! You *know* I do! Why are you being so horrid?'

'Oh it's not really being horrid,' she said, very offhand. 'It's more a question of being brave and going to take a look at things that scare you, things that work well but ought to work much better.' She made a pause, letting her words sink in. 'Like lavatories on trains, for instance.'

I saw the trap but couldn't help myself. 'How can lavatories on trains work better than they already do?'

'Well when you have a tuppenny and pull the handle afterwards, the lavatory just drops it onto the rail. It's a very dirty system, I'm afraid, and one day somebody is going to have to come up with an idea to stop the tuppenny dropping onto the ground. But that idea can only come from a scientist, a proper inventor, who isn't afraid of going and looking at it.'

'But I'm not afraid!' The words were out of my mouth before I could do anything about it. I had painted myself into a corner. I was caught good and proper. But that hardly mattered. The idea of a lavatory on a speeding train dropping a tuppenny onto the rails was a boy's dream come true. It was fascinating and disgusting and funny. I've been stool-minded all my life, and Mum got me off to a good start when she talked about barium meals and scrambled eggs. How to improve the working of toilets on trains, so that the tracks don't get covered with tuppenny? As Mum had so wisely said, you can only solve a problem if you can observe it with your own eyes.

The crusts of its fellows

I began to think I would have a good chance of solving the problem. At that moment I could think of little else. My mind didn't go in for modulation much. One obsession simply displaced another, even one with the opposite polarity.

Mum's problems went rapidly into reverse. Instead of being faced with a furious child refusing to go to the toilet on the train, now she had one who was mad with impatience to go. A whole trainful of kidney dishes offered to my throbbing botty wouldn't have persuaded me to stay in the compartment to which I had clung so desperately a few moments before. I still hadn't altogether regained my faith in Mum. To insure myself against further treachery I made her promise me something. She must solemnly swear. If I went to the loo on the train, she must promise to let me *see* the tuppenny dropping onto the tracks. When she swore her oath, I was ready to set off. I simply gritted my teeth against any discomfort which might follow. It was in the interests of science, after all. I could endure it. And I did just happen to have a mum who knew exactly how to carry me. Deftly she picked me up. She hung back for a moment at the edge of the concertina and then committed us to our passage across the metal waves. We picked our way safely through the groaning tunnel and from there to the lavatory.

Mum wanted to wipe the lavatory seat clean before she helped me sit down on it, but I over-ruled her. Scientists must accept the world as it is. I also reminded her that I needed to see the inside of the lavatory before I made my contribution to science. She propped me up so that I could see down the broad pipe to where a stained metal plate, held by a feeble spring, clanked and wobbled over the speeding rails. Then I gave the signal that she could sit me down now, to do my tuppenny.

I wanted to see what I had done even before I let her wipe me clean. I dare say we passed through some pretty countryside that day, and countryside was something I had hardly ever seen. But my enthusiasm was all for looking down the fœtid funnel of the lavatory, as my tuppenny, escorted by a feeble shower of water that could hardly qualify as a flush, went to join the crusts of its fellows on the trackbed of the Great Western Railway.

3

Permission to Die

The Canadian Red Cross Memorial Hospital, Taplow, wasn't built as a hospital, any more than it was built as a school. It was built as a grand country house – or rather it occupied converted buildings in the grounds of what was a country house. On the first day of the Great War, its owners had offered it to the army for use as a military hospital. The authorities had taken a quick look round and decided it wouldn't do. The house would require too much conversion to be immediately useful. They don't seem to have considered the offer very imaginatively. They looked at it, saw it wasn't actually a hospital as yet – no beds installed, no operating theatre – and more or less washed their hands of it.

Then the Canadian armed forces were made the same offer, and they saw the potential that had been missed by their British counterparts. The great house wasn't flexible, no, but it would serve perfectly well as a convalescent home. The surrounding buildings were much more promising. There were covered tennis courts, there was a bowling alley. These were large internal spaces that could accommodate hundreds of the wounded of the War.

At the end of the War, the family took possession again and the hospital melted back into outbuildings. When another war broke out, the hospital rematerialised, and this time it survived the end of hostilities. It was made over permanently as a hospital, as part of an ambitious restructuring of the estate, not entirely philanthropic since the post-war government was bearing down hard on the landed gentry. The house itself was gifted to the National Trust, though the family remained in residence. An early example of an arrangement that became commonplace, the rich divesting themselves of their assets but managing to stay in the saddle somehow.

That was the history of the place. As for the geography: it was essentially one enormous corridor. The house may have been a grand one, but our part of the estate wasn't exactly plush. All the wards were

Nissen huts. Even the chapel was a Nissen hut, a half-sized one.

The quarter-mile corridor started with Ward One, which was at the farthest and lowest end, and finished after Ward Twenty-Two. The main entrance was somewhere between Ward Fifteen and Ward Eighteen. The entire corridor sloped gently upwards in the direction of the main entrance. I think it was supposed to be evenly sloped, but there were little level bits outside each ward. The builders or designers made mistakes in the calculations somehow, because near the main entrance they must have realised they had to take the thing up quite a lot, but had almost run out of space to do it in. So there was a sudden, violent upheave as you came from the Ward One end. That part of the corridor was more like a ramp. Porters would have to put on a burst of speed to get a trolley up it. It made me feel a bit sick the first time I was jounced up the ramp, but then I learned to find it fun. Coming the other way, of course, the porters would have to dig their heels in to keep control of what they were pushing. Left to themselves, wheelchairs would tend to roll downhill to the end of the corridor, as if they were curious to find the exit there and to explore the grounds in their own right.

Immobility had been the mystical goal of my bed-rest years. As long as I stayed perfectly still in my garden of yellow roses, sooner or later the unicorn of perfect health would find me and lay its trusting muzzle in my lap. Of course immobility wasn't the Holy Grail but a poisoned chalice, or simply a cracked cup through which the last of my health drained away.

Staying perfectly still was no longer an obligation. So there was no obvious reason for me being put to bed in a side ward the moment I arrived at the hospital, in a sort of visual quarantine. Perhaps after years of seeing so little happen I fell into the category of a starving person, who must be prevented from stuffing himself with bread to protect a digestive system that might simply explode from the shock of nourishment. The digestive system in this case being my mind.

Mum and I had an early encounter with the nursing staff which gave notice of things to come. Along with my modest luggage she had brought along the fire-guard which had kept the bedclothes off my legs for so long. She was relying on maternal eloquence and her nursing background to make this improvised item acceptable to the hospital. It wasn't enough. She was listened to in stony silence, then told it was out of the question.

Mum's briskness always had a tremor in it, but even Granny might have struggled to impose herself on the nursing staff of my new home. I learned soon enough that Mum was right about the superiority of the fire-guardfire-guard to the adult-sized cradles issued there. They were hopeless. The volume of air they enclosed was so large that in any weather conditions short of the tropical my legs took ages to get warm. No reason was given for the unacceptability of the fire-guard, but I expect it was Manor Hospital all over again, a silent re-state-ment of the Weetabix Protocol. *They'll all want one.* We can't have that. As if it would be a bad thing for sick children to discover, that between warm ankylosed legs and cold ankylosed legs they had a pref-erence.

When she went home, Mum left the fire-guard behind in case some independent-minded member of the nursing staff saw its clear superiority for the intended purpose, and brought it back into service. None did. Perhaps none existed. The establishment regarded initia-tive as a symptom of organisational disease.

Junior Norns

After Mum left, I must have had a short sleep in my side ward. When I opened my eyes again, I was looking up at a little deputation of children. There were three of them. My new friends. They must have sneaked between the screens. 'Hello!' I said cheerfully, though I was already disappointed by what I saw. They were all girls, when I was counting on having some male company. I told myself that per-haps the boys here were shyer than the girls, though it didn't seem likely, or promising if true.

None of the girls returned my greeting or spoke to me in any way. They looked at me entirely expressionlessly. My stock of culture was not large. I had few tools for interpreting the world beyond the beloved *Snowflake*, some Beatrix Potter, a little Andersen and Grimm. My little supply of templates would not fit. I would need a broader swathe of knowledge to find a parallel for these girls – Scandinavian mythology, or Greek. I was facing a tribunal of junior Norns. These were the precocious Fates of the institution, who would spin me out, weave me and cut me off.

The girl in the middle spoke at last. She announced, 'He's not pale and floppy – he's very stiff and twisty,' and as if this bulletin gave them all they needed to know, they turned and began to move off. Their movement was ragged, I was pleased to notice, and I thought I could see the welcome gleam of a crutch.

'Wait a minute!' I called after them. After so long without contemporaries, I wasn't going to let them go without some attempt at communication. What they most looked like to me at that moment was an audience. I must entertain them. I decided that I would sing them a song, a special song.

This wasn't entirely an exhibitionist impulse. The last time I had been in a room with this many children, it had been the carol singers that Christmas time. Then they had sung to me, now it was my turn to return the favour. My turn. Fair dos. I started to sing, croakily at first, and then with more confidence. I knew from listening to 'Anything You Can Do I Can Do Better' that you don't have to have a sweet voice to make a song come alive. In fact I would have sung that song, itself, except that hearing one voice do both sides of the musical barney would have been too confusing.

The girls loomed back into my narrow field of vision. 'Mairzy doats and dozy doats,' I began, and went on through the whole cryptic but satisfying animal-dietetic saga. There was no sign of appreciation when I finished, so I explained what the words really meant. I switched from a sort of Ethel Merman impersonation to a version of Professor Joad on the *Brains Trust*. 'Mares eat oats and does eat oats . . . Do you see?' All silence was deadly to me just then, and I didn't notice any peculiarly fatal quality to this one. When I got to 'a kiddley divey too' I not only glossed the line as 'a kid will eat ivy too', but explained that a kid was a young goat. I didn't want to lose my hold on the audience by assuming too much knowledge.

I was just getting started on the natural history of ivy when the girl who had said I wasn't pale interrupted. 'We know the song, stupid. Uncle Mac plays it on the ruddy radio all the time. And *this*', she said, indicating the one on her right, 'is Ivy. I'm Wendy and she's Ivy. You'd better watch out for her. 'Cos you've got it the wrong way round. *She* eats *kids*.' The girl called Ivy, who wore thick glasses, bared her teeth and snapped at me, and the three of them laughed. Then they receded from my view in a slow collective hobble. 'Pleased to meet you,' I squeaked after them. My voice trailed away before I could finish with, 'I'm sure we're going to be great friends.' Skilled as I was in looking on the bright side, I couldn't persuade myself that we'd got off to much of a start.

After that first visitation I was left alone by the other patients. Every now and then nurses popped through the door to check on me, but otherwise I was left to my thoughts. I felt better if I thought about the earlier part of the day, before I actually arrived in the hospital, rather than my recent disappointments. From the years I had spent in the room with yellow roses on the wallpaper I had acquired some skill in controlling my mental activity. In replaying the day I concentrated on the train journey, my little adventure between confinements, and above all the ambulance ride that had started the journey in such style.

I felt there were important lessons for me to learn from what had gone on between the two men in the ambulance. I was determined to work it out. It was the word 'mate' that really struck me. 'Mate', as I'd learned from Mum, was what budgies did to make a chick and what a man did to a lady when he wanted to give her a baby, but this was clearly impossible here. Martin and Mikey were both men, and there was no taily-hole in either of them, so nowhere that a baby could be put in. But still, it seemed, they mated.

Suggestive shapes

The thoughts I was having about Martin and Mikey weren't to do with touch and excitement, they were to do with understanding how the world worked. In a sense they were scientific, but they were also hardly thoughts at all. They were more like stray wisps of feathery cloud, feathers of the mind drifting idly by, but clouds that gradually grew into suggestive shapes. I still had the idea that 'mating' was something painful for the man. The message relayed through Mum that Dad thought it very nice, as nice as I found the scalp-tickling contact of my Mason Pearson brush, hadn't really made an impression.

That was just British stiff-upper-lip. Certainly Mum had never given any indication that there was anything enjoyable for the lady about this activity. I decided that 'mating' was just a job that needed doing and you were pleased when you had got it out of the way, like heavy digging in the garden or building an aviary.

Still, there must be something which Mikey and Martin could do together. Even without holes, they must be able to mate to be 'mates'. Maybe the fact that they both wore uniform, like Dad, had something to do with it. Maybe it was only nice when you did it with another man in uniform. Maybe you had to tell little boys that it was nice to do with a lady, because if men only did nice things with men, people would stop having babies, which was ridiculous. Maybe little boys were tricked into believing it was nice, but they would grow up and become men and after having two or three children they would realise it wasn't nice at all. If little girls weren't nice, which was already beginning to seem a possibility, then how could grown-up ladies be nice? Even if they were nice I would never want to mate with them.

When I needed to do a tuppenny, a nurse brought a terrible thing, something which I thought had no place in my life. A bedpan. I tried to explain there was another way of doing a tuppenny which didn't hurt me, but they didn't want to know. There was to be no deviation from standard procedures, and there was no privacy, of course, for the agonies of excretion. The nurses could have learned better practice from Mum in a matter of minutes, until they were using a kidney dish as skilfully as she did, not only for my benefit but for everyone else on the ward, but they were doing everything by the book, which seemed to be their only ambition. Standard procedure was the gold standard as far as they were concerned. Never mind that it was a traumatic assault on the patient.

The bedpan was always cold, as if it had been kept in a 'fridge, but I could have put up with that. But my body had no flexibility. I couldn't support myself over a bedpan in a lying position (or any other). No wonder I moaned and made little groans. I wasn't making a fuss. It was hardly the Princess and the Pea – it was more like the Princess and the Mattress of Broken Glass.

From the nurses' point of view, my inflexibility actually made things easier, in terms of the laws of levers. All they had to do was lift me up by the ankles and jam the bedpan underneath me, and move on to the next patient while I tried to relax my bowels, ignoring the rampages of the pain in my joints. Then I would have to wait for the nurse to return, in her own good time, for the second stage of the ordeal: the wiping of my bottom.

The nurses weren't actively unkind. I thought of them as iron bedsteads in human form. There was no padding. There were no frills about their care. Some of them would wipe your bottom in a contemptuous way, others more or less tenderly. When they came on duty, they'd be assigned to particular patients, and I'd pray not to have an uncaring one, a bum-scraper who seemed disgusted by the whole business. It didn't help that the lavatory paper was the cheapest and most abrasive grade. Every sheet was stamped with the words 'Government Property', though it was mystifying that the Government should boast of its ownership – unless the Government wanted it back.

The ward where I was going to live was at the bottom of the corridor but at the top of the numbering system. This testified to the importance of Still's Disease in the establishment. Children with Still's were put in Wards One and Two, but they weren't segregated by sex. The numbers wouldn't have worked that way, since for some reason (as I found out with dismay) there were so many more girls affected than boys. Still's patients went on to Ward Three or Four after puberty, depending on gender. Ward Three for the boys becoming men, Four for girls becoming ladies. After that there was Men's Surgical and Women's Surgical. Further in the distance were some TB wards. For the time being, though, while they assessed my medical status, I lived in a little side ward off Ward One.

Any large institution is like a small town, and I had to meet the various inhabitants in turn, the separate sectors of the population. There were so many different aspects to the place to encounter and hope to understand. I had to get used to doctors, nurses, cleaning staff and teachers as well as my fellow patients.

I was under the charge of a doctor and a professor. The doctor was Barbara Ansell, pædiatric rheumatologist, and the director was the famous Professor Eric Bywaters, the one in the magazine article, who had no cure to offer. I saw Dr Ansell first. It was Ansell who first ran her experienced eyes over the body which was the only thing I had to show her. The nurse told Ansell my name, and she said, 'Hello, John,' brightly enough, but she asked no questions. She didn't need to.

One of the last things I had said to Mum before she left me at the hospital was, 'Where's the school?' I could see the hospital, but not the school. And she could only answer, 'It'll be here somewhere. You just wait and see.' She was right. In its own way that first meeting with Ansell was packed with educational matter. Learning doesn't only happen in the classroom. Medical staff have lessons of their own to teach.

Language lesson

It was from Dr Ansell that I learned something that had both a medical and a linguistic aspect. After she had examined me, she said just four words – both to me and to her colleagues – but they were four words with a great deal of teaching power in them. What she said was, 'The illness has raged.'

An exemplary sentence, one that deserves a place equally in a primer of grammar and in a text-book of diagnostics. The illness has raged. A demonstration of the implacability of tenses, and our language's preferred way of conveying that an action has been completed and now belongs to the past. The tense is the perfect. The illness has raged. As a medical professional, Ansell was saying that my case was a special one. Thanks to the years of misdiagnosis, everything that might moderate the effects of illness had been avoided, and every course of action which would aggravate them had been scrupulously pursued. In the absence of a cure Ansell and her commander-in-chief Professor Bywaters could only offer palliatives. My case was so severe that it was beyond the palliatives suitable for other patients.

The illness has raged. The perfect tense had implications that needed other tenses to spell them out. The patient cannot walk. The patient will not be walking any time soon.

There was one palliative in particular that Ansell relied on to relieve the symptoms of her patients with Still's. It was thought of as a miracle drug at the time, though it would be working no miracles for me. The illness having raged, my bones had hardened beyond the

166

point where cortisone could bring about a dampening of pain and restore an element of mobility, as it did for others. Cortisone the ur-, the proto-steroid, first-born of a dynasty that promised so much. My symptoms were beyond the reach of steroids.

Even with cortisone to lessen joint swelling the other patients on Ward One had difficulty walking. I don't want to exaggerate their easy station in life. Walking was not something that came easily to them. They didn't walk fast or smoothly. They needed help from special shoes, they needed help from the odd crutch or cane, but they could get about.

I couldn't. There's a spectrum in Still's Disease, just as there is with every other condition. I was stuck immovably in the ultraviolet. Lying down was all I could do. It seemed to be my talent and my fate. Ansell did all she could – she ordered built-up shoes for me, but even so I couldn't stand up unsupported, in the state I had arrived at the hospital.

There was only one thing Ansell could prescribe, which was physiotherapy. For the first few months of my time in that hospital I was lifted from my bed and wheeled on a trolley to appointments with supervised pain.

Physiotherapy took place at the far end of the long corridor on Mondays, Wednesdays and Fridays, from nine to eleven. Sometimes the physios came to the ward and put slings and springs on your bed, but mainly it was a trolley trip down the corridor, past the smell of boiled meats and dishonoured vegetables coming from the kitchen.

My view from the trolley was of miles of pipes snaking and hissing along the ceiling of the great corridor. The porters looked down at me and I stared up and past them. The pipes were lagged with different colours, though some weren't lagged at all. Some of them dripped water, either very cold or very hot. My first scald was a shock but I didn't say anything. I'd quickly understood that this was a place where complaining wasn't necessarily a good idea. Avoiding a scalding even became a kind of game. I learned to squirm away from the drips. The trolley trip became a sort of physiotherapy in itself, helping me to improve my squirming skills.

From time to time a loud voice echoed unintelligibly in the corridor. In fact it was the same lady's voice that could be heard in every room, so often that after a while I hardly noticed it – the Tannoy. I grasped at once that it was 'the Tannoy' not 'Miss Tannoy', though I couldn't help imagining the Tannoy lady sitting in a special room on a pile of cushions, eating chocolates to lubricate her voice while she spoke into her special telephone.

I liked the announcements best when I heard them in the corridor, because they were so blurred that you could imagine what you wanted to hear. I could half persuade myself that the Tannoy lady was saying, 'Jesus to the side ward, please, Jesus to the side ward. I repeat: Jesus Christ to Ward One. Thank you.' Just my luck to have a Visitor when I was otherwise engaged! I hoped he'd leave a note.

As I became used to hospital life and formed a more detailed mental map of the corridor ceiling and its ambushes, I turned dodging the drops into an organised sport. I would steer the trolley myself in a lordly way, not with my body but my voice. I was the captain and the porter was my crew. The captain doesn't need to steer the ship himself, or climb the mast, or drop the anchor. All he needs is the voice of command. A voice doesn't need legs.

So I'd call out, 'Left a bit!' or 'Hard right!' and if the porter was in a mood to play he might give the trolley quite a swerve. At first I issued orders more or less on a random basis, since I couldn't see where the obstructions and free spaces in the corridor might actually be. Little by little I became more sophisticated in my driving. In time I learned to detect the presence of superior powers by the way even a coöperative porter, responsive to my commands, would suddenly slow down and abandon any deviation from the straight. Then I would sing out, 'Good morning, Sister!' from where I lay, before her face even came into view above me, looking down as if she was on the point of telling me off, the moment she had managed to decide exactly what it was that I was doing wrong.

Years in a kiln

The physiotherapists weren't working out how they could get me to walk. That was far too ambitious. They were working out how to get me to sit. Without significant movement in my hips I could either stand – if supported – or lie down, but nothing in between.

The régime at the Canadian Red Cross Memorial Hospital, in line with the ethic of the period, was determined to get people to walk, however badly they did it. Wheelchairs were regarded as soft options certain to sap the fighting spirit. As assessed by this philosophy my case was paradoxical. It would take arduous months of physiotherapy before I would even be able to sit in a wheelchair for long enough to have my fighting spirit sapped.

The physiotherapy team weren't addressing the disease, they were trying to reverse some of the damage done by the treatment. Still's had affected my joints, and inactivity had made things much worse. Those years in bed had been a sort of kiln slowly baking my joints into hardness. Bed rest had caused my muscles to waste away, with the honourable exception of my quadriceps. The physios would do what they could with what I had left.

I had to get used to my built-up shoes. I had to learn how to use a wheelchair, and then in the distant future I was supposed to learn not to use it, to devise some approximation to walking.

It doesn't sound as if sitting in a wheelchair is something you need to learn. It's a chair, isn't it? You sit in it. It's not as simple as that if your hips are stuck in one position. My posture wasn't fixed so that my lower half continued the line of the upper – there was a bend of a sort, so that my legs were at an angle of perhaps 160 degrees to my torso. I couldn't sit, exactly, but I could perch on the edge of the seat. Because there was a little flexibility in the lower spine, I could make the limited bend appear greater than it was. I could even seem to be 'sitting comfortably', in true *Listen with Mother* style, but this was an optical illusion. All of it took effort. To start with, until my muscles became strong enough to hold me up, I could only sit in the wheelchair for short periods. Later when I went back home on weekend visits and even went socialising with Mum, I could manage reasonably well perched on an ordinary chair, as long as some kindly soul didn't come bustling along with a footstool, in which case my body went hurtling backwards and all impression of ease went out of the window.

If I had Jim Shaeffer to thank for giving me a watch that kept my right elbow marginally active, then certainly Dr Duckett deserves some credit for helping me resist atrophy in one crucial area at least. In the history of my health, though, he is a complex figure.

It was only much later that I understood that cortisone had actually been tried on me, and then abandoned, during the years of misdiagnosis and bed rest. Dr Duckett had tried prescribing cortisone at one point, and watched in amazement while I ran around as if there was nothing whatever the matter with me. Yet somehow he misliked the drug, despite the apparent miracle of its working. He didn't trust it. He told Mum that he wanted to discontinue the treatment – the results were just too dramatic. He was too experienced a physician to believe that any drug could just abolish an illness, when there was no question of curing it. It went against everything he knew about the relationship of the sick body with medicine.

The amazing thing was that Mum went along with him. Of course this was before she understood that a doctor might know less about what was wrong with her son than a magazine that someone had left in a dentist's waiting room (rare condition or no, he should have done a bit of homework). But Mum had been a nurse, however unsatisfactorily and for however short a period, and nurses normally have a healthy disrespect for the doctors after whose decisions humbler professionals have to clean up.

Even about the big issue of misdiagnosis she was remarkably forbearing. By rights Duckett should have been disgraced in her eyes. Of course it's always comforting to have someone to blame, but there was still an awful lot of taking-it-on-the-chin in the national culture.

Authority had prestige, right down to the level of village policeman and general practitioner. Even the postman had an aura vulnerable only to dogs. Mum accepted the mistakes of authority as having the force of fate, rather than anything as trivial as human error, and she never said a word against him.

In the earlier, lesser case of the steroids, she had taken his professional advice even when it was a substantial violation of common sense. Take the boy off these new-fangled drugs – they're doing him far too much good.

A dispersed function

Perhaps there was an extra factor at work. Sometimes it happens that a mundane communication taps into a deeper source of meaning.

A buried spiritual charge turns ordinary lower-case sentences into commands blazing with capitals and italics, all the curlicues of presence, so that a debatable proposition is instantly proven. Not that Dr Duckett was necessarily a spiritually commanding figure. The guru is a dispersed function as well as a real presence. The guru can requisition any tongue, speak out of any mouth at any time. And so Mum had followed Dr Duckett's directions, even though my immediate and seeming health relapsed dramatically as a result of her obedience.

My dreams of pushing Peter over, of being punished, of not wanting to go to bed in case I never got out again, all these were memories of a real period of two weeks when I was five. It's just that it was so unlike the experience of what came before and after that I meekly relegated it to the category of the nightly unreal.

Guru or no guru, Dr Duckett was a religious man, which in a strange way may explain his resistance to the wonder drug of the era, even when he saw its effects at first hand. Rather than actually restoring people to health perhaps he saw himself as ministering to the sick. He had the pessimism I have often noticed in practitioners of conventional medicine.

While I was in the hospital at Taplow he gave me a Bible. I had a Bible-cull a few years ago, when I was feeling particularly got at by the local Christians, and it's the only Christian book to have escaped. A whole box of holy tomes was lugged down to the charity shop, but this one survived the purge.

Only when I looked again at the book, at the time of that cull, did I see that my doctor's name was actually Ducat. Ducat like the money in Shakespeare. Ducat like the middle part of *educate*. His name was imprinted on my mind for all those years, yes, but misprinted.

And there were other misprints involved with this phase of my history. He had dated his gift – 14th May 1957 – and written simply 'Psalm 37:5'. I looked up the passage referred to, rather dreading that it might be that old chestnut, 'Which of you by taking thought can add one cubit unto his stature?' which despite its rather withering Old Testament feel comes from the Sermon on the Mount. In my judgement it's only later that the Sermon hits its stride, with the idea that we should take no thought for the morrow – one of those moments when Jesus was really on to something.

Dr Ducat's passage was a little different. Psalm 37:5 reads: ¶*Commit thy way unto the LORD; trust also in him; and he shall bring it to pass.* Inspirational too in its own way, I suppose, and certainly more tactful. Nice use of the semi-colon, too. I always loved the Gothic-looking backwards P which started the verse. I imagined it as a way of writing down the blast of a trumpet or ram's horn, to announce *Hear ye the Word of the Lord.* Typographical shawms or sackbuts – instruments made even more potent by the fact of my not knowing what they sounded (or even looked) like.

I was surprised to see, on the flyleaf under Dr Ducat's writing, two citations in my own sub-standard hand: 'Mark XII: 7' and 'Luke VI: 20'. I looked them up, wondering what it was about those passages that had so struck me. I didn't remember being particularly enraptured by the Bible at the time, even the pretty bits, and these seemed quite ordinary verses. Then I realised that it was misprints I was noting down: 'our's' and 'your's', both with apostrophes. Shame on Eyre and shame on Spottiswoode. Shame on Eyre & Spottiswoode both. Even at that age I was literal-minded, always on the lookout for typos. I couldn't help myself. It was a strongly rooted instinct. Blessed are the proofreaders, for they shall seek sense. They will read everything twice.

¶In fact in those days what I most enjoyed about the Bible was the richly plain typography and the layout of the verses. ¶I never lost my love for the little sign that introduced a new section. It seemed holy in itself. I was quite shocked the first time I saw it in an ordinary secular book, as if I had bumped into a bishop in full fig at the supermarket.

On the cortisone question, as it happens, I think Duckett (I can't get used to 'Ducat') was absolutely right. Cortisone betrayed my generation of Still's Disease patients. It stole their minds while it was supposed to be helping their bodies. One of the girls on the ward had a lively intelligence, a mental age of ten before she reached that birthday. Cortisone wore her away inside and out. When she was thirty she still had a mental age of ten, and she died before she got to thirty-one.

I don't regret my distinction, among Still's patients of my age, in being free of steroids except for those two hallucinatory weeks. I had a lucky escape. On that basis I have to be grateful, too, for the misdiagnosis of rheumatic fever, without which I would have been put on cortisone as a matter of course, to keep my bones soft. Nowadays the wisdom is to administer steroids for short periods only. They relieve symptoms without getting involved with underlying causes.

If I'd been prescribed the stuff at three, I'd have been on it for the duration, and I think cortisone would have done to me what it was doing to so many of the children on Wards One and Two at the Canadian Red Cross Memorial Hospital. It was giving them moon faces and weakening their resistance to other infections. By affecting the pituitary gland, which regulates growth, it kept them small and I'm convinced it stunted their mental growth also.

The same thief

You'll never read it stated in black and white that cortisone was the guilty party. I know because I've looked in all the right places. To me, though, it doesn't seem to be a coincidence that John Cromer, the one who missed out on the wonder drug, was the one who did some definite growing, and didn't have his mental age stolen by the same thief that took the pain away.

So I have every reason to thank Dr Duckett for his withdrawing of the wonder drug, whether his cavils were amplified by a mystical principle or not. Yes, I know, I hardly seem worth God's trouble. There has always been a small voice, when I think along these lines, asking the question internally, where on earth do you get the nerve to assume you qualify for divine intervention? Luckily there's also always been an internal voice, somewhat louder, asking me where on earth I would get the nerve to assume I don't.

At Taplow Dr Ansell became part of my daily, or at least my weekly life. She was strict, but then no one in hospitals was anything else in those days. She didn't tolerate nonsense, but there was no one there who did, and most of the things which excited my imagination received the label of nonsense. Still, Ansell was a definite force for good. She would say quite cheerfully, 'I know they all say "Here comes Old Bossyboots" when I come onto the ward,' which was perfectly true, though she wasn't old, not much older than Mum. And she was loved as well as feared.

173

I'm sure that if Ansell had witnessed my bedpan torments she might have come up with a solution, but of course I wouldn't be bed-panned while she was doing her rounds. I suppose I could even have told her about it, but I didn't think of that.

The only thing I didn't like about Ansell was the way she would talk nicely to me, asking how I felt and being completely friendly, and then she turned to the other members of the medical staff and started murmuring long words to them. I wanted to hear what the words were, and what they meant. If they were long and hard to pronounce, if they bristled with 'æ' and 'œ's, then all the better as far as I was concerned. Difficulty was an enticement not an obstacle. The easy things in life were hard for me, so why shouldn't the hard ones be easy? I longed to be an initiate. An initiate of what? That was less important at the time. The need precedes the object it selects.

Nose-blood petition

It was my bad luck that it was a point of principle back then, in medical circles, not to listen to the patient. It was virtually a sub-clause of the Hippocratic Oath.

I had the most violent nosebleeds in those early days at Taplow, abrupt cataracts of the vital essence. I connected them in my mind with the pills I was given, and asked the doctors if they might be the cause. They just laughed and said, 'Don't be so silly, John, it's only aspirin!'

This didn't stop me feeling that my body was registering objections on the cellular level every time I had a dose of aspirin. When enough signatures had been gathered, those objections issued as a petition, in the form of blood from my nose. And still nobody paid the blindest bit of notice.

Nowadays the rare reaction to aspirin in childhood is an acknowledged fact. It's called Reye's Syndrome. Back then its only name was 'John being silly'. Eventually they stopped giving me aspirin and the nosebleeds stopped also, but either nobody made the connection, or they didn't want me to know I had been cheeky enough to be right all along about what was going on in my body.

The nurse in charge of Ward One, including the side ward where I was kept for the time being, was Sister Heel. She had introduced herself to me, and I had noticed that her skin was creased and cracked like worn leather, like the brown shoes that Mum didn't wear for best. I hadn't really met her, though, in the sense of becoming acquainted with her personality. I didn't meet her in her essential form until she was out of the room, and I heard her giving a thorough scolding to one of her underlings.

In fact what I heard was a series of crashing noises, and Sister Heel's voice baying over everything. At first I thought that some poor trainee nurse was so terrified of Sister that she had simply dropped a tray of tea things, but it wasn't that at all. It was Sister Heel doing the smashing, with a fierce relish. The noise it all made would make a wedding party in a Greek restaurant seem quite muted in comparison. After a bit I could make out the words. What she was saying was, 'I've told you TIME and TIME and TIME AGAIN!' and each emphasised word coincided with a loud ceramic smash.

She was telling them that cracked cups were worse than useless and should be broken outright. 'A crack in a cup', she crowed, 'is an open invitation to germs.' Not that germs would dare to multiply in her presence, her very voice would sterilise them. 'If you wish to drink from unhygienic crockery, then you will do so in your own time and from your own dirty cups. No patient of mine will be exposed to infection because of the laxness of the staff. Is that understood?'

A voice hardly audible. 'Yes, Sister.'

'I couldn't hear that.'

'Yes, Sister!'

'Now clear up this mess and know better in future.'

The country might be on its knees after a heroic, self-sacrificial war, the National Health Service still struggling to be born out of the ashes of a vanished prosperity, but there was no excuse for a hospital cup having a crack in it.

In fact the economic aspects of the place were oddly unpredictable. We slept between linen sheets as a matter of course, like royalty, sheets washed and ironed in the hospital's own laundry. Ansell insisted on this extravagance – we were children, after all, who spent more than the usual amount of time in bed. The linen even had a wholesome taste against the tongue.

The discrepancy between the smoothness of the sheets we slept between and the roughness of the ones that were scraped against our tender little bums was part of the mystery of the place. In an institution where we had to have our bottoms wiped for us, by nurses whose tenderness was very variable, soft tissue would have made quite a difference, taking the abrasion factor out of the brusquer wipings.

Somehow Sister Heel was so terrifying she shot off the scale and blew back in at the other end, as a hurricane of reassurance. It made me feel better to know that she had the staff running round in small circles. She didn't have anything that corresponded to the modern term 'people skills'. She just shouted at the world until it fell into line, usually sooner rather than later.

Double dose of Senokot

Sister Heel wanted our 'bowels opened' daily. She would come round with Senokot for those whose bowels hadn't been shrewd enough to take the hint. So we learned to lie, to say we'd opened them even if we hadn't. This might work for a single day, but no longer. Then it was Senokot in a double dose. I wondered if this was the same as the castor oil which Mum remembered with such revulsion. Perhaps they'd just changed the name. Then I realised that if I didn't eat, I wouldn't do tuppennies, however much Senokot I was given, and I was very tempted to go without. No tuppennies – no bedpan torture.

It was extraordinary to learn that there was an authority even higher than Sister Heel. Matron was over and above everything, over all the sisters and nurses. She also seemed to have established a sort of dominance over the doctors. I heard that even Ansell went rather quiet when she approached. Matron was to Heel as Granny was to Mum. I could hardly imagine a person so formidable.

One day from my side ward I heard a cadet nurse sobbing in the little corridor, then a voice of familiar huskiness.

'Just learn to pull yourself together, my girl!' Heel was telling her roughly. 'I have no control over thermometer stock here. When you break one, you have to report to Matron to get a new one. Yes, of course you'll get a scolding. You will indeed. As did we all!'

That word 'scolding' was full of fascination for me. Mum had told me about what happened when hot liquid fell on the skin, about scalding and the rawness and blistering that followed. Bad scaldings never really healed. It stood to reason that a scolding was a verbal scalding, when someone else's mind boiled over on you, like milk on top of a stove. If ever I became too cocky, too knowing, too plain happy, I'd get a scolding. Someone would be sure to say, 'You're getting too big for your boots.' That's to say, too big for my built-up shoes. 'You need to be taken down a peg or two.' I was always being told about pride going before a fall. I didn't know why that proverb seemed to have my name on it.

It was thrilling to imagine Heel as a cadet herself, trembling before the mighty Matron. Interesting too that Heel, while informing the poor cadet about hospital procedure, was also delivering a scolding of her own. A scolding about a scolding, a scolding to tell her about the scolding she'd get from Matron. How fascinating! I reasoned that if Heel could scold the ward, and Matron could scold the hospital, then there must be someone who had the power to scold Matron, and calculated that there must be some kind of Super-Matron of all England who had the power to scold any matron in any hospital in the country. But who would have the power to scold her? My mind just naturally lost itself in such cosmological labyrinths.

So when I was told Matron was doing her rounds and would be visiting me in my side ward, I was distinctly nervous. It made sense that she would be completely terrifying. I hoped she would just take a quick look at me and go out again. I didn't think I could stand being on the receiving end of Matron's rough tongue. When Heel licked cadet nurses into shape, after all, they might sob for hours.

Then when Matron swept in at the head of a train of attendants it was a delicious surprise. She wore a purple uniform, which I immediately loved, and a starched hat which fitted tightly round her head, splaying out in a pleated fan around her shoulders like a peacock's tail upside-down. The world went very still when she came in. This wasn't an enforced or punitive silence but a rapt stillness, hushed and attentive.

'Good morning, John,' she said.

'Good morning, Matron,' I replied.

'Sister Heel tells me you were admitted last week, so I want to say how sorry I am that I have not visited you earlier. I hope all the nurses have been making you feel comfortable and At Home?'

They hadn't, or not all of them had, but Matron was so nice I wasn't going to squeal on the ones who wiped my bottom harshly. It would have made more sense to appeal for an improvement in the quality of the paper itself, but I didn't think of that.

'It's a little strange here,' I said, 'but I'm starting to get used to it. I'm very happy to meet you, Matron.'

'It's entirely my pleasure, John,' she said. 'I'm afraid that I am very busy at the moment, but I shall make time soon to pay a longer visit and get to know you better.'

'I would like that very much, Matron.'

'I hope you feel, John, that if anything is worrying you, or even if there is anything you do not understand – I hope you will send word to me any time you want. Say you have my express permission. Can you remember that, John? "Express permission"?'

'Yes, Matron,' I whispered. '"Express permission from Matron". Thank you very much.' I was really beginning to understand the phrase 'angel of mercy'. As the purple vision withdrew from my side ward with her retinue, I heard her murmur, 'What *beautiful* manners! Such a treat in this day and age. If only we could . . .' But then the end of the sentence was swallowed up by the sounds of the ward.

This was the longest conversation I had had with anyone in Taplow – and it had been with Matron! It was balm, it was soul-ointment, and I basked in the glow of it. I began to think that the Canadian Red Cross Memorial Hospital might be the right place for me after all.

Flakes of delight

Soon after that the assessment period came to an end and I was transferred to the ward proper. Some ministering angel or humane administrator had seen to it that Ivy and the girl who had threatened me with her, Wendy, were both a little way off. My nearest neighbours were gentler souls, Mary and Sarah.

Even before I took my place on the ward I had been initiated into the sorrows of the communal life. While I was still in my side ward a nurse had pounced on my sweetie tin, saying brightly, 'These'll go into the pool . . .' I was appalled. Why was this horrid nurse going to throw my sweeties in the swimming pool?

I wasn't much better pleased when I understood the workings of the system which operated in the hospital. Sweets were not private property. They went into a common hoard, to be shared out equally. I suppose this system was designed to benefit the less fortunate children, by taxing those with regular supplies of luxury choccies, but I wasn't wild about it. I would almost rather my personal sweets were ritually drowned in the pool than made into common property. My objections weren't ideological, really, it's just that I never liked the sweets I ended up with. I didn't think much of a system which dispersed my Milky Ways far and wide and repaid me in chunks of Pic-Nic, which I happened to hate.

The reply was waiting for any protest: 'Well, John, you're lucky to have sweets at all.' And I wasn't clever enough to say, 'But not as lucky as if you'd let me keep the ones Mum packed in my own little tin.'

In any case, there would have been no possibility of chilling and slicing the Mars Bars Mum brought, so as to turn the sticky logs into flakes of delight. Without access to a 'fridge the operation wasn't practical.

There was someone at the hospital who wasn't a doctor and wasn't a cleaner but something in between, and he did something to me soon after I arrived that I didn't like. He didn't seem to know my name, he just called me 'Sonny', but I had to do what he said. His name was Mr Fisk, and he took pictures. He had one of those moustaches that hang over the lower lip, like a weeping willow trailing its branches down towards the water. Mr Fisk was a fearful figure, not because he was nasty personally, but because it was nasty being photographed, naked and standing up as best you could, without shoes.

I had lost my taste for having my appearance captured since my triumphant photo-session with *Cyril Howes of Bath*. I was no longer a responsive model. If I didn't have my shoes on and a hand to hold I couldn't stand up, which seemed to vex Mr Fisk, but eventually even the rigid hospital régime took account of my circumstances and allowed me to wear shoes. Someone held my hand at the edge of the photograph, where it wouldn't obscure what they were interested in. It was never explained why there had to be photographs, and how the pictures that Mr Fisk took ended up in the hands of the doctors. It's not hard to understand, once you've been told. But you do have to be told.

I had the impression at that age that children were somehow automatically naked, as if it was a stage adults had grown out of. There was some sort of dividing line, and beyond that you need never be unclothed again. You might even be lucky enough to wear a uniform, but in any case being grown up would mean an end to nakedness. Till that happy day arrived, I would have to be photographed naked and childish by Mr Fisk four times a year.

While my wheelchair-sitting skills were still in their infancy, I started attending the hospital chapel. It was only another Nissen hut, half-sized at that, but it had a wonderful atmosphere. At first I thought you couldn't go to church unless you were able to sit up, but the monks told me that wasn't so. They volunteered to take me in on a stretcher. I remember being pushed along the corridor to the chapel on a trolley. It was a long way to go – a bit of an expedition.

In the little chapel I waited to hear a piano, perhaps even an organ, but there were no instruments. The singing was unaccompanied. I couldn't see the point, for about ten seconds, but then I got it. A different sort of feeling to the music. The monks were lovely. One of them said, 'If you can't manage the hymn book, I'll hold it for you.' He sat next to me on the trolley and it was wonderful. I didn't know whether he was really allowed to sit by me on the trolley, but I reasoned that although this was all hospital and the chapel was inside it, you could also say it was God's House and the hospital had no say-so. God would protect the monks from worldly scolding.

Invisible stubby quills

The monks were Benedictines, wearing brown tunics and scapulars with hoods, based at Nashdom Abbey which was either on the estate or very near. Their heads were shaved and I wanted to touch. Once I asked if I could, and the monk didn't answer but just bent his head down for me to explore. It was so delicious. I touched his shaven head.

I stroked the consecrated scalp. To the eye the surface was smooth but to the hand it was nothing but tiny prickles. It wasn't a polished shape like a marble sculpture, it was a field of invisible stubby quills. What I saw was only a small misleading part of things. I realised that touch was probably the best guide to the world, but that was where I was most disadvantaged. I would have to navigate by other means. Only on special occasions would the truth be palpable. I'd had the courage to ask to touch once, and once was permitted, once was ordinary human curiosity. Even Weetabix had been allowed once. More than once was something that would be frowned on in the long run.

Even so, I enjoyed the monkish tenderness and the atmosphere of contemplation. In those chapel services there was no one telling you to repent, or commit yourself, or put money in a dish. For once they didn't dissipate the essential mystical experience. If all Christianity lived up to that depth of presence, I'd be fonder of it now.

After its shaky start, my experience of social life on the ward could only improve, but the up-turn wasn't sudden or steep. It would be nice to think that bullying played no part on a ward of sick and disabled children, but it was more or less the foundation of our little society. The ringleader was the girl who had pronounced me stiff and twisty the day I arrived – Wendy Keach. Physical violence wasn't the basis of her power on the ward, but she showed that psychological torment can be just as effective. It certainly took the shine off *Peter Pan* for me, having such a nasty Wendy on the premises.

Wendy's lieutenant, the one who supposedly ate children, was Ivy Horrocks. How desperately we tried to be in good with the two of them! Otherwise we'd be on their list of victims. Neutrality was never an option. When I say 'we' I should really come clean and say 'I'. Not everyone was so cowardly.

There was a television on the ward, but it was only turned on for about half an hour a day. I remember seeing *Bill and Ben*, and a programme about the Abominable Snowman which scared me good and proper. There was a lot of talk among us about where the words on the screen went when they disappeared. The most popular answer was that 'little men' wound them round from the back of the set. Little men did a lot of odd jobs. Little men must also be responsible for cutting our poo into those little sausage lengths, though the idea of men living inside people's bottoms took a little getting used to. Nobody told us different. Little-man theory prevailed by default.

The thing I liked best of all about television was the way the image collapsed, when the set was turned off, into a mystical dot which hung there for a surprisingly long time. To date, the behaviour of the valves touched me more deeply than any programme.

The school was much harder to find on those premises than the hospital. This was a school in the fifth dimension, a shy and fugitive institution. The hospital was sure of itself while the school was tentative in the extreme. The hospital advanced to meet you, the school melted away at a moment's notice, abandoning its weaker claims. I wasn't well up on Broadway musicals – I knew only the one song from *Annie Get Your Gun*. Otherwise I might have been reminded of *Brigadoon*, and the village in the Highlands which appears for a single day every hundred years. Still, if there was no sign yet of school, there was plenty to learn. There was Ansell and 'The illness has raged', and there were other early lessons. I learned that I was something called Posh. My accent betrayed me to Wendy, but so did my choice of words. I said 'lavatory' for toilet. I soon learned to roughen up my vocabulary and even my accent.

I learned to use words like 'shit' and 'bum' instead of tuppenny and BTM. There's something to be said for the direct approach, after all. And of course tuppenny is only rhyming slang, isn't it? 'Tuppenny bit' equals 'shit'. I wonder if Mum and Dad even realised the vulgar roots of their genteel expression. Although it does add up in a way, the idea of spending-a-penny doubled.

Even after 'lavatory' had gone down the pan, Wendy found other ammunition. She never ran short. If for instance you have developed the charming notion, as a child beginning to speak, that the holes in your nose are called 'snorts' rather than nostrils, and if your parents have indulged your delightfulness by adopting the word themselves on the rare occasions when nostrils must be talked of, and if you then experience a drastic shift of company, forgetting that home words must stay in the home, then you will very quickly learn your mistake. Wendy snorted with derisive laughter, till the snot almost ran out of her nose-holes.

With the meagre materials to hand Wendy ran quite a little régime of terror. She was sly in extracting secrets she might use to her advantage. She was convinced that I had a middle name, despite my denials, and that it would be a goldmine of mockable ore when I was finally made to reveal it. She tricked me by claiming to have an embarrassing middle name herself – mine could hardly be worse than Buttercup, could it?

I felt almost sorry for her, in my folly, and I gave up my secret. I tried to give it some historical context by referring knowingly to the bouncing bomb, but I needn't have bothered. 'Wallis' became 'Wally', and that was what she called me from then on. Wally Snorts. Wally did not then mean 'idiot' as it does now, but still I flinched every time. I tried calling her 'Buttercup', though my heart wasn't in it, and she simply said, 'Did I say Buttercup? My mistake. My middle name is Jane. It's a rotten sort of name, isn't it?'

Somehow she heard about my meeting with the matron of the whole hospital, the empress in purple. She told me I was a poshie and a sissy and that I was 'sucking up to Matron', when I would never have thought of such a thing. It was an impossibility. It would have been like sucking up to God. After that she sometimes called me Little Lord Fauntleroy and sometimes Archie Andrews after a ventriloquist's dummy very popular on radio at the time.

That tells you all you need to know about the 1950s, really, that millions of listeners would tune in to a programme in which a man they couldn't see pretended to make his voice emerge from a dummy that was likewise invisible. Julie Andrews played the dummy's girlfriend, Beryl Reid his catty friend Monica. In the heyday of *Educating Archie* there was a whole little industry making souvenir mugs, ties, soap, confectionery and scarves. When clothes were still rationed, Archie had been given an allowance of 50 coupons a year to acknowledge the contribution he made to national morale.

Archie and his manipulator, Peter Brough, even performed privately for the late King and the princesses. After the show they asked him to take Archie's head off so that they could see how it worked. Later the King remarked that there had only been one beheading in his whole reign, and his daughters had insisted on watching the whole thing.

When the show made the logical transition to a visual medium, to television, it wasn't nearly so successful. People preferred the imaginary illusion to the real one. And they say the British have no taste for mysticism!

The Archie Andrews nick-name was particularly galling because I thought of myself as one of nature's ventriloquists rather than one of her dummies. I had pined for the teach-yourself-voice-throwing book advertised in the Ellisdons catalogue, but finally been stern with myself. It didn't fit my requirement that everything I sent off actually did something, preferably something spectacular, when it arrived.

Normal blue ink

When Mum wrote to me, she had a particular way of writing the address. She would use normal blue ink to write 'Ward 1' on the envelope, and then instead of 'Canadian Red Cross Memorial Hospital', she would write 'Canadian + Memorial Hospital'. But she'd change to red ink for the '+'. A red cross instead of 'Red Cross'. That was her special way of writing the hospital's name. She made it into a sort of game between us.

There was no guarantee that so wayward a variation of the address would be accepted by Her Majesty's postal service. It could easily have been returned. The Post Office were sticklers to a man, in those days before postcodes, after which stickling became more idiosyncratic, but they colluded with her little flight of fancy.

I learned to say 'C.R.C.M.H.', even to think it that way, always with capitals and the right pronunciation. C full stop R full stop C full stop M full stop H full stop. Then one day I was wheeled to an office in the hospital, where a clerk needed to fill in a form on my behalf. He asked me about my previous addresses, and then where I lived now.

Proud of knowing the right answer, I said 'C.R.C.M.H.,' complete with all stops. I looked up at the man, waiting for my pat on the back. Well done John! You've shown you're not hopelessly volatile but are able to listen gravely. Instead he said, 'That's rather a mouthful, don't you think, John? I'll let you in on a little secret. Up here we just write "CRX". Much easier, isn't it?' 'Affirmative,' I said, using Dad's forces form of words, which Mum found so exasperating ('Why can't you just say "Yes"?').

To tell the truth I was rather crestfallen to be corrected after so much brain-washing, but the clerk made it up to me by saying, 'Keep quiet about it, though – don't go telling the other kids on the ward.'

It wasn't altogether clear whether CRX, as I allowed myself to call it in my mind, was in Buckinghamshire or Berkshire. I badgered people to be definite. I didn't enjoy living with uncertainty in those days, and it didn't seem too much to hope that there was a definite answer in this case. But there wasn't. Letters could be sent to me either on 'Ward 1, Canadian Red Cross Memorial Hospital, Taplow, Bucks' or 'Ward 1, Canadian Red Cross Memorial Hospital, Taplow nr Maidenhead, Berks'. Post could be sorted in either place. In effect I spent several years of my life in a place with an indeterminate location. My first feeling was that I had a right to a definite answer, one way or the other, but then I came to enjoy the fact that things weren't so simple.

I liked the idea that I could go on holiday without moving. When I started writing a letter, I could ask myself, 'Where do I want to be today?' before I wrote the return address. The 'Bucks' form usually seemed clearer and more direct than the 'Berks' one, but my mood could change. Depending on which form of the address I used (always assuming my correspondent respected it), the letter of reply would pass through one sorting office or another. Action at a distance, always an attractive idea. The letter would pass under the eyes and hands of a different set of Post Office employees. One lot might process it more quickly than the other, but even if they didn't I would know the letter had come a different way. There was an extra edge of pleasure in the wait for the postman. Even at my most megalomaniac I had to concede that it was the same postman making the delivery, whichever route I had decreed for the letter to use.

There was a doubleness, too, about the name of the estate, or at least its pronunciation. There were two versions racked with class nuance, both of them at odds with the spelling. Mum said only sub-urban people said 'Cleeve-den'. Upper people always said 'Clivv-den' (just as Mum always said 'upper people'). The only thing both parties would have agreed on was that the name wasn't pronounced 'Cliveden', the way it was written, and they would have joined in laughing at anyone who knew no better.

In fact I remember Ansell saying 'Cleeve-den', which meant she was probably suburban, but then again she could be absolutely terrifying. I knew that suburban people were characteristically shy and uncertain (like Mum, deep down, with her longing to know what was right). So I began to realise that as long as you used enough force of character, you could be as suburban as you liked.

Cheese on toast

The third Norn in the welcoming committee, besides Wendy and Ivy, was Sarah Morrison – an entirely different character. She had been curious about me, like the others, and had joined their sortie but most of the time she went her own way. She was largely immune to the pressures of the Wendy gang.

I didn't find this out for a little while. We were cut off by illness from playing together, and from the natural mechanisms of community-building. Receiving hydrotherapy in the same pool, for instance, isn't necessarily a social opportunity, though in the right circumstances it can be. It was there that Sarah Morrison made friends with me, while we were waiting for our turn in the pool, by whispering that if you blew off under the water and took a good sniff, it was just like cheese on toast. When we were waiting to be taken out of the pool, she urged me to try it. She shuffled up next to me and then we both did blow-offs and politely took turns to have a sniff. The best part was feeling the bubbles of gas percolating through my trunks and tickling my spine as they rose to the surface. I couldn't bend over to get a proper noseful but I got an adequate sample. I didn't think the resemblance to cheese on toast was close, myself, but I wasn't going to spoil a friendly conversation, even one carried on in an up-draught of digestive gas. It was a rite of passage. I had always wanted a blood brother, though the ritual of cutting frightened me, but for the time being I was content with a blow-off sister.

There was another enthusiastic reader on the ward, little Mary

Finch. She was the single most straightforward person I have ever met. She came from Rutland, the smallest county in Great Britain, which seemed exactly right somehow. That this small and perfect person should come from a county not much bigger than a pocket handkerchief. Of course Still's Disease distorted her body, and steroids added a layer of blurring, but her character remained intact and in proportion.

Mary and I shared a passion for the Famous Five stories of Enid Blyton. Better than that, we had the same preferences in terms of the characters. Julian our top favourite, then Dick. Mary introduced me to the Pookie books – the adventures of a little winged rabbit. *Pookie in Search of a Home. Pookie Sets the World Right. Pookie and the Gipsies.* She had the lot. We never ran out of things to talk about. Having Mary on the ward took the solitariness out of reading. I was always saying to myself, as I read, 'Wait till Mary hears about this!'

We on Wards One and Two had nothing in common except the diagnosis we shared, so we negotiated our status by way of self-portraits with only a couple of characteristics, simplified identities. Wendy, for instance, characterised herself as a plain-speaking Northerner who had an older brother who would thump us so that we stayed thumped. It was hard to imagine him being able to add anything to Wendy's reign of terror. This brother who was the ace up her sleeve could hardly be more daunting than the aces she played every day.

It was some time before I realised that not all of us on those wards were in fact ill in the same way. I had noticed how few boys there were, and I hadn't succeeded in identifying any kindred spirits. There was one boy who seemed even less able to move than I did, as if he had been condemned in his turn to the bed rest I had escaped, keeping the horizontal population of England constant. His condition, though, seemed to be extreme weakness, rather than locked joints. To the extent that he could move at all he could move every part of himself. I would have been tempted to make overtures, though I would have needed help from the staff to approach him, if he wasn't always whispering the same thing to himself. I couldn't see him properly, but I could hear him whispering, 'Lamb . . . lamb . . . lamb.'

It was Mary who told me what was really going on. He had

arranged an army of toy soldiers on the bed, and he spent his time feebly knocking them over with the flick of a feeble finger, one after another, whispering the whole time, 'Blam . . . blam . . . blam.' I took against him over that, and not just because of my dislike of war games. I had the feeling that he was punishing his men for their inability to move, the moulded joints they couldn't help any more than I could help mine. Inevitably, Mary was more sympathetic. 'Poor boy,' she said. 'He's really very ill.'

Wendy was reliably more Gothic: 'He's done for. He's a goner. He's in the Death Bed. No one who sleeps in that bed lasts for long.'

Mixed population

She was doing what she could to make sense of a distinctly perverse arrangement. Professor Bywaters was an acknowledged expert on Still's Disease, but he had another interest also, a sideline. It seems absurd now to imagine that sick children could be put together simply on the basis of a doctor's twin clinical specialities, but that was how it was on Wards One and Two. Eric Bywaters was a big name, his wishes had force.

His other interest was childhood leukæmia. We were a mixed population for no other reason than that we had equal claim on his attention. The two classes of patient were nursed together, with no one actually explaining to them that they belonged to two quite different categories. The leukæmia children were going to die. The Still's Disease children weren't. They were likely to be in pain, and they were going to be deformed to one degree or another. You could go so far as to say that life had turned its face away from them (certainly that must have been how it seemed to many of their parents) but death wasn't staring them down.

So when Wendy had said on that first day, 'He's not pale – he's very twisty,' to the cannibal girl called Ivy, she was for once being scientific – in a rudimentary way – rather than merely baleful. Deep down she didn't buy the Death Bed notion, though it was a useful idea to frighten others with. She had understood from the first that some children were going to die, Death Bed or no Death Bed. She was establishing that I had Still's Disease and not the other thing, whatever it was. Information which could be obtained no other way than by going and taking a look. Sarah had been curious too, which was why she had joined the little party. Secrecy was the prevailing condition in that hospital. We were all in the dark. Why should patients be told about such things as the composition of the wards they were on? Patients who were children least of all. It was none of our business. For once Wendy Keach was ranged on the side of knowledge, against the ignorance in which we were left by the hospital. She was only assigning me to the correct tribe.

Professor Bywaters was a good man and a good doctor, but in those days being an expert in Still's Disease didn't actually mean you knew very much. The last I heard, he was still alive and alert. The mystery of Still's Disease is still alive too. There's a theory that it's an autoimmune condition, like the rheumatic fever I was originally supposed to have, but the jury is still out on that. Childhood leukæmia has given up a much larger proportion of its secrets. In the 1950s, when to say 'cancer' seemed no different from saying 'death', leukæmia was even more terrifying a diagnosis than it is now. It had a starkness.

Not all of us with Still's had quite the same symptoms. Ivy Horrocks was blind, although she was in the middle of a long series of operations which might do something to restore her sight. Her problem must have been acute iritis, caused by the disease from which we all suffered, with antibodies in her case attacking the eyes. Wendy told us Ivy was a witch who would put the evil eye on us, but that may just have been politeness on her part, wanting to establish her friend on an equal footing of malevolence.

I was fascinated by Ivy's books, of which she was very proud. They were made up of raised dots in enchanting patterns. In a genuinely rather witchy way, Ivy's eyes seemed to have migrated down her arms to her fingertips. Reading for her was now something that took place outside her head.

Sarah Morrison had senior status in the group, not because she was the oldest but because she had contracted the illness the youngest. She had been eighteen months old. She had been born in India, which meant she could eat the spicy food called curry without dying. She collected dolls. They were all from different countries and some of them had strange foreign names.

A girl called Geraldine, who was given to silent sobbing, could play chess, but as there was no one else who could, and no one who wanted to learn, her accomplishment didn't raise her status noticeably or even help her to pass the time.

Wally Snorts the Posh

As for me, I tried to sell myself as the son of an Air Force pilot war hero, but that made no impression, whether because an audience of girls wasn't susceptible to that brand of glamour, or because in our strange way we were a meritocracy, one of the few enclaves in the country at that time where it didn't matter what your father did as long as you said 'toilet' and not 'lavatory'. I was branded as Wally Snorts the Posh in Wendy's eyes, and I couldn't do anything about that, but I did manage to use Charlie to broker an enlarged identity.

I said that my best friend was a budgie who knew all my secrets, and that he would soon be coming to live with me on the ward. I knew perfectly well that pets of any sort were forbidden at CRX, but it was worth fibbing for the short-term advantage. Until I was found out, I could make any number of promises about what Charlie would do when he came to live on the ward, the words we'd teach him, whose bed his cage could be stood by at night. If they were really nice to me, that is.

Mary was my closest friend on the ward, not only because of her sweet nature but because we shared a passion for books. We would read Famous Five adventures together. We were always coming up with some altruistic scheme or other. The altruism was stronger in Mary, but I wasn't going to show myself up in front of her. Because I had a gramophone on top of my locker but no records, we decided to write a letter of appeal to Decca on behalf of the ward. It wasn't quite true that I had no records – there were a number at home that Mum would happily have brought in, but I didn't dare risk Wendy's contempt about my posh tastes. It seemed to me that Kathleen Ferrier singing 'Blow the Wind Southerly' was the quintessence of posh, and there was an aria from *La Bohème* that I also loved, but I wasn't going to risk that either.

The letter Mary and I concocted to send to Decca hit the jackpot.

They sent us a whole box of 78s. I suppose they were old stock, but I didn't mind. They were all operatic highlights. So I was even able to hear that aria without having to own up to my love for it. Of course it wasn't the repertoire the ward would have chosen for itself. Popular taste would have opted for Lonnie Donegan, Tommy Steele and Frankie Lymon. Frankie Lymon in particular hit the bullseye with a song about *not* being a juvenile delinquent. He preached a sermon that adults couldn't object to, and still he filled your head with thoughts of being bad.

Just when I was beginning to give up on the educational component of the institution, the school began to keep more than *Brigadoon* hours. Lessons started at last. There was no school-room as such – lessons were held right there in the ward. The first subjects I remember being taught at CRX were music and scripture.

Miss Reid sang songs in her reedy voice. There was a piano at the end of the ward. 'Please, Miss Reid,' I would say, 'will you pick up my pencil?' She bent over to do it, saying, not unkindly, 'I shall have to call you Dropper.' She taught us, 'Soldier, soldier, will you marry me?' but she blushed scarlet, as we knew she would, when we asked if anyone had ever proposed to her. After a moment when it didn't seem that she'd be able to speak, she said, 'Yes. Someone did once, as a matter of fact.' Of course we all cried out, 'And what did *you* say?' Though we knew the answer. If she had said 'Yes' she wouldn't still be a Miss and she wouldn't be teaching sick kids. It was still a surprise, somehow, when she said, 'I said No.'

Playing thickly

Miss Reid's lessons were fine, though she could only pick out a tune on the piano with one finger. What we really loved was when Mrs Pullen played thickly. Playing thickly meant using all her fingers, and all at once in great bunches. Playing chords. I looked longingly at the piano, which could make such a complex sound, but for some reason I was only ever assigned the triangle or tambourine.

In terms of equipment, the school at CRX was a step up from Miss Collins's portable blackboard, wiped clean by the hanky she kept in her sleeve, but only a step. A school within a hospital was unlikely to attract inspirational staff. It was a legal requirement that we should be educated. It would have been unlawful to strand us without lessons, even those of us who were not going to see another birthday. Yet there wasn't a strong sense of what we were being educated for. What, if anything, we were going to become.

The phantom school at CRX, so timid, so likely to vanish into the woodwork when a doctor appeared, didn't concern itself with discipline. No matter – Sister Heel took care of that, and it was still her ward when lessons, by her gracious permission, were taking place there. If we children talked after lights out, the procedure was: first, dire warnings. After that the offender's bed would be pulled into the middle of the ward. If we still hadn't learned our lesson, the bed was trundled into a side ward where we had to stay until morning. In the morning there would be a full-dress dressing-down from Sister Heel, a proper scolding. As we waited for morning we learned how cracked hospital mugs feel in the seconds before their public smashing.

Early in my stay in the hospital, an astounding thing happened on Ward Two. A boy with Still's Disease came down with measles, and when the measles cleared up so did the rheumatoid arthritis. The lesser illness carried off the greater on its back. Professor Bywaters was fascinated and did every test he could think of. He would have been happy for the boy to stay on the ward until the mechanism of this absurd cure was understood, but the boy no longer needed to be looked after. He wasn't a patient any more, and he wasn't going to loiter around. Gregory went home.

The mystical action of the measles cure was as mysterious as the way white wine lifts a stain of red, leaving the tablecloth none the worse for wear. And after all, the person who first tried that desperate bit of dinner-party alchemy must have been something of a mystic, or else only threw the second glassful in a fit of temper.

I spent a lot of time arguing with God about the measles cure. It seemed so unfair that Gregory was the one to get the luck. I tried not to bear a grudge, to resent him for his good fortune (not that I even knew him, since he was on Ward Two), but it was hard to accept things as they were. Why did it have to be Gregory who got to go home? Why couldn't it have been Wendy?

The professor tried to be methodical about this freak thunderbolt of healing energy. He wanted us all to get the measles, hoping that some or all of us would stumble on the same happy cancellation of one disease by another. I remember being indefatigably coughed on by feverish children. I didn't succumb, but quite a few did, including some of the leukæmics, who could hardly hope to benefit. There were no repetitions of the miracle cure, even among the Still's children. Freak lightning only struck the once. When the measles cleared up, they took nothing away with them except a little hope.

It doesn't seem exactly scientific, to expose sick children to measles on the off-chance that it will do them good. But ever since Fleming had waited for penicillin to re-occur naturally, after a promising mould was washed up by an over-zealous technician, the picture of scientific discovery had been changing. Now discoveries could be made by knowing what you were looking for and waiting for it to actually happen. It was less about genius taking a chisel to the materials of the universe, and more about a dance and marriage between a drifting spore and an opened mind.

I don't know if the term 'immune system' even existed in the 1950s. Certainly it wasn't in general currency. The mechanism of that freakish cure is easier to understand with its help. By analogy: a householder is fast asleep while thieves are stripping the house, packing his treasures into bags marked SWAG and throwing them out of a window to accomplices in the street outside, when he is woken by a bird flying down the chimney. Measles being the bird.

The analogy can just about be stretched to allow for the possibility that Still's proves to be an auto-immune condition. A sleep-walking householder is putting his own treasures into bags marked SWAG, throwing them out of the window into the empty street, when he's woken by a bird flying down the chimney. Measles still being the bird.

I remember asking Mum if I could have more pocket money if I caught measles. It vexed me that a boy called Wayne on Ward Two, who was only five, had two shillings a week pocket money, while I at eight had ninepence. When I complained about the manifest injustice, Mum had the good sense not to say, 'Don't get too jealous, John. Wayne has two months to live.' Instead she said, 'You've learned a very good lesson. There'll always be someone who's younger than you and gets more.' Taking a hard line. Still, when I said, 'Honestly, Mum, it'll take me till I'm twenty-four to save up for a tape-recorder,' she softened a bit and said, 'Oh all right. We'll meet you half-way.' There would be time enough for me to learn that Wayne had leukæmia.

Cross-bracing

Jim Shaeffer's two presents from the long-ago Christmas of fear and giving (of course the candy had been scoffed in short order) were invaluable in this new setting. They provided vital cross-bracing to my identity. The gramophone sat on the cupboard next to my bed, though I was strict about when it could be used – the nurses tended to brush against it and make the needle jump. I used to adore playing Lonnie Donegan's 'Gambling Man' but it tempted the staff to jive about. Some of them had such a heavy tread that they could make the needle skip just by galumphing nearby. 'You're not supposed to do that!' I told them, but it didn't do any good.

The Relide watch also enhanced my status. The boys and girls on the ward said it was 'Illuminous', but then the nurses called it that too. I tried for a while to correct them but it was much easier just to let them get on with being wrong. Radium was lovely because it glowed on its own. At any time of night. Staring at it during periods of sleeplessness was a great consolation.

I loved the fact that the watch was supposed to be serviced every thousand days – it was so precise and scientific an interval, but also like something out of a fairy tale. A princess might fall into a deep sleep for a thousand days, while a forest (or at least a herb garden) grew up around her. After the prescribed interval Dad took it to Maidenhead for servicing. When he brought it back I found that the dial had been replaced and I wanted to know why. Dad said it was nothing to worry about, but they'd had to change it because we weren't allowed to use radium any more.

'It's just the same, chicken,' he said, 'it's still your watch.' But it wasn't. He always called me chicken when he was being extra nice or when he felt in the wrong.

The numerals and hands on the new dial had to be charged by

holding them close to a light, and even so the effect didn't last long. You couldn't see anything at all, later on in the night. The old dial had actually made its own light. The radium markings were a kind of mind that could think its pale-green thoughts to the very end of the darkness. The new dial was only a memory, and not a very good one. It was in decline from the moment it was charged, fully informed with light. It could dimly remember the brightness from earlier on, but only for a little while. So it wasn't at all the same thing. In the darkest watches of the night my watch deserted me and went dark itself. I felt that some of Jim Shaeffer's gift had been filched from me. As if Dad was jealous, and trying to spoil things somehow.

Breakfast elves

There were some aspects of the running of the ward that were sociable, and even inspired. For instance: when it was someone's birthday there was jelly and ice cream for the whole ward, not just the lucky girl or boy, so we didn't resent each other's festivals.

Mum brought me squash for my locker. Though sweets must be shared, soft drinks could legitimately be hoarded. At breakfast there was a choice of cereals, so there was no direct repetition of the Weetabix trauma. In any case my taste had shifted by now to Rice Krispies. I particularly liked the three elves on the packet. I wanted to have elves like that, to keep as pets. Snap, Crackle and Pop would be useful little helpers for me, running errands and carrying messages, turning the pages of books. The other reason I wanted a little retinue of elves was so that I could pinch them very hard and make them cry out.

Behind the scenes Ansell must have been busy trying to solve the problem of my walking. Walking was an absolute passion and obsession of the establishment. In that respect also I'm sure it was of its time. Walking was more than encouraged, walking was absolutely insisted on. Not to walk qualified as a surrender to disability, a moral defect, but it was no good telling that to my joints.

One day Ansell proudly produced something that was supposed to help me with my walking. The first I heard of them was this tremendous clattering coming down the corridor. I thought this must be some sort of music class, a free-for-all percussion parade. What I was hearing seemed to be an unholy cross between drums and cymbals.

Then Ansell came into the ward brandishing a pair of bizarre devices. They were like sticks with tripod bases for extra stability. The effect was of very narrow pyramids with handles on the top. The tripods had an aluminium cladding which was what made all the noise, acting as a sort of amplifying chamber. Slowly it dawned on me that they weren't percussion instruments at all but intended as part of my rehabilitation. I hated them. I wouldn't even try them. It was bad enough being assigned the triangle or tambourine in music classes, without being made to advertise my sub-standard walking all over the premises with a one-man marching – tottering – band.

If I'd been taken to a room and quietly shown the tripods, and had their advantages explained, I might have approached them with an open mind. They had been made thin and light for my benefit, and the cladding was an ingenious way of bracing flimsy metal that would have been impossibly bendy otherwise. But when Ansell tried to show me how to use them, the din went all over the ward. I couldn't contemplate making all that noise. Imagine what it would have been like if I had ventured with those pyramids into that quarter-mile corridor! I couldn't afford having one more negative distinction being attached to me, on top of being Wally Snorts the Posh and having beautiful sucking-up manners. I'd given Wendy and her gang enough hostages already. The clanking which preceded the tall pyramids down the corridor had ruled them out as walking aids before I'd even set eyes on them.

Ansell wasn't best pleased to have her ingenious tailor-made John-supports rejected out of hand, and she told me I was spoilt, which was a bit of a slap in the face. I couldn't be expected to realise that these hateful objects were the end products of a careful design process, and were dreamed up specifically to meet my needs. Someone in a Workshop somewhere was probably very proud of his resourcefulness, and Ansell was certainly glowing with job satisfaction before I refused point blank to use those deafening devices.

I never heard that Ansell went on winter sports holidays, though of course it's possible. We on the ward were incapable of speculating about the life of the staff when they were off the premises. I wonder if Ansell wasn't doing a boisterous mime of skiing, using the pyramids as her poles, dashing them merrily against the lino, as she came rejoicing down the corridor to have her thoughtfulness turned down flat.

Ansell felt snubbed, and she snubbed me in my turn when I said I wanted the same walking aids as the others. They used things like spider legs, but she told me rather stiffly that they were too heavy for me. She was almost sulking, unlikely though that sounds. I could just about lift one of Sarah's spider legs, and I thought that it would give my arms good exercise to try walking with them. Anyway, she wouldn't let me. 'You're not strong enough, John,' she said with a sigh. 'That's the whole point. That's why we tried to get you something different.'

Behind the scenes she went on trying. The built-up shoes we all wore were very uncomfortable. One of the therapists who fitted them seemed to think that was as it should be. 'If they don't hurt they can't be remedial, can they?' she said. Blisters and calluses were commonplace. When we complained she padded them with cotton wool, entirely the wrong material for the job. In my mind I had a picture of something that would have the right effect, a sort of squashy wood which I had seen somewhere as a tile on a wall. Surely something like that could be cut to size? When I discovered, long afterward, that cork insoles were perfectly common items I was amazed all over again at the cluelessness of CRX in certain departments.

One day Ansell had my feet properly measured in every detail. She told me there was a man in Maidenhead who was going to make me a special pair of shoes which wouldn't pinch the way the National Health ones did. They were an incredible price, but somehow she had wangled the funding. She was a very powerful woman in the rheumatic field.

'What makes these shoes special?' I asked.

'They're Space Shoes, John. They're what people will wear in space. They're designed by scientists.'

She certainly knew how to appeal to my tastes. I was going through rather a space-travel phase at the time in terms of my reading, with a particular love of the Kemlo books (*Kemlo and the Martian Ghosts*, *Kemlo and the Star Men* and so on). Kemlo was a boy who had been born in space, and so he didn't need to breathe air. I tried to train myself to do without air like him, holding my breath for longer and longer periods, just as I had learned to inhale through one nostril during my bed-rest years. Of course this time it wasn't rough-and-ready *pranayama*. This time it really was John being silly.

Then the Space Shoes arrived, and I hated them. They were comfortable all right – it wasn't that. They were closely moulded to the foot, and gave excellent support. But it was like the percussion tripods all over again. The man who had designed them had forgotten that I needed to look vaguely human. I wouldn't have minded looking like a space man, but not a space monster. I refused to wear something that looked like a puffball mushroom. Wendy would show no mercy.

Ansell tried to talk me round. She even said, 'I can just see that space boy Kemlo wearing something like these,' which at the time I thought was simply a lucky guess. Of course it's more likely that she'd consulted Mary in hopes of finding a way to get me to like the horrible Space Shoes.

I wouldn't wear them. I was adamant. 'Sometimes, John,' said Ansell, 'I wonder if you really want us to help you.' I can't blame her. For the second time she was having to put away something that had taken a lot of thought and organisation. Since the Space Shoes had been made to my exact dimensions, they couldn't be offered to anyone else.

All in all, it looked as though I would be exempted from the painful duty of walking. Because of the virtual immobility of my hips it was obvious an ordinary wheelchair wouldn't help me. Instead I was issued with something called a Tan-Sad, a sort of raised baby carriage with a broad foot-plate and four fixed wheels. The manufacturers were pleased with their work, and had put a little plate on the Tan-Sad with their name on it, and a design of a rising sun.

The Tan-Sad was indeed the dawning of a new day for me. It didn't look inviting, but it was beautifully comfortable once you were in it. There were pillows and cushions aplenty. It was semi-reclining, so I could see much more of the world than when I was horizontal. I

could imagine myself lying down again by tilting my mind backwards, or sitting up straight by tilting it forward.

It had its draw-backs, of course. I couldn't get into it by myself,
but had to be lifted in and out. Because the wheels were fixed it
couldn't go round corners without being manhandled. It was forward
or backward, take your pick, but it was certainly a step up from
stretchers and trolleys.

Silent worship

At some stage I decided that Mary and I would be getting married.
Purity was the keynote of the married state as I imagined it. I was
strongly influenced by one of the songs that Miss Reid used to sing.
It was called 'Silent Worship', and I decided it was about the sort of
pure person I might marry:

> Did you not hear my lady,
> Go down the garden singing?
> Blackbird and thrush were silent
> To hear the earlies ringing

> O saw you not my lady out in the garden there
> Shaming the rose and lily for she is twice as fair.
> Though I am nothing to her,
> Though she must rarely look at me,
> And though I could never woo her,
> I will love her till I die.

> Surely you heard my lady
> Go down the garden singing,
> Silencing all the songbirds
> And setting the earlies ringing.
> But surely you see
> My lady out in the garden there
> Riv'lling the glitt'ring sunshine
> With the glory of her golden hair.

Mary's hair was more mouse than gold, but still the song seemed to
fit. She was the right sort of lady. If I was ever going to have a lady, it

would have to be like the lady of the song, the sort of lady who would never allow a man's taily anywhere near her. There would be none of that taily and pocket nonsense between us, but we would be great companions and we would help people by raising money for charity.

Of course the word wasn't really 'earlies'. At the time I heard Miss Reid sing the song, my vocabulary was lop-sided. I knew 'quadriceps' and 'blue cere', but I didn't know 'alley'. I wasn't going to put my hand up (or wave it, anyway) and ask about the 'earlies' with Wendy ready to pounce on any weakness, so I let God tell me what they were. They were ethereal spirits who were really really early getting up. They were so gentle and so fragile that their existence was more precarious than a spider's web. They could only be heard in crepuscular morning. The song of the Earlies took place between this world and the next, between darkness and daylight.

With the exception of Mary, and possibly Sarah too, the CRX kids were too low to be able to hear the Earlies. Wendy would pass boiled sweets round after her parents visited, and then when our mouths were full she announced proudly that she'd left her bum dirty earlier on and wiped the sweets against it. How would she possibly hear the Earlies? Her ears were sealed with wicked wax.

I told Mum about my plans and she looked thoughtful. 'Are you sure you wouldn't be better suited to Sarah?' she asked. She wasn't seriously weighing up Sarah as a marriage prospect. It was more that she and Sarah's mum had struck up a friendship of their own. Sarah's mum would come to visit driving a Volkswagen. I knew about this extraordinary car, because sometimes on her visits Sarah and I would be pushed to the end of that quarter-mile corridor to sample the delights of the WVS canteen, staffed by Mrs Carpenter of the Squashy Thumbs.

The squashy thumbs

Her thumbs really were squashy, and she always invited us to play with them. She would reach across a big red hand to us. Our fingers left little dimpled marks on her thumbs. They stayed visible for quite a while. I enjoyed the game so much it never occurred to me to ask why it happened. I only thought it must be nice to have a bit of plas-

ticine always with you. Possibly she suffered from a circulation disor-
der, causing some sort of œdema. At the time it seemed almost appropriate that someone who worked in a canteen should take on some of
the characteristics of dough, and I thought that the only ill people in
hospitals were the patients. I hardly understood that grown-ups could
be ill too. Didn't children have the monopoly?

After that we would be pushed to the entrance. Sarah's mum would
give a kiss to Sarah and a peck to me, and we would watch her driving off in her car, which looked so funny it made me laugh. 'It's
known as a Beetle and the engine's in the *back* and the boot is in the
front,' Sarah said proudly, which made me start laughing all over
again. We were too poor for a car, but I prayed that when we did get
one it would be a Beetle because it was wonderful in every way. Sarah's
mum gave me a ride in it once, but it was so uncomfortable I nearly
clicked my back and never wanted to go in one again. I reversed the
current of my prayers, pleading for any other car than a Beetle and
hoping that God would ignore my previous intercession.

As their friendship developed, sometimes at weekends Sarah's
mum would pick my mum up at the station and bring her to CRX in
the Beetle. Mum had nothing against Mary – no one could – but it
had to be admitted that her parents, stranded as they were in
Rutland, couldn't offer to give Mum useful lifts. That was how I
explained her preference for Sarah as a prospective daughter-in-law.

I knew my mum liked Sarah's mum Jacquetta, not because she had
plenty of money, I don't think, but because she had so much confidence. Sarah's dad had been in the Foreign Office and Jacquetta was
used to all sorts of people. She just naturally felt at home in any company, and that was something Mum admired and envied. Sarah's
mum was posh in a way Mum could never be, posh without effort.
Even Granny's sense of status had a strenuous edge to it, while true
posh, as I came to see, was almost blithe.

Without regular contact with her own mother, Mum's snobbery
was becoming somehow anæmic. I hadn't yet noticed it, but in those
years there was a Granny-shaped hole in my life. She wrote letters
from time to time, which sometimes enclosed postal orders, but the
postman brought me my only contact with her.

If I had been more on the ball I would have realised that the two of them weren't on speaking terms. Granny and Mum hadn't fallen out at the time of my misdiagnosis being revealed, but soon after. In a crisis family tension took second place, but it didn't go away. In fact the quarrel had been about something apparently trivial, but had taken a surprising turn. Granny had been going too far for most of her life. This time it was Mum who had trespassed into an area that was off limits, and Granny was slow to forgive. So slow that it seemed likely she would die first.

Guttersnipe in the making

Mum liked to talk about Jacquetta, and so did I. Jacquetta had given Mum her visiting card, which she proudly showed me. The address was 'I, Melmott Court, Cookham'. As a trainee snob, I pounced on this. I thought I had found a flaw in Mum's value system. I thought I had her cornered.

Of course, while I was in Mum's company I had to revert to my old choice of words, pre-eminently 'lavatory' rather than 'toilet'. I had to hide the fact that her apprentice snob was also a guttersnipe in the making. According to Mum, 'toilet' was roughly the commonest word in the world. Still's Disease was quite enough to be getting on with, thank you, without her son being infected with vulgar word choice. I was rapidly developing a habitual hesitation, almost a complex about what to call the room with the personal plumbing, rather a draw-back in a life where I must ask for help, more often than most people, to be taken there. I had reached a stage where every term sounded wrong.

Now I had a chance to return the favour of embarrassment. 'Mum?' I said, nice as pie. 'Didn't you tell me that decent people never live in numbered houses? Except of course in London, where there are so many houses that the GPO insists?'

If I'd hoped to rattle Mum I was disappointed. 'Quite true, JJ,' she said calmly, 'but if your address ends in Court it's *perfectly all right*.' It turned out that there was a whole intricate cult of addresses, seething with rules and exceptions. She felt about addresses roughly what traditional Japanese feel about tea, or their ancestors. 'It's the same with addresses which end in Park, and also Mansions.'

'How about Palace, Mum? Would that be a proper address?'

Mum put her head on one side. 'I think so.' On balance she was inclined to let an address ending in 'Palace' scrape into the paddock of privilege.

'But we live in Bathford, nr Bath, Somerset, and we have a number, don't we?'

'Well, yes we do. But we're in married quarters, you see, and with so many servicemen the RAF had to give numbers. That's quite all right. It isn't ideal, of course, and the neighbours − for instance Doreen Parsons, bless her! − are very suburban, but you can't always have everything, John. We won't live there for ever, you know, JJ,' she added. 'Things will change, you'll see.' And at least our street number was a single digit. Apparently that made a difference.

There were other subtleties. It was perfectly all right to have numbers if you were serving in the forces, or if you were in a nursing or medical college, or if you'd just left university and were quite poor, as long as you bucked up and got a proper address as soon as you possibly could.

It turned out that absolutely everybody who lived in America had numbers, but it was a big place and often your house number would be more than a thousand which in some strange way made it all right. There were upper people in America too, though it wasn't at all easy to tell them from the others.

Even at the time I sensed that Mum would have found a way of keeping Jacquetta Morrison among the poshest of the poshies even if her card had read, 'The Abandoned Railway Carriage, behind The Pigsty'. I hadn't been able to put even the slightest dent in her dreams.

Mum had lost a little of her authority in my eyes, somehow, along the way. At first I had been amazed that she could tell if I had disobeyed her orders and neglected to brush my teeth, but then I worked out that she gave my toothbrush a surreptitious stroke and scolded me if it was dry. The stiff bristles bore witness against me. After that it was easy to wet it from time to time.

In those days I really loved the *Just So Stories*. Miss Reid would read them with me, sitting on the edge of my bed. I wasn't sure that teachers were allowed to do that, whether they counted as doctors or only parents, but I wasn't going to say anything. A cuddle from her would have been nice, but I knew there was no chance. It was nice enough seeing her white nylon overall with the corner of my eye, and then having her big white botty approaching and flowing in from the left. Then she'd hold up the book and start to read. I wondered if the man had asked her to marry him before she had such a big bottom. If so, she must be kicking herself for saying no while she was still young and pretty. But if he had asked her when she already had a big bottom, how could she have turned him down? Logic didn't seem to help me to understand this important part of her life story. Perhaps she felt about tailies the way I felt about pockets. Not that keen. Perhaps it was as simple as that.

At about this time I wrote my own Just So Story by accident. It was all to do with Sarah's mum, and if it had really been written by Rudyard Kipling it might have been called 'How Muzzie Got Her Name'.

One day I had a real titbit to pass on to Mum, something that was guaranteed to give her pleasure. It was a lovely piece of intimate gossip about the Morrisons: I knew what Sarah called her mother when there wasn't anyone else around. I knew the special home private nick-name the daughter had for the mother. I told Mum what it was, and she seemed very pleased. I'd only heard it spoken the once, and then I felt as if I'd stumbled over a jewel. It was so sweet and private, part of a secret language, and I treasured the knowledge of it.

Sarah called Mrs Morrison 'Muzzie'. 'Mummy' was for the ward and the rest of the world, but when they were alone together it was 'Muzzie'. I spent a lot of time with them, on the days when Sarah's mum was the only visitor on the ward. When Sarah's mum brought Sarah a present, she always remembered to bring something for me, so that I didn't feel left out, but this was the best present she could possibly have given me, the sharing of the home word and pet name.

Mum enjoyed being in on the secret, but it was only going to be a matter of time before she revealed what she knew. Jacquetta Morrison was clearly an upper person, and everything about her was inherently interesting to Mum. Finally after the tea trolley had come round Mum said, 'I know Sarah's secret name for you, and guess how I found out?'

Jacquetta looked genuinely puzzled, and so did Sarah. They seemed to have no idea what we were talking about. Finally Mum and I had to announce the fact that Sarah called Jacquetta 'Muzzie', and still they looked blank. It became obvious that the name meant nothing to them. Mum covered her tracks by saying, 'John comes out with all sorts of things nearly all the time.' So much for loyalty.

'But I'm telling you the truth!' I stammered, getting very emotional. 'Sarah wanted a lift and you lifted her all wrong, and Sarah said "Oh, *Muzzie . . .* " But if you don't believe me, I don't care! I haven't told a lie, I know what I heard, Sarah said "Muzzie" – and if you don't want to believe me, I couldn't care less. From this time on I shall think of you as "Mrs Jacquetta Morrison, *Mrs Jacquetta Morrison*!!"' I don't know why I was getting so worked up, why the nick-name issue affected me so passionately.

I thought of Jacquetta as being old, at least compared to Mum, but that may have been partly due to the damage done to her complexion by the sun in India. Now she had a sort of faraway look and a younger, hesitant expression. 'I don't remember Sarah ever calling me that,' she said haltingly, 'but somehow . . . Well I don't see why you couldn't call me by that name, in fact it's rather . . .' True to her destiny as an upper person, Jacquetta was capable of letting a sentence trail away forever without reaching the final word 'sweet'.

I couldn't wait that long. 'So you *are* Muzzie?!' I said. By now I was blinking back tears of rage.

'Yes,' she said, 'I don't see why not. I am now. Muzzie. Yes. Why ever not?' From that day on, Mrs Jacquetta Morrison was never anything but 'Muzzie' to both our families, to me and Mum and Sarah too. The name bedded down beautifully and became second nature, and I certainly felt I'd earned the intimacy. Mum too was grateful for the existence of the nick-name, perhaps more than me. She liked Sarah's mother such a lot, but had never been comfortable calling her Jacquetta. It was an effort for her to embark on the presumptuousness of Christian names with such an upper person. Then Sarah's mum said, 'Oh, call me Ketter. All my friends do!', making it ever so much worse.

Muzzie meant to put Mum at her ease, but the task was impossible. For Mum, dealing with someone so posh meant scrambling over a whole series of hurdles at every meeting. Now this casually intimidating instruction turned every conversation into an even more daunting event, a pole-vault of social aspiration. 'Muzzie' was a lifeline. What a relief! – it sounded safe and familial.

Funny rattly gappy

What I said was perfectly true. I had heard the word said. What I hadn't taken into account was the larger context. In fact Sarah always called her Mum 'Mummy', whoever happened to be around. It's just that one day she had slumped a little in her chair, as happened from time to time, and needed lifting back into a more comfortable position. Her mum was there, and she was the best person in the whole world to lift her, but there were times when even Jacquetta Morrison didn't quite get it right, and this was one of them. She was lifting her daughter back into place into the chair, but not to Sarah's satisfaction.

Sarah complained bitterly when a lift was badly managed. There was nothing strange about that. We all did the same. It was painful. This time, being impatient, she started to protest before her mother had finished settling her. 'Oh *Muzzzzie*,' she said, almost groaning, 'you're doing it all wrong, now you'll have to do it all over again!' Her voice squeaked in a funny rattly gappy way while she was being lifted so ineptly.

She was the doll fanatic on the ward, with a large collection, but she had something in common with a doll herself. Her size was small even for that ward because of the early onset of the disease, and the subsequent impact of steroids. There are dolls that have little speakers in their backs, and they make an uh-uh-ah-ah-ah-uh-uh kind of staccato thrumming noise. Sarah's diaphragm, under pressure, produced a very similar effect.

'Oh *Muzzie* . . . ' I had misunderstood. I overheard a chance event and turned it into a splendid secret. Life on the ward was not eventful, and we got our excitement where we could. Sarah called Jacquetta 'Mummy' and nothing else. While Jacquetta was in the process of lifting her difficult daughter, Sarah's brain rapped out the words, 'Oh Mummy, you're doing it all wrong!' but those weren't exactly the words which came out of her mouth. She got out the 'Mu–' fine, but for the next bit Jacquetta must have been squeezing Sarah's rib-cage in a funny sort of a way, forcing the air out just as it got mixed up with an emotional sob (Sarah was so looking forward to sitting correctly and comfortably) and then it emerged as a sort of distorted sigh. There may have been some congestion in Sarah's lungs, as there often was. Anyway, the middle part of the word came out as a sighing 'ZZzz.' With that extra squeeze of Sarah's squeeze-box the consonant was mutated. A bilabial dental came out as a voiced alveolar fricative, and that's how Muzzie got her name.

Robot party trick

Muzzie gave me something in return for the gift of a nick-name, quite without intending it, just as I'd christened her by accident in the first place. She had always been generous on her visits, and careful not to leave me out of any present-giving. So one day she brought some new clothes for one of Sarah's dolls, and for me she brought a little robot of green plastic, only about four inches high. Plastic toys were just beginning to come in. They were more expensive than tin ones at that time, and had a correspondingly higher status.

Then Muzzie showed me what the robot did. From Bathford days and the Ellisdons catalogue I'd always been strongly prejudiced in favour of toys that actually did something. What the robot did, if you put it on a slope or slightly slanted surface – such as a propped-up book – and gave it a tiny push sideways, was totter downhill, rocking inelegantly from side to side.

I stared and stared at my robot as it did its party trick. Muzzie couldn't have made a better choice if my guardian angel had tugged on her arm in the toy shop and pointed it out.

The robot could walk. Not smoothly, not efficiently, but undeniably. It could walk. It didn't have hips or knees, it had nothing more than a sort of rocker arrangement for a foot, but under the right circumstances it could walk. And so could I.

The problem was for me to find a suitable slope. Of course there was the corridor outside, but that was too far daunting. I set my sights on the ramp to the day room, but even that was ambitious. I was afraid of falling over before I'd managed my first tiny step. I'd seen what happened if you got impatient with the robot and made the slope too steep. It tipped forward and fell onto its front, that's what.

I got a nurse to stand me up by my bed and be ready to catch me if I fell. Then I set about creating my own slope. It was largely a mental exercise. It was a variation of the way I had learned to 'lie down' or 'sit up' at will while reclining in the Tan-Sad, fiddling with the coördinates of reality since I had so little control over my own.

I charged up my body with a small pulse of energy, as if I was winding up an elastic band. I tugged my shoulder up a little. Then I leaned forward and to the side, getting the rocking motion going, and let the leg on the other side inch forward. That first stride was hardly detectable. It was only a stride at all on a technicality, but I was starting to believe that I could move by myself, on my own two legs. Without walking aids of any sort, neither the noisy ones nor the ones I couldn't lift.

My first expedition amounted to no more than six laborious inches. Then I learned to totter from bed to bed, and soon I was tottering around the ward. In my mind I used to stretch the distance ahead of me, and turn the next stopping point into a miniature runway, a landing strip that was waiting for me to touch down, so as to please the Dad in my head, the aviation wizard. The other kids' walks were fast compared to mine, their strides long. My stride could reach an inch and a half on a good day, but I learned to totter fairly fast. Soon I was everywhere, poking my nose into all sorts of things, peeping round corners. My walking was a sort of fiction, but it had me fooled.

One day I got as far as the swing doors, and a nurse coming the other way sent me flying. She knocked me over and she knocked me out. There were portholes in the swing doors, and she had looked through but not down. She would have had to stop dead, go on tiptoe and peer down to make sure that I wasn't there. My head was below her angle of vision, and so I went flying.

Even in an institution full of the disabled, and at a time when the received wisdom was that such people must be lured away from the seductive ease of their trolleys and wheelchairs, it was easy to be overlooked and bowled over. That might have been an advantage of the aluminium-clad tripods – they would have made my progress so noisy that no one could fail to hear me coming, and there would have been no collisions. It would still have been too high a price to pay.

Ansell sent me to Hammersmith Hospital for tests. She was worried about epilepsy. I remember having an EEG, with wires attached to my scalp and lots of flashing lights. It was wonderful. I convinced myself that they were hypnotising me, which was something I'd always wanted to happen. The Home Hypnosis Kit was pretty much my favourite item in the Ellisdons catalogue, but Mum would never let me send off for it. And now I was being hypnotised for free, on the National Health. Once Ansell was satisfied that I was free of epileptic tendencies, she relaxed her protectiveness. I was allowed to fall over as often as I liked.

I don't know what would have happened to me, as a non-walker in an institution that was fanatical about walking, if I hadn't come up with my own method, thanks to Muzzie's gift. That robot opened many doors for me. Even so, my progress was very slow. It didn't even look as if I was getting anywhere at all. Nobody paid me any attention. I seemed to be trapped for ever in the middle distance. And then – as I imagined it, anyway – the nurses would look up and 'suddenly' I wasn't there any more. Gone. Gone walkabout.

The best doors

It was high time I took a good look round the hospital. A robot my size would have made no end of clanking, but I could be pretty quiet. I was particularly attracted to doors with machinery behind them. The best doors had signs on them, saying things like PRIVATE, NO ENTRY or DANGER – ideally all three.

Doors could be a headache. All the same, I reasoned that any telling-off I got for straying into a restricted area would have to be diluted with praise for having covered such a distance. Deep down, wasn't I doing what I was always being told to do, walking at any price?

I was particularly attracted when a room was being fumigated, as sometimes happened, for instance if there had been a case of dysentery. The procedure involved sealing up the room with brown paper, and then releasing fumes from some sort of hygienic bomb. This was all very exciting, the combination of a bomb and a forbidden area, and I hung around as much as I could. I could never quite work out how the bomb was detonated inside the sealed room. Perhaps it was a time bomb. I just knew it would release something even more wonderful than a smell you could almost see.

Once I found my way into a broom cupboard full of mops and buckets and couldn't get out again. It was a surprisingly long time before anyone came looking for me. I was bit cheesed off about that. Weren't they supposed to be keeping an eye on me? I mean, anything could have happened, for all they knew. So by the time I started hearing voices calling my name I decided I wouldn't make it too easy for them – I wouldn't answer. The searching noises and calls became a bit desperate, and finally the cupboard door was flung open. If I'd been able to jump out like a jack-in-the-box I would have done it, but there was nothing to stop me shouting 'Boo!'

I was taken to Ansell, perhaps to get an earful, but Ansell couldn't stop smiling and said, 'Well, there's nothing wrong with his spirit, I'll say that for him.' I didn't even have to play my trump card, saying plaintively, 'But Doctor, I thought you said you wanted to get me walking . . .'

My marginal new mobility enabled me to give the nurses the slip, but it didn't have the same effect on Wendy and her charming gang. In fact they were able to escalate their campaign of terrors free from the inhibiting presence of staff. They would ambush me, or simply out-totter me. Their walking wasn't good, but mine was much worse. In these special Olympics I was never going to be a medallist.

Wendy Keach had a knife which she kept hidden under her dress while she was in view of any nurses but would point menacingly at me. I don't know if she wanted to do actual violence or simply to get me into a state. She may even have timed these little episodes so that the arrival of a nurse would 'thwart' her, but I had no reason to suppose she wasn't being serious when she hissed, 'Next time I will not miss.'

Ivy Horrocks's blindness dictated a division of labour, whereby Wendy looked after the physical side of things and Ivy was in charge of the psychology department. Ivy had a very effective trick of staring straight ahead of her while I toiled past her bed, and then suddenly focusing on me and hissing, 'Don't think I can't see you!' Even now I'm not sure how much she could actually see, but she certainly managed to get mileage out of her condition. Up close she smelled of wee, not because she was incontinent but for more complicated reasons. An earlier operation had restored her sight, but Mr Smiley the surgeon told her it was only for a few months at best. Then she would be blind again. The doctors advised her to walk around the ward as much as possible while her sight lasted, memorising the geography of the place. Then she would be able to get around later on.

It was a lot to ask of a child – to spend her eyesight, while she had it, preparing for a future in the dark. Ivy became despondent and withdrawn. When her eyesight failed she wanted a wheelchair, but was told off for that. Just because her eyes were worse, it didn't mean she was allowed to abandon the great project of walking. So she sat on an ordinary chair, and when she wanted a wee she would call for help from a nurse. Nobody ever said it was wrong to call, but it was certainly disapproved of. There was always a long wait involved, to rid you of any idea that the nurses were your personal servants. And by the time anyone came to help Ivy to the toilet, it was too late.

Once upon a time, I was told, Ivy had been a cheerful little girl. Everyone would call out, 'Oh cor blimey, 'ere comes Ivy!' when they saw her. It was only after the second blindness that she became so nasty and enlisted as Wendy's lieutenant. She took drastic measures to put herself beyond the reach of pity. She got her wheelchair in the end, but that wasn't enough in itself to reverse the changes in her character.

Strider

On a good day I could get into the toilet. There was no soap in the basin, so I decided I would make some. I just wet my hands and rubbed. Bubbles came, masses of them, until the whole basin was full. I decided I could do magic, and showed off very successfully to various of the girls on the ward. Then one day the talent disappeared and never came back. I suppose the most likely explanation is that there were soap residues all round the basin, and that was what was generating the magic bubbles, until one day some bathroom zealot made a proper job of the cleaning, but I'm not quite convinced. In the back of my mind there's always the possibility that the talent will come back.

A while after I had made my breakthrough by basing my movements on a toy robot rather than a fellow human being, I heard a couple of nurses talking about my being a 'strider'. I was thrilled that they paid such close attention to my progress, and tottered up to them to bask in the glory of it all. They went quiet and actually seemed embarrassed. It took a lot of wheedling to get them to explain what they had been saying.

Apparently I was known at CRX for my night noises. If your movements are restricted by day, they're not going to be any better at night. My sleeping posture was relatively inflexible – flat on my back. I hadn't known that my snoring was conspicuous, since nurses had tactfully been using the technical term. Not 'strider', silly, *stridor*. Medical Latin. A whistling noise produced during respiration.

There was no treatment proposed for my snoring. No clips were attached to my sleeping nose, no operation was undertaken to widen the passages, and for that I was grateful.

After I had been walking for a while the physios tried to get in on the act. I didn't take too kindly to that. I'd discovered my own technique for getting around, and now they wanted to horn in on all the glory, when they hadn't really helped.

They didn't even seem to understand the workings of my gait. If my stride was only a couple of inches, the actual height of each 'step' I took was minuscule. The physios measured it once and recorded it as a quarter of an inch. They told me that I must try harder, must increase the height of each step. They never explained exactly how increased height could be achieved with totally fused hips. I wasn't raising my leg at all, I was only leaning away from it.

'You do have a bit of movement in your spine, you know, John,' said the physio supremo Miss Withers, which was true but didn't make my hips work.

She was actually very nice, with a deepish voice and tufts of hair that sprouted from moles on her face. Never one to let a good style of nick-name go to waste, I dubbed her 'Withie Boy' and got everyone else to call her that behind her back. If she gave me pain she always said first, 'If it hurts too much let me know. The pain should not be allowed to become too great. Your body is giving you a warning.' This was an interesting interpretation of pain, though I couldn't take it all that seriously. If pain was a warning, then my body had been on red alert for years.

In some parts of the ward the lino hadn't been stuck down properly. It curled up half an inch or so, just enough to make it a perfect John-trap. When I was walking with the grain of the lino, by which I mean from the curl to the flat, the change of level added a little extra thrust to my totter. When I came from the other direction I would fall, often quite badly. I was always being told on those premises that pride came before a fall. It wasn't just pride. Absolutely anything could come before a fall.

My falling at that spot was a common enough event to spark controversy among the staff of the ward. Should they replace the lino, or should they train me to adapt to the ward better? It would be most inconvenient and expensive to do anything about the lino, and where would they put the children while it was being done?

It was decided that the cost of replacing lino to save me from injury was too great. The physios would take me in hand and make me, again in the same unspecified way, able to raise my foot above all obstacles. I don't think Withie Boy would ever have taken such a tough line, but she had 'flu at the time and her deputy, Miss Clipworth, was in charge. It happens very often that deputies are more authoritarian than their bosses. Flexibility seems a form of weakness unless endorsed at the highest level. So really it was the inflexible giving the inflexible a masterclass in being unbending.

Miss Clipworth watched me at my tottering and then asked me where I focused my eyes.

'Well, on the next bed, of course!' I said. 'If I see where my next stop is I can walk that far. I make believe it's a runway, and I'm a plane that can't land until it gets there. My Dad's in the RAF. It starts off hard, but it gets easier and easier as you go along because the distance gets shorter. That's how I worked out how to walk.' I felt rather proud of explaining my method.

'Then no wonder you keep falling over!' she said. 'What an absurd idea! If you'd wanted to learn how to walk properly, you should have come to me.'

She told me not to concentrate on the next bed, but to keep my attention on the floor. I obeyed, and keeled over after three steps. I lost confidence without being able to concentrate on the next bed, the vista that kept me going. She caught me, then roughly lifted me back to the vertical and told me to try again. The same thing happened again, and although she didn't let me fall I was very shaken. My heart was beating away like mad, and I started to cry. She said coldly, 'You're too old to cry – you don't want people thinking you're a sissy, do you?' If I'd been less upset I might have answered that most of them already did, but I just wanted to apologise for all the trouble one little person was making for everyone who tried to help him. It was frightening to realise that Miss Clipworth was angry with me. She was being rough, but that wasn't the worst of it, it was knowing that she despised me for the difficulties I was having.

I didn't hear the approach of righteous footsteps. All I knew was that I was caught in a whirlwind of starched uniforms. Sister Heel had snatched me from Clipworth, but it took me a few moments to grasp what was happening. I was still being roughly treated, but oh what a difference! Heel was absolutely cross, but not at me, she was cross at the way I had been treated. Her strong arms held me to her. It was painful in its own right, and there were sharp edges to the hug, her belt buckle perhaps and the watch she wore pinned to her front. It was a hug against a barrier of starched hospital linen. It was very far from anything you could term a cuddle, but in its own way it was sheerly loving.

Heel gave Clipworth something as close to a scolding as the absence of direct authority allowed. 'I don't know what you hope to gain, Miss Clipworth, by torturing your patients.' She was shaking with feeling as she said this. The tremors passed deliciously through me.

When Clipworth answered I could feel her emotion as a great wave of heat against my back, all that pride and shame and territorial resentment. 'Physiotherapy is my area and my responsibility, Sister Heel. You must allow me to know best in these matters.'

'Allow you to know best fiddlesticks!' cried Heel. 'This must be taken to arbitration.'

This was marvellous. I thought I knew CRX better than anyone by now, but I had no idea who or what Arbitration was. Sister went to her office, still holding me in her arms, and made a telephone call. Then she told me I should leave her. 'You can manage, can't you? I'm sorry Miss Clipworth is so disappointed in your walking. I think you've done rather well.' And this time the wave of heat came from inside me.

In less than a minute the Tannoy lady was announcing, '*Dr Ansell to Sister Heel's office, please . . . Dr Ansell.*' Soon Ansell was conferring with Heel in her office. At the time I was disappointed not to learn anything about Arbitration, but I knew Ansell would do the job just as well. I hung around the door and listened. This wasn't strictly necessary – when Ansell was on the ward, everybody heard her anyway. Soon Clipworth was summoned to the office. She must have been taking a series of deep breaths as she approached the show-down – this was *High Noon* in Bucks (or Berks) – or she would have scolded me as she passed. I hadn't been able to come up with an innocent reason for hanging around the office, and was picking off flakes of cream gloss paint from a crack in the wall.

What I heard from my listening post was a terrible piece of adult ganging-up – a coalition of Ansell and Heel against the physio. It was Heaven. Heel asked, 'Do you have any idea what effect your actions are having on the emotional development of the child?'

Clipworth must have known from the start that she was out-gunned but she shot back with, 'I'm simply trying to do the job I was trained to do. I am also aware of what it would cost to pull up the lino and re-lay it.'

Apostle of walking though she was, she had just made a false step herself. Heel let her voice go almost sugary as she asked, 'Since when have physios been so interested in the doings of the Costs & Maintenance Department?'

Taplow Tetragrammaton

I was reeling, outside the office, from all these new ideas. 'The Emotional Development of the Child' sounded wonderful, though I wasn't sure what it might mean. Still, it was something to do with Me. 'Costs & Maintenance' was another stunner. On my journeys along the corridor I had memorised every notice board in the place, and I had never seen one labelled Costs & Maintenance. I had learned, though, that CRX was mystically organised. There wasn't really any such thing as The School on those premises, either. It was an idea, a dream. It was conjured up when the stars were in the right alignment, and dematerialised when medical matters were in the ascendant. Costs & Maintenance, and also perhaps Arbitration, must have a similarly evanescent nature.

I was learning such a lot from the dramatic show-down in the office. I wish I had taken notes, except that my hand-writing was so poor I couldn't usually read it myself. In any case, all these revelations were just the prelude to a statement of fantastic brevity and interest. It was in the class of Ansell's 'The illness has raged', but you could argue that it was even more distinguished, since it contained a mere four syllables in four words, as against Ansell's rather slapdash and prolix five.

With Ansell laying down covering fire behind her, Heel produced a fantastic ack-ack of invective, making it clear that Ward matters were her province, and ending with this astounding fusillade: *'I am the Ward . . .'*

I am the Ward. *I am the Ward.* Something about the phrase resonated so deeply inside me I almost fainted. It was a connection more fundamental than memory

I am the Ward. This was the Taplow Tetragrammaton. It stopped the mind dead in its tracks, as a good mantra should. It sent a pulse of wonder through every brick in the place. This was an atom bomb of an argument against which nothing could prevail. I AM THE WARD. It had links with the Old Testament: *I AM THAT I AM* (Exodus 3:14). It joined hands with the New – *In the beginning was the Word* (John 1:1). ¶I AM THE WARD.

When Heel detonated this exemplary mantra, Miss Clipworth for all practical purposes ceased to exist. She must have crawled off somewhere, blackened and smoking, perhaps through a door marked Arbitration or Costs & Maintenance, or maybe she just melted into nothingness, falling between the cracks in the rucked-up lino. I don't think any of us ever saw or heard of her again.

It was only later that I worried about the hierarchies, about thrones, principalities and powers. If Sister Heel could atomise Miss Clipworth by saying 'I am the Ward', did that mean that if it came to a fight, Matron could flatten Heel by saying 'I AM THE HOSPITAL'?

I hadn't disliked Miss Clipworth, though it would be going too far to say I missed her when she was gone. There was only one physiotherapist I really disliked, in fact only one person on the whole staff, medical or scholastic: Miss Krüger, who worked on our walking and sometimes supervised solo sessions in the hydrotherapy pool. I hated and feared her because she was German. Dad always said that the Germans were an evil race. They were just naturally cruel and bad.

The rest of the staff pronounced her name as Krooger, but she herself used a different pronunciation, the vowel thin and gloating, the consonants as crisp as snapping bones.

In Miss Krüger's sessions, we would be made to walk without shoes, and without help from walking aids, the various crutches and canes. Miss Krüger was dark and short. I'm not a good judge of height, but I don't think she can have been much more than five feet – which could have worked in her favour. We liked to be looked after by people who didn't tower over us too much, but her therapy was anything but fun. At the beginning of each session she would say brightly, 'We have much work to do. We must make your ankles strong!' She would go down on her haunches in front of us, and hold out her hands, palm upwards, to encourage us to take steps, but if we did manage to hobble towards her, she moved backwards so that there was more ground to cover. None of us could ever reach that receding target. She'd say firmly, 'You must do it without help!' When we overbalanced she would catch us, but then she just set us to walking again, on legs that had no aptitude for keeping us upright but whose inflamed joints were sensitised to every little disturbance.

I didn't use walking aids like the others, so it wasn't a deprivation for me to do without such things as crutches and canes, but I couldn't keep myself vertical without the support of my shoes any better than anyone else. I'd topple again and again, until I thought I would prefer to fall over outright without being caught, as long as I was allowed to stay on the ground for the rest of the session. Miss Krüger would keep saying, 'Ups-a-daisy!' or 'Boomps-a-daisy!' as we lurched in our agony, breezy idioms which I came to hate since their actual meaning seemed to be 'Show me more pain.'

It wasn't that other physios (such as Miss Withers) made no pain, but Withie Boy stopped as soon as she could, and her own pain showed as a fact in the frown on her face. With Miss Krüger we went up on pointes like some tormented corps de ballet, and she made sure each of us had a solo. I had always had mixed feelings about the Little Mermaid in Hans Christian Andersen's tale, who chose human legs over a fishy tail even though each step would be like walking on knives. We had the sensation of walking on knives, all right, but our legs didn't even work properly. We'd been swizzled, getting all the bad bits of the bargain. I for one would happily have traded my legs for a mermaid's tail, which would have been hardly less useful and a lot more decorative. I'd like to see Miss Krüger try to get me walking on my tail! And at least I'd be able to do without a rubber ring in the hydrotherapy pool.

Hating the Hun

It was a relief to discover that we all hated and feared Miss Krüger. It wasn't just me. I felt better knowing I wasn't the only one who said hateful things under his breath, the only one who hated the Hun.

Although Clipworth had been annihilated, her arguments shredded and disposed of, somehow the lino didn't ever get taken up. Officially I was praised for being 'adventuresome', but there was some brisk back-pedalling on the let-him-walk-and-fall-over-as-much-as-he-wants idea. Suddenly a proper wheelchair materialised, and the Tan-Sad was held in reserve for long outside walks on rough terrain. I was told to stay in the wheelchair and only walk if nurse or physio or doctor was on hand. 'Besides,' said Miss Reid, 'we can't have you neglecting your Education, can we? And the staff have better things to do than to spend their time running round looking for you, you know . . .'

That was CRX all over. If I had asked for extra lessons, nothing whatever would have happened, but by tottering around the place like a madman I was able to force that wonderful sentence, 'We can't have you neglecting your Education,' into being. The best technique for getting something in the topsy-turvy world of CRX seemed to be to head firmly in the opposite direction. The most effective way of undermining the régime of the place was not to protest against its ordinances – like the walk-at-all-costs idea – but to carry them to extremes.

The feeling in those days seemed to be that rules were good things in themselves. For instance: hospital visiting hours amounted to eight hours a week, no more – seven to eight in the evening on weekdays, two to four in the afternoon on Saturdays, three to four on Sundays. These restrictions were strictly enforced unless you'd just had an operation or were actively and officially dying. Some of the kids asked rather tearfully about this. Mums and dads would have liked to visit more often, but many of them lived a long way away. Public transport wasn't reliable and there was no provision for family members to stay in the hospital. In general the presence of parents was considered an obstruction to the smooth running of the ward.

No one was allowed to sit on the edge of the bed except doctors, and they never did. Occasionally Ansell would sit on the edge of your bed, if she was explaining something important. This gave the lecture a special meaning and you listened particularly well to what she had to say, but it was a rare event. Again, the rule was waived if you were very ill or dying, so I suppose it was really quite a good sign if visitors weren't getting too familiar. The strictness of hospital policy meant that no one on Wards One and Two had visitors in the week except for Sarah Morrison, whose mum had moved to Cookham just to be near her.

Flowers were donated by posh ladies who felt sorry for us, making the ward a cheerier place. When it got dark Nurse came in and took them all off to another room and closed the door. Visiting hours were over for the day, even for flowers. When I asked the reason why, she said, 'They're dangerous at night. You're not allowed to be near them.' Mum got the science from Dad for me, explaining that plants absorbed carbon dioxide during the day and gave out oxygen, but at night they drank oxygen and emitted carbon dioxide. Normally this wasn't a problem, but the plants might take a bit too much and cause breathing problems for sick children. After this I was reconciled to the nightly departure of the flowers, though mainly with their welfare in mind. Surely they would be relieved not to be competing for air with the massed lungs of the ward.

The hospital restricted the hours for visitors, their seating arrangements and even their numbers. No one was allowed more than two visitors at a time. So if a kid had an auntie and an uncle and a mum and a dad visiting, two of them would have to wait outside in the main hospital corridor, which was cold and draughty. Each bed had two chairs, one on each side. Visitors were allowed to stand by the bed, or sit on the chair. Sister and her staff would police the system. A certain amount of hand-holding was allowed. I suppose that was how visitors knew this was a hospital and not a prison.

The hardship experienced by all those uncles and aunties over the years, waiting outside in such a spooky and comfortless place, must have come to quite a tidy sum of misery. It didn't compare with the sufferings of patients, but it was wholly unnecessary. Yet there was barely a murmur of grumbling. If families did speak up, they would be told firmly, 'We don't want to over-excite the patient, now, do we? Why not go to the WVS canteen and have a nice cup of tea? It's at the end of the corridor on the right.' Only a quarter of a mile away.

One day the visitors had exceeded their quota, and an officious nurse was doing her best to enforce the rules. There were also four kids who didn't have visitors. One of the aunties had the nous to say, 'Well, seeing as we are four relatives to one nephew, and the boy in the next bed has no visitors, why don't two of us be visitors to this boy, and then we can swap round, and we can all chat with him and he won't feel lonely? Besides,' she added in a whisper, 'even if Matron did swoop in, she would never know whose visitor was really whose, now would she?'

The ward held its breath while the nurse hesitated, and then she dissolved into a human being. Suddenly extra visitors were being hustled and bustled in. The ward rang with friendly chat and laughter, and boys with no visitor reaped the benefit. To crown it all, when the tea trolley came round, the rule of visitors being allowed tea but no cake went out of the window. It was madness, it was Liberty Hall. One boy ended up becoming very attached to his new uncle and auntie, and I think he went home with them for the odd weekend.

One day Mum told me that she and Dad were buying a house. At first I wondered what that had to do with me, and then I was suddenly terrified that they were moving far away on purpose so that they would never have to visit me again. It took me quite a while to realise that I'd got it exactly the wrong way round. They were moving to be near to me.

They must have done quite a lot of house-hunting on the sly, before I ever knew a move was on the cards. They didn't have much money, unlike Jacquetta Morrison who could just swan into Cookham and buy a house whose address ended in Court. Dad's pay at the time was barely a thousand pounds a year, so really it was a bit of a stretch. Mum and Dad had settled on Bourne End, which wasn't quite Cookham but was certainly a desirable place to live. Properties could easily fetch £10,000, which was far beyond Dad's reach. In fact riverside properties like the one they had found on the Abbotsbrook Estate could easily fetch higher prices than suburban Cookham – not that a village can have suburbs, but I'm sure that was how Mum would have viewed anything that wasn't in the heart of Old Cookham.

Somehow they had happened on a house that was much cheaper. It was only £3,000, though there was a reason for that. It had no electricity. The garden was so over-grown you could hardly see the house itself (which made it sound to my ears like Sleeping Beauty's castle). It had been occupied by two old dears who were nearly blind. Gardening was beyond them, but they made up for it in the kitchen. They spent all their time frying, or so it seemed. The kitchen was so encrusted with grease that it stank, and there would have to be many hours of scrubbing before the new occupiers could so much as make a cup of tea which didn't taste rancid. Every other room was dusty and decaying in a different way.

It sounded perfect. It had been called St Dunstan's, but Mum and Dad changed the name to Trees – which I thought was a bit of a cheat. If that was allowed, what was to stop common people decamping metaphysically from their numbered hovels by granting themselves decent addresses? Still, St Dunstan being the patron saint of the blind, he was no longer needed at that address. The trees, too, were worth celebrating. There were four or five poplars out at the front, as well as a cherry tree. I loved the poplars particularly, not just the way they looked but the sound they made. They sighed and swayed. There's no tree more in touch with its past lives than your poplar.

Bourne End was a little further away from CRX than Cookham, but it was in the same neck of the woods, and Muzzie offered to do a certain amount of ferrying. If there was any money left over it would go towards a car. Then I would be able to travel to this new home of ours at weekends without relying on lifts from other people.

When Mum and Dad had done a great deal of outdoor hacking and indoor de-greasing, the house looked very nice. The neighbour opposite, Arthur Foot, put up his easel one day, took his oil paints and painted a picture of it. He even gave them the painting, which was a lovely gesture. Arthur and Dad became good gardening friends, which is a curious sort of friendship, though in some ways better than the real thing. Mum had some sort of fraught acquaintance with his wife Dorothy. She knew her, in a phrase I found endlessly mysterious, 'to speak to'. I think she was shy of her. She wanted to spend all her time with upper people, but sometimes she felt she couldn't keep up with the uppers. Arthur and Dorothy Foot were always known locally as 'the Feet', a nick-name which Mum used nervously if at all.

Now that Trees had been made ship-shape I assumed Granny would be visiting. Mum soon squashed that notion. 'I don't need Granny getting under my feet,' she said, but she sounded almost wistful. I didn't dare ask any more questions about the family ruction which was keeping Granny away. Whatever it was, I assumed that it was my fault.

The only thing which was definitely disappointing about the new house had to do with the phone. The telephone at Bathford had a proper rotating dial, even if I wasn't supposed to use it except on special occasions. I remember one of Mum's friends had the number 4444, which was very tempting. I would be able to dial the whole thing without taking my finger out of the hole. It would be like dialling 999, but without having to wait for the house to burn down for an excuse. At Trees, though, there was no dial on the apparatus. You had to pick up the receiver and a little voice would say, 'Number please?' It was a bit of a step back.

Still, those first weekends in the house were wonderful. We all had to camp out, like joyful gipsies. We used paraffin lamps which had a lovely stink, though the light wasn't strong. Essentially, when it got dark, we went to bed. We had the radio, though, since it ran on a battery. I don't think I was ever quite so happy in that house again. As the house began to come together as a workable family residence, I began to feel that I was the only one still squatting. There wasn't enough money to do any real converting for my benefit. Perhaps I was meant to understand that a little inconvenience was a fair price for me to pay personally for the family up-rooting. The unwritten rule which operated in CRX seemed to be general: the disabled person must adapt to the world as it is.

It was a bit of a shock when I first heard Mum saying in company that the house had been bought 'because of John'. If it was my doing, shouldn't I perhaps have been asked whether I actually wanted them to up-root themselves? It was a bit much to make me solely responsible for something that was just announced to me from on high. Mum never stopped saying it, though, and I more or less got used to it.

Mum made friends quite quickly with a neighbour called Joy Payne, who was extraordinarily willing to put herself out to be helpful. She couldn't do enough for all of us. Soon she was driving Mum over to CRX on a Friday in her Vauxhall Victor estate. I loved how big and roomy that car was. I didn't know there could be anything so spacious. Of course her husband was chairman of Vauxhall Motors, or at least high up in the firm, so it wasn't quite the status symbol that it seemed to me then.

The Paynes lived in Otters Pool. How could you fail to love people whose house was called that? But Joy's real gift to me wasn't her house's name but her own. Joy Payne. How can you improve on that? What a lot of food for thought there was in those two syllables.

There was even a sweet that was popular at the time called Payne's Poppets, which reinforced the idea that Joy was a poppet as of right. One weekend Joy brought the Tan-Sad home with me and Mum – there was always room for one more in that Vauxhall. It folded up rather half-heartedly, and even semi-collapsed it was unwieldy. The

Tan-Sad stayed at Trees from then on, but it was much better suited for trips outside than for anything in the house. It was very unmanœuvrable, and it brought dirt in with it on its wheels.

Mum would sometimes take me into Bourne End in the Tan-Sad to do her shopping, hanging her purchases from the handles or tucking them next to me on the seat or down by my feet on the foot-plate. As a reward we would go into Mr Clifton's Toy Shop afterwards. There wasn't much in there which was up my street, but I would feel a tiny excitement before going in. You never knew, after all. Round the next corner of the shop there might lurk something which was just for me, perhaps a candle which burnt forever, or a tiny elephant which you had to feed real grass, chopped up very fine.

If I fell down during a weekend at home, if for instance I tripped on a carpet edge, Mum would help me up but Dad would take no notice. If we were alone in the room he'd pretend nothing had happened. He wouldn't look at me.

Informed wonder

It was very hard on him. He must have felt he'd been deprived of the son he was entitled to, but even so there were times when he forgot to be bereaved. Then he'd take me on nature rambles, pushing the Tan-Sad perfectly happily and collecting specimens from streams for me to look at. Hydra and daphne and rotifer: little worlds in water that he enjoyed explaining to me. 'That's a cyclops, John, see? A female – she's laden with eggs.' I could just make these creatures out with my naked eye, though Dad's powers of resolution were certainly superior. A new note came into his voice when he spoke about the natural world, one of informed wonder, and he became a different being. I liked him best when we were out and about away from the house. I don't know whether I wanted him to myself, or if he was genuinely different out of Mum's company. He seemed younger, almost a boy playing with another, the way he was before the War put the kibosh on his university career and reading biology.

One winter before Christmas, Mum said we should make a special trip to Clifton's, because he had things displayed which he didn't have at other times of the year. Mr Clifton had even said to her, 'Why don't you bring your son along to have a look when he comes home from hospital?'

I was excited, but mainly because Mum was. Deep down I knew that the toys in my dreams would never be found in a shop, but I got into the spirit of things.

The shop was chokker. There were loads of toys and games. I reckoned it would take at least an hour to have a proper look. All those extra things meant the space available for customers was smaller than usual. Mum got the Tan-Sad round as much of the shop as she could, and she went to fetch things from the parts I couldn't get to so I could see them properly. I was careful not to admire anything so forcefully that it ended up as a Christmas or birthday present. I had said I wanted a pet snake, and I knew this wasn't a popular request. I didn't want to be bought off with a Meccano set I couldn't use.

Then Mr Clifton came along and said, 'Your son is very welcome here, Mrs Cromer, but please, not at Christmas time! Why don't you bring him along for our January sale? We always have more space then, and there'll be some knock-down prices too!' He bent down to address me directly. 'That'll make your money go further, won't it John?'

'Yes, of course, Mr Clifton,' I said. I was as exasperated as anyone else with the intractability of the Tan-Sad, and I wasn't so very interested in the shop in the first place. All the same I didn't want Mr Clifton to feel that I thought he had a lot of tatty stuff in there, so I said, 'I can't see round that corner! Can you keep a few of those things for the January sale?' and Mr Clifton said he would see what he could do.

Mum pushed me outside into the fresh air, delightful after the fug of the shop. I thought that was an end of it, but as soon as she'd put the brakes on she went back in. My heart sank when I heard her shouting and wailing, while Mr Clifton pleaded with her not to misunderstand.

'Misunderstand? Misunder*stand*??' she wailed. 'Oh no, Mr Clifton, I most certainly do not misunder*stand*, in fact I under*stand* only too well. You don't want either my son or myself in your shop, that's what I under*stand*. Good day to you, Mr Clifton!' She pushed me home, sobbing all the way and entirely forgetting to buy bread and vegetables. After gathering her strength with a cup of tea she started on a telephone marathon, telling all her friends and neighbours, the Feet and the Paynes and of course Muzzie, exactly how awful Mr Clifton had been. 'I ask you,' she would say, 'can John help taking up more space than a healthy boy? Isn't he entitled to a little fun at Christmas too? Now he's very upset, and small wonder.'

John wasn't upset in the slightest. Except that John didn't enjoy being used as a sort of amplifier for other people's emotions, though he was having to get used to it.

I don't think Mum set out to organise a punitive boycott of Mr Clifton's Toy Shop, but more than one of the phone conversations ended with her saying, 'Well, if you think that's best. I wasn't going to suggest it. But that awful man can't say he didn't ask for it. See how he likes it, when the boot's on the other foot.'

I tried to soften Mum's attitude, but she told me not to make excuses for that horrible man. The next time she picked up the phone I found I was incorporated in her monologue all over again: 'John tried to tell me he didn't mind – as if he could pull the wool over a mother's eyes! He's such a sweet boy. He hates to see me upset.' Nothing is so crushing as a reputation for being noble, and I wasn't being noble at all. I just didn't care. If I'd been barred from a book-shop things would have been different. I'd have organised the boycott myself.

I'm not trying to suggest that Mum exaggerated the toy shop affair so as to be sure she would get plenty of offers of lifts to Maidenhead to do her Christmas shopping there. The emotional turmoil was its own reward and anything else was just a fringe benefit.

Dregs of humanity

What made things awkward for Mum was that Mr Clifton was such bad casting as any sort of villain. People who choose to run toy shops in genteel towns are rarely the dregs of humanity. When Mum next took me into Bourne End, she crossed the road with the Tan-Sad so that we didn't have to pass the toy shop, but Mr Clifton must have been watching out for us. He came trotting out of his premises and crossed the road to greet us.

He seemed very agitated. 'Ah, Mrs Cromer,' he said, 'I'm so glad to have caught you. I felt so bad after our . . . discussion the other day. I wanted to let you know that I've re-organised the whole shop. Everything's so much better now. I've put some hooks in the walls and arranged things higher up. The customers can see everything now – you've really done me a favour.' His smile was ghastly. 'Please come and see how much space there is, for *everyone*. And do please bring young Master Cromer.' Then he trotted back to the shop he had transformed to win back the favour of our scanty custom.

I wanted to see the new arrangement very much, and assumed we would call in on the way back from our shopping. Instead Mum chose a route which by-passed the shop altogether. 'Aren't we going to the toy shop?' I asked from the depths of the Tan-Sad. 'No, JJ, we're not.' She sounded very unhappy. 'I just can't face Mr Clifton after all the things I've said about him.'

I didn't get a Meccano set for Christmas, and I didn't get a snake either. I got nasty white mice in a wooden cage, on straw that smelled of wee. In fact they smelled like Ivy. I hated them. I wailed, 'Where's the present you said I would *like*?' The mice disappeared and were never seen again. Instead I was given a First Aid Kit. That was more like it. It had been planned as my birthday present but it was brought forward in double-quick time. It was a black box with a key and various dummy medications. Back at CRX I became the ward's community doctor, and soon ran out of supplies. I filled the empty bottles with dolly mixtures from the shop, carefully divided by colour. Dolly unmixture. Dolly mixtures unmixed by me and revealed as wonder drugs, placebo steroids without side-effects of any sort.

I thought perhaps Mum would take me to Clifton's for the sale in January, but still we kept away. I was back at CRX by the time I heard Mr Clifton had died of a heart attack, in February. I was sure it was my fault, at least partly. I could have tried harder to get Mum to accept the olive branch which Mr Clifton held out to her, with such pleading in his voice. I was supposed to be the one with the unreliable heart, but it was Mr Clifton who hadn't been able to stand the strain of trying to do business with the Cromers.

It wasn't just the Decca Gramophone Company who treated the unfortunate children of CRX to presents, or at least to surplus stock. There was a businessman, a tycoon even, who had invented a new sort of life-jacket, which you didn't have to inflate. It was the life-jacket of the future, destined to save thousands of lives. Little windows in the jacket expanded when wet. He gave the hospital a whole batch, for use in the hydrotherapy pool, for the poor children who couldn't support themselves in water in the normal way. Sister Heel and Miss Withers did a great job of building up these magic jackets in our minds. The staff would be able to pick one of us up and throw us into the pool, and we'd be absolutely fine. Even if we landed head down, the jacket would turn us right way up in no time, and then keep our heads safely above water.

It may have been clear to the staff at the time that this was at least partly a publicity stunt. It didn't occur to us. Private enterprise was tapping into a rich vein of pathos, but we who were that vein had no inkling. The new apparatus was tested, of course. The hospital authorities didn't take such claims on trust. It was tested on me.

I assumed that I was chosen because of my charm, intelligence and good humour, but although these may have been taken into consideration I was missing the point. I was the lucky volunteer because I hadn't been medicated with steroids. The illness having raged, my bones were almost ideally dense. My natural buoyancy was close to zero. I was the least floatable of an unfloatable bunch. This body pulls me under. In water my bones felt softer, all the same, like the canes which Miss Reid soaked overnight for basket weaving.

There were quite a few people gathered round the pool for the test. I don't think it was exactly a press call or photo opportunity – such things were in their early days then. The life-jackets were a lovely yellow colour. They were all technically Small, since they were being issued to children, but the one they put on me seemed very big just the same. It laced up, and there was so much cord left over that it went round me several times.

Miss Withers came into the pool with me. She was a real water baby. She loved it. On dry land there was no getting round her, but in the water she would turn a blind eye to a little bit of cheekiness. She could just about maintain her strictness when she was in the pool, but you could tell it was an effort. Not that I was being cheeky on this particular day. I was on best behaviour. Her hands were beneath me in the pool, and then she gave me a little push and I went under. Nothing much happened for a while, except that I started to breathe something that wasn't air. She hadn't given me enough warning, and I hadn't had time to take a breath. I thought perhaps that was the trouble. Maybe they were waiting for bubbles to break the surface before they decided it was time to rescue me. I tried to make bubbles but I didn't know how.

Then Miss Withers was lifting me up and I was spluttering in her arms. I was sorry that I hadn't been able to make the life-jacket work, but Miss Withers wasn't cross with me. She hugged me in a way that was rather painful, saying 'There, there.' Dad was away at the time, but I could almost hear his voice saying, 'For God's sake don't make such a fuss, he already thinks the whole world revolves around him.' Someone brought warm towels to wrap me in, and I began almost to enjoy myself. I can't have been under water long, but the air above the pool had changed, all the same, while I was away. Now it was agitated and swirling. The inventor in his dark suit was saying something about this not being a fair test. Not fair at all. My body was too abnormal for any life-jacket, past or future, to hold it up.

The hospital authorities must have been convinced by this line of argument, because the yellow life-jackets replaced the inflated rubber rings we had been using in the pool, except for me. I had failed to be saved by the life-jacket of the future, so my buoyancy would be guaranteed by an old-fashioned rubber ring. I didn't really mind. We weren't too closely supervised. There was always someone around, but staff might pop out for a few minutes without worrying.

One day I was playing with Mary Finch in the shallow end. In water our bodies were much more coöperative, much more responsive to commands, than they ever were on dry land. We could almost run, in a sort of slow motion. Mary 'ran away' and I 'chased' her. The difference between our speeds was nowhere near as great as it was when we were really walking.

Soon we were out of breath after all our squealing play. Mary lay on her back to float for a minute. I looked at her with love, but also with mischief. I couldn't resist the impulse to push her under. There was no danger – we had been told often enough how wonderful those life-jackets were, as long as your body made some sort of effort to be normal. Mary's face went below the surface of the water and stayed there. The yellow life-jacket seemed to be entirely ornamental. Her eyes were open and she was making little waving movements with her arms. Now it was terrible that I was only moving in slow motion as I tried to reach her. Finally I managed to get an arm against her and to give a lop-sided sort of push, and after that her face broke through the water and she was spluttering and crying and I was begging for her to forgive me. I felt I'd come close to doing something that God would hate me for.

Mary forgave me the moment she got her breath back. She wasn't capable of holding a grudge. We agreed that we wouldn't tell anyone what had happened. The life-jacket was a dud, but I couldn't tell Miss Withers or anyone else about it without admitting how I'd found out, by pushing Mary under.

Mum was very attuned to me in those days, and she persuaded me to tell her what the matter was. She was sworn to secrecy, but with Mum you could never quite be sure. Or there may have been other incidents in the pool that we weren't told about. One way or another, supervision in the pool area became much more continuous. Then one day our benefactor turned up on the television defending the reputation of his invention, saying that it was only a matter of a single batch being faulty at most. It happened to be at a weekend, and Mum and Dad were glued to the screen for once. Mum said I should look at the man's face very carefully, because that was what people looked like when they were lying. I imagine the product sank without trace, and possibly the company that made it as well. It was back to rubber rings for everyone all over again, not just me.

Even before I could go home most weekends, Saturday was always a super-special day as far as I was concerned. I would wake up and sing at the top of my voice, '*It's Saturday today!*' I bounced out of bed, or at least did what I could in that line, vibrating with joy till the nurses got round to me. I told everyone that if I ruled the world, every day would be a Saturday.

For me Saturday was a bright red colour, just as the other days of the week were chromatically coded. Sunday was a vibrant sunny yellow, Monday green, Tuesday a dull red, Wednesday a mustardy yellow, Thursday a blue so dark it was virtually black, Friday a bright blue.

This wasn't the true synæsthesia which is such a fascinating mystical hint, a loose thread in the fabric of perception left a-dangle, an unravelling which suggests that we could dissolve all our unreal categories. It was more a case of my emotions being split into different wave-lengths as they entered a prism, viz. the hospital week.

Saturday was a bright and joyful red because it was a day that held neither physiotherapy nor lessons. Sunday was yellow because, although it too was a day without pain or drudgery, it turned traitor at last by delivering me while I slept into the torments of Monday. There was a green streak at the bottom of yellow Sunday, if you looked closely enough. The colours of Monday, Wednesday and Friday were determined by those being physio days.

Reddish Tuesday was only a short-term reprieve, and Wednesday was the low point of the week, what with physiotherapy and lessons and so long to wait for the weekend. Thursday was almost worse, a day without physio but spent remembering the pain of the day before and anticipating the pain of the next – no more than the filling of a pain sandwich. Friday contained pain, but was shot through with the foreknowledge of the weekend. After Friday physio was the ordeal of fish and chips for lunch, a favourite with other kids but not with me. Once I bit into a piece of CRX batter, and a greasy globule burst in my mouth, some sort of abscess of oil. It ran down the back of my throat, making me retch. After that I just picked at the food, avoiding the fish altogether. So Friday contained hunger as well as pain, but at least it could be trusted to give me the weekend.

Most of the food at CRX was eatable. One dumpy little nurse would say, 'Wannit it all mashed up together?' and I'd say, 'Oh yes!' I watched with fascination as she went to work. Even the crispest pie would be reduced to mortar under her hand. The taste was oddly improved by the steamrollering to mush (though I wouldn't let her try with fish and chips). I suppose this was an underclass version of Mum's genteel microcosmal forkfuls.

Ninday

One morning Sister Heel announced that we would be getting an extra day. Perhaps she didn't mention this as a government decision, but that was my first thought. The government issued us with our toilet paper (horribly scratchy) and our orange juice (delicious, nothing ever as good after it was discontinued), why not an extra day? From then on my imagination got busy, going over and over it until the original information was entirely lost in the fanciful embroidery. I thought that the extra day would be added to every week, and asked what it was to be called. Sister Heel said, with only the slightest hesitation, 'Nin-day, John. The new day will be called Ninday.' Pleased with her quick thinking, she trotted off to her next round of duties.

I don't even know what lay behind her original announcement. Perhaps it was a rather feeble April Fool. I suppose it might have been to do with Leap Year in either 1956 or 1960, though the dates don't really marry up.

In my ignorance of the calendar and its pitfalls I became very excited and ran through the new list of days, calling out to Mary, 'So it'll be Monday (yuk!), Tuesday, Wednesday, Thursday, Friday, Saturday (yippee!), Ninday, Sunday . . .' I couldn't realistically expect every day to be Saturday, but doubling our quota of Saturdays was a good start.

'That sounds lovely, John,' said Mary, 'but perhaps we'd better ask Sister when the new day will be.'

Everyone knew that calling out for staff attention was not a good idea, but in my excitement I forgot and shouted, 'Sister! Sister!' When she appeared she wasn't best pleased, but without attempting to smooth her feathers in any way I asked, 'When's the new day going to be, Sister? I think it's going to come between Saturday and Sunday.'

'Oh no, John!' said Sister Heel. 'That would be a very bad idea. That would only make children lazy. The new eight-day week will help boys and girls work harder at school. The order will be Monday, Tuesday, Ninday, Wednesday, Thursday . . .'

My world went black. With six weekdays to cope with I knew I would be dead very soon. From my traumatised expression Sister Heel must have understood that her gruff style of teasing was not an indispensable qualification for the job of caring for sick children. She wasn't cruel, but sensitivity wasn't a quality much in vogue at the time. Perhaps she really thought she was doing me (or the ward) a favour in the long run by taking me down a peg. I didn't feel as if I was doing much more than keeping my peg above water, but perhaps I was more bumptious than I knew.

A fault he cannot mend

There's a certain amount of evidence about how I was regarded to be gleaned from my autograph book. Autograph books were a major preoccupation on the ward. Mine had a diamond-patterned cover and marbled end-papers. We children signed each other's, though that didn't really count as getting an autograph. It didn't count towards your score.

Sarah Morrison signed mine:

> When Johnny was a little boy
> He had curls, curls, curls
> But now he is older
> It's girls, girls, girls.
>
> With best wishes. Get better quickly. Sarah.

Not verse directly inspired by my character, I don't think, more a piece of ready-made doggerel. It's odd, all the same, that a message from a girl on the same ward, with the same diagnosis, should be so concerned about my health. I don't remember in what way I was ill.

Staff Nurse Hawes has written, 'I cannot dance but I can show you a few steps' – with a drawing of a ladder on a staircase. A. R. Putnam, whoever that was, has written:

> I wish I was a wiggley Bear
> With Fur upon my tummy

I'd crawl into a honey-Pot
and make my tummy, gummy,

    with best wishes.

There were a couple of rather embarrassing entries, which I didn't want Mum to see. One went:

Johnny had a little watch
He swallowed it one day
And now he's taking Epsom Salts
To pass the time away.

I wished I could excise that from the book without damaging the whole, although I did get the giggles from another risqué contribution, written by a pre-nursing student called Janice:

A rabbit has a shiny nose
A fault he cannot mend
Because his little powder puff
Is on the other end.

Some entries are rather lugubrious, as if there were times I wasn't expected to live much longer, which may very well have been the case. Nurse Fleming wrote in December 1957,

When your days on earth are ended
And your life is home-ward trod,
May your name in Gold be written
In the Autograph of God.

Of course that may just have been Nurse Fleming's way.

    Sister Heel appears on those pages with a joke of her own. She has written:

When in this page you look
When on this page you frown
Think of the nurse who spoilt it
By writing upside down.

Professor Bywaters did a creditable self-portrait in ink, using thick strokes of the pen to show a preoccupied man in waistcoat and bow tie, stethoscope in hand. He's done well to capture his own alert slouch and fierce eyebrows. It was kind of him to spend time with me, considering that I was an extreme case but not a medically interesting one. I had nothing to offer an expert.

There was a competitive edge to all our hobbies, including our autograph books. Even writing to Decca for gramophone records was done with an eye to my standing on the ward. Another favourite project was raising money for charity, though here annoyingly it was Sarah Morrison who shone, for the same reason she was such good company. She charmed people without effort, she had them eating out of her hand. It wasn't the same pure goodness as Mary's, but I had to admit it worked. There was a toughness to her, linked to the charm, which I admired and envied.

It was always me saying to Sarah, when the Wendy gang became unbearable, *I'm with you really, but I have to look as if I'm with them.* I could be a terrible toady sometimes, faced with the dark forces of Wendy and Ivy. Sarah never had to make excuses to me. She might be ostracised by the girl gang, but she wouldn't lower herself to be taken back into the group. I didn't have the strength to go it alone, though I could see quite well that Sarah's imperviousness worked in her favour. It was never long before she was accepted back, and she never grovelled or cringed. She actually raised her status by refusing to truckle, while I seemed to be a born truckler. I truckled with every breath I took, and that is not *pranayama* either.

A blessing and a leg-up

I remember one particular Friday afternoon with Mary in the hydrotherapy pool, when my interest in fund-raising had a short-lived renaissance. It was a couple of weeks before Easter, and there was a definite springy feeling in the air.

Mary and I had started talking in the pool, and we carried on while we were being dried off. She was trying to re-ignite my love affair with raffles. And suddenly we both got caught up in the idea of holding a bigger and better raffle than anyone at CRX had dreamed of before.

Mary and I had shown in the past that we were a good team. When a suggestion box was unveiled in the ward, Mary and I decided that what was needed to cheer everyone up was a bird table. CRX after all was a hospital in a forest. Wouldn't it be wonderful to have a bird table outside, so that patients could see it by going into the day room? We filled in our own suggestion slips, talked about nothing else to everyone, and we made it happen. A bird table was installed just where we'd said, and kept well supplied with bacon fat and crumbs. It was particularly lovely to watch in winter. The cost was five pounds, paid for by the League of Friends. I felt that Mary and I should have jolly well had our names inscribed on it, seeing that it was our idea in the first place.

If I had become disaffected about raffles it was because my previous venture in the field, judged by my own high standards, had been a failure. I had been very professional. I had bought a book of proper raffle tickets – or cloakroom tickets, at least. I had persuaded some of the nurses to give prizes, little packets of sweets and so on, and I made some of the smaller prizes out of modelling clay. I charged sixpence a ticket, three for a bob. There were bigger discounts on larger quantities. The tickets sold well. I felt I had a gift for this line of thing. You try selling a raffle ticket to a nurse who has already donated some sweets, so that she's paying for a chance to win back something she's already given away! I felt I should really take a commission, but Sarah explained you couldn't. I wasn't the first charitable administrator to feel that my work should be properly rewarded, but I managed to restrain myself and keep my hand out of the till.

When I sold the tickets in my boy's voice I said it was for the PDSA. I began to think that adults couldn't hear properly, because they kept saying, 'John's holding a raffle for the RSPCA.' When I tried to correct them they looked at me indulgently, as if I couldn't possibly know what I was talking about. One 'grown-up' even said, 'It's probably a branch of the RSPCA especially for children.' I was nearly in tears as I muttered, 'It isn't. It *isn't*! It *ISN'T*!! PDSA means People's Dispensary for Sick Animals and it's for people who are poor and have animals and can't afford to make them better.' Nothing I could say would change their stubborn minds. It was maddening that nothing seemed to be taken seriously unless it had something 'Royal' about it. That was the whole point of supporting the PDSA, because it didn't have the Royal Family giving it a blessing and a leg-up, only

Enid Blyton. The RSPCA had the Queen behind it, the PDSA only had 'Queen Bee', as she liked to be called.

At Taplow we were only a hop, skip and a jump from Windsor and the Castle, and it was partly that I liked the idea of cocking a snook at the Royals by supporting the other team. I don't know where I got this republican streak – perhaps I was fervently royalist in a previous life, now making amends. In the end I took my woes to the wise Sarah, who had a knack for talking to the daft beings called grown-ups. They took notice of Sarah. Nobody ever thought *she* was making things up.

I collected a total of two pounds, which was pretty good, but that was only the beginning as far as I was concerned. The raffle was a means to an end, and I'm ashamed to say that the end wasn't actually funding the treatment of poor people's pets, while slyly putting the Royal Family's nose out of joint. The end purpose of all this activity was to get my name in the *Busy Bee News* (Enid Blyton, editor). Queen Bee lived only a little further away from us than Queen Elizabeth, at Beaconsfield, which was maybe a hop, skip and two jumps away. She felt much nearer. She played a much larger part in our thoughts.

A stupid zoo

I reported my achievement to Queen Bee, and got back a form letter telling me it was a 'splendid effort'. When the next issue of *Busy Bee News* came out, though, there was no mention of my raffle on the 'Honeypot' page. This was the page set aside for Busy Bees who were not members of Hives as such, but had performed outstanding services or shown ingenuity. Barbara Ward had raffled a bunch of rhododendrons and sent in a measly 1s 9d – *she* got a mention. Jacqueline Wallace charged admission to a stupid Zoo in her dad's garage – a Zoo, if you please, consisting of a tortoise, some silkworms and a goldfish! The total take was a piffling £1, but she had her name in print for all time.

Of course when Sarah Morrison had organised a raffle, she not only won a glowing notice in the *Busy Bee News*, she got a hand-written letter from Queen Bee. She was invited to pay a visit to her at home in Beaconsfield. At this point I gave serious thought to the idea of hating Sarah Morrison. 'Queen Bee' wasn't just anybody, she was the most famous person in our lives. Sarah had been invited to meet Enid Blyton in person – and she didn't even like the Famous Five!

It was deeply unfair. Mary and I were the true devotees. I entertained the ugly thought that Sarah had only appeared in *Busy Bee News* because she'd mentioned in her letter that she had a fractured back. Which was true, but sneaky to put in your letter. I wondered if it was too late for me to write to Queen Bee again, saying that I was the worst walker in the whole hospital, and that sadly my condition was incurable. Then the iron entered my soul and I accepted defeat. I decided that 'splendid effort' only meant 'must try harder', but I didn't see how I could. It looked like the end of my charity work.

Then on that Friday afternoon before Easter, Mary Finch got me all excited again. She said she'd help out by doing some handicrafts – some modelling, maybe? She was a good craftsman, one who didn't blame her tools, though perhaps that was only natural as her tools were better than mine. I mean her hands. Her hands were far more dextrous, they were positively nifty. She asked, did I have any raffle tickets left? Well of course I did. She said we should make all the prizes have something to do with Easter. We could make cotton-wool bunnies. We could make bonnets. We could make daffodils from crêpe paper and glue and pipe-cleaners.

She really inspired me. She made me realise that we'd only been scratching the surface with our previous efforts. We needed to raise our sights, to be more ambitious. There was a world of pipe-cleaner modelling to be explored.

We would show ingenuity all right! We would set every Hive buzzing with envy. We would get the recognition we deserved if it killed us, if it left our fingers in ankylosed knots. What we were planning was so exciting. Raffle fever came back upon me doubled and redoubled, and Mary in her more selfless way became wildly keen too. Steroids give people a moon-faced look with prolonged use, but even when there was a touch of the chipmunk about her cheeks it didn't blur Mary's alert look. Cortisone couldn't filch the merry flicker from her eyes.

After sessions of hydrotherapy boys were dried off behind a separate screen from the girls. I was still wrapped in my towels on a slow dry.

Mary was being dried off much more rapidly, for a reason. She was going to have a long weekend at home with her parents, who lived in a big house in their pocket handkerchief of a county. They were picking her up later that afternoon. Even rapid drying had to be done carefully, to avoid jarring the joints, but the bustling of the towels to and fro around her shoulders made Mary's voice wobble in a delightful, musical way. She wasn't singing, exactly, though this was a very happy moment, but the wobble in her voice made her drag out a word like 'p-i-i-i-i-pe-clea-ea-ea-ner' as if she was one of the lady singers on the surplus-stock opera records Decca had been kind enough to send us, reaching the end of her aria. *One fine day. When I am laid to earth.* The towels massaged her vowels and stretched them out.

Mary had been looking forward to her long weekend away from Ward One, but just then she seemed reluctant to leave. What we were planning had really fired her imagination. 'John,' she said, 'I have to go now, but Tuesday first thing we'll carry on with this and start making proper plans. *Don't tell the others!* We'll really make them sit up and take notice. 'Bye! I'm really looking forward to it.' She waved and I waved back and she moved off, the energy of The Plan giving her a sprightly lift. But then her walking was always much better than mine.

That was the last time I saw her. The staff nurse (in a yellow uniform) who packed the medicines for her put the wrong ones in, or else wrote out the dose wrong. Her trusting parents faithfully kept on administering a lethal dose. When they realised things were seriously wrong they rushed her back to CRX. By then everyone on the staff was in a panic. Even the Tannoy lady sounded really desperate and upset. Mary was whisked into a side ward and the doors were shut behind her. We were told not to try and look inside. Geraldine did, and caught a glimpse. She said Mary looked like a ghost.

The ward was hushed that night, but I couldn't bear to keep quiet. I kept asking, 'What happened to Mary? What did she look like when she looked like a ghost?' I wouldn't shut up, however the nurses tried to silence me. I went through the whole procedure. None of it had any effect. I was given a warning, my bed was pulled out into the middle of the ward, and finally I was dragged into a side ward, where I stayed till morning.

I can't say I blame the nurses. My carrying on was upsetting the other children, the ones who were subdued rather than frantic. It was worse than the time Mary had gone beneath the surface of the hydrotherapy pool. This time she never came back to the surface.

I knew the next morning I would be getting a rocket from Heel. Fearful scoldings they were too. Their blast could be heard all over the ward. I was quaking when I heard her come on duty. One of the cadet nurses, who may not have known what had happened to Mary, sniggered, 'You're really in for it now!' Then Heel came in and just looked at me. She seemed to have run right out of scolding power. The batteries which supplied her with so much chastening energy had been drained of their charge. In a voice which cracked like her brown leathery face she asked if I had had a good night's sleep. I suddenly realised that if strict sisters could cry, Heel would be crying now. I understood that she wasn't allowed to cry, the same way Charlie, whom I missed like mad just now, wasn't allowed to have nostrils. She just walked quietly off and I was returned to the ward without even a pretence of punishment.

The lessons of another life

Mary was a pure creature, who would no more have taken a cut while organising a raffle than she would have rubbed sweets against her bum or done murder. I heard one of the nurses say she was 'too good for this world', which almost captured my sense of the thing. It wasn't quite right, though. The world was good enough to have Mary in it, but only just. Life had been lucky to have her. And, logically, perhaps she was better off out of it. I tried to understand that this was not a tragedy but a progress, which is what I believe to this day. Her soul needed only the lightest polishing, and I can't imagine her being required to learn the lessons of another life.

For a long time after she died, though, I was terrified. I thought it would be me next. It seemed to me that if Mary died, when her walking was so much better than mine, then my life must be hanging by a thread. I'd got it into my head that the reason we were always being bullied into walking was for our own good, because if we didn't walk we would die. As a theory it did at least fit the facts, and nobody had ever actually explained why walking was so over-ridingly important an activity for children who were so ill suited to it.

At this stage I was getting information and advice from two different quarters. Wendy and her gang were explaining that there's a Death Bed. That's why you die. Anyone who sleeps in the Death Bed will die. Mary slept in the Death Bed, and that's why she's dead. Nothing to do with any medicine. And now, according to them, I was sleeping in the Death Bed, the same bed in which Mary had died. The last time I had gone home for the weekend, the staff had switched the beds around. Hadn't I noticed? And now I was in the Death Bed and it was my turn.

I didn't believe Ivy and her gang the whole time, and Geraldine was saying something different, but it wasn't much more consoling. Geraldine was saying they tell us dirty lies. They told us Wayne was going to a different hospital, but if they took him to another hospital it was a funny stretcher they took him away in. Because on a normal stretcher you can see the bump of the person on top, but when they took Wayne away the top of the stretcher was flat and there was a bag hanging underneath it, and that's how we know he's dead and the staff tell dirty lies, so don't believe everything they tell you, not by a long chalk!

I got some comfort, during this period, from a hymn the monks sang in the chapel.

> This joyful Eastertide
> Away with sin and sorrow,

they sang. But I was deep in terror for a long while. I tried to be brave and fight my own battle, but it's quite hard when you've not long been old enough to take your own money out of your Post Office Savings Account and girls are ganging up on you, telling you you're in the Death Bed, you're going to die next and it won't be long.

I tried to put on a brave face when Mum visited, but she could see something was making me unhappy, and she asked ever so kindly. I crumpled and ended up telling her what the girls had been saying. That was all I told her, not about hearing little kids crying in the night, and then the next day they were gone, and what Geraldine said about the different stretchers and the lies.

After I'd opened my heart to her, or most of it at any rate, Mum went to see Sister Heel. She was in the office for a long time, talking. Eventually I was summoned to join them. My heart was pounding. I waited to hear what sentence would be passed on me.

Sister Heel had found again the scolding power she had temporarily lost. It filled her sails. She gave me an epic talking-to which included the words, many times repeated, 'John, you are not going to die! Is that quite clear? You are not! NOT!! NOT!!' It was the routine with the mugs all over again, except in reverse. She wasn't saying I was going to be smashed, she was saying I wasn't. I wasn't cracked. I didn't need smashing. I was safe.

Geraldine may have been right about the staff and doctors being a bunch of dirty liars, but Heel wasn't one of them. She always spoke the truth and we knew that. Now she talked at length about how she knew about dying. She had been with many people when they died, and yes it is very upsetting, especially when it is children. Especially when it is children you care for.

It was true that Sister Heel's face was brown and cracked, like the leather on Mum's favourite shoes, but that wasn't such a bad thing. Those shoes, after all, were past their best but Mum could never bring herself to throw them away. Heel talked in a funny way that was called an accent. She might even have come from the same part of the world as one of the cleaning ladies, Dora, who scowled and shook her mop when Wendy did a wee on the floor just to make work for her, but no one would ever play tricks on Sister Heel.

On the ward, dying was one of the most fascinating and most feared of all life's events, and here was someone talking with authority about it. She said Mary's case was quite different from mine. As for my idea that the less able you were to walk, the more likely you were to die – that was all my eye and Betty Martin. That was the purest codswallop from top to bottom. My cards weren't nearly up. My cards had only just been dealt.

What it came down to was that I didn't have Sister Heel's permission to die. An absurd argument, but at the same time the evidence supported it. Heel WAS the Ward, and everything within those walls was subject to her say-so. I wouldn't dare to die without her permission. This was a wonderful lesson, and a wonderful scolding to have from her. There was no trace of the oppressive Heel who had squashed me flat with the invention of Ninday. This was the fiercest scolding I had ever had, but I felt much better for it. I think the whole episode set me on the path of my life-long love affair with scolding. Scolding which is mostly awful but can be heavenly.

Calcutta superdragon

There have been a number of dragons in my life (Miss Collins, who was really a paper dragon, being I suppose the first), but Sister Heel showed herself to be only partly dragon. She was partly St George. If she didn't slay the dragon of mortal fear in my boyhood self, then at least she boxed its ears and made it hang its head. Perhaps the social conditions for the creation of dragons don't exist any more – the War that was then so recent, rationing more than a memory, strong public services. When a phenomenon like Mother Teresa comes along, we're all baffled – but the Calcutta superdragon rang a bell with me.

One day Mum simply arrived with Gipsy, not because she had forgotten that pets weren't allowed but because she thought it more important to cheer me up. She must have felt that she had earned her own immunity from Sister's scoldings, but I wasn't so sure. The first I knew of Gipsy's presence was a wonderful scrabbling noise, as she lost her footing on the highly polished floor. All the children on the ward gasped in wonder as Gipsy came skidding and skating into view. The moment she had righted herself she made a dash towards me, where she leaped not onto the bed (her training was too good for that) but onto one of the chairs left out for visitors.

Mum had intervened successfully with Sister Heel about whether I had permission to die, but now I was afraid it had gone to her head. She seemed to think that she and Sister had an understanding. I winced and waited for the explosion, as the Heather imbalance in her character inevitably led her to overstep the mark. It wasn't more than a minute before Mum trespassed in a big way. She waited until Sister Heel came by my bed, and then she said, without even a token apology for Gipsy's presence in the second visitor's chair, 'I think John needs cheering up, don't you? He misses his budgie Charlie, and Charlie's not the same without him. Can't Charlie come for a weekend?'

It was an awful moment. I was going to lose face with everyone, not just Wendy and Ivy but Geraldine and Sarah, because Sister Heel was about to destroy the budgie fantasy for good, the fantasy which had bolstered my position on the ward for so long. Wendy must have smelled blood, because she called out, 'Yes, Sister, John keeps saying his budgie's going to come and live here. He goes on and on about it.'

Sister Heel frowned and said, 'What have you been telling people, John? Everyone knows pets aren't allowed on the ward.' In the pit of my stomach I could feel my status going on the slide as my lies were exposed to the world. I heartily wished that Mum hadn't chosen to meddle with things she didn't understand. Why didn't she stay at home where she belonged? If she wanted attention there were always waiting rooms and bus stops.

Then Heel said, 'Still . . .' At this point it was as if someone else had taken over the operation of her mouth. She said something completely unexpected. From the look on her face, she was at least as surprised as the rest of us.

It was like the ventriloquism lessons from Ellisdons that I had wanted to send off for. This was precisely the effect I would have hoped to achieve, but at my first attempt and without benefit of a single lesson! No one saw my mouth move while the magic words were uttered – not only that, but Sister obligingly moved her lips to coincide with the incredible syllables. 'I suppose a weekend wouldn't hurt.'

This first attempt at throwing my voice was a total success, even if all of us were startled by what Sister Heel had said. She herself looked stunned, like a medium coming out of a trance, violently shaken by the departure of her spirit guide. I suppose it's possible that the whole scene was cooked up between Mum and Sister Heel, but I don't really think so. It was hardly Mum's style to make nice things happen and take no credit. Besides, Heel was genuinely astonished by what she heard herself saying.

What happened next, of course, was that she fell in love with Charlie. At the end of the weekend one of the other nurses asked when he would be going back. She said, 'He's not. He'll cheer the whole place up. It's not just John who will benefit. Budgies should be prescribed on the National Health, that's what I say.' Naturally enough, the next question was, 'But isn't it against the rules? Won't they make him leave?' And the answer to that one was, *'Just let them try!'*

Before entrusting her budgie to the care of the dragon, Mum had issued dire warnings about not leaving any windows open if ever Charlie was allowed out of his cage. Sister Heel took her seriously. A window decree went out to the nurses, constantly repeated and underlined. At the best of times Heel regarded nurses as inherently unreliable, leaky vessels needing to be topped up with frequent scoldings, and she dreaded them exposing Charlie to the temptation of freedom.

At first it was an enormous treat when he was let out during rest time – for us as well as for him – but then it became part of the daily routine. Soon he was flying freely around the ward, which was an ideal half-way house for him. The outside world was too hostile for him, and the rooms at Trees a little cramped. Within this converted Nissen hut Charlie could fly from one end of the ward to the other and really spread his wings. First he would sit on the curtain rails, and then he would honour the kids with a personal appearance. He sat on little girls' heads and made them giggle with delight. He was only a runty blue budgie, but he brought as much colour to the ward as a whole flight of kingfishers, darting and diving in the arrowhead formation.

Heel was right about the general benefit. Charlie made a huge difference to the emotional health of the ward. He had miraculous powers. I saw it happen any number of times. There was no shortage of witnesses to the wonders he worked. Every time he landed on a finger he made someone St Francis for a moment.

He was everybody's friend, but he would come to me when I called him and sit on my finger. No lover's nibbling kisses on the lips could be more tender, no secrets chirped in my ear could be more sacred. Gang hostilities were forgotten from one moment to the next as I became the most popular boy on the ward – also the only boy, admittedly, in my little Still's group at the time. I certainly made the most of the boosting of my status.

God in the telephone

Miss Reid taught Scripture as well as music. The first thing she told us was that God was everywhere. A marvellous lesson. God wasn't

245

just in the sky, God was in the walls and in the telephone. This was the first thing anyone had said to me about God which made any sense. God was omnipotent, omniscient, omnipresent. I was very happy with that assessment.

Latently I had a huge reservoir of love towards teachers. My tutor Miss Collins hadn't tapped into that. If anything she had capped it off for a time, even if the reservoir was still there, fed by invisible springs. It made sense that teachers should be greater even than doctors or scientists or priests, since didn't doctors and scientists need to be taught? My academic love burst out in fierce little gushes at CRX.

Then one week Miss Reid taught us about sin. She read something about gardening from the Bible and explained what it meant. There was wheat and there was chaff. Wheat was like Shredded Wheat at breakfast – wheat was good. But chaff was useless, worse than useless. It would go into the fire to be burnt. There were some things called tares as well. Tares were even worse than chaff.

These bulletins really shook me. I felt myself go very red in the face. Miss Reid seem to be looking directly at me as she expounded her botanical model of the moral universe. Guilt flared, because I had used bad words, I had forgotten to say my prayers as often as I did in the Bathford days, I had neglected to brush my teeth but had wetted my toothbrush to fool Mum. I had ganged up with Wendy against Geraldine. I thought also about general and specific thrills. My admiration for uniforms, my games with taily. I knew then that I was going to Hell.

Sin requires privacy, and there was little enough of that at CRX. There was no private space, unless you count the lockers that few of us could open ourselves, and no private time. The closest thing to either came during rest time after lunch when we were encouraged to take a nap. The curtains weren't drawn, but sometimes screens would be pulled round our beds. One day a nurse said, 'You were doing something with yourself during Rest, weren't you?' And I said, 'I don't know what you're talking about.' I was hardly going to say, 'Have a heart. It's my only chance to have a proper talk with taily.'

Not that my investigations were very advanced. They were just that – investigations, carried out in a scientific spirit. Apart from the mystery of the 'I', unaffected by pleasure or pain, which was a mystery which couldn't be broached with anyone I had ever met, tailies and what they wanted were life's biggest enigma.

Sometimes I made a low wall with the bedclothes, with taily in the middle. I made it rise up stiff by thinking of boys playing with their legs round each other, then thought of nothing and watched as taily went down. It was so interesting to see that it didn't go down smoothly, but in little steps – bob . . . bob . . . bob . . . – with a sort of elastic bounce. If I intervened with my mind before countdown had reached zero and taily had hit belly I could stop it from snoozing and make it wake up again. It was lovely, in a body which seemed to want nothing to do with my wishes, to have mental control of this little joystick.

I assumed that my taily was the only one of its kind, with this hydraulic capability. Everything about me seemed to be abnormal, so it would be rash to assume that anyone else's taily had anything in common with mine. I couldn't ask the doctors or nurses. I couldn't ask my friends because they were all girls, and all sick boys did when they made their walls of bedclothes was put their toy soldiers all over the place and go blam-blam-blam . . . It seemed obvious that their tailies weren't like mine, otherwise they wouldn't build ramparts in the bedclothes for anything as stupid as blam-blam-blam. They'd be exploring bob-bob-bob just like me.

I felt that I was definitely damned for the fire, and almost wished they would just get on and do it now. Put me in the hospital inciner-ator, so that the smoke that had once been John could drift past the windows for the metaphysical diversion of another sick child. Miss Reid told us about holy people being granted visions by God. I closed my eyes and squeezed them together as tight as possible and asked for a vision. For a few moments I saw some pink and blue flowers, and there was a garden, and I even think Mary was in it, but the picture wouldn't form properly. I decided I was not good enough to be granted a vision by God, which meant I was certainly damned.

At the same time some stubborn internal voice was protesting that they'd changed their minds about God. I hated U-turns more than anything. Don't do a tuppenny in the bed whatever you do. Now we're going to stick something up your botty and make you do a tup-penny in the bed. Don't move whatever you do. Be a good boy and stay absolutely still. Now walk, walk, walk. Walking is what life's all about! Now here's a wheelchair – don't walk without permission.

Hated parties

Now they'd played the same low trick on God. One week God was all-powerful, all-knowing and everywhere, the next he was a fraud and a failure: partipotent, partiscient and partipresent. I hated those parties. I wanted to go back to the omnies. I felt at home with the omnies.

If God was omnipresent he was in my taily as well as the telephone. He was taily as well as being everything else. I didn't think God would let anyone go to Hell. And if God was everywhere, he was in Hell too, and then how could it be Hell? What did 'Hell' mean?

I was rescued from all this religious negativity by the very person who had got it started, Miss Reid. Christmas came round, tinsel and streamers were hung all about, a beautiful tree was brought into the ward, and all the kids went '*AAaaaah!!*' Miss Reid sang,

> All poor men and humble,
> All lame men who stumble,
> Come rest ye nor be ye afraid.

This was a song called 'Poverty'.

Hope flared in my heart like an Ellisdons' Mount Ætna. I wasn't as poor as Wendy and her family, but I wasn't far off. Sarah was rich, but she was pure which was the same as humble. I felt sure she was 'poor in heart'. She had no interest in tailies unless it was in one of her disconcertingly dirty jokes, so that raised her score. As for 'lame' and 'stumble', well I passed that test with flying colours. Lame men hobbled around from place to place, but I was much more lame than the lame. I spent much of my time falling over. The time I spent falling over redeemed the time I spent talking to taily.

Miss Reid looked significantly at me when she sang about the lame men who stumble, just as she had when she was talking about the wheat and the chaff, but this time she was beaming with compassion. So yes, I was chaff and due to be burnt, but I was on my way to being poor, scoring top marks in the stumbling section, and as even Reid said, Jesus was most merciful and loved to rescue people. The song went on,

> Then haste we to show him
> The praises we owe him;
> Our service he ne'er can despise

which clinched it. Jesus would see me right.

That Christmas Mum had the brainwave of giving me a tiny book – *The Smallest Bible in The World*, allegedly. Perhaps she got it from Ellisdons. At first it looked as though its teeny pages were covered in minute blobs, but Mum gave me a magnifying glass as well, and then I could read every letter. She followed it up for my birthday with a matching Webster's Dictionary.

I didn't enjoy being small myself, but I loved small things.

I loved the poem about Solomon Grundy. Everything from womb to tomb sorted out in the course of a week. I didn't think it was morbid, I thought it was wonderfully tidy. It appealed to my taste for the small and definite. I hadn't yet developed my love for the vast and indeterminate.

As for objects, the smaller they were, and the more they contained, the better. I had a blue money-box that was done up to look like a book, until you saw the coin-slot in the side where the pages should be. There was even a cut-out circle where you could post in a rolled-up banknote (fat chance!). Written on the cover was the motto *Great Oaks from Little Acorns Grow*, which more or less consecrated my fascination with little things, but I also loved acorns in their own right. They didn't have to grow into oaks to prove their value to me. From the divine perspective but also from mine, they were already what they were meant to be. Acorns had nothing to prove to either of us.

I loved my tiny Bible and my tiny dictionary, but really I didn't care what little books were about or where they came from. It was the dimensions I loved. They were books to swallow whole, to remember word for word. It's a fact, though, that little books tend to have designs on their readers, and a lot of my favourites were from the Jehovah's Witnesses. Dad rolled his eyes when he saw them, and said, 'My God! Now he's reading *tracts*!' I didn't let him put me off the little books I loved.

The next plot from us at Bourne End was a sort of big hut called a chalet. The Freemans lived there, Magda who was Austrian and Ozzie who wasn't. Their son Pippo (his real name was Philip) ran around with no clothes on, which Mum thought was completely beyond the pale. They seemed to push him out in all weathers, naked, though it wasn't clear if he was being actively punished or simply seasoned like a boy of wood. Magda certainly believed in the benefits of the cold.

Although the Freemans weren't upper people as Mum understood such things (in fact precisely because they weren't) she had a clearer grasp of how to behave towards them than she did with, say, our posher neighbours Arthur and Dorothy, the Feet. The way to behave with a family like the Freemans, with their chalet and their Austrian ways and their driving their shivering Pinocchio of a son out into the cold, was to get on the phone to the National Society for the Prevention of Cruelty to Children, day in, day out, till they finally sent someone to check on the goings-on in that sinister household.

She did this very early on in her life in Bourne End, even before the re-wiring of the house was finished. Heather people can't leave well alone. It was the only way Mum knew of settling into a new home. To make a cat feel at ease in new surroundings, you butter its paws – by the time it has licked them clean, it will have settled in. To work the same magic with Mum, all you needed was unconventional neighbours and the phone number of the NSPCC.

The visitor from the Society gave the Freemans a clean bill of health. There was no cruelty going on at that address. Mum found this out when she phoned up again, to learn the result of the swoop. She was shocked, rather disappointed by the fallibility of the organisation. 'Don't they have eyes in their heads?' she wanted to know. 'Those awful parents must have made their boy lie.'

I'm afraid I got the giggles. I was in an odd, hectic mood, something which came on me abruptly every now and then. My thoughts rushed after each other so fast they seemed to collide. 'I don't think so, Mum. We'd know if he lied, wouldn't we?'

'Would we? How?'

'His nose would grow!' I thought this was the funniest thing any-one had ever thought of.

'You do talk nonsense sometimes, JJ.' Which had already been remarked on at CRX. She bent down with a sigh to pick up a Liquorice Allsort which she had accidentally flattened beneath her foot. I quite see that I could sometimes be exasperating to live with.

I was going through a Liquorice Allsorts phase at the time, though I preferred to decant Bassetts' noble confectionery from the packet into my own containers, tubes passed on to me by Mum and also by Muzzie. I was teaching myself to flick them into my mouth – other-wise I'd have had to use a fork – and my accuracy was improving, but a few inevitably ended up on the floor.

At CRX we were regularly lectured on the evils of eating sweets. After the years of wartime and post-war rationing, parents found it hard to turn the clock back by rationing their children's sweet intake. The CRX dentist, Mr McCorley, ranted particularly against Opal Fruits when they came in. He thought them highly pernicious, with their squishiness, their way of moulding to the teeth and clinging there while their stinging sweetness was absorbed by the tongue, as if they were sticky slugs actively sensing the tender pulp behind the enamel – but Liquorice Allsorts were little better in his book.

Sarah's sweet habit contributed to some quite severe decay. Mr McCorley gave her some fillings, numbing her mouth with cocaine. She must have had an allergic reaction – what she told us about it made me fear the dentist more than anything. When it was my turn to have a filling, years later, McCorley asked, 'Shall I deaden it with some cocaine?' and I said, 'No thank you, it doesn't agree with me,' like the vicar refusing an offer of sherry.

The cocaine would have been made up in paste form, labelled FOR DENTAL USE ONLY and kept locked in a safe between treatments. Altogether a missed opportunity.

Revenge of a sort

I have to say Magda Freeman was remarkably good about the whole business of Mum's denunciation to the NSPCC. She didn't hold a grudge. She can't have been in much doubt about who peached on her, but she didn't stop being neighbourly. Peter and I liked her, much to Mum's annoyance. Perhaps that was revenge of a sort.

Magda knew the way to our hearts. Later, when Peter was a Boy Scout, she gave him things to do in Bob-a-Job Week. He did her weeding while I sat by in the Tan-Sad. There was nowhere I could go without my brotherly engine. When she gave Peter his shilling at the end of the afternoon, she gave me tenpence of my own, for supervising him. And I wasn't even a Boy Scout! Which meant I didn't have to pass on the money to a charitable destination. If I had known I was getting paid to watch Peter work, I'd have enjoyed it more, and I'd have tried to wear a proper supervisory expression.

If I'd been told that an Austrian was a sort of German, I wouldn't have been so trusting. Mum certainly missed a trick there.

We had a television at Trees by this time, although Mum didn't let us watch ITV on it. I far preferred the commercial channel when watching at CRX, and pestered her about it. She explained that reception would naturally be good at CRX because of the transmitter up Hedsor Hill. On the Abbotsbrook Estate, on the other hand, which was after all near the river, the 'other channel' was so fuzzy it was unwatchable. There was no point even trying to tune in. Why she thought closeness to a river interfered with reception I don't know. There was more involved than picture quality, clearly. Mum wanted to keep ITV out of reach on principle. Borrowing her terminology from radio, she called it 'The Light Programme', as opposed to 'The Home Service' (the BBC). Sometimes she complained that 'your father has been watching the Light Programme again!' which should have tipped me off to the possibility of watching ITV at home sooner than it did.

By Abbotsbrook stream on the way towards Marlow there was marshland, fascinating to Dad but of no interest to Mum. I only remember her coming that way with us the once, and that was for her own reasons. She had broken a mirror and was trudging behind us with the shards in a bag. Seven years' bad luck! The size of the mirror doesn't make a difference, apparently. This one was only a hand mirror, though quite a large one. Instead of accepting the sentence of doom passed by her belief system, Mum was trying to weasel out of it. The bad luck could be neutralised, according to the small print of her faith, by putting the pieces in running water. So she had kept them in the bath, with the tap running, and now she was going to dispose of them safely in the river. Somehow I had even less patience for Mum's superstitiousness when she tried to dodge the bad luck she had invented.

Our party made an incongruous caravan: a rationalist (Dad) pushing a mystic (me), with an irrationalist bringing up the rear. I don't remember if Peter came along, but if he did he would have added to the philosophical variety, being in those days pretty much a pagan.

On every other occasion Dad and I explored those parts alone. There were places I would rather have gone, but Dad was very methodical, preferring to examine a single habitat under different conditions. I was fickle and impatient – so the moment I heard from Miss Reid that sundews, plants that ate insects, grew wild on Chobham Common in Surrey I wanted to go there right away. I couldn't get it out of my mind. As soon as I got home for the weekend I started pestering him, while he was still unloading the car, and he snapped at me. 'Get out of my hair, you pesky little nit!' he said, and I went crying to Mum.

The car was new, or at least new to us, a Vauxhall estate of our own. Perhaps the transaction was smoothed in some way by dear Joy Payne. Estate cars were a very new idea then (though nothing less would have accommodated the Tan-Sad) and Mum cautioned Peter and me against boasting about ours. I don't know who she thought we would try to impress. It was really only her old worry about the word 'estate' with its two meanings, the upper and the working class. Casual acquaintances might not realise right away that this was an Abbotsbrook Estate car.

'It's so unfair!' I told Mum when we got inside the house. 'When you and Dad told me about sundews it made me cry because I felt so sorry for the fly. Then when I got used to the idea and asked where I could find one you both said you hadn't the slightest idea. Then I go and find out on my own where I can get one, and now he tells me I'm a pesky little nit who gets in his hair. It's not fair!'

Lessons in Dad

'Well JJ,' Mum said, 'I can see I'm going to have to give you some LID. That's Lessons In Dad. It's a matter of timing. You must learn to hold back and then pounce. If you ask him while he's rushing about, of course he's going to say "No"! All he wants to do is get out into the garden. I'm afraid you'll just have to let another week go by now. By then I promise you he'll have forgotten the entire affair. Wait till next Friday and then pounce. I'll make an apple pie and after that I'll give him sweet milky coffee (ugggh!) and a couple of chocs left over from last Christmas. They're Black Magic. Your father never grew out of his liking for sweets, you know . . . Wait until he's all relaxed and floppy and then spring it on him.'

I had first heard of the sundew plant in the Bathford days, when the thought of a plant eating a fly like that made me burst into tears. Perhaps I was a cannibal in a previous life – that would explain so much dietary fastidiousness in this. Then I had a conversation about them with one of the nurses at CRX, who said that it moved 'ever so quickly' to catch its prey. I'd become more of a man of the world by then. There were more than enough flies in the world, after all, and it made sense that there should be plants whose job was to eat some of them.

My interest had a scientific tinge to it. Perhaps this was an area where I would make discoveries and breakthroughs. It would be such a triumph to breed a variety which ate wasps, for the benefit of people like Sarah who reacted really badly to their sting.

And still I hadn't seen one. By this time I had cross-examined the nurse who was an expert in sundews (at least compared to me) many times. I just asked the same questions time after time. I reasoned that if you kept on hammering away, sooner or later you were bound to hit the jackpot – even if the coins often cascaded towards you from a completely unexpected direction. It was especially encouraging when the victim said, 'Honestly John, I've told you absolutely everything I know or can remember on the subject. There really isn't anything more that I can remember.' That always meant that they knew plenty. That wasn't the moment to let go, but rather to intensify my mental grip.

One day I was reaching the end of a rather fruitful interrogation session – I'd established that the colour was a little more golden than I had suspected, and that the plants tended to have ten rather than six wee fisted rosettes. Then I heard a little voice edging politely into the conversation with, 'Excuse me for interrupting, John, but I could not help overhearing your conversation with Nurse Burrows. I gather that you have developed quite an interest in the sundew plant!'

It was Miss Reid of all people, whose previous botanising had been so ominously symbolic. I was afraid she was going to take these wonderful plants away from me before I had even seen one, to cast them on the everlasting bomfire. 'Are they tares, Miss?' I asked timidly, bracing myself for the worst.

'Of course not, John,' she said. 'Why would you think so? They're wild flowers.' Reid moved so smoothly between the world of the Bible and the world of nature study that I expect she didn't know she was doing it, but I couldn't really be blamed for feeling confused.

'I don't honestly know an awful lot about them,' she went on, 'but I can tell you where they grow in the wild. I thought you might be interested.' She settled on the very edge of the bed. Miss Reid had her needlework bag with her, and fished out a piece of embroidery. It was soothing to watch her work at it. She glanced up at me from time to time, but there was no danger of her fixing me with the meaningful gaze of judgement.

'Chobham Common is only a few miles away. I believe', she said as she pulled a thread tight, 'that two varieties grow there – the round-leaved and the long-leaved. If you are lucky, you may also see some butterworts growing there. You told me last week that your family now has a car. Perhaps you could ask your father to drive you there one weekend.'

Two varieties of sundew, and butterworts thrown in by nature's generous hand! If that wasn't worth Dad's petrol money, what was? No wonder I thought that the cake of the coming weekend was iced and fully decorated, with Roman candles set around the edge sending up globes of hot light in my honour.

971 centimetres a second squared

Mum's wait-and-pounce plan worked like a charm the next week. Dad's system, charged with sugar and caffeine, couldn't muster resistance to the plan. Once we got going, Dad really enjoyed himself, and we brought back some sundews as trophies. I feel a bit guilty about that, but there were no protected species then.

Chobham Common was a special expedition, and the marshland by the river was for every day. Dad made it his mission to show me that even a familiar habitat could spring surprises. He was good at spotting something in nature and pointing me towards it in the chair. Then he would navigate my eye by landmarks towards what he wanted me to notice. He was very good at getting me to see what he saw. It's a useful knack. There's no use just pointing at something (in this case, something that nature has taken trouble to tuck away) if you don't share an eyeline with the person you want to see it.

There was a bridge that we had to cross, on our way to the marshy patch which was Dad's passion. It was very narrow and had no railing, really closer to a broad plank than a bridge proper. The Tan-Sad, as I well knew, had four small wheels and was very awkward to manœuvre. I started to fret as we came up to the bridge. There was only about half an inch of leeway each side. 'I'll fall, Dad,' I whispered. 'It's too narrow.'

'No you won't,' he said. 'You will not fall.' His voice was very firm, very reassuring. 'What's over there is well worth going to see. You won't find it anywhere else in these parts.'

I put my life in his hands. Then the right side of the chair slipped over the edge of the plank bridge. I started falling sideways at a great rate – at the rate prescribed by gravity (971 centimetres a second *squared*). I saw myself going into the marsh. Then Dad grabbed the chair as it fell and held its weight. With a great effort he wrenched it back onto the bridge. We were both panting with terror and relief. I could hear him behind me. 'Not bad, eh?' he said, trying to sound jaunty. 'That's jungle training for you. Lightning reflexes. I told you I wouldn't let you fall, didn't I?'

Once we had reached the marshy bit, he pointed out what I thought were pinky worms that had come out of the ground and had climbed up some nettles to greet the morning sun. They weren't worms at all. Dad said, 'What you see there is called dodder, John.'

A fascinating plant if ever there was one, a parasite which grows on the heads and stems of live stinging nettles, shedding its own roots the moment it finds a host. It would have been greater dodder we found, *Cuscuta europæa*, which taps into the sap of the nettle using suckers. It's a specialised relative of bindweed (as indicated by its family, the *convulvulaceæ*), that demure invader, bane of gardeners everywhere.

I was my father's son. I couldn't help being fascinated. Dad said, 'Worth crossing a few bridges for, eh, chicken? And I told you I wouldn't let you fall, didn't I?' I managed not to say, *but I did! I did fall. I just didn't fall all the way down or all the way out of the chair.* I was beginning to get a sense of adults and the promises they made. Promises weren't all the same. When it came to reassurance, Dad's promise-you-won't-fall was nowhere near as cast-iron as Heel's you-don't-have-permission-to-die-it's-against-hospital-rules.

Softening agent

Sister Heel herself was perhaps less flinty than she had been, the agent of softening being Charlie. Love had transformed her routine. She came on duty as promptly as ever, but after a quick riffle through the paperwork in her office she would slip out into the grounds. We could see her through the ward windows picking the groundsel which grew in such quantities as a weed on the Cliveden estate. Heel had become a budgie expert in her own right. Nurses would be given lectures on the digestive systems of budgies, not strictly part of their medical training, I suppose, but good for their general knowledge. Only Heel was allowed to give him greens. She cleaned his cage on a regular basis, scrubbing tirelessly away, as if she was one of the cleaning ladies on her own ward. She replaced his sand-paper and brought him cuttlefish out of her own pocket. Cuttlefish and the finest millet money could buy.

She talked to him constantly and taught him many new things. As soon as she opened his cage door, he was on her shoulder talking to her. He gave her love-nibbles on the lips, and told her deeper secrets than he had ever told me. Soon he was putting his head right inside her mouth, to retrieve a tasty bud of groundsel coated in saliva. For a bird who had been rejected from the egg and never known a mum of his own species, of his own family or even his order, I have to assume that this smother love was budgie Heaven.

Birds know nothing of the womb. They can hardly want to return to a place where they have never been, unless somehow they remember being processed into life by the mammal machine, in lives gone by, suckled and weaned, licked clean by a rough tongue. That was what Heel was offering Charlie when she opened her mouth so invitingly – a womb to be returned to, a warm dark cave of belonging, wet with seeds and endearments.

The time came when Heel had a week's leave. She left instructions that Charlie was not to be allowed out of his cage while she was away. One day she even turned up out of uniform, just to make sure he was all right, and that her edicts carried weight in her absence.

Charlie's cage was waiting in her office on her first morning back. She said, 'Good morning, Charlie,' and he chirped back, 'God, you're a dirty bugger!' If her face hadn't been shoe-leather brown, it would have turned scarlet. She muttered, 'I'll give him what for.' A trail led straight to the culprit – Charlie imitated his intonations all too well.

We on the ward had known all about Dr Benny's small revenge on Sister Heel, not a personal settling of scores, I don't think, just an attempt to bring the dragon down a peg or two. We knew what Charlie had been learning during his private lessons. His vocabulary had always been large, but now it was being expanded into unknown regions. We were amazed that any doctor could imagine he would have the last word in a confrontation with Heel, but nobody listened to us.

In CRX the pecking order was strict. Even the lowest doctor ranked higher than the highest sister, but that was only the theory. On Ward One, even registrars quailed before Heel. We counted down the hours till Dr Benny's next shift and his fatal rendezvous with Heel's 'what for'. A cadet nurse, almost as thrilled and alarmed as we were, tipped us off about his hours.

Heel laid no blame on the innocent bird. Her love for Charlie was now close to obsessive. It was hard to think of anything he could do that wouldn't instantly be forgiven. More love grated out of her mouth than ever before. Even deeper secrets were exchanged, while his beak dabbled in her mouth to retrieve the seeds of love.

By the time Dr Benny came on duty we felt thoroughly sorry for him. He put on a brave face at first, pretending not to notice Heel's basilisk stare, sweeping past her to attend to a patient immediately. Did he think she would hesitate to use the Tannoy? It wasn't long before her voice crackled over the system like a whip to summon him to her office. Ten minutes later a bedraggled and crestfallen man stumbled out. He crept off to a little side room to stitch together the rags of his composure. Someone said he had been crying.

Soon Charlie was spending more time alone with Sister Heel in her office, and less with us in the ward. He was learning to concentrate on genteel topics and a seemly vocabulary. He was still my bird, but that was becoming a technicality. If Heel and I had been at opposite ends of the ward, and Charlie had been let out of his cage in the middle, I was no longer sure which way he would have flown.

Sometimes Charlie gave our hands a peck, but Sister was always able to make out it was the child's fault, which suited us fine. And Charlie knew better than to peck her. I prayed a little tearfully to God about Charlie's transfer of affections, and God simply said, 'When Charlie flew out of the cage, your main wish was that he should be all right. Remember? So tell me, is he happy now or not?' God had a point. I had to face the fact that Charlie was very happy indeed.

When I started to have solo sessions in the hydrotherapy pool with Miss Krüger, I began to understand more about her approach to her work. She would hold me so that my face was just on a level with the surface of the water, and then she would tip me gently back, so that I was just under it. She would hold a position that let the water just begin to trickle into my nostrils. It's possible to shut your mouth and hold your breath, but it's not possible to close your nose in the same definite way. Sooner or later you have to let your breath out in any case.

When I started to choke and splutter she would push me under a little deeper and then bring me up to the surface, coughing and spluttering. Not close to the fact of drowning but brought up close to the idea of it. Nothing about her face gave away what was happening – that she was claiming the power of life and death over me.

There was no therapeutic basis to the group sessions on dry land, when she made us walk without the support of our shoes, but she didn't want us to know what she was doing. Here in this more private setting she wanted me to be in on it. She was making it very clear how fine was the line separating life and death. She could see that I didn't want to cross over just then. She never said anything. She never murmured, 'It didn't happen that time . . . but next time, who knows?' She didn't need to.

While the jaws grind shut

The first time Miss Krüger held me under the water, I shut my eyes. The second time, I kept them open and tried to read her expression, hoping to see something recognisably human. I imagine people being bitten in half by a shark have the same need to look in the creature's eyes while the jaws grind shut, simply hoping to see a feeling on that face that they can imagine sharing. Wanting the reassurance of knowing that for the shark, too, this is an emotional experience.

In this respect Miss Krüger had more to offer than a shark would. She smiled – her face was quite lively. She even wrinkled her nose in a way which on someone else I might have found adorable. I think she must have liked her victims to keep their eyes open. It made the experience more intense for her, though there was nothing that she let show. I say 'her victims' although I don't know in a definite way that I wasn't the only one to get that treatment in the hydrotherapy pool. But I don't flatter myself. I wasn't special. I didn't talk about it, and I didn't ask anyone else, but I'm sure my case was not isolated.

Assuming that I wasn't singled out in the pool, then perhaps it was part of Miss Krüger's pleasure that our group should both know and not know what was going on. The child being smiled down on in the pool, fighting the urge to thrash in a way that would do no good and be painful in its own right, could be in no doubt about the nature of what was happening. The children in the walking group, going up on pointes one after the other – 'Ups-a-daisy, try again' – knew how much it hurt, but not that it was the opposite of therapy. After all, the occupational therapist wasn't feeding off our pain when she told us that remedial shoes had to hurt if they were to do us any good (I give her the benefit of the doubt). Miss Krüger was something else entirely. Individually, in the pool, we all knew we were being tortured. As a group, made to walk without support on chronically inflamed joints, we had no idea. Walking was the fetish and watchword of the place. It always hurt. Miss Krüger's exercises didn't seem as obviously insane as they should have.

Physical punishment wasn't part of the régime at CRX, but it wasn't easy to tell. This was because the régime itself subscribed so fervently to an agenda which forced children to fit in with an able-bodied world at whatever cost. Pain wasn't administered with specific intention, but it was certainly part of daily life. There was a certain amount of incompetence too, perhaps. The lady who fitted us with built-up shoes, grudgingly stuffing them with cotton wool if we went on complaining, might not have dared to say in Dr Ansell's hearing that they were meant to hurt, but we weren't sensitive to these cross-currents of hospital culture. We didn't know that there were two schools of thought at the time, one of them less severe.

Tough love, love so toughened as hardly to be recognisable as such, was part of the mission of the hospital from its foundation. Those converted Nissen huts were impregnated with a tradition of untender tending. Nancy Astor herself, mistress of Cliveden, was very much present in the early days of the hospital, in that first War. Her speciality was the unsympathetic handling of those, desperately scarred or damaged, who couldn't be rallied by the conventional means. They were at death's door. She merely held the door open and bowed ironically, hoping to shame them. *After you.* She thought of it as 'gingering them up'.

It may be that the nursing staff had reservations about this approach, which strayed rather far from Nightingale principles. If so, they were hardly likely to say anything. Not only was Nancy Astor their landlady, she was their employer. Nancy and her husband Waldorf paid the wages of the Medical Officers, nurses and orderlies. They were stuck with her, this lay matron who came alive around the dying.

Her bedside routine regularly included unstrapping her watch and placing it on a patient's bedside table. 'I bet you this watch', she'd say, 'that you'll be dead this time tomorrow. You've pretty much thrown in the towel. I'll leave it with you for now – it's a nice little watch. I don't know if you're hungry. Probably not. Still, they say a condemned man is allowed a last meal, so order anything you like from the kitchens. I'll make sure you get it. And I'll be back for my watch this time tomorrow.'

Her style was harder than Heel's, her method more paradoxical.

Instead of withholding permission to die, she gave it freely, so as to goad the moribund into defying her.

She lost that bet and that particular watch, but I wonder if there were some bets she won that we don't hear so much about, disfigured amputees who couldn't quite be gingered up the Nancy Astor way. Sometimes she went in for a refinement of the same approach, a sort of jingoistic shock therapy. Hearing from the nurses that a couple of young airmen with burns all over their faces and bodies had lost any will to live, she approached their bedsides and bent down so they could hear her, through the grease that kept the bandages from touching their war-cooked flesh. 'You're going to die,' she said, 'and so would I if it meant I didn't have to go back to Canada.' Sprinkling salt on their wounds, for their own ultimate good. 'If you were a Yank or a Cockney or a Scot you'd live, because – unlike you – they've got guts.'

The mutilated boys tried to defend their country against these insults, as best they could through charred lips. In this way they were tricked into regaining the will to live, gingered up in spite of themselves. Brusqueness and an almost contemptuous mobilisation of the life force were part of the fabric of the place.

I was a veteran of pain by that time, as we all were, and had had various types of relationship with it. The best sort of relationship to have with pain is a contemplative one, when the pain itself is constant, and distance from it can be maintained by homespun meditation and yoga breathing. Then it's easy to remember that pain is unreal, and the 'I' which burns underneath everything is made of a substance impervious to it.

At other times the pain pounced without warning, when for instance Mum was doing her Noh-drama rough-housing and my back clicked. Then the relationship was necessarily confrontational, until I could bring my thoughts under control. But this was the first time that a person had intruded on my relationship with pain. This was my first experience of pain with an agency. Pain with an agent: cruelty. Miss Krüger claimed an obscene intimacy, by watching us in our pain, and making us watch her watching. It hadn't been cruel when Dad had gone on reading his paper when I fell over practising my walking – all he wanted was for me not to be in difficulties, and the closest he could get to that goal was refusing to acknowledge them, absenting himself from the scene. That wasn't cruel, but this was. This was cruelty itself.

Miss Krüger's solo pool sessions were mainly about power, and her group lessons were about pain, pain that was distilled and extracted from us for another person to consume. Ankylosed joints were being asked to take our weight without other means of support. It was no different from getting people with freshly broken ankles to walk on them. One day Geraldine bit quite deeply into her tongue, trying not to scream. The sight of blood seemed to sober Miss Krüger up. It may even have frightened her. It's possible that she was squeamish – an odd characteristic in a sadist, but not unheard-of. Some of the blood got onto her smock, and she was very distressed by that, less by where it had come from, I suppose, than where it had got to. The violation of the proper order wasn't blood dripping from a child's chin but the same substance compromising a uniform, contaminating the wearer.

It may be, though, that there was a part of Miss Krüger which didn't consent to her actions, and which was suddenly made aware that things had got out of hand. The dream of cruelty can become too real even for the person who is making it happen. For a while Krüger certainly watched herself. She eased up on us for a bit – she was almost like a real physio. And then she started all over again. It was stronger than her. It was the deepest part of her, and the part of her that did not consent to it was effectively smothered, or held under the surface of some interior pool until it stopped struggling.

Deep down she wanted to save me

In the pool Miss Krüger could almost have been modelling herself on the bogus priest in that rather scary film *Night of the Hunter*, who has LOVE tattooed on the knuckles of one hand, HATE on the other. In Miss Krüger's case the words appearing in phantom form on the knuckles of her clean, well-cared-for hands would have been DROWN and SAVE, perhaps with a question mark – SAVE? – to make the symmetry perfect. Even when she was pressing down on my chest with one hand, after all, she was continuing to support me with the other. Otherwise I would have sunk like a gasping stone. Perhaps the whole ritual was about her and not us at all. Perhaps it was more to do with frustration than cruelty. It may be that deep down she wanted to save me, and how could she do that without drowning me a bit first?

The other part of her programme, though, the agony ballet in group physiotherapy sessions – I can't devise any nuanced reading of that. That was just a routine of atrocity.

And still we failed to realise we were being tortured. I'm not sure we ever really got the message, as a group. We never talked about it. We weren't attuned to our own violation. In the culture of the time, the real danger to children wasn't abuse but spoiling. The fear wasn't that children might be cruelly treated but that they might not learn manners. They might cry themselves to sleep after torture by physio, but at least they would write proper thank-you letters, a minimum of three paragraphs long, to relatives they rarely saw, for presents they hadn't liked.

So many aspects of our lives at CRX were painful or humiliating that it was hard to be sure when something had no other purpose. Being photographed naked by Mr Fisk four times a year, for instance, was something I dreaded, since no one had taken the time to explain what it had to do with being ill, or how those photographs ended up being pored over by the medical staff. My sense of dread wasn't nuanced enough to make a real distinction between Mr Fisk and Miss Krüger. It's just that Miss Krüger's visitations happened more often.

The whole doctrine of walking at any cost had the effect of making us feel our pain was beneath notice, so it was hard to be aware of the difference when it was being actively cultivated, when we were being mined for the pain we could be made to yield. One of the defects of the prevailing wisdom that you had to be cruel to be kind was that it masked so well those who were being cruel to be cruel. It's hard even now to draw a meaningful line between a régime of obtuse doctrinaire rehabilitation and straightforward abuse. This was a characteristic of the system which Miss Krüger shrewdly exploited. Even the authorised therapies prided themselves on ignoring the desires of the patient.

I can't answer for anyone else, but it never occurred to me to grass Miss Krüger up to Heel. That wasn't a thinkable option, it was strictly taboo in the culture of the hospital. Even if I had been tempted, the timing wasn't right. Sister Heel was full of budgie love and budgie thoughts. Charlie's loving beak was pouring endearments in her ear which would drown out any complaints.

I did worry, though, about Mary, and whether her short life had included episodes of torture in the pool. She had gone up on pointes with the rest of us in group sessions, but I didn't know about the pool. I tried to remember if she had talked about Miss Krüger, but if she had I had already forgotten. I told myself that she couldn't have sat there so happily, elaborating schemes for raffles, on the last day we spent together, if the pool had meant pain and horror to her, as it already did, partly, for me. She had a very forgiving nature, but forgiving Miss Krüger without making a protest would have been a crime against herself.

Couldn't bear to see children suffer

With a bona fide sadist on the premises, it seems odd that we had any fear left over for anyone else. It was Ivy who had first told me stories about Vera Cole. I'm certain that she believed what she was telling me. She was passing on fears that she shared, not infecting me with something to which she was immune.

Vera was a lady who killed children. The story always went that she'd been seen just lately in the hospital, looking through a list of names she held in her hands. She was very smartly dressed in a fur coat and wore gloves. She wasn't heartless, it was just the opposite. She couldn't bear to see children suffer. She wanted them to be out of their pain, and so she slit their throats and drank their blood. We all believed absolutely in Vera Cole. There were even a couple of cadet nurses who talked about her. Of course they seemed old to us, but cadet nurses were hardly older than children themselves.

I wonder if there was some tiny basis in truth behind the story. Perhaps there really was a Vera Cole in the newspapers at that time, or someone with a similar name, who'd been involved in a child's death with a hint of mercy killing. I can imagine someone like Wendy embroidering a few nasty extra touches – she maintained, for instance, that it was boys that made Vera Cole so sad, and that she got into bed with them for a special kiss before she ended their pain. Still,

I don't think any of us had the imagination to make the whole thing up from scratch. The details about the clothes make me wonder if there isn't an echo of Cruella de Vil from *101 Dalmatians*. The book, of course. The film hadn't happened yet.

So we could talk for hours amongst ourselves about the danger we were in from Vera Cole, who had been seen in the WVS canteen only the other day, but we said nothing about the sadist into whose hands we were passed on a regular basis. It complicated things that Miss Krüger was German. I had been brought up with a strong anti-Teutonic reflex, and I'm sure I wasn't the only one. Dad was always saying that the only good German was a dead German, and hadn't he done his bit in the War to produce exactly that improvement of character? But if Germans were inherently cruel and evil, then we couldn't be surprised by Miss Krüger's actions. In fact it seemed obvious that if a German physio had been hired, then it was to do precisely what Miss Krüger was doing.

We didn't have the independence of mind to notice that certain things only happened when Miss Krüger was in sole charge of us, when no one else was in the physiotherapy room or the hydrotherapy pool. An outsider might have thought it significant that although we were competitive about our autograph books, as about everything else in our rather restricted world, none of us asked Miss Krüger to sign them, but that was the only ripple which showed even faintly on the surface.

You say nugget here

Sarah had been very kind to me after Mary died. She told me once about guardian angels, and how we all had one. She was sure that Mary had been made a guardian angel, but it would be selfish to want to know whose.

In fact if I had a guardian angel on those premises it was Sarah herself. She watched over me and helped me protect myself when my home-conditioned reflexes let me down. At home Mum sometimes let me have one of her favourite chocolates as a special treat. At CRX similar sweets turned up in the communal confectionery hoard. When I was asked which ones I wanted, I said, 'I'd like some nougat, please,' pronouncing it 'noo-gah'. Almost before I had said it Sarah made a warning hiss and muttered urgently from the side of her mouth, 'You say *nugget* here,' before Wendy could get wind of my latest poshie blunder.

As we all grew up, Wendy's weak points became easier to notice. She was invincibly ignorant – not stupid by any means, but very badly informed. She thought, for instance, that the sun was only as big as it looked. Which meant it was as big as a farthing. I knew from Arthur Mee's book that the sun was 93 million miles away, and I made my case in the strongest terms. I also moved a coin away from her and asked how big it looked now.

Wendy didn't exactly cave in, but she changed her story. She maintained that you couldn't possibly see something that was so far off, but she did allow the sun a little discreet expansion. The sun was now as big as Ward Two – not Ward One, but as big as Ward Two. Which was, admittedly, the larger of the two wards. But not of cosmic dimensions. I wished that I could bring *The World We Live In* into the ward, to have Arthur Mee back me up, but I didn't trust anyone, patients or nurses, with anything precious.

Sex was another area of intellectual vulnerability for Wendy. Wendy was adamant that when a lady had a baby it came out of her belly button. There was consistency to her theory, since she thought a man made a baby by putting his willy 'in a lady's belly button' in the first place, but I had an eloquent supporter on my side. I didn't even need to go into detail, because Sarah Morrison had a book. Muzzie must have been very advanced to supply such a thing. Sarah didn't contradict Wendy directly, she was too politic for that. Instead she just read aloud from her book: 'When humans mate, they lie on their sides facing each other . . .' Funny that there was no leeway in her book for missionaries and their positions.

It was sweet enough that Wendy was too dim to know about tailies and pockets. Even better that the street arab of the ward, our resident guttersnipe, had fallen back on the word 'lady'. She went all posh herself, when she was threatened and flustered.

What would life have been like if Wendy had been better informed about the universe and the marriage bed, if there hadn't been a necessary limit to her tyranny? It was a question that used to haunt me, my scaled-down equivalent of the one that could still make people of my parents' generation shiver: what if Hitler hadn't attacked Russia?

I also wondered from time to time what life at CRX would have been like without Sarah. One day she told me that she was unfortunately unable to propose to me, since that task fell to the man. I immediately proposed, and she accepted. Sarah told Muzzie, I broke the news to Mum and everybody was delighted. I held Sarah's hand and Muzzie and Mum, surprisingly emotional, gave each other a hug and a kiss. When I went to do the same to Sarah she said, blushing slightly, 'We mustn't get any closer than this until the day.' Muzzie and Mum clapped their hands and burst out in peals of laughter. I didn't quite know why.

Sarah and I would have our own house, made a bit smaller just for us – but not too small, so our parents and other visitors wouldn't bump their heads. Sarah could develop her talent for charity work, and we would work away like beavers for the PDSA (not the RSPCA). We would probably form our own Hive. Then I'd have a much better chance of getting a proper mention in the *Busy Bee News*, though my resentment of Sarah's greater success in such matters had evaporated long ago.

I could just see it. There we would be in our own sweet little house, and organising a Grand Fête. I would be phoning up design firms and explaining to the manager, for the sixth time that morning, exactly what a circumflex was (a recent discovery of my own).

'Think of it as a word meaning F-E-S-T-I-I-I-I-V-I-T-Y,' I explained, tired but delighted I'd learnèd to put a warble into the word to bring it to life. 'It used to be "Feste", but that's not too easy to say so they dropped the awkward "s". The circumflex is just a reminder that it used to be there.'

'Well, now you put it that way, Guv,' the design manager would say, 'I think I shall remember the word "Fête" for the rest of my life. The way you put it, Sir, seems to make it stick in my mind somehow. Wish I'd 'ad a teacher like you when I was a kid, Sir.'

During all this Sarah would be answering the phone on the other line. I'd spotted that Heel had two phones in her office and coveted this nerve centre of modern communications. To the caller she'd say: 'Just one moment please, I shall have to ask my husband,' and then to me, putting her hand over the mouthpiece, 'M'dear . . .' (I would have quickly weaned her off such gooeyness as 'Darling'), 'It's Mr Millthorpe from Cookham Dean. Submissions for stalls closed yesterday, of course, but he has a family of performing voles – in fact a whole vole vaudeville, or so it seems.'

I would make a delighted face and give a thumbs-up, as this was just what I had been looking for, but then I would change it to a frown and make a wavy signal with my hand instead. Sarah, experienced in our business and perfectly attuned to my little ways, would take the cue and say, 'Well, I'm afraid your application is in late, Sir, and we are absolutely chock-a-blocko, but I've put in a word with my husband and he *thinks* he can manage to squeeze you in somehow, even if he has to stay up all night working out the details.' I would yawn at the very thought of it, and then (yawns being so very contagious) Sarah would yawn too, apologising to the grateful caller as she signed off with, 'We'll see you on the day.' I would remind her about the importance of proper supervision for the queues. Mum had once seen Ken Dodd jump the queue for the fortune teller at a CRX fête. She sometimes laughed at his jokes even after that, but lost all respect for him as a person.

Newts up-stream of their ladies

Sarah and I would soon work out that all this taily stuff really wasn't practical or necessary. Dad had shown me books about the animal kingdom, and I had learned that there were methods of carrying on the species much more appealing to me personally than putting tailies in ladies' holes. Newts, for instance, simply swam up-stream of their ladies and dropped off a parcel for them to collect! I wanted the physical side of marriage to be run on a similar, postal basis, otherwise I wouldn't have any part of it.

Our beds would be close enough for us to hold hands before going to sleep. For babies we had plenty of options. By the time we were grown up, everybody would probably be doing it all by packages and parcels. Besides, Mary had become an angel by now, and she would help us. She was far above feelings of jealousy and being left out. She would probably be a senior angel by then, so we were well connected.

We would be high on the waiting list.

All I had to do to link up with this marvellous future was to survive my solo sessions in the pool with Miss Krüger. I was scared, of course, though there were weeks when nothing happened – either because she was adding psychological torture to the mix, until I was almost longing for the drowning to start, so that it would be over for the week and I could think of something else, or because there were other staff around and she couldn't get up to her tricks. I had enough sense to know that she was risking her job, German or no German, if she actually drowned someone.

Then suddenly, from one day to the next, Miss Krüger was gone, and she didn't even drown anybody! Gone under a cloud, a pink fluffy angora cloud, disgrace raining down on her head. It wasn't her perversion that got her dismissed, the sessions of ankylosis ballet when no one else was around, the drowning therapy in the pool. It was pilfering that was her downfall. She had stolen three balls of pink angora wool from another nurse. They were found in her locker. And she didn't even knit! So perhaps it was simple spite. If she'd stuck with sadism and not been tempted by spite, she would have been more secure. She would have kept her position.

I suppose it's possible that the theft was only a pretext for dismissing her, to prevent uglier things coming to light, and the real reason was some cruelty that had been witnessed or reported. If so I think even in the 'fifties we'd have been asked about her ideas of treatment. What she'd done. Unless the principle of Least Said Soonest Mended which ruled our house so fiercely held sway on the ward also. And perhaps in this case it actually was for the best. I was very happy to know that I would never see Miss Krüger again.

There were weeks now when the phantom school's existence within the hospital was almost continuous, weeks when that shy woodland creature hiding in the buildings seemed tame enough to come and eat out of my hand. The headmaster, Mr Turpin, known of course as Turps or Old Turpentine, began to take a closer interest in me.

I loved the smell of turpentine, and a little of that tenderness rubbed off on Mr Turpin. When Sarah did oil painting by numbers, she thinned her paints with turpentine even though everyone said you shouldn't do that.

When he first met me Mr Turpin said doubtfully, 'I suppose he might earn a living as some sort of clerk.' It's true I had a little move-ment in the elbow of my writing arm, but it was hardly something I wanted to do for eight hours a day. He said it before he had seen my hand-writing – there were only smudgy dashes where the letters should have been. 'It's a shame you can't be a doctor,' he said, rather insensitively, 'your hand-writing would be perfect for that.' Turps must have seen my wounded expression, because he brought in an art teacher from Ward Three, who let me be as smudgy as I liked.

She gave me a brush and some water-colours and said to try and draw a cornfield. When I'd finished, the teacher said, 'Your painting is very like van Gogh, John!' which made me very happy. As Art pro-gressed, she gently gave me a few tips. She got me to look out of the window and see if I could spot any straight lines. 'The moment you see any straight lines in nature, John,' she said, 'be sure to let me know.' That was tactful. She suggested I watched her paint a bit, just to get a few ideas, and I lapped it all up. Two weeks later, when I'd finished another painting, she put it alongside the 'van Gogh' and said, 'See how much better the new one is, John!'

When I looked at them both, the improvement was very notice-able. In fact the first one was awful, but my teacher hadn't said so. She had used words of encouragement and helped me climb out of my own mess. This enlightened style of teaching was entirely new to me. There's an old proverb that goes, 'The harvest called learning requires the rain called tears.' My art teacher at CRX gave me my first indica-tion that the sun might get a look in from time to time.

Mr Turpin must have seen some potential for study in me. He taught me English, managing to get through the barrier of my child-ishness. His biggest challenge came the day he said, 'Today we're going to do some poetry.' He gave me a book and said we were going to read 'To Autumn' by someone called John Keats. He'd got as far as the first two lines before I collapsed into laughter. 'Season of mists and mellow fruitfulness,' he read, 'Close bosom friend of the matur-ing sun'. I just howled. Oh what a lovely writer John Keats must have been. Bosoms bosoms bosoms. And how grown-up Mr Turpin was to be able to say 'bosom' without laughing.

Mr Turpin looked at me kindly and smiled. I said, 'Is it a poem about BOSOMS, sir?' and collapsed back into my laughter. Even before I'd come to CRX I'd known that 'bosom' was a real word and also a rude one, though the home word we used was 'boozzie'. Turpin explained that 'bosom' was a word of many meanings. He didn't make the mistake of any actual reference to biology. I think he repeated bosom-bosom-bosom many times in an attempt to lull me into being bored with the word, but it made no difference. It was just as funny every time. Eventually he said we'd move on, and the rest of 'To Autumn' got rather more of my attention than the opening lines.

I was almost totally blind to the lost songs of spring, although I thought the barrèd clouds blooming the soft dying day were great, since I learned from Turps about how you could use accents in a word to make another syllable. I decided that accents and funny letters would become a speciality for me from then on. Deep down my pleasure was more typographical than literary.

Bosom bosom bosom

At home I would walk around the house saying *bosom bosom bosom*, cunningly incorporating the word into proper sentences, to see if anyone in the family could keep a straight face. As it happened, Mum wanted a word with me on a very similar subject. She told me that Muzzie was going to have an operation because her bosom had grown far too big. The phrase 'Muzzie's boozzie' was full of giggly music, but I soon understood that this was a serious thing. I tried to pass the word to Muzzie that I couldn't see anything wrong with her boozzie. In fact I liked it. It made her into a lovely pillowy sort of mum for Sarah, while my Mum was more a straight-up-and-down sort of mum. Muzzie was like a great walking cuddle, and I was sad that she wanted an operation to take away something that was so much part of her, as far as I was concerned.

Life was very fine with Miss Krüger gone, until we were told that her replacement was coming. I had a dreadful thought. Maybe the new one would be German too. I had to know. I asked Heel, because I knew she would tell me the truth, and she said, 'As a matter of fact she is, John. Miss Schmidt. Why do you ask?'

Then the sun was altogether hidden, and I went into a decline which mystified those who had charge of me. There was no one to connect my withdrawal with the impending arrival of a new pain-choreographer. The new physio would be a Miss Krüger with fresh tricks, that's all. I knew it. Only this one would be smart enough to keep her thieving mitts off other people's knitting supplies, and she'd make us dance as we'd never danced before.

I had a week of misery, unable to eat or tell anyone what the matter was. I was a perky little bird in the normal run of things, but the news knocked me right off my perch and I stopped singing. Also eating. On the ward if you didn't open your bowels, you'd have to take Senokot, but if you didn't eat you were just told not to be so fussy.

The day of my first session with Miss Schmidt I was back with the old Miss Krüger-pool feeling – let's get this over with. I heard her before I saw her, because she was wearing clogs, and Mum said only people from Yorkshire wore clogs, so my first question was, 'Are you from Yorkshire?' even though I was fairly sure Yorkshire wasn't in Germany, and she burst out laughing.

Within ten minutes of meeting her I was singing again. She was a jolt of joy and a living delight. Apart from anything else, she did massage. It was Heaven. My body wasn't exactly being pampered, but it was being worked on in a respectful way. It was being talked to, not punished or even lectured for its failure to coöperate. Miss Schmidt started me on a whole series of love affairs. One of them was with massage, and another was with the language she spoke. She would chatter in German while she kneaded subtly away. It sounded lovely, and I couldn't take my eyes off her. She said, '*Machst du mir Kuh Augen?*' 'What does that mean?' I asked. She wouldn't translate what she had said until I had repeated it back to her and got it by heart, and then she told me it meant, 'Are you making at me cows' eyes?' Then I understood, although I told her that in English we said sheep's eyes.

In German the look of love seems to be bovine rather than ovine. Neither image flatters the love-struck. Of course I was making cows' eyes, sheep's eyes, at her – take your pick. I looked at her the same way Sister Heel looked at the budgie who made life worth living, ray of feathered sunshine. If I had been Charlie I would have been displaying the posture I had taught Heel to recognise: head plumage standing up, side plumage fanned out. Eyes closed to slits. Happiness in full feather.

I had so many reasons to be thrilled and goggling. Because Miss Schmidt had a lovely clear complexion, because her hands knew how to talk to my body in a way that wasn't any sort of scolding, because she was German and even so she wasn't holding my head beneath the surface of the hydrotherapy pool.

I got up the nerve to ask her what her first name was. It was Gisela. She let me call her that. Adults letting children call them by their first names wasn't common in those days anywhere. In hospitals it was as rare as undercooked vegetables.

On our second or third session, Gisela starting reciting something with a soothing, tantalising sound and rhythm. I asked her what it was. It is a poem. A nursery rhyme. And I said: 'Teach me please!' What I meant was for her to tell me what the poem meant, but again she did something much better. First she taught me the poem as pure sound. My favourite part sounded like 'Gink a line'. Only later did she supply the meaning, and by then the German words had put down little radicles of their own. They had begun to be rooted. Once again it turned out that medical staff had lessons of their own to teach.

The poem went:

Hänschen klein
Ging allein
In die weite Welt hinein:
Stock und Hut
Steht ihm gut,
Ist ja wohlgemut.
Aber Mutter weinet sehr,
Hat ja nun kein Hänschen mehr,
Da besinnt Sich das Kind
Läuft nach Haus geschwind.

The meaning, when she told me, was something like:

Little Hans
Went alone
Into the wide world beyond:
Stick and hat,

He's very pleased with himself.
But Mother is crying bitterly,
She hasn't got little Hans any more.
The little boy thinks again
And runs very quickly back home.

She couldn't have chosen a more illuminating text. I liked the image of Little Hans with his stick. I had a stick of my own, not to walk with but to point to things or nudge them towards me. Also to scratch my head where I couldn't reach.

It became even more marvellous when Gisela explained that Hänschen was a double diminutive of John. She explained this to me with hand gestures rather than words. First she pointed at me, and said 'Johann'. Then she put her thumb and index finger an inch apart, and said, 'Hans'. Then she brought them so close together they were almost touching, and said, 'Hänschen'. Hänschen was Little Johnnie. Hänschen was a Johnlet, a mini-John.

Horizontal vertigo

My hatred of everything German began to turn into its opposite. The language made such satisfying demands on the tongue and the lips and the palate, while German fingers brought deep relief and warmth. Soon I was listening out for her footsteps in the corridor. The clop of her clogs made my heart lift even before I could see her. It was wonderful for me to lie down and have Gisela conjure delicious pangs from my flesh.

She in her turn was impressed by the National Health Service of which she was now a part, saying simply, 'In Charmany your parents would have to pay.'

The standing-up parts of our sessions weren't quite so much fun. I had a sort of horizontal vertigo after Miss Krüger's lessons. That time left scars. I clung to the wall and resisted any attempt to coax me into walking. Small distances seemed absolutely terrifying. Gisela would crouch a little in front of me and sing out, 'Come just so far, Hänschen,' and I would make myself trust her. As I tried to do as I was asked, I experienced something that was either a hallucination or a revelation of the true nature of matter. It seemed to me that as I inched my foot forward, the ground came into existence to meet it, and dematerialised again the moment I took another pace and moved on. This was either an intuition of quantum physics or a side-effect of eating Liquorice Allsorts.

I would manage the daunting distance to Gisela. But then she would move away the same distance and tell me again that I needed to come just so far. So I would say, 'I think you lied to me, Gisela,' and she would say, 'I lied from love.' Sensibly she broke the daunting task down into manageable slices of effort. Then finally she would turn me round and say, 'Look! See how far you have been!' And the distance would be impressive enough for her loving lie to disappear from my mind.

I became ambitious under her influence. A tricycle was the next adventure. I learned to move the pedals through part of their arc, and then to back-pedal so as to do the same thing again. I really wanted to ride a bike, but was told it was impossible. I didn't see why. My determination won approval from the faction that regarded refusal of a wheelchair as the greatest virtue in someone like me.

It seemed to me that riding a bike would be relatively easy. Riding it, as opposed to starting or stopping. When the pedals were horizontal I would jiggle down against the ratchet for an inch and a half, then back-pedal slightly and repeat the process. Setting a rhythm was crucial. I managed to get another inch or two of drive down onto the pedals by lifting my bottom up.

So Shmitty would always walk beside me. Walk and then run. One of the joys of riding a bike in CRX was that so much of it was on a slope. I could get up a fantastic speed in some corridors. Shmitty would be panting, saying that she had never had a patient who made her work so hard.

Of course riding the bike was insanely painful, but there came a time when the joy and sensation of freedom it brought reached a certain level, and drowned the pain. Or rather, it was still pain but it changed key, and when I had got the bike moving properly the pain was in the key of triumph. It was well worth it, even though my legs felt very locked and deadened after Gisela lifted me off at last.

I had a cactus on the ward. It did nothing. It did nothing in a really

276

big way. It was inert even for a cactus, and cacti aren't the most entertaining of plants. It didn't help that I was watering it. Watering it
and then, when that didn't seem to do any good, watering it some
more. I dare say I'd only been given the cactus in the first place
because of its ease of maintenance. If so, my needs were misunderstood. I didn't want something that survived despite my neglect. I
wanted something that thrived entirely because of love and care.
Somehow my rage to make things grow escaped people's notice. I
wanted active responsibility for life, not mere curatorship. In those
terms, having intervened and failed (by watering a desert plant,
thereby killing it) was a better outcome than learning the bad lesson
of laissez-faire.

I was serving notice of an important character trait, the need to
keep something alive beside myself. Into that disobliging cactus I
poured energy that would have sustained a whole extended family, a
menagerie, a harem. It was Gisela who broke the news to me, saying,
'Your cactus I think is dead.' We lifted it from the pot and the stench
of rotten vegetation was overwhelming. But the cactus didn't die in
vain. I asked Gisela to translate a special sentence for me into
German. I wanted to know how to say, 'You smell like my old cactus.'
Gisela laughed, but it wasn't the sort of laugh that means no. She told
me I should say, '*Du stinkst wie mein alter Kaktus.*' She coached me
until my pronunciation was perfect. Then I'd say it to doctors I did-
n't like, under my breath at first and then with more confidence, out
loud. It was my revenge for the way they were always producing
incomprehensible sentences of their own.

I didn't know it, but some of the doctors were trying alternatives
to cortisone. In 1958 we had all been prescribed phenylbutazone,
under the trade name of Butazolidin. I memorised every medical
word I came across, and I'd taught myself to read upside down, so I
could decipher what the doctors were writing down. It was no good
asking them – they wouldn't tell you. Poor Geraldine went all red
and itchy, so the drug was stopped for everyone. It's true that it can
kill white blood cells, it can hurt bone marrow in some people, it can
lead to aplastic anæmia. Certainly its side-effects were more obvious
than those of steroids, and they could be severe in ten per cent of people. It's just that I can't help feeling it was a better drug for the ninety

per cent who could tolerate it than what they were on. It certainly wouldn't have stunted them.

I'm not talking selfishly at this point, since I wasn't on cortisone in the first place. It's the rest of my generation that I wonder about. Cortisone was insidious. Cortisone was the worse drug in the long run. Still, phenylbutazone was banned outright in 1970, so I'm in the minority on that one.

I was put on Enseals after the Butazolidin fiasco, and stayed on them for a very long time. Enseals were coated aspirin. The outer shell came off after it had passed through your stomach, lessening the chance of hæmorrhage in the stomach lining. Presumably it did less damage to the jejunum, duodenum, and so on down the line.

Gisela didn't teach me German in any systematic way, but she'd often get me to say something during one massage session and explain its meaning at the next, when it had sunk in as pure sound. It's a teaching method that I've become rather attached to. She knew how to intrigue me with arcane and archaic knowledge, appealing to the latent cabbalist in me. It's as if she intuited my special interest in surplus or non-standard letters – residue of the battle over 'Æ'– and showed me the old-style umlaut, which was two angled flecks over the vowel, like double inverted commas. Also the old-fashioned sign for a doubled consonant, a line over (for instance) the m in *Som̄er*.

Physio's pet

I concentrated as hard as I could during official lessons, and wished there was school from morning till night, but learning from Gisela was different. I absorbed sounds first and meanings later, while her wily hands kneaded and released. Her massage was the only treatment I had received to date which had no other object than to make me feel better. Very few of the procedures designed for me were ever explained, but here was one that explained itself. I'd always wanted to be a teacher's pet, but there was never a teacher I could worship without reservation. Now I settled very happily for being a physio's pet instead.

During weekends at home Mum continued to give me her own style of instruction, mainly on social matters. Bourne End was a world where she was beginning to get a toehold. It had never been run-down, but now it was becoming increasingly smart. There were rumours that an actor or two was thinking of moving in. It wasn't clear whether this was a step up or down for the area.

We lived on the Abbotsbrook Estate. She trained me not to say we lived 'on an estate' but to spell out our status clearly. Our cleaning lady, Mrs Ring, did live on a council estate, and there was a world of difference. I wanted to be like Ring. I loved her directness. Mum and Dad were always saying they were short of money, and I found out that Ring's rent was fourteen shillings a week. I decided that if we lived in a council house we might pick up the habit of saying what we meant.

I was developing a class-consciousness which was a distortion of my parents' already distorted view of things. I never liked 'our kind of people'. I was convinced that a room full of working-class people would be really quite exciting. If a working-class woman didn't like Doreen Parsons from Mum's Bathford days, she'd call her a miserable cow, not 'Oh you poor sweetheart!' I thought Doreen Parsons would really rather be called a miserable cow, because later on, if she changed her ways, she might be told she was a Little Gem or something like that. If the first comment was sincere, then so would be the second.

If Mum and Dad were saving money on where they lived, Ring could still pop round every day, do a bit of cleaning and then have a cup of coffee (she didn't drink tea) and a chat with me. We would often have a good old chinwag while Mum was out, and I was looking forward to more of the same. Small talk and comfortable silences. 'I saw that *Night of the Demon*,' she might say, 'That was nice, yeah . . .'

One day Mum caught me slumming with Ring, leaving the ends off words, saying 'Mmmmm' with the appropriate intonation rather than 'Yes' or 'No'. She gave me stick. 'You are not to talk to Ring like that. It's fine for Ring, but Ring is Ring and you are you. You couldn't live with people like that. Not really.'

Then one day in the village, with Mum pushing the Tan-Sad, we saw Ring and her young son Graham, which for some reason Ring pronounced 'Grarm'. They didn't see us, so we shadowed them for quite a while. It felt strange to be spying on her like that, but it was a treat for me not to be noticed. Suddenly Ring told Grarm off and then whacked him. In fact she whacked him first, saying 'Take that!', and told him off afterwards. The whacking was just to get his attention. Then she marched him off, still howling. For the first time I saw the draw-back of expressing your impulses without restraint.

Mum was shrewd enough to capitalise on my shock. 'That's what happens with some people. If that was me, I'd have said, "John, darling, I *have* asked you more than once not to do that . . ."' I didn't say I'd rather be whacked and have done with it. I couldn't fetch the words up in all sincerity.

According to Mum the danger and the problem wasn't with the working class, though, it was with suburban people and the nouveaux riches. The Delamare family who lived nearby were a good case in point. 'I'm not fooled by the French veneer for one minute,' said Mum. 'Their very name is a trick to make you think they're upper when they are most certainly not.' It was Suburbans who felt uncomfortable with the working class, since that was where they had come from so recently.

Mum said that with each month that passed, it was getting harder to tell who was who. Many suburban people were intelligent, and some of them were even 'nice'. They were getting university degrees, moving into schools and hospitals and working out the rates on your house. They weren't dunces. In fact Suburbans tended to have extremely high IQs, and they adapted very quickly. More than anything they wanted to be thought of as Uppers. They would go to any lengths to achieve that imposture.

However, upper people mustn't despair. There were secrets that would always elude Suburbans. At this point Mum reverently led me to the tabernacle of her particular cult, her stationery box. She put it on the table, tapping it with a proud finger. This was what decent people stood for. This was pure embossed justification. She opened the lid.

'Just take a look at our printed notepaper, JJ,' she said, pulling out a sheet. 'Some things can't be counterfeited.' I did as I was told. Our printed notepaper had the address on the right-hand side with a downwards slope:

> Trees,
> Abbotsbrook,
> Bourne End,
> Bucks.

I already felt a little let down by that fourth line. Bucks? Why were we being so shy about the full glory of our home county? Returning from one of our first trips in the Vauxhall, I was sure I had spotted a signpost as we crossed the border which announced 'The Royal County of Buckinghamshire'. 'Why can't we put that on all our letters,' I asked, 'and make everyone who writes to us put it on the envelope?' I must have been taking time off from my anti-monarchism that day.

I argued and argued. 'Why not? Why can't we? We can if we want to!' I was only silenced by Mum shouting, 'Well we just can't and that's all there is to it.' I went into the deepest possible sulk for some time after that. Again I discovered that the best way to undermine an idea was not to oppose it but to put your heart and soul into endorsing it.

In fact my eyes had deceived me, hardly surprisingly considering my awkward position in the car and my restricted ability to turn my head. It turned out that Buckinghamshire wasn't the Royal County. That was Berkshire. My geography wasn't up to much – how could it be, when I spent so much time immobilised? I loved maps, but was vague about how they connected up with the larger world of which I had seen so little.

Later I worked things out to my own satisfaction. Everyone knew that the Queen lived in Buckingham Palace, so the link between royalty and Buckinghamshire was fundamental. It was unnecessary to spell it out any further. Leave that sort of crudity to the desperate parvenu that was Berkshire.

Whichever was the Royal County as between Berkshire and Buckinghamshire, I also realised that the two addresses of CRX, one in each county, allowed it an indeterminate status. In a republican mood, I could use one return address, but on days when I thought the Queen was really rather pretty I could be gracious and use the other.

Re-entering the notepaper debate, I asked, 'Shouldn't "Bucks" at least be "Buckinghamshire"?' Mum said it was important not to show off when it came to printed notepaper. Not that it would be wrong to put in the full name of the county, but if she did that there would be too many letters in the word and then she wouldn't be able to have her 'Little House'.

I asked her why she didn't ask to have it printed like this:

Trees,
Abbotsbrook,
Bourne End
Buckinghamshire

I liked a nice justified left-hand margin – and then Mum could have the county spelled out in full.

'Jay-Jayee . . .' Mum said, and I was happy to see that she was in a tender mood. When she was like that it was wonderful. I could forgive her any mistake in the world, and I was more than happy to fight against the whole suburban world if that was what she had wanted me to do.

'Jay-Jayee,' she said again, with a playful smile curling up one side of her mouth, 'I don't think you've been listening to a single word I've been sayee-ing, have you? Take another look at the notepaper. Can't you see Mum's Little House?'

We seemed to be playing some sort of game, which was good, but however hard I looked at the subtle eggshell paper with its bold blue printing, I couldn't see anything which resembled a 'Little House'. I knew the secret was right in front of me, a thrilling feeling. The Queen's Velvet watermark was winking at me invisibly. I didn't need to hold the paper up to the light to see it. I knew it was there, and there was something else there too, just waiting to be seen. I was on the brink of great things, but I couldn't see a Little House anywhere.

'All right, Jay,' she said. 'Let's tackle this from a different angle. Now let's see. Take a piece of paper and draw me a little house.' I hoped she was going to give me a sheet of notepaper to do my drawing on, but art work was never my strong point and I couldn't blame her for being thrifty. She tore a sheet off an ordinary white notepad, but then she handed me her Parker fountain pen filled with blue Quink, which made me feel that this drawing would be special after all.

Chemical storms

I felt honoured because Mum had always drilled into me that fountain pens adapt to the writer's hand. You should never write with a pen that belonged to somebody else, and you should certainly never lend yours to anybody.

Taking the sacrosanct pen I drew a little box, put in two windows and a door, and topped it with a roof. I added a chimney with smoke coming out. For me a house without a chimney hardly counted as a human habitation. People need smoke – it's a mystical given. 'Very good!' said Mum. I looked at my little house which was very good, apparently, if not quite good enough to deserve the Queen's Velvet in her Historic County of Buckinghamshire. 'Now,' she said, 'take away the walls, windows and doors and tell me what's left!' I couldn't exactly take those bits away, so I shifted the paper and made a few more quick Parker strokes. I said, 'It leaves a roof and a chimney with smoke coming out.'

I still couldn't see anything in Mum's headed notepaper like this pictogram, so I screwed up my eyebrows and scratched my head with my stick. Mum's puzzle was turning out to be quite a poser. Perhaps I'd under-estimated her brains. To give myself more time to think, I popped open the tube in which I kept my Liquorice Allsorts and flipped one up into my mouth. My aim was much improved by this time, practically perfect.

Mum gave me an encouraging smile. 'Try looking at how the telephone number is done,' she said, so I had another good hard look. On the left of the page I read:

Bourne End 1176

though it didn't look like that at all. It wasn't horizontal. It sloped as steeply as the corridor at CRX just by the main entrance. If that 'Bourne End 1176' was part of the Queen's Highway in the Historic County there would be a sign before it bearing a giant exclamation mark and the words CAUTION / STEEP HILL / 1:3.

If Dad was driving up that hill he would pray that it was a good dry day and that the Vauxhall had a decent amount of tread on its tyres. He would give the throttle all he'd got even before he reached the 'B', and then he just might make it to the '6' at the end of the ramp, pointing all the way up to the moon. The blood was pounding in my ears as I imagined the scene and I felt almost faint.

The telephone number sloped upwards like this: /, and the way Mum had the address printed out made an imaginary line sloping like this: \. When when you put them together you saw something like this: ∧.

Bingo Jai-Jaiya Hallelujah and Allah-Be-Praised! I had seen the roof of the little house at last. My imagination must have been severely inflamed, because for a moment I could see an imaginary chimney and imaginary smoke coming out too. I was incoherent with excitement for a good ten minutes. Mum was pleased to have made a convert but still rather taken aback. I seemed to be even more obsessed about the importance of the right stationery than she was. I told her that we must get the house notepaper redesigned. After the present batch had run out, we were going to have the address done just the way she had it, but with one vital addition – a printed house-top with a chimney, and smoke coming out of it.

I wanted to start writing letters there and then to all and sundry, so as to use up the old stock of notepaper, now obsolete. At that moment I felt I could write letters tirelessly all day, until there was no paper left. 'Let's starting writing lots of letters, Mum!' Good though her mood was, Mum wasn't going to indulge me any further. 'Don't be silly, JJ,' she said. 'I've got my notepaper just the way I want it. And it's not cheap. It's not for wasting on letters that aren't important.' She wouldn't let me use so much as one piece, and this threw me into a stark depression.

She took back her Parker pen, as if she regretted breaking her own rules by letting me touch it, boxed up the Queen's Velvet and put everything away. The only consolation for me was that she tucked my very ordinary sketch, done on very ordinary white paper, into the box as well.

I felt completely exhausted after all the stationery excitement. My moods went wildly up and down. Emotions fizzed like sherbet on my tongue and then tasted of ashes. At the time I thought that childhood was like this for everyone. One more reason to wish for it to be over, although another part of me was terrified of growing up. I wished there was a way to stop being a child that didn't involve becoming a grown-up.

Moods are complex constructions, chemical storms. Part of that chemistry was to do with sugar intoxication from my Liquorice Allsorts. A child's metabolism is finely balanced, easily knocked off its kilter. The tube from which I shook them was involved. It was a metal screw-top Smith Kline & French tube passed on to me by Mum or Muzzie. It was much harder to open, and much more satisfying, than the packet they had originally come in.

I didn't pay any attention to what had been in those tubes before. It was something prescribed without a murmur, after all, to anyone who was feeling a bit run down, a popular general pick-me-up. A standard tonic – Muzzie called it 'petrol for the nerves'. It was benzedrine, racemic amphetamine, and the powdered residue from the tablets had settled on my Bassett's Liquorice Allsorts, dusting each one with a stimulant coating. That was why I so often chattered nonsense at a terrific rate, and then felt sullenly exhausted. No wonder my mood would lift off like a rocket and come down like a stick. Muzzie, Mum and I were all on speed. In that sense we were all upper people.

Forces both inside and outside me seemed to push me towards a new and alarming stage of life. My taily was whispering in my ear, telling me secrets deeper than anything Charlie knew. It was pointing the way into the future, with a slight leftward slant. When everyone in the ward was on rest time taily showed me how to enter a heavenly and forbidden world. When I manœuvred a cold pillow between my legs and pressed taily against the cool flaxcloth, it showed me how to be a player in a silent orchestra.

I had never seen a man's taily, and could only imagine what such a thing would look like. There seemed no likelihood that it would match mine in any respect. At CRX there was little opportunity for groin-watching. The staff were mainly female, and the men I saw, whether doctors or porters, wore white coats or overalls. It was at weekends in Bourne End that I could look more closely at the middle parts of men.

A warm tie pointing upwards

What I liked best of everything I saw was pressed black trousers. I loved the neat seam running through the middle of the shapely lump. I thought the taily would be equally neat and pressed and cloth-like. More like a warm tie pointing upwards than anything made of flesh.

The beautiful young men in my fantasies were still the ones I had admired with Mary. I'd been faithful. They were the ones from the Famous Five: Julian for preference. I imagined him asking me along on an adventure, to a cave or some such place. Then he would send the others (including Timmy the dog) out on a recce. Julian would clear his throat and say, pretending calm, 'You know why I sent the others away, don't you?'

My heart hammering, I'd say, 'To uncover the mystery?'

He'd smile as he opened his arms and legs to me at last. 'The only mystery here is you and me . . .' I had Dick in reserve for when Julian's aura was exhausted. In third place, as emergency fetish, Rollo the gipsy from the Rupert annuals. The gipsies, oh. The raggle-taggle.

My loyalty to old friends might seem rather pitiful, as if I was hallucinating on vanilla ice cream in the absence of stronger stuff. It's true that like everyone else in the 1950s I wasn't exactly bombarded with sexually inviting images, but this line of thinking doesn't do justice to my imagination, or to Enid Blyton's either. I wasn't surprised when I read up on her later, to find that the Queen Bee was a rather racy figure in her own way. Tennis parties in the nude and so on. I don't think she was actively beaming arousing thoughts down the hill to me from where she lived, but she was a livelier figure than she has been given credit for. Her characters were bound to reflect that sensuality, once she left Andy Pandy and Big Ears in the nursery and started writing more freely about the Famous Five.

Masturbation corrupted my character, but only incidentally. It wasn't the act itself, but the extremes I had to go to in order to practise it undisturbed. I didn't even do tuppenny in private, so how was I going to talk to taily without eavesdroppers? Rest time was an oasis only in theory. Now we were older none of us did more than doze, and I had the feeling of female ears tuning in to every little move. The solution was to break the rules. Only if I misbehaved seriously and often would I be exiled to a side ward, where I would have the leisure to explore taily properly.

I had to learn taily's language. Masturbation for me has to come from the shoulder, apart from the odd finger-flick. More satisfying, usually, since my hips could generate virtually nothing in the way of thrust, was to hold the sheet against myself. I learned to excite myself without actual touch, using a stream of charged images to urge myself on to the dry lightning, the thrilling discharge of nothing yet. Thanks to Ansell, the electrical storms of pre-adolescence were provoked by contact with the finest Irish linen.

It was a different sort of sin against those linen sheets that most often got me banished to a side ward in the first place. Early on in my time at CRX I had learned that linen was more or less edible. I could suck a patch until it went soft and then chew a bit off. Then I'd spit it at the wall to see if anyone noticed. Paper was also useful for this purpose. First I chewed it to soggy pap and then spat it at the wall. Once it had dried, it stayed stuck there remarkably firmly. But linen was my spitting material of choice. It's a paradoxical textile, resistant to high temperatures but vulnerable to friction and nibbling. I have to admit there was an addictive aspect to my bad habit. I was drawn to those sheets like a moth to a flame, like a moth to a winter woollie. The staff might not notice the spat-out whitish lumplets on the wall, but they could hardly miss the nibbled edges of the sheets. I hope that Ansell never knew how I insulted the luxury textile that she insisted we have, a two-pronged assault with teeth and taily.

Later on in my school career I learned that I wasn't alone in the animal kingdom – weaver birds, house martins, ants and termites all used the same technique. By then I had grown out of my vice, but I felt retrospectively vindicated. I wasn't such a masticatory anomaly as I had seemed to myself and others. I may even have been inspired by my budgie in the first place. Charlie was a dab hand at chewing things, including cloth and paper. On one famous occasion he had made short work of a ten-shilling note Dad had left unattended, chewing it into little balls of brownish pulp. It was a tremendous feat, on a par with a human being chewing up (and spitting out) the Bayeux Tapestry, but Dad didn't appreciate it.

By this time I knew the rules of CRX. When my body became a man's, or at least stopped being a boy's, I would be moved to Ward Three. The prospect terrified me. It wasn't that I loved the girls on Ward One, but I had decided I didn't like boys either. I had overheard a nurse saying, 'They're all Teddy boys in there.' Mr Turpin the headmaster was the form teacher of Ward Three, and I didn't mind him, but he didn't sleep on the ward. I knew because I asked him, and he said he went home to Mrs Turpin. Teddy boys were exactly as terrifying as teddy bears were wonderful. Teddy boys were wild. They came out at night. How could Old Turps protect me then? I decided I would be better off staying where I was.

Mrs Pullen, who played the piano thickly and sang, 'Where there's a king with a golden crown, riding on a donkey,' now taught me English and Essays. She tried to soothe my terror by telling me that she also went to Ward Three to teach. I couldn't understand how she could go there and live. The Sister of Ward Three was known to be a dragon – and don't even think of looking for a heart of gold beneath those scales. It didn't help that I was told, 'No nurse will wipe your bottom on Ward Three, so you'd just better work out a way of doing the job yourself!'

I'd stay where I was, Wendy or no Wendy. One of the compensations of the school being such a secondary presence in the institution was that it had no power to coerce. If I dug my heels in, they couldn't make me move. So Mr Turpin went on coming over to teach me in Ward One. He must have thought I was being very silly, but he didn't make me feel bad about it.

In fact Wendy had in some strange way lost her power. It wasn't exactly that she had mellowed. Her body turned out to have another trick to play on her, besides the one that had brought her to CRX in the first place. She had always had a strange dentition, though as she didn't make her way in the world by smiling it wasn't the first thing people noticed. Her front right tooth (left when you looked at her) was almost twice as wide as its neighbour on the other side of the median line. It had a groove in the middle, if you looked closely, but no real division.

Disturbed odontogenesis

Double teeth are caused by disturbances during odontogenesis, the lovely word that only means the birth of teeth. They run in families. A geminated tooth is one where two teeth grow together, though each one still has a root canal. In true fusion, the tooth germs unite before the calcification process has begun, and the result is a tooth with a single root canal. There's also a variant known as concrescence, when the fusion occurs in the embryo when the cementum layer of the root is forming. The technical terms of dentistry have their own special magic – really, the whole vocabulary is glorious once you lift the veils of fear and pain which shroud it.

Wendy couldn't wait to lose that big tooth, that monster gnasher. When it finally happened she was delighted. She wouldn't have expected compensation from the Tooth Fairy in exchange for a body part she detested so much. If anything I imagine her leaving a tip under the pillow to cover the cost of disposal. She waited for the adult teeth to erupt, hoping they would be separate and normal. None came.

This is a classic pattern. A double baby tooth is associated with a missing adult tooth. Wendy was very upset, but there was nothing she could do about it. The Tooth Fairy giveth and the Tooth Fairy taketh away.

Time drew Wendy's teeth. It became possible to imagine feeling sorry for her, in the same way that it's possible to imagine the square root of minus one, even after Mr McCorley had fitted her with a relatively convincing false tooth. Two false teeth, actually, so Wendy got at least part of what she wanted.

Despite not wanting to grow up, I had come to enjoy testing authority in small sidelong ways. I loved to have the last word. One day there was a film on the ward telly, with a group of men on an adventure. When one of the men was wounded, a lady who had come along (even though she'd been told this was an expedition for men only) tore a strip off her skirt to dress his wounds, using some disinfectant which she kept handy. He flinched and looked the other way while the music went very lovey-dovey indeed.

When night-time came (in the film) I couldn't help myself. I called out to Staff Nurse, 'Come quickly, come quickly!' Then when she'd trotted up looking rather flustered, I said, 'See! It's night-time, and look! They're sleeping in the forest. Why doesn't someone come along and take those trees away? Don't they know it's dangerous to sleep near all those plants?'

Staff Nurse seemed a little flummoxed, but said the difference was that the people weren't in hospital. I said, 'One of them has just got wounded and that's almost the same.' Then she got quite shirty and told me about the Upas Tree. The Upas Tree gave out a gas which stupefied an already sleeping man. It would then bend its branches down, pick you up, digest you while you were sleeping and you would never be seen again. Within a day everyone would have forgotten that you ever existed. I should be grateful I only had daffodils and buzy lizzies to contend with, and not ask so many questions.

Of course the upas tree, *Antiaria toxicaria*, isn't like that at all. Only the sap is poisonous, a sort of toxic milk, and you'd be waiting a long time before one got round to eating you. Even so, I was delighted. I admired carnivorous plants unreservedly, and the idea of a carnivorous tree thrilled me to the core.

My hand-writing was resisting all efforts to improve it. I didn't see why I had to write things down. I wanted to live my whole life without having to make silly marks. If things were forgotten then so be it. The forgetting made way for new things to come along. Finally Turps had the idea that I should learn to type instead. Perhaps he had noticed my love of fiddling with knobs and buttons.

'Typing', said Miss Reid grimly, 'is only for those who have learned to write properly first!' As if this was tea-time, and typing was the cake reserved for those who had eaten up their bread and butter. I hated arbitrary objections like this – why couldn't she just scream, 'No you can't! Over my dead body will you learn to type! You're a pesky little nit!'? That would at least be honest.

'Oh I don't know . . .' said Turpin. 'Why don't we let him try and see how things go?'

I suppose he was exercising his authority. Turpin and Reid weren't exactly the best of friends. They'd had a minor territorial barney a few weeks before, so perhaps their backs were already up. Mr Turpin had come along to give me an English lesson, using a book by Ronald Ridout which I had loved. Reid had been very sniffy about it, saying she would never recommend that book.

Now Miss Reid went very red in the face, which didn't suit her. 'As you wish, headmaster,' she said. 'Teaching him such a skill, though, would lie Outside The Orbit Of My Assistance.' It's a lost art, I'm afraid, speaking in initial caps. 'One must be careful not to set a precedent.'

I didn't know what a precedent was, but it certainly felt like a variation on a theme of Weetabix. Allow him to type and they'll all want to do it. Ward One will become a typing pool. 'Perhaps you can find someone else.'

'As a matter of fact I have someone in mind who I'm sure will be happy to help.' I noticed that he too was red in the face. 'Mrs Rhodes.'

'I need hardly remind you that Mrs Rhodes teaches on Ward Three, and John is refusing to go there. If he wants to continue in his childish ways, then he shouldn't expect to get adult things like typewriters as well!' Her reedy voice was displaying an unattractive range of overtones, but I didn't care. Turpentine and Reid were having a row, right there in the ward, and it was all over me!

At this point Turpentine went on the attack. 'I don't suppose it's occurred to you, Miss Reid, to put yourself in John's shoes?' said Turps. 'If you hadn't been doing your best to hold him back for four years, he might be on Ward Three right now!'

This was outrageous, of course. He could just as easily have said it was to her credit that I didn't want to leave her class. Poor Miss Reid had little enough status, and now it was being trampled on. A typewriter was imported from Ward Three, and so was Mrs Rhodes to teach me how to use all my fingers. Miss Reid learned a new skill of her own – looking straight through me. After all we'd been through together, the sins, the songs, the botany.

Mrs Rhodes had her work cut out. I remember her training me to type the word 'alone' correctly, dividing the work between my hands, rather than pecking haphazardly, but there were limits to what I could do. My hands were not like hers, and not only because she had long nails painted red.

I instinctively knew that if the point of her long fingernail hit anything hard, then it would give her a nasty jolt, and that if the hard thing was the key of a typewriter (manual, naturally, at that date), then it would just plain hurt. Even so her typing was rapid and bossy. Not only did her clattering fingers hit the right keys, but on each stroke the pointed nail would fit tenderly for an instant over the rounded key, like a cap designed to fit it, before the next command came from Mrs Rhodes' brain and her fingers darted away to flirt with another key.

Between us we lowered our sights. Using all my fingers was not a possibility. She and the machine were made for each other. It didn't respond to my advances in the same way. Since I had no movement in my left elbow, it was my left thumb and index finger which had the best access to the keyboard. In that position the smaller fingers were angled away from the keyboard.

On the other hand I could move my right elbow, so it made sense to exploit this splendid power, letting the fourth and fifth fingers take charge of the right-hand sector of the typewriter. I became a dogged and very happy four-finger typist, tapping out reams of drivel. It's just that the four fingers I used were a motley bunch of digits, not crack troops like Mrs Rhodes deployed, with their scarlet shields, but ragged volunteers. Yokels with pitchforks, really.

For a while I could keep change at bay by sheer force of will. I could refuse to move to Ward Three and I could hypnotise Turpentine into coöperating. But then it turned out I couldn't stay in Ward One. None of us could.

CRX was being struck by an administrative earthquake. We would all be moving, the girls and I. We wouldn't be going far, though. We would only be moving from Ward One to Ward Two, and everything else would stay the same. I wasn't drastically upset. It didn't seem too much of an upheaval. Perhaps there weren't enough Still's patients any more to justify two whole wards. Now Ward One was going to become a maternity ward.

It wasn't as if we had many possessions, and we weren't expected to shift them ourselves. People cling to their routines, of course, whether they choose them or not. We would be exchanging one configuration of bed and wall and window for another, unfamiliar but essentially the same, and that was that.

Except that the move got mixed up with other things. Sarah told me that when the nurses were changing Ivy's knickers, there was yellow sticky stuff in them, which meant her periods were starting. This held terror for me. I didn't want my periods to come. My taily had been developing its own ideas about what to do, and I was frightened that sticky stuff would come out of it, maybe blood. Nearly everything else about me seemed to be abnormal, so I couldn't take anything for granted. The most surprising thing, really, would be for me to follow the standard pattern.

I asked Sister Heel if I would be allowed to stay on Ward Two, or if this was all a trick to move me to a men's ward. She could normally be relied on to tell the truth, but she hardly seemed to hear me. She told me she had been a nurse for a long time. She thought this would be a good time to retire. Her voice was unusually soft, as if she was already retiring in instalments. It felt as if she was washing her hands of me.

Then when we were safely established in Ward Two I learned something about the move that made it much more serious. Ward One was being turned into a maternity ward, yes, fine. People had babies, I knew that. People had babies all the time. Mum was going to have a baby too – that I knew. She'd told me about it, I had it in the back of my mind. She wanted to have a little girl. Perhaps it would happen this time. I didn't see anything wrong in that. A baby girl might make her happy. I didn't have strong objections.

It was putting all the information together that made things unbearable. All the little propositions combined into a terrible theorem. Mum was going to go into Ward One to have her new baby.

There was something primal about my revulsion, no question of that. It made my skin crawl, the idea that Mum would be full of baby and so near. Couldn't she go and have her stupid baby somewhere else?

There was also an intense social discomfort. The different rules of home and hospital meant that there was a dividing line between them on my mental maps. What linguists call an isogloss, a contour representing changes in language. On one side of this line was 'toilet', 'close' and jeering at the posh. On the other was 'lavatory', 'stuffy' and sneering at everything common. It was awkward enough when the two worlds were a few miles apart, but in a little while there were going to be only yards between them. The isogloss would slice right through CRX, the isogloss would hang above me like a curtain of ice, quivering in every breeze, as if it was going to fall on me and slice me in two. The ice curtain was horribly permeable to sound. If the hospital was quiet Mum would be able to hear me saying 'toilet' to the little ruffians I shared the ward with, and Wendy would be able to hear me talking posh to her ladyship. I'd catch it coming and going. I'd be mocked and chastised by all parties. It made me feel sick just thinking about it.

The obvious thing to say would be that I was jealous of the baby that was coming. That wasn't how it felt. I wished the baby well. I wished the baby well away. It certainly didn't occur to me that tailies must have been busy in pockets, one taily in particular. If I was blotting out an intolerable truth for the sake of my sanity, I did a good job.

It felt as if there was almost nothing in my life I could control, and now everything was bearing down on me. I was counted precocious by the modest standards of CRX, but I hadn't read Edgar Allan Poe at this stage. If I had, I might have found my nightmare well expressed in 'The Pit and the Pendulum'. The walls gliding towards me, ready to crush me in my bed or push me into an abyss. The isogloss playing the part of the pendulum with its wicked blade, swishing in wider and wider arcs as it approached my bound body. Swishing one way with a whisper of 'Nugget'. Swishing back with a murmur of 'Noo-gah'.

I tried to explain to Sarah but for once she didn't get it. She couldn't imagine not wanting Muzzie near her, and wasn't a baby the best news in the world? It's reading too much into the past to suggest that this was the first time I wondered if she was keeping up with me mentally the way she had always done before.

When Mum was actually in the hospital waiting for the baby to come I was almost hysterical. Liquorice Allsorts were my only comfort. A nurse came to say that Mum was coming to say hello. I couldn't bear it. I tried to scramble off the bed to intercept her. Whatever my joints felt about it, I wanted to totter down the corridor to head her off before she got to Ward Two. The nurse told me to lie down and be patient. Everything was fine and my mum was on her way.

Then she came in, with the glow that pregnancy can give, eerily amplified in her case so that she seemed unnaturally calm and loving. Not herself at all. The nurse said, 'Doesn't your mum look well?' Yes she did, but it didn't suit her. It wasn't her. The baby had put something strange inside her.

She asked me how I was and she called me 'darling' – Gran's word, but with its briskness replaced by something tender. 'How do you like your mum coming to stay in your hospital? Isn't it great fun?'

I couldn't speak. To speak in full hearing of both Mum and the cruel girls on the ward, to choose between pretending to be common and remembering to be posh, was not something I could do. All I could think of to do was to cough and mumble, 'Sore throat,' while Mum and the nurse looked at each other at a loss. No wonder they were baffled. I'm baffled myself when I look back. I was a boy whose body was distorted by an illness that would never go away, I was living in a hospital, and here I was transparently faking a trivial ailment. One thing I had no experience of was pretending to be ill. Funny that I made such a fuss.

Disastrous convergence

When the baby was born I did my best to prevent the disastrous convergence of the two worlds that I tried to belong to, by saying that Mum would be tired out and it would be better if I went to see her in my old ward rather than have her come to my new one. Luckily childbirth was still treated in those days as an illness in itself, and new mothers were discouraged from putting their feet to the floor for some time after the birth. Then they really did feel ill and weak when they finally got up. So bed rest came to my rescue for once. That was the only time it did me any good.

I brought with me the game of Flying Hats I'd won in a competition in the hospital. I don't even remember what the competition was, and the game wasn't really what I had my eye on in the matter of prizes. I wanted the loom that was also on offer. Looms were felt to be beneficial at CRX, in some way therapeutic, and I would have liked to have a go on one, but this particular model was unwieldy. It needed two hands to work it. It was described as 'easy to operate', but it was only easy to operate if you used both your hands. It required considerable motor skills to work it, which made it a completely perverse prize in this context. Presumably someone had one to spare and was getting rid of it, in a nice way.

It wasn't nearly as good as the special loom Wendy Keach had, whose shuttle you could flip over one-handed, but she wasn't about to let me have a go on that. In the end I settled for the Flying Hats. There's a picture of Lord David Astor bending down to give me my prize. He owned the *Observer* newspaper. He didn't like Cliveden very much, I don't think. He certainly didn't spend much time there.

Mum and I played Flying Hats as best we could, though I was still as much of a Dropper as I had been when Miss Reid gave me that name, after having to pick up so many pens and pencils. Mum wasn't supposed to move more than the minimum, so if we dropped hats a nurse had to retrieve them. It's not a very thrilling game at the best of times. At the end of it, though, Mum hugged me, in the barely-touching way she'd mastered by then, and said, 'We do have fun, don't we, John?' It was so out of character it gave me the shivers. Everyone kept on and on about how she glowed, but what if I didn't like the new light in her eyes?

I said I had to go to the toilet, partly as a way of testing this new Mum, to see if there was any trace of the old one left. The old Mum would never have let the word 'toilet' pass, but this new one just said absently, 'Of course you must,' and promised not to take her turn at the game until I had come back.

Audrey. The new baby was called Audrey. It was a girl. Good news. Lucky Mum. She was tucked away in a cot, snoozing.

Later Audrey woke up and a nurse handed her to Mum. This little baby was a stranger. I felt she had nothing to do with me – but the woman who held her was also a stranger. I felt that Laura Cromer had disappeared and been replaced with a substitute, one who could only have fooled people who didn't really know her, like the nurses on the ward. Despite a superficial resemblance, this person had nothing in common with my mother. She had already seemed strange while the baby was inside her, but having the baby taken out had left the strangeness still there. It hadn't brought Mum back. I felt sure that Dad would feel the same way when he saw her, but he greeted her and the new baby as if there was nothing unusual going on except having a new person in the family.

While new motherhood was still working its alarming miracles on her, Mum made a suggestion to me. She'd heard that Sister Heel was going to retire, and she knew that Heel was unmarried and lived alone. How did I feel about giving her Charlie as a retirement gift? Wouldn't that be wonderful? My first reaction was to think, 'What a cheek! Give away your own blooming budgie!' But she had done that already, when she gave him to me. She couldn't help herself. She was baby-happy, swollen with the joy that a new life brought.

Even so, the moment she said it, I knew it was the right thing to do. I'd already said good-bye to Charlie once, after all, when I first went to CRX. If the only thing I wanted for Charlie was to see him happy, then happy he certainly was, and he made his mistress Heel happy into the bargain. The truth was that I had grown out of him rather, quite apart from the fact that for all practical purposes he was Heel's already. Handing him over for good would be a legal detail. I was only transferring title.

I still had to nerve myself a little. It was another irrevocable change, even if I was making it happen myself. My voice even cracked when I asked her whether she would like to take Charlie with her as a retirement present. Her voice almost didn't work for a moment. She was close to tears. The dragon had long since unmasked herself and we were almost friends. Then she said that she would be honoured.

Soon after that she was logging off on her last duty, walking quietly out of the ward. She had warned us that she hated good-byes and would rather everyone behaved as if it was the end of a normal day. Except for the birdcage in her hand, of course. That wasn't normal.

I wasn't very good in those days at following people in my mind when they left the room. There seemed no end to their options – it was dizzying. Perhaps as an ex-toddler confined to one room, I was slow to learn that if you leave a space you must enter another one (the whole thing is an illusion, but the illusion is roughly consistent). It wasn't that I had thought of other people as toys in a box to be put away. I felt like a toy in a box myself, that no one was allowed to play with. Still I found my mind could follow Sister Heel, budgie cage in hand, all the way home, right up to the moment when Charlie hopped into her mouth at last. He need never come out again.

I soon got my old Mum back. Audrey wasn't the sort of baby to sleep through the night if she could help it. The unreal or just unfamiliar light began to die from Mum's eyes.

After that, Mum had her little girl. She had what she wanted. If she still wasn't happy, it wasn't a matter of there being something actually missing from the pattern, more that she didn't have the knack.

I hadn't seen much of Peter for a while, but that began to change when he came to see the baby and decided it would be fun to take charge of my wheelchair. I was very happy to have a chauffeur. He found it heavy work at first, so we just pottered round the CRX grounds. He wanted to find a secret passage – he was sure it was just the place to have one. The best we could find at short notice was a manhole cover that hadn't been put back properly, so that it lay at an angle. We decided that this must be the entrance to an underground labyrinth. It was far too heavy for Peter to lift. The Famous Five would have made a better job of uncovering a mystery.

Peter got quite a taste for pushing me around, though controlling the Tan-Sad, when I came home at weekends, was much more of a challenge. It must have been about this time that some adjustments were made to Trees which made life easier for me and for everyone else. There was an L-shaped bedroom annexe, with a ramp. Even so, the extension was always a bit bleak. There was no carpet, for fear that the Tan-Sad would track in mud from outside. There was just lino. I told Mum I had seen enough lino at CRX to last me a lifetime, but she was adamant that she didn't want to spend all her life cleaning up after me. There was a utility room, too, so Mum also benefited from the re-modelling, and a second bathroom on the ground floor, so that I didn't have to be carried upstairs to have a bath.

As Peter grew more skilled at handling the Tan-Sad, we began to make little expeditions round Bourne End. It was rather unnerving, being stared at. At CRX I was often invisible, which wasn't always a bad thing, and when I was out with Mum her adult aura neutralised curiosity. I don't know whether it was worse for me, protected from noticing most of the stares thanks to the immobility of my neck, or for Peter who was spared nothing. I don't think it was much fun for either of us.

There were compensations, of course, times when we could stare in our turn. One day we saw a dog with its head in what looked like a loudspeaker – actually a ruff to stop him scratching a healing wound or biting out stitches. We thought it must be a joke or some strange sort of advertisement. As if the dog from the record label, listening raptly to recorded sound, had finally climbed into the gramophone to find out where exactly His Master's Voice had taken up residence. We thought it was killing.

In the open air the whole business of pushing and being pushed worked against conversation, but when we stopped for Peter to get his breath back we had some fine chats.

He had obviously been giving my situation some thought. 'You should go to an ordinary school,' he said. '– you can come to my school if you like. It's all right. Except you're getting too old.'

'Yes, I'll be too old.' I had been dreaming of a proper school, all the same.

'And you should be able to go to prison. If you robbed a bank you should go to prison like everyone else.'

'They'd probably put me in the prison hospital, which isn't at all the same thing.' I hadn't given the question any thought before this moment. Now I began to feel cheated of my right to do time, hard time.

'What a swizz. But I was thinking . . . if you did rob a bank, the police should count to a thousand before they started chasing you. Then you'd have the same chance as everyone else.'

He was ahead of his time, really, was brother Peter. His philosophy of handicap was sophisticated in its own way. Equal rights plus a few courtesies.

With Peter's help I was able to resume my interrupted career of mischief. One day we got into rather a lot of trouble, but after all, I was owed. There had been years when I hadn't been in any position to get into trouble at all.

Being unsupervised and out of doors was intoxicating in itself. Fire was the specific lure, as so often – I've never understood why fire in the afterlife seems to be relegated to Hell, and defines it. As far I'm concerned, without fire it can't be Heaven.

Peter made a very willing lab assistant. The special equipment for one particular set of investigations was the empty tin of a Fray Bentos steak-and-kidney pie. I didn't approve of the pie, and had eaten only a little of the pastry, but I heartily approved of the tin. It was circular and had sloping sides. When washed up it made a very decent crucible. Peter had been hoarding candles for some time on my instructions, and now he wedged them all in the tin and lit them in rapid succession. Soon they started to melt together and flame became general. We had made one giant candle with multiple wicks. Then under my direction he fed more combustibles into the flames, scraps of old wax and torn-up bits of cloth, until the whole tinful was boiling and getting really hot.

We weren't being irresponsible. We were conducting our experiments outside in the open air, the way we knew we were meant to. We were behind the shed in the garden. The tin was safely on the ground, and we weren't touching it.

There was only one moment when the experimenter couldn't avoid getting close to the tin, and that was the moment when he was going to pour onto the tiny inferno a tablespoonful of cold water. The experimenter was really me, but Peter had to do the pouring. Doing things at arm's length isn't practical for me. The arm isn't a standard unit of measurement, and mine don't really count. I would operate Peter by remote control. I gave him the timing, saying, 'Ready . . . set . . . GO!!!'

Light blue touch paper and retire immediately. I'd given him a proper briefing. He knew that he had to pour the spoonful of water in with a single rapid motion, then run like hell.

Gratifying little bomb

It all worked quite beautifully. Nothing happened instantaneously. There was a fractional pause which allowed Peter to make his escape. In that pause, the seething wax seemed to be assessing the cold water that had been dumped into it with a sort of elemental incredulity. It held its breath. Then it exploded. There was a marvellous caustic burp, a great rising cloud of steam and ash, and boiling wax was richly deposited on our clothes and any flesh they didn't cover. I had the glorious sensation of having challenged Nature to a duel and survived. It was a draw. It's true that there was a scrap of cloth which landed on my lap still burning, but Peter easily patted it out. He was as exhilarated by our discovery as I was myself.

It was all throughly worth while. From candle-ends and a pie tin we had fashioned a gratifying little bomb. I suppose Peter must have been a bit worried about the incendiary wax-shower and the burning shreds in flight, because he confessed to Mum in dribs and drabs while she was putting us to bed. He was always a good boy. She said nothing about it. She didn't seem to take it in. She just smiled absently and said, 'I'm glad you two amused yourselves.' As if we'd been playing Scrabble.

The next day we did it all over again. Only this time a boy staying with neighbours insisted on being in on it. Parents didn't keep children on a tight rein in those days, even in cities, and the Abbotsbrook Estate was no city. We *told* him it was dangerous. We *told* him it was only for big boys. I suppose Howie was about five – not nearly old enough to understand science. We told him to stay far back but he wouldn't listen. Howie said if we didn't let him see he'd tell his mother we'd hit him.

That was too much for me, and I said, 'You'll really tell your mum that *I* hit you?' And he said, 'No I won't.' He pointed at Peter. 'I'll say that *he* hit me and you *bit*.' So we let him stay. Of course we didn't let him pour the water into the tin, but he stood right next to Peter, watching, and he wasn't so sharp at backing off.

He got very little of the wax on him, but of course he went howling off to his mother, and then she came round screeching, 'How *could* you burn my baby?' If Howie was five then he wasn't a baby, or alternatively, if he was a baby she shouldn't have let him out of her sight, should she? She wasn't being at all reasonable.

Howie's mum told the whole saga to Mum and soon Mum was bellowing, 'What in the world did you think you were doing, burning poor Howie?' A scolding can be just as bad as a scalding because you just have to stand there and pretend it doesn't hurt. However unfair it is.

Mum absolutely denied that we'd told her the day before what we'd been up to. 'Do you really think', she said, 'that I'd have let you play with fire if I'd known what you were doing, with or without Howie being there?' It's true we had been puzzled by how calm she was the night before. I suppose we twigged that she hadn't taken it in, but we'd told her just the same. Wasn't that the point? It wasn't our fault that she was hypnotised and not listening. And what were we supposed to do when Howie started pestering us and wanting to be in on the experiment? Tie him up?

We had discussed tying him up, as a matter of fact, Peter and I, but Howie was the sort of child who runs to his mother about everything, so he'd be off complaining about *that* the moment he was set free. So really it made quite as much sense to let him witness our experiment and take his chances. He might learn something, even if it was only to listen to what bigger boys said.

I couldn't seem to get the hang of how I was supposed to behave. Everybody kept on about how awful it was that I couldn't do normal things, but the moment I made a normal bomb they came down on me like a ton of angry bricks. Mum's face even looked like a brick when she shouted. I'd seen her plucking her eyebrows, anyway, hundreds of times, so I couldn't understand all the fuss about Howie's. She always said they grew back overnight.

Somewhere in this turbulent epoch I managed to find the time to fail my eleven-plus. Quite why we were all put in for this ordeal I don't know. The results wouldn't have made a difference to our futures either way – it's not as if there was a grammar school and a secondary modern both reaching out for us, waiting for our results to see which institution would get lucky. I dare say participation in the eleven-plus charade was (like the entirety of our education) no more than a legal requirement.

I failed the eleven-plus. I don't remember the details. Apparently I wasn't as clever as everyone said, or at least not good at getting my brain across to people I didn't know, who didn't know me. I don't even remember whether I used a pen, writing fast and with doctorish illegibility, or the typewriter, readable but painfully slow. Either way, in the separation of sheep from goats, I was officially a goat. I think we were all goats at CRX.

Not that it held me back. The eleven-plus was a sort of dummy exam, in my case at least. Failing it didn't hamper my progress, any more than passing it would have moved me on. It turned out that a new school had already been thought of, to provide secondary education tailored to my needs, or my body's.

I'd understood by then, without knowing the word, that Dr Ansell was an assimilationist. She felt that the disabled should – wherever possible – go to mainstream schools. She said she'd heard all the arguments about bullying, the sheer vulnerability of the handicapped (as we were then, before we became disabled), and she didn't think much of them. In practice it didn't happen. People got on with their lives. The arguments about bullying were all pretexts for a sort of fearful apartheid. It was touching that she assumed bullying would be a new danger for a child who had been a citizen of her little kingdom.

Even so, no mainstream school was proposed for me, by Ansell or anyone else. Perhaps I was just too disabled. I fell foul of the small print, of that 'wherever possible'. Ansell had a splendid motto, very enlightened for the period: 'Every child has his own disease.' Even so, my own disease seemed horribly classic. I was text-book – but an old text-book, a pre-war or even Victorian text-book, from before the arrival of steroids.

What I was offered wasn't a normal school. Still, if it was a school at all, if it wasn't a hospital lightly disguised, then it could only be more normal than what I was used to. 'More normal' would have to stand in for normal.

I had exhausted the educational possibilities of the school inside the hospital inside the Nissen huts in the grounds of the stately home, but I hadn't exhausted everything the place had to teach me. One thing I completely failed to spot during my time at CRX was that the place itself was one colossal clue. There were esoteric secrets on the premises beyond the ken even of the Famous Five. I didn't know that Nancy Astor was a Christian Scientist. Of course I also didn't know who Nancy Astor was, or what she had to do with CRX. I didn't know that she was the first woman to be elected an MP – well she wasn't, so I have that excuse for not knowing it. She wasn't the first woman to be elected an MP (who was a member of Sinn Féin campaigning from prison in Holloway) but she was the first to take her seat in the House.

I also didn't know at the time what a Christian Scientist was. If Christian Scientists had bombarded CRX with anything like the fervour of the Jehovah's Witnesses, I'd have been better informed. Nancy hadn't been raised in the faith but had seen the light of Mary Baker Eddy. Her husband Waldorf had seen it too, if only because it was bounced off the reflective surfaces of the formidable Nancy. If Nancy had taken up ritual cannibalism, Waldorf would most likely have gone along with it, not tasting the human sacrifices, necessarily (perhaps refusing with a wave of the hand when the plates were brought round), but ready with a toothpick afterwards, to help Nancy dislodge the human gristle from her teeth. So both of them adhered to a faith that says the pain is unreal – and then the moment a war comes along they volunteer their house as a hospital. It's more than a gesture. They pay the wages of thirty-odd people, Lady Astor helps on the wards.

She had her own style of nursing, admittedly – if she didn't rub salt into servicemen's open wounds, she certainly grated ginger over them. What she didn't do was tell them, as a good Christian Scientist should, that their pain was caused by Error and not real. If pain is unreal, why take pains to relieve it? Indifference would seem the better response.

So even in the foundation of the institution in which I lived for so long, with its two addresses and two pronunciations, there was a huge clue about the double nature of pain and the double nature of everything else. Both real and not real. Or (if that makes it simpler) neither. Neither real nor unreal.

Old Turps, the same headmaster who had been able to propose nothing better for my future life than work as a clerk, came to see me before I left the hospital. I didn't forget that he had indulged my phobias and kept me safe from Teddy boys as much as he could. 'If you go on to do great things,' he said, 'I hope you'll give us a mention' – consider it done.

Somewhere in this phase of life I had made an advance in my prayer technique. My relations with divinity were calmer. I'd stopped bargaining so nakedly. Now I was praying that if I was going to have pain in this life, and it seemed that I was, that I should have the pain all at the beginning, compressed, so that I could relax and enjoy what came afterwards. The way I phrased it to myself, and to God, was that I wanted to have all the gyp in a dollop. 'Gyp' came from *Mrs Dale's Diary*, I think, to which Mum had become addicted.

This was a real break-through for me, to be praying for what I already had. It was definite progress. My prayer wasn't disinterested, to be sure. It was a sort of bet, but when later in life I read about Pascal's Wager I felt rather sniffy about it. I didn't think it was particularly impressive, either intellectually or spiritually. Pascal's idea was that it made sense to believe in God and judgement, since if you were wrong there was no penalty, and if you were right there was a reward. Either you won or you didn't lose.

I see now that he was conducting a sort of mental experiment, which may even have included elements of teasing. At the time I felt it was really just cowardly to trick yourself into belief. My approach was a little subtler. Prayer showed no signs of being able to take the pain away, so I would devise a new style of prayer which would be self-fulfilling. It would seem already to be being answered, day by day. I had asked for pain, and here it was, but I could tell myself it came on my terms. I awarded myself the privilege of meaningful choice despite my absence of options. I took pain on myself, now, not as an ordeal or a sacrifice but as something more in the nature of an investment.

Dolls of the world

The Cromers and the Morrisons kept in touch for some time after I left CRX, though Sarah and I stopped being so close. The last time I saw her was as late as 1972. She was living in a Cheshire Home near Crystal Palace. The spark that made her Sarah seemed to be missing. She knew who I was, but I couldn't interest her in very much. She didn't always answer a question, and if she did it was as if she had to push the words out against some sort of internal resistance. Then her voice would tail away. Even Muzzie couldn't always get through to her.

Sarah lay in bed with her eyes on her prized possessions. Her doll collection had grown enormously. Now she had a magnificent mahogany cabinet with glass doors to house them all. Her ambition was to have a doll from every country in the world on those shelves. She was nearly there. I think there was only one more doll needed to complete her miniature United Nations.

The only signs of a new interest were the Crystal Palace supporters' scarves draped across the top of the cabinet, and I couldn't be sure they were Sarah's. They might have been something the carers had thought of to bring a bit of life to the room.

Sarah had more to say to her dolls than she did to people. Every now and then a carer would put a doll in her hands and then she would prattle away, almost like the Sarah I had known. She seemed to know what all her dolls were doing with their lives. They all had names, of course. She even knew what they did when she was asleep herself. She might call for Rita to be exchanged for Serafina, or Pushpa for Gita. Holding the doll in her arms, she would listen intently to what she had to say. She would say a few motherly words herself, give the doll a cuddle and then call for it to be put back in exactly the right place. Then she would call for another one.

The helpers at the home entered into Sarah's world whole-heartedly. This was greatly to the credit of the institution and its staff. It was also rather creepy. Maria said, 'Sarah! You haven't mentioned or spoken to your little Eskimo girl for ten days – I hope she's not starting to feel left out?'

'Oh yes Maria you're so right!' chirped Sarah. 'Oh do give me Polly straight away . . . Oh Polly darling, yes it's true I have been neglecting you, but I didn't mean to. It's just that you've been so good, you see. That doesn't always pay, you know! I'm afraid I've been terribly busy trying to keep the peace between Sally and Salim. Come and have a quick cuddle. I won't let you get too warm . . . What? Yes, I know you'd like me to keep you in the 'fridge, but if I did that I couldn't see you! And be fair . . . I have put you in the part of the cabinet that's nearest to the window and the fresh air. I'm afraid that will just have to do . . .'

I felt fatally grown-up compared to Sarah, and very sorry for her. I wanted to buy her that one last doll, but at the same time I had qualms about putting the finishing touch to someone's life's work. Her life's work was what it seemed to be. Best to leave her to get on with it. With the United Nations complete, what would Sarah have to look forward to? Academic question, as it turned out, since she died a few months later.

One isolated case isn't any sort of scientific sample. I have no evidence to back up my indictment of steroids, as they were administered in the 1950s and '60s, beyond the fact that my friend Sarah had a mental age of ten when I met her in the 1950s, and the same mental age in 1972. The drug had stopped her bones from hardening as much as mine had, but at the cost of making other things soft as well. By the time she died, Sarah had been prattling to her dolls for a good fifteen years. Steroids had stopped her growing up. They'd even stopped her from out-growing her toys. Thanks to the medication she was given, her second childhood came hard on the heels of the first. They were like the sentences tough-minded judges sometimes pass on hardened criminals when they want to make an example of them, running consecutively without remission.

4

No Such Word as Can't

There were definite things I wanted from a new school. At CRX the hospital was the sun and the school the moon. A lot of the time it had hardly been visible. It was a pale, almost theoretical presence. Education was required by law rather than pursued with passion. I wanted a place where lessons wouldn't just be fitted in around the routines of a hospital, where education wasn't always giving way to medical science.

The new school had a strange name. It was called The Vulcan School. It also had a sort of subtitle amounting to a technical description: 'A Boarding School for the Education and Rehabilitation of Severely Disabled but Intelligent Boys'.

When I had been told about Canadian Red Cross Memorial Hospital all I needed to know was that there was a school on the premises. Then I was happy to be on my way. After CRX I wasn't quite so trusting. I had learned to be afraid. Mum and Dad had to do a little selling of its advantages. There were three main attractions to Vulcan School, as they presented it to me:

1. It's in a lovely old castle, like something from a fairy tale. A famous explorer used to live there, but now it's a school for boys like you.

How like me? Exactly like me?

No, but boys who need a bit of help getting around and doing things for themselves.

2. The headmaster, Mr Raeburn, is the brother of the lady who does the puppets on television. Yes, that's right, Margery Raeburn pulls the strings for Andy Pandy.

3. Guess who helps the school to get money? Uncle Mac!

All of this was true. Farley Castle was indeed a crenellated pile, although built in the eighteenth century as a folly, rather than earlier on as a defensive stronghold. It had been owned by Colonel 'Mitch' Mitchell-Hedges, an adventurer and explorer (less romantically a collector of English silverware), who had lived there with his adopted daughter Sammy. The legend was that he never had less than half a million in cash on his person at any time.

The school had been founded by Marion Willis and Alan Raeburn. Alan had a special feeling for disabled boys – he had lost the use of his legs during the war when a tank rolled on him. And yes, his sister Margery held the strings of Andy Pandy and made him move. It wasn't a particularly dazzling piece of puppetry. Andy Pandy didn't move a lot more fluently than I did.

Points 1 and 2 didn't make this funny-sounding school seem all that attractive. Number 3 had more weight. Uncle Mac, alias Derek McCulloch, Chairman of the Board of Governors of Vulcan, was the most immediately familiar figure outside family for any British child of the time. He presented *Children's Favourites* on the radio (though plenty of people still said 'wireless'). He was the voice of Muffin the Mule. Uncle Mac pervaded Saturday mornings at CRX. We would listen raptly to the Light Programme when he was on. Admittedly much of the silence on the ward every Saturday morning was explained by the fact that one or more of us had written in to the BBC with a request for Uncle Mac. There wasn't an official league table, but everyone knew Sarah Morrison had had her name read out on the radio more than anyone else. That was Sarah all over.

Uncle Mac's catch-phrase was the way he signed off at the end of a programme: 'Good-bye children . . . . . everywhere.' It was the pause that made it so distinctive – that drawn-out ellipsis. Definitely five dots rather than three. Uncle Mac's radio programmes were central to our experience of radio and of life on the ward, and a school whose board of governors was chaired by this avuncular mystic couldn't help getting a boost in my mind.

The songs that Uncle Mac played came to carry a huge freight of emotion by association. Hearing one of your favourite songs on a

Saturday morning could make a difference to the whole weekend. I liked Danny Kaye's 'The King's New Clothes', because it was more or less rude. I liked 'The Three Billy Goats Gruff' because it was frightening. I liked 'Sparky's Magic Piano' because it showed someone else believed in magic. I liked 'The Animals Went In Two by Two' because it was easier than reading the Bible. I liked 'The Runaway Train' because of the happy ending (*the last we heard she was going still . . .*). I liked 'Mairzy Doats and Dozy Doats', despite its failure to win me friends at CRX, because it was in a sort of code. I liked 'The Teddy Bears' Picnic' because I thought they would be waiting for me in CRX woods, providing I could dodge the Teddy boys from Ward Three.

I liked 'I'm a Pink Toothbrush, You're a Blue Toothbrush' because the guru Max Bygraves helped me see that love doesn't mind if you're different. I liked 'A Windmill in Old Amsterdam' because there was no resisting the idea of mice in clogs. I liked Lonnie Donegan's 'My Old Man's a Dustman' because it meant I could sing in Cockney, even in earshot of Mum, without getting a scalding. I liked 'Little White Bull' for the same Cockneyphile reasons – I was careful to pronounce 'little' with the proper glottal stop as 'li'ul' – and also because I was in love with Tommy Steele. I kept asking Mum when I'd be old enough to have my hair dyed blond to match his. I liked Rosemary Clooney's 'This Old House' (she didn't realise how much she loved the house, and would be *really sorry* when she left it) because it served her right.

I loved 'Dem Bones Dem Bones (Dem Dry Bones)', for reasons that had nothing to do with the words. What got me was the bounciness of the rhythm, the thrilling male voices calling out in gospel style, and the percussion that mimicked clockwork, either running down or being wound up. *The hipbone's connected to the – thighbone, the thighbone's connected to the – kneebone.* I made no connection between the bones in the song and my own, which were very connected indeed.

Mum and Dad told me that Uncle Mac had lost an eye and part of a lung in the Great War, and then lost a leg in a car smash-up between the wars. I thought he must be clumsy as well as unlucky, but it was as if they were giving me a present. 'Isn't that wonderful?' they asked. Not wonderful that he was disabled, exactly, but wonderful that he led such an active life no one would know. He didn't let missing a few bits and pieces hold him back. It took a bit of getting used to, the idea that Uncle Mac and I were supposed to have things in common. I wasn't missing any bits, but so far being disabled was doing a grand job of holding me back. I was too disabled to be a doctor or a scientist or anything important, but somehow I didn't seem to be disabled enough to cut any ice with the *Busy Bee News*.

The Tin Triangle

The new place had to be better than CRX. 'I expect you'll miss having girls around,' said Dad, with a roguishness that wasn't really his style. He made it sound as if being the only boy in a group of girls, all of us disabled, made me a sultan with a harem. No I would not miss having girls around (I was forgetting my engagement to Sarah, of course, and being disloyal to Mary's memory). However bad boys could be, they could never be as spiteful as girls.

I made out to Mum and Dad that the Uncle Mac factor was the clincher, but there were other things going on in my mind. Peter with his love of planes filled me in on the school's name. The Air Force had three V-bombers – the Vickers Valiant, the Handley Page Victor and the Avro Vulcan. The Vulcan was their longest-range bomber. It could fly 4000 miles at 50,000 feet. It was also known as the Tin Triangle (which made me think of those less inspired pieces of technology, Ansell's tailor-made walking pods). As far as Peter was concerned, I couldn't do better.

For a long time, too, I had prayed to God for a boy companion whom I could love and who would be my special friend. I had strong ideas about this, not all of them derived from Enid Blyton. Boys played together and chummed up. When they had a scrap they would always seem to end up rolling on the ground, two as one, their legs interlocked and their arms wrapped round each other. My special friend was going to be physically normal or almost normal. Of course at the beginning we would spend a lot of time in tender loving embraces, but when passion had ripened into something more mature, the real quest would begin. It would be daring and danger-ous. He would fight the enemy on the physical plane and I would take care of the ghosts, spirits and ghouls. Vulcan School would be the ideal place to find this soul-mate, among the Intelligent Boys. The place was clearly the answer to my prayers.

My mind gave Vulcan School the thumbs-up, but my body had other ideas. It started playing a mean trick on me that I thought was ancient history. I had chewed those linen sheets and spat them out, I had frotted myself against them ecstatically, and now I was wetting them like a baby.

Rather surprisingly, bed-wetting attracted no punishment in CRX. My sheets were changed without complaint or reproach. I could even enjoy the state between waking and dream, that strange shoreline that can seem deeper than the sea. I could luxuriate in the feeling of warm wetness seeping all around, knowing the sheets would be changed before the pee got uncomfortably cold. I was very ashamed, all the same, and knew perfectly well that at Vulcan School this would never do.

I also snored incurably, a vice which I thought I could get away with in the absence of other night-time vices but hardly in combination. I was confident that boys, intelligent boys, would be more understanding and generally nicer than girls, but bed-wetting and snoring would hardly be a passport to big-boyhood. I was well enough versed in the literature to know that in boys' schools they gave you nick-names. They would be bound to come up with something that would advertise both my vices. I badly wanted to start with a clean sheet but I was sure I was doomed to swap Wally Snorts for something worse.

Snoring and wetting the bed. No great inventiveness would be required on the part of my fellow intelligent boys. They would call me 'Snorwetta' but no, 'r's and 'w's didn't really go together like that. They'd just drop the 'w' and I'd be known as . . . Snoretta.

A boy who sounded like a piggy version of Henrietta. I would never be allowed into proper boyhood, Julian-and-Dick boyhood. I'd be chained by girlhood again, as I had been at CRX, where a posh accent was considered girly. Ansell and some of the other staff had always said I sounded nice and not girly at all, but I hadn't been living and sleeping with Ansell, unfortunately.

The missing tweeny

In my time of limbo between institutions, when I hung between a hospital set up by someone who didn't believe in pain and a school that might have been named for my benefit by Bomber Command, there was one memorable day. The Mad Major put in a personal appearance at last – he was invited to lunch. Who by? It can only have been Dad. There was a conciliatory edge to his usual patterns of behaviour in the run-up to the event, as if he knew he had arranged something that went well beyond the call of marital duty.

Peter and I knew it was an important occasion. Each of them kept complaining about the fuss the other was making about something very ordinary. Mum said, 'I don't know why Dad is so keyed up about seeing this dull old friend of his,' but it wasn't every day she folded napkins into the tricky Bishop's Mitre shape, following the instructions in her old copy of Mrs Beeton's *Household Management*. The book was a cast-off of Granny's – in fact it was less a book than an oppressive hint, printed and bound. It was an old edition, old enough to list the duties of the 'tweeny', which included cleaning the back stairs. Every time she opened up the book Mum must have reproached herself for having neither a tweeny nor back stairs to turn her loose on.

Meanwhile Dad was saying, 'I don't know why your mother has to make such a song and dance about a visit from an old comrade-in-arms. Still, you know what she's like.' Indeed we did, but we also saw the look in Dad's eyes which meant he was wondering if he should ask her if his tie was smart enough. He might even be considering the drastic step of wearing the cuff-links she had given him for Christmas. Peter asked, 'Is he really mad? Is he doolally loony? Will he bark?' Mum said she wouldn't be surprised.

'Shall I call him Major Mad or Mad Major? Which is proper?'

That was going too far for Mum. 'Neither is proper, neither is polite. You'll call him . . .' – suddenly she didn't seem certain herself – 'Major Draper.'

'Kit is pretty relaxed about the "Mad Major" routine, m'dear,' Dad broke in. 'So he should be, with some of the things he's done in his time. And do you know, he's working on his life story for a book? It should make fascinating reading.'

Mum answered only with a sigh and told him to get out from under her feet. The most consistent strand in all the stories about the Major was his unreliability, and Mum took it for granted that he would be late. She had started issuing ultimatums soon after breakfast on the great day, saying, 'I hope you don't expect me to wait lunch for him – we eat at one sharp.' And then he arrived, soon after eleven o'clock. We could hear the gravel of the drive being displaced by unfamiliar wheels. Peter made to dash out, but Mum restrained him. Dad went out alone. The welcoming committee was a one-man show.

When the Major came in, I was shocked to see how old he was. He was closer to Granny's age than Dad's. I wasn't old enough myself to understand that someone who had held a pilot's licence since 1913 couldn't be any younger than that. I suppose he was in his late sixties. He was tubby, with a face that managed to be flabby and big-chinned at the same time. He was mainly bald. He wore thick glasses. His teeth seemed strange.

He looked from me to Peter and back again, as if he wasn't sure which was which. I've loved people for less – but the pantomime has to be done exactly right. He passed the test. Finally he fixed on me and said, 'You must be the son and heir.'

He turned to Peter and said, 'And you must be the runner-up.' There was a gleam around his teeth which was kindness, perhaps. The same gleam flickered in his eyes, behind the lenses which unkindly piggified them. 'I even think there may be a baby somewhere near.' This was a joke, since Audrey was just then screaming the house down. 'I know one of you chaps loves school and the other's not so sure. That's you, I fancy?' he asked, looking over at Peter. 'I'm shoulder to shoulder with you about that, old man. Hated every minute. Couldn't wait to get outdoors and into the open. Perhaps you feel the same way?' Peter was tongue-tied. Mum wasn't much better, when she came in carrying Audrey. She was at a double disadvantage, trying to quiet a baby and wearing her apron, red-faced from the heat of the kitchen.

The Major had hardly arrived before he swept Dad off with him to a nearby pub for what he called a 'sharpener or two', saying brightly that they'd be back in good time for lunch. This time Peter couldn't reasonably be restrained from dashing out to see the Major's car.

Unusually, Dad took control of the wheelchair – something normally that happened only on our nature-study expeditions with the Tan-Sad. Otherwise, though, I would have been stranded inside the house, and I enjoyed the rare paternal push.

The Major's car was an old-fashioned one with running-boards. He let Peter stand on one of them when he started off, driving very slowly and looking back anxiously to make sure he'd jumped off safely. Peter made a show of falling over and rolling in the dirt, but luckily he did it very unconvincingly, after a clean landing, so the Major and Dad could drive away with clear consciences.

Nothing had actively gone wrong as yet, but Mum was too far down the path of having a bad time to retrace her steps at short notice. By the time Dad and the Major rolled happily back just before one, she was seething. Dad seemed puzzled by her antagonism, but it was too late for him to be taking Lessons In Mum, though I could have taught him a few. It would certainly have been better tactics on the men's part to arrive shame-faced and contrite at half-past. There's nothing a martyr likes less than being ritually installed among the kindling, not tied to the post but grasping it firmly behind her back, and then no one having the common politeness to strike a match.

Ra Ra Rickerar

Normally I sat at the head of the table, since that was the only position from which I could follow events without the great effort of turning my head. Mum had decided that Dad should replace me just this once. In other circumstances Dad might have enjoyed this assertion of his theoretical dominance, but even his very moderate sensitivity to atmospheres was sending him danger signals.

I didn't mind losing my place, but I didn't want to miss out socially, and I had made Peter promise to install me in my wheelchair facing directly at the Major. The Major looked up in surprise as Peter trundled me in and lined me up at him like a small piece of artillery, primed ordnance which at this range could easily take his head off. Then he gave me an oddly shy smile, a wavering flag of good nature.

Mum's bad mood was clinched by the Major offering to say grace before the meal. 'We're not much for grace in this house,' she said, but the Major paid no attention. He offered to say Chinese grace on this special occasion – 'maybe the kiddies will like that.' He winked as he said so, a funny sort of wink. When Dad winked it was only the eyelid that moved, but when the Major winked he screwed up one whole side of his face. Of course he was right. We would love to hear Chinese grace. I adored everything to do with foreign languages, with anything I couldn't understand, and Peter wasn't going to be left out, now or ever.

To prepare himself for the high office of saying grace, the Major grabbed the napkin sitting on his side plate, in its smart Bishop's Mitre fold, and popped it on top of his shining head. It perched there unsteadily, so that he had to put up a hand to keep it more or less in place. He put his hands together and closed his eyes. We did the same, not really.

Then the Major moved his wrists apart so that it was only his fingertips touching, and his hands made a strange pyramid-like shape, which Peter copied. Even I had a go. His eyelids trembled as he looked out from under them, at our even more transparent pretence of inward raptness. Then he intoned in a great whisper: '*RA RA RICK-ERAR – REE PO NEE – FATTER KITTY WHISKERS – CHIT-TAPON CHITTAPON – CHINESE CHOO-CHOO!*'

That was Chinese grace. We howled with joy. We made him say it again. It was even better the second time, when we knew what was coming. We made him promise to say it one more time, before pudding. Twice more, please! Please!

After Chinese grace, we were his creatures absolutely, but Mum's face was coldly set as she busied herself with the soup ladle. Soup was partly a concession to me, since vegetarian soups didn't call attention to themselves in a way Mum wouldn't allow. On the other hand, I had to use a mug to drink it, which drew attention to my difficulties with spoons and liquids. I had offered to do my very best with a bowl, on this more formal occasion, but Mum must have realised that I would make an even less elegant impression methodically flicking celery soup over myself, very little of it reaching my mouth. My presence at table would always entail a certain amount of embarrassment.

Soup suited the Major perfectly. Before he started eating he removed his false teeth and put them on his side plate, discreetly

317

draping his napkin over them. He can have had no idea what his hostess suffered, watching that square yard of crisp linen being insulted. Mum gazed accusingly at the gleaming fabric, come down in the world so quickly, passing from Bishop's Mitre to theatrical prop to denture-cosy in a few short minutes.

After the soup the Major re-installed his teeth, catching my eye as he did so. In fact he brandished them at Peter and me, before he fitted them back inside his face. We were thrilled and delighted, though of course there was some disgust mixed in there too. It certainly made a change from Sunday lunch as it was played out week by week.

The Major had been doing without a napkin during the soup course, but now he picked it up by one corner and shook it open. He didn't even look at it, let alone make appreciative comments on Mum's deftness, the trouble she had taken, or the elegance of the result.

In theory she should have been able to balance her vulnerabilities. If she was outraged by the Major's infantile behaviour then she should have cared less about the possibility of me embarrassing her with my soup-mug or other utensils. But a sense of proportion was never really her style, and she experienced no difficulty in multiplying the negative emotions.

Peter was fascinated by the Major's dentures. 'Did you smash up your teeth in an accident?' he wanted to know. 'Did you have a plane crash?'

'Well, yes and no, young Peter. I did smash up my teeth against the control panel of a plane, yes. I didn't crash the plane, though. It crashed all by itself.'

'Wasn't there anybody flying the plane?'

'Not really, no. It's rather a long story . . .'

It was one we had to hear, of course. It turned out that the Major had been suffering rather badly from 'flu on the day of an air display. He hadn't wanted to disappoint the spectators. He didn't want to be a wash-out – and then he had simply passed out in the middle of a stunt. It was as simple as that. So the plane had crashed, but *he* hadn't crashed it. He had an alibi, being unconscious at the time.

The crash was no sort of reflection on the Major's flying abilities, apparently. He hadn't lost control of a plane, after all, he had only lost control of that other tricky piece of apparatus, Major Kit Draper, and his unreliable consciousness. It wasn't so much a crash as a faint in a plane, when he had happened to be at the controls. It didn't make him a duffer. A man could stand up and look himself in the face after a smash-up like that. Once he had healed up enough to walk about, of course.

To the civilians in his audience, this sounded rather an odd account of falling out of the sky, with so much emphasis on his unspotted record as a professional airman. Still, Dad was nodding sympathetically along, whether out of Services solidarity or because this really is the way pilots think.

Married to the skies

It's possible that Mum had made a huge moral effort at the beginning of the day, and had decided to give the Major the benefit of the doubt. Even if she had started out with an open mind, though, it would have snapped shut as sharply as her powder compact any number of times during the meal.

The Major did his best. When Mum brought the main course into the dining room, roast lamb, he had a compliment ready. Women at the time were known to live for compliments. Unfortunately the Major was a 'man's man' without much talent in that line.

He said, 'That looks absolutely delicious, Mrs Cromer, Laura I should say –' And then his face went waggish, '– though to judge by your waistline, you won't be eating much of it yourself.' There was a slightly uncomfortable silence. He had said something a little too true, when we were expecting soft soap and flannel. Mum was always forgetting to eat. There was a stark contrast between the way she plied us with food and the amount she took in herself, and she was beginning to look too thin for her own good.

During the main course (while I ate my vegetables) Peter asked our guest if there was a Mrs Mad – 'I mean a Mrs Major,' he added, rather embarrassed.

The Major said, 'Oh, I'm married all right – have been for years. Absolutely devoted.' Dad looked distinctly startled by this information. The English eyebrow is a peerless instrument for conveying extreme states of mind. Then the Major went on, 'The only thing is,

I'm married to the skies! As a matter of fact, this book I'm writing, that's what it's going to be called. *Married to the Skies*. It has a good ring, don't you think?' Mum gave a little snort, disguised as a momentary difficulty with chewing. It was clearly her feeling that the skies were welcome to the Major. Who else would have him?

While Mum was clearing away our plates and preparing to bring in the next course, the Major was unwise enough to mention that his favourite pudding was the rum omelette to which he'd been introduced in Barbados during the Second War, which was served in flames. After that, there was no holding Peter and me. I don't know which of us started it, but soon Peter was pounding the table with his spoon, and we were both chanting, 'Burning pudding! Burning pudding!' We were in an incendiary mood, and Mum's trusty apple pie didn't suit our mood.

The Major didn't stay long after lunch. He may even have had some dim sense that he had not made a good impression. It's unlikely that he realised he had blotted his copy-book on every one of its lines. He had sided with Dad and the pub against the sherry Mum had got in for the occasion (special glasses washed and ready). He had sided with her children and hilarity against her and decorum. He had failed to notice the starched compliment of her napery. He had sided with her figure against her food.

There was nothing he could do to reverse the trend of the meal. If he had brought someone back from the dead after pudding, Mum would have said he was just showing off.

She was sufficiently aggrieved to vent some of her feelings before the Major left. He was just starting up his car, and Peter was already jumping up and down, hoping for the earlier treat to be repeated. She leaned over his window and said, distinctly, 'Major Draper, do you mind not offering Peter another ride on your running-boards? We prefer him not to be given treats that John can't share.' The Major looked off at an odd downward angle while this chastisement registered, and his crumpled old face wore a baffled frown.

'Quite right too,' he mumbled, as he slid the car into gear. I thought for a moment he was going to say, 'Thank you for having me,' the way we had been taught, even (or especially) when we'd had a very bad time indeed.

The ban on excitements I couldn't share was a principle coined for the occasion. If it had been enforced, after all, Peter would have gone very short on treats – but Mum wasn't above resorting to foul play when the situation called for it.

Dad must have seen that there were bridges to be mended, or he would hardly have volunteered to help with the washing-up. On this special occasion she washed and he dried. Normally he refused, by saying, 'M'dear, if you use water of the proper temperature everything dries by itself. Why don't we wash up turn and turn about?' And Mum would reply, 'You forget, Dennis, that I've seen the results of your washing-up. I'd rather do it myself and have some confidence in the results.'

Now he was humble as he rolled up his shirt-sleeves and picked up the tea-towel. The intention may have been to make peace, but as they did the washing-up together they had one of their few actual rows. Normally they shared the house without being together very much. They could both be in the garden at the same time, but each in a separate kingdom, Dad doing a bit of digging while Mum gathered herbs. Dad always had the refuge of the shed and the garage.

They could go for months without sharing a routine, but now they were locked together for the duration of the chore. Neither of them had the option of quietly moving off or pretending not to hear something. If in the course of conversation Mum chose to give him a good scrape, as if he was a plate encrusted with dirt, there wasn't very much he could do about it.

'Your friend the Major', she said, 'has a bit of a nerve talking about the War, I must say.' It was true that the Major had referred to global conflict, but only as a backdrop to his activities, not really as a historical event in its own right.

'What do you mean, m'dear? Kit served his country as much as anyone.'

'Everyone knows he was practically a Nazi.' She pronounced the hated word, as quite a few of her generation did, with a soft 'z', to rhyme with a word Dad sometimes used for the lavatory, and which she claimed to find supremely disgusting. The khazi.

'You've got Kit all wrong – he was a double agent. He was pretending to sell aviation secrets to the Nazis but it was all above board.

When they approached him he went straight to British Intelligence. It was all given the go-ahead by the head of MI5. Percy Sillitoe. The Top Man.' That phrase still had a little residual power in our family.

She said, 'So why did the Nazis think he'd help them in the first place? Why did they go to him? No smoke without fire. Oh, I remember now. Wasn't it because the Major had already given lectures saying how wonderful they all were?'

Dad looked very uncomfortable. He rubbed away at the dish he was drying, looking intently at one spot, as if Mum might have left a speck. 'That was in peacetime, m'dear. Honest mistake. Can't hold that sort of thing against a fellow. He was short of cash at the time, and they gave him three pounds a lecture. He only did it for the money.'

His second family

He must have known he was serving the Major up on a plate, ready for carving. 'All things considered, Dennis, I'd rather he spoke up for the Nazis because he believed in them. And as for money, some people will always be short of it.'

Mum herself was thrifty, and would ration her treats or even forfeit them if need be. Dad, though, regarded his pleasures as sacred, and had never been able to limit his consumption of cigarettes. Mum would often tell him he had smoked his way through a whole house. Sometimes she would bounce the comment off me – 'John, your father has smoked his way . . .' Turning a house into smoke was a rather mystical achievement, to my way of thinking, but I had enough sense to realise that Dad wasn't being praised.

Now she returned to the attack. 'I expected your friend the Major to be shabby, Dennis. I make allowances – but that man was actually rather dirty.'

'Don't be hard on him, m'dear. He's fallen on hard times – going through rather a bad patch. Perhaps this book of his will change his fortunes.' This time Mum's sniff was undisguised.

So Mum got the last word over the kitchen sink, or at least the last sniff, on the day the Major came. Really the meal could hardly have gone better, from her point of view, unless Dad had dropped one of the best plates while doing the drying-up.

Yet she didn't really seem to relish her triumph. Of course, the Major was an impossible friend for any married man. No wife could sincerely enjoy having him as a guest, even a wife more tolerant and secure than Mum. But still he left an uneasy atmosphere behind. I suspect that the wrong thing about the Major from Mum's point of view wasn't his supposed treasonable sympathies. It wasn't as a Nazi that he set the alarm bells ringing but as a bachelor. He didn't represent the menace of Fascism but the temptation of the single life. Rolling up any time he pleased, disparaging good food, treating folded napkins as if they were no better than fancy hankies. And if the Major was Married to the Skies, then so had Dad been. Mum had tried to come between him and the clouds, and so had I, but it wasn't at all clear that we had succeeded. We were his second family, and the Raff was still the first.

School for plastics

My new school was hard to find, as if it took its resemblance to an enchanted castle seriously. The Cromer party in the Vauxhall got completely lost. The name of the school felt unnatural on the tongue, which inhibited us from asking directions. After we had gone round in circles three times Mum asked a farm worker where Farley Castle was.

The farm worker said, 'OO-arr! That'll be the school for plastics will it? Your littl'un goin' there be he? Well good luck, Sonny, that be a right rum place and no mistake!'

Some allowance has to be made, in the way this story has been embellished in the passing on, for the incrementally yokelising tendencies of Mum's ear and class assumptions. I was too keyed-up myself to listen properly, but the man's speech did seem pretty rough. It's just that I think I'd remember if he'd actually been chewing straw or scratching his head with the tines of a rake.

When we finally set eyes on The Vulcan School, that first day, Mum cried out, 'It really does look like a fairy-tale castle, doesn't it, Dennis? Don't you think so, John?' Well, yes I did, but not everything that happens in fairy tales is nice.

When the Vauxhall drew up on the school gravel Mr Raeburn came out to greet us, with his co-principal Miss Willis. Raeburn had distinctive eyes, grey with just a hint of blue. I had been alerted to his disabled status, which was presented (as usual) as a wonderful treat for me, as if he had let his legs be crushed by a tank just to make me feel at home. He managed his sticks very well, making progress in a series of fluent lurches. It was actually Miss Willis, vast and motherly, who moved more awkwardly.

I would have liked to leap out of the car to shake hands, but if I had been able to do that I wouldn't have been accepted as a pupil in the first place. I had to wait to be helped. Raeburn and Miss Willis didn't make me feel awkward by crowding round the car, but they couldn't avoid making me feel awkward by hanging back politely until I was helped to the upright. It was a sunny day, and I had to screw up my eyes to make out with any clarity these looming blobs of authority.

It was important to me to walk unaided at this point, asserting my marginal claim to biped status. I did my level best. I even had a crack at shaking hands. Then I had to accept the convenience of the Tan-Sad, since the gravel was wide and there was a lot of ground to cover.

When I had left CRX I was asked to return the wheelchair in which I had spent most of my time in that place, but there was no demand for the Tan-Sad, so I kept it. I was hoping my new school would provide a superior vehicle.

A young man came up to us, and was introduced to me as Roger Stott. Raeburn said that he would be showing me round and answering any questions. He seemed unnecessarily tall and handsome.

'Are you a teacher, Sir?' I managed to ask, and he laughed and explained, 'No, I'm one of the ABs. Able-bodied pupils. I have asthma. That's usually what's wrong with the ABs. Apart from having to do most of the work of running the school.'

No one had alerted me to the fact that there would be physically normal, strapping great boys roaming all over my nice disabled school. When Roger Stott looked at me, I felt as I had at CRX when Mr Fisk first took his pictures, agonisingly naked, though he had large eyes with a lot of warmth and sparkle in them. He had celebrity looks, somehow, without actually reminding me of anyone.

Roger pushed the Tan-Sad, and then with him behind me I felt more or less clothed again. There was a lot to see. The estate wasn't in the Cliveden class, but it had nine acres of grass and woodland. There was no other house in sight of the Castle. Pupils had no sense of being overlooked. That was very much what Raeburn and Miss Willis had been looking for when they placed their advertisement in the *Sunday Times*, and the then owner, Colonel Mitchell-Hedges, had responded. There were trees, Spanish chestnuts and oaks, screening the grounds from the road, and great masses of rhododendrons. There was also a yew hedge, tall and very gloomy, with the edges of a sign just visible, half over-grown. Roger told me it had YEW HEDGE – POISONOUS TO HORSES written on it, but disappointingly the few horses that passed through never seemed tempted to try it.

Are you sleeping with me?

I had decided that I had only one slim chance of escaping the fateful nick-name of Snoretta, and that was to make friends instantly – before bed-time. I had only a few hours. I was in a hurry to establish who would be sleeping within range of my snoring and the whiff of my pee, so I asked Roger Stott the question whose importance dwarfed all others. 'Are you sleeping with me?'

I blushed and rapidly translated the question into what I thought was the universal school idiom. 'Are you one of the chaps in my Dorm?' 'I don't know where you're going, exactly,' said Roger. 'If you're Blue Dorm, then yes. But don't worry about that – we'll get you settled in later. Right now I'm here to show you around. You'll soon get used to it.' I tried. All the same it was frustrating not knowing who would be in my dormitory yet, the all-powerful peers, my judges.

Roger showed me the area at the front of the Castle where games were played. There were a couple of go-karts which were brought out on special occasions. To start with, he said, they had been fitted with governors to limit their speed. The boys had gone on strike until they were removed. There hadn't been any serious accidents, though one boy had panicked and forgotten how to stop. Luckily he had the sense to run into the bushes, not out of the drive and onto the road. It was reassuring to hear that there was room for mishap and possible disaster at this new school. The normal dangers.

325

There was archery, too. Roger Stott looked at my arms rather doubtfully and said that wheelchair shinty – hockey for hooligans – might turn out to be my game. I thought this was an activity in which I would be pushed by an AB, perhaps by Roger himself, and tried to look forward to it.

He showed me the area round the side of the Castle where cars were parked. For school expeditions there was a Bedford Transit van, but it had no room for wheelchairs. I could look forward to being manhandled into the back, while the folded chairs were loaded onto a trailer knocked together by a local garage.

Then Roger Stott took me inside and showed me a sort of cubicle, a fairly dismal space but one without which the Castle could hardly last a day as a school for the disabled. This was the lift. All the dormitories were upstairs.

Farley Castle may have had the privacy Raeburn and Miss Willis were looking for, but it was desperately short of amenities. You could say it was a folly twice over – once when it was built and all over again when it was converted, in the teeth of its unsuitability for the purpose, into a school for the disabled. The school itself was disabled, and there were aspects to living in a fairy-tale castle which came close to a living nightmare. CRX had been much more practical in disabled terms, being an enormous bloody bungalow straggling along a corridor, with treacherous slopes and any number of traps but no actual stairs.

The lift at Vulcan wasn't even big. It was nowhere near big enough to serve the needs of such a place, and had been squeezed in by the sacrifice of half the space of the back stairway. It had a weight limit of only 350 lb. Roger Stott explained that it was very slow, when it worked at all. 'When the engine's kaput,' he said, 'old Rabies has to crank the mechanism by hand. I can tell you he gets awfully red in the face!' Old Rabies! I was thrilled to be at a proper school at last, with official nick-names and everything.

When the school started up, there hadn't been a lift at all. Admittedly there had only been one pupil, so it was hardly a problem. This was the legendary Kim Derbishire, prime mover in Vulcan's creation myth. I would hear a lot about him in the days to come. Kim was pretty much able-bodied, having only infrequent epilepsy and mild spasticity in one arm and a leg. He could help with washing-up, cleaning and even carpentry. In keeping with the active role he played at the school, he had always called the co-principals Marion and Alan. Roger said he still visited the school every so often. One day I might meet him.

As he showed me the hall where we would be taking our meals, Roger passed on some of the colourful history of Farley Castle. There was a Grey Lady who had lost her lover while alive, and came looking for him every so often after her death. When a new boy arrived at the school, she had the habit of seeking him out to ask if this stranger had any news for her. You'd think I'd have grown out of childish scares by this stage, after the years of nonsense about Vera Cole, but I was thoroughly alarmed. It was going to be hard enough to keep the bed dry that night without a supernatural visitation.

Roger went into a little more detail. 'The Grey Lady drags her chains behind her as she searches for her loved one. I don't know why she should be dragging chains, myself, the daft old thing . . . in fact, I've heard it said that her chains sound more like someone rattling an old sweet tin full of keys and coins. And she's learned to imitate the voices of the boys.'

'However does she manage that?' I asked. I wasn't cottoning on very quickly to Roger's kind hints of reassurance. He had to spell things out more clearly.

'The Grey Lady visits after lights out on the first night of term. About 9.30. And when all the new boys are quaking in their beds, she recites her poem. It's not a bad poem, actually – I suppose she's had plenty of time to get it right. Then she gives out the most blood-curdling howl. It's so loud it almost sounds like a whole lot of people howling.' He lowered his voice. 'And you'd better be a good little chap, and scream along with the rest of the new bugs.'

He took pity on me, that's what it comes down to, and initiated me into the hoax. Did he really say 'new bugs', or was that something I'd picked up from my reading? Perhaps it was something I demanded to be called, on my first day of secondary school, my first real school-day, the ritual insult that certified my belonging.

I don't exactly remember when Mum and Dad left, which suggests that the induction process was smoothly managed. I had no sense of being abandoned. And as evening drew on, I was buoyed up by the knowledge of the Grey Lady ordeal which was in store for all the unsuspecting new bugs but me. I was also so tired that I thought I might sleep through her visitation anyway.

At supper I had a chance to assess the full range of the school's intake. There was a large handful of able-bodied boys like Roger Stott, who helped with the actual running of the place, and there was a small handful of boys who could do next to nothing for themselves. These were the ones with degenerative disorders, who needed help even to eat. It was Vulcan's proud boast that it imposed no upper limit on the severity of its pupils' condition, though they should at least be stable. That was hardly the case with these few wan souls, fading away almost visibly. The mouths to which food was lifted in patient spoonfuls hardly reacted to the approach of nourishment.

Roger poured me a glass of water from a large jug, but he didn't meet my eyes. I wasn't disappointed by that – though if I was going to drink without help I was going to need a more manageable vessel, something with a handle. It fitted in with what I expected from a real school. Roger had broken a rule by telling me about the bogus haunting. I cheerfully accepted that he might never acknowledge me again.

As bed-time approached, I found that Roger hadn't been exaggerating when he told me that the lift was hopelessly slow. The problem wasn't simply the speed at which it moved. There was only room for one wheelchair at a time, and even so the foot-plates had to be removed. Some of the boys needed electric wheelchairs, which didn't have removable foot-plates, so those pupils had to be transferred to a pushing chair for the journey up a level, while their chairs stayed below or were carried upstairs separately. The Tan-Sad, despite its lack of motor, was actually bulkier than an electric machine, so I had to be transferred myself. The master in charge looked at it with something like fascination. 'That's a very interesting buggy you've got there, I must say. Perhaps you won't mind swopping it for something a little nippier?' I wouldn't mind at all. In fact I couldn't wait.

Even in a pushing chair riding in the lift wasn't comfortable. Passengers with working knees could tuck their legs neatly away, but I had to be propped up almost vertically to fit in the cage. Vulcan was a small school, but it took a good three minutes to get even a pushing wheelchair into the lift and up to the first floor, so the evening transfers (and of course the reverse journeys in the morning) took up a great deal of time.

My new home was in fact the Blue Dorm, and Roger was the AB assigned to it, which was thrilling, but I knew better than to presume on his acquaintanceship. My peers must judge me, and Roger would not intervene. As I lay in my bed after lights out in my new home, getting used to the dark and fearfully trying to gauge my bladder's intentions, a voice spoke out. It wasn't the Grey Lady making an early entrance. There was nothing other-worldly about the voice or what it said. It came from the boy in the next bed. What he said was a single word. He said, 'Rip.' I thought I knew what he meant, I certainly hoped so, but I didn't dare to respond.

A purty fair shake-down

There was a pause, and then another voice said 'Ned.' Then I knew for certain what was coming next, and I said 'Kelly' at the same time as the fourth boy in the room. Some sort of game had started, but I didn't know what kind, or what came next. I waited in high excitement. Then the first voice said, more confidently, 'Waaaal, this seems like a purty fair shake-down, pardners . . . think the posse heard us?' And we were off.

Television had ridden to my rescue. God bless television. Television had taken the pressure off my bladder. Those little dorms were natural settings for story-telling and play-acting. A television series gave us our cast list, and we were off. What a relief after all my fears! We rode the range. We guarded the wagon train. We pronounced 'coyotes' to rhyme with 'winter coats'. From that night on, the cue for the game was always the same. One: Rip! Two: Ned! Three: Kelly! I was completely caught up in our Western universe by the time the Grey Lady came for us with her box of coins and keys.

Her poem went like this:

I am the Ghost of Farley Castle
For fifty years wrapped up in a parcel.

329

> The string was undone, I was let loose
> And now I'm out to COOK YOUR GOOSE!

I couldn't wait to get the dutiful screaming out of the way, and to head back to Indian Territory. The sheets were coarse after the linen at CRX but the company was kind, and the sheets stayed dry. It turned out after all my fears that I didn't normally even need a pee in the night, but if I really got desperate I just called out for Roger Stott's help. Nocturnal enuresis put its ugly head below the parapet, and I stopped worrying about waking up wet. I think it's the worry that makes the wetness.

Roger's tenderness in alerting me to the ghost hoax seems to me, looking back, like the first gentle waft of the new decade. Just because he had been severely scared on his first night in a new place (presumably) was no reason to pass the trauma on. It was 1961, but the 'sixties were a decade which was a long time getting started and a long time dying down.

In other respects Vulcan was lodged firmly in the 1950s, perhaps even earlier. There wasn't a school uniform as such, but if a boy was able to wear a tie, he was expected to do so. If you couldn't tie it yourself, like me, then an AB would do it for you. The knot had to be pulled good and tight. I asked if there were any exceptions, and it turned out that there were, but they didn't cover my case. Exceptions were made for those with tracheotomies. If you were breathing through your neck rather than your nose, you were exempted from wearing a tie. So we were spared the sight of ties fluttering in the tracheal breeze or being inhaled dangerously into a makeshift orifice, where a door had been opened in a boy's throat.

Asthmatics didn't have to wear ties, but were expected to sport cravats instead. If they were having a particularly wheezy patch they could go to a matron, who might let them off altogether. Then they could go open-necked.

One particular boy called Paul Dandridge had been so badly affected by polio that he could only breathe by gulping down air – we called it his 'frog breathing' – and not at all at night without the aid of a respirator. He still had to wear a cravat, unless perhaps he was officially exempt but had decided to set a good example.

330

When the weather was warm we were allowed to loosen our ties (providing there were no important visitors). If we had lessons outside or went on expeditions, the more indulgent teachers would let us take them off. By 'take them off' I always mean 'get someone else to take it off', of course. And all this in a school whose whole reason for existing was to make daily life easier for disabled boys!

I had only been at Vulcan for a week or so when I woke up with a pain in my lower right side. I hadn't really settled in at the school, and I was already feeling rather sorry for myself. Is it possible that I was missing CRX? Perhaps even Ivy and Wendy seemed reassuring figures from a peaceful past, and a place where I had known the ropes. Here I was all tangled up in them.

First a nurse came along and was sympathetic, and then an unfriendly one came and told me I must be namby-pamby to be making such a fuss about a little stomach ache. I'd been called many things at CRX, Posh and Dropper and Archie Andrews, but I'd never been called namby-pamby and I was offended. The physical pain got no better, and I couldn't eat. The second nurse, who was called Judy Brisby, came back to see if I was still being namby-pamby, but I said I wanted to see the first one, the nurse who had been so much friendlier. Judy Brisby told me firmly that I was mistaken if I thought there were any nurses at Vulcan at all. Didn't I understand that this was a school and not a hospital? There were matrons here, day matrons and night matrons, little matrons and one Big Matron who was in charge of all, but there were no nurses of any description.

I could muster enough bolshiness, despite the pain in my side, to point out that there were matrons at hospitals too, so it was a funny word to choose if you wanted people not to think of hospitals. I also said that if there were only matrons in the school then I wanted to see the *other* matron. In fact the biggest available matron.

Judy Brisby muttered that I should learn to stop answering back if I knew what was good for me, but she did eventually do as I asked. When the Big Matron came, she was very nice, but she didn't have the incandescent authority of Matron at CRX. I couldn't imagine her saying, 'I am the School!' under any circumstances. That was clearly the prerogative of the co-principals, of Raeburn and Miss Willis. Still, the Big Matron, who was called Sheila Ewart, did manage to see that I wasn't malingering.

I hate to admit it, but Judy Brisby wasn't altogether wrong. I had been conditioned by my long residency in a hospital. It hadn't occurred to me that there wasn't a medical staff at Vulcan. It really was what I had said I wanted: a school. Getting what you want always takes a bit of getting used to.

On the other hand, I was right about thinking I had a pain in my side. Sheila Ewart called out the local GP, who was Vulcan's only medical resource. He in turn called out an ambulance to take me to hospital, since I had appendicitis.

The ambulance took me to a hospital, all right. It took me all the way back to CRX. I was back in those very familiar surroundings. No better cure exists for nostalgia than abrupt return to the idealised scene. In my case I was also helpless and in pain, which worked to restore defects of perspective. I was in a familiar hospital but a strange ward – Men's Surgical, I think. Very soon I was nostalgic for the new school I hardly knew.

Apparently the appendix was severely inflamed and had come close to bursting during surgery. On the other hand, I've never met anyone who's had appendicitis without being told the same story. Perhaps it's a standard piece of description, medical boiler-plate which makes both doctors and patients feel they've been caught up in a heroic intervention.

I came round from the anæsthetic with a lot of pain. I was warned that defæcating was going to be very painful. 'Oh, and another thing,' the doctor said. 'Don't laugh whatever you do. That hurts a lot.' I thought I would be able to avoid laughter. I could barely muster a polite smile for the doctor, and I was safe from any fiercer pangs of amusement.

I had been looking forward to getting a scar, which was one of the few consequences of illness that had eluded me to date. It was a long wait. The incision stubbornly refused to heal. I ended up being 'off' for the rest of term. It particularly grieved me that my first school report was such a wash-out. There had been no such things as reports at CRX, so this was my first ever, and I had wanted a glowing testimonial to my intelligence, charm and powers of application. I wanted a written record of my virtues. No one could promise me an actual career, so I set great store by distinguishing myself in the school equivalent.

I can't blame the authorities at Vulcan – I'd only had a handful of lessons, after all. The most the co-principals could say in all conscience was that I seemed 'an alert and cheerful boy'. They looked forward to getting to know me better.

Pecking obedience

I was soon bored to tears at CRX, though Ansell was kind enough to look in on me. I put sustained pressure on Mum to give me a convalescence present. I had my heart set on the miracle toy of the period, the Doodlemaster. 'It's suitable for anyone from eight to eighty and it'll give me hours of instructive amusement,' I told her, familiar with the sort of things it said on the boxes toys came in, and knowing the royal road to a parent's heart and pocket. She gave in before I drove her round the bend, but only just before.

It's impossible to convey at this distance the mystique of the Doodlemaster. The best way of describing it might be as a Stone Age video game. It looked like a flat little television of red plastic, with two white knobs. Between them these knobs controlled the movement of a stylus which pressed on the underside of the screen and scraped off an aluminium-powder coating to make patterns. Your design was restricted by the impossibility of either correcting mistakes or lifting the stylus off the screen. When you had finished your drawing, after everyone had politely goggled at it and guessed what it was, you turned the Doodlemaster upside down and gave it a good shake, to redistribute the silvery grains ready for the next drawing.

This was an absurd choice of toy to beguile my convalescence, though I had only myself to blame. What it was in essence was a wrist-humbling apparatus. Children with two fluent and flexible arms and hands were reduced to the level of robot toddlers with crayons bolted to their fists. Each wrist was demoted to providing a single element, vertical or horizontal, of a complex movement. It took even gifted students hours to be able to produce a passable diagonal, let alone a flowing curve. Those fabled Zen Masters we're always hearing about, who think nothing of drawing a perfect circle with a single brush-stroke, would have been driven to foaming fury by the frustrations of the machine.

My wrists were humbled already, and it was hard labour for me to get even a straight line out of the Doodlemaster. Soon my fingers ached with futile twiddling. My right hand was the more adept, since the elbow on that side had movement, but accomplishment on the Doodlemaster was necessarily on the level of the weaker arm. My right wrist had no power to raise my level. Instead the left one dragged me down. It was even more humbling when I had to ask passing nurses to turn the fiendish device upside down on my behalf, to give it the ritual shaking that prepared the screen for my next abject failure of doodling.

Essentially it was a machine that simulated disability, by making a simple accomplishment daunting, and I was the last boy in the country to need that challenge just then. I already knew what it was like to have cursive shapes clear in your mind, and to produce only jagged scratches. That was my experience of hand-writing. I so much preferred the pecking obedience of a typewriter to anything my fingers could manage unaided.

The Doodlemaster passed automatically into the suppler hands of Peter, without actively being given to him, when I came home from hospital. Soon he could do a passable Egyptian pyramid, while my drawings in that line were more in the stepped, Mayan style. They were ramshackle ziggurats. Peter would sit with the Doodlemaster and the toddling Audrey both on his knee, allowing her to work one knob with both little fists. It was clear that soon even the baby of the family would out-perform me on my convalescence toy.

Shortly afterwards the makers of the Doodlemaster were taken over by an American company and the device was renamed the Etch-a-Sketch. My only consolation in the whole episode was that at least I owned a first-generation machine.

Audrey was a very watchful child. She had a lovely smile, but from the moment she discovered her frowning muscles those were the ones she used most. From the start it was as if she had set herself to cracking the code of the strange family in which she found herself. I wished her luck with that ambitious and deceptive project.

If Mum had hoped for a child who would never leave her orbit, unlike her boys who were bound sooner or later to join the world of men, then she was disappointed almost from the start. Mum proudly announced Audrey's first word as 'Mum'. In fact it turned out to be 'merm', her version of 'worm'. She loved the worms in the garden, and would bring them indoors at every opportunity. Dad was delighted by her interest in the natural world, though of course it was too early to tell if she was a little biologist or just a little madam. I don't know whether Audrey ever ate her beloved merms, or even ate much dirt, but sometimes she would come in with her mouth streaked with mud. Perhaps she knew by instinct what would agitate Mum most.

Mum was having a hard time with Audrey just then, during my convalescence. This was a toddler who was just beginning to get into everything, and would resort to tremendous tantrums if thwarted. Mum couldn't do anything with her. I had the brain-wave of taking some of the microscopic sweeties called hundreds and thousands, dividing them by colour (which was a bit of a fag, admittedly) and then arranging them in separate compartments of my Junior First Aid Kit – one of my most treasured possessions, a Christmas present which I was slow to out-grow. Then I would look at the bawling Audrey, make great play of selecting the colour appropriate to her mood, and balance a single tiny pill on my finger.

She would come over to take it from me, calmer already. Her mood sweetened and stayed sweet. I had discovered some sort of colour cure – call it chromotherapy by placebo. Cromer therapy, even. The effect was so marked that Mum thought it somehow abnormal. She asked me to stop dosing Audrey with magic beans, and got Dr Flanagan to prescribe something instead. Flanny gave her Distaval, the brand name of thalidomide. Which worked perfectly well, I admit. It's a valid drug as long as you aren't pregnant.

It must have been at about the same stage of my convalescence that Peter taught me a huge lesson. He was being given a lesson himself at the time, and I don't think he ever knew how much he taught me that morning. It was a Saturday, and he was enduring the piano lesson which was perhaps the low point of his week. Dad was reasonably musical, and even played the organ for services in Little Marlow Church. The vicar was a Mr Jayne, who had the mannerism of ending prayers with the formula, 'a-through Jesus Christ Our Lord'. I pointed this out to Peter, and from then on we listened out for that moment, beginning to giggle before there was anything to giggle at. It sound like a holy sneeze.

At Dad's insistence Peter was sentenced to piano lessons, but he didn't prosper at the keyboard. Now I listened in on his lesson, though that makes it sound as if I made a positive choice. It was more that I didn't go to the mighty effort of moving out of earshot. From CRX I knew the layout of the keyboard, and even the names of the notes, but of course I was never in the running for lessons of my own.

There was a note in the music which Peter was playing that never quite happened. He seemed to hit every possible note on either side of it, and then his teacher would say 'Again,' not with irritation but with a sort of suppressed sigh. Irritation would have been more bearable.

In my mind I felt I could see his hand making the required stretch. In fact I could see my own hand – my hand as it should have been – striking the note fair and square. It seemed very unfair that I had the musical awareness and Peter the working parts.

I lived with this comfortingly tragic view of destiny for perhaps as long as ten minutes. Then it occurred to me that Peter might be seeing in his mind exactly what I saw in mine, his hand reaching for the right note. It's just that he couldn't make his mental image into a reality. In that respect we were as one. Despite their differences of constitution the brothers were looking down at an identical disobedience. Was it likely that I was the only intuitively musical soul in the family, and the only one who couldn't address the keyboard competently? Life wasn't fair, it seemed to me, but its unfairness followed certain rules.

This was my opportunity to realise that there was no difference between our two ways, Peter's and mine, of not being able to play the piano. We just weren't very musical as a tribe, we Cromers, even Dad. I think he liked the organ because all the stops and controls reminded him of a cockpit. It was a primitive flight simulator. Returning to my own case: there was no buried treasure of talent buried in my disqualified body. Underneath the disability my inability was intact.

Of course none of this was neatly thought out. It came in a rush of conviction, a brain event like the opposite of a stroke, a reverse aneurysm. My awareness of one aspect of 'reality' had been closed off by a sort of self-imposed mental clamp, which had now simply fallen away. I felt the free flow of blood through a fresh set of thoughts. Shortly after that, to his profound relief, Peter stopped taking lessons.

On top of its sheer folly, my demand for an appendicitis present had ruined the economy of Christmas. The Doodlemaster pretty much broke the bank. For Christmas proper, and birthday proper, I had to make do with a modest book token. I think I bought myself a bumper dose of Narnia, but however exciting the stories I read at home, I couldn't wait to be back at Vulcan. Already I was nostalgic for those days which only really began at lights out, when the curtain went up on the latest improvised instalment of Western adventures, staged by our little after-hours sagebrush repertory theatre in deepest Berkshire. Bandit country.

At New Year Mum took me to the Theatre Royal, Windsor, as a treat. She had bought the tickets months ahead. I loved going to a show and wasn't in the least fussy, though Dad said it was only ever drawing-room comedies at the Theatre Royal, which I'd hate. I wouldn't, I wouldn't, I wouldn't.

This wasn't an expedition to the panto but an evening of music and laughter with Flanders and Swann, performing the songs from their revues *At the Drop of a Hat* and *At the Drop of Another Hat*. I knew and loved some of their songs from the radio ('Mud Glorious Mud' for one, 'The Gas Man Cometh' for another). Musical pleasure, though, wasn't the only reason for the outing. Michael Flanders was in a wheelchair, and I'd never even known. I hadn't seen a picture.

Mum had even got up the nerve to arrange for us to call on the artistes in their dressing room after the show. It was good to realise that although Swann was musically the driving force of the partnership, Flanders had the charisma. Donald Swann was a skinny little chap like a little bird who twittered with pleasure whenever Michael Flanders, burly and bearded in his wheelchair, said anything. Flanders rumbled sweetly, and Swann gave a little embellishing trill from his branch when the big man had finished speaking.

Soon Flanders was saying, 'Now I think I'd like a confab with this young man. Boys' talk.' Donald Swann took the cue and started buttering Mum up. 'The purpose of satire', I could hear him saying, 'is to strip away the veneer of comforting illusion and cosy half-truth – and our job is sticking it right back again!' With the advent of *Beyond the Fringe* I suppose their sort of material was beginning to seem rather tame. Mum laughed rather nervously. She didn't enjoy clever talk.

Michael Flanders was a sort of ambassador for disability, and a very good one since he was both sweet and sharp. He said to me, 'You may already have noticed, young man, that the world and his wife think it's wonderful when people like you and me manage without wheelchairs, and rather a poor show if we can't. Pay no attention. We can't all be Douglas Bader, can we?' he said, and then added in a whisper, as if it was a great secret, 'And not all of us even want to!' He told me that Bader's doctors had written on his medical notes, 'Refuses to use a wheelchair', with a tick. 'If I'd been his doctor,' Michael Flanders told me, 'I'd have written *silly ass* instead.' He made it into a huge joke and a lovely conspiracy against the cult of Mr Tin Legs.

Michael signed a photograph for me, and even wrote a message on it so that I wouldn't forget what he had said. What he wrote, in clear, firm, very legible hand-writing (unlike mine) was 'REMEMBER: TWO LEGS GOOD, FOUR WHEELS BETTER!' The only problem with the whole inspiring visit was that the dressing room hardly had room for two wheelchairs at the same time. Mum and Donald Swann more or less had to clamber round us, which took some of the fun out of Michael Flanders' morale-boosting message.

When the spring term began, I was anxious in case I had lost ground in lessons, but much more concerned that the nightly wagon train of narrative might have moved on without me. I needn't have worried. Those slow-moving stagecoaches could be overtaken by the most lumbering wheelchair. Even the Tan-Sad would have gained on them.

In fact there was danger of the situations becoming stale. The show-downs were repetitive, and you could see the double-crosses coming a mile off. Then one night our cowboy theatre witnessed an artistic break-through. There was something missing from the nightly adventures of our desperadoes, but no one had quite worked out what it was. Then one of the other boys said to me, 'John, you're very good at all the parts, but the story's going round and round in circles. Would you mind playing a lady or a mum?'

This was my chance to take the reins. I plunged right in. I started playing Mum, who broke up fights between her boys when they got too fierce and served vast amounts of imaginary food, steaming hot and lovingly described. Then I began to experiment in the temptress vein, making kissing noises that went on and on while everyone in their separate beds listened enraptured.

I found the freedom intoxicating, now that I could take the story in any direction I wanted. It seemed incredible that we had been content with all-male stories for so long. I suppose that's the way with a lot of primitive art forms. Greek tragedy only had one actor for quite a while. Sumo wrestling started off as a sort of dance representing the contest between a man and an invisible god (who always won) for a very long time before someone had the brave notion of adding another wrestler to bring the crowds in and put bums on mats.

After that first night of playing female roles, I was rarely back in trousers. And though I could take the story anywhere I wanted, in practice I paid the proper homage to the basic drives, sex and hunger.

Hunger was the more pressing interest. School food was fairly basic, sometimes aspiring to wholesomeness, sometimes flirting with inedibility. It turned out, for instance, that over the Christmas holidays the 'fridge had broken down. The butter had gone rancid, but it wasn't thrown away, despite the horrible taste. We were told that expert opinion had been consulted, and no harm would come to us from eating it. They put that butter on the table for a month. We could smell it coming. Everyone switched to dry bread until the rank yellow grease was finally taken away.

To compensate for this joyless attitude to catering, we were always interrupting the narrative for someone to come in with a bowl of hot food. Never mind that the tension of the plotting slackened to nothing. This was fantasy of a different but no less necessary kind. One of the other boys improvised a bowl of hot chilli one night. 'What's chilli?' I asked. 'It's spicy stew,' he said. So I said crushingly that

Chile was in South America, and that cowboys would eat the same food as the Indians, and Indians ate curry. I didn't miss any chance to throw my weight around. After that the cowpokes settled down to big bowls of curry and crackers and coffee.

I suppose I got a little cocky, a little drunk on acceptance. This has been a recurring fault with me, testing the limits of acceptable naughtiness. Minor matrons would do a head count last thing at night, before closing the door. One night I managed to wriggle round so that my feet were on the pillow. I got a smack on the bum for my trouble. Quite without warning. But that was just peremptory, there wasn't any sadism in it. I was more surprised than hurt.

I never really got used to the multiplicity of matrons at Vulcan School, matrons of all moods and sizes. At CRX Matron had been an overwhelming figure and a name of great power. As a Hindu in the making I should have rejoiced at the multiplication of deities at Vulcan, but the reality was different. It was like the moment in *Fantasia* when Mickey Mouse, sorcerer's apprentice, hacks the enchanted broom to pieces – only to find that each separate splinter reconstitutes itself as a new broom, toting a pair of pails in a maddening imitation of life.

Protective fugs

The Blue Dorm in Farley Castle was on a corner of the building, and I think it must have been on the north side. In winter it was bitter. I remember Raeburn explaining that a dorm was for sleeping in, not living in. He thought that waking up in a cold room encouraged a boy to move about a bit, to get his circulation moving at a good rate and warm up naturally. Quite how a boy with his joints ankylosed was supposed to initiate this beneficial process was never made clear. Winter mornings in the Blue Dorm were hellish.

The shock to my system was total. In Bathford days Mum had kept my room good and warm. At CRX Sister Heel made sure the radiators earned their keep. I had spent most of my winters in a series of protective fugs. Not any more.

Waking up and being able to see your breath was only the start. The first job for the staff was to get boys out of bed and onto the toilet – and the Blue Dorm's toilet was in a turret. It was the only toilet in the school whose door was too narrow to admit even the slimmest wheelchair. If the dorm was a 'fridge then the turret was a deep freeze. I'm not convinced that even Pippo Freeman from Bourne End, that boy of seasoned wood, could have stood up to the rigours of the cold in the Blue Dorm's turret.

I wouldn't wish the experience of defæcating when your body can't stop shivering on anyone. Then there was the wiping of the bum with hard dry crackly paper. The sensation ranged from awful to perfectly bearable, depending on the niceness of the matron on duty. Sometimes I was just left on the seat. After I'd opened my bowels I just got colder and colder, because the matron who had put me on the seat had forgotten all about me. My bum would go numb. I could call at the top of my voice from that cold turret, but no one heard me. Perhaps no one wanted to. I thought about what it would be like to die on that toilet seat. One day I even decided that it would be better to die than to be left like this. I wondered, if I did die, how long it would be until anyone noticed. I seemed to be getting more and more unimportant every day.

Once it was a kind matron, Gillian Walker (always called Gillie), who forgot to come and get me off the toilet. She was the nicest of the nice, a rose in the spiky desert of the Vulcan garden. I remember once I wanted a mosquito bite on my ankle scratched, and it turned out there were different moral approaches even to this small request. Gillie's school of matronly thought held that carers should only do what was best for the boy (and scratching would only make the irritation worse), while there were other matrons that would oblige without comment. I remember Gillie Walker saying with real dismay, after I'd gone behind her back to be scratched by another matron, 'But John, you don't understand, I care a lot more than Mrs Lewis does!' She was actually quite upset.

When Gillie remembered me at last, having obviously become involved with another boy's needs – it wasn't as if she'd gone to the pictures – she came running. She cried, 'Oh John *darling*, you must think me absolutely *beastly*! I'd understand if you never ever forgave me!' It was easy to say, 'Of course I forgive you, Gillie,' and even to add, 'I could forgive you anything.' It really didn't matter as long as

341

there was some tenderness in there somewhere, even though I was numb and sore and had pins and needles in unexpected places.

It was obvious that Gillie and the Big Matron, Sheila Ewart, known as Biggie, were aware of the indignities we were undergoing. They set themselves to soothing us with kind words and gentle touch.

Judy Brisby, though, had a different approach. She was the one who had dismissed my appendix pains as namby-pamby wallowing. While Biggie and Gillie tried to take the edge off the Spartan conditions, Judy preferred them good and sharp. She used the morning routine as an opportunity to transfer her own inner pain to the boys. I had a sense of this even then. During the bum-wiping process a boy had the chance of reviewing his karmic bank balance with her over the past week. The more sycophantic and dishonest he had been, the better for his bum's sake. I learned to be a toady, which was the part I felt I had to play for a long time after I left the school. My motto had become *You wipe my bum, and I'll kiss yours.*

On a winter morning it was the duty roster which determined how the day would begin, whether discomfort would be intensified by cruelty or melted away with tender words. Biggie would come in smiling, and say, 'Time to get up, boys.' The smiling wasn't forced, and it never stopped. She'd rub her hands together and say, 'It's very chilly bom-bom today, boys!' still smiling. She loved to say that — chilly bom-bom. To make a game of the awful cold. 'Yes, it's very cold indeed this morning. I'll get you boys up one at a time. The others can stay in bed until the first boy is finished. Now then, someone has to be first, I'm afraid, so who will it be? John, you've had a lie-in for a few days so it's your turn to be first. OK then, bedclothes off! Come on then, let Biggie give you a little cuddle, but we can't stay here all day, can we? That's better.' And she'd push me along to the dreaded turret.

'Oh my dear, yes I know it really is a horrid cold toilet seat, isn't it? Just stay in your wheelchair for a minute. Let Biggie sit on the toilet for a few seconds first to take the chill off . . . There, that's a little better isn't it? Oh this horrid paper! Let Biggie rub it together like this to soften it a bit . . . Let Biggie breathe on it to take the edge off. I really must see Miss Willis about having a little heater put in these toilets.' It was one of Biggie's quirks that she put the word 'little' in almost every sentence. 'They're bitterly cold, even for me, and I've been up since six o'clock and had my cup of tea . . .' Motherly she clucked away, wondering if it was right for boys to have such hardship, and what the inspector would say if he paid a visit in the cold season. Biggie was a bustler if ever there was one, a bustler and a prattler, and the nasty moments passed without our even noticing.

A Judy Brisby start to the day was different. No boy would be allowed extra time in bed. If Judy Brisby was going to get us up we had no warning at all. The bedclothes were whisked right off all of us, not just the first to be got up. Lying in bed shivering without bedclothes was just as bad as being plonked on a frosty toilet. Small bodies can't retain their heat, as Judy Brisby must have known, particularly small thin bodies, which was all we were likely to be on the Vulcan diet. I was one of the smaller ones, but none of us was exactly pink with warmth on those mornings.

Any boy who complained about the shock of the cold soon learned to put up with it. Complaints only led to even harsher treatment in the toilet, to vicious scrubbings with hard paper. I'm sure I'm not the only one who lay there fantasising about a contraption that would lift the bedclothes back onto our bodies while Judy was out of the room. Professor Branestawm was the man for the job. I loved the books in which he appeared. I liked logic to fly free, without the downward tug of common sense. Professor Branestawm would design us a subtle system of ropes and pulleys which would yank the bedclothes off again at Judy's approach, so that we were helplessly exposed to the cold. The way she liked us to be. Meanwhile the contraption would vanish into the walls.

Tooth-cleaning was also a fearful event. Boys who were able to brush their own teeth were at a definite advantage here. I was an in-between. On a good day I could manage it, but when the weather was really cold my joints seized up altogether, and I couldn't reach. I went through the motions as well as I could, knowing the consequences if she singled me out. I had a special toothbrush, but it wasn't all that special. It was special in a very ordinary way. It was only a normal toothbrush with a stick (a piece of dowelling) tied to the handle to extend my reach. Apart from the question of reach there was also the problem of getting the right angle.

She caught a boy slacking once, as she thought, and seeing that he wasn't able to reach very well, she said: 'Don't you even know how to clean your teeth properly? Let me show you – and pay attention everybody!' She put a good squeeze of paste onto the boy's brush, then pulled his head back by his hair. She told him to open his mouth and started brushing. Or rather I should say she started agitating her hand. Her mouth twisted itself in a frenzy, while she transferred her sense of her own inner dirtiness into the mouth of the boy. He whimpered a bit, but she hissed, 'Quiet!' and increased the vibration rate. 'This is the way to clean out a boy's dirty mouth!' she said. 'And the only way you can tell when it's really clean is to draw blood!'

Draw blood she did. When she told the poor boy to rinse his mouth the basin was streaked with pink. Blood trickled from his lips. 'There, that feels much better, doesn't it?' Judy Brisby demanded. The poor boy agreed through his mouthful of minty blood that yes, it was better now. Ever so much better. I don't think she necessarily intended to draw blood, but when she saw the bleeding she declared it a good and necessary thing. It was either that or put the brakes on, maybe even apologise, and she wasn't going to do either of those things.

After we'd all been cleaned and delivered downstairs by way of that sluggish lift we had our breakfast, which was cold whatever the weather. Bread-and-butter and marmalade and Puffed Wheat. Only the tea was reasonably hot. There were four people at each table, one member of staff and three boys, and on the table there was a toast rack which held four half-pieces of wholemeal toast. This was for staff only.

Mostly the staff ate their full entitlement of toast. It was a small enough perk in an unglamorous job. But Biggie always made sure that three of her pieces of toast were given away, and so did Gillie. Judy Brisby's table was run differently. She would take a tiny nibble of her toast and then sit there, chewing very slowly, as if lost in her thoughts. Of course she knew exactly what she was doing. She could make that slice last all day. She would certainly stretch things out so that she was still on her first piece of toast when the table was cleared and we had to get ready for lessons. Not that the other slices will have gone to waste. I dare say the kitchen staff were rationed as much as any of us, but if they turned up their noses at the cold toast we so much coveted then it will have gone to the pigs.

One of the asthmatic ABs, called David Lockett, a tremendous animal lover, kept pigs. It wasn't the school's project, he did it entirely on his own initiative. He had special permission, and he looked after them with superb devotion and efficiency. David always said that he was going to be a farmer in Australia, and since ABs weren't automatically debarred from pursuing their ambitions, as most of us were, there's no reason to think he didn't manage to do what he wanted.

Judy Brisby was sly enough to realise that if no one ever got a bite of her toast we would learn to ignore her nibbling routine. So there would be a small act of sharing every now and then, always in favour of the boy who abased himself most shamelessly in front of her.

My toady self

One breakfast time I qualified. As an avid reader of Æsop's fables in CRX, I had learned the moral that if you praise the crow's beautiful song you can steal the titbit (a piece of toast, say) when it opens its beak to sing. The toast had long since lost all its original warmth, of course, and Judy had smeared it with the thinnest possible scrape of butter, the most grudging dab of jam. As I ate it I tried to feel that it held at least a symbolic warmth, the memory of its charring, but all I could taste was my toady self. My mouth was full of the bitter juices of sycophancy.

After breakfast I could feel that the worst part of the day was behind me, and that Vulcan School was really an OK place to be. I made a solemn vow, in the days of the Blue Dorm, that when I left school I would never again expose this body to the indignity of receiving a cold shock first thing in the morning.

The cold at Vulcan was always presented by the authorities as having a healthful, bracing aspect. It didn't occur to me that this, like many other features of the school, was really a matter of economics.

Mum had explained to me that Cromer, the name of the man she had married and consequently my surname, was a resort town in East Anglia where it was always cold and windy. There had been a vogue in early Victorian times for healthful bracing resorts, where the north wind could be relied on to blow away all thoughts of lounging and to impose a régime of brisk walks, well wrapped up. 'But who'd want to go to a place like that?' I wanted to know. She couldn't really give an answer. She had never gone there herself.

I suppose I should pay a visit one of these days – see Cromer and die. I'm not interested in family history, not really believing in either family or history. I'm in two minds about geography, come to that. Anyway, it stands to reason that my forebears weren't called Cromer when they lived there – they got that name at the next town they moved to, when they were the people *from* Cromer.

The turret of the Blue Dorm made Cromer seem like Barbados, but the Spartan conditions weren't entirely meant. Feather beds would sap the moral fibre, certainly – but feather beds were also expensive. When I had left CRX and come to Vulcan I had moved, without real-ising it, from the care of an institution with resources to one without. The difference was masked by their shared ideas about the young, and the dire consequences of mollycoddling. Thrift was the over-riding style of things, so that actual poverty didn't show up so much.

The Canadian Red Cross Memorial Hospital, set up on a historic estate, had been richly endowed from the first day it was offered to the authorities. The Astors had provided more than the premises, paying the wages of staff. When the National Health Service was established, CRX was smoothly absorbed into it. CRX was a benefactor with a lit-tle body fat on it – Sister Heel's gleeful mug-smashing and Dr Ansell's matter-of-fact insistence on linen sheets for children were extravagances that could be indulged. If the toilet paper was hard, that was because the soft variety was morally suspect, not because it cost too much.

Old Boys' reunion in the sky

The Vulcan School was different, the Vulcan School was skin and bones. It had only the most tenuous and long-delayed claim on pub-lic resources. The school opened on personal loans, with one pupil, and laboured to build up to official size and status. It was hard for local authorities to send pupils until this critical mass was reached. Things that might be classed as necessities, such as a lift so that wheelchair-bound children could ascend to the dormitories upstairs, were installed only as funds allowed. Vulcan was an undernourished orphan taking in others of its own kind, without having secured its own place in the world.

From the school's point of view I imagine even David Lockett's pig husbandry came in handy. There were pigs to sell every now and then, and that can only have helped a bit with the money side of things.

Fund-raising was an issue that loomed large. We were strongly encouraged to attend church regularly at Swallowfield. This was a soft ultimatum. Raeburn and Miss Willis cultivated social contacts there, vital for funding. I didn't enjoy the rough ride there and back in the Bedford Transit, with the wheelchairs bumping along behind on the trailer.

I wanted to be in the choir, like some of the other boys. That would have livened up the services for me. I enjoyed singing and I don't think my voice would have let the side down, but I didn't qualify. It was discrimination of the most blatant kind – shocking, actually, in an institution that was supposed to give disabled boys a full life. I could sing, but I couldn't get into the choir stalls at Swallowfield Church, and that was a good enough reason, apparently, to keep me out of the choir.

So I day-dreamed through the services. If I didn't already have a sense of God I wouldn't have picked one up there. Every now and then, though, Reverend Cook the minister would preach a sermon that hit me for six. I remember him explaining the Persons of the Trinity in terms that really fired me up. 'Think of the sun,' he said. 'There's the sun itself, its light and its heat. They are three, but they can't be separated from each other. We can't begin to imagine the Sun without its Light and its Heat, yet the Light comes from the Sun, and the Heat from the Sun – and you could also say that its Heat comes from its Light.' My mind was intoxicated with this way of considering the world in its invisible and visible aspects.

Then unfortunately he changed gear, and started to explain the same theological point in terms that he must have thought were more accessible to the Vulcanians in the congregation.

'Perhaps another comparison will be more useful,' he said. 'Let's say that a man sends his boy to school, as a boarder, not so much for him to have a good time – though he is glad that he should, as long as he gets it by working hard and keeping out of mischief – as because it is

347

the best education and training for him, to fit him for something higher later on.

'The father wishes his boy to keep straight, and to have a good influence over his friends, and in his house, and (if possible) in the whole school as well, and is pleased if he finds the boy is shaping that way. He keeps in touch with him by writing, so that the boy has no excuse for forgetting what his father wants, and how much he cares about it!

'Another thing that helps the boy very much is that he had an elder brother at the school. The school was in a very bad state when he came there, but his work in it (particularly in the last part of the time that he was there), and the work of the friends whom he had influenced, made a great and lasting difference to it, though it is a very long way from being what it might be. The boy has the example of his elder brother to live up to, though he knows he will never even come close. The elder brother has not in any way ceased to take an interest in the school – he keeps in touch with it and comes back to it. He is just as anxious as the father that the boy should be a good influence on his house.

'Besides this, the boy has another person to help him, whose influence is entirely in the same direction. He has a good friend whom he can always get at and consult, and who is really always giving him advice in an unobtrusive sort of way, setting him on the right lines and keeping him there. Of course the boy doesn't always take the advice he is given – he may well put it on one side, because it is hard or unpleasant, or because the other fellows at the school will laugh at him if he follows it.

'Even so, I'm sure you will agree that a boy who has all this help available to him has no right to turn out a failure. At the end of his time at school he ought to have a record he can be proud of, one that will make him a credit to the Father and Brother and Friend who helped him. He should be fit for higher work when he comes to leave the school at last . . .'

This contorted allegory left me more confused than ever. I suppose it might have worked better in the Catholic tradition – then at least there would be a place in the scheme for a Matron. The school analogy didn't please me half as much as the solar one, partly because I no

348

longer felt the need to personify God, as I had in the days when I thought of him as the Knitting Pattern Man. I didn't visualise a man with a white beard – if anything I visualised a beard without a man, a Cheshire Cat kind of deity.

It didn't appeal to me to think of Heaven as an Old Boys' reunion in the sky, though I idly wonder how many old school ties the Trinity would be sporting – one? Three? Perhaps even two, since it was a moot point whether God the Father had actually attended.

Trevor the human suitcase

On Sundays when I did take fire from the Reverend Cook for a while, there was no one to share the feeling with, and my excitement would have died by the time we got back to the school. I liked the idea of drinking communion wine, but it made me feel sick to see old biddies slobbering into the chalice. I certainly prayed that the Holy Ghost was effective against germs.

Every Sunday after church Mr Yeo the church warden would come back with us to the school, take his jacket off, roll his sleeves up and bathe two or three of the less portable boys.

Then the school was given a Thames Valley Leyland bus, a single-decker, by the Handicapped Children's Aid Committee. It could carry both boys and wheelchairs, so the Bedford Transit was retired from duty. Raeburn devised a derrick that enabled boys to be hoisted through the door at the front of the bus without leaving their wheelchairs. We would then be tied securely to bolts in the floor. Eventually BEA gave the school some old aircraft seats, which were installed by a coach firm in Reading. I remember watching Miss Willis bouncing on her seat on the way to church, her face at peace, her bulky handbag on her lap. I might have found the sight less reassuring if I'd known then, as I do now, that she carried a carving knife in that bag. This was in case there was a crash, and she had to save us by cutting the straps that secured us to the floor.

The only exciting moments in church were when things went wrong. There was one boy, Trevor Burbage, with polio so severe that it almost seemed he needed holding together by artificial means. He had a calliper on one leg, but that was only the beginning. He had to wear a device called a Milwaukee brace, a sort of metal corset with a rod going up to the back of his head and a frame under his chin to hold his head in the correct position. The brace even had a sort of handle at the back of the collar – like the handles you see on heavy luggage. He was practically a human suitcase.

One Sunday at church he fell over during a hymn. No one worried about him – his mother made him wear a riding hat at all times, and we were confident that it would have absorbed the impact. Trevor was merry, talkative and entirely impervious. Miss Willis passed a hymn book down to him and he went on lustily singing from underneath his riding hat. In deference to the formality of church the ABs waited till the end of the hymn before they lugged him to his feet.

Outings and expeditions were a major part of what Vulcan had to offer, though one of Raeburn's favourite destinations seems a little odd in hindsight. He used to take parties of disabled boys to watch the passing-out parades at the Army Apprentices School at Arborfield. Perhaps there was an element of nostalgia for him in these visits, bitter-sweet memories of his own training before it was cut short with the crushing of his legs. More likely, though, he wanted us to notice what happened at least once on every occasion, more often when the weather was hot. These were literally passing-out parades. Cadets holding a motionless pose would simply keel over in a faint. Perhaps Raeburn thought it was useful for us to know that even perfect bodies could let their owners down. Or perhaps he just enjoyed seeing it happen. We certainly did.

Whipser-Nade

A more important occasion for me personally was a visit to Whipsnade Zoo. It wasn't even my first exposure to the Zoo – I'd been there before, on a trip from CRX, but this was the important occasion.

I remember being proud on the previous visit that I knew to give the name two syllables, along with Sarah, while Wendy and her crew said 'Whipser-Nade'. Even the nurses at CRX made the same mistake. All the same, that first visit wasn't a happy one. The Elephant House had a wall in front of it, which adults could look over, while children had to be lifted. I was waiting my turn to get a view when some non-CRX kid jostled in front of me and scrambled up on the broad foot-plate of the Tan-Sad to see for himself, as if I was more parapet than person. He trod heavily on my foot, which swelled up and was sore for a good ten days.

I don't even remember whether I got to see the elephants that day. It hardly matters. I don't have an elephant's memory, but some things will stay with me as long as this body does. I experienced what it would feel like if an elephant stepped on your foot, not even noticing, and that's not something anyone forgets.

On this second visit everything was different. I saw a keeper with a snake round his shoulders. He was wearing it. It must have been a young python, recently fed and pleasantly drowsy. Everyone else was hanging back and saying it gave them the creeps, but I wanted to wear a snake too. There was no bravado in this, for once, it was a physical longing entirely separate from the desire to impress. I put my hand up, and I think the teacher in charge must have made a more obvious signal because the keeper came over to me right away.

As often happens to me when I want something really badly, I swallowed my voice and the keeper had to lean over to hear. Then even before I had asked if I could have the snake on me, the python moved its head my way. It was as if it understood. As the keeper helped the snake to unwind from him and wind onto me, he said, 'Don't worry, 'e's perfectly 'armless!' though I hardly needed reassurance. The rest of the Vulcan party laughed uneasily. I'm not even sure they got the feeble joke.

With a snake round my neck, I felt crowned and complete. There was an instant bond. I understand that this requires explaining. Snakes have found an ecological niche for themselves where legs would only get in the way, and we're prejudiced against such a radical bit of stream-lining. I myself have warmed to the world of the cold-blooded, starting from that moment at Whipsnade, with the snake warm round my neck.

Cold-blooded is a rather loaded term, of course. Just go to the desert and see whose blood is hotter, the snake's or the human being's. See for yourself which organism struggles to keep to a comfortable operating temperature. The more respectful word is ectothermic. The point is, that every time I say *python* or *cobra*, I'm like a well-bred teenaged girl saying 'pony'. With that undertone of crush. Pash. Thrill.

It wasn't a spiritual lesson I had at Whipsnade. It's easy to say that the snake, limbless but absolutely whole, was there to show me the way. The immature python round my shoulders would never have as much dexterity as I did even with my clumped fingers, but its adaptation to life was absolute. Who would dare to say or even think that a snake was disabled? All perfectly true and perfectly irrelevant. What I felt wasn't a sermon in reptile guise but a piercing sensation, a deep satisfaction that was also an intensification of longing.

Charman clean and Charman dirty

The main satisfaction within the walls of Vulcan was still the night-time story-telling. After I had broken through the gender barrier, there was no holding me. First of all the temptress became German. It helped that my range of German cliché was a little wider than ve-have-vays-of-making-you-talk. I remembered Gisela Schmidt, for instance, saying that CRX was 'not *Charman* clean, but clean'. Also 'In Charmany your parents would have to pay.'

There was Charman clean and there was Charman dirty. I made the temptress say, 'I want your hand to squeeze my bosoms,' but she wasn't a cheap trollop, she was a woman in love. After the bosom-squeezing was done (with the dorm chorus providing any number of unlikely pneumatic noises) she said tenderly, 'Oh *Darlink* I *luff* you.' That went down a storm. Effectively I was the Marlene Dietrich of our little after-lights-out repertory theatre.

I don't think I can have seen any of Dietrich's films on television at that time, but whenever I've happened to tune in to one since, it has seemed like familiar territory. So perhaps there was some subliminal memory of *Destry Rides Again* or even *Touch of Evil* in those ignorantly erotic improvisations, some whiff of Tanya (Tanya with her chilli!), of Frenchy, in those love scenes, those *luff* scenes which came so close to getting out of hand. When the temperature started getting too high I would interrupt my flagrant self and her lover in the character of Mum, knocking on the door with a feast of curried stew and thickly buttered bread, and endless cups of tea.

Then over time the mother figure mutated into Miss Willis, the mum who was actually on the premises. I incorporated some of her mannerisms into my performance. For instance I consciously let my cheeks go slack, to duplicate the unmistakable Willis wobble.

Marion Willis and Alan Raeburn were very much the mum and dad of the school. In a sense they were like a couple of newly-weds who had fallen in love with a derelict castle while on honeymoon and had bought it on impulse, without being able to change a fuse. Farley Castle was their folly *à deux*, though of course they weren't married. Marion was older, and bulk limited her romantic appeal. They were no less a couple for that. They were married to the same vision, a vision which led them into areas of which they had previously known nothing.

The qualifications that Mr Raeburn and Miss Willis had for running a disabled school were really very simple. She was a teacher, and he was disabled. After the War, Alan Raeburn had studied at Cambridge, then gone to Barts Hospital to train as a doctor. He contracted TB, which closed off that particular career path. He was working half days in a local office when he and Marion got to know each other. He had a car, an adapted Morris Minor, but no garage, so Miss Willis let him share hers. They started talking about the tragic mental thwarting of intelligent disabled boys. The Education Act 1944 was a step forward – it imposed an obligation on local authorities to provide schooling for the handicapped, but grammar-school education was not available. They decided that was the standard they would aim for.

If Farley Castle wasn't technically derelict when they acquired it, still everything needed looking after. The bottom kept dropping out of the Aga. It didn't take much to block the outside drains, and it took ages to clear them. Manholes ran in a chain from the front door and outside the kitchen windows, all the way to a cesspit in a neighbour's field. The manholes were so widely separated that sometimes one set of rods wouldn't reach, and the co-principals would have to borrow a spare set from the Post Office at Farley Hill. Once, in fact, the postman was persuaded to break off from his round of deliveries to lend a hand with the unblocking.

353

There were always problems popping up to surprise the co-principals. They had some woodland cleared on the other side of the road from the school, but the workmen hired to fell the trees had ignored the instruction to refrain from making bonfires. Neighbours rang up to complain that smoke was working its way underground towards them. I remember more than once watching with incredulous delight as firemen tramped gingerly over hot ground, tracing the fire by little spurts of smoke popping up in front of them. What a boost for my pyrolatry! Perhaps in the next life I'll come back as a little rogue flame, and not as a person at all.

I had been wildly excited, after all, when I had read about the will-o'-the-wisp, nagging Mum and Dad to take me to see it, until it was explained to me that it wasn't something you could see on demand. It was more an event triggered by certain circumstances. The real wisp would only appear in haunted marshes at night-time when there were few people around to be scared. I had hopes, though, that methane would combust spontaneously from all the tuppenny in the Vulcan School cesspit. That would be good enough for me.

The roof leaked after heavy rain. The co-principals would hear about it from a staff member on the receiving end of the drips, who would have had to hold up an umbrella in bed. The slates on the roof were brittle. The battlements weren't held in place in any sensible way, they simply balanced there. Leaning against them would be enough to send them toppling.

Once Raeburn, inspecting the loft, found five starlings drowned in the water tank. With a heavy heart he summoned the county's Medical Officer, expecting to be told to close the school down for a period. He wasn't looking forward to the equivalent of evacuating a small town of dependent people. Luckily the MO of Berkshire merely advised the boiling of drinking water for a week or two. After all, no one had been poisoned so far, had they? No need to panic.

It was a strange experience to watch Raeburn climb the ladder to the loft. Miss Willis would stand below him, since he had no sensation in his legs, grabbing each foot in turn and placing it on the next rung. She had to do this both going up and coming down. Raeburn's sister Margery might have been a professional puppeteer, but on these expeditions into the unknown areas of loft and roof it was Miss Willis who seemed to have usurped that rôle. Alan might not be putty in her hands, but at loft-inspection time he was at least half puppet.

Civilisation and the cripple

Raeburn took a kindly interest in me, and said he would give me private walking lessons. So at eleven o'clock most mornings we met in a classroom for twenty minutes. Supporting himself with an expertise which was beyond me, he helped me in the gentle art of challenged walking, telling me I was quite safe, not to worry, and assuring me I could not fall. His touch was very tender and I felt safe with his strong arms making a little cage around me or a bar for me to hold. I remember I could touch and hold that strong arm-sinew as much as I liked. Looking back, I realise he must have kept an arm free to hold on to his sticks, but I don't remember it, and fortunately at that time logic drifted in and out of my world.

When the classroom was busy we met instead in his study. One day he caught me looking at a book on the shelves whose spine I could read. Its title was *Civilisation and the Cripple* – poignant juxtaposition. I don't know if he was referring to that book at all, perhaps even paraphrasing, but at that point we had by far the most searching general conversation that I had had with anyone to date. Everyone was always telling me I was clever, except the eleven-plus examiners, but no one before him treated me as an adult. I suppose he was using me as a sounding board for his own inspirational little theories.

I remember him saying, 'You and I are the judges of civilisation, in a way. If civilisation means anything it means looking after the weak, not getting rid of handicapped children by exposing them on the mountainside, as I'm afraid the Ancient Greeks did, for all their culture, and not by throwing useful human beings in the dustbin, as we sometimes do. Funnily enough the Aztecs – those are the chaps who used to live in what we now call Mexico – uncivilised people in many ways, but they looked after disabled people very well. They had the idea that people with . . . um, with deformities, were holy in some way, you know, dear to the gods.'

Nothing could have been better calculated to get me wildly excited, what with my blocked dreams of religious vocation, an occupation where it seemed my face fitted only in the little book where uniforms folded neatly down round a stuck-in photograph. 'So were the handicapped people made into priests?' I asked. 'I'm not sure about that, John, but I'll try to look it up for you.' Perhaps he did, but he didn't ever mention the Aztecs to me again.

Since then I've learned that Aztec enlightenment had its limits. They had a rather narrow definition, as it turns out, of the value of the disabled. Not so much intrinsic worth as usefulness in a crisis. The disabled were emergency supplies of sorts. The Aztecs looked after their deformed citizens with great care until there was a solar eclipse, and then put them right at the top of the list of the human sacrifices, to have their hearts cut out and their skin removed. A compliment of sorts, since only the choicest hearts and freshly bleeding hides could tempt the day-star out of hiding, but not easy to take in the right spirit.

Raeburn had changed tack before I could ask any more awkward questions about the Aztecs. 'I know you're interested in animals, John – well, sometimes naturalists find a bone, a lion's leg-bone, say, and they can tell by looking at it that this bone had been broken but healed. What they can tell from that is that the other lions in the pride looked after the injured one, feeding it when it couldn't hunt for itself, or else it would have starved before it could recover. Of course there are animals that have no feeling for their fellows, perhaps most of them don't, but human beings do. They just have to be told how best to help. And if you and I in this country aren't helped to make the best of things then I don't think much of anything else our country does.'

So we were judges of our society, not the judged! This was an intoxicating idea. I could go round with a little book, noting down who had helped me and who hadn't. Mr Turpin at CRX had said I could be a clerk, which I hadn't fancied – but it would be a different matter if I was attached to the Recording Angel's office.

My karma banks at Coutts

Most thinking about disability that I knew at that point, and even mine, circled warily round the idea of punishment. Miss Reid had started it all by going on about wheat and chaff and tares and Hell, even if she had relented when she saw how miserable she made me. And still, what she was really saying was that I would scrape into Heaven if my life on earth was enough like hell. What sort of merciful God would arrange things like that? The whole thing was a big mess.

Mum and Dad had confronted this question in a conversation once, when I wasn't quite out of earshot. Either that, or my memory has decided to have a part of my thinking played out in the voices of the people I knew best.

'I'm sure you know, m'dear, that many people think of handicap as a sort of punishment . . .'

'He's only a little boy, he hasn't *done* anything!'

'Don't jump down my throat, m'dear! I'm only saying what some religious people think, I didn't say I agreed with them. It's not an attractive idea, it may be a lot of nonsense, but that's how some people think.'

'But, Dennis, he's done nothing. So perhaps it's our fault? We're the ones being punished?'

'It's not so bad, m'dear. And I don't know what you'd do without him . . .' Dad gets marks in my book for blocking Mum's move to take on all the guilt of the world.

Disability as punishment for actions in a previous life – there's no point in pretending there isn't a side of the mind that responds to these punitive simplicities. I can't seem to muster the proper outrage at such suggestions.

Since then, though, I've discovered a different application of the concept of karma. By this interpretation, disability at birth or in early life is a highly specific condition. It relates to an earlier life in which one displayed mystical powers. The physical difficulties are only the residue of a sage or mage over-taxing his spiritual strength in that previous life. Not really a punishment – more of an overdraft, and on a rather swish account at that. *My karma banks at Coutts, don't you know. Lovely people – they're very understanding. And even in this day and age the statements are written by hand!* I find this idea terribly attractive, but if I claim to be open-minded, and I do, then I can't dismiss the harsher doctrine either.

I felt very close to Raeburn after our talk about being the judges of civilisation, but on that same morning I said something I regretted for a long time. It wasn't what I said, exactly, but the way I said it. Raeburn asked me if I could feel below my waist. Proud that the sense of touch was one area where I wasn't disabled, I set my chest out proud and said, 'I should hope so, Sir!'

I hoped to increase my standing in Alan Raeburn's eyes. He stood there saying nothing for a long moment.

'Some people can't, you know,' he said at last. I looked at those grey-blue eyes, which didn't seem to be focusing on anything in the room. I had disappointed him by thinking only of myself. He must have had hopes of my showing a stronger streak of enlightenment. I had failed the very first test. Obviously it was right for me to tell the truth, but why couldn't I have said, 'Yes, sir,' without feeling the need to boast?

Secret lovers

It was then, all the same, that Raeburn and I became secret lovers. Our love affair carried me through term after term in that austere school. Of course I don't mean that any impropriety occurred between man and boy. We were secret lovers, not in the sense that Romeo and Juliet were – because of the consequences if they were found out – but the way Cyrano and Roxanne were secret lovers. Because the infatuated party didn't dare to say anything and the infatuator (if that's the word I want) was entirely in the dark. Our love was the purest sort of secret, so secret that he didn't have a clue.

I turned out to be better at hero-worship than at friendship. My experience of the girl gang at CRX had made me suspicious of groups. I loved the story-telling after lights out, but I didn't actually become particularly close to my dorm-fellows. I enjoyed the prestige which performing brought. It was possible for people to listen in from the corridor outside, so that I might have a larger audience than the obvious one. This hadn't escaped me. After a few weeks of term one of the teachers suggested that I study German, on the basis that my accent was good, and really how could he know that except through being told by someone who listened in?

I was vain of my closeness to Raeburn and boasted about it to

358

Roger Stott. He was perhaps more surprised than impressed. It was his idea that Raeburn gave priority to the pupils who had been recently disabled. Certainly they were the ones with the gravest problems of adjustment.

It made sense that they would be Raeburn's special domain because he belonged, more or less, to their category. His adjustment was more directly inspirational for them than for us. Those of us who had long since passed the point where we had been disabled for half our lives just got on with it. None of us envied the recently disabled for their past privileges, and we tried to be patient with their present resentments.

There was a caste system at work in the school, but one with a great deal of complexity. Seniority in the school was a factor, but much less so than difference of diagnosis.

The obvious distinction was between the ABs and the others. For all I know there were nuances of asthma that determined relative status among the ABs, but from underneath the divide it looked pretty much like Us and Them. Among Us, though, there were any number of distinctions that could affect your place in the hierarchy. Those without wheelchairs looked down on those who had them – even if, like Trevor Burbage the human suitcase, they needed so much support that their upright status was more or less fictional.

If you were in a wheelchair then it buoyed up your status if you had sensation below the waist, like me and unlike paraplegics. Paraplegics among themselves perhaps preened themselves on the strength of their arms. On a boy-racer, what-car-does-your-dad-drive? level, electric wheelchairs were more desirable than ones without motors, but they went along with the more severe difficulties, so their social meaning wasn't altogether clear-cut.

Spastics – there was no respectful 'cerebral palsy' label then – who were free of uncontrollable spasms out-ranked those with the more extreme type of the condition, the one named athetoid. Those with degenerative disorders were ranked lower than those of us without. We almost set up a new Us and Them barrier at this point, to make it clear that their futures were so different from ours that it was idiotic to lump us together. The degenerative boys lived in their own narrowing tunnel.

Raw social status, class as the world saw it, was a minor issue. We may vaguely have known that Paul Dandridge, the one who did the 'frog breathing' and needed a respirator at night, was from a very poor background, while Abadi Mukherjee in the same dorm had parents who were terrifically rich (they ran a large Indian business called the Appa Corporation), but we didn't care. I imagine the co-principals cared to a certain extent, since the Mukherjees paid full fees, but from our point of view, Abadi out-ranked Paul by virtue of the mildness of his polio. The mildness of his life outside school (the first-class air travel to Bombay in the holidays) was neither here nor there, though I suppose we noticed the lavishness of his pocket money. If it meant one thing to us, India meant poverty – yet Abadi was the richest boy in the school.

If an AB who didn't often have to use his inhaler was at the top of the caste system, and a boy with muscular dystrophy was at the bottom, then Still's disease gave me a fairly reliable, not unduly fluctuating status somewhere near the middle of my world. An affinity of physical condition could give me more in common with a given person than brute closeness in age. Given that he was a year ahead of me, and also an AB, Roger was remarkably friendly. Age gap plus mobility gap should have created something of a personal chasm, but his good nature bridged it.

He always tied my tie in the mornings. As time went on the exact nature of his good looks became clearer. He bore a striking resemblance to George Harrison, except that the Beatles had hardly even formed at the time so it didn't mean anything yet. As the decade developed, he found himself benefiting not only from good looks but the extra dividend of looking like the kid brother of a new kind of celebrity.

Dry bed-wetter

There was a hidden aspect to our friendship. Roger and I were both bed-wetters. I had grown out of this bad habit very recently, but on some deeper level I wasn't free of it. There's more to being a bed-wetter than the physical symptoms. Part of the condition is the pain of being picked on and being made an object of derision. I was a fellow bed-wetter in spirit if not in fact. I was a dry bed-wetter like a dry drunk, someone who could fall off the wagon any night.

Judy Brisby gave Roger the harshest, most abrasive scoldings. Her words were caustic soda, they made his face go bright red, not a healthy skin tone but one denoting damage. The epidermis was outraged. Roger had to change his sheets while she watched. She seemed to enjoy humiliating him in front of younger boys. All the while she barracked him about the cost of laundering his sheets. You would have thought it was coming out of her own pocket. To hear Judy Brisby talk, Roger was wearing the sheets out and should be thoroughly ashamed of himself. As if that was the problem, Roger not being ashamed enough.

One boy who was always very friendly to me was Julian Robinson, who had polio, but I had no idea of how to behave nicely back. It should have helped that he too had a father in the Raff. In fact Dad knew Julian's dad and said that Robinson was a good chap. He must have meant Robinson Senior, but it seemed to follow that Robinson Junior was a good chap too. I was rather under the sway of Dad's view of things at the time, but in a rather perverse way. I decided to feel superior to Julian Robinson simply because my dad out-ranked his.

Julian seemed rather a little boy who mostly sounded like a little girl. I'd prayed to God to send me a special friend called Julian, but this wasn't the one I had ordered. He was gentle and quiet, not the sort to push himself forward, full of secrets and fantasies. I managed not to notice that we might be rather compatible, and dismissed him as a kid.

At the end of the second term a number of us had a pow-wow about things to do when we all came back after the holidays. Lessons were so deadly boring it was unbelievable. The teachers were ogres and sadists. We all said so, and perhaps I was the only one who found many of the lessons thrilling, and some of the teachers lovely. I said, 'Who's got a chemistry set? When we come back, why don't we all bring our chemistry sets with us?' The idea made an instant impact. I had visions of lovely smells to come, much pungently holy smoke. Smoke always a mystical substance, however foul.

Life in Bourne End was more fun now that Peter was strong enough to push me greater distances. The funny looks we got when we were promenading round the town made us at first subdued, then mildly defiant. We started singing an old song that had been played to death on the radio. It went, 'Edie was a lady, although her past was shady . . .' We sang it all round town, but it was more fun to ramble a bit further.

Just beyond the border of the Abbotsbrook Estate was the railway track. It was always a thrill to cross that line, in case the train came speeding along. We heard stories of boys putting pennies on the line, waiting for the train to come along and flatten them till they were paper-thin. Peter had seen such transubstantiated pennies, and very much wanted to own one. Mum absolutely forbade it. 'If a policeman sees you', she said, 'you'll have to go to prison, or at least a Remand Home.' I knew by then that prison would always be a hopeless dream on my part, but I agreed to set Peter a good example. Besides, there were other ways to get into trouble.

A little further along there were some house-boats, some of them very smart, and further on there was the UTSC, the Upper Thames Sailing Club, which was ultra-posh. The yachts looked so very pretty that it was a kind of meditation to go and watch them, but there was a sign with a stiff warning, that only permit holders were allowed Past This Sign. Very official and daunting. Peter said it would be all right once they 'saw the wheelchair'. People seeing the wheelchair always helped. They'd let us in to watch the boats any time we wanted. The wheelchair was an Open Sesame – but not to this Marina of Wonders. They saw the wheelchair and still they told us to clear off. We were just as bad as other boys, undifferentiated vermin, and in retrospect I take this as a compliment. I wasn't singled out.

Sometimes when the coast was relatively clear we'd venture in. Once we were spotted and shouted at. Peter speeded up, since this was obviously one of those occasions when 'You there, come here at once!' meant 'Run like hell'. We ran all the way through the UTSC, past the warning sign posted to deter vermin coming in the other direction. Now we were in exile. We couldn't return the way we came and had to go home the long way round. We were expecting a scolding from Mum, but she turned round and rang up the UTSC to scold *them*. She said we were merely doing what all boys do, all hearty and adventurous boys (and I admit I glowed at hearing this description).

362

If anything had happened to us, she would have held the Club entirely responsible for its callous attitude. 'Haven't you ever been young?' she wanted to know.

One day we found a twisty road that wound up a steep incline. How Peter managed to push me up there I'll never know. I was no great weight, but the Tan-Sad was a real handful. We thought if we just carried on we would soon reach the sea.

We took with us an *I-Spy* book about the countryside, wanting to identify many unusual things, so as to get a high score and perhaps send our findings to Big Chief I-Spy who would send us a certificate and publish our names if we were the champion observers. We longed above all things to spot a Colorado beetle, not only because it carried a whacking great point score but because you had to report it to the police if you did.

There was a pretty spooky feeling about that steep and winding lane, and particularly about a little house some way up and on the right. We called it the Witch's House, and the rule was that you weren't allowed to speak until you had passed it. Otherwise you'd wake the Witch and she'd cast a spell on you. After we had passed the Witch's House and it was safe, Peter would open his mouth and sing loudly, 'Meadie was a lady' and I sang back '. . . although her past was shady'. Edie had become Meadie, for some reason.

We would go up Elm Lane and into Chapman Lane towards Flackwell Heath. There was a haunted wood further up on the left where we used to go and make a den. One day Peter was grubbing about in the leaf mould and found an old wooden foot. It was rotting away. We were sure that Meadie had in fact had a false leg. She'd left it in this wood (Meadie had now become the Witch). She was bound to be coming back for it, probably any minute now. We gave ourselves a good scare, and Peter got me back down the twisty lane as fast as he dared. We vowed never to go back there alone.

Instead we took Dad with us to show him the haunted wood. We saw no evidence of witchery – we couldn't even find Meadie's wooden foot again, which made us think she'd taken it back. Instead we saw something just as other-worldly and far more beautiful, a great cloud of cinnabar moths fluttering in dappled sunlight. Dad explained that there was plenty of ragwort there (genus *Senecio*, family *Asteraceæ*, *jacobæa* the most likely species), the exclusive host plant of the cinnabar moth's caterpillars. There must have been a massive hatching.

Peter rolled his eyes when Dad explained about nature, but I couldn't get enough. He explained that ragwort, which is related to groundsel, is poisonous to livestock, especially horses – it attacks the liver. The plant has a bitter taste which alerts animals not to eat it, but still it can get through their defences. Either a single early leaf (in which the bitter taste may not have developed) is eaten as part of a mouthful of grass, or else a clump of leaves is eaten and then spat out, but then inadvertently returned to by the same animal or another. The bitter taste dissipates once the leaf is dead, but the toxicity remains.

Meanwhile the cinnabar moths, immune to the toxin and also impregnated with it, broadcast with their beautiful red colour the protective status of their poisonous, their magnificent untouchability.

Fun with Gilbert

I wasn't sure the others in the dorm would remember about the chemistry-set project, but on the first day of the next term we all had our sets laid out on the beds to compare well before lights out. There were a number of different makes. Julian had a Lotts Chemistry Set and I had 'Fun with Gilbert Chemistry'. The picture on the box made Julian's set look very grown-up. My picture wasn't too bad but the word 'Fun' on the box made my set seem childish, and 'Gilbert' was hopeless. I could see Julian brightening up when he saw Fun with Gilbert, and my heart was glad.

Once you had the boxes open, the situation wasn't so clear. Julian took the lid off his set, and showed off its range of little cardboard cylinders with plastic insert lids. Perhaps he didn't know that the little barrels containing his chemicals were made of cardboard, but I did. I knew, but I was biding my time.

My set opened up properly, on hinges – it didn't have anything as make-shift as a lift-off lid. The hinged lid on 'Fun with Gilbert Chemistry' doubled as a protective cover, and there were two sturdy drawers beneath. The right-hand drawer held twenty-one glass bottles of a decent size, labelled and stoppered with metal screw caps. The left drawer was divided into two tiers, the top one holding slender test tubes full of chemicals. They too were labelled, and stopped with cork bungs. Not wanting to waste space, Gilbert (whoever he was) had thoughtfully put two grades of litmus paper behind them. The bottom half of the set had a shelf with holes in it to hold test tubes. With a lavish hand Gilbert had thrown in eye droppers, filter papers, instructions and tweezers. There were also some strips of magnesium ribbon.

I just about managed not to crow, 'Mine's better than yours!' I decided that Gilbert and his Chemistry Set were quite able to speak for themselves. I just watched Julian give a miserable gulp. For a moment I even felt a little sorry for him. I said, 'I expect yours is much better than mine really.'

I wasn't being at all frank with my school-mates. What no one at Vulcan knew was that during the holidays Dad and I had already gone through all the experiments in Lotts. Dad was highly enthusiastic about chemistry. It gave him the chance to play under cover of supervising his son. When Mum said, 'John's going to do chemistry this afternoon,' it really meant that Dad was going to do all the experiments, and John was going to watch. 'Gives him a real chance to learn, m'dear,' he said. 'Too damn dangerous for him to attempt on his own!' When he was in his playful vein, he tended to monopolise toys.

I didn't mind too much being made to watch him playing with my chemistry set. Mum said, 'I've told him he's got to clear up all the mess and put it away afterwards,' talking out of the side of her mouth the way she did when she was feeling subversive. 'And don't worry, I've kept next Tuesday afternoon clear for us. When Dad's at work, you and me are going to do chemistry. I'll have to do the experiments, but as I don't understand the first thing about it you don't need to worry. I'll do exactly what you say.' I was already fairly excited by doing chemistry with Dad, even if it meant just watching, so the idea of doing it with Mum as well, in secret on a Tuesday afternoon, was heavenly.

Dad did seven Lotts experiments that Saturday afternoon, with me watching, and we weren't any too impressed by the results. We decided to be more adventurous the next Saturday. It had been raining all week, and when Saturday came the sky was very dark. There was a tremendous rainstorm, which created ideal conditions for doing chemistry – but even compared to the previous Saturday, our experiments gave poor results. Because of the raised atmospheric humidity the strontium nitrate had caked like lumpy sugar. The copper sulphate was distinctly gooey and the Congo Red was not only gooey but had turned anæmic. 'This company cheats,' said Dad with a thrilling sternness. 'It's only our second time using the set, and look what a tiny pinch of powder is left!'

He didn't know about the intervening Tuesday, when Mum was my lab assistant, but the point held good. The quantities were measly. There was an element of triumph and point-scoring in Dad's denunciation of Lotts. When we had been shopping for chemistry sets Dad had wanted to buy 'Gilbert', but Mum had put her foot down. She said we couldn't afford it – 'Not with you on forty cigarettes a day, Dennis! We shall have to settle for Lotts. That's what Renee Utterson has bought for her boy Tim. I understand it's very good.' And that was why it had been Lotts.

Now, though, he had Mum just where he wanted her, thoroughly on the defensive. Dad made her squirm by saying, 'What is it you're always saying, m'dear? "You get what you pay for"?' She had to admit that Lotts had been a bad bargain. The price of the better set was still high, but now that Dad was involved the resources could somehow be found. Gilbert had won, in a fair fight.

Dad's interest waned as we had known it would, and Peter started to join in. Over time we became rather adventurous. When a standard experiment seemed uninteresting we added chemicals according to intuition. How could it be a proper experiment, we argued, if someone had done it already? We would end up with our adding a bit of everything we had to the crucible, and marvelling at the frothy bubbling mass that resulted. I always overdid it with the Flowers of Sulphur. I would be in ecstasies sniffing the little whiffs of acrid vapour being puffed into the air as the little blue flame began to spread over the powder like a mould on cheese. 'What's happening here', I would explain with great joy, 'is essentially what goes on inside a volcano.'

I wasn't far wrong. After one experiment got out of hand and left a scorched crater in our wooden table, Dad banned the use of the meths Bunsen burner. Then the emphasis shifted to chemical gardening. We spent weeks watching rusty nails, copper sulphate crystals and shards of ammonium dichromate growing horns and feathers in a solution of isinglass.

Lotts for Tiny Tots

So when it came to a show-down between Lotts and Gilbert in a duel of stinks and bangs, I already knew the winner. I was being a proper little schemer.

Back in the Blue Dorm we fixed a chemistry session for Saturday afternoon. Willis, Raeburn and the rest of the teaching staff seemed unconcerned. I dare say they didn't know much about chemistry and didn't want to be shown up. The authorities gave us permission, saying that as long as we had an AB with us, they supposed it would be all right.

It rained heavily on Friday and again on Saturday. There was a damp smell in the air and there seemed to be moisture oozing out of the walls. Even before we started on the duel there were several abrupt flashes and bangs from the wiring, then a brief power cut accompanied by a subliminally acrid smell. God was doing some experiments of his own, helping the Gothic setting along.

'I think we should do Julian's experiments first,' I said. Pure wickedness on my part. 'His set has the most grown-up picture.' So the Lotts Chemistry Set went on trial first. And guess what? The strontium nitrate had caked like lumpy sugar, the copper sulphate was so gooey it had started seeping into the cardboard tube – you could see the bluey-green stain even from the outside – and the Congo Red had lost much of its colour. It seemed to be in need of a transfusion. 'Oh dear,' I said, all helpfulness and dismay. 'That's not at all how it's supposed to look, is it? I expect there's a bit of cochineal in the kitchens. Perhaps we could try asking Grace if she'd let us add some of that . . .?' Tireless Roger Stott, the AB in charge, offered to find out, but we soon decided that the best thing was just to get on with it.

We were in the big dining room. Before the adventure Biggie had said it was extremely chilly for May, and had given instructions for a big log fire to be made in the huge grate. In theory we boys were unsupervised and on our own, but Biggie kept popping in and out to see if everything was all right. In fact she couldn't stay away. She seemed to have a fascination with our chemistry. Now she surged in, as if she had detected Julian's distress from the other end of the premises, and brought the level of wickedness in the dining room right down. 'Julian, perhaps we could pop your set nearer to the fire? Then while it's drying you boys can try some of John's experiments.' Julian was sniffling quietly. I had kicked him where it hurt, right in the chemistry set. Biggie went to give him a cuddle, and the sniffling turned to full crying.

I was beginning to feel sorry for Julian myself, but the situation I had set up wasn't entirely within my control. A boy called Norman Spencer saw his chance to be spiteful, and said sneeringly, 'Nah! "Lotts" means "Tiny Tots"! Chemistry sets that don't work specially made for boys who cry!'

'Now that's Quite Enough!' snapped Biggie. Single-handedly she was keeping alive the knack of capitalising the spoken word. 'I've told you boys not to Tell Tales, not ever! And that rule also covers chemistry sets. Specifically!! Come on Julian, darling . . . Come over with Biggie and we'll sit by the hearth near all those damp chemicals – not *too* near, mind you! Why, I'm sure that after half an hour everything will be as right as rain . . .'

I had the stage to myself and got busy. My experiments worked wonderfully. Biggie went *Oooh!* and *Aaah!* along with the others as my flash paper disappeared into thin air, my invisible ink glowed brown when we warmed up the paper, my hydrogen popped and my violet iodine solution cleared in an instant when I gave the magic command. At the moment when my magnesium ribbon ignited in eye-searing fashion, the hope on Julian's face finally died.

His set had dried out by now, all the same, and Biggie encouraged him to put on his own performance. She had become thoroughly involved and did her best to make his display a success. She even told boys that they should pay as much attention to Julian's experiments as they had to mine, which I thought was taking fair-mindedness rather too far. In any case our audience had had enough of chemistry by now. Boys started drifting off into other parts of the building, and I left too. It's not in my power (in this body) to slip out unobtrusively, but I didn't see why I should stay out of politeness when the contest had so clearly been won. The last words I spoke to Julian that day, under my breath but quite loud enough for him to hear, were, 'Enjoy your Tiny Tots.' It pains me now to think that I had been as spiteful as anyone. If I had put as much effort into treating Julian nicely as I did into stage-managing his public humiliation, I could have shrunk my ego down to manageable dimensions and transformed my own experience of the school.

Corrupt cylinder

At this point I was equally drawn to making myself popular and unpopular. If there were sausages for supper, in which case we had two per person, I would eat one and slip the other into a pocket, with a slice of bread wrapped round it to catch the grease. O sausage both holy and debased! Corrupt cylinder of nameless flesh and bland padding, but undeniably modular. Easy to transport.

Then in the dorm I'd stow it under the pillow and once the lights were out, slyly retrieve it. I'd croon 'Nar-nar-na-nar-nar' under my breath, that jeer of triumph which must be one of the oldest things in language. *I've got something you don't have.* I'd make sure to eat the sausage as loudly as possible, with the maximum possible chomping and slurping.

Outrage and uproar. Physical mobility being in short supply in the dorm the other boys had little chance of grabbing a bite (though Roger Stott would have been in with a chance), but they could certainly vent their frustration in scream and song. Matrons came thudding, and I had an appointment the next morning to explain myself and the mayhem I had caused.

I didn't cringe. I explained that this was something that was *supposed* to happen. 'It's called a midnight feast,' I said. 'It's in all the books.' I made my case. The dorm feast might not be in the calendar, but it was every bit as necessary as Hallowe'en. The snack of misrule was an indispensable part of life in a proper school.

I managed to turn something which started as a piece of selfish swank into a community crusade. Of course there had to be confab at every level before the justice of my assertion could be confirmed and something less ramshackle arranged. Midnight feast was schoolboy anarchy, but these schoolboys couldn't be anarchic without help from the authorities to be defied. It wouldn't have been possible for anyone but an AB to raid the kitchens, for instance. Raeburn, Willis, the matrons – everybody must have been in on the planning stages.

So one night there was salad for supper. Everyone complained about rabbit food, and nobody really ate a great deal. Then an hour after lights-out matrons came in with torches and bowls of crisps and slices of cake. Biggie was queen of the feast, but still somehow invisible.

There are puppet shows where the operators are in full view. It's only convention that makes them disappear. That was how it worked in the dormitory, after the first moment of stunned surprise. We understood perfectly that the staff were not socially present. They were the conjurors of the treat, but they were not part of the event. It would have been wrong to thank them. They weren't really there, but the food really was.

It was a magic feast, like something out of the Arabian Nights, even if the genies weren't very light on their feet and blocked the light of the torches they brought. And genies as they return to their bottles don't normally murmur, 'We'll be back with flannels and toothbrushes in half an hour.'

A scar I could be proud of

When I had come back to Vulcan after the appendix, once I finally had a scar I could be proud of and show off to selected fellow pupils, the Tan-Sad had stayed put in Bourne End. The reclining position it enforced had made it impossible for me to come close enough to a desk for lessons.

Waiting for me at Farley Castle was an Everest & Jennings wheel-chair. Despite the classy name it was the standard National Health Service issue at the time. It wasn't electric, but it could be converted. What this meant in plain language that an E&J motor (on order, rather a waiting list I'm afraid, John) could be bolted in place on the silver-chrome chassis to power the chair, the bulky battery tucked in at the back. Of course the NHS supplied the chair but not the motor.

With so little mobility in my hips I had never really been able to sit, though I learned to impersonate sitting well enough to put others at ease. On visits with Mum to friends of hers in Bourne End I would be able to settle myself in most chairs. I would perch my bum on the edge of the seat and lean back, keeping balance with my feet.

The Everest & Jennings was hardly more practicable. For longer trips around the Castle I could be pushed by Roger Stott my pet AB, the George-Harrison-in-waiting, his features soon to be plastered on most of the bedroom walls in the world, but he wasn't my servant, or even designated as my helper except by his good nature. I needed to be able to move the chair myself, even if only to adjust its position relative to the desk once Roger had delivered me to a lesson. I learned to do this by leaning over and pushing against the tyre minimally with my hand, but my leverage was small and the required position precarious.

There weren't seat belts for cars yet, so there were hardly going to be seat belts for wheelchairs. My guardian angel must have been working overtime during this period, which was perhaps why she (if mine was Mary Finch) didn't have energy to spare to deal with human threats to my well-being. With Judy Brisby.

One thing that always annoyed me when I was finally settled at my desk was the paper. Foolscap. Why did the school insist on dishing out that particular size? It was so tall that if I tried to write anywhere near the top of the sheet I would inevitably crease and crumple the bottom half. On the other hand, it was both wasteful and odd-looking if I started writing half-way down. Out of the question, of course, to cut it in half for my benefit. The only concession offered was that I could use a typewriter. Although I was thrilled when Raeburn praised my competence on the machine (saying I was 'quite the touch-typist'), I was stubborn enough to persist in writing by hand. I preferred the typewriter, but in my perverse way thought it made things too easy for other people. It was only fair that the teachers should struggle to decipher my markings. I had struggled to make them.

After CRX, the standard of the teaching at Vulcan was thrillingly high. Of course there was the odd journeyman duffer, whose idea of teaching was to read things to us out of text-books, but there were also bright sparks on the staff, and teachers who weren't threatened by having bright sparks in front of them as pupils.

At CRX the school had been an after-thought, here it was a real priority. One boy, Cyril, would turn up to lessons pushed on his bed, lying on his stomach, the only position he could manage. But turn up he did. Later he was adopted by a husband and wife on the staff.

There was sincere encouragement for good work and jocular threats for bad. One threat I can remember came from more than one teacher in that first year at Vulcan: 'If you can't do better than that, you'll have to go to Lord Mayor Treloar!' I had no idea what Lord Mayor Treloar was – not any sort of hell-hole or bedlam, I don't think, but simply a hospital with tuition (at Alton in Hampshire) rather than a real school like the one I was privileged to attend. The threat was effective despite its lack of clear meaning. I put my head down and I worked.

When it got around that I knew a little German and my accent was good, I was told I was just the right age to start learning in earnest. Learning German was never quite as effortless as it had been while Gisela Schmidt's hands were working their wonders, but I made a good start. The knotty aspects of the language were like clenched muscles in themselves, tense nodes which had to be pummelled into relaxation. The drowned cactus of CRX flowered and fruited in its own sweet time. One thing I liked, with a love of definiteness which I've well and truly got out of my system since, was the way it was pronounced just the way it looked on the page. With French it seemed that you had to say what you didn't see and you couldn't say what you saw.

Not far short of trollops

One day during a walking lesson with Raeburn I voiced a worry I had had for some time.

'Please, Sir,' I said, 'can you tell me about Vulcan? I mean the Roman god the school is named after.'

'Well, John, he's the god of fire and also of its human uses. So fire the element, and metal-working. He was known as the blacksmith of the gods. Not the most glamorous activity, I know, but an essential one, very much so for the ancients. Is that the sort of thing you want to know?'

'Not quite, Sir. I was asking more about his family background.' Which wasn't quite the phrase I wanted. I knew what the brochure said about Vulcan, the official line: *This god had been hurled from Olympus by his father and become crippled, but he had doggedly pursued the physical skill of metal-working, becoming the smith and armourer of the gods, and also renowned for his intellect.*

'I see.' Raeburn's grey-blue eyes were looking straight through me. 'Well, John, I'm going to treat you as a grown-up. Why don't you tell me what you've heard, or what you've read, and I promise not to fob you off with flannel. Does that sound fair?'

'More than fair, Sir. I suppose what I'm asking about, sir, is really Jupiter and not Vulcan at all. Is it true that when Jupiter saw Vulcan as a baby, he thought he was so ugly he threw him out of Heaven? Really he wanted to kill him, but the baby was immortal so he couldn't, so instead he grabbed the baby by the leg and threw him out of Heaven so he fell all down the sky. So he's lame where Jupiter hurt him. He's only handicapped because his dad hated him and couldn't actually kill him. Is that true?'

'That's what the myths say, yes. But you must have noticed that none of the gods is exactly normal. They're none of them well-balanced, even the Greek ones. I suppose Athena comes close, but she's always playing favourites and she cheats when she gets the chance. Apollo seems to play fair, but even he's a bit of a pill. I'm speaking frankly now, John, and telling you things that may not be in the Tales you've read, which water things down a bit. The gods are in and out of bed with each other the whole time – and with mortals. Sex-mad, the lot of them. Some of the goddesses aren't far short of trollops. And as for Jupiter, who should be setting an example, he's pretty much the worst of the lot. So we shouldn't be too upset that poor old Vulcan doesn't live up to our hopes. Do you see, John?'

'Yes, Sir.'

'We racked our brains to find a good name for the school, I don't mind telling you. Marion was all for "Nelson" – one eye, one arm, changed the course of history and all that – but I thought we'd end up spending all our time explaining we weren't running a training college for naval cadets. So I was rather bucked when I thought of Vulcan. There's also the Greek version of the same god, Hephaistos or (to the Romans) Hephæstus, but I thought the school would have quite enough trouble making its way in the world without being difficult to spell.'

Even so, I was thrilled by the idea that if he had decided differently I might have been attending a school with the honorary twenty-seventh letter in its name. Already I was fighting the temptation to write his name with the same embellishment, as *Ræburn*. 'But now you know more about the goings-on on Mount Olympus than dear Marion does, and I'd be grateful if you kept it that way. She'd be upset, you see, if she thought that the name we came up with for our school had made any one of our boys unhappy. She's devoted to you all, you know.' As I was devoted to Alan Raeburn.

In the summer of 1962 it was decided that my health was stable enough for the family to go on holiday. Our destination was Looe in Cornwall. Peter and I were thrilled. We had no idea what to expect from a family holiday, and the name of our destination was fantastic. For ages we'd ask, 'Are we really going to [th']Looe for a week?' sounding the article as much as we dared. Loo was an even lower word than toilet. Peter said we might end up staying on Khazi Street, but we knew that was too much to hope.

When she married Dad, Mum must have been thinking of the foreign postings which would take her thousands of miles away from the mother she couldn't quite reject. Looe wasn't quite what she bargained, a poor substitute, almost a booby prize. I put the kibosh on world travel by becoming ill, which was hardly fair on her. I remember Granny saying once that Mum had married a uniform, and if that was true then she was fully entitled to the travel documents stowed away in its inner pockets.

The choice fell on Looe because friends of Mum and Dad had a guest-house there. Dorrie Mason was a former resident of the Abbotsbrook Estate who had retired to Cornwall after her husband died. Running a guest-house had always been her dream. Mum said it was an ideal situation. Staying with old friends meant that you got the best of both worlds, family atmosphere and reasonable rates.

It was a punishing drive in the Vauxhall, and we were starving when we arrived. Dad greeted our hostess with, 'Awfully good of you to let us all stay here, Dorrie.'

'Why wouldn't I, Dennis? That's why it's called a guest-house! And so much nicer with old friends.'

Dorrie Mason was like Aunt Fanny in the Famous Five books, only more motherly. Her language was down-to-earth if not downright rollicking. Mum sometimes let Peter and me watch *Coronation Street* on the Light Programme – in fact she made us watch it, saying we shouldn't be protected from knowledge of what low-class people were like. The Northern accents were hard to make out, and Dorrie's was nothing like them, but there was a directness that I loved and recognised. Dorrie pounced on Audrey, who had slept for most of the journey, and swept her into her arms, delighting her by kissing her tummy with a noise like a whoopee cushion.

When she left the room to make tea, Mum whispered to Dad, 'I don't remember her being quite like that when she was our neighbour.' Dad nodded wisely and said, 'Shall I tell you what's happened, m'dear? She's reverted to type,' and Mum nodded in the same style. Away from the genteel breezes of Bourne End Dorrie had become blowsy and coarse-grained.

Dad made conversation perfectly smoothly, but Mum was really quite put out by Dorrie's class back-sliding. 'She's just stopped making an effort, that's what it comes down to,' she said later. Dorrie had thrown out her fish-knives and gone native.

Peter and I fell in love with the whole set-up immediately. We had arrived late and very much hoped for a hot meal. 'I've not got a lot in the larder, ducks,' said Dorrie, 'but I'll see what I can do.' What she could do was make fried-egg sandwiches. When the plate was put before her Mum just stared at it. Of course Peter and I ate like pigs and chirped out, 'Can we have these at Trees, Mum?'

All through our stay Dad kept trying to offer help. 'Let me give you a hand with all that, Dorrie,' he would call out. 'This is all really very good of you, you know!' and Dorrie had yelled back, 'Nonsense, Dennis, you stay right where you are – you're on holiday, remember!'

At breakfast the next day Mum, who hadn't slept well, tried her best to find Dorrie's fatal weakness. She cast a critical eye over the room's décor, but though the colours were brash and the patterns clashed, the house was spotless. The tea was also scolding hot, just the way Mum liked it, and served in green Beryl Ware, the only crockery Mum was really at home with.

Dorrie made an entrance carrying a large oval ceramic dish with many fried sunny-side-up eggs arranged at its centre, surrounded by many slices of lean back bacon. 'Toast coming right up, love,' she said. 'Won't be a jiff.'

Mum muttered, 'I wonder if she can cook anything except fried eggs,' and it's true that we ate so many eggs that week it's a wonder any of us had a bowel movement ever again. Mum cheered up when she saw that Dorrie had forgotten to warm the plates, whispering, 'By the time it all gets here your eggs will either be cold or hard or both. You know how you both hate that! Really she's hopeless! She hasn't a clue! I'm sorry about this, boys.'

Dorrie came sailing in with the toast and butter, saying that she would just nip out for the plates. While she was out of the room Mum said to us, 'Everything is going to be cold by the time you get it. The only trouble with staying with friends is that you can't complain when things go wrong. Never mind – if you really can't face it we can get some food in the town later on.' In the event we ate so quickly that the temperature hardly mattered. The butter spread like a dream. By the time Dorrie produced home-made marmalade Mum was thoroughly out of sorts.

I could never decide whether Dad's interventions in her moods were mean-spirited or just badly timed. Now he said, 'Isn't it good to be staying with friends, m'dear?'

When Dorrie came in to tidy up the breakfast things she asked if we were having lunch in Looe or would prefer to eat in the house. Peter and I yelled out 'Here!' but were smartly over-ruled.

Even in town we kept on singing Dorrie's praises. We weren't consciously rebelling against Mum's way of doing things, but I doubt if that made it easier for Mum to bear. When we were offered ice creams or a funfair ride, we would ask, 'When can we go back to Dorrie's?' The guest-house was supposed to be a basic lodgings, a base from which to explore the sights and sounds of Looe, but as far as we were concerned it *was* the sights and sounds of Looe. It was good that

Audrey was too young to defend her preferences, and could be trotted off unprotesting to the beach.

Positively indecent

I suppose Dorrie played up to us, offering a performance of rustic joviality, but she put her heart into it, and her daughter Celia made a fine supporting player. Celia had put in a brief appearance on our first night in Cornwall, but long enough for me to realise that she had nothing in common with the shy girl I remembered from Bourne End, who hid behind her hair. She had blossomed, and her clothes hadn't quite kept pace.

'Cee-li-aaaah,' Dorrie had barked out in her saloon-bar voice, 'I want to see you wearing different trousers tomorrow. You're looking positively indecent.' She looked at Peter and me and rolled her eyes. 'That girl!' she said, completely unembarrassed, as she bustled off to put the kettle on. Celia was an unalterably genteel, Bourne End sort of name, but Dorrie made it sound almost obscene by the way she dragged out the syllables.

The following morning, when Celia made her entrance, there was nothing amiss with her grey flannel slacks, but a hole had mysteriously appeared in the back seam by the time she got up from the table.

'Cee-li-aaaah!' Dorrie called after her, 'Do something about that hole in your bum, or you'll be giving these nice boys the wrong idea!' Mum didn't know where to look, although when she was pushing me around in Bourne End and saw a botty or a boozzie that was a little out of the ordinary, she'd be sure to nudge me so we could share a little laugh. Now, though, she said, 'I'll just go out and get a breath of fresh air,' a polite reproach wasted on Dorrie, whose sensibilities had been blunted by years of shameless biscuit-dunking.

Celia galumphed up the stairs and came down a few minutes later wearing a gleaming pair of tight-fitting white trousers. She twirled in front of us. Again there was a hole in the rear, though a much smaller one.

'I thought I'd fixed that,' said Dorrie, 'but my stitches don't hold.' Then she said straight out to Celia, 'When I see a hole like that in your bum, it makes me want to stick my finger up it! Know what I mean, boys?'

Peter and I were deeply glad that Mum was out of the house, inhaling the moral breeze. We also decided to spend as much time nattering with Dorrie as we possibly could. She was very happy to oblige. At the end of a meal she would say with a wink, while she was clearing the table, 'We'll have coffee *later*, boys,' the italics perfectly audible. Having coffee *later* meant having a natter with Dorrie while we drank it. She would also light up a succession of cigarettes. The nattering was continuous, though there were little pauses in the flow when I think Dorrie was fighting the urge to offer us one of her smokes.

A boy-friend in the wood-work

It was no part of Mum's holiday plans for her sons to spend their time revelling in the smutty talk of a sea-side landlady. She became tearful, though Peter and I were unsympathetic. Couldn't she wait to cry till we got home? Dad wasn't indulgent either, telling her to buck up, m'dear, buck up and enjoy the rest of the holiday – but then he too was crying inside when Dorrie served up the bill the night before we left.

It turned out that the hospitality of old friends didn't come cheap. Dad said, 'I feel such a chump for helping her clear the table – I should have charged the ghastly old bird by the cup and plate!'

We travelled home in the Vauxhall in an atmosphere of rancid gloom. Audrey made a great fuss, while Mum and Dad argued about who should give up which pleasure, to pay the high price of staying with old friends. Mum was considering giving up her own occasional cigarettes, but it seemed a futile gesture if Dad was still puffing away. Mum had only ever smoked her way through a shed.

In the car, Dad said, 'It's pretty obvious that there was a boy-friend somewhere in the wood-work. Thank God she didn't show show him to us – at least we were spared that. Shows the woman hasn't lost her senses completely.'

Mum shuddered. 'I hardly dare think what such a creature must be like. But I can imagine the state of his finger-nails.'

Dad had more or less cheered up by the time we were in mid-

Devon. 'Do you think that woman does much reading, m'dear?'

'I shouldn't think so, Dennis. Why do you ask?'

'I was just thinking . . . if it wasn't so obvious that she never opens a book from one year's end to another, I'd say she'd been reading far too much H. E. Bates.'

Mum laughed nervously, as if she didn't quite follow. It was understood that since she didn't drive she should beguile the time for Dad on long journeys with undemanding conversation. She was under instructions to talk but not to prattle. The border between these activities is hard to establish.

If Mum didn't take up conversational space then Peter and I would infallibly get on Dad's nerves by reading out every road- and pub-sign we passed, just as we had on the outward journey ('Wethered, Dad!', 'Arkells, Dad!').

Sometimes it was painful to listen in to Mum's strained talk, but this time I was glad I had. I made a note of the name. If H. E. Bates wrote stories about people like Dorrie and Cee-li-aaaaah then I wanted to read them. There was a public library in Bourne End, and I was already a regular customer, though it was Mum who liaised with Mrs Pavey, the excellent librarian, ordering books for me and bringing them home in her bicycle basket.

Dad raised an eyebrow when he saw my library copy of *The Darling Buds of May*. He said it was Bates's earlier work, stories written under the pseudonym of Flying Officer X, which was really worth reading, but I didn't care. I was gorging on warmth and earthiness until it almost revolted me. It made Enid Blyton seem a little feeble, and though I felt a pang of disloyalty I over-rode it. I needed to know that there were people like Dorrie and the Larkins, who didn't hide their feelings as a matter of course. At this point books were telling me more about life than life was.

I needed to know there was life beyond Bourne End. I couldn't afford to keep life at arm's length – my body would do that all by itself. I hugged to myself the idea that if I escaped Bourne End and let myself run to seed like Dorrie, constipated only in the literal sense (those fried eggs), in all other respects lusty and open to impulse, there might be a boy-friend somewhere in the wood-work for me too. I would never tire of looking at the dirt beneath his finger-nails.

Peter and I wondered when we should start pestering Mum and Dad to take us to Dorrie's in Cornwall again. We didn't get very far. The excuse they gave was that Gipsy had pined for us while she was in kennels, and had lost a lot of weight. Dorrie didn't accept pets, which Mum thought was a bit of a nerve, abandoning the consistency of her position in the heat of the moment. If Dorrie did accept pets, Mum would have had to find another excuse to fob us off with.

A ban on limbo-dancing

Back at school for the autumn term, I continued my worship of Alan Raeburn. I would write out my fantasies about him (using the intimate spelling *Ræburn*) – and very innocent they were too, cuddles and caresses. Even so, the moment I had finished writing I covered the paper with my strong UHU adhesive and folded it over, so that my love would only be discovered at the end of time, the secret bursting from its chrysalis of glue.

All the same, I allowed myself to worship one other teacher. Mum had told me that how well you did at a given subject depended on how well you got on with the teacher. If you liked him a lot, then you could learn anything without even trying. By that criterion Mr Nevin could have taught me anything from quantum physics to origami.

Nevin was a Canadian, tall and rugged, who taught English. He was a great lover of the outdoors, of adventure and canoeing, and he took me out in my wheelchair a lot. One minute he could be talking about gerunds and parsing sentences, then we would be in the woods making a fire. He would turn over a log and call me over to see the larvæ of a stags'-horn beetle. He was a man who was whole and could turn his hand to just about anything. Every other person I had ever met in the world seemed twisted in some way. I had never realised until I met Mr Nevin just how straight, noble and god-like a man could be. I wasn't ready for a guru but I was more than ready for a hero. I could ask him anything and he never minded. Why should he mind? There was nothing he didn't know.

There were plenty of woods around the school, and we would spend a lot of time there, though I don't think we can have been alone together quite as much as my memory likes to think. Mr Nevin built big bonfires, using brushwood and leaves to start with, then moving on to logs. We had a proper camp fire, up to the highest cowboy standards. In winter Mr Nevin would produce warm wraps for us both, and cups of steaming drink to keep out cold.

His stories were full of nature, and of the wonder of all things Canadian. The way the leaves turned yellow, crimson and even blue in the autumn. About (a word, incidentally, which he pronounced as 'aboot') how cold it got there. If we thought our winters were cold, we didn't know what we were talking about.

Dad was good at talking about nature, but not much interested in my thoughts and feelings. Mr Nevin was strong in both departments. He had the knack of drawing me out without seeming to pry, though it was only near him that I was shy in the first place. His own physical poise played a part in this, the sense that he was completely at ease in the world. I told him I had learned about sundew plants when I was five, and had cried over the sad fate of the insect trapped inside. Then I thought about how helpless and immobile normal plants were, and how superb it was that a few of them had learned to pounce.

He leaned back while I spoke, entirely relaxed. Weak sun threw patches of light on his face, and then he said, as if it was the most natural thing in the world, 'Well if that interests you, John, we have pitcher plaants aplenty . . .' He lengthened the 'a' in 'plants' but didn't twist it as Americans seem to do. 'When I go home during the holidays I'll bring one back for you if you like. I'll have to hack it out of the ice, of course, but I'll bring it back. Maybe we could set up a little garden for you at your height. When spring comes you can look after it and watch it grow.'

What could Raeburn offer me compared to this? Here was a man in the fullest sense of the word, a lover of the outdoors, knowledgeable, humorous, strong.

I asked him could I have his address in Canada and he said, 'Sure,' and wrote it out like this:

Ben Nevin
Rothesay
New Brunswick
Canada

'Is that *it*, Sir?' I asked, and though he nodded I still couldn't believe it. When I looked at the few addresses I had in my collection, my adoration grew. My own address was:

John Cromer, Esquire
Vulcan School
Farley Castle
Farley Hill
Swallowfield
Nr Reading
Berkshire
England

I lived in a tiny little country but I needed eight lines to tell the postman where to take my letters. Ben Nevin lived in a vast land, but all he needed was four lines. Take away his name and the country, and that left two. I couldn't get over it. I cross-examined him, and he guaranteed me he had given me his full and correct address, just as it appeared on his passport. Even so my faith was weak. In the hols I wrote him a letter to test the theory. My love grew to infinity when I received a reply. I cherished the fact that his name differed only by a letter from Ben Nevis, the highest point in Great Britain (though a dwarf peak by Canadian standards), our little local Himalaya.

A man whose beauty exceeded that of all other men was going to return to a vast country where he was so well-known that just three words on an envelope would find him, and part of his time he might be hacking out a pitcher plant just for me. I realised he might never do it, but I told myself that it didn't matter. The fact that the idea had occurred to him even for a moment was intoxicating.

The fantasy which grew up around Ben Nevin was strong and total. Relatively few actual climaxes were involved, and they were never of the quick-lurk-in-a-corner or moment-snatched-in-the-lav sort. That would have sullied the purity of my feelings. The moments of truest arousal were in the great outdoors, Mr Nevin's natural habitat. I had learned the lessons of CRX well, and could quite discreetly bring myself off (my orgasm still dry at this stage) under the blankets my idol had so thoughtfully supplied. He never noticed. My powers of concentration increased, and eventually I was able to take my pleasure with my hands decorously visible above the blanket. I don't know why the phrase 'mental masturbation' should be such a disparaging one, when the skill is so useful and privacy hard to come by.

Mr Nevin set up a sort of garden on a low table (when I told Dad about it, fair play, he was inspired to do the same). Even so, it wasn't ideal – there was only so much of the area I could reach. I dreamed of a much wider garden, with bays at regular intervals along it for wheelchair access, a sort of flowering arcade.

The mealtime rule at Vulcan was that elbows were never to be rested on the table. I can't say I was bothered – my elbows don't have that inclination. It's like a ban on limbo-dancing as far as I'm concerned, an infringement of my liberty, obviously, but not something I can work myself into a lather about.

Ben Nevin, though, invariably rested an elbow on the table. Sometimes two elbows, when he was making a resting-place out of his interlaced fingers for his strong chin. There was a certain amount of grumbling behind his back about this, which I did my best to squelch. Why was Ben Nevin allowed the satisfactions of this bad habit when we weren't? The answer was so terribly obvious. Because he was Ben Nevin, and we weren't.

I imagined living with Mr Nevin in Canada after I grew up. Then I spoiled the fantasy for myself by realising that a woman would come along and ruin everything by marrying him, so I tried very hard to give up that particular dream. It was true that we could manage in Canada very nicely, but I thought it pretty unlikely that he would ever take up with anyone as small as me.

Mr Nevin was generally loved, but I discovered with a shock that Raeburn wasn't necessarily popular with the boys. Some of them made fun of the fact that he hadn't really been injured in the War. It was *during* the War, but not in the War. A tank had rolled on him while he was doing his training at Sandhurst. For some of the boys this meant he wasn't a proper hero. I didn't think it made a difference.

The Board of Education

Another thing on which I disagreed with some of my fellows was 'The Board of Education' – the same wooden paddle with a cartoon of a boy printed on it which I had seen so often while browsing in the Ellisdons catalogue. Alan kept the Board of Education on his desk, or else he tucked it into his back pocket while he did the rounds of the school. His knees knocked together and his feet were splayed out as he walked with his canes, so that the Board bobbed almost merrily in his back pocket. To me this was only proof that the co-principal of Vulcan School loved getting toys and tricks through the post as much as I did, but I couldn't ignore the fact that the B of E was an object of fear to many of the pupils. I didn't understand it, though, and one day I asked if he would let me take a look. Cheerfully he handed it to me to inspect.

It was light in weight but very strong, and very comfortable to hold. Looking at the grimacing manikin having his bottom whacked on the Board, I decided to whack my own spare hand with it. It didn't hurt a bit. I just wondered if there was a secret thing on it, some wonderful button which made it spring into action. The finest and most characteristic Ellisdon products had some such gimmick. Eventually I returned it to Raeburn, still baffled by its appeal to him and its menace to everyone else. In my best junior-boffin voice I asked, 'Exactly what does it *do*, Sir?' and he simply replied, 'I hope you never have to find out, John . . .'

At the school, it was Raeburn's rôle to demonstrate to the boys that there were few obstacles that could not be overcome with the proper attitude. His watch-word was, 'If I can do it, so can you.' He was more than a teacher, he was a living lesson.

Miss Willis was more the educational philosopher of the pair. She felt that every boy should be encouraged, even goaded, into achieving as much physical independence as was possible in his particular case. Encouraged – or goaded. The goading idea, with its Nancy Astor overtones, ran deeper with her than with Alan. Marion felt that a boarding school was well placed to help disabled boys, because their families had a regrettable tendency to cocoon them. She didn't know a lot about my family, in which the cocooning was very erratic. Marion's watch-word was, 'There's no such word as can't.' I spent a lot of my time at Vulcan School muttering between clenched teeth, '*Can't* is a perfectly good word.'

Sometimes there were film shows put on for us. *Reach for the Sky* came round rather more often than was natural – the Douglas Bader story. It was a homily in celluloid, preached on the foundation text of the school. The Germans could have tortured him for days without him admitting that there was such a word as can't. They would have had to take the pliers to Kenneth More's tongue. We didn't much care for that film. Julian Robinson got a big laugh by saying that if ever they made a film about the food served at the school, it should be called *Retch for the Sky*.

Marion Willis was the one with contacts, and the skill at exploiting them. One particular Friend of Vulcan was Bernard Miles, the actor and impresario. He arranged for boys from the school to attend performances of *Treasure Island* at the Mermaid, the theatre he had founded in London. He himself played Long John Silver, with one leg fairly obviously tied up behind him (which was disappointing) but with a real parrot, which was just about the most marvellous thing I'd ever seen in my life. His Long John Silver was very well done – rather frightening, a study in charm and greed. He'd sidle up to his victims and almost lean on them for support while he slid his knife in, murmuring soothing words the whole time. 'That's it,' he would say. 'Let it slip in gently, boy . . . *All will be darkness soon.*' Could this terrifying villain really be Miss Willis's friend?

Some of us went to see Mr Miles back-stage – the braver ones – and were disappointed that he abandoned the rough accent along with the wooden leg and the parrot, whose cage had a cloth thrown over it to promote silence. It was all 'Marion, how lovely to see you!'and 'Darling, it's been an age!' He conveyed intimacy by way of a paradoxical formality, calling her Ma-ri-on, as if he'd never heard of the name before or only seen it written down.

It wasn't that we expected him to lean stabbingly on Miss Willis, though that would certainly have been something to talk about in the school bus on the long ride home. We got used to it. His voice was like dark sweet beer. In fact he spoke the words for the Mackeson advertisements. The voice had come to merge with the product it promoted.

Something about the production which excited me almost as much as the parrot was the way they used dry ice from canisters to reproduce sea mist. It seemed (predictably) mystical to me. I almost strained my tongue reaching out to try and taste it. I convinced myself that I could detect the other-worldly flavour on my tongue, an essence of clouds.

I asked Mr Miles, posh in his dressing room, if you had to make it or if you could buy it. He was helpful and informative, though he warned me a grown-up might have to do the actual buying. Then of course I was pestering Mum and Dad for them to get me a canister of my own. There must be shops that sell it, otherwise how would theatres buy it?

Square balloons

It was like the time I spotted a square balloon at a CRX fête. It was floating straight up all by itself, so I knew it was filled with something cleverer than air. Dad explained to me about helium, and when I went on and on at him he promised to get me my own square balloon later on, perhaps hoping to shut me up. He didn't know me very well if he thought I would forget. When I say square – technically I suppose cuboid. Straight edges, that's the point. I put him under pressure to do the rounds over the next few months. Gamages. Hamleys. Harrods.

I had particularly high hopes of Harrods. Dad must have cursed the day he told me that Harrods could get you absolutely anything you wanted, even an elephant. I reminded him of that more than once. He could hardly say I didn't listen to what he said. And hadn't he told me that if you sent a telegram to Harrods, you sent it to *Everything, London*? Wasn't a square balloon part of Everything? Wasn't a canister of dry ice part of Everything? I had seen these things with my own eyes. I wasn't making them up. They existed.

There was also another expedition to the Theatre Royal, Windsor, this time to see the pantomime. I loved the frumpy Dame who was a man dressed up. It was wildly funny. There was one bit of dialogue I particularly remember.

Page-boy: 'What's your name?'

Dame: 'It's Gertrude. But you can call me Gert, and leave off the rude part.'

We howled. We thought that was absolutely killing. Marion

Willis's middle name was Gertrude. Those of the party with flexible necks craned round in their seats to look at her. She had turned the colour of a letter-box.

From then on she acquired the nick-name Gertrude. In my mind I sometimes called her 'Marion Gertrude', or rather 'Marlon Gertrude'. I'd noticed early on that the co-principal of Vulcan School signed herself 'Marlon G. Willis'. I asked her why she didn't dot the 'i', and she said that in a signature you could do things like that. No one could tell you how you should sign your name. No one could over-rule you. This little revelation gave me one more reason to embrace the chore of writing by hand.

Even on the premises, Miss Willis had a talent for creating an atmosphere on special occasions. She enjoyed choosing a decorative scheme – sea creatures, say, or Spain – and went to a lot of trouble to make everything look magical. True, the high ceilings of the castle meant that her efforts didn't have the impact they would have had in more compact quarters. I particularly remember one combined Hallowe'en and Guy Fawkes, when for once my reactions weren't entirely conditioned by the presence or otherwise of high-grade fireworks. The build-up towards the end of October was intense. We boys were given the job of hollowing out pumpkins for the Hallowe'en aspect of the festival.

Actually it was mostly mangel-wurzels that were dished out, which were so cheap they were almost free. The extracted guts completed their life cycle by being fed to David Lockett's lucky pigs. I was fortunate enough to get a pumpkin, but even with this softer fruit I needed a certain amount of help. I knew exactly the effect I wanted to achieve. Making the nose, eyes and mouth was extremely satisfying – I made sure there were peggy teeth with the right air of menace. I was very particular that the top of the lantern was the top from my pumpkin and not another one, feeling that some of my fellow pupils were being negligent in not minding which lid went where.

Grace in the kitchen, who had taken our pumpkin guts to turn into a big pie, also made parkin and special biscuits. There were gingerbread men and toffee apples, baked potatoes and French bread. There was even a special bonfire cake. I think the whole presentation topped even Mum's Scrambled Egg Boats when she pulled out all the stops on Bonfire Night. I loved the smell the candles made, as they toasted the pumpkin flesh from inside.

I made a secret wish that all the lights would be turned off so we could see the dancing faces, and almost the moment I made the wish, Marion Willis made it come true. I went into a trance looking at the flickering show. Even when bed-time came I didn't want to leave. Since boys had to be taken up one by one in the slow lift, bed-time must have been an arduous business for the staff. But that night the kind matrons let me stay where I was for as long as possible, worshipping the lights. On that lovely night I may have been the last boy in the whole school to be put to bed.

We know what we're doing

Whatever the quality of the school celebrations, I wasn't going to miss the fireworks at Trees, and the only festival my family did consistently well. Since the triumph of Fun with Gilbert, my Bible had been *Chemistry Experiments at Home for Boys and Girls* by H. L. Heys, MA (Cantab). It was first published in 1949, making it my exact contemporary. I loved even its epigraph, which tapped into my hunger for primary experiences: *'Why,' said the Dodo, 'the best way to explain it is to do it.'*

Even better was the passage which read: 'A recent Annual Report of His Majesty's Inspectors of Explosives announces a large increase in the number of accidents caused by the illegal manufacture of fireworks.' A whole career path opened up in front of me, bathed in a flickering chemical light. It was obviously just the job. *This is Inspector Cromer of HMIoE. I'm afraid I must impound those home-made Roman Candles. They will be disposed of in controlled explosions by properly trained personnel.*

We know what we're doing.

I still wasn't allowed to light fireworks or handle sparklers, and I suppose I can see the sense of that. Things that have to be done at arm's length come too close.

The only dissident at those festivities was Mum, who turned into the personification of a damp squib. Once she said, after what had been one of Dad's best displays, 'I really don't know why your father bothers. The Queen has the best fireworks – I thought everyone knew that. He'll never even come close.' She took a sort of pride in missing the point.

Gipsy would howl from the kitchen, not so much because she was scared of flashes and bangs as because she felt abandoned by her people, though able to smell them strongly through the door. Solitude is what dogs never get used to, though they put on brave faces.

Peter and I made lists of fireworks and marked them out of ten. We ranked them by a definite system.

The brand names of fireworks had an appeal distinct from the products themselves. There was a thrill in even the plainest: Standard. Then there was Brock's, with its overtone of badgers. I never felt quite the same about Astra fireworks, though, after I learned they weren't the Air Force's own make – the RAF motto of *Per Ardua ad Astra* was inculcated very young in a household like mine. Then there was Pain's. I thought that the name must be some sort of message. It was spelled differently from Payne, our neighbour Joy's name, but I had the sense that a similar hint was being dropped. Once or twice a glazier's van came to the Castle, with the motto *Your Pane is Our Pleasure* painted on its side, which may also have been significant. I tried to turn the pain in my joints into firework patterns, bright tracings against a background awareness like dark velvet, to go *ooh* and *aah* rather than *ow* and *yikes* and *make it stop*.

There was a separate set of ratings based on pure performance. Half our marks went for colour and half for sound, and there were bonus points for variability – doing unexpected things such as splitting off, changing colour, going from being pretty to being noisy, or starting off noisy and subsiding into prettiness. Brock's were the tops – plenty of good colours and the best bangs. Standard were perfectly respectable fireworks, though at a level below Brock's. Peter and I gave Pain's the thumbs-down. The colours were so poor and bleached. They were anæmic – a potent word from my memories of CRX. They needed iron injections in the bottom and lots of spinach in their diet.

One year our neighbours the Paynes attended our firework party, and contributed a massive piece (at the top of the entire Pain's range) called an Air Raid, which needed to be nailed to a tree. The rumour ran round the party that it had cost £5 3s 8d. It came with an instruction leaflet suggesting that you might like to run indoors after lighting the touch paper. For the adults it must have been like re-living a bit of the War. I'm surprised they didn't start looking around for an Anderson shelter.

The 'Air Raid' scored full points for noise, but Mum had hustled us indoors, so we could hardly assess it for variability or for colour. In the absence of direct evidence, I had to assume that the Pain's colours were as drab as ever, although it earned a few points for effort. (I knew from school that marks for effort were always insulting.) I hope this cocky dismissal of an expensive present didn't get back to the Paynes.

Nerve punches

I was an older creature now than I had been when Miss Krüger had ruled CRX with her terror. Now I understood that cruelty was not an official part of education, even in a disabled school. I began to wonder if I could mention Judy Brisby to Mum without breaching the schoolboy code – Judy Brisby and what she did.

She liked to demonstrate what she called 'nerve punches', agonising blows to the upper arm which left no mark. She gave one to a very strong boy called Terence Wilberforce (who had slight polio in one leg, I think), and told us with quiet pride that it would go on being extremely painful for a full two weeks. She also said the boys who learned to take it from her would in time be taught the proper technique for delivering such punches. Then they could find others to practise on. I don't think anyone took her up on the offer to join a prætorian guard of nerve-punching thugs. Toadying could only go so far, and beyond the occasional piece of cold toast from her breakfast entitlement, Judy Brisby had nothing whatever to offer.

Even her nerve-punch technique wasn't as perfect as she made out – she left a dark mark on Terence's arm like a tea-bag. Terence called the mark 'PG Tips', but it took all the bravado he could muster, and he flinched if he thought anyone was going to touch it.

Judy Brisby seemed to have the confidence of the school authorities, but I'm certain there were staff members who realised that something wasn't right. I remember dear Gillie Walker, who had a very sunny disposition and used to rush into my arms and call me 'Darling', saying to us in an undertone when the subject of Judy Brisby was mentioned, 'I don't know how you boys tolerate her.' Looking back, I would say that darling Gillie, though the nicest of the nice, was far from being the bravest of the brave. We shouldn't have had to tolerate Judy Brisby. There was nothing to stop Gillie reporting her, unless the rules against telling tales were as strict among matrons, those brooms promoted from splinters, as they were among the schoolboys they were supposed to protect. Even when it came to denouncing a sadistic colleague.

In the end I said nothing to Mum. I wasn't strong like Terence Wilberforce, and I took some comfort from that. With her medical training Judy Brisby must surely be able to understand the risks. She wouldn't dare to give me a nerve punch because it would kill me. On the other hand she gave one to Trevor Burbage (the human suitcase) once, saying calmly, 'Let that be a lesson to anyone who wants to write letters to their parents about how mean certain people are.'

Judy Brisby's campaign against Roger Stott's bed-wetting wasn't helping him to break the habit. Of course it wasn't meant to. Having made his problem worse she referred him up the power structure, and turned the headmaster into the executive arm of her cruelty.

My feelings for Ben Nevin contained no element of fear, unless awe is by definition the benign form of fear, but my perception of my other secret lover Alan Raeburn became clouded over. The Board of Education, that innocent, sinister object, to be seen on his desk or protruding from his back pocket, began to pose a threat, and my knowledge of its origin in the Ellisdons catalogue wasn't enough to protect me from fantasies of disaster.

Now at Judy Brisby's bidding Raeburn was warning Roger Stott that if he didn't snap out of that dirty habit double quick, it would be time for extreme measures. The Board of Education would be convened on his backside.

A few bed-wets later Roger was told to go to the Headmaster's office, to be given a lesson he would never forget. A small group of us gathered quietly nearby. The noise of the whacking coming from the office was terrifying, and when Roger came out, he had tears streaming down his face. He couldn't say anything, and his bottom hurt so much he couldn't sit. He just went off somewhere by himself and cried for a long time. I felt very forlorn and wished there was something I could do for him, but I had no help to give. I was also terrified that even if this beating 'cured' him, it might somehow bring the habit back to me. I wasn't wrong. Nocturnal enuresis came back from the past to torment me for a period after that.

This was like a death sentence for me. I had seen what had been done to Roger, and I knew that my own body was very fragile. I didn't see how it could survive that level of corporal punishment. So the you're-going-to-die feeling, which I thought I'd left behind at CRX, of Death Bed and Vera Cole all lumped together, came back to haunt me again.

I needn't have worried. Raeburn had telephoned Dr Ansell at CRX to ask if he could beat me in the same way as he beat everyone else – which was very decent of him – and she had said, 'Not under any circumstances.' So I was exempt, though I didn't know it at the time. Raeburn had wanted Ansell to rubber-stamp the Board of Education, but bless her, she wouldn't do it.

Low blows on our flesh

The next boy to be called up for a beating was James O'Brien, another asthmatic AB but a very different kettle of fish from gentle Roger. I think he was from Irish gentry. He never had less than £20 in his pocket, a staggering sum. There was another boy, Jeremy Fraser, who got a letter from his mother every two weeks with a ten-shilling note in it. That was affluence enough by our measure. Julian Robinson did the sums in his head and announced that this added up to £3 per term. I went dizzy at the thought. Jeremy Fraser was rich all right, but James O'Brien was stinking. Rolling in it.

He even had a job all ready for him when he left school, working for his father. James was a rather cocky boy who showed little respect for any of his teachers. He had no fear of Raeburn and his Board of Education. He even laughed at Raeburn in his study, who beat him until the Board broke. Raeburn said it made no difference as he had a spare, but we all reckoned he was shaken by what had happened. James became a hero, not perhaps for the best of reasons.

Still, it gave me some comfort to know that the Board couldn't duplicate the *Fantasia* trick known to matrons and enchanted brooms. Reconstituting itself full-size many times over from the splinters.

Not long afterwards Raeburn had an accident. He fell over and took a nasty knock. Subsequent investigation revealed that his sticks had been sawn apart and then carefully glued together to make a seamless join. The co-principals rattled their sabres and put it about that this was a dirty low-down rotten snivelling cowardly thing to do to a man who couldn't walk properly. They were confident that the perpetrator would be unmasked in short order by a boy with the proper loyalty to the school and its co-principal.

We didn't sit down and discuss how obscene this suggestion was, that we were expected to expose the saboteur of canes. Its vileness was glaring. The Board of Education was no respecter of disability, it had landed low blows on our flesh, and now we were expected to take the witness stand on its behalf. There were those of us who personally couldn't stand James O'Brien, but we didn't have the slightest intention of exposing him. No one came forward. Nothing could be proved anyway, and we showed how well we had learned our lesson about not telling tales. We had been indoctrinated, fully absorbing the ethos of the school. Closing ranks was all the loyalty we knew.

I felt a little sorry for Alan Raeburn, all the same. My love was still there under the layers of UHU glue, even if it was always ebbing and flowing between him and my other secret lover Ben Nevin, but now I felt ashamed that I had ever wavered in my devotion to this man with the blue-grey eyes who had told me secrets about the gods of Olympus and trusted me to be discreet. His lack of popularity made me feel that it was a duty for me to stick up for him, if only in my mind.

Knickers at half-mast

The winter of 1962–3 was one of the coldest of the century. The temperature didn't rise above freezing for months. Yet I don't remember the Great Freeze as being any worse than other winters at Vulcan – in fact it was rather more endurable. We heard a lot about extreme

393

conditions. Birds for instance were starving to death in their hundreds of thousands. It's just I don't remember it being any colder. It wasn't that I had become used to low temperatures. Heaters were found for the dormitories (they didn't reappear the following year). Even Judy Brisby suspended her habit of pulling the bedclothes off every boy, not just the one whose turn it was to be washed first. No heating was possible for the lavatories, of course, but a stricter régime of watchfulness was instituted, so that there was no chance of a mishap. It wouldn't be good for the fund-raising that was such a perpetual headache for Raeburn and Miss Willis for a severely disabled thirteen-year-old such as myself to be found frozen to death on the lavvie, knickers at half-mast round his blue and useless ankles, *rigor mortis* subtly replacing *rigor vitæ*. Not quite the pretty tableau at the end of Hans Christian Andersen's *Little Match Girl*. I still think the coldness of the Blue Dorm lavatory in winter was an absolute beyond the understanding of Kelvin. Weather conditions, extreme or mild, had no power of addition or subtraction there, though the temperature had a moral aspect. Biggie when she entered could raise it ten degrees.

In all weathers we had fire drill, but that was lovely. It catered to my need to be held. Raeburn and Miss Willis took the risk of fire seriously, as was proper for those in charge of a large old building full of boys who couldn't save themselves. There was a fire escape running from a room in the north-west corner of the Castle, and alarm bells at each corner. My love of fire was close to unconditional, but stopped short of a desire to be burned alive, so I would have taken part in these disaster rehearsals willingly enough in any case. In fact fire drill was a treat rather than a labour, thanks to the large chute that ran from a first-floor door at the south-east corner of the building down onto the lawn.

The more able-bodied boys would simply throw themselves down the chute, howling with pleasure, to be caught at the bottom or land on piles of cushions. On one occasion a nervous boy hung back, perhaps frightened by the howls of those ahead, and clung so tightly to the top of the chute that Raeburn had to detach him by main force. In the event his shrieks of distress had changed, by the time he was halfway down, to screams of joy.

Those of us who were more disabled would ride on the laps of teachers, deafening ourselves and our companions with excited noises as we rushed downwards in the dark to the small circle of light at the bottom. In the event of a real emergency I imagine the staff would be expected to re-enter the building, if possible, to help a new batch of disabled boys to reach safety, while those already rescued grumbled about the unfairness of grown-ups having extra turns.

With my luck, I tended to go down the slide on the laps of people I didn't care for, so that the joy of the sensation was diluted by resentment of the company. More than once it was Mr Lewis the history teacher who was my fire-drill partner. He was so bony it was like going down the chute on an iron bedstead. What I wanted more than anything else never happened – for Ben Nevin to take me on his lap and plunge with me down the chute. If it had happened, I would have been very tempted to die of happiness before we reached the bottom. As Hindus know, the last moments of a life affect the beginning of the next – it's not a full stop, hardly even a comma, the sense runs on – and with such a death I'd have a head start on the next go-round, or would be promoted to bliss without the chore of further flesh.

Motes of fantasy sifting

Perhaps it was because the reality of the school had so many sharp edges that fantasy flourished so strongly there. Motes of fantasy sifted in through every chink in the windows (and God knows there were plenty of those) and drifted under the beds. I'm inclined to think that there was something congenial to fantasy in the air, or in the water, or in the soil of the place. The Castle had been a fantastical edifice from its foundation. Realism never really got a look in. Farley Castle was a castle in the air that had only touched down for a moment. Soon it would float away again. Raeburn and Miss Willis would never succeed in tethering it, unrealistic as they were in their own way.

This was a period when a new strain of fantasy was emerging, preoccupied with spies and gadgets. The James Bond novels had been around for quite a while, and now a film had been made of one of them. Everyone claimed to have seen *Dr No*, though I don't know that they could have. Perhaps some had elder brothers who were able to give an account of the high points. Even I learned, when asked which was my favourite bit, to say, 'The bit where the lady came out of the sea,' and to look as sly as I possibly could.

The strangest places could be colonised by fantasy. One was the cramped lift, along with the shaft in which it moved. It was feature-less, unless you count a plaque acknowledging the contribution made by The Commonwealth Fund for Crippled Children. Even Judy Brisby had the grace, when she saw me looking at it, to say, 'It's not the nicest word, is it?'

The lift was a sort of non-place in which we spent a lot of time over the years. It was just waiting to be transformed. A whole mythology came to encrust the lift-shaft, and I can claim to have given it its start. I seemed to be able to spin the most fantastic yarns after lights out, and there was no reason to be inhibited by daylight. Perhaps my style was a little cramped in our cowboy fantasy with its frequent pornographic excursions, our buckskin Kama Sutra passion play. It sometimes made me feel a little type-cast as a personified bosom, a *yoni* ready for any *lingam*, the girl who gets swamped with hormones while she's cooking, and has to fit in a passionate love-making session with a hunky cow-boy in the pantry, timing things so she can repeat her climax as many times as possible, before emerging without a hair out of place when the mistress returns in her wagon or the cakes start to burn.

By day I could mine a new vein of dreaming. There were nooks and crannies in the brick-work of the lift-shaft which gave imagination a finger-hold. My idea was that you could use the crannies to deposit and pick up letters as part of an international network of spies. You would have to roll them up very tight to poke them through the con-certina grille of the lift itself. It became a challenge and a thrill for the more able-bodied, spiced by the prospect of losing a finger as the cage ascended or descended. I wasn't physically able to make the drops myself, but I explained the system to people who weren't in on it. 'I'm not supposed to tell you this,' I'd say, looking around with as much suavity as I could muster. 'I'm an agent myself. It's worked by com-pressed air. Every so often they turn the pumps on, and all the letters disappear with a great WHOOSH! I've seen it happen.'

It was certainly true that some letters seemed to disappear soon after they were left, while others lingered, but that was easily explained. Not everyone had cranny-posting privileges, and unautho-rised personnel would have their messages ignored, just as if they had posted a letter without a stamp.

The secret between his legs

I had stiff competition in the secret-agent fantasy line. The reign-ing champion was Julian Robinson, the boy I'd humiliated so meanly, whose chemistry set I had crushed with the overpowering excellence of Gilbert's Fun. Lotts for tiny tots. He was very far from being a tiny tot by now. He must have had a growth spurt, or a series of them. Of course I had my growth spurts too, but you would have needed a micrometer to measure them.

I remember one story that Julian circulated, about the Yanks proudly sending British Intelligence the smallest tube in the world, so small you could hardly see it. Our back-room boys sent it back with a thank-you note, inscribed on an even smaller tube tucked inside the original one. We absolutely believed stories of this sort, confident that spies and super-scientists jostled each other to get to the post, to find the packages marked TOP SECRET in large letters. We ourselves jockeyed for position in our wheelchairs when Miss Willis floated into the hall, holding a stack of letters in her left hand and peering down her half-moon glasses as she laid them out on the big table.

Our jingoist sense of superiority to everything American co-existed very happily with its opposite, and the night-time story-telling con-tinued to have a spurious Old West setting.

When Julian and I were on our own I was supposed to call him QM. I think he had simply combined the abbreviations of the two geniuses in the supporting cast of the James Bond stories, Q the inventor and M the tactician. Putting x and y together in algebra meant you were multiplying. Julian was multiplying the powers of the boffin and the director of operations.

His powers were certainly on the rise. Every time I looked at Julian, he seemed to have out-grown his last pair of jeans and to be freshly installed in new ones. I became swept up in his make-believe of espionage, but at the start my interest was less the hidden microfilm than the secret between his legs.

I wanted to explore his private parts, so that I could at last understand what normal ones looked like. I'd seen one set of genitals, on a
boy being given a shower, and very hairy and darkly dangling they
were too, but he was multiply disabled and it stood to reason that his
parts would be abnormal also. Julian, though, was an increasingly
strapping lad apart from the effects of polio on his legs. I was sure his
parts would be normal. He was also a physically affectionate boy,
something I enjoyed in its own right but which also gave my objective a real chance of success.

His whispered instructions about our missions had a lot in common with the sweet nothings of lovers. 'I've taken delivery of a special
gun,' he breathed in my ear. 'It needs to be installed somewhere no
one will ever think of looking for it.' I gave an important nod. 'I know
just the place,' he went on. 'Inside your walking stick.'

Of course! It wasn't actually a walking stick, or rather I didn't actually use it for walking. It was the stick I carried in the wheelchair
with me for poking and prodding and nudging myself along. He was
right. No one would dream of looking in there.

'The procedure for installing is rather complicated. I'll take your
stick away and do the conversion outside, away from you-know-who.'
I had no idea who. He was gone for a long time, about fifteen minutes. When he brought it back I didn't think it looked any different
at first, but then Julian showed me the notch I would have to press to
fire it. He made me promise not to use it indoors unless there was a
real emergency.

Did I really think that Julian had installed a gun in my stick? I
think I did. It somehow felt different after that, warm from his hand,
heavier, more laden with consequence. He had an extraordinary ability to lead people into his little world, though of course everyone's
world is exactly the same size.

Hook, line and sinker

Next day he gave me a briefing. 'Your assignment', he whispered,
'is to keep an eye on Mr Atkinson. Top security. Of course you know
he's a Russian spy? We've been watching him for some time now . . .'

Mr Atkinson! It was the last thing I expected, yet it made perfect sense. Mr Atkinson had been hired to teach us German, which he wrote and spoke very well indeed. I got on well with him, and my German improved by leaps and bounds. He always looked so dapper in his smart suit and open-necked shirt. His hair was curly and lay very close to his head, so that it looked stuck on. It was white – not just grey but entirely white – and yet his face was as smooth as a lady's, almost as if he didn't need to shave.

Atkinson had been sent to spy on us boys, disguised as someone who wanted to help us. Raeburn and Willis had fallen for his tricks hook, line and sinker, and so had I. That was the worst part of it. He'd been pally and friendly with me, and I'd been pally and friendly right back. I was such a chatter-box (everyone always said so) that I might have told him just about anything. My face started to burn with shame.

'Are you sure?' I stammered. 'How do you know?'

'Oh come on! As an agent I expect you to do better than that!' said Julian. 'Don't tell me you haven't noticed his upward-sloping curly *R*s? It's a dead give-away!'

Upward-sloping curly Rs! I'd done more than notice them – I'd raised them in class, I'd chattered about them for twelve whole minutes of a lesson to pass the time. I adored them, I'd adopted them as my own. I'd even been scolded by Willis for using them. Miss Willis had strong ideas about hand-writing, saying for instance that script which sloped backwards was a sure sign of someone who was afraid of life. After that, my script sloped forward so much the letters almost fell on their faces.

I only used my special *R*s when doing homework for Mr Atkinson. He also pronounced perfect German 'r's, though he wasn't German. He pronounced them like a native, like Gisela. I should have realised that an Englishman cannot do that. I'd come close to hero-worship, and now I realised that I'd been played for a fool.

At the same time I was thrilled. At CRX I'd felt a twinge of sadness when I finished reading *Five Fall into Adventure*. It lent life and colour to the ward. I knew that adventures never really happened, but I'd dared to ask for a real adventure for myself. And now it had been granted – granted with a vengeance. My prayer had even included a pal called Julian, and God had sent that. I'd asked for him to have blond hair to remind me of Tommy Steele, and Julian's was dark, but I couldn't expect God to attend to every detail when he was so busy.

I thought of some of the things I must have said to Atkinson, which the situation just made seem even more frightening. Raeburn was a military man, he would know what to do – but how to contact him? He might just as well be miles away. Dad would also know what to do, but fate had separated me from my family. Even if I broke the rules and 'told', no one would believe us. The truth was that Atkinson was a very cunning agent indeed.

'He has a gun of his own, of course,' added Julian smoothly. 'It's a small Beretta. Point four oh two. First thing I noticed. That's why I told HQ you had to be armed. If you do have to shoot Atkinson I'll take full responsibility.'

I started to get frightened then, which had the advantage of bringing Julian closer. He hugged me awkwardly, but said, 'Pull yourself together. British agents don't cry.'

'But it's only my second day . . .' I whined.

'These people we're up against are ruthless. They'll use your weakness against you.' This I could understand. This was just the sort of rubbish that filtered down from the fathers of our generation. 'Don't worry,' he said, 'nothing will happen that I can't handle. That's what I'm here for, after all . . .'

He had been on the blower to his boss at HQ, and there was a plan in place. Atkinson would be kidnapped the next Monday. He would be detained at HQ for three days, interrogated and then brainwashed. Atkinson was very dangerous, but it had to be admitted that he was an extremely good agent. It would be a shame to eliminate a man of that calibre, so HQ (after taking advice from Julian, of course) had decided that it was worth taking the risk of recruiting him to be one of ours, once he had been brain-washed.

The funny thing was that Atkinson did disappear on the Monday. Miss Willis told us that his sister had been taken ill suddenly and he needed to visit her. She hoped that things would be back to normal in a few days. She read out this announcement from a piece of paper, peering down at it through her half-moon specs.

My admiration for the boy agent Julian went from strength to

400

strength – it was a treat to see how even Miss Willis had fallen for the cover story. I just wished I'd been a senior enough agent to be trusted with it ahead of time. On Thursday Atkinson was back, looking just as dapper, and continuing to write his upward-sloping curly *R*s in just the same way, but somehow he was milder. Something had happened to him which was the opposite of what happened to my stick when the gun was installed. He had been hollowed out. More had been taken out during interrogation than had been put back in.

All the same, I got a reward for my part in the successful conclusion of the Atkinson affair. QM used his influence to get me a promotion. He was now my immediate superior. I was to report only to him.

Usefulness in the field

Julian told me I would be put on an assignment within a week. I was very excited, but I also had doubts about my usefulness in the field. 'We've already thought of that,' he said. 'GHQ says you're to be issued with a hidden tape-recorder. It will be planted in your body at some stage. It may be grafted on while you're sleeping – we do a lot of our work that way – or I may install it myself. *Keep it on you at all times!*' I promised I would. Of course, since it would be grafted onto my body, I wouldn't be able to do anything else.

I was looking forward to getting my tape-recorder, but I wasn't sure that I wanted a secret agent to install it in my body while I was asleep. What if I woke up in the middle of installation? And if I woke in the night I would wonder if an agent had already been, to leave his equipment inside me. I much preferred the plan that Julian – QM – would install the apparatus himself. If he did, he would have to get close to me, and after all, I did have a mission of my own.

It turned out that HQ wasn't able to send an agent that week. Some sort of show in the Balkans. So Julian was authorised to take care of the installation himself, in an empty classroom at the end of the school day, when no one else was around. It was vital for both missions that secrecy was observed, otherwise the whole operation would turn into a fiasco. QM reminded me that the security of our country depended on vigilance, and I took my new job very seriously.

Julian came over to me and leant his crutches against the wall by my desk. I put the brake on my wheelchair to give him something stable to hold on to. I tingled from having him so close. Julian always wore a nice shirt and nicer jeans. His clothes looked fresh and smart, however long he wore them. He had a nice fresh smell and kept himself very clean, although the facilities at Vulcan weren't wonderful. I could never quite work out how he achieved this level of grooming. Perhaps it was all part of an agent's training.

He was holding himself up on the arm of my wheelchair, to the left of my legs. I wondered what the promised secret tape-recorder would look like. I was also gazing at those crisp new legs. I was familiar with Julian's back view, and his snug young bottom. Now I was close to the cleft at his front, and trying my hardest to see what was there. There didn't seem to be very much. Then by good luck I was given another means to explore the equipment.

'It would be best if you close your eyes now,' said Julian. 'HQ's very anxious that you don't witness the transfer. What you don't know can't be tortured out of you.' This was a less welcome thought. Julian put his left arm over my right shoulder and then leaned back slightly while I closed my eyes. He was very strong. His strength ran through me. I felt a pressure on my forehead which must have been his thumb. He pressed and twisted, almost to the point of pain, then told me to open my eyes.

Nothing felt different, but my heart was pounding as if he had given me a stimulant injection. Julian's warm breath was falling on my face. The tape-recorder might be inside me or it might never have existed, but there were other things in the world that cried out to be investigated.

'This is a solemn moment,' I said. 'We should recognise its importance with some sort of pledge.' I stumbled over the words. 'You know, a hand-shake or a hug. Maybe even a kiss . . .'

I was afraid that I had gone too far but Julian didn't hesitate. 'Good plan, Agent Nesbitt,' he replied. Why he called me Agent Nesbitt I have no idea. 'You have an inventive mind. GHQ will like that. I reckon it should be a hug and a kiss on the ear, and while I'm doing that, I'll pass on some Top Secret Info!'

Julian hadn't lost his extraordinary ability to bring others into his fantasy world, but he was also responding to mine. We were like two master hypnotists putting the moves on each other, or just two schoolboys, both equally suggestible, getting carried away.

While I waited for the Top Secret Info to be poured into me, I had my own scheme of espionage. The plan was to get Julian's leg between mine, and when I had him close to fumble at his cleft just as fast and as furiously as I could. If any treasure was there, I would be sure to find it, even with the somewhat primitive data-gathering equipment available to me. Because of the inflexibility of my wrists, there was no possibility of me turning my palms towards Julian's crotch. I would have to make do with the backs of my hands.

My assignment within an assignment had its share of risk, but the strong taboo against telling tales, which left me vulnerable at other times, was strangely protective here. I said a quick prayer, hoping that God was indeed omnipresent. Then he must also be in the devil who was tempting me today.

I was an undercover agent, true, but I was certainly a beginner. There was something I had overlooked in my eagerness to go under-cover. I parted my legs and waited in rapture for Julian's left leg to come mounding and pressing against my genitals. The leg never made it that far. As it approached my knee, I felt not pleasure but a bolt of pain.

Chaperone and chastity belt

I could only open my legs the merest crack. I was having a good day in terms of flexibility, and I expect I managed a few inches, but of course a few inches at floor level isn't the same distance when you work up to the knee. A rolling pin could hardly have fitted between my upper legs, let alone the neatly trousered leg of this strong thirteen-year-old boy.

We were in a school for the disabled, everything in the establish-ment catered to our difficulties and our special needs, but in the heat of secret-agent fantasy it had slipped my mind that I had Still's Disease and that he had polio. I hadn't forgotten, exactly, but at that moment I didn't remember. I knew perfectly well that Julian wore callipers, but this too had disappeared from my consciousness at this point.

The progress of his braced left leg towards a tryst with my taily and dependent scallywag was sharply arrested by my knees. Instead of warmth and love I felt the hard press of metal and leather. The flash of pain was produced by his heavy callipers scraping against my legs. I winced, he lurched backwards and the exchange of secret information was over before it could begin.

My attempt at seduction was foiled by a double mechanical impossibility. My hips were immobile while his legs were floppy, needing to be braced mechanically for him to walk. What made me feel even more stupid after the event was that I'd so often watched polio boys having their callipers put on. Some of them needed help from the little matrons, others learned to fend for themselves. Julian pretty much put them on for himself. The contrast between strong upper bodies and wasted legs made those boys seem like mythical beasts, minotaur colts.

I had even examined Julian's callipers in the early days of secret-agent fascination, while he explained the various modifications HQ was going to install. I tried to hold one when it was off, but it was too heavy for me to lift for more than a moment or two. I liked the idea of being close to a boy who had switches and hinges on him, as if Professor Branestawm had had a hand in designing him.

Each calliper consisted of two parallel metal bars which ran down each side of the leg. The bars were hinged at the knee and could be set to lock or unlock. To hold the calliper in place a series of leather straps and buckles ran crosswise and round the leg. It was vital that the hinge of the calliper coincided with the hinge of each knee, in order to avoid terrible pain when Julian wanted to bend his legs. For walking, the bars were set at lock. There was a release catch on each side of each knee, so in order to bend his knees for sitting down at meals or lessons Julian – and all the other boys with callipers – had to set four release catches, and then repeat the process in reverse for standing up.

Julian's jeans were able-bodied items of clothing, but I could see that they didn't wear out in the normal way. His legs weren't mobile enough to manage much in the way of scuffing, but the hinges of his callipers were always nipping the cloth round the knees.

He'd told me often enough that putting the callipers on was an elaborate business. Gillie Walker and Biggie were the best 'putteronners' – the love they had for their work meant their hands became sensitised to the boy's requirements. All the straps had to be set at the right degree of tension. If the strap was set too loose the leg would wobble and shift inside the cage, making it dangerous or impossible for him to walk. If the strap was set too tight, then the circulation of blood would be impaired. An already difficult job was made even more taxing by the fact that the boys were growing fast, none faster than Julian, and the weather played its part. A boy's leg would be smaller on a cold day and so need more strapping. It would expand in warmer weather. Additionally the leg would be much colder (and smaller) at the beginning of the day and hotter and larger at the end. So Julian and the other polio boys could often be seen fiddling with their callipers at various points in the day.

All this had gone out of my mind while I waited for the embrace of knowledge. I hadn't yet learned that there are points in the body where energy gathers in debased forms unless it is released by the proper procedure. Julian and I were alarmingly clogged in our adolescent chakras with thickly sedimented desire, but ankylosis was my chaperone and Julian's polio was his chastity belt.

Life became easier for calliper users a little later, when Velcro started to replace leather straps. Velcro had been around for some time, but its use in callipers came as a separate little break-through.

When I'd first seen this new material which mimicked couch grass, I'd fallen in love with it. I'd not personally had any great problem with manipulating zips. I even fancied myself something of an expert, but it had been an easy matter to convince Mum, who was always a dab hand at needle-work, that Velcro would be easier for me. She got to work with a vengeance. When the magic closures had been installed, I spent hours opening and closing the gap at my groin. I thoroughly enjoyed the tearing sound as the male and female surfaces were torn apart. In time, as the novelty wore off, I would forget to close the flies before the trousers were washed. After only a few adventures in the maëlstrøm of the washing machine, the male component of the Velcro would be festooned with stray fibres, bonded into unorthodox unions which allowed no divorce. There was no getting rid of the fluff once it had become embedded. The initial sharp rip of the tearing when the fly was opened would soften to a dull scrape.

405

Mum would scold me on the eve of my regular returns to Vulcan. 'You must make *sure* that you join the Velcro zip before it gets washed – just see what fluff and what-not has got in!' It was already too late. Gaps appeared in the fly opening as the male hooks lost interest in the arranged marriage intended by the manufacturers. They preferred to hook up with the low-life denizens which flaunted themselves in the vortex of the washing machine's drum.

The Cromer Cocklebur

When I learned the circumstances of this material's invention, it was a shattering disappointment. It was so obvious that it should have been me that made the break-through.

George de Mestral, Swiss engineer and outdoorsman, got the idea for Velcro from cockleburs caught in his clothes and his dog's fur. How could a seed-case show the same affinity for his tweeds and for his dog's coat? He detached a bur from his trousers and examined it under the microscope. It was covered with tiny hooks.

That's all it took – ingredients which I also had to hand: dog, cockleburs from the burdock that grew so plentifully round the Abbotsbrook Estate, microscope. An eye that noticed oddities and a mind that followed them up. How many significant inventions are born so painlessly? It should have been me – surely it would have, if George de Mestral hadn't beaten me to it by taking that fateful walk the year before I was born.

I had looked to chemistry as my medium for making a mark on the world, not entirely foolishly. Joseph Priestley and John Dalton, after all, were amateurs without laboratories or extensive materials. William Perkin was only eighteen when he discovered a wonderful new dye while experimenting at home with his own chemicals.

An invention, though, was a greater achievement than a discovery. It could have been me, looking up with a smile from the microscope and murmuring to my select audience (a dog with matted fur, trying in vain to remove its infestation of hook-balls), 'I tell you, Gipsy, I will design a unique, two-sided fastener, one side covered with tiny stiff hooks like these burs and the other side with soft loops like the fabric of my trousers. I will fund and research the whole enterprise myself. I will call my invention "Velcro" by combining the words *velour* and *crochet*. It will out-shine the fallible zip in the excellence of its fastening ability. Shortly I will be selling six million metres a year.

'On second thoughts, since I don't think in French, and therefore have no particular reason for devising a portmanteau name combining the words in that language for *velvet* and *hook*, I will select a trade-name which will enshrine my name in glorious company. The Cromer Cocklebur Closure. The Cromer for short. Accept no substitute. In the future, when people want to get out of their clothes, they will simple undo their Cromers . . .'

I suppose this scenario would have benefited from Peter being present, pushing the wheelchair. And since the burs would be unlikely to leap up onto my clothing, perhaps it would fall to Peter to say, slapping ineffectually at his trousers, 'Drat these bally things! They're not sticky when you touch them, but they stick like mad to fabric and pelt! I wonder how that comes about?' He was a Cromer too, after all. He could share in the glory, before he got down to the chore of brushing Gipsy's coat. Leaving me to say the fateful words, 'Hold on a minute. I've got an idea. Let's take a proper *scientific* look at one of those things . . .' Though of course I'd also have to invent a time machine, so that I could pop back in time and steal a march on M. de Mestral, before he could steal a march on me.

Miss Pearce

For quite a time Velcro was the sole possession of the disabled, who loved it and were grateful for it. Then it was adopted as a fad by people who could manage zips and buttons perfectly well.

Installing Velcro in my trousers was elementary. It didn't stretch Mum's abilities as a seamstress. By now she had got to know Dorothy Foot a little better. Dorothy was a wonderful dressmaker, who started holding actual classes, and Mum told Dad she wanted to join.

He wouldn't have it at first. 'Mm. Bet that's going to cost a packet, and where d'you think the money for it will come? From muggins here. What's wrong with knitting? You're good at that – go and buy some more balls of wool, and I'll treat you to a new pair of needles. We can run to that!'

Mum shed actual tears at his callousness. 'A little sewing and dressmaking class would be a perfect opportunity to meet people,' she said, 'and I know I'd be good at it. You know, I might get good enough to make shirts. Dorothy says that's really hard, but she feels I've got it in me to do it. It would make such a difference if I could make shirts that really fit.'

'Mine fit fine,' said Dad.

'You're not the only person in the world, you know,' Mum said, and I imagine she tipped her head towards me. I pretended not to be listening.

Later she poured her heart out to me. She still did that then. 'It's true I'd need a sewing machine and material and all sorts, so I suppose Dad is right. We don't really have the money. It's always there for his cigarettes, though . . .' By now Dad was just starting to smoke his way through his second house.

Then he gave in after all. Perhaps it was the prospect of her being able to tailor shirts to my short arms which made him relent. When the sewing classes started, Mum found herself in a happy period of her life. In the end, those classes led to us acquiring a sort of house guest, even (if only in Mum's eyes) a new member of the family.

She would come back into the house proud of what she had learned, bubbling also with the gossip that went with the sewing. She was newly plugged in to the grape-vine. It was as if she had been on a long holiday, rather than to a neighbour's house for a few hours. All of us in the house felt the benefit.

It wasn't long before Dorothy announced that Mum had learned all she needed to make clothes for other ladies. There was more involved than skill, however. 'I knew it,' said Dad when Mum passed this on.

If Mum was to do herself justice, she couldn't just take her tape to make measurements, write them down, and come back later with the garment. That would be slap-dash and amateurish. To set herself up as any sort of professional she needed a proper dressmaker's dummy. There may have been a fancy dressmakers' term for such contraptions, to justify their vast expense, but if I was told it I have forgotten.

Mum showed Dad the catalogue and he went red in the face when he saw the prices. He said she could have the cheapest one there was, and half the money would have to be repaid when she started earning from the new hobby, if that day ever dawned. Mum hankered after one rather better than the basic model, though she wasn't competing with Dorothy, who owned one which was very much *de luxe*. In the end I think she took a deep breath and ran down to the Post Office with her savings book and drew on that slim reserve.

Mum was very excited after placing her order at last. I could sympathise, remembering my own Ellisdons frenzies. She would phone up the catalogue headquarters on a regular basis to see if it had come in. When she was told at last that it had, she asked the man to be sure to hold on to it. Her cheque was on its way. The man told her not to worry. 'Tell you what I'll do,' he said. 'To put your mind at rest I'm going to get a special marker pen, and I'll write *Mrs Cromer* on your model.' 'Oh would you? That would be so kind.'

Mum was very happy. At last the box arrived. I was in the next room when she opened it, and I could hear from her voice that something was wrong. It was obviously not the one she had ordered, after all. 'Oh for Heaven's sake!' she called out to me. 'You'll never guess what they've done, JJ. They've sent me one with someone else's name written on the back, and not "Cromer" at all. This one should have gone to "Miss Pearce", whoever she may be.'

Mum seemed to be in a sort of agony. There was obviously something she wasn't telling me. She picked up the phone and asked Dorothy if she could come over straight away. Mum didn't say much on the phone, but Dorothy got enough of a whiff of emergency to drop everything and come over.

As she came in Dorothy called out politely, 'How are you, John, keeping well?' but then she went very quiet when she saw what was in the box. She said, 'Would it be all right if I sat down and had a cup of coffee and a biscuit, Laura dear?' This escalation to refreshments made me realise that I was eavesdropping on some sort of summit conference, even if I still had no idea what it was all about.

I punted the wheelchair round as gently as I could, so I could catch a glimpse of what was going on in the kitchen. I had made a little progress since the Bathford days. I wanted to know what was happening right away. I no longer had the patience to wait until later, when I could peck at Mum's beak and be fed a meal of regurgitated gossip.

'What do you think has happened, Dorothy?' Mum was asking in a troubled voice. 'And what should I do about it? I'm in a frightful bind.'

'I don't see that you are, dear, And it's perfectly obvious what has happened. You ordered a Morris Minor and they delivered a Rolls-Royce instead! That's what has happened. There's nothing this model won't do.' I could see it now, a headless torso of wire and struts. Dorothy Foot started adjusting handles and pulling little levers. 'It's a marvel. Every single part of it adjustable. With this to work with, there'll be no holding you – you'll be the top dressmaker in the county!'

'It is so beautiful,' said Mum. 'I think it's almost as good as yours.'

'Nonsense, dear. I know what I'm talking about. Mine is a Bentley at best – a Bentley that has seen better days!'

'But what am I to do? I can't keep it.'

'I don't see why not. If it *was* a Rolls-Royce when you had ordered a Morris Minor then you wouldn't have much joy of it. It would have to stay in the garage and you'd never do more than gaze at it. But this never needs to leave the house. Hang on to it for dear life! It'll be the making of you.'

'But I can't!' Mum wailed. 'I have to send it back. I could never afford to pay the difference. I'm putting my neck out even to get what I ordered.'

'At least wait for them to ask for it. Promise me that. It's not your mistake, it's theirs. For all we know this Miss Pearce is a perfect horror and they've done this to put her nose out of joint. In any case, you're storing their property for them – you should charge them by the day! Just sit tight and wait to hear from the catalogue people, that's my advice. Don't go to meet trouble half-way.' Going to meet trouble half-way was usually Mum's method, but for once she seemed to be wavering.

'And if you take my advice,' Dorothy went on, 'you won't mention this to Dennis until it's settled one way or the other. Men choose the strangest moments to be righteous citizens.'

So Mum tucked Miss Pearce away in the spare room and said nothing. How Dad failed to notice her state of high excitement over the next few days I'll never know. Her flesh burned with the suspense of it all. If she had an actual corpse concealed in that room, rather than an innocently headless form which could assume every curve and contour of the female state, she could hardly have radiated guilt across a broader spectrum.

After two weeks, when the coast seemed to be clear, Miss Pearce emerged from the shadows and took her place in the front room. Dad was introduced to her at last, though he wasn't altogether taken with her. 'It's an ugly thing, really,' he said, with his practised unawareness of Mum's feelings. 'Is this going to be out in full view the whole time, m'dear? Couldn't you tidy it away when you're not using it?' He didn't see Miss Pearce's beauty. But Mum couldn't bear to let Miss Pearce out of her sight.

At first I couldn't see what the fuss was about myself. Miss Pearce was an amorphous nothing, a headless cage of wire with some prominences in front. But Mum's state of rapture was contagious.

The newcomer was always 'Miss Pearce'. Mum broke one of her own rules, which was that cherished possessions were known by the names of their manufacturers. Granny wasn't exactly unmaterialistic, but it would never have occurred to her to think that her consumer choices said anything about her. They wouldn't dare. Her things were the best simply by virtue of her having chosen them, but Mum agonised over every purchase. She was an early subscriber to *Which?* magazine, which came to play a huge part in her mental life. Proust had the Almanach de Gotha and Mum had *Which?*.

When the household acquired a sewing machine, it was always 'The Bernina'. On hot days Mum made iced coffee in the new 'Kenwood'. The oven was always 'The Rayburn', though she was anxious for it to be known that ours was the model which burned solid fuel, not the electric one.

Finding brand-name fuel to load into it was less easy. 'Coke' soon got the thumbs-down, and for a while she raved about the wonder fuel anthracite. Finally she said that removing the clonker (she always said 'clonker' rather than 'clinker') simply wore her out, and why on earth couldn't 'they' invent a fuel which simply burnt away to nothing?

Dishes had to be washed up with Squezy, elevenses was more relaxing with a cup of 'Nescafé'. The pronunciation soon shifted to 'Nescaff', which was what Muzzie had said, Muzzie being posh enough to play the game of common. Mum would slake her thirst with 'a Kia-Ora', and replenish her energy with a couple of 'Yeast-Vite'. And when she felt like a good gripe, she'd complain about our lawn mower, which was always going wrong. 'Your Dad never listens to me', she would say. 'If he'd bought an AtCo right from the start, as I advised, life would have run much more smoothly. Arthur Grant over the road has had one for years, and never had any trouble at all with it.' Only disgraced products forfeited their right to the maker's name, but Miss Pearce was never disgraced, and Miss Pearce was always 'Miss Pearce'.

Soon pretty ladies began to call to see Mum, and she would take them to a private place and come back with a full set of measurements. Then Miss Pearce would creak and grind as Mum winched and cranked her into the shape of the pretty lady. 'I can wind her all the way down to the size of Miss Susan Small,' she said, 'and all the way up to Bessie Braddock!' These were the Alpha and Omega of the womanly form post-war, a famous model whose waist measured eighteen inches and a portly and truculent Labour MP.

As the dress took shape she would come in with it every so often to show me the tricks of the trade. 'See here,' she would say, 'I don't have to call Alison to come in for a fitting. I've made this exactly to the correct measurements but see –' and here she would drop the dress onto the form '– it doesn't look quite right, does it? We have to have more of a tuck just here . . .' Then she would take the dress away for adjustments. The next time the dress met Miss Pearce the fit would be perfect. It showed what a good worker Mum was that the dress draped just as flatteringly on the satisfied customer as it had on Miss Pearce. Soon another lady would be told about Laura, how clever she was and how reasonable, and it wasn't long before Mum had a little clientèle all her own.

Miss Pearce was certainly the most precious thing in Mum's life at this point. She was dove-grey and cream – Quaker colours. She was a Quaker missionary sent into our home to dispense her sober joy. She was a frame on which Mum could drape her dreams. In fact we all felt warmly towards her, for bringing contentment into the house, though our feelings were more casual.

There's no doubt that if the house had burned down, it was Miss

Pearce that Mum would have rescued from the flames. I'm not saying that she would have neglected her family duties. She would have got me and Audrey and the pets out of there somehow (there were cats by this time as well as Gipsy, no longer young), but then she would have gone back in for Miss Pearce. Everything else was replaceable, but not the mistaken delivery which had brought so much happiness. On the whole Mum might have preferred to stay in the house with Miss Pearce, as the curtains caught and blazed, resting her head on that unrejecting breast.

A spiritchull baby

At this period I was equally thrilled by science and religion, without seeing a conflict. I got very excited about Billy Graham, who was on one of his gospel crusades, scorching the soul of middle England. There was a lot about him in the papers. I was just curious. The Bishop of Reading had come along the previous year and confirmed a batch of us, handing out Books of Common Prayer, and I had enjoyed that. His hands were nice and warm, but I didn't see why I shouldn't have a look around at the other options on offer.

The history teacher, John Wooffindin, organised an expedition to catch the show. That was how he put it, 'to catch the show', a clear enough indication that he wasn't a fan. I think he was trying to inoculate us against charisma. He was giving us our shots.

I can't remember now if the venue was in Reading or Slough. What I remember is thinking, when the great man made his entrance, 'Why does he have all that stuff on his face?' The make-up was not subtle, and very distracting. All the same I felt the desire to join in, to be swallowed up, the ancient surge of cult attraction, as well as a more cynical interest. The Reverend Billy Graham had power and I wanted to bathe in it.

Billy Graham's voice was a shout with a croon cradled inside it. He said, 'You'll be a spiritchull baby. You will need to be handled with tender care. Now, you can go away or you can come forward – Are you ready? If you're in any doubt, come forward.' Bright lights, loud music – it was all very unlike the Church of England. That last suggestion was particularly alien. Translated into Anglican, it would have come out meaning just the opposite: *If you're in any doubt, go away and think about it. We wouldn't want to rush you.*

Well, I was ready. I didn't mind the rush. I wanted to be a spiritual baby. I wanted handling with tender care. In fact John Wooffindin may have been dismayed that quite a few of us volunteered for the spiritual-baby treatment. Those of us who were in wheelchairs had to catch the eye of one of Graham's underlings – were they acolytes or marshals? Either way, it wasn't difficult. Those boys were certainly attuned to the presence of the disabled.

I noticed, though, that despite being in the middle of the Vulcan group I was somehow filtered out and led to one side. I felt flattered, as if I had been selected for something special, away from the flood-lights. The acolyte-marshal who had taken charge of me was ready with his Bible. He was handsome if a little sweaty. They all looked like brothers, rather piggy brothers. 'What's your name?' he asked.

'John.'

'Are you ready, John, to accept Jesus Christ as your personal sav-iour?'

'He may be or he may not be.'

'Don't you know what it says in the Bible about those who do not believe?' He had passages already marked in red. The frighteners. I forget which particular one he showed me, but it had the words 'ever-lasting' and 'fire' in it. And that, essentially, was the Billy Graham method for winning over the waverers. Scare them out of their wits. Doubt was not acceptable in a spiritual baby. There was to be no cradling of doubt. Doubt was simply flattened by the charismatic steam-roller.

For some reason I didn't find it difficult to stand my ground. 'That's stupid,' I said. 'If that's your God you can keep him. What's your name?' Actually he was wearing a name badge. 'Timothy? If you're so sure of everything in this world and the next, why do you bite your nails?'

He was very thrown by this, and blushed bright red. 'I don't,' he said, tucking his hands behind him.

'Then who does?' I asked, very pert. After that I was returned at fair speed to the rest of the Vulcan party. I don't think any of us had a more positive experience of the Billy Graham show than I had. If so, we didn't talk about it, any more than I talked about my feelings when I realised why I had been taken aside away from the bright lights. I hadn't been selected, I had been de-selected. There had been a rapid and worldly sifting. Not all people in wheelchairs are alike. Some of them may (just possibly) stand up and stagger marvelling into the light, pledging themselves to Billy Graham and God's holy word. And some will not, whatever the voltage of the preaching. I was not going to bring glory to the crusade. The silly thing was that I wasn't expecting a miracle myself, I didn't even want one, but I was a bit miffed that they had ruled one out. What business was it of theirs to restrict the powers of the God they claimed to represent?

Years later I read Sartre's remark when someone was going into ecstasies about the piles of crutches left behind at Lourdes after miracle cures – 'No wooden legs, though, eh?' I paraphrase. The communist atheist was being no more cynical than Billy Graham and his acolytes. I myself came no nearer to Lourdes than Bath Spa, but what it comes down to is this: my faith was less conditional than Billy Graham's. I put no limits on divine power.

If God wanted me to be conventionally shaped then I would be. In non-dualistic thinking, moreover, there are no divisions to be found, no line to be drawn between the human and divine, John and God. It follows that if I wanted to be conventionally shaped then I would be. And I'm fine as I am.

The visit to the waters at Bath dates back to the early days of my illness. Bath was very near. All I remember is being wrapped up in hot towels like a little dumpling, in great pain but loving being at the centre of attention.

A Raff neighbour in Bathford had a son, Tim, who fell in the gym at school and sustained brain damage. His speech and coördination were impaired. They gave him a board to spell words out on. He was like a human ouija-board. His mother, Sheila, was very religious and must have been Catholic, because her church got up a collection and sent Tim to Lourdes. I heard about it and wanted to go too, though Lourdes didn't help Tim, externally at least. And there was nothing wrong on the inside in the first place.

Tim got tricycles from the National Health (though Mum said 'Government') which he kept smashing up, going too fast. We drifted away from them. I dare say Mum's heart wasn't in pursuing the acquaintance. Heathers don't seek out the company of fellow unfortunates.

And Bath Spa did my symptoms no more good than Lourdes did to Tim. But that's not the point. The issue isn't effectiveness, it's commitment. When you live in Bathford, Lourdes is a pilgrimage, but Bath Spa is hardly even a day out.

Palace of laps

One of the major events of my time at Vulcan was that QM came to visit. The real QM, not Julian Robinson, boy agent. The Queen Mother. I say 'major event' not as a royalist but as a student of spiritual power. She spoke to me and softly shook my hand. She wore a lilac outfit and a hat with a little veil. Her make-up was a work of art. She made Billy Graham look like a circus clown.

The graduated eye contact of royalty is a fascinating thing to experience. I felt her attention even before her gaze arrived. She spoke her words of greeting, which were full of meaning without having any actual content. I had planned to speak up, and to ask a question. We hadn't been encouraged to make conversation, but she seemed quite a chatty type. 'Marm,' I was going to say – I knew you had to say 'Marm' – 'is it true that you once met Archie Andrews?' Putting her in her place just a bit. I was still slightly sore about the way the PDSA was out-ranked by the RSPCA, just because of a few royal patrons. Then the moment came and there was no need. There was no gap to be filled.

When the Queen Mother's eyes moved on, I had no feeling that her gaze had left me. If her attention had had depth as well as breadth, she'd have been a considerable guru rather than a local totem, with only the powers proper to its sphere. Her serenity was strictly secular.

The strange thing was that one of the school cats followed her round for the whole of her visit. Cats have their snobbery, God knows, but it doesn't coincide with ours. Still, this cat must have sensed something special. It was actually the least regarded of the school's many cats, the one grudgingly given the name of Anon, only one step up from actual namelessness. The cat-naming skills of our group were rudimentary – we ran out of names after Catty, Kitty, Tabby, Whiskers and Fluffy. From a feline point of view a school full of wheelchairs must be Heaven, a palace full of laps. The school cats were lazy and spoiled. They wouldn't budge for anybody, but Anon showed that a cat really can look at a queen, even at a dowager ex-empress.

After her visit the Queen Mother sent gifts to the school at regular intervals. Her generosity took the form, each time, of a big box of chocolates, which everybody loved – really big, so that everyone at the school could have more than one dip – and a rather beautiful porcelain vessel, blue and white, which contained slimy black dots with a fishy smell, like tadpoles gone wrong. To me those nasty little eggs seemed even more disgusting than tinned fish, which I had always hated. Very few of the pupils or staff members tried them. Some of those who did retched. The contents of the pretty jar ended up going into David Lockett's pig-swill. This was the crowning extravagance in the topsy-turvy economy of the school: rancid butter for the boys, caviar for the pigs.

I don't expect the QM specified the contents of the food parcel – I dare say she just said, 'Send those lovely boys something nice.' It was some equerry or other being too posh for his own good.

I dreaded Tuesday evening meals at Vulcan because it was always cold pilchards on toast. I hated that food with all my heart. To start with we were told to eat it up or go hungry. That was fine by me. That suited me down to the ground. I was very happy to go hungry. I was attuned to the notion of fasting – in Bathford days hadn't I gone without stuffed marrow the day after Scrambled Egg Boats?

Then the rule changed to 'You've got to eat it *or else.*' Then we were told what 'or else' meant. Eat it or be force-fed. Judy Brisby was very keen to implement the stricter system. She could hardly wait to find the first resisting suffragette.

On the night the new rules came into force I was in despair. There was no possibility that I was going to eat that disgusting food. Soon everyone else had finished theirs. I noticed that David Driver had a boiled egg and some toast. It looked delicious. On the other hand, David had muscular dystrophy which was going to kill him soon anyway, which must have been why he was excused pilchards and

417

likewise force-feeding. He was so weak it wouldn't have taken much to finish him off. He didn't have the strength to raise his arms to his face without help. There were special pivoted arm-rests on the side of his chair to help him get some leverage, but even then it was a huge effort for him. He always needed help at meal times.

Eventually I was the only pupil left in the dining hall. Even David had done his best by the boiled egg and had been wheeled away. Judy Brisby said to the kitchen staff, 'Just leave him there until he eats it all.' I waited for a very long time, sitting and staring at that awful fish. Its juices had seeped into the toast, which had swollen and turned into unspeakable mush. The kitchen staff finished their shift and left. Then Judy Brisby was back. She checked all the doors of the dining room, in case there were stragglers or someone coming back for something.

She came close. 'I'm warning you', she whispered, 'that if you don't eat this on your own, I'll just have to force-feed you. I'll pinch your nose shut so you have to open your mouth. And then I'll jam the food in with my fingers if I have to. I'm going to count to five, and then I'll start. You can't say you haven't been warned.'

I didn't say anything but I didn't feel at all brave. I was telling myself she wouldn't dare give me a nerve punch, but the woman leaning over me didn't seem short of nerve. She even seemed excited by what was going on.

If she counted to five she did it quickly and without moving her lips. Then she did indeed pinch my nose. She kept her promise. She pulled my head back as far as it would go, and somehow she got my mouth open. Next second she was stuffing pilchards down me and ordering me to swallow. I wouldn't even chew it. When she told me again to swallow 'or you'll get "what for"', I spat it out. I had been quite a good spitter at CRX, practising on chewed-up corners of linen sheet, but I excelled myself now. The squalid mouthful of mushy fish went everywhere. Much of it went sailing over the table and on to the floor.

My defiance made Judy Brisby truly terrifying now. She simply picked me up from the chair and strode out of the dining room. Her rage wouldn't contemplate the delay of the lift. She passed it by and carried me up the stairs and to the Blue Dorm. At the top of the stairs she held me upside down over the stair-well. Only her death-grip on my ankles stopped me from falling. She was beside herself. She hissed, '*Now* will you? *Now* will you?' She was panting with fury and exertion. Now would I what? The pilchards were miles away by then. This was no longer about pilchards. At last she got her breathing under control, dragged me back over the banisters and took me to the dorm. When she was a yard or so from my bed, she stopped and simply threw me towards it.

Her aim wasn't good, or else only part of her wanted me to land safely. On my way through the air towards the bed my hip hit the side very hard. I howled in pain and couldn't stop. Judy Brisby went out, and I went on crying.

Then Judy Brisby came back with Biggie, the Big Matron in charge of all the others, Sheila Ewart, nothing but kindness from stem to stern. Even the nicest matrons were strict at Vulcan, though, and Biggie had her own fixed principles. In her book there was nothing worse than telling tales.

Judy Brisby had obviously told her about what had been going on. Now she put on a show of tender concern, saying, 'Well why didn't you *say* you didn't like the dinner? David Driver doesn't like it either, so he had boiled egg and toast. You could have had that if you had wanted it! Lot of fuss about nothing!' As if all I was crying about was not liking the food. Little cry-baby fuss-pot.

I looked tearfully at her and knew she had won with her lies. There she was, lying in front of dear Biggie, and Biggie was swallowing it all down. There was nothing I could do about it. Nothing at all.

Of course I took Biggie too literally. When she talked about not telling tales, she meant she didn't want to hear petty accusations among the boys. Who had drawn on whose book, who had called whom a 'thrombosis' (which was our roundabout way of saying 'bloody clot'). Being hurled through the air by a member of staff came into a different category. She'd have wanted to hear about that, but I didn't know it at the time.

I couldn't make a phone call without the help of a member of staff, so how could I grass Judy Brisby up? Telling Mum wouldn't do much good either. She knew the number of the NSPCC off by heart, but when it came right down to it she was better at telling her neighbours how they should behave than knowing what to do herself.

The hip gave me pain for some time after the event, but I didn't dare ask to see a doctor about it, in case he asked me questions whose answers would get me into more trouble.

All over PG Tips

Judy Brisby was lucky in her timing. I had made up my mind to confide in Mum, no matter what, the next time I went home for the weekend. Not to tell tales but to ask what to do, and to hope that she would take it out of my hands. But by then something had happened which made it certain that I would keep my trap shut.

It turned out that I wasn't the only Cromer to be having a bad time at his school. Peter was attending Lord Wandsworth College in Long Sutton, near Hook in Hampshire. The school was founded in 1912 with funds from the late lord, who wanted to help full or half orphans – children who had lost at least one parent. The school's whole purpose was tender, by that token, and of course the years after 1912 were absolute prime years for the creation of orphans. The supply began to dry up after the Second War, though, and after that time fee-paying pupils untouched by bereavement began to be accepted.

There were still traces of the founder's mercy in Peter's time. Permission was granted for pupils to keep certain pets. They had to be animals (such as rabbits and guinea pigs) that didn't need to roam free. There were even a couple of lizards. Peter didn't have a pet himself, but he had a powerful connection with animals. The fact that the pets which were tortured at the school belonged to other boys didn't actually make a difference to him. The rabbit with the lacerated ears. The guinea pig with the scorched fur. The lizard whose shed tail did not deceive its giggling predators. Their pain lodged in him. He had no ability to disown it.

His sense of justice was soothed when the bullies turned their attention on him. They would drive drawing pins into his arms and legs. Then they started on beatings which became general and promiscuous. The site they chose for this torture was an old bomb shelter in the grounds. They told him when to come there, and he came. They didn't need to come and fetch him. He took all he could take, and then he simply walked out and went to the railway station, took a train and explained to the ticket-collector that he had to go home.

That was one advantage I enjoyed at Vulcan. Judy Brisby never expected me to go to her to be ill-treated. She came to me.

When Peter arrived home after his train journey, there was bruising all over his body. The boys at Lord Wandsworth had been only partially educated. They hadn't learned the trick of the nerve punches. Their tea-bag marks were very visible. Peter was all over PG Tips.

There were bruises on his soul that took much longer to heal. It showed how deeply the bullying had gone that he hadn't said a word to me about it. Any more, I suppose, than I had told him about what Judy Brisby got up to. We protected our tormentors while we could, and never owned up to the taint of pain while we had the choice.

Our GP in Bourne End Dr Flanagan (Flanny) said that Peter's injuries were certainly serious enough for us to sue Lord Wandsworth College. She said she would be happy to give evidence and back him up in court. Flanny was very far from being a soft touch. She was brisk and efficient and didn't have much time for the niceties. It's a fact that medical school is designed to grind down idealism into heartless competence, but Flanny must have been well on her way already. She had a head start.

In the end Mum and Dad decided against legal action, perhaps because Peter would be exposed to further damage, perhaps because suing was not quite nice. They settled for having the fees waived for that last traumatic term. Peter never went back. He had plenty of experience at standing up for me, none for defending himself. He was a gentle boy, eager to belong, a magnet for bullying.

I realised right away that there was no possibility of grassing Judy Brisby up after what had happened to Peter. I might have been able to live down the taboo of telling tales, but now I would be known as a copy-cat as well as a sneak. Copy-cat tale-telling had to be the worst crime in the whole book.

I was stuck with Vulcan for the duration. I wonder how many other pupils thought of grassing Judy Brisby up, and either pulled back from the brink or weren't believed. I certainly remember when unsinkable Trevor Burbage, the human suitcase with the riding hat, decided to 'run away' from the school.

The pretext was that he had been given thirty lines by the German teacher Mr Atkinson, and it's true that Trevor could be very cheeky. He would pretend to misunderstand things, just to be provoking. *Es gibt drei Türen . . .* 'Are the doors dry, Sir? Does it mean Wet Paint or something?' That sort of thing. He said he'd rather run away than copy out the lines. 'I'm not staying in this dump,' he said. There must have been something else driving him, though, mustn't there?

We asked him, 'What will you do for a living, once you get away from here?' He said, 'I'll be a lorry driver's mate. That's the ticket for me! I can't drive but I can be the driver's mate and see the world.' He set off in his privately bought wheelchair, which out-ranked mine – but then his grandmother had money and was always buying him out of trouble at the school with timely endowments. It was called a Wrigley, like the chewing gum to which a few boys were addicted, though they spat it out discreetly if Miss Wilding hove into view.

The Wrigley went too fast to pass Government safety tests. It had proper inflatable tyres, instead of the solid rubber ones on my E&J. Raeburn was normally the person who charged the batteries, but we made sure the ABs gave Trevor a top-up till the last possible moment. Then he was off. He'd left a note with me in an envelope but I wasn't allowed to show it to anyone until he had made his get-away. We were blood brothers, so I couldn't refuse it or grass him up.

There was no special reason for us being blood brothers, except that we had dared each other to make the cuts and then couldn't manage to back down.

The next morning Miss Willis drove off in a panic to track him down. She was back in five minutes. He'd got as far as the bottom of Farley Hill. He was tired and hungry but he had seen the world. He came back to a hero's welcome, and I have no idea why.

Grit buggered the relays

I had been waiting so long for the motor and battery required to convert my Everest & Jennings to self-propulsion status that they had joined the category of things which can exist only in language, like hen's teeth and sky-hooks, the horns of the hare and the children of a barren woman.

I had learned to get around reasonably well without a motor, in the end, graduating from pushing against the tyres by hand to using a stick to punt myself about. In fact I had mixed feelings about the new arrangement, not because Roger Stott was a handsomer engine than any substitute (I couldn't see him while he was pushing anyway), but because he was more reliable than the mechanism which replaced him.

Grit of any sort buggered the relays on an Everest & Jennings, and it couldn't cope with some surfaces. If you wanted an electric wheel-chair which could be driven over gravel, for instance, you had to go private and fork out. The Everest & Jennings was almost Government issue, with all that that implied – like the hard toilet paper at CRX. If you wanted the equivalent of soft toilet paper in self-sufficient invalid transport then you would have to throw money at Messrs Wrigley (as Trevor Burbage's grandmother and others had).

The E&J was controlled by a sort of tiller, a T-bar which came up from the top of the motor and passed between my legs. It had two speeds, plus neutral and reverse. The tiller would be fitted on after I had been installed in the chair, and I needed someone to remove it before I could be helped to dismount. There was a twist grip mounted on the right-hand bar of the T. If the grip had been on the left bar then, with the short-comings of the elbow on that side, I wouldn't have been able to operate it.

Once all the pieces were in place I was the proud owner/driver of an electric wheelchair. Having a powered vehicle allowed me to pretend that the controls had got stuck, so that I could run over the feet of members of staff, always with a cheery cry of 'Awfully sorry, Sir! These bloomin' chariots take some getting used to!' In an ideal world I would only have trespassed on the toes of teachers I actively disliked, but in this life my opportunities to make mischief have been limited. There is an obligation to make the most of them. I wasn't about to restrict my fun by being fussy and high-minded, so if even the divine Ben Nevin came within range, his god-like toes were fair game for the crunching.

For years I had only had a postal Granny, and then suddenly she was back in the picture, flesh and blood. The first I heard of it was a passing mention from Mum. 'The strangest thing has happened,' she said. 'You know that Mediterranean cruise that Caroline is going on – you know, Muzzie's Caroline – well, your Uncle Roy's going on it too. Pure coincidence. And we were saying, Granny and I, wouldn't it be wonderful if they liked each other? Caroline's a lovely girl, delightful, and at least she's not tall.' It was all-important in that generation that wives be shorter than their husbands.

I had met Caroline a few times when she came to visit Sarah in CRX. She was as cheerful and as buxom as her mother.

'Roy would be a bit of a catch,' Mum said, 'even though he's a bit older.' I was so surprised by the mention of Granny that I missed the ominous overtones of the word 'catch'. Dad had been a bit of a catch in his day, after all, a catch who didn't much want to be caught. There was always a catch, wasn't there?

I couldn't remember the last time Mum had referred to her mother. 'When did you see Granny?'

'Oh, we spoke on the phone.'

'Was it you who called her? Or did she call you?'

Mum frowned. 'I don't remember.' Was I really supposed to believe she could have been in doubt about something so crucial? I didn't believe her for a moment, but Mum could be stubborn when she chose to. Since she had never admitted to a breaking-off of relations, I could hardly expect details of a reconciliation.

As far as I can piece it together, Granny had been pulling a few strings ever since Audrey was born. She wasn't going to be accused of ignoring the birth of her first, her only granddaughter, but nor was she going to melt like a sentimental old lady, forgiving offences promiscuously. Amnesty on strict conditions was more her style. So she sent along a shawl, an apostle spoon and a christening mug, and there was a cheque tucked into the accompanying card, but the card itself was blank.

That cheque was like a hand-grenade of solvency waiting to go off. Sooner or later Mum would pull the pin and money would explode into the bank account she shared with Dad. Granny would hear the echo of the blast when she next cast her eyes over her bank statement, and she would know that Laura hadn't been able to live up to her injured pride.

The extension to the house must also have been funded by Granny, though I don't know how it was negotiated. Extensions don't grow on Trees, and I should have realised that the family exchequer was being topped up. Granny still kept her distance, but Mum must have hated the being beholden.

Money has a way of estranging even as it reconciles, which of course was one of the things that Granny liked about it.

The conversation about Roy and Caroline marked a further phase of warming in family relations. The Cold War was almost over. Granny and Mum were united at last by their compulsion to meddle.

Granny took to staying the odd weekend at an Otel on the riverside not far off, a rather grand one in fact, the Compleat Angler at Marlow. Rooms there could easily cost ten pounds a night. It was one of her favourite quips to say that Cockneys should be encouraged to run Otels, 'since they can at least pronounce the word properly, unlike so many people these days'. I was keen for Granny to come and stay with us in the house, but there were limits to détente.

A summons to join Granny at the Compleat Angler would come for the whole family or, according to her mood, for Peter and me, or just one of us. These occasions were balanced on a knife-edge between treat and ordeal. A knife-edge, or a fork-point – since the use of cutlery turned out to be something of a mine-field.

Granny developed the habit, while staying at the Compleat Angler, of sending a taxi to pick up Peter and me for our meal at her expense. The taxi was expensive but not extravagant, since it served a double purpose. Quite apart from conveying her grandchildren the few miles required it delivered a satisfactory snub to Mum and Dad.

The first time Peter went there for a meal on his own, he ordered a prawn cocktail. He had only just conveyed the first spoonful safely into his mouth when Granny came out with her whiplash whisper: *'One uses a fork!'* He came home from his evening with Granny more or less gibbering with etiquette trauma. Another time we were both there, and it was my turn to order the prawn cocktail. I did my ankylosed best with a fork. This time Granny seemed almost puzzled, saying, 'Wouldn't it be easier with a spoon? The rules don't apply to you, John. You may eat it in any way you please.' I had noticed, though, that my exemption from rules was a precarious dispensation. It was best not to rely on it.

Granny always ordered the same way, and usually the same thing. 'I'm going to plump for the lamb and mint sauce,' she would say. 'What would you like, boys?' Granny always 'plumped' for things. I would usually plump for an omelette. Peter plumped for steak.

In fact Granny didn't have much of an appetite. When the main course arrived, she would say, 'You boys carry on. All Granny does is make a little road right through the middle.' She did exactly that, while Peter stuffed himself. I didn't do badly either, in my weight class. After she had made her little road across the plate, Granny would put her knife and fork down and say, 'Well, I'm *defeated*.'

Granny gave Peter a little lecture on what to look for in a good restaurant like the one at the Compleat Angler. She told him to watch the waiters, to see how their job should really be done. 'It's not just a matter of serving from the right and taking away from the left, though that's part of it. It's an attitude, an attentiveness, which holds lessons for everyone. It should never be difficult to catch a waiter's eye.'

Granny waited until every last waiter had his back turned, dealing with other diners, and then murmured, 'Excuse me!' Immediately one of them appeared at her shoulder, leaning forward with a neutral readiness. 'Would you be so kind as to bring me a fresh fork, please? This one has rather a mark.' 'Of course, Madam,' he murmured, 'right away.'

'Do you see, boys?' she said. 'Some may say that being a waiter is a lowly career, but there's nothing more important than seeing that people are properly fed. I myself ran a British Restaurant during the war, and it was no small thing to organise. Once I had my staff properly drilled – I had to make do with waitresses, of course – the whole mood of the place changed. It became a pleasure to be there, even if the food was basic at best. We created the right atmosphere, do you see?'

At the end of the meal Granny announced, 'Peter, I think waiting would be a suitable job for you, in due course. I'll look into it. The best waiters are of course foreign. It might be necessary for you to be trained abroad – Switzerland, perhaps, if not France itself.'

426

Peter managed to keep his feelings hidden until we were in the taxi on the way home. He despised waiters absolutely, hating in particular the way they walked. When we were home, he did an impression of a waiter's walk, wiggling his bottom absurdly. How could Granny give so much as a penny to those waltzing ninnies, let alone tell him he should become one of them?

'Don't be too hasty, Peter,' I said. 'The old lady may be on to something.' I was thinking of something quite different, about how nice waiters' bottoms looked in their tight black trousers. Their short jackets could almost have been designed to draw attention to those bottoms, and I liked the fact that you were allowed to inspect them quite closely before you plumped for your omelette.

Granny never referred to the long absence of social contact. She didn't seem actively happy to see us, but then that was never her style. Mum for her part had a sort of masochistic glow, as if a stone was back in her shoe that she had never really learned to do without.

Perhaps the attempt to make a match between Roy and Caroline was just an excuse for something that would have happened anyway, but I remember meals at the Complete Angler where strategy was discussed. Dad had no interest in the romantic plotting, and stayed away.

'We must be very careful how we handle this, Laura,' said Granny. 'I rather think it will be like stalking wildlife in Africa. We should keep ourselves well and truly down-wind of Roy and, for that matter, Caroline as well.' It simply wouldn't do to clash batch and spinst together like a pair of cymbals.

Damp powder

Despite the subtle seethe of planning behind the scenes, nothing much came of the cruise. Caroline had followed her mother under the surgeon's knife, and was now by all accounts much less top-heavy. She wasn't fully used to her new centre of gravity, all the same, and part of the idea behind the cruise was that dancing on a boat made everyone's movements reassuringly clumsy. She would be able to take to the floor without embarrassment. I think that was how the whole curious business was explained to me.

427

Anyway, it didn't work. Either romance fizzled out early or the powder was damp from the beginning. Granny had listed the subjects in which Roy took particular interest, and Mum had passed them on to Muzzie. Caroline had lightly read up on them, being careful not to show undue independence of mind, but even so Roy was not to be taken out of himself. As Caroline reported to her mother, who passed the news on to Mum, 'It was all jolly hard work, and Roy was strange. He was always polite and courteous to me, but his attention always seemed to be on . . . another man.' Mum left the insinuating three dots intact when she passed this information on to me. I think it must have been a marginally censored version which reached Granny. I can't see Mum retaining that punctuational innuendo.

I was slow to connect Granny's reappearance with the fact that Dad had resigned from the Air Force. Wing Commander Cromer came back down to earth, with something of a bump. It was no small thing, as he discovered, to be looking for a job at forty-plus. He held onto his rank, of course, but it was a rather different thing to be a Wing-Co at an altitude of zero feet. There was no reason given for this drastic change of life. I doubt if I even asked. The reasons grown-ups gave for things never made sense to me anyway. Mum didn't say in so many words that she put pressure on him. All she said was that a family needed a father. He couldn't expect to go on a foreign posting and then walk in whenever he felt like it for a hero's welcome.

Granny's antennæ registered the shift in the family's finances, and the new relationships it made possible. Mum and Dad would find it much harder to say 'no' to any offers she might care to make. They might even be made to beg. I swear she could smell an overdraft the way ogres in fairy tales smell an Englishman's blood.

Mum and Dad were faced with the problem of what school to send Peter to now. One possibility was Sidcot School in Winscombe, North Somerset. We all went along along in the car for Peter's interview. From the first breath I found the atmosphere of this school wonderfully comforting – it was an old Quaker foundation, though at the time I wouldn't have understood anything by that. I was very happy for Peter if it meant he could have a new start in such welcoming surroundings, though I felt all the more isolated in my own schooling.

The headmaster of Sidcot, Mr Brayshaw, was both absent-minded and very much on the ball, a combination rather common among school-teachers. I thought he was beautiful. He gave Peter a sincere welcome. Peter was shy and I suppose traumatised, so he hung back. Mum was nervous and horribly humble, while Dad was almost truculent. You could almost hear him thinking, 'Don't think your authority impresses me, I've got some of my own if it comes to that. I'll hear you out but that's all. Just don't expect me to kow-tow.' In Dad's book kow-towing was worse than being a sneak and a copy-cat and a bad sport all put together.

When Mr Brayshaw set eyes on me, he included me in the conversation quite naturally. He was wonderfully warm. He was like the dream uncle I'd always wanted, and more. In this lifetime I've suffered from a severe shortage of uncles. Roy was a dud uncle, really.

As he gave us the tour Mr Brayshaw kept saying madly positive things like, 'Now there's not really much of a step here,' and, 'This next classroom may be difficult, but I am sure we can find a way if we just put our minds to it . . . You know, we really only go in there in the winter. Most of the time the class just comes outside and sits under that tree over there, so that would be fine for John . . . I'm sure something can be arranged before winter comes . . .'

With much rambling and pottering he mapped out his vision of Sidcot School with John in it. The greatest problem as he saw it was the inaccessibility of the dancing class, but it was clear that if I had my heart set on learning to dance it would be made to happen somehow.

Mum was in a panic and going 'ahem' like mad, making the humble artificial double cough that meant she needed to be asked to speak, but Mr Brayshaw hadn't risen to the rank of headmaster without knowing how to ignore a parent. He conducted the whole interview as if I was the only candidate to be considered, as if that had been the morning's only task and theme.

When we wound up back in the headmaster's study, Mr Brayshaw asked if we had any questions, just as if Mum hadn't been trying to butt in for the last half-hour.

'But Mr Brayshaw,' she cried. 'It's John's brother Peter who is applying to come to Sidcot, not John himself!'

'Yes, I'm well aware of that, Mrs Cromer,' he replied, 'but I thought it would be rather nice for Peter if he could have his older brother with him, don't you? It's perfectly practical. He's not on any dangerous medication, I take it? So it's not a matter of medical supervision, just washing and dressing. Not a great deal of effort, I should have thought. Doesn't seem much of an obstacle, as obstacles go.'

The twinkle in his eye made me jump up and down from my seated position, exploiting the residual flexibility of my spine. I waved my arms about and shouted out of turn, 'Oh Mum, wouldn't it be wonderful? Mr Brayshaw wants me to be with Peter! Please, please, oh *please* say yes!!' Please let me escape from Judy Brisby and from the Board of Education. Please let me sit under a tree surrounded by love and understanding, where the harvest called learning will be brought on by steady sunshine. This was more like it. This was the old tune of No Such Word As Can't played thickly on Sparky's Magic Piano, not picked out with one finger. I was being offered something I would never have dared to ask for myself.

To Mr Brayshaw Dad said, 'Well, we'll have to think about that.' But the moment we were in the car, he told me, 'It's not on. It's a lovely dream, chicken, but it's not on.'

'But you said you'd think about it!'

'I've thought about it. It's just not on, and that's that!' How I hated those words. I was no longer a child, I wouldn't thrash and scream and say, 'You lied, I'll never trust you again.' I sat and thought about what could be learned from this unprecedented afternoon.

I looked at Mum and Dad in the car, bickering routinely over the map. For the first time in any of our lives we had encountered something genuinely unusual – disability being treated as unimportant, neither here nor there. And what was Mum and Dad's reaction? Social embarrassment. Revelation had been greeted with fidgeting and changing of the subject. I vowed that the next time a path opened up in front of me, I would put the Everest & Jennings into the higher of its two gears and head straight for the gap. Then woe betide any toe which got in my way.

For a moment I had been grazed by happiness. Even so, I was happy that Peter had escaped his Colditz Castle and would be treated tenderly in a new school. I myself had learned something about 'reality'. When the building-blocks of the world, those things we consider facts, seem to be most firmly chamfered and grouted one against another, then – exactly then – is when the wall will shiver and turn to liquid. I just had to be aware that when every obstacle had disappeared from view, Mum and Dad would invent new ones. With the path cleared in front of them and brilliantly lit, they would stay exactly where they were, pretending it hadn't happened and there was nothing they could do about it, except to put the car in reverse and drive glumly home.

That I had been accepted as a pupil of a normal school to which I hadn't even applied was a miracle. It was a full miracle, despite the fact that it hadn't happened. Mum and Dad wouldn't let it happen, and miracles don't insist. That isn't the etiquette.

The divine invitation is written on creamy card so thick no human hand can fold it – that is so. Its embossing stands so proud it casts a shadow. Also true. But nothing whatever happens unless you RSVP. Divine intervention isn't a unilateral business. Miracles are consensual. I vowed that next time one was offered I would not cringe with the rest of my tribe. I would claim my place in the summer sun, under that tree.

Sidcot School turned out to be as good a school for Peter as it might have been for me. There was a lot of care about the place. Mum went to visit once and didn't announce herself to Peter. She crept along the walls until she could see him talking to another boy. He had a cup of coffee in his hand and was standing very straight. The two boys were talking man to man. Then Mum showed herself and Peter turned back into an awkward little boy again.

The only trouble he got into at that school was when he was caught making wax copies of keys. He wanted the power to slip through the fabric of an institution, even one where he was happy – simply to melt away. He wanted to have the power of locking doors between himself and misery, in case misery came back to get him.

He was punished in an adult Quaker way, without anger, by the simple withdrawing of privileges. He accepted this punishment, also in an adult way, without complaint, with understanding. Dad was never prouder of him than in that manly acceptance of chastisement.

I wish Dad had been a little less keen on self-suppression in his children, but then he was busy suppressing himself at the time, so at least he was being consistent.

It wasn't long before Dad got a job, though it wasn't a great success. His employer was Centrum Intercoms, and he was supposed to be a salesman. He just wasn't pushy enough, and in any case he didn't really believe in the product. It was the wrong sort of product, for one thing. Communication wasn't really Dad's thing, in fact it was close to being the opposite of his thing.

There has never been anyone with so little of the salesman's temperament. The more he praised a product to a potential customer, the more he despised it in his heart, and over time the contempt seeped back into his patter. There was a pile of paperwork to be done, until one day he simply walked away from the job. He came home exultant, and Peter and I giving him a great welcome. I imagine Mum's feelings were more mixed. The less earning power Dad had, the greater the place Granny could claim for herself in our lives.

Shooting the rapids

The most constant thing in my life at Vulcan, apart from lessons, was the saga after lights-out. By now it was very markedly eroticised. Gunfights and cattle-rustling had been eclipsed by a sexual free-for-all. Over time I had developed my own way of describing things. I knew the word 'penis' but wasn't sure if the other boys did, so I said 'John Thomas' instead, which was how the nurses in CRX had referred to those parts. I still used the words 'taily' and 'scallywag' in my head most of the time, but was trying to out-grow them. I certainly wouldn't use them in these surroundings. I knew and liked the word 'vagina' but felt it would tend to make the proceedings a bit clinical, when the whole point was to be outrageously dirty.

I was a sort of orchestral conductor, drawing out the filthy music in everyone's head, the dorm itself my instrument. I gloried in my powers. I could send my audience to sleep dreaming of hot steaming home-cooked food, or I could get the room so keyed up it was as if the whole humming chafing collective was going to break loose and shoot the rapids.

No one else ever played ladies' parts, but I often doubled up. One night we realised we were a villain short. It was decided that Terry would play that, though he was usually Rip, till he said he'd get muddled if Rip had a fight with the villain. I volunteered to be Rip and the lady. Then one night I was not only Rip and Mum/Miss Willis but also a bar floozie with big bosoms. One scenario started with Rip making love to the floozie (me making love to myself in two vocal registers). Then the villain – Terry – was going to come along and punch Rip on the nose and fight him and knock him out. To start with I was going to scream as the floozie (quietly so no matron would hear) because the villain was scaring me, but then he would seize me in his strong villain arms and I would be overwhelmed by passion. Our love-making would have to be quick. We knew that we were destined to be parted. Perhaps the posse was thundering towards us even as we kissed. Opposite sides of the fence, a love that could never be, and yet this violent throbbing moment was perfect in every way, a memory to take with us for the rest of our lives.

I had to find the right voice for each character. As the action became more complicated it became necessary to sketch it out ahead of time. Before the scene began I had to give the dorm a certain amount of briefing, bossy little impresario that I was.

'Give me plenty of time to get going on the love scene,' I told Terry, 'before you come in and start making trouble . . . I've got some really juicy ideas for tonight. Then in the show-down – punching noises, everybody, plenty of "what the – ?" and 'I'll larn ya!"' Punching noises I wasn't good at. Roger Stott was the expert at those. 'Okay, pardners, let's roll.'

Love was my speciality, though. For me, the sexiest of all words was *darling*. I experimented with its pronunciation, shifting the stress between the syllables, alternating dárling and darlíng. 'Oh darlíng, I luff you – yes, darlíng, touch me in every place, oh, oh, oh I wish you had more fingers on ze hand and more hands on ze body. Now take your John Thomas and push it deep into my crack . . . and when it's in there, please take one of your fingers – any one – and slide it into my botty and I'll push my finger into your botty also, oh dárling, I am in so much love I could die like this . . .'

The holiday in Looe with Dorrie had left a legacy, undoubtedly. In our cowboy stories the formula 'This town ain't big enough for the both of us' had pretty much been made obsolete by 'When I see a hole like that in your bum, it makes me want to stick my finger up it – *know what I mean, boys?'*

Sometimes for variety I told a ghost story instead. I improvised freely, and though my plots didn't always hang together I could certainly brew a spooky mood. One night, just when I was saying, 'And then SUDDENLY – !!' with no real idea of what the sudden thing might be, there was a terrific twang and a strong smell of burning. Something skittered across the floor, and a number of boys cried out in fear.

We called a matron, who turned the lights on. There was a mark on the floor which looked as if it was caused by scorching. By daylight we could see more clearly what had happened. Raeburn had left one of the Wrigleys on the re-charger. The fuse had blown and then somehow bounced across the floor. By then, though, my supernatural authority was unassailable. Facts couldn't dent it.

Amnesia was killing Paul

One of the boys was so scared he said he wouldn't sleep another night in that haunted dorm. It was Stevie Templeton, known as Half-Pint. The nick-name wasn't really to do with his height (relatively few people at Vulcan were standard in size or shape). It was because his father ran a pub. So Stevie was moved to another dorm, and Julian was moved in.

I don't know if there was anything fishy about this dream come true. Julian didn't claim in so many words to have arranged the whole thing with HQ, by booby-trapping the fuse of the charger, pressing the remote-control button when he heard (through a hidden microphone) that my story had reached a suitable stage, but he certainly took credit for the transfer.

I felt a little guilty about having driven Stevie from the dorm, if that was what I had done. He was an athetoid spastic, unable to control his movements, and Julian was much quieter company. No question about it, there was a certain amount of relief.

It wasn't just the charger. None of the wiring was reliable. At

Vulcan we were always having our own power cuts, on top of the general ones. Once one happened in the middle of the night. People went on sleeping. What else would they do? Why bother to wake up, just to find that the lights aren't working?

Paul Dandridge, a year senior to me, slept on in his dorm like everyone else. The difference was that he started to die the moment the power went off. He was the severe polio case who did 'frog-breathing' during the day. He literally swallowed air – with a distinctly froggy expression – instead of breathing as other people did. At night, of course, he couldn't swallow air the way he could during the day. When he fell asleep his breathing would stop, so at night he was connected to a respirator.

The respirator made no sound when the power went off. Just the opposite. Its hum and swish died away. The dorm was quieter than it had ever been since Paul arrived. Paul just stopped breathing – or rather, he didn't start. It was all very peaceful. Then Abadi Mukherjee, in the next bed, woke up.

Not only did he wake up, he understood immediately what was happening. Only a few seconds had passed without power, but already amnesia was killing Paul in his bed. He was dying of forgetting to breathe. Nothing had replaced the mechanical wheeze of the respirator that had stopped, not Paul's day-time gulping, let alone the smooth rise and fall of a normal boy's sleeping chest. Abadi had very little time to reverse this trend of dying.

In a way, though, it wasn't all that dramatic. He didn't need to give Paul the kiss of life or anything. All he had to do was wake him up, so that he could be reminded to breathe. Abadi didn't even need to get out of bed to do it. His polio was much less severe than Paul's, but he couldn't simply spring out of bed. Just as well he didn't need to. All he had to do was shout, for Paul to live.

After that night they became inseparable. From being friends among other friends they became a consecrated couple. What could be more natural? Even if Paul Dandridge was poor and from the East End of London, and Abadi Mukherjee was very rich. His parents, they who ran the Appa Corporation in Bombay, paid full fees for him. In effect Abadi became Paul's primary carer, despite being so very far from AB status himself, and it was a job he did very well.

435

All this was completely marvellous, and I did rather resent it. Although Abadi was a year above me, we had always had wonderful chats, particularly on scientific themes. Abadi took sugar in his tea, for instance, while I didn't, and he had the idea that there is a moment when you withdraw the spoon after stirring when the tea eddies faster than ever. He wouldn't be persuaded that this was a violation of natural law, acceleration in the absence of propulsion. We had a lot of fun wrangling over that.

Averages and statistics were also fertile grounds for debate. I told him that if a single person was immortal, that would be enough to raise the life expectancy of the whole human race to infinity. This is perfectly true (nought and infinity always make sums wonky and mystical), though he wouldn't have it. But now he didn't have time for me and my quibbles. His bond with Paul was all the go.

If I had my nose put out of joint by the intensity of the new bond between Paul and Abadi, it was only partly because I was cheated of a few satisfying quibbles. On a more general level the whole thing seemed so very unfair. Ideal friendship on a base of mutual self-sacrifice was just what I'd always longed for, and had looked for specifically in my experience of Vulcan School, and now somebody else had got it instead of me. There was even the element of class contrast for which I had always hankered, though Granny would hardly have recognised Abadi, heir of merchant princes, as an upper person.

I was always trying to imagine how I could behave on a large unselfish scale despite my un-coöperative body, and now Abadi had had heroic action served up to him on a plate. It had been so easy for him. Wake up, and shout. I was considerably more disabled than Abadi, but even I could have done that. It was as if I had been cheated. How hard was it to notice that a respirator had gone quiet, anyway? Paul's respirator wasn't a full-body one, the famous iron lung, fully enclosing the patient. It was something called a cuirass respirator, and it was powered by a modified vacuum cleaner. All Abadi had done was notice when a vacuum cleaner stopped roaring in his ear. I managed to forget, for the greater purpose of drumming up a grievance, how deeply I slept myself.

It was as if someone had snaffled all the soft centres from the existential chocolate box, and I began to feel very sorry for myself. I was useless. I couldn't have a simple spy camera installed in my head without getting my knees hurt.

I was coming down with a particularly virulent strain of self-pity, a common condition in early adolescence. Who really cared about me? Who would miss me if I just disappeared? And why did I have to do history when I was no good at it?

I wasn't even going to be made a prefect. In books about schools you could be a prefect as long as you were good at lessons and loyal to the spirit of school. At Vulcan you could only be a prefect if you were an AB, or at least a lot more able-bodied than me. It was so unfair. It was unfair to umpteen decimal places.

Peek Frean Peek Frean

On top of which I had been let down by the pen-friend I had been assigned, so that I could polish my German while she improved her English. We had only just started our correspondence, and her English was very formal. She sent her warmest compliments to my esteemed parents, for some unknown reason. Still, I thought we had a lot going for us as pen-friends. She was called Waltraut Bzdok. I imagine her family was originally Czech or Polish. I absolutely loved the name. In my bed-rest years I had hated the way words when you repeated them lost all meaning. The words on the biscuit tin just dissolved with repetition, as surely as if they had been bodily dunked in tea. Peek Frean Peek Frean. Waltraut Bzdok was different. She was immune to the Peek Frean effect. However often you said her name to yourself, it retained its gritty integrity. Cross-braced by all those sturdy consonants, it ran no risk of dissolving. That name was like a piece of heavy engineering, scoring highly on both tensile and compressive strength. It was impervious.

We were getting on so well I decided to send her a present to seal our friendship. I bought some shampoo from the village shop. Then the postmaster spoiled everything by saying I wasn't allowed to put something in the post that might leak.

We had a hideous sort of conversation, which went like this:

POSTMASTER: 'What is the nature of your package?'

437

JOHN (sings out happily): 'I'm sending some shampoo to my pen-friend in Germany. She's called Waltraut. Waltraut Bzdok. I think her family may have come from Czechoslovakia originally.'
POSTMASTER: 'International postal regulations prohibit the despatch of items other than those certified leak-proof. They endanger legitimate packages.'
JOHN (doubtfully): 'Perhaps I could wrap them up better? Pad them somehow? With tissue paper?'
POSTMASTER: 'Send bath cubes. Girls like bath cubes. Even German girls must like bath cubes.'

I couldn't out-run his decision, even though Mum always said that if you were a lady bath cubes made you go itchy between the legs. I bought some anyway, once my finances had recovered from the extravagance of buying shampoo I couldn't send.

The postmaster must have been right about what girls liked, because Waltraut was thrilled. She wrote a letter saying that when she opened the parcel she thought that she would have been dreaming. I should tell her everything about myself. To begin, where was I studying at school?

I took a lot of trouble over the letter I wrote. I found out that the German for 'disabled' was *behindert*. I can't say I liked the look of the word – the associations of being *hindered* and *behindhand* were too raw, somehow, in an unfamiliar language. I persisted with it, though, and told Waltraut among many other chatty things that I was studying at a *Schule für Behinderte Jungen*. And of course I needn't have worried about niceties of language. Pen-friends aren't bothered by little things like that. The message got across perfectly, and she didn't write back.

So I made my decision. One afternoon I took the Everest & Jennings out into the woods. I would lie down and fade away into the forest din. I left the wheelchair and managed a controlled fall, holding on to branches while I lowered myself to the ground. Then I rolled away from the chair into some leaves. That was actually hard work, even with the help of a slope. There I waited to die, or be discovered by a passing woodsman who would bring me up as his own. I wouldn't be missed – and I certainly wouldn't miss any of that lot.

438

In another part of my mind, I knew perfectly well that I would be missed. The dorm after lights-out would be hushed, if not out of respect then out of an inability to manage without me. Nobody else knew how to cook up such treats of story-telling. Nobody else had the nerve to tackle ladies' parts, or the virtuosity to play both sides of a fight or a love scene. Did they think fingers got up botties in the heat of the moment all by themselves? They'd soon discover otherwise. There was an art to it.

After about two hours, I heard voices calling my name, gradually coming closer. When I heard a familiar voice shouting, 'Oh my good Lord!' I decided to live after all. I closed my eyes. It was Biggie, bustling fit to burst. The doctor was called – he gravely prescribed bed rest. Bed rest my old friend, but with a difference. There was a big pile of DC comics like *Superman* and *Eerie* that I could read while my schoolmates studied.

I enjoyed the privilege more than the content of the comics. My favourite publication was still *Judy*, my favourite serial (and character) 'Backstroke Babs'. It didn't excite adverse comment at Vulcan that a thirteen-year-old boy should read a girls' comic, or if it did, the objection was soon neutralised by the sheer excellence of the story, when I was gracious enough to let *Judy* pass from my exclusive possession. It beat the boys' comics hollow. The plot was well-constructed, the situations not too repetitious and the psychology a cut above the competition. This was a proper story. It showed real people and their sneaky nasty plans.

Even at home in Bourne End, *Judy* had a readership. Peter wasn't expected to be much of a tough lad, and he was attending a Quaker school, but there would still have been social consequences if he had read *Judy* on the premises. Even at Trees he continued to swear allegiance to the *Dandy*. Yet while I was devouring a new issue of *Judy* (leaving 'Backstroke Babs' till last, naturally), and he was turning the pages of the *Dandy* hot off its presses, it was perfectly plain that his heart wasn't in it. It was all he could do not to ask what was happening to Babs in the latest instalment. Finally I would let him read it for himself, while I cast a patronising eye over the antics in the *Dandy*.

On dry land Backstroke Babs used a wheelchair, but in the swimming pool she was in her element. She was her school's strongest swimmer, always turning the tide in competitions and thwarting the plans of those who envied her talents and her popularity, her utter niceness. It's a little strange that I don't remember the exact nature of Babs's disability, considering my unsought connoisseurship in this area of life. Was she paraplegic? She'd have had to be a bloody good swimmer all right, to churn her way past the able-bodied, disregarding the way her legs let her down in the pool. Even if it was polio the set-up was remarkably unlikely. So perhaps I realised that this was consoling fantasy – better not to examine it too closely.

I didn't lose face in the school after my 'accident' in the Vulcan grounds, though I amply deserved to. No one was rude enough to point out that since the tiller had to be lifted off before I could dismount from the E&J, the tableau in the woods could hardly be anything but a planned event.

Nor was 'suicide' a possibility. How, exactly, was I supposed to have climbed out of the wheelchair in my self-destructive despair? I had to have help.

Julian Robinson was the obvious candidate. He was very happy to remove the tiller and help me clamber out of the machine. For once I blessed the rigidity his callipers gave. He held me up and we tottered a few feet together, until I could get a grip of the branches and make my controlled fall. We had agreed beforehand that he wouldn't help me with rolling down the slope unless I really got stuck. Realism was important. It was a matter of pride. The last little bit of effort makes all the difference between slap-dash work and something you can be proud of.

Julian didn't ask why I wanted to give the impression that I had come to grief in the woods. He was bound by his temperament to join any conspiracy that offered itself. He wasn't fussy.

Madly propitious

The calliper fiasco had created a certain embarrassment between us, and I still hadn't satisfied my curiosity about Julian's private parts. Then only a few weeks later he was served up to me on a plate. Quite suddenly the circumstances were propitious, so madly propitious that nothing could hold me back, and it happened in the unlikely setting of the Blue Dorm. Not only that, but it was with everyone in attendance, everyone taking part in my sexual exploration of the boy whose humiliation I had once engineered in the duel of the chemistry sets.

Roger Stott was sitting on another boy's bed, helping him stick stamps in an album. There were a couple of boys from another dorm too, paying a visit. There was an atmosphere of great ease and licence. Julian was in his bed writing a letter. His callipers had been stood down for the day. Perhaps they had been cutting into him. He was defended by nothing more daunting than the winceyette of his pyjamas. Suddenly I knew that I must get into bed with him. I called out, 'Julian! Julian! I bet I can stop you writing that letter.'

He didn't even raise his eyes from the paper. 'And how do you imagine you're going to do that, John?'

'Well, if my bed was next to yours,' I said, 'I'd be in there with you in a moment and I'd find a way to break your concentration!'

'It wouldn't make the slightest difference,' he said, 'and besides, there's no way you could get over here.'

'Oh couldn't I?' I said. 'Just you watch!'

Roger had finished his business with the stamp album, so I signalled him to come over to my bed. I whispered to him that he must carry me over to Julian's. Without a word he picked me up and carried me over, putting me on the bed right next to Julian – who went right on writing his letter, just as if nothing had happened. I whispered to Roger that I needed to get under the covers.

He pretended to be exasperated, saying, 'If I do that there'll be no end to it. Next you'll be complaining that I haven't tucked you in properly,' and I said, 'Yes of course I will. You're getting the hang of this.' Next minute Roger was holding me up in the air again and asking one of the bystanders to pull back Julian's sheets and blankets to let me in. Julian was doggedly writing his letter and not acknowledging my existence at all. Soon I was tucked up next to him while the other boys at least pretended to carry on with their activities.

'You see I'm going on writing this letter exactly as I said I would, don't you?' said Julian breezily. 'Your being in the bed hasn't made the slightest bit of difference to me . . . Except that now I've run out of things to write . . . What shall I say?'

'Say . . . "John is lying on top of me . . ."' I said. 'Good idea! That'll do,' said Julian, happily scribbling away, 'and incidentally I don't think it'd make a scrap of difference even if you were . . .'

'What makes you so sure?'

'It'd take a lot more than that to break my concentration.'

'Don't say I didn't warn you, that's all.'

'Go ahead then.' He actually said, in the blithest possible voice, 'Do your worst, Cromer.'

People are always talking about the cover of darkness, but what I had working for me in the Blue Dorm was the cover of light. The cover of light made everything perfect. No one could have suspected that my intentions towards Julian were anything other than honourable. We were playing a game. I was overjoyed that my plans were coming to fruition at last. Without waiting for him to change his mind, I made to mount him.

The logistics of the thing meant that I might just as well have tried to climb Everest. There was no way that I could get on top of him. I got as far as wriggling onto my side and trying to swing my leg over his. No good. Then Roger Stott, the lucky boy who more and more saw George Harrison in the mirror, and who had been watching with a grin on his face, gave a sigh of mock exasperation and said, 'And now I suppose you'll be asking me to lift you up and put you on top of him?' I waggled my head to say Yes.

Mount Julian

As he lifted me up and I began my descent onto the well-cushioned territory called Mount Julian, I gave thanks to Roger Stott, the guardian angel of my wayward desire. He was helping me be a bit of a devil. I could appreciate in a more general way that Marion Willis and Alan Raeburn had been very much on the ball when they had opened the school to ABs. It had partly been a tactic, to cast their net as widely as possible, and to maximise the money coming in. ABs could have managed well enough at any school, but for the proper working of Vulcan as a complex organism they were indispensable. Without them, there would have been a much higher staff-to-pupil ratio, and consequent squashing of a lot of fun and freedom. What matron, however enlightened, would ever have had the nerve to lift

442

me onto another boy, purely to serve the sparky mood of the dorm?

The next few seconds were a feast of sensation, and I gorged myself. My previous fantasy had run aground because I had failed to factor Julian's callipers into the equation. Now I had learned my lesson, and delayed my pounce until the callipers were off. Bravo John! Sound tactics. On the other hand, I hadn't thought things through properly. I hadn't fully understood what it meant that his callipers were now off. After all, they were worn for a reason.

The legs which had been so hard and unyielding in the castle class-room still had the reflected glamour of motion and masculinity, but without the hated supporting brackets they had no power. I had fantasised about interlocking my legs with man-boy or boy-man, but now that I was in the desired position Julian couldn't play his part. For once the assignment was beyond the schoolboy agent QM. For all I know, Julian was throwing all the appropriate switches in his brain, but the wasted poliomyelised muscles in his legs couldn't respond to the messages, though they still had a full range of movement. My case was the opposite, so that once again there was a fatal dove-tailing of disabilities. Messages from brain to legs came through loud and clear. Willing muscles pulled in the proper planes. Ankylosed joints refused to budge.

Nevertheless there was much that I could achieve in these seconds. I was lucky in having Roger Stott as a willing collaborator. My body didn't usefully respond to my commands. Roger's could and did. I was pulling his strings very nicely, but he was also following his own mischievous agenda, at a tangent to mine. We weren't moving as one, which would have been boring. We were improvising some sort of unprecedented dance, full of cross-rhythms.

Throwing myself open to the spontaneity blossoming in the room, I raised my little fists and brought them down on Julian's chest, shouting, 'You will stop writing that letter. You will *stop* writing that letter! If you don't stop writing I shall beat you up.'

'That's it John, you tell him!' said Roger. 'I'll make it easier for you . . .' He put his arms round my waist and lifted me slightly, and soon we had become marvellously syncopated. As I raised my hands a few inches, Roger lifted me a little and when I brought them winging down he gave a downward thrust at the same time to amplify the movement. I was a tender battering ram, storming the walled town that was Julian Robinson with the help of a passing volunteer army.

We soon got into the swing of it. Julian let the letter slip out of his hands and called out in a show of panic, 'Oh no please, don't do it! I surrender. I'll do anything you want. Just name your price!'

By now I had captured the attention of the entire dorm. Someone said, 'Come on John, do some of your "Darling I luff you" stuff now.' 'Naahhh!' said someone else, charitably. 'He always gets stuffed in the play. He should be underneath.'

'Oh don't be so old-fashioned!' said the first voice, 'he can do anything he wants. Just give it to him, John!'

Roger obligingly moved his arms down to my hips and started using my fused pelvis to hump Julian's body. I took advantage of those seconds to tell him I wanted to mate with him. The word which I had heard used by an ambulance man all those years ago still had power over me. I mouthed the words as if they were part of the play, though I was perfectly sincere. I pretended to be only pretending to mean them. I also used those precious moments to explore Julian's body with my hands.

It wasn't easy. As I was bounced up and down I was reminded of the flicker books other boys used to play with – they resisted my fumbling – where a series of still pictures turned into a miniature film when riffled with a competent thumb, some jerky chase or other. I needed to assemble these moments into a fuller portrait. I would have liked to take my time over the exploration, but I knew I had only seconds before the mood of the room changed. Ideally I would savour each new sensation, comparing it with what I had thought it would be like. I would let each batch of information be smoothly absorbed before moving on to the next one. Pretend to be playing with his tummy, admire the firmness, comment on the muscles, let your hand go down further accidentally on purpose, see if he flinches away, if his reaction is neutral it might mean he didn't want you to think he enjoyed it. Take your time, as much as seems decent, a whole day if you can spare it. Later in the sequence, put your hand between his legs and give a gentle nudge, in order to feel . . . whatever was there.

That was the problem I faced. I still didn't have much idea about what I was going to find. For all I knew, tailies might get smaller and smaller as you grew older until they'd diminished to a residual bud. In any event, my chances to explore his body had to take place in flicker-book flashes. As Roger held my botty and plunged it down onto Julian's body I was able to feel *something*. The problem was interpreting the data. It was the first time that I'd been on top of another human being since I was running around making bomfires in 1953. Now my ankylosed joints were being pumped on top of the minotaur boy. His top half was perfect. The bottom half was a mystery waiting to be solved.

My brain must have been working as fast as it had for many years – probably since I had lain in bed in Bathford listening to 'the song where the lady wins in spite of not knowing about pies', also known as 'Anything You Can Do, I Can Do Better'. The camera in my head was taking pictures at a huge rate. Flash-bulbs were popping. My hand was being squashed in rhythm against Julian's body. My thumb on his firm tummy slipped into a little hollow that I knew must be the belly button. I'd located the central dent of his anatomy. Now I should try to slide my thumb southward an inch or two at a time. *Blow the thumb southerly, south or south-west. My lad's in the dorm whom I love best . . .*

It's not usually possible for me, with my fixed wrists, to lay my palms against the parts of the world that interest me, so I've learned over time to transfer tactile sensitivity to the backs of my hands. I've done as much mental re-wiring as I can manage, and I've learned to interpret the data that streams in from surfaces which nature left only meanly supplied with pleasure sensors.

Roger, bless him, was working me in a reasonably slow rhythm, though it wasn't as slow as I would have liked. I would have liked to freeze time at the bottom of each plunge, deadly earnest at the centre of the laughing group. As things stood, each downward thrust gave me barely half a second's time to explore. I located Julian's legs, and wondered at the exquisite softness of them. If I could get the secret of those legs and how to copy them, Julian and I could set up in business. We'd make cushions which would sell in every country of the world. We could charge any price – but there was no sum of money that could make me want to let go of what I was touching, this glorious prototype. It was the most astounding sensation. Inwardly I wept, while busy gloating, that such tender softness must spend its days imprisoned by leather and metal. How much I would have loved to drift off to sleep resting against those legs!

Our high jinks in the dorm were getting rather rowdy. Miss Willis's voice called up from the bottom of the stair-well to ask what on earth was going on. Roger froze in the middle of a thrust, just when my pioneering arm was investigating the uncharted territory between Julian's soft legs, and called out that everything was fine. 'It's just boyish high spirits, Miss Willis,' he shouted. 'Nothing I can't control.'

Then he said, more quietly, 'Settle down, everyone – play-time over,' but he was merciful enough to leave me snuggling against Julian.

'Come on,' said Julian. 'You spend so much of your time mothering us and feeding us, I think it's about time I gave you a cuddle. Come here, my sweet baby, come to Mummy! Let Mummy make a fuss!' He took me in his arms and kissed me, and moved me about quite a lot with those strong arms, making sure not to rest any weight against me.

Soon we heard Biggie and Gillie setting off up the stairs to tuck us in and turn the lights out. The boys who had strayed in from elsewhere scattered to their proper dorms. Roger scampered over to pick me up and carry me back to my bed. There was a flurry of sheet-straightening and tucking in of blankets.

There was no adventure story after lights-out that night. It would have been an anti-climax. I stayed awake for a long time, with my brain fully engaged in the sifting of new information. I couldn't swear to it, but I thought I had managed to locate Julian's penis, in the last half-second before Miss Willis called out and Roger Stott froze. If I had, then my ideas about the world would have to be revised one more time. The dwindling-bud theory of sexual development would have to be abandoned. It wouldn't wash.

While I waited for sleep I imagined that there would be many more exploring times to come. My expedition into the interior of the manly groin was only just under way. I understood, though, that conditions would never again be so favourable to the project. Just that one time, everyone had lent a hand with my homework. With a lot of help, I now had my mental Julian flicker book bound and safely shelved.

I know there's a theory that experience works by contrast – without the lows you wouldn't enjoy the highs. By that logic Judy Brisby was necessary for me fully to appreciate that night in the Blue Dorm with Roger and Julian, with a whole innocently whooping crowd helping me to stuff my face with forbidden fruit. I disagree. Riding the rollercoaster of Julian's body was a peak independent of any trough. It was mystically separate, and strangely, for that reason, it didn't blot out my awareness of Judy Brisby, her cruelty lurking in the institution like dry rot that undermines everything, a fruiting body hidden in the walls.

Bloody Assizes

It would have been some sort of fitting end to that evening if Raeburn had burst in and walloped us all. In fact it was a few nights later that the wrath of the Board of Education was visited on the Blue Dorm. I suppose we had been making a ruckus, and we'd ignored Miss Willis when she shouted up the stairs, 'Quiet in the Blue Dorm!' We would simmer down for about a minute and then start up again. We forced her to take more drastic action. 'Now you'll be sorry!' she shouted up the stairs again, 'I'm going to report you!' We knew what this meant. There might be two co-principals but only one used physical means of discipline. She was threatening to summon Old Rabies and unleash the B of E.

Miss Willis didn't really approve of physical punishment, and usually she was just bluffing, but this time she made good on her threats. The next thing we heard was the same voice shouting, 'Now Mr Raeburn is coming to give you little rowdies "What for"!!'

Raeburn came lurching into the dorm and got to work walloping bottoms. He turned the lights on and told us all to roll over onto our tummies. Then he went round giving a single tremendous thwack at each bedside.

I did as I was told. I could turn onto my left side but not the right, because of the way my right elbow stuck forward. Using my head to give a little more momentum I could end up on my tummy, more or less. It wasn't comfortable, and I had a bit of panic in case I suffocated against the pillow, not being able to raise my neck fully clear of it. Still, I did it. I presented myself for punishment, wondering if I'd be able to stand up to it, or if this would be the death-blow that even Judy Brisby hadn't dared to deliver.

Then Old Rabies was by my bed. I felt his warm hand against my buttocks through the material of my pyjamas. 'Is that your bottom?' he asked, without anger, almost tenderly. Under the circumstances it was a strange question. Did he have doubts about it being a bottom, or doubts about the bottom being mine?

'Yes,' I answered, my mouth completely dry. *Thwack!* went the Board of Education. The noise was terrific, and the pain was non-existent. He had given the bed a mighty blow with the B of E. Then he said sternly, 'Let that be a lesson to you!' and moved on to the next bed and the next rowdy bottom to be given 'What for'.

I lay there wishing I had known ahead of time that he wasn't going to hit me. Then I could have paid proper attention to the feel of his hand against my bottom, something that I'd fantasised about for so long. As it was, I rushed through the sublime moment anticipating a dreadful one. That's always the way with sensation. It claims to be so absolute, but everything depends on the context.

Even now I'm not sure if he hit the other boys. Perhaps none of us got a whack and no one wanted to own up, but I'm inclined to think that the Board of Education claimed some victims. There was a certain amount of blinking back tears after he had left, and also a certain amount of hatred, which is the immediate as well as the lasting product of physical punishment. So perhaps I was the only one to get a placebo beating, just as I imagine I was the only one to get a loving pat on the bottom, like a little caress from the hanging judge, right in the middle of the Bloody Assizes.

Adult essence

By this time my mind was no longer entirely a child's, and my

448

body was making the same pilgrimage towards maturity. My orgasms weren't as dry as they had once been. They had begun to produce a few pearls. The adult essence didn't make its appearance suddenly, from one day to the next, and dribbles could be dissipated. Creamier compounds could be rubbed over the hands until they disappeared. Although there were obsessive hawks in the school, none was so vigilant or well-trained as to spot minor signs like the dandruff snowflakes fluttering from a boy's hands . . .

A lot of the time the fibres of my pyjama trousers simply absorbed the distillate, which turned them crisp and made the matrons frown. It's true I collected Redoxon Effervescent 1000 mg tubes from my blood brother Trevor Burbage, Trevor the unsinkable, the human suitcase with the riding hat. Purely in the interest of science I would sometimes shut myself away with a Redoxon tube, so as to decant the seminal treasure, what little there was of it. I'd stopper it up and keep it in my pocket to see what happened to it over time. The results were not pleasing.

So there was sexual practice, in the form of these solitary adventures, and there was sexual theory, in the form of the nightly play, now inconceivably orgiastic. Apart from that single night in the Blue Dorm there was no convergence between the two.

In any given week so many cowboys and foreign visitors had played with my bosoms and emptied their testicle consommé into my ravenous vagina, that I was a little bored with it all. We had worked our way through every possible heterosexual permutation. What changed the proceedings was a troubling new presence in the audience.

Soon after flicker-book night in the Blue Dorm, Roger Stott told me he was being moved out. 'They say it's temporary, just for a week,' he said. He was rather cast down by it, as if he was being punished for something done wrong. I asked who was being moved in. Luke Squires, that's who, and he wasn't even an AB.

Luke Squires was mildly spastic and in the year above us. I'd seen him around – he certainly stood out. There was something about the way he handled his wheelchair that was absolutely distinctive. It seemed to glide him from place to place, and to arrive perfectly smoothly wherever he wanted to be.

Anything that could be done in a wheelchair Luke could do outstandingly well. He was something of a sports star at Vulcan, equally gifted at basketball (a certainty for the school team at the Stoke Mandeville games) and wheelchair shinty, a game which seemed entirely unburdened with rules. Normally it's paraplegics who have the wheelchair sports pretty much sewn up, having the strong working arms needed to generate speed and power.

The Vulcan team enjoyed challenging the staff, whom they thrashed on a regular basis, as they did any able-bodied team rash enough to borrow wheelchairs and accept a challenge. The home team's familiarity with the chairs gave them a huge advantage. All this sporting activity had no great appeal to me personally, I mean as a spectator, but at least it wasn't absurdly contrived, as some sports events at the school were. Watching one boy attempting what was called archery, when in fact someone else was holding the bow and he had to be pulled bodily backwards in his wheelchair to draw it, it was hard to see where exactly the element of sport lay. It would have made as much sense to catapult him forward, using the tension stored up in the bow, as it did to pretend he was firing it. It might also have been more fun.

It was hard to believe that Luke's lower body wasn't under the same control as his upper, but of course it wasn't so. When he got up from the wheelchair he could hardly stand. He wasn't athetoid – his spasms weren't dramatic – but his movements were greatly impaired.

In a gulch of the badlands

I had a pow-wow with Julian about how I should behave in Luke's presence. I could hardly stop leading the night's radio play of erotic adventures, but I'd surely get into trouble if I carried on in the usual way.

'I can tell you one thing,' said the boy agent QM, '– I don't think much of La Willis's tactics. She's being very obvious. You can't just parachute a spy into enemy territory without papers or any sort of cover story.'

Julian was spy-mad, but that didn't mean he was wrong in this case. It was very clear that a spy was what Luke Squires was. He was trusted by Miss Willis, and he was being sent to discover just what boyish-high-spirits were getting up to, amid the excited murmuring after lights-out. I just didn't know what to do. Acting normally would mean putting on a pornographic vaudeville in which Miss Willis herself, lightly transposed to a brothel in a gulch of the badlands (what was a gulch? what were badlands?), did a star turn.

For once Julian couldn't advise me. 'I can't get through to HQ,' he solemnly told me. 'I think the signal's being jammed. Of course there's always a possibility that Squires is a double agent anyway.'

'How do you mean?'

'Let's just say he might not be as reliable as the Willis seems to think. I've heard of a few interesting messages being intercepted from the lift-shaft.'

Hold on! Hadn't I made that up, the stuff about the message drop in the lift? As so often with Julian Robinson, I began to lose track of the distinction, arbitrary anyway, between fantasy and the other thing.

Julian told me that in the absence of guidance from HQ he accepted full responsibility for whatever I decided to do – but I couldn't help feeling that this came to the same thing as his washing his hands of me. He also warned me that if contact was re-established by lights-out, HQ would be listening in to the show for once. Normally the privacy of the dorm after bed-time was respected, and the tape-recorder in my head was de-activated. I'd insisted on HQ's word of honour about that. Tonight, though, was too significant an occasion for the privilege of privacy from surveillance to stand.

I made one last attempt to disentangle myself from Julian's fantasies. I didn't know who was a spy in what sense (and for who?), what was a game and what might not be.

'Julian,' I said, 'what happens to the tapes in my head? When they're full up, and HQ needs to listen to them?'

'They get changed while you're asleep.'

'Then there's another agent in the dorm, isn't there? You're not the senior operative at all!'

'Yes I am!' he said. 'There's only me! I change them myself.' Then I knew that I had him. Pride had gone before a fall, as Miss Reid of CRX had so often promised. We both knew that once Julian's callipers were off he wasn't going anywhere.

It was strange, even so. Under torture – and QM had alluded darkly to that possibility – I would have said that there wasn't a tape-recorder in my head and never had been. But I still half believed in the gun in my walking stick.

By the time the lights were turned out that night, I had decided on my plan. Defiance. It would be business as usual in the honky-tonks of the Old West. Business as usual, plus over-time.

I pushed the storyline recklessly in new directions. I started off playing the serving wench who timed her cake-baking to allow for a quick fling in the pantry with the stable lad, making sure that the romping was properly finished before the mistress of the house returned or the cakes caught fire. Of course, we weren't fools about narrative. To keep the tension going, the mistress had to return some days while we were still in the act. I also played the part of the mistress, the technical challenge adding considerably to my sense of unreal delight. I marched in and caught us red-handed, and I acted all strict, as though I was Miss Willis herself. Normally the other boys in the dorm would have been in hysterics about that, but with Luke listening in they kept mum. No one would even help me out with sound effects. I had to do all the sex groaning myself.

Sump of dirty dreams

I smacked her/my bottom, almost in silence because of my deficient smacking skills, but making up for it with enthusiastic 'Take that!'s and 'How dare you!'s. I pleaded with myself and begged for mercy, and said I would do anything not to get the sack. Then at some stage I (as Miss Willis) spotted the bulge in the stable boy's trousers and scolded the wench, saying the worst fault to be found in a working girl was selfishness and the inability to share lovely things. Did she think it was really fair for a poor working lad to be fiddling around with a callow girl who hardly knew one end of a man from another? If she was going to behave in this manner behind my (Miss Willis's) back, it would be well for her indeed if she were to take a few lessons from an older woman and at least have the common decency to learn how to share, and to do a good job into the bargain. Heaven knows where I got all this fine and juicy stuff. The collective unconscious is a sump of dirty dreams, and I just lowered my little bucket into it.

The greater mystery, I suppose, is that all the time I thought we were being secret and absolutely disgusting (not realising that the Kama Sutra was way ahead of us) I had never thought to include any element of my own fantasies into the performance. In an all-boy school, the filth I produced was rigorously heterosexual, and now that I felt I had exhausted those possibilities, I broke ground in a new area. Far from feeling my way towards what actually aroused me, I moved further in the other direction.

The wench's first lesson was to hand the boy over to me (Willis) while I put him through his paces until I had him moaning with delight. The moans would have been better done by third parties, but there was no helping that. It was my first real experience of a resistant audience, and it made me lose confidence. I dispensed with the boy and made love to the wench, but my heart wasn't in it. I wasn't quite sure what I was doing. At some stage I told the stable boy to make tea for us and took the wench to bed with me.

For once the story fizzled out. There was a silence of a fairly ghastly type, and then Luke spoke very quietly. 'John?' he said, and my heart sank. 'You're every bit as entertaining a performer as I've been told. But perhaps there are one or two things we should discuss.' His manner was off-hand, except that murmurs after lights-out can never be off-hand, and everyone in the dorm knew he was a man on a mission. 'If you have nothing better to do,' he went on, 'might you meet me for a few words after school tomorrow? Would it be convenient to meet by the bus?'

If the mood of the dorm had been put into words at that moment it would have been *Now you're for the high jump!*, with a certain amount of satisfaction. Ungrateful beasts. And I wasn't so sure about the high jump anyway.

The meeting-place meant that there was a high degree of secrecy involved. The bus was round a corner and easily fifty yards from the front entrance of the Castle. It was an old London Transport Leyland (Raeburn drove it, which can't have been easy). But then Julian was always saying that there were microphones planted all over Vulcan School, to monitor our conversations. It made sense that an older boy would know where to go to avoid being overheard. And why care so much about privacy if he was only going to dish me with Miss Willis?

453

In all the mixed feelings about Luke's invitation and what it might mean, I was overlooking one practical difficulty. I only realised it in the morning. The Everest & Jennings was a decent enough machine, but it wasn't suitable for all surfaces. It certainly wouldn't go over gravel. Not very handy, now that perhaps the most important appointment of my life, demanding absolute privacy, was due to take place on the far side of fifty gravelled yards.

Perhaps this would be the one day when the low-specification machine would simply zing along, gravel no obstacle. That was Plan A. If Plan A didn't work, I had no Plan B. I certainly didn't want worldly Luke, who might be wanting to talk man to man, to find me stranded like an over-sized pebble among the little pebbles of the drive.

When the Everest & Jennings ground to a halt on the gravel, grit buggering the relays in the usual way, I found I did have a Plan B after all. Plan B was to wave my arms feebly about and shout 'I say' in as loud a voice as I could muster. And amazingly, my cries of P. G. Wodehouse distress were heard. An AB spotted me from an upstairs window and came to help. I couldn't believe my luck. It was Roger Stott, the motive power for my sexual assault on Julian. He had shown great despatch and discretion then, and surely he would be equal to any demand I made on him now.

Roger called out of the window and said he'd come and help. He brought a pushing chair with him, to transfer me. When I explained that I was meeting Luke out by the bus he raised his eyebrows, those George Harrison brows, but he didn't pass comment. Rather pathetically I said, 'It's all rather hush-hush.' Then he said something that was rather alarming, bearing in mind I had been impersonating Miss Willis as a prodigious insatiable harlot less than twenty-four hours previously: 'He's rather one of Marion's pets, isn't he?' Well yes, but I clung to the thought that if all he wanted to do was denounce me there were better ways of going about it than making a rendezvous by the school bus.

The school's ABs paid quite a price for their over-class status. They might seem effortlessly superior to us, but they were being exploited all the same in a way that wasn't necessarily to be envied. They were a mild form of slave labour, expected to help with the running of the establishment in a way that would have been unthinkable, surely, in a mainstream school. Even so, there was an obvious difference between an AB like Roger, who would positively offer to help, and the ones who undertook their tasks grudgingly and never did favours.

Roger even offered to join me later if I wanted help getting back to the Castle, which was sweet although it may also have shown some curiosity about my meeting. Would half an hour be long enough? I had no idea, but I thought I'd better say yes. I was getting wildly excited and even a little panicky. Would Luke even come? Perhaps I'd be left alone with the pounding of my suspect heart.

In fact he arrived when I'd hardly been waiting a minute. Luke Squires was as much a good-looking boy as Roger Stott, but in a different style. He was sleek with secrets. He had fair hair, which was always tousled, but tousled just so. And if Roger was the sort of incredulously handsome teenager who can't resist looking at himself in any reflective surface, even the back of a spoon, Luke had the ability to glide past a mirror on his enchanted wheelchair without raising his eyes to it, and still to take in all the relevant information.

Lesbian Sandwich

As he approached I noticed again how smoothly he managed that wheelchair, but this time I also noticed what made his mastery of it possible. Luke was the only boy in the school to have the large wheels at the front of his wheelchair, and not the back. Most boys had to do some delicate finessing when it came to even a little bump, but Luke just lazily glided over, the little back wheel following obediently in the slipstream of his smooth momentum. Luke didn't wheel along, he flowed. I'd been feeling pretty good about my electric wheelchair, even if it was the most basic model, but now Luke's grace made me feel like a bumbler all over again. Not that his chair would have done me any good, without the strong, supple, only marginally spastic arms that powered it. Of course it was his air of sexual knowledgeability that gave his simplest actions a tantric aura.

I wanted so very badly to learn from him. At this stage in life I wanted instruction in cabbala, with a bit of the Apocrypha mixed in, and I suppose that was near enough what I got.

His first words were purely shocking. 'Good afternoon, John. I have a question for you. Don't you think that Marion – sorry, *Miss Willis* – looks exactly like an iceberg of blubber? *Whipped* blubber, to be exact. Like whipped cream, you know.' I was shocked, but also made wary. If this was one of Marion's pets, then he must be laying a trap for me. For once there might be an actual tape-recorder in use, tucked into Luke's smart trousers. It was best to say nothing. 'Mind you,' he went on, 'I'll say one thing for her. Fat people usually stink, you know, but the Willis is clean as a whistle. Sometimes when I'm close to her I take a good sniff while she's looking the other way. Nothing but freshness and soap – and my nose is *very* sensitive.' He flared his nostrils with quiet pride.

'By the way,' he went on, 'you put on quite a show last night. That was hot stuff.' His tone of voice suggested a cool critical verdict rather than an audience's rapturous acclaim. It took me down a peg as well as up. 'Do you know the word for what you were describing last night?' I blushed with proud shame, and said, 'I suppose you mean "smut". Smutty talk.'

'I mean women coupling with each other.' Since I'd invented this activity (as I thought) I could hardly know what it was called. Women had coupled with each other in my improvisation only because the dramatic possibilities, and the men, had been milked dry.

'Why don't you tell me?' I was a little sullen as well as curious. Luke had started with a compliment, but had moved rapidly on to doing what the whole world did, making me feel small.

'That was a Lesbian Orgy,' he said. 'And you did a good job.'

'Lesbian Orgy,' I repeated, copying the assurance of his tone.

'You do know,' said Luke, 'that Lesbians exist, don't you?'

'Yes of course.'

'In fact . . . Lesbians are closer than you might think.'

'How do you mean?'

'I mean Miss Dawkins and Miss Salisbury. That's what I mean. They're lovers. L-O-V-E-R-S.' He did a beautifully rendered double-take, to convey his surprise at my unawareness. 'You really didn't know, did you?'

Miss Dawkins was one of the nicest of the matrons, usually work-ing nights, and Miss Salisbury was a junior physiotherapist, blonde and absent-minded. Marion favoured physios who made us work rather than moving our limbs for us – all part of the goading agenda – but Miss Salisbury was a bit of a softie who would sometimes go easy on us and manoeuvre recalcitrant limbs without expecting too much effort from the patient. She wasn't a Gisela Schmidt, though. There was no massage.

'What makes you so sure?' I asked.

'I'm surprised you haven't noticed yourself. It's not that hard to work out. They always arrange to have the same weekends off. That's the give-away.' While I was absorbing this fascinating information, Luke started to fill me in about lesbian love. 'They make love all weekend. They forget to eat. Very slowly they take their clothes off. If it's cold, they sit by the fire. If it's warm, they go into the garden. They lie down and rub each other's bosoms. Then Miss Dawkins puts her tongue in Miss Salisbury's ear, while Miss Salisbury puts her tongue in Miss Dawkins' ear. That's called a Telephone Call. Lesbians have very long tongues. Then Miss Salisbury puts her face in Miss Dawkins' lap, and Miss Dawkins puts her face in Miss Salisbury's lap, and they stay like that for hours. That's called 69. That's called a Lesbian Sandwich.' He smiled. 'So now you know. There's a lot goes on in Farley Castle. It pays to keep your eyes and ears open.' The implication was that it all went on with his knowledge, perhaps even depended on his approval.

All the time he was talking he cupped his hand round his groin. His black trousers looked new. He was very smart and well scrubbed in a white shirt and black tie, but it was the trousers that held my eye, as they did on the waiters at the Compleat Angler. At first I couldn't believe he was really making that cupping movement round his groin, so I kept having to take another peek to make sure. There was no mistake.

'Do you like my trousers?' he asked. 'They have a permanent crease.' Pretending not to be too interested I asked, 'What's a permanent crease?'

'It means that you can wash them as much as you like and the crease will never go, even if you don't iron them. They're also drip-dry. My mother ironed them anyway, so the crease is even sharper – come closer and see. You could slice ham with those creases.'

It was at this point that I noticed that an additional reason for Luke's unique posture was the fact that he didn't have any side arms on his wheelchair. With side arms, he wouldn't have been able to get his strong hands easily onto those huge front wheels, would he? He was a brilliant boy. At that moment I loved and envied him so much for his ability to flow around in all directions and all classrooms with his bulge on display.

The permanent crease was a wonderful thing, sharp as a mountain ridge. He glided in closer to me so that I had a better view. I rested my hand on his knee for a bit, and followed with my eye the two ridges as they ran up his legs till they were overshadowed by the genital tumulus, round barrow pulsing with secrets.

Again he squeezed his groin with his long flat hand. 'Why do you keep doing that?' I asked.

'I need to dissipate the extra heat,' he said smoothly. 'It's an area of the body which generates more heat than the rest. Here, hold my hands for a minute – feel how cold they get from pushing on these wheels.' I held his hand, and it was indeed very cold, and rather calloused, too. He went on to say that when the school's new block, so long in the planning, was finally built, he would have a lot of extra pushing to do to cover the extra ground. I asked him if he had seen the plans and he said, 'Of course,' as if the go-ahead for construction could hardly be given without his say-so.

His hands would get even colder as he made the journey in the open through the empty spaces between the Castle and the new block, so he had developed this technique for making heat flow out from the central knoll in his lap. He took my hand and pressed it there and yes, it was true that a wonderful amount of heat radiated out from that place.

I was thrilled but also dismayed. For years I had worn black flannels and complained about the cold, and now Mum had bought me grey corduroys to keep me snug. Now I was mortified that I hadn't persevered with the black flannel pants which looked so good on Luke.

'I have to go now,' he said. 'I'll be missed. There are spies everywhere, you know,' and he gave me a wink. 'If there's more you need to know, you know where to find me.' Then he manœuvred himself elegantly backwards and glided off on his marvellous wheels. They made only a hushed crackle on the gravel. I waited where I was for the arrival of my endlessly patient human taxi.

Luke had spoken by daylight and outdoors about matters which had been restricted in my experience to darkness and the sanctuary of the dorm theatre. He had spoken with great authority, whereas I made things up as I went along. And after he had taken my breath away with new vistas of perverse knowledge, he had offered to answer any questions I might have in the future.

When he described the Lesbian amours going on among the staff of the school, Luke had specified the slow taking off of clothes, but when I visualised the scene later I imagined it played out with the women fully clothed. Miss Dawkins' glasses steamed up, and Miss Salisbury was split and mended under her physio's smock by dry orgasms like my Enid Blyton ecstasies over Julian (the original Julian) and Dick.

Soon after that, Luke Squires's reconnaissance mission in the Blue Dorm came to an end, and Roger Stott came back from exile. We waited for repercussions from Luke's report to Miss Willis, but nothing seemed to happen. All the same, he became a figure of fascination for me.

The Vulcan School was an austere place, but every possible delight was put on show by prodigal Luke in his wheelchair. Without sound or fuss, gliding by on silent wheels, he seemed to be in many places at once.

It's never much of a problem to feast your eyes on the trousered groin of a wheelchair occupant, since his bottom and legs are already on a kind of tray. If you're at a distance of only two or three feet and at the same level yourself, there's much less of an angle for your eye to swivel through, if it so happens that you wish to inspect the nether regions. The same intensity of ogling directed at a vertical schoolboy would be bound to draw attention.

For Luke, that tray was offered to the world in uniquely tempting style, thanks to those large front wheels which tilted the dish up a little higher, at the front, than the horizontal. His one-of-a-kind wheelchair gave as tempting a view of his legs and neatly trousered bum as anyone could wish for. On top of which his hands were always framing his privates, plumping them up for inspection. Once you had noticed this, it was shameless, actually. I was amazed that he got away with it the way he did.

In the James Bond books, Bond always felt very sexy when he saw or felt the *Mound of Venus* at the base of a lady's thumb. I wondered if those books would have been written differently if Ian Fleming had had a chance to view the far more tempting hill of potential resonating between Luke's legs.

My fascination with Luke didn't affect my devotion to my two secret lovers, the adults Raeburn and Nevin, nor the subtle flow of preferential feeling involved there. In fact my two adult passions weren't really at odds. The two sets of feelings had elements in common – admiration, curiosity and a sort of rage to be touched – but they were drawn on different accounts.

Your groin area

Then Gillie Walker was sent to sound me out on a delicate matter. We were known to have a liking for each other, to get on, and so she had been delegated. 'John,' she said, ever so casually, 'it has been noticed that your hand often rests at the bottom of your tummy, by your groin area . . .' The passive construction didn't fool me for a moment, nor was it meant to. The noticer was very clearly Marion, who noticed certain things and not others. She didn't notice the virtually continuous priapic display made by Luke Squires, but she'd spotted something amiss with my very ordinary posture. Gillie went on, 'I don't expect you to inform on another boy, but is there something you'd like to tell me?' The idea seemed to be that I had become abnormally sensitised to my genital chakra – as if that was something that could only come from outside.

I hadn't been expecting this interrogation, but in a tight corner my brain worked fast. When I opened my mouth the words flowed very smoothly. 'Honestly, Gillie,' I said, 'have you taken a look at this arm? Roll up the sleeve and do a proper inspection. I want you to. My left elbow doesn't bend – do you see? – so the hand just naturally falls where you say. As I'm sure you've noticed, it never happens with the other hand, because the elbow on that side actually works.'

Gillie gave me a warm smile. 'I knew there would be a good reason,

John. I had every confidence in you, of course. I never doubted you for a moment, but I was duty bound to ask. I'm sure you understand.'

Of course I understood. I understood that Luke Squires was protected by his very blatancy. He couldn't keep his hands off his parts. He practically raised his cock in class when he knew the answer to something, in preference to his hand, and Marion Willis saw nothing. No one said a dicky-bird. No one came to grill him, but when I gave my unglamorous parts the occasional rearranging tug, there was consternation and court-martial.

My funny turn

Peter and I were more or less getting the hang of mealtimes with Granny at the Compleat Angler. One of the waiters at the Otel was her favourite, absolutely her pet, even though he was Spanish and she believed that the language of good food was French. This waiter loved to tease her while he was serving, and she loved it. After Granny had made her little road through the food, and then put her knife and fork down saying, 'Well, I'm *defeated*,' he waved his finger at her charmingly. 'Madam,' he would say, 'I hope you realise that when I take this back to the kitchen they will mince it up and feed it back to me! I don't know what I am going to do with you, Madam!' Granny absolutely ate it up. What this Spanish waiter was saying was outrageously cheeky, it was no way to treat a lady and so on, but she absolutely loved it, she couldn't get enough.

After lunch Peter and I played chess in Granny's room. Then something happened that wasn't supposed to. He started to win. A bishop and a knight killed my queen, and my king was next for the chop. I knew Mum was prone to fainting, and I thought, I've never fainted in my life. This would be a good time to start.

I was carried through to the bed. Peter and Granny picked their way through the scattered chess pieces. I heard Granny saying, 'It must have been the heat.' She bathed my face with a cold flannel for twenty minutes. Then she said, 'Granny has decided to buy you a special sort of wheelchair. It's called a Wrigley.' Obviously she had been approached beforehand, but my funny turn may have tipped the balance. It did no harm for her to be reminded of my frailty. It wasn't blackmail, exactly. I wouldn't say it was any darker than greymail.

I was delighted by the news, though I could only let my pleasure show as a faint smile through the simulated blur of weakness. A hundred and sixty smackers! I dare say Granny withheld a fraction of the sum on principle, or imposed terms in some way, but I never learned the details.

Peter was delighted too. 'We can have a lot of fun with that Wrigley,' he whispered. 'And don't worry. I made a mental note of the position on the board. I know exactly where everything was. We can finish that game any time you like.'

The plans for the expansion of the school must have been given Luke's approval, because quite dramatic building works were under way. Phase One involved erecting a couple of staff houses – before then, there was no accommodation for staff, just a group of caravans installed behind the yew hedge outside the kitchen windows. It wasn't ideal, with no facilities for washing or bathing except by slipping into the Castle through a side door. In winter the caravans were cold, but electric fires being left on would scorch the carpets and fill the grounds with the lovely rustic smell of burning plastic.

Then a wing was built to one side of the Castle, containing a dormitory block and a dining room. Finally there was a new block of classrooms, shaped like an H. The dorms were supposed to be ready for the start of the school year, but no such luck. In the September half of them could just about be used, but there were polythene sheets flapping all over the place, and breeze-blocks and bags of cement were stacked up against every wall. Luckily the weather was mild. Raeburn and Miss Willis advertised in the parish magazine for households which could take the less severely disabled boys in. The rest of us were issued with hot-water bottles.

The new block provided much better facilities for teaching, but more importantly it also offered a much greater range of places where surreptitious meetings could take place. Julian Robinson still said there were microphones hidden everywhere, and that the new buildings had actively been wired for sound, with tape-recordings made of every word spoken, but his authority in such matters took a dive when it was discovered that his Sean Connery autograph contained three spelling mistakes. Whatever the risks, the new block with its nooks and crannies gave promise of fruitful encounters. The new spaces were open to being colonised by forbidden activities. The smell was freeing in itself, of new wood and fresh paint.

The transformed school no longer contained Ben Nevin, who had gone back to Canada. It was a sort of bereavement, but he gave me a wonderful present before he left. It was a Chinese box, beautifully enamelled, which he'd picked up on a visit to Hong Kong. Best of all, it had a secret compartment. Unless you pressed at exactly the right point, you'd never be able to open it. It wasn't roomy, as secret compartments go, but big enough to hold a folded piece of paper on which I'd written in my best hand, which was still pretty bad, *Given to John Cromer by Ben Nevin at Vulcan School. A GREAT MAN.*

I would have mourned Mr Nevin more keenly if Judy Brisby hadn't left at the same time. That was a present finer even than a Chinese box with a hidden compartment. Hearing the news gave a definite spring to the tyres of my wheelchair. It wasn't that her leaving compensated for his, exactly, but it certainly made it harder to wish for the clock to be turned back.

Judy Brisby hadn't been found out and dismissed in disgrace, rather the opposite. She left the school without a stain on her character, and she had the gall to get married too. She had found someone her own size to give nerve punches to, someone to make beg for cold toast at breakfast. At first it seemed surprising that her husband was a soldier, but I suppose it meant he was used to taking orders.

No one could have measured up to Ben Nevin, so it was splendid in a way that his replacement should be such an abject duffer as a teacher – the sort whose idea of teaching is to read long passages out from a book. Mr Gilchrist was Irish. We thought he was old, meaning I suppose that he was in his forties. Somebody must have tipped him off about my imperfect control of my wheelchair, because I never managed to run over his feet, though Heaven knows I tried. He was annoyingly nimble, and perhaps accustomed to unpopularity.

I was shocked when I learned Mr Gilchrist's first name was Christopher. He had Christ in his name twice over and he was still horrible. I thought perhaps the Christs had cancelled each other out, like terms on opposite sides of the equals sign in algebra. In my book he had no redeeming features.

I remember that for Geography the book was green. Once he was dictating something about winter wheat under snow, and how the snow gave the seeds a chance to breed. Of course he meant 'breathe', but the Irish accent made it unclear, and *breed* was what I wrote down. I had my doubts, but didn't dare ask. He wasn't the sort of teacher you could ask about things – I suppose that means he wasn't worth anything as a teacher, really. If I'd been an AB, he would have clipped me round the ear, but in common with the other more or less severely disabled boys I wasn't supposed to have my ear clipped. So he crept up behind me with a pencil rubber in each hand and rubbed them both up and down my sideboards really hard, whispering, 'Some say that having this slower pain is worse than having your ears tweaked,' again in that thick Irish accent, so that 'worse' sounded like 'worras'. I had no reason to doubt it.

It wasn't just Ben Nevin and Judy Brisby. At the point when the school expanded its premises, there was a whole-sale change-over of staff, so that very few of the matrons who had been at the school when I arrived still worked there. I enjoyed these new faces rather than regretted the passing of the old. New people could be conned, by virtue of their unfamiliarity with the place, into letting me get away with little ruses that would formerly have been stopped dead in their tracks.

I did miss Sheila Ewart, Big Matron, the original Biggie, who left the school at this time. She was replaced by Mrs Wemyss (pronounced Weems), who was never known as anything but Mrs Wemyss. When you are spelled Wemyss and pronounced Weems, nick-names are unnecessary.

From a wheelchair, you tend to look up people's noses. In Mrs Wemyss's case, there was usually something to see. She had a resident bogey, more often than not, waggling as she spoke. It bobbed up and down as the breath went in and out.

I was learning that anyone in authority has at least one hobby-horse. Mrs Wemyss had two, hot breakfasts and tonsils. On the first subject she would say, 'How these boys can be expected to learn anything at school without a hot breakfast inside them is simply beyond me. In summer it's one thing, but in winter? Quite absurd.' She instituted porridge and campaigned for bacon and eggs.

464

Her line on tonsils was less humane. She thought they were a mistake. Everyone would be much the better for having theirs out. She had strong ideas about the best post-operative diet: dry toast. 'My goodness, don't you cry when you eat your first piece! But you get better quickly. At my last place of work there was an Italian man who was crying his silly eyes out when I made him eat his toast. Next day what happens? He thanks me from the bottom of his heart, for helping him get better so much more quickly than the patients being pampered with jellies and ice cream. Such a soppy thing to give a tonsillectomy patient!' Temperamentally she was well suited to the school's philosophy of care that stopped well short of spoiling.

Ponky-doodle

I appreciated the porridge very much and enjoyed the occasional fried egg but hung stubbornly on to my tonsils. One of the minor matrons who joined the school at this time was Millicent Baxter, thin and pretty, very lively. She had a stylised way of sniffing when she was near some of the boys. Whatever else Vulcan was, it was a place where boys reached physical maturity far away from their mothers' tender nagging. Some of us positively hummed. She would raise her chin and tilt her head to one side, to take two thoughtful sniffs. There was nothing censorious about it. She might have been trying to memorise the scent of a flower strange to her. Then she might casually say, to an Egyptian boy who was sometimes distinctly aromatic, 'Nabil, have you had a bath today? We're getting a little . . .' She never said *smelly*. She never said *whiffy*, *rank*, *stinky* or *high*. She never even said *pongy*. What she said was *ponky-doodle*.

Her other mannerism was what she said instead of swearing. Just when it seemed that the temptation to say 'Bloody' was too much, and she'd gone beyond the point of no return with those satisfying opening consonants, that 'Bl–', she would make a great effort and say '–ue pencil!' instead. Blue pencil. The censor's blue pencil crossed out the expressions she didn't allow herself to utter.

In theory the new buildings were perfectly tailored to our needs, but there were plenty of little flaws. Miss Willis often told us about the bell-push she had seen at a Local Authority building, for the dis-

465

abled to ring for assistance, but placed far too high for anyone in a wheelchair to reach. This was one of her little sermons. Even so, on her home ground she hadn't been able to anticipate every problem. There was a metal ridge, for instance, to the front entrance of the dormitory block, which no electric wheelchairs could cross, and only the most skilful manual wheelers could jerk themselves up and over. A temporary wooden ramp was commissioned so that the premises could be properly accessible while the repairs were pending.

Trussed, basted, oven ready

Judy Brisby had the nerve to visit the school to flaunt her happiness. She even came into the classroom and said she had an announcement to make. She was going to have a baby. Why, exactly, were we supposed to care?

There was dutiful applause from two or three pupils. I was one of them, toady to the last, but since all I can do in the way of clapping is to pat the back of the left hand with the front of my right I hardly swelled the accolade. Julian didn't even go through the motions of clapping. As the applause was dying away he said, 'Poor kid!' not loudly – but loudly enough.

'Would you mind repeating what you just said?' snapped Judy Brisby, remembering the power of her days as a matron. 'I think we'd all like to hear it.' But her power was only a memory.

'Certainly,' said Julian with a smile. 'I said: "Poor kid!"'

She was trussed, she was basted, she was oven ready. The boy agent QM had defeated the fiend from Smersh (or did she answer to Spectre?). He was fully entitled to blow the smoke casually from his strong index and middle fingers, the double barrels of his Beretta. He had earned the double-o prefix, his licence to kill. He was ooQM as far as I was concerned, outright head of the Secret Service, but nobody missed Judy Brisby and she was never mentioned again.

I try to avoid passing severe judgements on my fellow beings, but I have to admit I'm pretty unforgiving when it comes to Judy Brisby. I take a rather vindictive line with her. I hope she has many future lives. There – I've said it. No taking back.

Luke Squires was much on my mind, but I also kept my distance

466

from him. He would roll past me from time to time in his nifty wheelchair and squeeze his groin as he went by. I was terrified of getting caught if I responded. At the beginning of the new term senior boys had circulated warnings that 'any boy found indulging in homosexual practices' was to be expelled. Then Terence Wilberforce and another boy were caught in the act by Miss Salisbury and told to report to Raeburn. Miss Salisbury had a nerve turning them in, I thought, when she spent so much of her spare time head down in Miss Dawkins' lap. Terence and his co-accused went in prepared for the worst, hoping for pain rather than expulsion. They would prefer a beating, however savage, to the end of the only education they could hope for.

A group of us mustered outside Raeburn's study. If poor bedwetting Roger Stott couldn't sit down for days after being on the receiving end of the Board of Education, what would be the punishment for taboo practices with another boy? From the other side of the door came a silence we took to be ominous. Time went by, and someone set his ear against the solid wood of the door. He could hear murmurings from within, but not what was being said.

The suspense was killing. It was torture being outside that door, not knowing what torture was in progress on the other side of it. If it was worse than what we were going through, then it was terrible indeed. Finally Terence hobbled out of the office – but as he had hobbled in, that didn't signify. He was moving quite normally and smiling. Had Raeburn tried to wallop their bottoms? Had he broken the spare Board of Education in the frenzy of his walloping?

No, Raeburn hadn't walloped them. Not at all. He had offered them a small sherry. They were close to being adults, after all – wasn't that what this chat should be about? Then he explained that nothing shocked or surprised him, after being in the Army. Boys of their age were naturally curious. However, Marion did get rather upset by this sort of thing, and she wasn't alone in that. He advised them to be careful, and ended the interview by saying that if they had any questions on this particular subject, to come and see him any time at all. At the start of the day I had been thanking God Almighty that I hadn't been one of the boys caught in the act, and I ended up almost blaming Him for depriving me of that glass of sherry and the friendly chat.

So perhaps the risks weren't impossible to contemplate after all. I tried to imagine the best place to explore the warming mound in Luke's lap. There were so many new nooks and crannies to the new premises. Luke must have rubbed his hands together (against his groin, naturally) when he saw the plans – if that ever really happened – to see so many protected new spaces. Exploitable little pockets for potential sensuality.

After any number of delays and teething problems the new dormitory block was opened, and so was the new classroom block. Initially being a pupil of Vulcan had really been like living in a castle, but now the main building was the hub, and the new dormitory block and the new classrooms were like two arms spidering out in opposite directions from the original school.

Marching papers

The new dormitories were on ground level, which was a manifest improvement. It was never anywhere near as cold as it had been in that castle turret. The facilities were better, with one bathroom between each pair of dorms. I was being given a bath there one November day when shouting seemed to burst out from a number of places at once. All I could hear was, 'Kenny's dead!' which made me very sad. I had liked Mr Kenny the maths teacher. He had beautiful hand-writing on the blackboard. His emotions were always close to the surface. In one lesson I couldn't concentrate because my knee was so sore. He asked me why I was finding the lesson so difficult and I explained. After the lesson he stroked my knee and said some sort of prayer over it. He told me about a spiritual healer called Rebecca Beard. He had read her book *Everyman's Search* and was convinced she was on to something. There were tears in his eyes.

It wasn't that sort of touch which had got him into trouble, though. Mr Kenny had been dismissed (wrongfully, to my way of thinking) for hitting Bernard Baines, a provoking lad who dressed as a Teddy boy and listened to Buddy Holly on his Grundig tape-recorder. In any case Bernard had hit back with far greater force and given Mr Kenny a black eye, as well as his marching papers by grassing him up. Now Mr Kenny had ended his life, and his death would lie on Bernard's conscience with all the weight (I was sure about this) of a feather. Still, the school would remember him, and I would return the favour of the prayers he said over my hot and angry knee.

Of course it wasn't Kenny at all. It was Kennedy, the American president, who had died. Mr Kenny moved to Australia and wrote me nice letters.

One strange thing about the new dorm was that our filthy radio plays stopped dead, or (putting it another way) never got started after the change of address. The new environment had an acoustic that deadened our fantasies. Perhaps the Castle itself really had been an accomplice – the Grey Lady herself needing a few cheap thrills to beguile the tedium of non-existence. Or else it was simply that I had begun to lose interest and was looking for an excuse to let it drop. Without me to cook, mother and whore my way through the narrative every night, the carnival was over.

To make love like Ten

These days I was more interested in Luke Squires, though I was also fascinated by a new pupil called Jimmy Kettle. He hardly seemed like a pupil at all. He was older than me, fifteen or even sixteen, and American. James Charles Kettle III. He was certainly old enough that he needed to shave – I remember that. He hardly seemed to need any education, since he was sophisticated to a terrifying degree. This isn't normally a character profile which fills teachers with admiration, but Jimmy had no trouble in getting away with it. Teachers never resented him missing their lessons – it was rather the other way round. They were surprised and delighted if he chose to turn up, but also almost nervous. It was as if they knew they must perform at the peak of their powers to have a chance of holding his attention.

Jimmy didn't feel the need to stay at Vulcan for the whole term. He was free to pick and choose his school-days. His home was in Paris with his glamorous mother, who was often away on her travels. She was rich enough to treat the school more or less as an Otel for her son on those occasions, and the school was poor enough to accept such a pupil on any terms whatsoever. Jimmy was spastic, not quite athetoid but certainly on the borderline of that unhappy state. He was less able to control his involuntary movements than Luke, especially when he was tired. On the other hand, he enjoyed the advantage over Luke that his spasms didn't affect his legs too much, so his walking was reasonably assured. He didn't need a chair. Luke and he didn't get on, which was virtually inevitable. They were fighting to monopolise the very small amount of spastic mystique available.

It would be quite wrong to imagine that I played these two fascinating young men against each other. I wouldn't have known how.

I was used to being thought of as clever, but I cheerfully passed the brainy laurels over to Jimmy, as long as he let me talk to him, which he seemed happy to do. His accent took a little getting used to. It was some time before I realised that it was genteel Boston trying to sound Southern. Jimmy wanted to be an actor, and it didn't seem an impossible dream, compared to many on the premises. He jigged in rhythm while he spoke. The tremors in his hands could be built into dramatic gestures. It didn't seem out of the question that he might act a part in a play without breaking character.

On stage he might be able to gain a greater mastery of his physical instrument, as long as he didn't get too tired. He was confident of success, saying that actors didn't need to use their own energy. That was what the audience was there for – as an energy source. It was only rehearsals that he would need to worry about, in terms of draining his batteries. Performance would replenish them.

Somehow he made it possible to imagine him appearing in a play which required him to come down a grand staircase in evening dress, carrying a brimming glass, and not spilling a drop.

Jimmy Kettle had one absolute obsession, deserving the solemn label of monomania. He wanted to do everything like Ten. Everything came back to that. He wanted to drink like Ten, he wanted to smoke like Ten, he wanted to make love like Ten. He mentioned Ten not ten times a day but ten times a minute. He worshipped Ten.

Ten was Tennessee Williams. Hence the over-lay of Southern accent. Ten, rather than Tenn, because that was how highly he scored with Jimmy. In fact he wrote it down in numeral form, as 10. Ten out of ten.

There were no obstacles in the way of his drinking and smoking like 10, since his mobility and his funds were both more or less unlimited. The grounds of Vulcan were large, and it wasn't as if a posse was despatched every time he missed a class. He was allowed to go his own way. If anyone objected to his conscientious programme of dissolution, they would be likely to find the co-principals' hearing, normally so sharp, blocked with earmuffs paid for by Mrs Kettle's very welcome cheques.

The cutest scrunched-up face

Making love like 10 wasn't quite so straightforward a prospect as the drinking and smoking. Jimmy's own tastes were conventional, though hardly late-blooming. He offered to take me to Paris, and to let me have a turn with his favourite companion. 'Her name is Minouche,' he said, 'and she's got the cutest scrunched-up face. And don't worry, you won't have to pay. It'll be my treat.'

When I said I didn't care for girls in that way he seemed delighted, saying, 'I'll take you where the queers go if you like. You've no idea what goes on in the Place Pigalle.' In fact he regarded his own sexual conformity as the greatest obstacle in the path of what he most wanted, close friendship with 10 himself.

Though one hundred per cent heterosexual, he would make an exception for Tennessee Williams, and wouldn't make a fuss about it. 'If 10 wanted to sleep with me, I'd do it like a shot. It would be the least I could do,' Genius had its privileges, after all, and so does charm, which was just a part of what Jimmy had.

He kept issuing invitations to Paris, saying, 'Ma Kettle would be sure to make you welcome.' It pleased him to refer to his glamorous mother invariably as 'Ma Kettle', as if she was a hillbilly chewing black-eyed peas on a porch somewhere, her quid of chewing tobacco parked during the interruption of the meal in the lap of a dress that had once been a potato sack.

After learning that I wasn't a potential customer for Minouche, Jimmy lent me a book of stories by 10 called *Three Players of a Summer Game*, which he said was far 'fruitier' than anything 10 could get away with on stage in our retarded little country (no offence). *The Darling Buds of May* was already quite a step up for me, and I struggled with

10's book, though I could dimly see that there was a vitality in it not altogether different from what H. E. Bates admired in his Larkins, though turned to different ends – less likely to produce a family of six. Jimmy took pity on me and would drop quotations from 10 into our conversations. He set out to shape my mind, in a way that no teacher had really bothered to do.

Jimmy read to me from his favourite stories in the book I was so slow to read. He conducted the reading with broad hand gestures which somehow damped down the involuntary movements in his arms. I remember in particular him declaiming, 'He is a drinker who has not yet completely fallen beneath the savage axe blows of his liquor,' and, with an almost Shakespearean grandeur, 'the dark and wondering stuff beneath the dome of calcium . . .'

We wept together over 'One Arm' – Jimmy's tears the more surprising since he knew the story so well. In another story, a man and a woman take to going to depraved bars together – although they're both interested in men. It's just that they're both more likely to be successful if they work as a team. The man calls what they're looking for 'the lyric quarry'.

Later, on a cross-country holiday, they make a detour to a place called Corpus Christi 'to investigate the fact or fancy of those legendary seven connecting glory-holes in a certain tea-room there' (it turned out to be fancy or could not be located). Jimmy explained that a tea-room was a public lavatory, and a glory-hole was a hole made in a cubicle through which a man might push his parts if he so cared, leaving the rest of himself unseen.

I was amazed. I rocked back on my heels. I'd never heard of anything so sporting in my entire life! Such an arrangement would have made it so straightforward for me to satisfy my curiosity about the male equipment, quite without embarrassment since I couldn't be seen. After all this time, I had glimpsed one set of parts briefly in a shower, and touched two others very fleetingly – Julian's in flicker-book fragments, and Luke's when he had pressed my hand to his over-heated groin. On that second occasion I had been naïve enough to concentrate my attention on thermal output rather than anatomical glory. It's true that Luke's groin seemed to generate heat in the same way that Jim Shaeffer's luminous watch radiated light before its re-painting.

472

'But Jimmy,' I said, 'this is an unbelievably filthy book. Where did you buy it? Who would publish such a thing?'

Jimmy thought for a moment. 'I bought it in a London bookstore – near Soho, now you mention it. Called Hatchards.' He riffled through the early pages of the book. 'And it's published by a smutty crew who go by "Secker & Warburg", of 7 John Street, WC1. Soho again, I guess.'

I had heard of Secker & Warburg and had considered them respectable. It seemed most likely that there had been no one in the office to tell them the meaning of 'tea-room' or the real source of the glory in a glory-hole.

We wanted to set up a croquet lawn at Vulcan in 10's honour (croquet being the 'summer game' of his title). The authorities weren't convinced. I don't know how seriously the co-principals considered our suggestion. The grounds of the school were extensive, but level terrain was at a premium. The co-principals may have decided that suave control of a mallet was beyond all but a handful of the boys, or they may have spotted right away that this was closer to a literary allusion than a real plea for sporting facilities.

Jimmy hated television, though the medium didn't exactly dominate life at Vulcan except on special occasions. The television set was in the old hall near the great fireplace, and viewing hours were restricted. Jimmy would remind me of 10's *bon mot* that TV stood for 'tired vaudeville', as every single pupil except him rushed through their evening meal on a Thursday, waiting for the word of dismissal which meant we could scurry in all our various styles of locomotion towards the television and *Top of the Pops*. It was the only time of the week when he made me feel that I tested his patience.

Soft wheat

Jimmy treated me like a grown-up, which was a new feeling. By this time, though, I had some downy hair on my top lip. This was called 'bum fluff', which was a lovely idea. I liked to imagine nice curved bottoms planted all over with the same soft wheat.

Shaving seemed an attractive idea, all the same. Lots of the other boys were doing it, and it made sense for me to serve my own apprenticeship in face-scraping. I set out to acquire the proper equipment. One of the achievements of the Raeburn–Willis régime was the provision in the hall of easels on which newspapers were displayed. The papers would be slid under a string running down the centre of the easel, and after that they could be read with minimal assistance from the hands. Those who really couldn't manage by themselves could always ask someone else to turn the pages. As Raeburn said, 'Why should the reach of a boy's mind be held back by the reach of his arms?'

It was on Saturdays that I paid most attention to the press. There were any number of special offers advertised on a Saturday, and I hadn't lost my taste for retail action-at-a-distance, familiarly known as mail order. I still sent off for the Ellisdons catalogue, though it was no longer so perfectly on my wave-length. I noticed that in these degraded days Ellisdons now offered a reproduction of the Brussels Squirt Boy, whose more usual name is the Manneken Pis.

It was from the *Daily Mail* one Saturday that I sent off for an electric razor of my own, costing 25/-. I liked the *Mail* because Dad despised it, just as I treasured my *Reader's Digest* annual all the more after he told me its motto should be 'Let Us Do Your Thinking for You'. There was one article in the annual, called 'The Eyes which Nothing Can Escape', about the tracking powers of the Aborigines of Australia, whose title gave me a shiver I now recognise as religious.

Of course, when the electric razor arrived it needed a certain amount of modifying, so that I could actually use it. My arms were at the wrong distance and the wrong angle. The school handyman, who was called Mr Wilby, was rather capricious – sometimes he would do things right away, and sometimes he seemed able to put simple tasks off for months. This was the background to one of the school sayings – *Boys will be boys, and Wilby Wilby Wilby*. On this occasion he made no difficulties and came up with a satisfactory solution. In fact it was the same solution as the one he devised for my toothbrush. He lashed it on a stick with the help of a bracket, and then I could manage. Then I could reach my face with it. Soon I was shaving my top lip with the best of them.

Special toothbrush, special electric razor. In my case 'special' usually turned out to mean 'on a stick'.

It stands to reason that if I could spend enough time with Jimmy to be lent books and (theoretically) prostitutes, then Luke Squires could have made my acquaintance in the same above-board way. If he didn't, it was because he didn't want to. He positively preferred the hole-and-corner. The underhand was his element. Perhaps he thought Jimmy's approach rather pedestrian, and Luke was anything but pedestrian. He flowed past in his unique chair, often only glimpsed from the corner of my eye before he vanished. He had told me that I knew where to find him, but then he took care to make himself a liar by disappearing the moment he was sighted.

Even a chance meeting would take a lot of planning. Everything had to take account of school time-tables, and things grew complex when the boy you wanted to bump into was in a higher class, having his own friends and his own priorities. I couldn't just knock on a door and arrange a meeting.

Chance did its own mischievous time-tabling, most memorably one morning by the serving hatch where the morning milk or coffee was dealt out. I had needed to pass some urine fifteen minutes before the end of a lesson, and had been given permission to go to the toilet. I went along the corridor to the sliding door in the assembly hall and did what I had to do. I didn't linger over it, but by the time I had finished there were only seven minutes left of the lesson. When I opened the sliding door of the classroom with my stick, the teacher said there was no point in my coming back in now, disrupting everybody's concentration just to sit at my desk for those few minutes. I might as well wait in the assembly hall. That's where I was when I heard the bell, and the rush of wheelchairs preparing to escape from classrooms. Of course the able-bodied boys were first out.

Roger Stott was there in a moment, standing at the counter. Then Luke came gliding along. I'd noticed that he always stood up out of the chair, supporting himself with his arms on the bar counter. He liked the chair to be pushed aside so he could have a chance to stand. He managed very well as long as he could lean against a wall. Roger managed things very diplomatically, ministering to weakness without advertising his strength. He never forced himself on the people

475

he was supposed to help, but stood casually to one side when a boy wanted to emerge from his chair, in place to lend a hand if the boy lost his grip and was in danger of falling over.

So there was Luke, propping up the shelf of the milk bar while we all waited for the hatch to open. Chairs and ABs were piling up behind us. Luke was at the front of the queue, directly in front of me, while Roger, tactful chaperone of the disabled, stood to one side. I looked at Luke's bottom from the vantage-point of my wheelchair. It looked as if it had been squashed flat by the long hours he had spent sitting. I was overwhelmed by pity for the pressures of its restricted life, and the desire to give it comfort with a good old grope.

It was quite an ambitious project, but not impossible. I knew all the boys in the queue would have their eyes fixed on the hatch, through which came the clatter of preparations and the tempting smell of powdered coffee. Staff members were served their coffee elsewhere. Luckily my wheelchair had automatic brakes, or the attempt at seduction would have had no chance at all. As it was, I could nudge smoothly forward and then lock myself in place. I wasn't worried about Roger Stott noticing. After the letter-writing scene in the Blue Dorm I knew that he wouldn't be shocked – he might even get a kick out of helping perverse excitement along. It's wonderful how quickly, on the right occasion, an innocent vessel can fly the Jolly Roger and the chaperone turn procurer.

Normally a groping hand must have the palm as its main sensor, that being where the nerve-endings are concentrated. The only way I could have brought my palm into contact with Luke's buttocks was if the Willis–Raeburn Alliance had provided a couch for the purpose in the assembly hall by the serving hatch, on which boys could be installed face down for exploration. This was unlikely, for all Raeburn's broad-mindedness, and in any case the protruding legs of the waiting boys would block the coffee queue. Besides, where would the challenge be then, the sense of achievement against the odds? Stolen apples not only taste sweeter, they are ravishingly smoother to the touch.

I would rely as usual on the backs of my hands, cast against type as conduits of ecstasy. I didn't even try to look around to check who might be able to see what – not that my unyielding neck would have helped very much if I had. I was relying on Roger to stand where he would screen us from the idly curious. I murmured sorrowfully, 'How creased your trousers are, just here on the seat,' and embarked on a full slow grope along Luke's bottom. I tried to move the backs of my hands with a sensuous waggle.

Gilding the tousled strands

Luke turned his head round on its flexible neck, and when he saw me supporting him by the seat he smiled. At that moment the serving hatch was yanked open and light streamed around his head, gilding the tousled strands of his yellow hair. I was overwhelmed with sensory riches. The chakra in my groin was singing and dancing, and I was dazzled by the way light seemed to be streaming right through that beautiful head, not just round it.

Luke murmured, 'That's very helpful – my legs get tired so quickly. Do you mind just staying there for a moment while I adjust my balance?' I took this for licence to extend the radiant moment of groping. Not only did the sunlight seem to be streaming through Luke's head, it seemed to be streaming through mine. Eventually Luke signalled that he needed to sit down. I edged the Wrigley backwards, and Roger helped him back to his own chair. I established myself at a table to recover from the excitement. Roger brought over my coffee a few minutes later, but I hardly needed to drink it with the way my body was humming to itself. Roger nipped smartly back to the hatch, since as a helper he was entitled to any milk and coffee left over in the kitchenette. Luke, of course, had disappeared. I seemed to have exactly half of the wherewithal to establish magical control of him. I had the spell to make him vanish. That was infallible. All I needed was the spell to make him appear – out of the wood-work. I began to get an idea about that piece of conjuring.

There had always been gaps in the curriculum at Vulcan, it seemed to me. I was always top at languages, and very full of myself until Trevor Burbage mentioned that his sister studied the hardest language in the world. It was called Sanskrit. I was incensed, and persuaded him to accompany me on the long trek out to the school sand-pit. Then I scratched marks in it with a stick. 'That's sand-

script,' I said grimly. 'It's not so hard.' Trevor said rather patronis-
ingly, 'There's a bit more to it than that, you know, John.'

'Please can I have a Sanskrit teacher?' I asked Miss Willis, Mr
Raeburn and even Ben Nevin, who was still there at the time. No I
couldn't. The school was in desperate straits. It was no time for
extravagant spending. Mr Nevin had done his best for me. He ordered
A Sanskrit Grammar for Students, by A. A. MacDonell (Third Edition,
1927), for the library, and told me I could keep it as long as I liked.
But that wasn't at all what I wanted.

Even when there were teachers and facilities my rage for learning
was denied. One of my grudges against the school had always been
that I wasn't allowed to have piano lessons. My musical grounding as
a listener had begun early and was reasonably good. It went back to
Bathford days and the Deadwood Stage a-riding all over the hills, and
the couple of swells who had to get away from the City Smells (always
made me laugh like mad!), not to mention Ten Tiny Fingers.

On the serious side there was Mozart's Clarinet Con-chair-toe and
also Puccini's *La Bohème*, which I found difficult at first. It was in a
language I didn't understand, but I knew when a good bit was coming. A lone lady cried out about half-way through, 'Fo-do kala fa-za-
mee,' (as I heard it) and I said to Mum I must learn those few words
properly and what did they mean? Mum said she didn't know so we
made some up which went 'I've got a pain in my tummy'. At the end
they all joined in and sang thickly, and by the time it got to that bit,
I was flying. (All this thanks to Jim Shaeffer's gramophone).

CRX had built on this modest foundation, but Vulcan seemed to
do its best to quash my enthusiasm, despite such a promising background. When I said I wanted to play the piano, I was offered a choice
between the tambourine or the triangle. Then a lady came and played
a marimba for us once. It was so beautiful. It had a lovely golden-
brown resonance. The sound just hung there glowing. Deciding that
this was nearly as good as a piano, I said could I have one to play, and
they said yes. Yes! But when it arrived it was only a rotten little xylophone, with no resonators. It wasn't even a true xylophone since the
bars were metal. It was just a horrible little thing with a tinny sound.
I felt stupid just being near it. When I mentioned the piano again,
explaining I knew the names of the notes already, they said it simply

wasn't on. My hands didn't have sufficient span. I would be wasting a teacher's time.

My love for the piano was unkillable, and I played it whenever I had a spare moment. No one gave me a lesson, no one showed me how, but I worked out a few things for myself. There was a music room in the new classroom block, so I could get access to the piano there relatively easily.

Joan Baez the guilty party

It was true that the only comfortable span I had on the keyboard was C– G, a fifth (with the left hand), but if I did ten minutes of exercises or ran the hot tap in the toilet and soaked my hand in it, I could manage a sixth (C– A). On a really good summer's day I could reach a seventh on the white keys, although it meant that my right hand had to take a break from picking out the melody to force the reluctant fingers apart. At that extremity of my stretch the fingers in the middle, the ones between my thumb and little finger, froze and refused to bend, so I couldn't play any notes in between. At the furthest limit of its working, the whole hand threatened to close down, and once again I had to despatch the right hand to assist, this time with unlocking.

Mind you, of my two hands it was the left that had the talent. The right hand was far more restricted, and could only manage two notes at the same time if it played them with the index and little fingers. I'd have been much better off with the capabilities of my hands reversed, or else with a piano re-strung for my convenience, the bass on the right-hand side, where I could pick out single low notes, and the treble at the disposal of my more agile left hand.

Even so, I learned some chords and worked out for myself some passable arrangements of simple pieces and a few popular songs. The great thing about a good tune is that the whole thing can be present even in the barest bones. It struck me, though, that something was still not right. Every time I took my fingers off the keys the music died as though it had never been.

Then I discovered the sustaining pedal. With that discovery came a new world of sound and resonance, and I revelled in it. There was a draw-back, naturally: with the sustaining pedal down I could only play the bass notes, the ones for the left hand. If I tried to get my right hand into play to carry the tune, my foot slipped off the pedal and the sound died again.

I'm fond of my toes. Sneakily they've held on to quite a bit of movement. They can manage quite a vigorous wiggle at short notice, but since they're the only moving parts of my legs I can hardly expect them to make up for the deficiencies of the rest. I could usually manage to hold the pedal down, but there was no question of pumping it up and down, not with the toes alone. I could use my leg as a wedge but not as a working lever. I used the sustaining pedal like the Shift Lock key on the typewriter when I wanted to treat myself to a binge of capital letters.

Although the staff kept snootily silent about my efforts, I wasn't actively barred from playing. Sometimes I might find another boy by my side, listening in. If it was faithful Roger Stott then I'd ask him to keep an eye on my right foot, and when he saw it waggling, to work the sustaining pedal for me. Once again he acted as my personal remote control. It was amazing what a difference it made to the wholeness of the music.

My favourite piece to play on the piano in the Music Room was something called 'Plaisir d'amour'. It was more or less respectable – call it semi-classical. I think it was a proper piece of old-fashioned court music, re-hashed for the folk craze then in full swing. Joan Baez seems the right name in this context. I think she was the guilty party.

Once, though, while I was playing 'Plaisir d'amour' on that piano, a choir of little matrons formed up behind me, three of them, and started crooning, ''cos I can't . . . help . . . Falling in Love, with, You . . .' It's the same tune, or near enough. I think it was re-vamped (re-re-vamped, really) and given new words for an Elvis Presley film. Hearing the joy in those little matrons' voices made me want to give it all I had, and so I played the tune again from the top, somehow managing to ignore the pounce of pain in my back.

The Wrigley was an altogether superior item to the E&J, in terms of speed and reliability, but it had one major draw-back. You could easily swing the foot-plates of the E&J to one side, so as to have access to the piano pedals. The Wrigley was a much sturdier piece of equipment, without being highly strung. It could move at a hell of a lick, though the reflexes of the staff were disappointingly swift and I hadn't yet scored any direct hits. They all took evasive action, as if they'd taken a special course in wheelchair avoidance. If I'd managed an impact, the effect would have been considerable, for just the same reason that the Wrigley hampered me so much at the keyboard. Its footplates were rigid. There was no possibility of approaching the piano's controls. At a posher school, of course, I might have had a crack at a grand piano. Everyone knows grands have more leg-room.

Quite apart from its effect on any listeners I might have, 'Plaisir d'amour' could put me into a trance. Luckily for me, the bass part didn't play chords all at once. They were broken up in triplets, and since the tempo was slow I could strike them one by one without straining my left hand. Then my right, for all its inadequacies, could float the tune on top. When the sustaining pedal was down, everything blended into a coloured pattern you could almost see. Without Roger Stott (or some other stand-in) to hold that pedal down, it was a futile exercise. The level of beauty did a nose-dive. I might just as well have been a chicken pecking at the notes. The Wrigley brought any number of improvements to my life, but it blighted my little career as a pianist.

I'd already noticed that Luke always seemed to turn up when I started playing 'Plaisir d'amour'. If he was the genie of the school, then that tune was the rubbing which called him out of his magic lamp. I dare say that comparison came to me because we had done *Ali Baba and the Forty Wheelchair Thieves* as our school play one year.

He had wanted to learn to play 'Plaisir d'amour' himself, so I reversed my wheelchair out, to let his in, but I couldn't seem to teach him and after a while he asked me to start playing again. The Sunday after our mystical moment by the serving hatch, I was playing the piano in the Music Room and mourning the decline in my performing skills.

Plaisir d'amour

I started playing 'Plaisir d'amour' without even knowing I was doing it. Before I had finished the first verse Luke was sitting beside me. He put a gentle hand on my shoulder and said I should stop playing. He could see that I was in pain. This was a side of him I hadn't seen before.

I explained the draw-back of the chair, and how it was cheating us both of the sounds we wanted to hear. He thought for a moment and then said, 'Do you think you could manœuvre yourself so you're sitting on my lap? I know my chair doesn't have arms, but I promise to hold you safe.'

I was a bit doubtful, but I was also flooded with memories of sitting on laps as a little boy, and how sad I was when the doctor said I wasn't allowed to do it any more. I looked at those wonderful legs in their black trousers with the permanent crease, and I found myself saying, 'Well, we won't know if it works unless we try it, will we? I must admit, it would be a relief to be able to play without getting back-ache.' It wasn't every day I got the chance to be the Sit-Upon Boy.

Luke positioned his chair in front of the piano and put the brake on. I moved mine clear of the piano and locked the wheels in position. I was thrilled and frightened by the prospect of transferring onto his lap, but the fear soon left me. I didn't have to totter more than a few inches before I felt his strong arms holding me.

His lap was on a gradient and I realised that with luck I would be able to adjust my sitting height by which part of it I sat on. I came down carefully at about the mid-point of his thighs. It was a perfect piece of upholstery, positively the Rolls-Royce of laps, but when he moved forward I still couldn't get my foot to wedge the sustaining pedal properly.

'I think if you could pull me up and back about another inch, Luke,' I said, 'I'll be as snug as a bug in a rug.' This had been one of Gillie Walker's favourite expressions, and of course I was using childish language to camouflage an adult yearning. He put his arms round me and pulled me back onto his lap a little more. This position was higher, and this quadrant of his lap a lot softer, but still I couldn't address the pedal properly. Now I asked if he could move the whole chair backwards and then forwards again so I could have another go. He released the brakes and slowly slid the Chair–Luke–John complex backwards before surging softly forward again. The position we reached was almost ideal. My foot had been too far from the pedal, then too near it, but it just dropped down perfectly. The sustaining pedal was on and I could feel that my bum ended where Groin Hillock began.

'I need to be just a little higher,' I said. 'Any chance you can pull me back just another half-inch?' Luke pulled me further onto his lap and then every part found its place. Luke's unique heat-generating crotch exerted gentle pressure beneath me.

'Now just play,' he said in my ear. 'I've been wanting to hear it like this for a long time.'

Snakes' tongues sampling the breeze

And so had I. My left hand went into the rhythm of the 1-2-3, and as the little waltz started its lilt, Luke's wonderful hand came over to my crotch and gave gentle squeezes in time to the tune. The sun shone through the windows and the notes were properly sustained for the first time.

The tune went round again, but already it sounded different. I thanked God that I had rejected my new grey corduroys in favour of some old black flannels, even though their crease couldn't compare with Luke's. Their Velcro would yield at a touch, almost at a thought. Velcro is tantric. After a few more refrains, I seemed to hear lower notes in the waltz, a sort of basso profundo *oom-pah-pah* as I felt his cock swelling a little more into the crease of my bum. Sonorities and sensations changed places, as if the piano had turned into a vast theatre organ. I marvelled that as Luke's member rocked in place, it kept such perfect time with the bass notes under my fingers. The tune spiralled onwards by itself. I lost all idea of being responsible for it. In fact I stopped playing – 'I' stopped playing – but those fingers kept on striking the correct piano notes, and the right foot maintained its engagement with the sustain pedal.

When I say 'he squeezed my crotch', 'he stroked my balls', all that is defective description. Luke's hand was like an Eastern musician, who would think it rather unsophisticated to play a note directly. When I struck the A above middle C on the keyboard, I produced a note approximating to 440 hertz, the imprecision due only to the tuning of the instrument. Luke's hand was doing something altogether more artful, withholding a note till I could think of nothing else. It would be clumsy, misleading, far too bald, to say simply 'he touched me' in this place or that.

First of all the palm of his hand rested lightly on my knee, then a little more heavily until my leg had grown accustomed to the weight of the hand and much of the supporting arm. Then his four fingers raised themselves, gently waving in the air, like snakes' tongues sampling the breeze, while the thumb of the hand probed and pressed into the tense quadriceps muscle above my knee, coaxing the tension there to drain away. The thumb continued its gentle kneading, and then it seemed to extend itself out of the hand, growing in length until it burrowed almost painfully into an area of the relaxing muscle a little higher up my thigh.

It was as though the end of his thumb had hooked itself in that part of my leg, and was sending out roots. The palm and the thumb seemed to be acting independently, thanks to the flexibility of Luke's elbow and wrist, and yet collaborating on a single master plan. The thumb didn't actually pull the palm further up – it merely shortened itself, and the mesmerised palm followed in a silent trance, the four serpent tongues of the fingers, meanwhile, fluttering blindly as they tracked the pheromones to their source.

Luke's hand eased its lazy way higher up my leg like a serpent edging along a knotty bough, and when the four tongues encountered the beginning of my balls, they fluttered in the air a little more, then gently came to rest. The thumb extended itself again, hooking itself into my groin, and the palm smoothly followed. His hand nestled there, warm and heavy. I could feel it grafting itself into my leg.

The fingertip tongues danced nonchalantly in the area just above my penis, and I was sure that they were sensitive to the extra heat from that area about which Luke had spoken so eloquently. I closed my eyes and waited for them to make actual contact. My hands were playing the piano without intention, only achievement. They needed no help from eyes or conscious brain.

Nothing happened. The tactile moment never arrived. I opened my eyes again. Luke's fingers were now more like summer swallows, perhaps, than snakes. They dived and swooped and banked in perfect formation, describing intricate overlapping parabolas in the air around my cock, but they never landed. I marvelled that they could perform such elaborate manœuvres in so limited a space. My genital chakra could sense their fluttering through the cloth of my trousers, and my mind was a hot and mystical cave resounding with the single sentence, '*For God's sake grab it!*'

Luke's fingers landed at last, but some way away from my cock. They started a prodding dance on my thigh muscle, varied with a series of subtle flicks, as those tantalising digits began exploring the notional barrier of the Velcro closure.

Luke's chameleon fingers had undergone another transformation within the animal kingdom. Now they were so many kitten snouts trying to find their way under a sleeper's quilt on a winter morning, burrowing for a weak point in the thermal seal, wanting to snuggle up in the warmth within.

Luke's ring finger made a little opening at the base of the Velcro, its sensitive tip entering lightly as though delicately tasting the damp air within. Once it had gained entry, the little finger followed. There was just enough space for the abductor muscles to team up and make the opening larger. Then the fingers boldly peeled back the material so that my cock stood free. They still hadn't touched it.

Within two trances, the musical one and the sensual one, I experienced a moment of doubt. I wasn't sure I wanted to be so vulnerable in a public place. We would have only seconds of notice before someone came into the room. I wasn't convinced I would have time to stow myself away so as to produce the appearance of normality, or at least of an unconventional duet not exceeding the bounds of the musical. Removing my hands from the keyboard would itself draw suspicious attention, but could I really rely on Luke to restore order to my trouser-front?

Just when I was most torn between arousal and dithering, Luke resolved the matter by touching my cock at last. Then another instrument entered the symphonic poem. I felt his tongue on the back of my neck. Luke started sucking and kissing the skin, and all the while his hands cradled and stroked my parts into bliss. I was being fondled by a master of the groping arts. '*Plaisir d'amour*' was a waltz, and Luke's hand was a perfect dancing partner for my genital cluster. *ONE-two-three*, he marked the rhythm. *ONE-two-three. COCK-ball-ball.*

485

Now was the moment, the moment as perfect as it would ever get. I felt an orgasm was the least tribute I could pay to its splendour, but Luke turned out to be a groping master in the esoteric mode, endless deferrer of release. He worked his tongue round to my right ear, and next moment he was whispering to me: 'This isn't the right time or the right place. Trust me. I know what I'm doing.'

'What? What? When and where, then?'

'Not here and not now. I'll let you know.'

And with that there was diminuendo. The music died under my fingers. Luke had cast his spell, and he must have known that by this stage I was willing to follow him anywhere. Tenderly he assisted me back to my own chair, then smoothed out the extra creases in his pants, creases that had been made by me. Re-adjusting his bulge to assume a more dignified position, he gave me a quick squeeze between the legs and a peck on the cheek, and then he was away, gliding out of the Music Room. I followed on some time later, wondering when the right time and place would come together to round off the tune. On my way out of the room, awkwardly punting, I came upon Millicent Baxter, who looked down at me rather oddly. It was only later that I realised there was a wet patch at the front of my trousers. Millicent's sharp look was explained. Incontinence wasn't an unusual event on those premises, but it had never been part of my portfolio. I hope at least it wasn't ponky-doodle. Millicent's nose was very sensitive.

Scratched at by rabbits

One facility that was lacking even in the extended school was a swimming pool. The co-principals decided that such a construction would be a great asset. Their plan was simple: an oblong of lawn was marked out, forty foot by thirty. The projected pool was supposed to have a shallow end four foot deep – not exactly my notion of shallow – and a deep end of six foot six. The idea was that it should be dug by hand, with the available resources. So the male teachers dug, the male cook dug, a party from the Army Apprentices' School at Arborfield dug.

Eltham College, where Miss Willis had taught before Vulcan, sent senior boys over to help on the pool for a week at a time. Any pupil of

Vulcan who could control a trowel from a standing, sitting or even a lying position was put to work as well. That let me out. The net impact of all this digging was hardly noticeable to the naked eye. Even after weeks of dogged excavation the patch designated for the swimming pool looked as if it had been scratched at by rabbits rather than actually dug.

Eventually a bulldozer had to be hired. The driver seemed to find it droll that Alan and Marion should imagine such a huge project was within their powers, but he was careful not to mock the work that had been done. So was I. I just about managed not to go round saying 'There's no such word as *can't*, eh?' under my breath.

There was some sort of arrangement between Vulcan and St Paul's School in London, not just for pool-digging but regular visits. Senior boys would come and lend a hand for a week or two. It was like having a new consignment of lovely ABs, fresh blood. They were terribly obliging.

Once on the bus I yelled desperately, 'Oh no! I've dropped my sixpence!' A St Paul's boy called Gordon, of whom I was particularly fond, went down on his hands and knees to search for it down on the dirty floor of the bus, saying sweetly, 'Don't worry, John, it's not going to get away! If you dropped it we'll find it.' The search seemed to go on and on all the same, until at last he said, 'John – I've found it! It was right here at the back!'

Which it couldn't have been, really, since I didn't have sixpence in the first place. That was the whole point of making such a fuss, to turn the big heart of this lovely boy into my own private mint for sixpences. Best to use it just the once, though, and not wear it out.

When the pool was finally dug, the next mighty project began: filling it, using two garden hoses. It took about a week. The water supply was a cause of friction with the village at the best of times. The water tower was only a few hundred yards away from the school, and looked pretty against a background of woods, but the pumps laboured to raise water up to the tanks in the Castle. The school learned to be a good neighbour, and not to starve surrounding areas of their water supply.

For disabled swimmers a cold pool was never going to be much good. It would be virtually useless outside high summer. Once I was near the pool and overheard a conversation between Miss Willis and a workman about how much topping-up the pool was needing. Evaporation was a problem, and the solution Marion favoured was building a huge greenhouse over the pool. Up to that point I had been more or less indifferent to the pool, though most of the other boys got excited, at least when the bulldozer arrived. But now I began to thrill to the possibilities. In a greenhouse of that size I could go to town planting African and Australian sundews, and maybe even some Nepenthes. The pitcher plant which Ben Nevin had hacked for me out of the living ice of his rugged homeland was doing well, but I knew that many carnivorous plants need pampering.

In the end Uncle Mac persuaded some friends to pay for roofing over the pool and the installation of proper heating. Even before that he was firmly ensconced in the pantheon of the school. Although radios were strictly forbidden in the dining room, an exception was made for *Children's Favourites*, or any other programme on which the universal uncle appeared. I was just getting to the stage of being ashamed to admit that I still liked some of the songs he played on his programme.

I think the swimming pool was a bit of a disappointment, all the same, even when it was properly heated. The successes of Backstroke Babs from the *Judy* weren't easy to reproduce. Disabled boys might experience much less difficulty with movement in the water, but they weren't going to win any prizes in competition against the able-bodied. 'Backstroke Babs' turned out to be a fairy tale after all. It was a likeable variation on the Little Mermaid, in which Babs struck a reasonably shrewd bargain, moderate helplessness on land but getting to show off with the help of her tail in the pool.

The time and the place

It would have been wonderful if the communications centre in the Vulcan lift-shaft had really worked, delivering mail with a whoosh of compressed air. It would have been the perfect medium for Luke to send me a message about the consummation of our involvement. As it was, it was Roger Stott who handed me a folded slip of paper which read, over the initials L.S., *Woodlarks. The time and the place.* Luke's hand-writing was well-formed but sloped backwards. If it was Miss Willis's idea that backward-sloping script was a sure sign of someone who was afraid of life, then here was the refutation. I can't help feeling that graphology is a terrible load of old rubbish.

Woodlarks was a special holiday camp to which Vulcan sent boys. I knew that Luke had been there before. Until I got his note, the idea had never held any attraction, but that soon changed. Then I was on fire to go, and pestered Mum and Dad to let me. They must have been puzzled by an enthusiasm that was rather out of character for me, but went along with it happily enough. I can't remember if they had to contribute financially, or if the school bore the cost. Despite all my pleas, Mum insisted on replacing the Velcro on my trousers. Every time I had a pee I made a noise like ripping sheets, which didn't seem a particularly favourable omen for a week away in which I was counting on losing what little virginity I had left.

Before Woodlarks, though, I had a date with destiny, or I suppose it was an attempt to head destiny off and buy myself a little time. I was fine with shaving at school. I even enjoyed it. But I had an absolute horror of shaving at home. Even the thought of it made me go red in the face. My electric razor stayed at Vulcan. No question of taking it home.

The only thing I had which gave me a tiny bit of privacy was the Chinese brick I'd been given by the great man Ben Nevin. It was only about four inches by five, and two deep, so of course the secret compartment was much smaller than that. I'd learned where to press to make the compartment open, but I'd had more sense than to show the trick to anyone else – even Peter – or to reveal that there was a trick involved. As far as anyone else was concerned, it was just a wooden brick with some decorative patterns cut on it. Purely ornamental.

Finally one day I got up the courage to go into town on the Wrigley, on my own. I was desperate. I couldn't bring the box with me. Then I headed for the chemist's. I think it was called Pedley's. There were a couple of steps outside the shop, so that was as far as I could get for the time being. I had decided to nobble an old dear, and get her to run my errand for me. You never had to wait long in Bourne End for an old dear.

When an old dear came along, she didn't make difficulties. I gave

her the money and told her what I wanted. I said it was for my mother
– though what sort of mother sends such a boy out on such an errand?

While the old dear was in Pedley's I had second thoughts about her
suitability. She had whiskers herself. If that still counted as bum fluff
I might give bums a wide berth after all. And what if they took one
look at her and gave her Extra Strength Formula?

The old dear came through with the goods, though, and I could
nip back home before I met anyone I knew. Even a small tube of
Immac wouldn't quite fit into the internal compartment of the
Chinese brick, but if I squashed the bottom of the tube over I could
just about jam it into place. As the level of the cream in the tube went
down, of course, the compartment could accommodate it more easily.

I think it worked. I think it made a difference. I was lucky that my
facial hair was only on my upper lip so far, not on my chin. So that's
what I did in the holidays, while the shaver stayed at school. I used a
depilatory ointment to suppress the teenage changes. It was quite a
business.

I was at the limit of my mobility. I had to put Immac on my right
fore-finger, and then rest my hand on my stick. Then with a combination of leaning-down and pushing-up movement it could just
about be made to happen. It was very tricky.

It's hardly surprising that I was ambivalent about growing up,
about becoming a man, because neither I nor anyone round me had
the slightest idea of what being a man might mean in my case. But in
there with all the queasiness was a certain excitement, a certain
anticipation. It wasn't really me that had the horror of the adult male
and his body. It was Mum. I dreaded the changes to come because of
their consequences, not for themselves. I felt I had more mileage as
Mum's Little Boy than I ever would as Mum's Little Man. And Immac
kept me on the right side of that barrier for a few extra months.

When I did irrevocably move from one category of life to another,
from boy to man, then she too would be evicted from one compartment and forced into another. It may be that terror of her own ageing
was what lay underneath that whole painful passage between us.
Mum always said that she wouldn't be able to stand being fifty,
though that was still comfortably a decade off.

Woodlarks camp was only about half an hour's drive away. In a funny way I was nostalgic for the old Bedford van. Not that the school's Leyland bus was new. It must have been built in the 1940s. But I had come to prefer travelling separately from my wheelchair. There was always the possibility of sitting on someone's lap. In the wheelchair I felt my erection was terribly noticeable, unless I adopted the hand position which had got me into trouble in the past.

Luke, of course, since he had been there before, knew the ropes at the camp. I was beginning to realise that he was the sort of person who was born knowing the ropes. The camp was run by ordinary lovely boys in their late teens, wearing jeans and the chunky suède lace-ups called desert boots. I suppose one or two of them may have been in their early twenties. It was all I could do to take my eyes off their ordinary jeans.

Luke and I were the oldest disabled boys in the party, allowed to stay up after the tinies had been stowed away in their tents. Luke and I had a tent to ourselves, which was an immensely exciting prospect.

Luke called our helpers 'lads', and talked to them relentlessly about girls. Almost his first remark was, 'Who have you got lined up for us tonight, then? I like blondes, but my friend John here prefers brunettes.' He got them talking about their girl-friends and occasional conquests, doing a very smooth job I must say. Buttering them up a treat. I tried to join in, even though all this girl talk was getting me down. I was baffled that Luke showed so much enthusiasm. Fucking fucking fucking. Every sentence seemed to need at least one *fucking*.

There was a proper camp fire. We had baked beans washed down with mugs of tea. We had marshmallows, impaled on twigs and toasted by the fire. They were almost too hot to eat, fiery puddles of sugar that would fall off the twig if you weren't careful. We learned to blow on them to cool them down – even when they were already in our mouths. We would pull our lips back and try to balance them on the tips of our teeth. Somehow the taste buds seemed to send their most intense messages of sweetness when they were fighting for their own survival.

The lads had brought a radio with them, and I remember the ordinary god-like boy who undressed me for the night singing along with the Ivy League. The words should have been 'I can't sleep at night, tossing and turning',' but he changed the last phrase into 'too much wanking' instead, and gave me a wink.

The helpers were planning a sneaky pub visit and said Luke was welcome to join them if he liked. They thought he looked old enough not to be challenged (which I didn't). It was an agonising moment. If he'd said yes it would have entirely scuppered my evening and possibly my whole life, but at the last moment he said, 'You know what, lads? I'll stay with John. You go on ahead. Save a girl for me!'

Before they left they put us to bed while the fire died down. Our sleeping bags were laid out side by side, with a ground-sheet underneath. I liked the lads, but I didn't enjoy being helped into bed by them, though at least my pyjamas didn't let me down. Mum's needlework skills meant they were tailored to fit, not clumsily altered. The lads eased us down onto the ground and into our sleeping bags. I said I was still a bit hot from the fire, so I didn't need to be zipped in just yet. I thought this was a brilliant piece of strategy. I wanted the shreds of my virginity to fall away quite silently, without effort. The wheelchairs certainly cluttered up the tent, and it was a relief when the helpers took them away.

That ecstatic clench

Luke said, 'I thought those lads would never go,' but I didn't dare to put into words what I felt or what I wanted. I wanted a cuddle. I wanted to interlock legs. The convention of the evening seemed to be that we talked about girls, though, and I stuck with it doggedly. I was wittering on about a girl I knew in Bourne End when Luke cut in with, 'Why are you talking about this Trish girl?' He was already sliding smoothly towards me.

'Well . . . she lives in Bourne End and she seems to like me. I was thinking I should start seeing her.'

'Good idea. Now I'm going to suck your cock.' All I could say was, 'Why in the world would you want to do that?' It was no part of my sexual imaginings. He lifted the undefended flap of my sleeping bag away from my body.

'You'll like it. In fact you'll love it. Everyone likes the way I do it.'

Everyone? Who was everyone? 'Who, for instance?'

If Julian was right and everything connected with Vulcan was picked up by hidden microphones, then on the tape this would have sounded like spirited resistance, but in fact Luke had already taken my cock out of my pyjamas and was holding it by the base, giving it little shakes. Checking it for the wobble of half-heartedness, I expect, and finding none.

'Oh, you'd be surprised. Chris Hudson, for one. He can't get enough.'

How would I ever be able to face Chris Hudson? Not that I knew him at all well. He was a nice boy from Birmingham whose parents ran a shop. He stole, or rather things tended to disappear while he was around. I always kept an eye on the Ben Nevin box when Chris was in the vicinity.

It's hard for someone in my position to defend himself from pilfering, whether it's a Chinese box from Hong Kong that's likely to go missing, or his own genitals, being swallowed by someone he's been chasing for months.

Luke started doing what he wanted, which he was so confident would bring me pleasure, but I could hardly assimilate the sensations. I was so used to pressing myself against the sheet. All that slipperiness, that feeling of a membrane, was very alien. His lips closed round my penis in a hermetic seal. Air was as likely to get into that ecstatic clench as it was to penetrate the rubber gasket of Mum's pressure cooker. I couldn't understand how he was able to breathe, and I was worried that my excitement might explode in his mouth, and choke him or poison him.

Then Luke had the brain-wave of using his hand to help things along. I muttered, 'I'm sorry, I'm sorry,' as I came, thinking I was spoiling everything, but he amazed me by swallowing greedily. He lay there licking his lips, and even humming a tune. It was 'Tossing and turning' again.

'I'll be back for more of that, John,' he said. 'You kept me waiting long enough.' Whatever Luke lacked, it wasn't confidence.

Before long, the helpers came back from their pub expedition, if they'd really gone. Perhaps they were being tactful to leave us alone together. I'd opened Pandora's Box at the ripe old age of fifteen, and I still hadn't seen any penis but my own. It was stiff again and poking out of my pyjamas, and I thought it was a monster, an in-between creature like a basilisk, something unholy and unnatural. It wanted more. But I still wanted a cuddle, and didn't understand how it was safe to do what we had done, but not safe to hold me as I wanted to be held.

For years after that night the smell of marshmallows toasting would give me an erection. Caramelisation of any description was likely to set me off. I had to steel myself against arousal when pudding time came round at the Compleat Angler. I'm not sure I'm safe even now.

It didn't take me long, that night, to make sense of the novel idea and experience of being fellated. I decided that for a number of reasons it was a good thing. No evidence was left behind, so no one would know what had gone on. If the practice caught on at school, we could keep the staff in ignorance indefinitely of what went on in the sucking academy when they weren't around. There was also a more mystical aspect. Part of me was now in Luke. Everywhere he went he would take a little bit of John with him. I had no illusions that his interest in me was deep or exclusive, but that too was a good thing. Every time he enjoyed himself so expertly with another male, we would both be bonded to another being down the chain . . .

In the morning I woke with my feet out of the tent, wet on dewy grass. The ground must have been on a slight slope, and I'd gone sliding downhill. I couldn't pull myself back without help.

The rest of the Woodlarks week wasn't nearly as much fun. I didn't enjoy sleeping on the ground. The discomfort didn't bother me all that much – it wasn't as if the beds at Vulcan were anything but basic. I just didn't like the knowledge that I couldn't get up without help. At a pinch I could get out of a bed unaided, but not up off a floor. When I was older and read Kafka's *Metamorphosis* it brought it all back to me, that helpless beetle feeling. I especially didn't like being helped in intimate things by the ordinary lovely boys. I preferred the school matrons because I was more relaxed. It didn't seem so crush-

494

ingly important that they should like me. I wondered whether looking after us was a punishment, and if so what the lads had done to
deserve it, looking after disabled boys instead of being out with the
girls they liked so much. You always wonder what helpers have done
to draw the short straw.

On other nights Luke wanted to repeat the activities of the first,
but I wouldn't let him. If he persisted I would pretend to be having a
bad dream for the benefit of the people in the other tents, shouting
and mumbling until he was scared off. Then of course I had to hold
my bladder all night, because I could hardly wake Luke up and ask
him to pass the pee bottle without offering something in return. I
resented the idea that I was a sort of buffet for him to nibble at whenever he felt peckish. After our elaborate courtship on the school premises I felt I deserved better than to be treated as a sort of midnight
feast in a sleeping bag.

I certainly learned to fuck that week, though. By the end of it I was
the fuckingest fucker who had ever fucked. Every sentence was stuffed
with *fucking*. I didn't know what the word meant, but its rhythm was
a very addictive addition to my conversational repertoire. When Dad
was driving me home in the car I told him that having a camp fire at
night was fucking great, food cooked outside was fucking tasty –
mind you, the ground was fucking hard for sleeping. I loved my new
word. It could make itself at home in any part of a sentence.

Dad didn't say anything. He pulled over and parked with care, signalling and using the mirror, and then he gave me a good clout on the
ear. I was stunned, and really didn't know the reason why.

Dad seemed to calm down once he'd shut me up so effectively.
When we were nearly home he said, 'Be sure to try out your new word
on your mother. I'm not sure she's ever heard it . . .' Did he think I
was born yesterday? If he wanted to upset Mum, he could fucking
well do it himself.

The tensions between Mum and Dad weren't exactly tucked out of
sight, even though they were never talked about. Raeburn and Miss
Willis managed to maintain a façade much more skilfully. We pupils
of the school were unaware of any differences between them. It's true
that someone had once heard her saying, 'Alan, please don't,' when he
was about to let loose with the Board of Education, whether from

495

squeamishness or real disapproval. Otherwise the co-principals kept up a united front.

Then suddenly all that changed, and each of them dealt the other a terrible wound. Each felt betrayed, though the betrayals were different in kind, one professional and one personal.

Old Rabies is tying the knot

The rumour came round the school's bush telegraph, so that I felt like somebody near the end of the circle in a game of Chinese Whispers, hearing a formula so garbled it bore no relationship to the original. 'Old Rabies is tying the knot with Ponky-doodle.' What on earth could that mean? A little later it was made official. Alan Raeburn was marrying Millicent Baxter, she of the sensitive sniffer and the blue-pencilled swear-words. There was going to be a party laid on to celebrate the happy event.

By chance Kim Derbishire, the school's first pupil, primal Vulcanian, was paying a visit just then. He attended the party. To me he was a figure from legend. I was trying to get the meat of a walnut out of its shell, wrestling with the little vice provided for the purpose. A crotch wrapped in brown corduroy entered my field of vision. The very limited movement of my cervical spine made it hard for me to look at tall boys' faces. It was a pain in the neck. It was much easier to look at their groins. With an effort I followed this particular pair of trousers up to the shirt and beyond, to his smiling face. He reached into the nut dish and picked up a handful. There was a noise like bones crunching and I realised to my amazement that he was breaking them in one hand. He handed them over to me with a gallant flourish, and then he quietly continued his walk round the dining tables. He was like an ambassador or minister, but to me he was little short of a god.

Kim radiated sex appeal, not musk but aura. Everyone except Miss Willis knew that Kim was having nightly trysts in the school library with one of the new helpers, little Dagmar Bosch from Oberammergau who hardly came up to his shoulder. It wasn't hard to pull the wool over Marion's eyes when it came to her pets. And if Kim didn't get enough of a frisson from having sex after lights-out on the premises of his old school, he could tickle himself even further with the thought that Dagmar's brother had played Christ in the Oberammergau Passionsspiel.

Marion's eyes had been shining all evening at the engagement party for Millicent and Alan. Emotion wasn't necessarily out of place on such an occasion, but of course it depends on what the emotion is. She seemed very restless, moving from place to place, but she happened to be near me when the speeches started, and I could hear quite clearly what she said.

'Oh Alan, please, don't do this to me. I can't bear it.' Then with a sob she hurried away.

It was the smallest possible outburst, swallowed up by the noise of the party, a genteel death-rattle kept well back in her throat. Teachers learn to project as a matter of course, clarity of articulation an occupational requirement, but this was something that her divided larynx fought with, half to shout out to the castellated roof-tops and half to swallow down like a cyanide pill. Even in a culture that hated scenes above anything, where murmuring 'For God's sake, m'dear, don't make a scene' could bring all but the most hysterical or actively foreign to their senses, it didn't count as an unwarrantable parading of emotion.

'Oh Alan, please, don't do this to me.' Very similar words to what she had said when Alan had brandished the Board of Education that time, and just as ineffectual. Alan turned a deaf ear to Marion. He hadn't laid down the B of E then, and he wasn't going to give up pretty Millicent Baxter now.

Marion uttered only a handful of words, unheard by the man to whom they were addressed, and then she dashed from the room. It was hardly Dido's lament.

Seen from another angle, of course, Dido's lament was exactly what it was. The wail of a woman departing from love and life. *All will be darkness soon . . .* It was even the *'Liebestod'* from Wagner, but played in the key of *Brief Encounter.*

All the same, Miss Willis would not have wanted to think of herself as Dido. Dido was selfish. Dido didn't look beyond her own needs. She was a distraction on the way to Æneas's true destiny (as I had learned at Vulcan) which was the journey to Italy and eventually the founding of Rome. By this reckoning Dido wasn't Marion. Dido was Millicent. Dido put love before duty, and did all she could to divert a great man from his true course.

In the version of the story being played out at Vulcan School, Dido was triumphant. Dido won. She detained him on his way to where he was meant to go. She would want children, she would want a home. Marion Willis was keening from the other corner of the triangle, voicing all the spectral sorrow of a city that would not now be founded, the lasting utopia where the disabled and able-bodied would find common ground, and where Miss Willis would wake up next to Alan Raeburn, kiss him and hand him his canes.

A house of divorce

Superficially the school kept running as before, but everything beneath the surface was different. If it was true that Marion and Alan were the mum and dad of the school, then beyond a certain point we were all living in a house of divorce. Raeburn and Willis were our Shiva and Parvati, and now there was grief in Heaven.

The finances of Vulcan had always been precarious, but by this time they were becoming desperate. The governors began to realise that even an extra ten boys or another appeal (rather soon after the last one) wouldn't be enough to resolve the difficulties. They began to look into the possibility of setting the school up on a different basis. One idea was that the Department of Education and Science, which had declared the school an invaluable asset, might step in with a grant. This turned out to be wishful thinking. There was no precedent for making such a grant to a school outside the state system. Nor would the department take over the running of the school, turning it into a national resource and funding it out of national taxation.

This would have been the fairest and most logical way of proceeding, but again unprecedented. Instead the department brought pressure to bear on the County of Berkshire, successfully in the end, to take over a school which drew most of its pupils from outside the county. A price was agreed that would enable the school to pay off its debts.

Alan Raeburn opposed all the suggested alternatives. He would have preferred the school to close down rather than lose its independence. He felt particularly betrayed that Marion took another point of view. He fought a long rearguard action against the changes. First he resigned as co-principal, leaving Marion in sole charge. He was the only governor to vote against the proposed take-over by the County of Berkshire, and when – eventually – the motion was passed he resigned from the committee, severing his connection with the school. After that he and Millicent moved north.

It's hard not to side with Marion Willis on the level of economic realism. Closing the school would deprive future pupils of the closest approach to mainstream education they were likely to get, quite apart from throwing the present school population back into a system with a marked tendency to let them down – which was why the school had been founded in the first place. There were personal consequences, too, attached to the defiant line Raeburn was advocating. Alan and Marion would have been left with huge personal debts, and the whole little army of sponsors and patrons would have been badly let down.

It's easy to imagine that her emotions were involved, all the same, in the decision to take the school in a direction that Alan would never have been able to accept. I don't mean that she was motivated by revenge, to pay back one betrayal with another. She was different after the engagement party, that's all. Once upon a time she would have voted with Alan without question, and to hell with the consequences. Bankruptcy wouldn't have frightened her from his side. Now Millicent was by his side instead, and he couldn't count on Marion's loyalty in the old way. They had been more than friends once, and much more than allies, but he had re-drawn those lines in a way which excluded her. It wasn't Alan and Marion against the world any more, and it could never be the same way again.

The secret marriage between Alan and Marion was real, as was proved by the wounds it left, the pain of its ending. He came to regard her as a traitor who had allowed his dreams to be sold off, and she saw him as a sort of bigamist even though their association had been purely professional. He had made her no promise.

The magnetic hill

I tried to avoid Luke Squires after the week at Woodlarks camp, an adventure which had been mainly a disappointment. He wasn't easily avoided if he wanted to see you, though, any more than he could be found if he had decided to disappear. I was leaving the new toilet block one day when he appeared before me. He swerved his wheelchair to a halt in front of mine, as if it was a police car smoothly intercepting a car making its get-away after a bank robbery.

'This is the third week of term,' he said lazily. 'And we've hardly had a chance to see each other . . . There are lots of things we have to catch up on . . .'

Even now I don't know why he was pursuing me. Perhaps he was so unused to anyone saying no to him that it piqued an interest which would otherwise have died down.

'What catching up is there to do?' I asked, rather lamely.

'Well, there's the problem of my German,' he drawled carelessly. 'Miss Willis likes me a lot – you know it, I know it, the whole school knows it. But she says the days are long gone when you could get good marks just because a teacher likes you. She says that I must stop being so lazy, and get down and do some work.' His hand played over his knee and thigh, coming to rest on the magnetic hill between his legs. 'But it's a tough language, you know. The way all those words keep changing depending on what they are doing or what is being done to them. It's very confusing . . .' His prehensile wrist–hand complex gave two or three thoughtful squeezes to his crotch, while I tried to keep my eyes on his face.

'Then Miss Willis had a brain-wave. She said, "I don't know why you don't get more pally with John Cromer. He's easily the best student of German we have and I'm sure you would both benefit from chumming up together". . .'

I was impressed all over again by Luke's shamelessness. If this didn't take the Peek Frean! He had recruited poor trusting Marion into his scheme. Miss Willis had the saving grace of many autocrats – she was quite unable to tell the difference between like-minded lieutenants and charmers who would tell her exactly what she wanted to hear. She was supremely vulnerable to double agents.

Now Luke began to imitate Miss Willis's speech, just as I had the first night I became aware of him. '. . . "I know it's a little hard, my dear. . ."', he said, '"no boy ever likes to receive help from a boy junior to himself . . ."' He squeezed his crotch again, so that it swelled by a good half-inch. '. . . "But in this day and age there comes a time for everyone when they have to bow to someone younger than them-selves. Besides, I think that you two would be very good for each other. John has a keen brain, but he doesn't make friends easily. You on the other hand are strong and frightened of no one, but a little mental sharpening would do you no harm at all . . ."'

Luke was a brilliant instinctive strategist. There he was, acting out the part of Miss Willis and speaking perfectly loudly, not caring if anyone heard. He knew exactly what he could get away with. He was parroting educational platitudes all the time he was arranging an assignation with me, while pretending to be carrying out the sole principal's wishes!

I felt his charm but fought its pull. What was it about me, really, that he wanted so much?

'Well,' I said, trying not to let my voice shake. 'If you really feel I could be of any use to you, I'll gladly help you with your German. When shall we start?'

'Well, I'm a bit tied up tomorrow,' he said, still in a Willis tone of voice, 'but I've plenty of time for the day after. Check and see if you've some time then. Tell you what, go for a pee about fifteen minutes before the end of class on Thursday. I'll do the same, and we can meet up in the toilet and make a study schedule . . . I'd better get back to my class,' he went on, rather as if he was teaching it.

He surged off in his wonderful chair, taking my assent entirely for granted. Just before he reached the corridor, he span his chair grace-fully round and called out, 'Don't forget your *Deutsches Leben*, old man!'

I wondered what would happen if I didn't turn up. I could say that the teacher wouldn't let me go to the loo, or just tell Luke flat out that I wasn't interested. It's true that Luke was prone to wild rages, but I wasn't actually afraid of him.

Up to a certain point Luke would be quiet and soft-spoken, but if he lost his self-control then there was no going back. His face became so contorted he could hardly be recognised. He would clear the room. People didn't stick around – the sense of danger was palpable. Mr Nevin had sometimes been able to handle him, speaking gently and taking him by the arm. Biggie could also sometimes get through to him. Each of them had riddled him with bullets of pure love. After they had left the school his rages were much more intractable.

If Luke decided to thrash out, it wasn't the legs you had to watch out for but his strong arms. Charged up with energy from the heat source in his groin, Luke's fists could pack quite a punch. Sometimes two or three members of staff were needed to subdue him. Judy Brisby had boasted once that she could calm him single-handed with her nerve-punching technique, but she was thrown off like a straw doll, and ended up bruised herself. Threats had no effect on him.

Impressive but not contagious

If I wasn't actually afraid of Luke, then there's no denying that I was tense when the appointed day arrived. I made my excuse to the teacher at the agreed (actually the dictated) time. It was only as I approached the sliding door that I realised that I had forgotten to bring my copy of *Deutsches Leben*. I was stymied. I couldn't go back and collect it, or the English teacher would certainly wonder why I needed a German text-book in the loo. There was no turning back.

'*Kann ich dick helfen?*' Luke said in greeting, with that slow drawling smile. I was so flustered that I failed to consider the possibility that he was playing with me. It's well-known that the English have a real problem with the soft German 'ch', but I had Gisela Schmidt's example to follow. In that school I was accounted sharp, but it didn't occur to me that Luke was pronouncing the second word of his sentence exactly as he intended.

'It's not "*dick*", it's "*dir*",' I corrected him. '"*Helfen*" takes the dative because you're giving help *to* someone.' I was relieved to see that he had his copy of *Deutsches Leben* with him, pressed lightly against his groin. At least one of us had an alibi.

I had assumed that he had thought of a discreet place for our explorations, but he seemed to think the toilet block was a discreet enough venue. It was a newly built facility but already seemed neglected. There was a constant hissing and spluttering from some sort of maladjusted cistern, and water lay in pools on the floor.

The door to the block slid and could not be locked. There were urinals for the ABs, and I suppose for some pupils like Julian whose callipers meant that any unnecessary sitting down was a chore. There were also cubicles, which had locks and could accommodate a wheelchair. One wheelchair, not two. Luke's solution was to lever himself out of his chair and install himself inside, supporting himself on the door. From there he called out, 'Come on, John! What are you waiting for?'

Doubtfully I approached the toilet in the Wrigley. There was room for me to get past Luke's distinctive machine, but I still wasn't keen. Luke's sense of invulnerability was impressive but not contagious. Anyone coming into the toilet block would guess how matters stood from the silent testimony of that chair.

In even the most benign scenario of discovery, there would be no sherry. Raeburn was still on the staff, pending the vote on the Berkshire take-over, but the reins were held in Marion's sole hand. I was aware as Luke got down onto his knees before me – and how would he explain the damp patches on his smart trousers? – that St John was only two classrooms away savagely tweaking some poor kid's ear, and if that's what you got for making a mistake, Heaven knows what he would do if he knew that boys were being indecently gross and grossly indecent right now in the school's new toilet block.

It was probably true that anyone asking permission to go to the toilet this late in a lesson would be told to wait for break, but I knew that ABs like Roger Stott who helped serve elevenses sometimes jumped the gun, leaving before the bell was actually rung. So I felt absolutely unsafe while Luke got busy with the symbolic transfer of fluids. On the level of sensation I probably enjoyed it more than I had at Woodlarks, when I had hardly been able to take in what was happening, but this was not a peak experience. Luke's excitement made the Wrigley rattle, but I didn't even get a glimpse of what he had hauled out of his trousers, while he tested to the limit the manufacturers' claims about their permanent crease. I tried to project more congenial images onto the cubicle walls, jungles, mountains and clouds, or even the tent at Woodlarks, impregnated with the erotic scent of marshmallows. Nothing worked. The ambience of sanitary porcelain and leaky water-works could not be blotted out.

Luke gasped and shuddered. He had got what he wanted before the bell rang or the first AB was sighted, but he was too smart an operator to delude himself. He knew that I would want no repetition of our session of private study. Those few minutes in the toilet block were the first and last seminar that we had, and his performance in German O-level, good or bad, owed nothing to me.

Departure of fantasy

Though my carnal rendezvous with Luke Squires was hardly a high point of my life at Vulcan, I reconciled myself to the venue, at least. Julian Robinson and I had several encounters there in my last year at the school. Julian had the great advantage over Luke that he didn't use a wheelchair. There was no evidence left outside the cubicle to betray us, and the level of risk became acceptable to me.

Julian had shed his secret-agent fantasies by now. There was no disguising of our objective any more, yet our explorations had very little flair. All that would happen in that cubicle was that Julian would unzip himself and present me with his cock, almost thwacking it down on the side bar of my wheelchair. Here at last was another penis for me to examine. I played little arpeggios on it, marvelling at the texture, so hard and so soft at the same time. This was all very satisfactory – my penis was clearly standard issue, give or take. After prodding and poking at Julian's for a while, though, I'd learned all I could from it. Its academic interest out-weighed its potential for pleasure. Any actual sexual act would have been very hard to stage-manage, with Julian's callipers locking his knees in place and my wheelchair getting in the way, and so little room to manoeuvre.

By mutual consent, Julian's parts were tucked back in his jeans. Then we would debate how best to leave the toilet block without arousing suspicion. The departure of fantasy didn't announce the advent of realism. We agreed that the best alibi for our risky intimacy would be to stage a fight in the corridor. So once we were out in the open I would steer the Wrigley so as to graze him, and he would cannon into the wall and shake his fist at me while I cruised at high speed back into innocent company. This routine became slick with much practice – you go that way and I'll go this – but I don't see how it can ever have fooled anyone. Nothing in fact could be fishier than these shows of hostility.

There were lots of possible reasons for the way both sets of liaison, with Luke and with Julian, fizzled out. The toilet block wasn't an ideal setting, but then nor was the Blue Dorm when Julian was trying to write his letter, and I was impersonating a perverse puppet who bossed people around and made them laugh. Nor was the music room, when Luke and I had played '*Plaisir d'amour*' as a duet for lovers with a piano for our pimp and our alibi. Looking back, I have to acknowledge what those two scenes shared, a sort of blatancy that made me feel safe as well as excited. Perhaps anyone brought up without privacy is likely to turn into a voyeur or an exhibitionist or both.

I also had a growing preference when it came to the objects of my affection. Although Ben Nevin had left and my feelings about Raeburn were more mixed than they had once been, I had pretty much decided that boys weren't what I wanted. I wanted a man, and I had my eyes on Mr Kirby the physics teacher. He had the right smell.

I had watched dogs smelling each other, and admired their unembarrassability. I longed to smell people, though not their bottoms particularly. Mr Kirby gave me a golden opportunity once. He was doing an experiment which needed careful watching, and while he was absorbed in the task I had a good old sniff. The lab window was very near and I didn't dare lean over for too long. When I had returned to the vertical there was still no one visible through the window, and I thought I had got away with it.

At lunch-time that day, though, a boy called Philip Battersby came up and asked me if I thought Mr Kirby had a nice bottom. I said I hadn't the least idea. He said, 'Well you were certainly getting a good look at it in the lab this morning.' I didn't know what to say, and Philip made the most of this rare event. What would he have said if he had realised I was sniffing rather than peering? Mr Kirby smelled of Quink and cinnamon.

For ever in the minds of men

Mr Kirby had a side-line in astronomy. Patrick Moore of *The Sky At*

Night came to deliver a talk with slides, and jolly good it was too. I remember that at one point he stamped on the floor twice, and then told us how far the universe had expanded in that second between his stamps. We were a good audience. Everyone went *'Ooohh . . .!'* absolutely sincerely.

There was a little reception given for him after the talk. I'd read some of his space novels for boys and badly wanted to chat with him, but Patrick was only interested in Luke, who was laying on the charm and praising the space novels. Which I'd told him about in the first place. I didn't get a look in, and nor did anyone else. On his way out Patrick Moore told Miss Willis that Luke had real promise as a novelist and she absolutely beamed. Little parcels arrived for Luke for some time after that, books, cards and bits of meteorite. Perhaps it was then that I began to get tired of the relentlessness of Luke's overtures to the world at large. Luke Squires, novelist or con-man in the making.

I wasn't going to miss the star-gazing evening Mr Kirby had arranged, even if the only star I was interested in was Mr Kirby himself. On a star-gazing evening the lights would be turned off in the classrooms, and over much of the rest of the school, to allow our night sight to develop. It was easy to slip away even for those with compromised mobility. There was an awful lot of lurking relative to the amount of actual astronomy. The few times I tried to join in with the proper, star-gazing part of the evening I couldn't see a darned thing.

I had a rechargeable torch, rather a treasure when such things were very new. It may even have come from Ellisdons. They were nickel cadmium batteries, really very primitive. Their working life was not long. After a few weeks I had to keep charging it continuously, and even then it gave the dimmest possible glow.

I went into one of the classrooms and perched by the door in the Wrigley, beckoning Mr Kirby with my dim torch. I was a little glow-worm of desire, signalling with my feeble beam, to a physics teacher who was perhaps attuned to other wave-lengths of light, or wasn't going to risk burning the wings of his flammable career. Come-hither looks don't work well from a wheelchair, even to those with their night sight at its clearest, their antennæ fully unfurled. All you can do is waggle your eyebrows. Mr Kirby came a bit closer, but wouldn't commit himself. Then he faded into the further darkness.

All the same, I was determined not to return to the dorm, no matter what happened. I wouldn't willingly submit to curfew while my desires were in flood. I wheeled disconsolately into the new wing, ending up in the sixth-form common room. I wasn't entitled to be there, since I wasn't in the sixth form, though I could be invited in by someone who was, like Paul or Abadi. A certain amount of smoking went on. Now it was deserted.

I knew that before long I would be hearing my name called in exasperated tones. I had to give myself some sort of alibi, to explain without disgrace why at a late hour I was nowhere near my allotted sleeping-place. In the common room I simply stood up and fell back into a deep chair I couldn't get out of. That was alibi enough and to spare. No one would question the likelihood of my miscalculating in this way, though for years I had known at a glance – it was a survival skill – whether a given step, door or chair was Johnable. I closed my eyes and waited in weary disgust for the search party. Instead I heard the whispering spokes of a distinctive wheelchair as it pulled in neatly next to the upholstered dungeon into which I had flung myself.

Luke Squires had found me, and in a position which I suppose cried out to be exploited. He lifted himself out of his chair and onto his knees. If I couldn't get up from the chair, I could do no more than squirm while he infiltrated my Velcro. I said, 'Go away!' but it came out as an ineffectual mutter rather than the howl of outrage I intended. 'Fat chance!' he said. He gloated, very much in the manner of a villain in a penny dreadful. He gave a stage laugh and crooned, 'Now I have you in my power!' and stroked the bottom of his face, where the villain's beard would be.

Oh well, I thought, why deny him his fun? Let him get on with it. At least something was happening. There ensued an oral act. Luke said afterwards, 'You're always good value, John. You can't have wanked for a fortnight. I love the way the stuff banks up. I've never been able to wait longer than a week, but it's worth it when you finally do it.'

I hadn't actually been abstaining at all – but it was a ridiculous conversation to be having with the debaucher who'd just set my clock back to zero anyway. And that was the end of my sexual life at that special school for ordinarily delinquent boys, who couldn't get into half as much trouble as they wanted to.

I was erotically stale-mated, with no adult taking the slightest bit of interest in me. Jimmy Kettle would be ashamed of me – 10 himself would disown me, for my lack of daring and imagination. My feebleness in tracking down the lyric quarry. I was also disappointed in Luke Squires. I could hardly pretend that I was his lyric quarry either, if that phrase meant anything at all. I was just a sort of human lolly for use in emergencies.

Jimmy Kettle was as full as ever of drive and determination (even if one of his strongest ambitions was still to fell himself with the savage axe blows of liquor). He told me that I was the only adult apart from him among the pupils of Vulcan, and that this could mean only one thing. I would go crazy if I stuck around. His opinion counted with me. Of all the fantasists at that address, Jimmy was far the most realistic.

He was writing a play of his own now, though he wouldn't let anyone look at it. His pseudonym for the purpose was James Delaney. When he was satisfied with the play he would send a copy to 10, which wasn't intended as any kind of career move. It was pure homage.

Jimmy was realistic about his prospects as a first-time playwright. He told me that a first play, however brilliant, might have to wait six months, or even a year, for a Broadway production. He was setting his sights on the West End, where the field was less crowded and the waiting time shorter.

Somehow I got a glimpse of Jimmy's play, a single line and not even a line of dialogue, just a stage direction. I don't remember how I managed this – it seems a bit fishy, somehow. Normally it's easy for other people to hide things from me, so perhaps Jimmy let me see that one line on purpose.

It certainly told me a great deal about what he was doing. The stage direction read: *Night. Sound of the respirator.* Not much ambiguity there. Jimmy was writing about Abadi and Paul. Not only had those two found each other, and the heroic action which would transform both their lives, but now they had found their Homer too, the bard who would make their story live for ever in the minds of men.

I remember one more school expedition, with Alan and Marion presenting a united front for the sake of the children. It was actually rather an ambitious one, to Amsterdam. We were on a tram when Raeburn said something about us being on the Queen's Highway. Of course I piped up and said we're not in England so there's no queen. 'Oh yes there is!' he said smartly. 'It's Queen Juliana, and we're on her Highway now, so we will obey and oblige Her Majesty in any way we can!' I thought it was rotten luck that our school holiday had to be in just about the only other European country that had a ruddy Queen.

The Sit-Upon Boy

We went on a tour of the canals by boat. Most of the boys fitted in the seats very nicely, but not John with his all-but-fixed hips. I couldn't see a damned thing except the sky. Then Raeburn called out from the aisle on the other side, 'Would you like to sit on my lap?' It was a wonderful reunion with Alan, bringing back all the emotions I had felt for him at the beginning. I didn't want the canal tour to end, so that I could go on being the Sit-Upon Boy. It was only afterwards I remembered that he didn't have sensation below the waist, so it can't have meant anything much to him being the Sat-Upon Man.

Contact with Miss Willis was a little more traumatic. At the end of the trip she was helping me down some steps in a wheelchair single-handed. Not the Wrigley, of course. For the trip I was in a pushing chair. She would balance the back wheels on each step and then lower me down to the next one.

It was a mad thing for someone of her size to undertake. Of course she slipped and down we all tumbled, Miss Willis, John Cromer and all. I could see nothing. I had broken Marion's fall, or rather the wheelchair had. She had somehow moulded round me and the Wrigley, blocking out all light.

I was pinned under her mighty bosom. It was very soft. Her body was all forgiveness, not at all authoritarian. I became aware for the first time of her subtle perfume. I could confirm at first hand what Luke Squires had said about her freedom from pong. She smelled of soapy flannels and rubber ducks.

I was rather shaken up, but it was worse for poor Marion Gertrude.

She wept with pain and shock, retrieving a hanky from her sleeve to wipe her eyes and blow her nose. I was still buoyed up by the thrill of sitting on Raeburn's lap, and her sufferings didn't make as much impression as they should have.

Almost Mum's first words on my return were, 'Well, I hope you're going to sit down and write them a thank-you letter. They've gone to a lot of trouble for you, you know.' All the same she was surprised when I picked up a piece of paper and put it in my typewriter straight away. She preferred her scoldings to be ineffectual, so that they could be repeated without limit.

'Dear Mr Raeburn and Miss Willis,' I wrote. 'Thank you so much for taking me to Holland for such a wonderful holiday. I shall remember it for ever, especially the canal trip.' I was going to return the carriage of the typewriter, and underline the last four words, but decided against it. Extreme caution was called for. My Alan fixation was Top Secret, and I had to get a message past the guards, namely Mum and Miss Willis. Mum checked over my letter – she vetted everything I wrote, there was nothing I could do to stop her – and said it was fine, sealed it and stamped it. So my love letter got past at least one of the guards . . .

I was ashamed to learn when I went back to Vulcan that Miss Willis had broken three ribs in the accident with me. She wasn't really well enough to be running the school, but as she said, if she didn't do what had to be done, who would? Seeing Marion, dishevelled and unwell, somehow holding onto the reins made me feel guilty that I had been the cause of her misfortune. For a while I thought nothing but tender thoughts about poor Marion Gertrude.

Eventually Marion's injuries healed, but the psychological damage done by the rift with Alan was more intractable. She began to feel threatened when pupils showed too much initiative, a rare enough event in a disabled school and one which she might have set herself to welcome. That after all was the rationale of the school, to protect disabled boys less than their misguided families would tend to do. She didn't repudiate her philosophy of goading into independence, but she began to show signs almost of smothering.

Abadi Mukherjee got it into his head that his great friend Paul
Dandridge should see India. He wanted to show him a different
world. The practical difficulties were enormous, but Abadi wasn't
deterred by them, and neither was Paul.

Marion did everything she could to discourage them. She didn't
quite have the nerve to say that there was such a word as 'can't' after
all, but she made it pretty clear that there was such a word as 'should-
n't' and such a phrase as 'would be mad to'.

She told Abadi that Paul would die in his care, but this argument
didn't even begin to work on him. If it hadn't been for Abadi Paul
would be dead already, wasn't that so? That historic reprieve made
him invulnerable. Neither Abadi nor Paul responded to her threats.
On their side strings were pulled, appeals made, until Air India
offered them free plane tickets. Abadi's parents were very wealthy, so
I suppose the fact that free tickets were so welcome must mean they
weren't helping.

Marion's heart must have sunk when she discovered that the mad
trip seemed to be going ahead despite her objections. Then it got
worse, much worse. Abadi turned down the airline tickets and
decided to go overland. He would feed, bathe and change Paul. At
night he would run the respirator off the car battery.

Abadi's passion had always been driving, which he claimed he'd
been doing in India since he was eight. We'd heard that his grandfa-
ther was an enthusiastic driver who had once run over eighteen beg-
gars in a single day (he didn't say if they were all in a clump, or if they
had been picked off individually), so it was in his blood. He would get
his licence, and then he would make it happen.

It took him a long time to get sponsorship for the trip. In fact it
took years. He managed it in the end and off the pair of them went on
their mad adventure. When they reached Delhi, Mrs Gandhi came
out to welcome them. I'm not sure she was Prime Minister at this
point, but certainly a figure on the world stage.

I had mixed feelings about the overland-to-India saga. Sometimes
it seemed to me that Abadi and Paul were making things too easy for
their chronicler James Delaney/Kettle, by throwing in Acts Two and

Three free of charge.

The Skull of Doom

The infestation of fantasy which was such a distinctive feature of
Vulcan School did us no harm, when it was a matter of James Bond
paraphrase or even rip-roaring buckaroo porn. It was only when Miss
Willis's damaged emotional state was stirred into the mixture that
mischief was done. The last manifestation of fantasy that I witnessed
in my time at Vulcan was decidedly Gothic, and it did real harm to at
least one vulnerable person.

Miss Willis set the rumour mill going well ahead of time. More
than one person asked me, 'Is it really true there's a visitor coming to
give a talk who's got a real ghost in a box?' I had to say that I didn't
know, but it didn't seem very likely. I was still regarded as an authority on the supernatural. One little fuse-poltergeist and you're an
expert for life!

I was intrigued enough to ask Luke who our visitor was, but all he
said was, 'Nobody special – just some old duck,' which made me
wonder if he enjoyed Miss Willis's confidence as much as he once had.

On the appointed afternoon we assembled in the main hall.
Marion's voice rang out in plump authority. 'Boys of Vulcan School!
It is a great pleasure to introduce our guest – and my personal friend
– Miss Anna Mitchell-Hedges. Anna was living in the Castle before
most of you boys were even thought of. It was her father the Colonel
who placed the advertisement in the paper which Mr Raeburn and I
answered all those years ago. Of course Anna knew the Castle as it was
before we made our recent modifications, but I hope she gives her
approval!' To which Anna Mitchell-Hedges returned a twisted smile.
'Anna and her father spent their lives travelling the world, surviving
many dangers and discovering many things. In her time she has given
a pedicure to the Duke of Windsor, and she has also landed the heav-
iest hammerhead shark ever caught by a woman – weighing fifteen
hundred pounds!

'She has brought one of her treasures to show to you today, a treasure which is much older than even the oldest part of the Castle. Please
make her welcome, boys!'

We made her welcome, this strange, rather sunken creature with grey hair and a cold and grating voice.

'Thank you, Miss Willis. It is a joy to me to see that what was once my home is giving hospitality to so many fine boys.' It was odd to hear her speaking so coldly of joy. Her smile was like a winter night. 'Now I must have darkness, total darkness.' Presumably Marion had been briefed about this requirement beforehand. She went over to the windows and tugged the curtains scrupulously across. Then she went over to the door and turned the lights off.

In the darkness we could hear a succession of thrilling, slightly sinister noises. Miss Mitchell-Hedges' voice came again in the darkness: 'And now, dear friends, some music.' There was a heavy click, and a tape-recorder started to play some music. I recognised it. It was the frightening music from *Fantasia*, from the bit with the spooks. 'Night on the Bare Mountain'. It didn't frighten me. If there was anything that did give me a moment of goose-flesh, it was Anna Mitchell-Hedges saying the words 'dear friends'. She didn't sound as if she'd ever had a friend in her life.

She made the music quieter, so that she could speak properly over it. 'And now for some light . . .' But she didn't ask Miss Willis to turn the lights in the room back on. Instead she clicked on a powerful torch which she was holding just beneath an object on the desk in front of her. The light shone through the object. The light was red. There was a red lens on the torch. The only light in the room came from that torch, and reached us by passing through what was sitting on the desk before her, facing us with its grin. Miss Mitchell-Hedges made small passes with the torch, so that the red light wavered and cast changing shadows.

This was the moment, after the clunks and the click and the spooky music, when I started to hear another sound. A low continuous banging, with a moan inside it.

It was also the moment when Anna's voice took on an oddly crooning quality. 'What you are looking at, dear boys,' she said, 'and what is looking back at you, is an object full of value and danger. It is valuable because it is one of a very few in the world. The British Museum has another such object, but that has not been authenticated. And it is dangerous because of what it can do to those who under-estimate it.

What it has done, indeed, to those who have shown it disrespect.

'The Skull maintains an unvarying temperature of seventy degrees, no matter what its surroundings. It changes colour, even against a neutral background. Sometimes it goes a cloudy white, sometimes a dark spot expands until the whole Skull goes black.

'This terrible, beautiful artefact was made from a huge piece of rock quartz, worn down into its shape by efforts that must have taken hundreds of years. The Mayans had no chisels, boys, they did not have so much as sand-paper. What they had was sand. The crystal was worn down by hand. Think of that! The sand wearing down both the crystal and the hands that rubbed it, year after year. They must have been slaves, I think, who did the rubbing, knowing that if they did their work well and finished the task that had been set their ancestors, then the blood of their descendants might moisten the stone and satisfy its thirst . . .

'This is the Skull of Doom, made by the Maya people of South America. I was led to discover it in 1924. It has knowledge beyond our own. In ancient sacrifice it was used to bring about the death of tribal enemies. The Mayans would spill blood on it to make it work. Human blood.

'Once you have been cursed by this Skull, there is nowhere for you to run to in this world. Or the next.

'One man who spoke out against the power of the Skull developed a fever in three days and died. Another fell down a mine-shaft, a third went insane. One man in Africa was struck by lightning – out of a clear blue sky. Even to think bad thoughts about the Skull can bring sickness and death.'

The banging with the moaning inside it was getting louder, making a strong contribution to the oppressive atmosphere. I was sure I hadn't secretly thought anything wrong about the skull, but I can't say I felt very relaxed about it. While Miss Mitchell-Hedges was talking she let two fingers of one hand, the index and the little, slide down the front of the Skull onto its eye-sockets, interrupting the red light from the torch. The effect was eerie – all right, it was downright frightening. She was covering up the empty eyes of the Skull, but she seemed rather to be producing two searching beams of darkness. The gesture had something in it that was unlike a person touching an object: There was a sensual element, as if flesh was touching flesh, gloating at the contact. She was really milking the mood. If you like a captive audience, the disabled are always going to be at the top of your list.

'As you know, boys, Farley Castle used to be my home. The Skull lived here with me for many years. It knows the building well. It would be wise for each of you to remember that something of the Skull has always been here. Something of the Skull will remain here, even after it returns to its case and travels home with me to Reading.'

At this point in her spook show she nodded to Miss Willis, who was waiting by the light switch and restored the room to its normal state. Anna Mitchell-Hedges turned off the torch and pressed the Stop button on the tape-recorder. She had a little colour in her face now, as if she had had a transfusion under cover of darkness. She seemed a little drunk, even, on the fear she had summoned up.

'In a moment the brave ones among you may inspect the Skull at close quarters. Do you have any questions?' This formula always creates a silence. Miss Willis raised her hand.

The sound in the room which had been bothering me for some time was still going on, but now I knew what it was. Little 'Half-Pint' Stevie Templeton, athetoid spastic, who could be jumpy and twitchy at the best of times, was jumping up and down very violently in his wheelchair. Sometimes on Sunday afternoons Mr Wooffindin the English teacher would read to us from *The Lord of the Rings*, and Stevie would become very agitated when he heard about the Dark Riders, but this was something else again. Poor Stevie! She was pouring fully a quart of anguish into that half-pint pot.

Little cries and moans of pain and bits of words he couldn't articulate came stammering out of his mouth. He was sobbing and dribbling with terror. He was knocking his head hard against the metal sides of the wheelchair. There was blood.

Roger Stott called out from his seat, 'Miss Willis?' The look she gave him wasn't one of her warmest. 'Roger, you must have the courtesy to wait your turn before you ask our guest a question. What must she think of our manners?'

'But Miss Willis, Stevie is shaking. Really shaking.'

She didn't even look over to his wheelchair. 'I'm familiar with Stevie's condition, thank you, Roger. To resume: Miss Mitchell-

Hedges – Anna, if I may – what is the most useful thing to take with you on expeditions to the wild parts of the world?'

Stevie Templeton was beside himself, and no wonder. If he was too frightened to stay in a dorm with me after a blown fuse had made a ghost story seem a little too real, then what chance did he have of coping with Anna Mitchell-Hedges' carefully orchestrated spook show?

Even at that age, I could smell a prepared question, a put-up job. To her credit, Marion must have glanced over to Stevie and seen that something was wrong, just as Anna was getting into the stride of her answer. Anna raised her voice to cover the noise he was making.

Boiling without fire

'Yours is a good question, Miss Willis, and one to which I have given much thought over the years. My answer is the same as my father's: Eno's liver salts. It is useful in two ways. It settles the stomach and is a tonic to the system. But it can also serve in an emergency to impress savages. Nothing makes a greater impact on the primitive mind than the white man's ability to make water boil without using fire. That is how they understand the effervescence of the salts. If any of your audience remains unconvinced, your ability to drink the boiling water you have made without being scalded will certainly do the trick. If you decide to administer the salts to a native for their original purpose of soothing an upset stomach, you would do well to intone a spell beforehand, to account for the coldness of the liquid. Anything sonorous will do for a spell. On such occasions my father would recite the Twenty-third Psalm, not for sense but for rhythm.'

A handy tip in its way, but by this time few of us were resonating on Anna's wave-length. Even while Anna Mitchell-Hedges was answering her question Marion started to sober up. At last she saw that Stevie Templeton was doing more than shaking in the ordinary way and she whisked him from the room. She didn't appear again, but I can't say that Miss Anna Mitchell-Hedges seemed to miss her. She had thoroughly enjoyed herself.

I wasn't sure about taking up the offer to inspect the Skull at close quarters, but I certainly felt the artefact's fascination. Everyone else seemed to be giving it a wide berth. At last I Wrigleyed up to the desk which Miss Mitchell-Hedges had used for her nasty *son et lumière*. She smiled at me. 'Young man,' she said, 'have you come to consult the Skull of Doom? You may touch it. You may speak to it.' I found I wasn't afraid. I came right up to the desk and gazed at the object. There were still people in the hall, but they melted away and then it was just Mitchell-Hedges, the Artefact and Me. She whispered, 'In fact there is no need to speak. The Skull is fully telepathic. If you merely think towards it and listen carefully, you will hear what it has to say. Simply gaze on eternity.'

The Skull was very deep and beautiful. I looked at it, touched it, caressed it and felt very honoured. The witch from Reading murmured in my ear, but I wasn't really listening. As I gazed at the Skull, I felt the pain of Stevie Templeton, now dying away, and I knew without having to ask that the Skull would never have an interest in frightening a nervous little boy who had a huge task simply getting from one end of a day to the other. The Skull wasn't baleful in itself, though it served Miss Mitchell-Hedges well in that respect. There was any amount of knowledge hidden away in that crystal chamber. Things seen and unseen swirled within its depths. As the Skull's aura resolved more clearly in my mind, I began to have the surprising thought that it was actually female rather than male. In some strange way the Skull was a lady.

For a moment I thought of owning the Skull, but only to be able to spend time with it alone, and to give it a less ominous name. At the same time I realised the emptiness of treating it as a possession. I communed so deeply with the artefact that I began to think Miss Mitchell-Hedges knew nothing about it, apart from its ability to amplify her fantasies of control through fear. She was really just another Judy Brisby, a Miss Krüger too fastidious to touch her victims, and I had grown beyond the reach of such people.

From my vantage-point I could also see that the Skull was not in fact made from one piece of crystal. The lower jaw was detachable, held on with a piece of wire. At some stage an upper tooth had been chipped, one next to a canine. I wondered whether a clever dentist might not be able to make a little quartz crown for it.

Anna Mitchell-Hedges wrapped the Skull in cloths before putting it back in its case. 'I wonder where Marion has got to?' she asked, but she didn't really seem concerned. She seemed pleased with her after-noon's work. Her act was essentially ventriloquism, with the element of misdirection being crucial. Archie Andrews would have been shocked, though, by what was really going on. The crystal jaws of the Skull didn't move, but everyone was looking at it, and meanwhile Anna Mitchell-Hedges had bitten into a schoolboy's bone marrow, while Miss Willis looked foolishly on, pleased to have a friend who had cut the toe-nails of the Duke of Windsor, until the damage got out of hand. It was clear that she got a kick out of the fear and pain she caused Stevie Templeton. It couldn't have been more obvious if she had gone over to him and licked the blood from his wheelchair.

She packed the Skull away and drove it back to Reading. With no real idea of where or how she lived, I visualised a gingerbread maisonette with a garden whose herbaceous borders were decorated with arrangements of children's bones, and a basket in the hall for the Skull like a dog's, except when it was allowed up on Anna's lap while she watched Bruce Forsyth presenting *Sunday Night at the London Palladium*.

Abrasive enterprise

The Skull of Doom had been shaped over generations by sand held in the hands of slaves. For years now I had been engaged on an abra-sive enterprise of my own. Ever since the interview at Sidcot School, when I had been accepted without needing to apply, I had been deter-mined that I would go to a proper school, a normal school, a grammar school. I'd realised by now that there had never been a possibility of being sent to Lord Mayor Treloar. I was one of the best students in the school. It meant something to me, too, that Jimmy Delaney/Kettle thought I would go mad if I stayed at Vulcan.

The lump of rock quartz that I needed to abrade into shape was Dad's resistance. I needed to wear down a mass of No into a sliver of Yes. My only tool was my tongue. I had to keep on at him. It was bad enough from his point of view when I pestered him for dry ice or square balloons, but now I was committed to the campaign of attri-tion. I wouldn't let it go. All I needed was a recently built grammar school. Then it would have lifts. Dad might claim that there was no dry ice and no square balloons to be had in any shop, including Harrods, but he could hardly maintain there were no grammar schools in Berkshire with lifts. Sooner or later he was bound to say, 'I'll make this phone call if it means I get some peace. If it means you'll finally shut up . . .'

It helped my cause that Dad was back in employment. Through old RAF contacts he had landed a job in the Personnel Department of BOAC, our national airline. Broadly speaking he was in a good mood. It suited him down to the ground. It was as close to a Services job as could be had on Civvy Street, stiff with officiousness and protocol.

I knew that Miss Willis wouldn't be happy to see me go, but I hadn't prepared my arguments. The summons to the sole principal's study was peremptory. She was hoping to catch me off guard, and to nip my independence in the bud.

I found it odd to be there without Raeburn. His presence was still strong. If anything she seemed to be trespassing on his sanctum. This after all was where Raeburn had given me some of our walking lessons, told me about the Aztecs and their enlightened ways, and asked me whether I had sensation below the waist. This was also where he had given two sexually experimental boys their small glasses of sherry, and told them that they must be discreet and not worry Miss Willis, who was old-fashioned about such things. Behind her I could still see the spine of *Civilisation and the Cripple*.

'I think you have been happy here, John, so I don't know what to make of this misguided idea of changing schools. What is it that you want, John? Really?'

'I want to go to a proper school.'

'This is a proper school.'

'I want to go to a grammar school.'

'This is a grammar school in all but name. Our educational programme is ambitious. It's odd that I should have to make mention of the fact to someone who has benefited from it for some years now. Vulcan has a precise name, corresponding to a precise function. This is a special boarding school for the education and rehabilitation of severely disabled but intelligent boys. And you are severely disabled, John. You need a high level of care. You are also intelligent, but not more intelligent than a number of boys who have gone on to success

519

in their exams, and who have started to find their place in the world. Are there subjects you would wish to study that are not provided for here?'

'Chemistry, Miss Willis. Chemistry is an important subject. And I want to play the piano.'

'If you are serious about chemistry I will see what can be done. As for the piano, it is not Vulcan School that disqualifies you from it. You can't simply ignore your limitations if you are to make the most of the opportunities you have.'

'Miss Willis, I want to go to a normal school.'

Marion smiled. 'No school that is able to meet your needs could be described as normal, John. I am an educationalist, and you must trust my expertise. If there was the remotest possibility of disabled boys thriving in any old school, do you think that Mr Raeburn and I would have gone through our various ordeals to set up this one?

'You are already a pupil at an exceptional school. Why throw away what we have achieved together? Is it perhaps that you want the academic company of girls? Because I can tell you that girls may be a disappointment, if you are hoping for special friendships and tender sympathy.' She was barking up the wrong tree there, of course. Perhaps she was referring indirectly to her own school-days. In her bleak smile could be read a certain amount of suffering.

'I want to go to Burnham Grammar School. Not because there are girls there.'

'And who will devote themselves to your care at this school? To put it at its most basic, who will take you to the lavatory there?'

'I'll manage.'

Marion said, 'John, I've come to know you better than anybody over the years, to understand your qualities – which are considerable – and also your limitations.' She settled back in her chair. 'John, you know your little adventure in the woods? The time when no one could find you, after your "accident"? It was as plain as plain that you were just begging for attention. I said nothing about it. Perhaps you don't realise that I have to divide myself into many little pieces to look after you all. And perhaps this application to another school is an exercise in the same vein, a way of making yourself important.'

In a sense I'd never before had a conflict with authority. I'd been indoctrinated by Mum and sensitised by Dad to his withholding of feeling. I'd been tortured by two generations of carers, by Miss Krüger at CRX and Judy at Vulcan: strong hands had held me under the surface of the hospital pool, strong hands had dangled me over the school stair-well. In my time I'd been scolded, roughly hugged and taken under a few wings. I'd had passing battles of will with Granny, which had been invaluable training, but this was actually the first time a whole personality had been nakedly opposed to mine, on something like equal terms.

Miss Willis expected the force of what she said, or simply the authority she embodied, to carry the day. To prevail because either she was right or because she was Miss Willis. It was almost intoxicating, to have her voice address me at its deepest, with the Kathleen Ferrier throb giving her an extra authority, and her clean-and-not-really-like-a-fat-person's smell taking me back to the time she broke my fall on the steps.

Of course she was right that I craved attention. She wasn't stupid. Even in my days of bed rest, with my day-dreams of having a steel ball in the room, which I could move around with the force of my mind – the whole point of the fantasy was that everyone would be impressed. Not that I had powers, but that everyone knew about it. In the absence of acclaim a steel ball was a duller toy than most.

The Little Mermaid had always been one of my favourite stories, but I always bridled at the bargain she made, to walk in agony and have no one know her suffering. I had no objection to suffering in silence, as long as everyone knew about it.

The weather-vane of Marion's rhetoric changed quarter. I had stood up to the breezes of reproach and wheedling, now she would try some colder blasts. Her voice took on a hard edge. 'In a school other than this, you would not be treated with understanding. You would be humiliated and mocked. Never accepted. I have watched you spread your wings here, with our help, but that doesn't mean I must watch as you throw yourself off a cliff and try to join a flock which will peck you to death. You can't judge the world outside by our splendid ABs.

It can be a cruel place, and weakness is no protection. Weakness can even be an incitement to cruelty.'

Of course, it spoiled her case that the world over which she ruled was crueller than she knew. Judy Brisby hadn't been detected in her various assaults. She had left the school as an unspotted professional, as a loving wife and mother-to-be.

In fact there was only one person reprimanded for bullying in my years at Vulcan, as far as I know, and that was me. We were used to our own little tortures. Chinese Burns were common currency, given and received without much comment. I was almost proud of the first one I got. It was painful but also a mark of belonging, like a phantom bracelet. Eventually I found someone even weaker than me, a worthy person to receive an amateurish sort of Chinese Burn in his turn (my hands not really being up to the task of twisting the skin of the wrists in two directions at once) – and I got a proper scolding for it. It even turned up on my report: 'John really must stop bullying boys weaker than himself.' Unfair, unfair! The action was technically difficult and it was quite a feat to manage it at all. But oh no, suddenly grassing people up is perfectly all right and I'm a menace to society. Never mind that no one ever got a word in their reports about the Chinese Burns they'd given me.

And after all, as the whole Skull of Doom episode showed, there was a little nerve of cruelty unknown to Marion herself which pulsed in her from time to time. If she was *in loco parentis* for all the children, then by letting little Stevie Templeton be frightened until his athetoid twitching became frantic and he cut his head against the metal of his wheelchair, she was responsible for the hurt he suffered. She was hurting him as directly as if she had knocked his head against the metal herself.

'It's natural, John, and even admirable that your reach should exceed your grasp . . .' She faltered for a moment, realising the ineptness of her chosen words. I looked down at my hands, which got equally poor marks for reaching and grasping, and then gazed defiantly up at her, so that she went quite red. There's startling imagery dozing in all our expressions – I mean, 'flogging a dead horse'. Why ever not? It's the only sort of horse I'd condone flogging. Language is full of these pitfalls, and I can't pretend they've ever bothered me, really.

Arms and legs. They're basic, aren't they? The last thing I want is for people to hamstring the language, put their words in shackles, out of a misplaced and cringing tact. Still, I wasn't going to let that stop me using any weapon I could find, in the struggle with a benefactor who was blocking my way so that she could help me indefinitely, and heal her own wounds in the process.

'One more thing, John,' she said. 'I've been looking through your academic record. Perhaps we've made a mistake. That does happen. Very rarely. Or perhaps it is you that is mistaken.' She made a show of shuffling the papers on the desk she had somehow taken over from Raeburn. 'Did you in fact pass your eleven-plus?'

Her cheeks might wobble but her voice was strong. Even so I began to see that her eyes behind their glasses looked small and frightened. I could hear her breathing. She wasn't puffing out her cheeks, as I would do when I imitated her for the entertainment of the Blue Dorm, but she was making little panting noises, as if she was an invalid with damaged lungs trying to blow out a birthday candle set too far away from her.

I felt guiltily sorry for her at that moment. I had to remind myself what she was actually doing. The candle in front of her was my hope for a normal education. That's what she was doing her best to extinguish. 'No, Miss Willis, I didn't. But Burnham Grammar School will take me anyway. It's all arranged. I have a letter from my parents.'

This means you

Then her voice changed, becoming rougher but also, horribly, softer. 'John, I can't let you go,' she said. 'I can't let you go.' Remembering what she had said at Raeburn's engagement party, I understood that she was no longer speaking as an educationalist with special expertise but as something else. Call it an educationalist scorned. There came a point where she wanted to hang on to me, to keep me near, and not necessarily for my own good. If I moved to a main-stream school, that was something other than a success story and a vindication of the Vulcan ideal. It had become a personal rejection, and she had had quite enough in that line. *John, I can't let you go* was like a melancholy reprise of *Alan, don't do this to me*. Dido again.

Dido made monstrous by grief. The proud Carthaginian queen step-ping onto the pyre and holding me in her arms as it was lit.

Then she recovered her poise, and the vocal softness disappeared for good. 'One thing I will say. If you go to this school where they know nothing about you, you will come crawling back to me on your hands and knees. You will beg to be taken back where you belong.'

'Then I will come crawling back to you on my hands and knees. And when I do you can say whatever you like.'

It gave me courage that she still didn't know about Kim and Dagmar Bosch from Oberammergau, and their trysts in the library. She didn't know that Luke Squires met Terence Wilberforce on the go-cart track any night when there wasn't rain. And hang it all, after the trip to Amsterdam, she had told us to do paintings of the tulip fields using a ruler, if you please! I had ignored her and been held up to shame. 'But Miss Willis,' I had said, 'there are no straight lines in nature.'

'Allow me to know best, John. I saw any number of straight lines in Holland, and so did you.' Allow her to know best? Not any more.

Marion tried to regain control of the conversation by dismissing me, saying, 'You can go now, John.' I deliberately misunderstood, and said, 'I know, Miss Willis, that's just what I've been saying.' I wasn't going to give her the satisfaction of ordering me out of the room. The battle was won, and this was just a skirmish over who had the right to dismiss who. Or as she might have put it, asserting her authority to the last – who had the right to dismiss *whom*, John. I'd go in my own good time. It turned out I was the one with the mobility after all.

I closed my eyes in a curious state of peace. I no longer even felt like a pupil of the school. I was already for all practical purposes an old boy. Miss Willis might be sitting there in front of me, holding her head in her hands, but in reality I had already left. I was reverting to a technique older than anything I'd learned at Vulcan, the almost subliminal mode of movement that had served me so well at CRX. I could see a door opening on the far side of Miss Willis, glowing with possibilities, and I had only to get to it. All I had to do was to start taking tiny steps and I would somehow arrive at my destination before anyone really noticed that I was on my way. It had worked any number of times in the past. The length of my 'stride', to call it that, might only be an inch and a half, and for any amount of time I seemed to be getting nowhere. Yet the next time Marion Willis looked up I would be long gone, tottering securely into a corridor full of possibilities, where every door was very promisingly marked *Private* or *No Admittance. Absolutely no unauthorised personnel.*

Danger. Trespassers Will Be Prosecuted.

Keep Out. This Means You.